Colleen McCullough

THREE COMPLETE NOVELS

Colleen McCullough

THREE COMPLETE NOVELS

TIM

AN INDECENT OBSESSION

THE LADIES OF MISSALONGHI

WINGS BOOKS
NEW YORK

This 1998 edition is published by Wings Books®, an imprint of Random House Value Publishing, Inc., 201 East 50th Street, New York, NY 10021, by arrangement with HarperCollins Publishers, Inc.

Wings Books®, and design are registered trademarks of Random House Value Publishing, Inc.

Printed in the United States of America

Random House
New York • Toronto • London • Sydney • Auckland
http://www.randomhouse.com/

Library of Congress Cataloging-in-Publication Data
McCullough, Colleen, 1937-
    [Novels. Selections]
    Three complete novels / Colleen McCullough.
        p.   cm.
    Contents: Tim — An indecent obsession — The ladies of Missalonghi.
    ISBN 0-517-20166-6
    1. Man-woman relationships—Australia—Fiction.
    2. Mentally handicapped—Australia—Fiction.   3. Women—Australia—Fiction.
    I. Title.
    PR9619.3.M32A6   1999
    823—dc21   98-19504
                                                                              CIP

10 9 8 7 6 5 4 3 2 1

CONTENTS

TIM

For

Gilbert H. Glaser, M.D.

Chairman, Department of Neurology
Yale University School of Medicine

with gratitude and affection

One

Harry Markham and his crew arrived on the job at
exactly seven o'clock that Friday morning, Harry
and his foreman Jim Irvine sitting inside the pickup cabin and
Harry's three men in the open back of the truck, perched wherever they could find a level space for their behinds. The house
they were renovating lay on Sydney's North Shore in the suburb of Artarmon, just behind the spreading desolation of the
brick pits. It was not a big job, even for a small-time builder like
Harry; merely covering the red brick bungalow with stucco and
adding a sleepout to the back veranda, the kind of job Harry
welcomed from time to time because it filled in the gaps between larger contracts.

The weekend promised heat and endless sun, if Friday morning was any indication; the men piled out of the pickup grum-
bling among themselves, plunged into the gloomy tree-shielded
aisle of the side passage and shed their clothes without a twinge
of self-consciousness or shame.

Changed into their work-shorts, they came round the back
corner of the house just as the Old Girl was shuffling down the
backyard in her faded pink chenille bathrobe, circa 1950, carefully carrying a gaudily flowered china chamber pot in both
hands, her head a twinkling mass of tin butterfly hair wavers,

also circa 1950. No new-fangled rollers for Mrs. Emily Parker, thank you very much. The yard slipped gradually into the maw of a gravelly clay canyon which had once been the source of a considerable number of Sydney's bricks; now it served as a convenient place for the Old Girl to empty her chamber pot every morning, for she clung doggedly to the habits of her rural origins and insisted on her potty at night.

As the contents of the pot flew in a solid-looking arc of pale amber toward the bottom of the brick pit, she turned her head and eyed the nearly naked men sourly.

"G'day, Miz Parker!" Harry called. "Oughta finish this today, I reckon!"

"And about bloody time, too, you lazy lot of bots!" the Old Girl snarled as she came slopping up the yard again, quite unembarrassed. "The things I have to put up with on account of youse! Miss Horton complained to me last night that her prize pink geranyimums is all covered with cement dust, and her maidenhair fern got squashed flat when some useless coot buzzed a brick over her fence yestiddy."

"If Miss Horton's that prune-faced old spinster next door," Mick Devine muttered to Bill Naismith, "then I bet her bloody maidenhair didn't get squashed by a brick only yestiddy, it up and died years ago from no fertilizer!"

Still complaining loudly, the Old Girl disappeared inside with her empty chamber pot; a few seconds later the men heard the energetic sounds of Mrs. Emily Parker cleaning her chamber pot in the back veranda toilet, followed by the swoosh of the toilet cistern discharging and a sound of ringing china as the pot was hung on its diurnal hook above the more orthodox repository of human wastes.

"Jesus Henry, I bet the bloody grass is green down in that brick pit," Harry said to a grinning crew.

"It's a bloody wonder she ain't flooded it out long before now," Bill sniggered.

"Well, if youse asks me, she ain't the full quid," Mick said. "In this day and age and with two proper bogs in her house, she's still peeing into a guzunda."

"A guzunda?" Tim Melville echoed.

"Yeah, sport, a guzunda. A guzunda is the thing that guzunda the bed every night and that you always put your flaming foot in when you get up in a hurry," Harry explained. He looked at his watch. "The Readymix Concrete truck ought to be here any tick, I reckon. Tim, you get out the front and wait for it. Take the big wheelbarrow off the truck and start ferrying the mud back to us as soon as the blighter shows, okay?"

Tim Melville smiled, nodded, and trotted off.

Mick Devine, absently watching him go and still pondering on the vagaries of Old Girls, started to laugh. "Oh, struth! I just thought of a beaut! Listen, you blokes, at smoke-oh this morning you just follow my lead, and maybe we'll teach Tim a thing or two about guzundas and such-like."

Two

Mary Horton screwed her long, very thick hair into its habitual bun on the back of her neck, thrust two more pins into it and eyed her reflection in the mirror without joy or sorrow, or indeed much interest. The mirror was a good one, and gave back her image without flattery or distortion; had her eyes been engaged in a more personal inspection they would have seen a short, rather stocky woman of early middle age, with white hair as colorless as crystal pulled cruelly away from a square but regular-featured face. She wore no make-up, deeming it a waste of time and money to pay homage to vanity. The eyes themselves were dark brown and snappingly alert, no-nonsense eyes which echoed the decisive, slightly hard planes of her face. Her body was clad in what her fellow workers had long ago decided was her equivalent of army uniform or nun's habit; a crisp white shirt buttoned high at her throat, over which the top half of a severely cut gray linen suit slipped smoothly. Her hemline was decently below her knees, the skirt cut generously enough to avoid its riding up when she sat down, her legs were sheathed in sensibly thick support hose, and on her feet she wore black lace-up shoes with solid block heels.

The shoes were polished until they twinkled, not a speck or

a spot marred the white surface of her shirt, no crease sullied the perfection of the linen suit. To be at all times absolutely impeccable was an obsession with Mary Horton; her young assistant at the office swore that she had seen Miss Horton remove her clothes carefully and put them on a hanger before she used the lavatory so they would not become creased or disarranged.

Satisfied that she measured up to her inflexible standards, Mary Horton nudged a black straw hat onto the upper margin of her bun, stuck a hatpin through it in one movement, drew on her black kid gloves and pulled her huge handbag to the edge of the dressing table. She opened the bag and methodically checked to see that it contained keys, money, handkerchief, spare Kotex pad, pen and notebook, appointment diary, identification and credit cards, driver's license, parking lot gate card, safety pins, straight pins, needle and thread box, scissors, nail file, two spare shirt buttons, screwdriver, pliers, wirecutters, flashlight, steel tape measure in centimeters and inches, box of .38 cartridges, and police service revolver.

She was a crack shot. It was a part of her duties to do Constable Steel & Mining's banking, and since the time she had neatly winged a felon as he scuttled away with Constable Steel & Mining's payroll under his arm, there was not a criminal in Sydney with sufficient intestinal fortitude to tackle Miss Horton on her way from the bank. She had yielded her briefcase so imperturbably, with such composure and lack of protest, that the thief had thought himself perfectly safe; then as he turned to run she opened her handbag, took out the pistol, leveled it, aimed it and fired it. Sergeant Hopkins of the NSW Police pistol range maintained she was faster on the draw than Sammy Davis, Junior.

Thrown on her own resources at the age of fourteen, she had shared a room at the YWCA with five other girls, and worked as a salesclerk in David Jones until she completed a night secretarial course. At fifteen she had commenced work in the general typists' pool at Constable Steel & Mining, so poor that she wore the same scrupulously laundered skirt and blouse every day and darned her cotton stockings until they contained more darns than original fabric.

Within five years her efficiency, unobtrusive quietness, and remarkable intelligence took her from the general office to the post of private secretary for Archibald Johnson, the managing director, but during her first ten years with the firm she continued to live at the Y, darn her stockings over and over again and save much more than she spent.

When she was twenty-five years old she approached Archie Johnson for advice on investing her savings, and by the time she was thirty she had made many, many times her initial outlay. Consequently, at the age of forty-three she owned a house in Artarmon, a quiet middle-class suburb, drove a very conservative but very expensive British Bentley upholstered in genuine leather and paneled in genuine walnut, owned a beach cottage on twenty acres of land north of Sydney, and had her suits made by the man who tailored for the wife of the Governor General of Australia.

She was very well satisfied with herself and her life; she enjoyed the small luxuries which only money permitted, kept almost totally to herself at work and at home, had no friends save five thousand books which lined the walls of her den and several hundred LPs devoted almost entirely to Bach, Brahms, Beethoven, and Handel. She loved gardening and cleaning house, never watched television or went to the movies, and had never wanted or had a boyfriend.

When Mary Horton let herself out of her front door she stood on the stoop for a moment, screwing up her eyes against the glare and checking the state of her front garden. The grass needed mowing badly; where was that dratted man whom she paid to barber it every Thursday fortnight? He had not come

6

for a month, and the closely cropped green velvet surface was becoming tussocky. Most annoying, she thought, really most annoying.

There was a curious thrumming in the air, half a sound and half a sensation, a sort of faintly heard *boom, boom, boom* that seeped into the bones and told the experienced Sydneysider that today was going to be a very hot day, up over the century. The twin West Australian flowering gums on either side of her front gate fluttered their blue, sickled leaves limply downward in sighing protest against the hammer of the heat, and Japanese beetles clicked and rattled busily among the suffocating masses of yellow flowers on the cassia bushes. A bank of magnificent red double oleanders flanked the stone-flagged pathway leading from the front door to the garage; Mary Horton set her lips together tightly and began to walk along it.

Then the duel began, the struggle which recurred every morning and evening of summer. As she drew level with the first beautiful, blooming bush, it began to shriek and caterwaul in an incredible volume of shrilling sound which rang in her ears until it set her head reeling.

Down went the handbag, off came the gloves; Mary Horton marched to the neat green coils of the garden hose, turned its faucet full on and began to drench her oleanders: Gradually the noise dwindled away as the bushes became saturated, until there was only a single basso profundo "breek!" emanating from the bush nearest to the house. Mary shook her fist at it vindictively.

"I'll get you yet, you old twirp!" she said through clenched teeth.

"Breeeeeek!" answered the cicada choirmaster derisively.

On went the gloves, up came the handbag; Mary proceeded to the garage in peace and quiet.

From her driveway it was possible to see the mess that had once been Mrs. Emily Parker's pretty red brick bungalow next

7

door. Mary eyed the havoc disapprovingly as she hefted up the door of her garage and glanced idly toward the sidewalk.

Walton Street's sidewalks were lovely; they consisted of a narrow concrete path and a beautifully kept, very wide stretch of lawn from path to curb. Every thirty feet down each side of the street there grew a huge oleander tree, one white, one pink, one red, one pink, in successive quartets that were the pride of Walton Street's residents and one of the chief reasons why Walton Street was generally a prizewinner in the annual *Herald* garden competition.

A massive concrete carrier was parked with its idly revolving drum slapping against one of Emily Parker's sidewalk oleanders, and a chute was discharging gluey gray gallons of concrete on to the grass. It dripped from the sad, petrified branches of the tree, it ran and oozed sluggishly into pools where the lawn was uneven, it slopped onto the paved path. Mary's mouth was a thin white line of vexation. What on earth had possessed Emily Parker to poultice the red brick sides of her house with this disgusting substance? There was no accounting for taste, or rather the lack of it, she reflected.

A young man was standing bare-headed in the sun, dispassionately watching the desecration of Walton Street; from where she stood some twenty feet away Mary Horton gazed at him, dumbfounded.

Had he lived two and a half thousand years before, Phidias and Praxiteles would have used him as model for the greatest Apollos of all time; instead of standing with such superb lack of self-consciousness in the backwater of a Sydney street to suffer the oblivion of utter mortality, he would have lived forever in the cool, smoothly satin curves of pale marble, and his stone eyes would have looked indifferently over the awed heads of generations upon generations of men.

But here he stood, amid a slushy concrete mess on Walton Street, obviously a member of Harry Markham's building crew, for he wore the builder's uniform of khaki shorts with legs rolled up until the lower curve of the buttocks was just visible, the waistline of the shorts slipped down until they rode his hips. Aside from the shorts and a pair of thick woollen socks turned down over the tops of heavy, clumping workman's boots, he wore nothing; not shirt or coat or hat.

Momentarily turned side-on to her, he glistened in the sun like living, melted gold, legs so beautifully shaped that she fancied he was a long-distance runner; indeed, that was the cast of his whole physique, long and slender and graceful, the planes of his chest as he swung toward her tapering gradually from wide shoulders to exquisitely narrow hips.

And the face—oh, the face! It was flawless. The nose was short and straight, the cheekbones high and pronounced, the mouth tenderly curved. Where his cheek sloped in toward the corner of his mouth on the left side he bore a tiny crease, and that minute furrow saddened him, lent him an air of lost, childlike innocence. His hair, brows, and lashes were the color of ripe wheat, magnificent with the sun pouring down on them, and his wide eyes were as intensely, vividly blue as a cornflower.

When he noticed her watching him he smiled at her happily, and the smile snatched Mary Horton's breath from her body in an uncontrolled gasp. She had never gasped so in all her life; horrified to find herself spellbound by his extraordinary beauty, she made a sudden mad dash for the haven of her car.

The memory of him stayed with her all through the crawling drive into North Sydney's commercial center, where Constable Steel & Mining had its forty-story office building. Try as she would to concentrate on the traffic and the coming events of the day, Mary could not banish him from her mind. If he had been effeminate, if his face had been merely pretty or he had exuded some indefinable aura of brutishness, she could have forgotten him as easily as long self-discipline had trained her to forget anything unwelcome or upsetting. Oh, God, how beautiful he was, how completely, appallingly beautiful! Then she remembered Emily Parker saying the builders would be finished today; driving on doggedly, everything in the quivering, shimmering mist of heat around her seemed to dim a little.

Three

With Mary Horton gone and the garden hose rendered impotent, the cicada choirmaster in his oleander bush emitted a deep, resonating "breeek!" and was immediately answered by the diva soprano two bushes over. One by one they came in, tenors, contraltos, baritones, and sopranos, until the beating sun charged their little iridescent green bodies with such a singing power of sound that to attempt a conversation within feet of the bushes was useless. The deafening chorus spread, over the tops of the clattery denizens of the cassias to the flowering gums, across the fence to the oleanders along Walton Street's sidewalks, and into the row of camphor laurels between Mary Horton's and Emily Parker's back gardens.

The toiling builders hardly noticed the cicadas until they had to shout to each other, scooping trowel-loads of concrete from the big heap Tim Melville kept replenishing and throwing them—*slurp!*—against the chipped red brick sides of the Old Girl's bungalow. The sleepout was finished, all save a final coat of stucco; bare backs bending and straightening in the swing and rhythm of hard labor, the builders flowed steadily up and around the house, bones basking in the wonderful warmth of summer, sweat drying before it had a chance to bead on their silky brown skins. Bill Naismith slapped wet concrete on the bricks, Mick Devine smoothed the splashes into a continuous sheet of coarse-grained, greenish plaster, and behind him Jim Irvine slithered along a rickety scaffold, sweeping his shaping trowel back and forth in easy curves that imparted a swirling series of arcs to the surface. Harry Markham, eyes everywhere, glanced at his watch and shouted for Tim.

"Oy, mate, go inside and ask the Old Girl if you can put the billy on, will you?" Harry yelled when he gained Tim's attention.

Tim parked his wheelbarrow in the side passage, gathered the gallon-capacity tin billycan and the box of supplies into his arms, and kicked a query of admission on the back door.

Mrs. Parker appeared a moment later, a shadowy lump behind the veiling darkness of the fly-screening.

"Oh, it's you, is it, love?" she asked, opening the door. "Come in, come in! I suppose you want me to boil a kettle for them 'orrible warts outside, do yer?" she went on, lighting a cigarette and leering appreciatively at him as he stood blinking in the gloom, sun-blinded.

"Yes, please, Mrs. Parker," Tim said politely, smiling.

"Well, all right then, I suppose I don't have much choice, do I, not if I want me house finished before the weekend? Sit yourself down while the kettle boils, love."

She moved around the kitchen sloppily, her salt-and-pepper hair crimped into an impossible battery of waves, her uncorseted figure swathed in a cotton housedress of purple and yellow pansies.

"Want a bikkie, love?" she asked, extending the cookie jar. "I got some real grouse choccy ones in there."

"Yes, please, Mrs. Parker," Tim smiled, pawing in the jar until his hand closed on a very chocolatey cookie.

He sat silently on the chair while the Old Girl took his can of supplies from him and spooned a good quarter of a pound of loose tea into the billycan. When the kettle boiled she half-filled the billycan, then put the kettle on to boil again while Tim set out battered enamel mugs on the kitchen table and stood a bottle of milk and a jar of sugar alongside them.

"Here, pet, wipe yer hands on the tea towel like a good bloke, will yer?" the Old Girl asked as Tim left a brown smear of chocolate on the table edge.

She went to the back door, stuck her head outside and bawled, "Smoke-oh!" at the top of her voice.

Tim poured himself a mug of coal-black, milkless tea, then added so much sugar to it that it slopped over the top of the mug onto the table and set the Old Girl clucking again.

"Christ, you're a grub!" she grinned at him forgivingly. "I wouldn't put up with it from them other bots, but you can't help it, can you, love?"

Tim smiled at her warmly, picked up his cup and carried it outside as the other men began to come into the kitchen.

They ate at the back of the house, where it began to curve around the newly erected sleepout. It was a shady spot, far enough from the garbage cans to be comparatively free of flies, and they had each arranged a small, flat-topped cairn of bricks to sit on while they ate. The camphor laurels between Miss Horton's backyard and Mrs. Parker's leaned over them thickly, with a shade dense enough to make resting there a pleasure after working in the baking sun. Each man sat down with his mug of tea in one hand and his brown paper bag of food in the other, stretching his legs out with a sigh and snorting the flies away.

Since they started work at seven and finished at three, this morning break occurred at nine, followed by lunch at eleven-thirty. Traditionally the nine o'clock pause was referred to as "smoke-oh," and occupied about half an hour. Engaged in heavy manual labor, they ate with enormous appetite, though they had little to show for it on their spare, muscular frames. A

13

breakfast of hot porridge, fried chops or sausages with two or three fried eggs, several cups of tea, and slices of toast started each man's day off around five-thirty; during smoke-oh they consumed home-made sandwiches and slabs of cake, and for lunch the same, only twice as much. There was no afternoon break; at three they were gone, working shorts thrust into their oddly medical-looking little brown bags, once more clad in open-necked shirts and thin cotton trousers as they headed for the pub. Each day led inexorably to this, its culmination and high point; within the buzzing, latrine-like interior of a pub they could relax with a foot on the bar rail and a brimming fifteen-ounce schooner of beer in one fist, yarning with work-mates and pub cronies and flirting sterilely with the hard-faced barmaids. Homecoming was total anticlimax after this, a half-surly submission to the cramping pettiness of women and off-spring.

There was a rather tense, expectant air about the men this morning as they sat down to enjoy their smoke-oh. Mick Devine and his boon companion Bill Naismith sat side by side against the high paling fence, mugs at their feet and food spread out in their laps; Harry Markham and Jim Irvine faced them, with Tim Melville nearest to the back door of the Old Girl's house, so he could fetch and carry when the others demanded. As junior member of the team, his was the position of menial and general dogsbody; on Harry's books his official title was "Builder's La-borer," and he had been with Harry for ten of his twenty-five years without promotion.

"Hey, Tim, what youse got on yer sandwiches this morning?" Mick asked, winking heavily at the others.

"Gee, Mick, the same as always, jam," Tim answered, holding up untidily hacked white bread with thick amber jam oozing out its edges.

"What sorta jam?" Mick persisted, eyeing his own sandwich unenthusiastically.

"Apricot, I think."

"Wanta swap? I got sausages on mine."

Tim's face lit up. "Sausages! Oh, I love sausage sandwiches! I'll swap!"

The exchange was made; Mick bit clumsily into the apricot jam sandwich while Tim, oblivious of the grinning regard of the others, disposed of Mick's sausage sandwich in a few bites. He had the last wedge poised to eat when Mick, shoulders shaking with suppressed laughter, reached out a hand and grasped his wrist.

The blue eyes lifted to Mick's face in a helpless, childish question, fear lurking in them; his sad mouth dropped slackly open.

"What's the matter, Mick?" he asked.

"That bloody sausage sandwich didn't even touch the sides, mate. How did it taste, or didn't you keep it in yer mouth long enough to find out, eh?"

The tiny crease to the left side of Tim's mouth quivered into being again as he closed his mouth and looked at Mick in apprehensive wonder.

"It was all right, Mick," he said slowly. "It tasted a bit different, but it was all right."

Mick roared, and in a moment they were all writhing in paroxysms of laughter, tears running down their faces, hands slapping at aching sides, gasping for breath.

"Oh, Christ, Tim, you're the dizzy limit! Harry thinks you're worth at least sixty cents in the quid, but I said you weren't worth more than ten, and after this effort I reckon I'm right. You couldn't possibly be worth more than ten cents in the quid, mate!"

"What's the matter?" Tim asked, bewildered. "What did I do? I know I'm not the full quid, Mick, honest I do!"

"If yer sandwich didn't taste like sausage, Tim, what did it taste like?" Mick grinned.

15

"Well, I dunno. . . ." Tim's golden brows knit in fierce concentration. "I dunno! It just tasted different, like."

"Why don't youse open that last bit and take a real good look, mate?"

Tim's square, beautifully shaped hands fumbled with the two fragments of bread and pulled them apart. The last piece of sausage was squashed out of shape, its edges slippery and sticky-looking.

"Smell it!" Mick ordered, glancing around the helpless circle and wiping the tears out of his eyes with the back of his hand.

Tim brought it to his nose; the nostrils twitched and flared, then he put the bread down again and sat looking at them in puzzled wonder. "I dunno what it is," he said pathetically.

"It's a *turd*, you great ding!" Mick answered disgustedly. "Christ, are you dim! You still don't know what it is, even after taking a whiff of it?"

"A turd?" Tim echoed, staring at Mick. "What's a turd, Mick?"

Everyone collapsed in a fresh storm of laughter, while Tim sat with the small remnant of sandwich between his fingers, watching and waiting patiently until someone recovered sufficiently to answer his question.

"A turd, Tim me boy, is a big fat piece of *shit!*" Mick howled.

Tim shivered and gulped, flung the bread away in horror and sat wringing his hands together, shrinking into himself. They all moved away from his vicinity hastily, thinking he might vomit, but he did not; he just sat staring at them, grief-stricken.

It had happened again. He had made everyone laugh by doing something silly, but he didn't know what it was, why it was so funny. His father would have said he ought to be a "wakeup," whatever that meant, but he hadn't been a wakeup, he had happily eaten a sausage sandwich that hadn't been a sausage sandwich. A piece of shit, they said it was, but how could he know what a piece of shit tasted like, when he had never eaten it before? What was so funny? He wished he knew; he hungered to know, to share in their laughter and understand. That was always the greatest sorrow, that he could never seem to understand.

His wide blue eyes filled with tears, his face twisted up in anguish and he began to cry like a small child, bellowing noisily, still wringing his hands together and shrinking away from them.

"Jesus bloody Christ, what a lot of bastards you dirty buggers are!" the Old Girl roared, erupting from her back door like a harpy, yellow and purple pansies swirling about her. She came across to Tim and took his hands, pulling him to his feet as she glared around at the sobering men. "Come on, love, you come inside with me a little minute while I give you something nice to take the nasty taste away," she soothed, patting his hands and stroking his hair. "As for you lot," she hissed, sticking her face up to Mick so viciously that he backed away, "I hope you all fall down a manhole arse-first onto a nice iron spike! You oughta be horse-whipped for doing something like this, you great myopic gits! You'd better see this job is finished today, Harry Markham, or it won't be finished at all! I never want to see you lot again!"

Clucking and soothing, she led Tim inside and left the men standing staring at each other.

Mick shrugged. "Bloody women!" he said. "I never met a woman yet what had a sense of humor. Come on, let's get this job finished today, I'm sick of it too."

Mrs. Parker led Tim into the kitchen and sat him on a chair.

"You poor flaming little coot," she said, moving to the refrigerator. "I dunno why men think it's so bloody funny to bait dimwits and dogs. Listen to 'em out there, yahaing and yawhawing, real funny! I'd like to bake 'em a dirty great chocolate cake and flavor it with shit, since they think it's so bloody funny! You, you poor little bugger, didn't even throw it up again, but they'd be spewing for an hour, the walloping great heroes!" She turned to look at him, softening because he still wept, the big

17

tears spilling down his cheeks as he hiccoughed and snuffled miserably. "Oh, here, stop it!" she said, pulling a tissue out of a box and taking his chin in her hand. "Blow yer nose, booby!"

He did as he was told, then suffered her ungentle ministrations as she tidied up his face.

"Christ, what a waste!" she said, half to herself, looking at his face, then she threw the tissue into the kitchen tidy and shrugged. "Oh, well, that's the way it goes, I suppose. Can't have everything, even the biggest and best of us, eh, love?" She patted his cheek with one ropey old hand. "Now what do you like best, love, ice cream with choccy syrup all over it, or a big bit of jam pud with cold banana custard all over it?"

He stopped sniffling long enough to smile radiantly. "Oh, jam pud, please, Mrs. Parker! I love jam pud and cold banana custard, it's my favorite!"

She sat opposite him at the kitchen table while he shoveled the pudding into his mouth in huge spoonfuls, chiding him for eating too fast and telling him to mind his manners.

"Chew with yer mouth closed, love, it's 'orrible looking at someone slopping their food around in an open mouth. And take yer elbows off the table, like a good boy."

Four

Mary Horton put her car in the garage at six-thirty that evening, so tired that she could hardly walk the few feet to her front door without her knees trembling. She had pushed herself furiously all day long, and succeeded in deadening all sensations save weariness. Mrs. Parker's house was evidently finished; the red brick exterior had entirely gone, replaced by wet, green-gray stucco. The phone began to ring as she closed the front door, and she ran to answer it.

"Miss Horton, that you?" rasped her neighbor's voice. "It's Emily Parker here, pet. Listen, can you do something for me?"

"Certainly."

"I've got to go out now, me son's just rung from Central and I've got to go and pick him up there. The builders finished this arvo, but there's still a lot of their stuff in the backyard, and Harry said he was coming back to clean it up. Just keep an eye on things for me, will youse?"

"Certainly, Mrs. Parker."

"Ta, love! Hooroo, see youse tomorrow."

Mary sighed in exasperation. All she wanted was to sit down in her easy chair by the picture window, put her feet up with her before-dinner sherry and read the *Sydney Morning Herald*, as was her nightly custom. She went through to the living room and opened her liquor cabinet tiredly. Her glassware was all Waterford hobnail, exquisitely graceful, and she took one of the long-stemmed sherry glasses from its place on a polished shelf. Her preference was for a medium-sweet sherry, which she mixed herself by pouring half a glass of dry Amontillado and topping it up with a very sweet sherry. The ritual completed, she carried the glass through to the kitchen, and then out onto her back terrace.

Her house was better designed than Mrs. Parker's; instead of a back veranda she had a high, wide patio of sandstone flags, which fell away on three sides as a terraced rock garden to the lawn fifteen feet below. It was very pretty and in the heat of summer very cool, for an overhead trellis covered one side of it completely with a roof of grapevine and wistaria. In summer she could sit beneath the thick green canopy, shielded from the sun; in winter she could sit under bare gnarled branches and let the sun warm her; in spring the lilac clusters of wistaria made it stunningly beautiful, and in late summer and autumn the trellis hung heavy with great bunches of table grapes, red and white and purple.

She walked soundlessly across the flagstones in her neat black shoes, for she was a cat-footed kind of person and liked to approach people silently so she could see them before they saw her. It was sometimes very useful to catch people off guard.

At the far edge of the patio was a balustrade of white-painted wrought iron in a grape pattern, just two or three feet of it on either side of a flight of steps leading down to the sweeping stretch of lawn below. Noiseless as always, she stood with her glass balanced on the top of the balustrade and looked toward Mrs. Parker's backyard.

The sun was dying down to the horizon of the western sky, which she faced, and had she been the kind of person whom beauty moved, she would have been awe-struck at the prospect before her. Between her back terrace and the Blue Mountains twenty miles away there was nothing higher; even the hills of Ryde did not obstruct her outlook but rather enhanced it, lending it a mid-distance perspective. It had been well over the hundred during the afternoon and even now was close to that, so there were no clouds in the sky to score a splendid end to the day. But the light itself was beautiful, deep yellow and faintly bronzing, tinting the greenest things more green and everything else amber. Mary shaded a hand over her eyes and scanned Mrs. Parker's backyard.

The young man of the morning was sweeping a cloudy heap of cement dust toward a pile of trash and builder's remains, golden head bent absorbed over the simple task, as if he liked to give everything, even this, all his attention. He was still half-naked, still as beautiful, perhaps even more beautiful in the last limpid light than he had been in the first prickling sharpness of day. Drink forgotten, Mary stood in lost loneliness watching him, not aware of herself, not conscious that she was possessed by an emotion alien to her whole being, neither guilty nor confounded. She simply watched him.

The sweeping finished, he lifted his head and saw her, waved a cheery hand in her direction, then disappeared. Mary jumped, heart in mouth, and before she could stop herself she had crossed to the row of camphor laurels between the two back gardens and was slipping through a space in the paling fence.

He had evidently completed whatever he had been set to do, for he had his workman's bag in his hand and was pulling his street clothes out of it.

"Hullo," he said, smiling at her without a shadow of self-awareness, as if he had no idea of his own beauty or of its inevitable impact on others.

"Hullo," Mary replied, not smiling; something wet touched her hand, and she glanced down to see her sherry slopping over the rim of the forgotten glass.

21

"You're spilling your drink," he observed.

"Yes, isn't that idiotic of me?" she ventured, trying to fix her features into a pleasant mask.

He had no answer for that, but stood watching her in his bright, interested way, and smiling.

"Would you like to earn a little extra money?" Mary inquired eventually, staring at him searchingly.

He looked puzzled. "Eh?"

She flushed, her dark eyes surveying him a little ironically. "My grass needs cutting badly and my man hasn't been in a month, I doubt if I'll ever see him again. I'm very proud of my garden and I hate to see it like this, but it's extremely difficult to get someone to cut the grass. So I thought, seeing you here working overtime on a Friday, that you might be in need of a little extra money. Would you be able to come tomorrow and cut my grass? I have a tractor mower, so it's really more a question of time than effort."

"Eh?" he repeated, still smiling, but not quite so broadly.

She twitched her shoulders impatiently. "Oh, for heaven's sake! If you don't want the work, say so! I merely want to know if you'd like to come and cut my grass tomorrow. I'll pay you more than Mr. Markham does."

He walked across to the gap in the paling fence and peered through into her yard curiously, then nodded. "Yes, it does need cutting, doesn't it? I can cut it for you."

She slipped back through to her own side of the fence and turned to face him. "Thank you. I appreciate it, and I assure you I'll make it well worth your while. Just come to the back door tomorrow morning and I'll give you your instructions."

"All right, Missus," he answered gravely.

"Don't you want to know my name?" she asked.

"I suppose so," he smiled.

His veneer of permanent amusement flicked her on the raw, and she flushed again. "My name is Miss Horton!" she snapped. "What's your name, young man?"

"Tim Melville."

"Then I'll see you tomorrow morning, Mr. Melville. Goodbye, and thank you."

"Bye bye," he said, smiling.

When she turned at the top of her patio steps to look back into Mrs. Parker's yard, he had gone. Her sherry had gone too, the last of it spilled when she absently turned the glass upside down in her hurry to escape that innocent blue gaze.

Five

The Seaside Hotel was a very popular drinking place among the citizens of Randwick. They came to it from all parts of the big, sprawling suburb, from Randwick proper and Coogee and Clovelly and even Maroubra. It served an excellent brand of beer, beautifully chilled, and there was plenty of room to spread, but whatever the reason for its popularity, there was not a moment of its opening life that was not busy and cheerful with the noises of contented beer drinkers. Several stories high, it had walls of pure white stucco, and between them and its Alhambra-like row of arches across the front, it looked something like a massive hacienda. Perched two hundred feet above the ocean that lay in front of it and not half a mile away, it commanded a magnificent view of Coogee Beach, one of the smaller surfing beaches in the eastern suburbs. Most of the drinkers stood outside the public bar on the long red veranda, which was plunged into deep shade from three in the afternoon. On a hot evening it was a perfect spot to drink, for the sun set behind the hill at the back of the pub, and the sea breeze puffed in off the luminous blue Pacific without a thing to hinder it.

Ron Melville was standing on the veranda with his two best drinking mates, his eyes alternating between his watch and the beach far below. Tim was late; it was nearly eight o'clock and he ought to have been there by six-thirty at the outside. Ron was more annoyed than worried, for long experience had taught him that worrying over Tim was a good way to train for an early heart attack.

The short Sydney twilight was at its peak, and the Norfolk Island pines bordering the sandstone beach promenade had turned from dark green to black. The tide was coming in and the surf was getting up into a roar, spreading itself in a spent sheet of bubbles far up the sloping white sand, and the shadows were slipping further and further out across the water. The buses came down the hill alongside the beach park, and the bus stop was on the corner far below; Ron watched a bus squeal to a halt at the stop and passed his eyes over the disembarking passengers, looking for Tim's unmistakable yellow head. It was there, so Ron turned away immediately.

"There's Tim on that bus, so I think I'll go in and get him a beer. Another round?" he asked casually.

By the time he emerged again the street lights were turned on, and Tim was standing smiling at Ron's mates.

"Hullo, Pop," he said to Ron, smiling.

"G'day, mate, where've you been?" his father demanded sourly.

"I had to finish up a job. Harry didn't want to come back on Monday."

"Well, we can do with the overtime."

"I got another job, too," Tim said importantly as he took the glass of beer from his father and downed it in one long gulp. "That was great! Can I have another one, Pop?"

"In a minute. What other job?"

"Oh, that! The lady next door wants me to cut her grass tomorrow."

"Next door to who?"

"Next door to where we were today."

Curly Campbell sniggered. "Did youse ask her where she wanted her grass cut, Tim? Inside or outside?"

"Shut up, Curly, you drongo!" Ron snarled irritably. "You know Tim don't understand that sort of talk!"

"Her grass is too long and it needs cutting," Tim explained.

"Did you say you'd do it, Tim?" Ron asked.

"Yes, tomorrow morning. She said she was going to pay me, so I thought you wouldn't mind."

Ron stared at his son's exquisite face cynically. If the lady in question had any ideas, five minutes with Tim would squelch them. Nothing cooled their ardor faster than discovering Tim wasn't the full quid, or, if that didn't turn them off, they soon found out that trying to seduce Tim was a lost cause, since he had no concept of what women were for or about. Ron had trained his son to flee the moment a woman got too excited or tried some sexy little come-on; Tim was very susceptible to a suggestion of fear, and he could be taught to fear anything.

"Can I have another beer, Pop?" Tim asked again.

"Righto, son. Go and ask Florrie for a schooner. I reckon you've earned it."

Curly Campbell and Dave O'Brien watched his tall, slender form disappear under the arches.

"I've known youse for twenty bloody years, Ron," Curly said, "and I still haven't worked out who Tim gets his looks from."

Ron grinned. "I dunno either, mate. Tim's a throwback to someone we've never heard of, I reckon."

The Melvilles, *père et fils*, left the Seaside a little before nine and walked briskly down past Coogee Oval to the row of brightly lit milk bars, fun parlors, and wine shops at the far end of the beach park. Ron herded his son past them quickly as they cut from Arden Street across to Surf Street, making sure that the hungry glances Tim evoked in the lolling tarts and trollops had no chance to develop.

The Melville house was in Surf Street but not in the post

26

section on top of the hill, where Nobby Clark the jockey lived. They walked up the one-in-three pitch of the incredibly steep hill easily, neither of them so much as breathing heavily, for they both worked in the building trade and were in superb physical condition. Halfway down the other side of the hill in the hollow which lay between the ritzy top and the far hump of Clovelly Road they turned into the side gate of a very ordinary brick semi-detached house.

The female Melvilles had long since eaten, but as Ron and Tim let themselves in the back door Esme Melville came out of the living room and met them in the kitchen.

"Your dinner's ruined," she said, without much indignation.

"Go on, Es, you always say that," Ron grinned, sitting down at the kitchen table, where his place and Tim's still lay undisturbed. "What's to eat?"

"As if you care when you're full of beer," Esme retorted. "It's Friday, mug! What do youse always eat on Friday, eh? I got fish and chips from the Dago's as usual."

"Oh, goody! Fish and chips!" Tim exclaimed, beaming. "Gee, Mum, I love fish and chips!"

His mother looked at him tenderly, ruffling his thick hair in the only kind of caress she ever gave him. "It wouldn't matter what I gave you, love, you'd still think it was your favorite. Here youse are."

She slapped heaped plates of greasy, batter-coated fish and soft, very un-crisp French fries in front of her men and went back to the living room, where the television set was in the middle of the umpteenth re-run of *Coronation Street.* That glimpse of English working-class life was fascinating, and she loved it; she would sit there thinking of her nice big house and garden and the fine weather and the tennis and the beach, pitying the inhabitants of Coronation Street from the bottom of her heart. If you had to be working-class, Aussie working-class was the only one to be.

Tim didn't tell his mother and father about eating the turd sandwich, because he had forgotten all about it; when he finished his fish and chips he and his father left their empty plates on the table and entered the living room.

"Come on, Es, it's time for the cricket summary," Ron said, switching channels.

His wife sighed. "I wish you'd stay out a bit longer, then I might get to see a Joan Crawford picture or something instead of sport, sport, sport!"

"Well, if Tim gets a bit more part-time work, love, I'll buy youse your own TV set," Ron rejoined, kicking his shoes off and stretching himself out full-length on the sofa. "Where's Dawnie?"

"Out with some fella, I suppose."

"What one this time?"

"How the hell do I know, love? I never worry about her, she's too smart to get into trouble."

Ron looked at his son. "Ain't it the dizzy limit, Es, the way life turns out? We got the best looking boy in Sydney and he's about fourpence in the quid, then we go and get Dawnie. There's him, can only sign his name and count to ten, and Dawnie so clever she can win university gold medals without even studying."

Esme picked up her knitting, looking at Ron sadly. He felt it, poor old Ron, but in his own way he'd been real good to Tim, watched out for him without treading on him or treating him like a baby. Didn't he let the boy drink with him, hadn't he insisted Tim should earn his own bread like any normal boy? It was just as well, because they weren't as young as they used to be. Ron was almost seventy and she was only six months behind him. That was why Tim had been born simple, the doctors told her. He was twenty-five now, and he was the first-born. Well over forty, she and Ron were when he was born; the doctors said it was something to do with her ovaries being tired and out of practice. Then a year later Dawnie was born, perfectly nor-

28

mal, which was how it went, the doctors said. The first one was usually the hardest hit when a woman began having children at over forty years of age.

She let her eyes dwell on Tim as he sat in his own special chair by the far wall, closer to the TV than any of the other chairs: like a small child, he liked to be in the middle of the picture. There he sat, the loveliest, sweetest boy, eyes shining as he applauded a cricketing run; she sighed, wondering for the millionth time what would become of him after she and Ron were dead. Dawnie would have to see to him, of course. She was devotedly fond of her brother, but in the normal way of things she would get tired of studying one day and decide to marry instead, and then would her husband want someone like Tim around? Esme doubted it very much. Who wanted a grown-up five-year-old kid if he wasn't their own flesh and blood?

Six

Saturday was just as fine and hot as Friday had been, so Tim set off for Artarmon at six in the morning wearing a short-sleeved sports shirt and tailored shorts with knee socks. His mother always looked out what clothes he was to wear, cooked his breakfast and packed his daytime food, made sure his bag contained a clean pair of work shorts and that he had enough money to see him through any possible difficulty.

When Tim knocked on Mary Horton's door it was just seven, and she was sound asleep. She stumbled, bare-footed, through the house, wrapping a dark gray robe around her sensible white cotton pajamas, pushing the few stray wisps of hair away from her face impatiently.

"My goodness, do you always arrive at seven in the morning?" she muttered, blinking the sleep out of her eyes.

"That's when I'm supposed to start work," he replied, smiling.

"Well, since you're here I'd better show you what to do," Mary decided, leading him down the patio steps and across the lawn to a little fern-house.

The ferns disguised the fact that it was actually a repository for gardening equipment, tools, and fertilizers. A small, urban-looking tractor was parked neatly inside the door, covered with a waterproof cloth in case the roof ever leaked, which of course it didn't, since it belonged to Mary Horton.

"Here's the tractor, and it's got the mower already attached. Can you operate it?"

Tim took the cover off and stroked the tractor's shiny surface lovingly. "Oh, it's a beaut!"

Mary suppressed her impatience. "Beaut or not, can you work it, Mr. Melville?"

"Oh, yes! Pop says I'm awfully good with machinery."

"Isn't that nice?" she remarked waspishly. "Is there anything else you're likely to need, Mr. Melville?"

The blue eyes regarded her with puzzled wonder. "Why do you keep calling me Mr. Melville?" he asked. "Mr. Melville is my father! I'm just Tim."

"Heavens!" she thought, "he's a child!," but she said, "Well, I'll leave you to it. If you need anything, just knock on the back door."

"Righto, Missus!" he said cheerfully, smiling.

"I'm not a Missus!" she snapped. "My name is Horton, *Miss* Horton!"

"Righto, Miss Horton," he amended happily, not at all disconcerted.

By the time she returned inside she was wide awake, and had abandoned any thought of snatching two or three more hours in bed. In a moment he would start the tractor, and that would be the end of it. The house was centrally air conditioned, so was cool and dry no matter what the humidity and temperature outside were, but as she got herself some toast and tea Mary decided that it would be very pleasant to eat on the terrace, where she could keep an eye on her new gardener.

When she carried her little tray out she was fully dressed in her weekend at-home uniform of a plain dark gray cotton dress, as creaseless and perfect as everything about her always was.

31

Her hair, which she wore in a long braid for sleeping, was dragged into its daytime bun. Mary never wore slippers or sandals, even when she was at her beach cottage near Gosford; the moment she got out of bed she dressed, which meant support stockings and stout black shoes.

The mower had been purring smoothly from the backyard for twenty minutes when she sat down at a white-painted wrought-iron table by the balustrade and poured herself a cup of tea. Tim was working down at the far end where the yard tipped over into the brick pit, and he was going about it as slowly and methodically as he had seemed to work for Harry Markham, getting down from the tractor as he completed a strip to make sure the next one would overlap it. She sat munching toast and sipping tea, her eyes never leaving his distant figure. Since she was not given to self-analysis or even to mild introspection, it did not occur to her to wonder why she watched him so fixedly; it was enough to realize that he fascinated her. Not for one moment did she think of her fascination as attraction.

"G'day there, Miss Horton!" came the raucous voice of Mrs. Parker, and the next moment the Old Girl flopped her violently colored body into the spare chair.

"Good morning, Mrs. Parker. Would you care for a cup of tea?" Mary said, rather coldly.

"Ta, love, that sounds real nice. No, don't get up, I can find another cup meself."

"No, please don't. I have to freshen up the tea anyway."

When she returned to the patio with a new pot of tea and some more toast Mrs. Parker was sitting with her chin in her hand, watching Tim.

"That was a good idea, getting Tim to mow yer lawn. I noticed yer usual bloke hasn't been for a while. That's where I'm lucky. One of me sons always comes over to mow me lawn, but you've got no one, eh?"

"Well, I did as you asked yesterday and checked to see that everything was all right regarding the builders and their mess. That was when I met Tim, who seemed to have been left to clean up on his own. He was quite grateful for the offer of a little extra money, I think."

Mrs. Parker disregarded the last part of Mary's statement. "If that ain't typical of them rotten buggers!" she snarled. "Not content to make the poor little blighter's life a misery during the day, but scooted off to the pub and left him to do their dirty work! They had the hide to tell me they was all coming back to clean up! I've a good mind to knock a couple of hundred quid off of Mr. Harry Markham's bill!"

Mary put down her teacup and stared at Mrs. Parker, puzzled. "What makes you so indignant, Mrs. Parker?"

The yellow and purple pansies swathing Mrs. Parker's ample bosom heaved. "Well, wouldn't you be? Oh, I forgot, I didn't see youse last night to tell youse what those miserable bastards did to the poor little bloke, did I? Sometimes I swear I could kill every man that was ever born! They don't seem to have a skerick of sympathy or understanding for the underdog, unless of course he's a drunk or a no-hoper like themselves. But someone like Tim, what does a decent day's work and keeps his end up, they don't feel any pity for him at all. He's their butt, their whipping boy, and the poor little coot's too dill-brained to realize it! He can't help it if he was born simple, now can he? A terrible shame, though, ain't it? Fancy a boy what looks like him not being the full quid! I could cry! Well, anyway, wait until I tell you what they did to him yestiddy morning at smoke-oh. . . ."

Mrs. Parker's nasal, common voice whined on as she told Mary her horrible little story, but Mary only half-listened, her eyes riveted on the bent golden head at the bottom of her yard.

Last night before she had gone to bed she had culled the shelves of her library, searching for a face that looked like his.

Botticelli? she wondered, and finding some of his reproductions in a book she dismissed the artist contemptuously. Those faces were too soft, too feminine, too subtly cunning and feline. In the end she had given up the search, quite unsatisfied. Only in the ancient Greek and Roman statues had she found some hint of Tim, perhaps because his kind of beauty was better illustrated in stone than on canvas. He was a three-dimensional creature. And she had wished bitterly that in her ungifted hands there had resided the skill to immortalize him.

She was conscious of a terrible, crushing disappointment, a desire to weep: Mrs. Parker's presence had faded to the back of her thoughts. It was a kind of ironic anticlimax to discover now that Tim's tragic mouth and wistful, wondering eyes led inward to a nothing, that his spark had been snuffed out of existence long before there could possibly have been tragedy or loss. He was no better than a dog or a cat, which one kept because it was good to look upon and blindly, lovingly faithful. But it could not think, it could never answer intelligently and draw out a shivering response in another questing mind. All the beast did was sit there, smiling and loving. As did Tim, Tim the simpleton. Tricked into eating excrement, he had not vomited it as any thinking being must; he had cried instead, as a dog would have howled, and been cajoled back into smiling again by the prospect of something good to eat.

Childless, loveless, destitute of any humanizing influence, Mary Horton had no emotional yardstick whereby to measure this new, frightening concept of a mindless Tim. As retarded emotionally as he was intellectually, she did not know that Tim could be loved because of his stunted mental growth, let alone in spite of it. She had thought of him the way Socrates must have thought of Alcibiades, the aging, unlovely philosopher confronted with a youth of surpassing physical and intellectual beauty. She had imagined herself introducing him to Beethoven and Proust, expanding his careless young mind until it encompassed music and literature and art, until he was as beautiful within as he was without. But he was a simpleton, a poor, silly half-wit.

They had a pungently evocative way of expressing it, smacking of the earthy callousness so typical of the Australian; they translated intelligence into money, and expressed the one in terms of the other. He who was poorly equipped mentally was "not the full quid"; a value was set upon his intellectual powers, expressed in parts of the dollar or in the vernacular, *quid*. He might be worth as much as ninety cents or as little as nine cents, and still be not the full quid.

Mrs. Parker was not aware that she held only a small part of Mary's attention, and chattered on happily about the insensitivity of the average male, drank several cups of tea, and answered her own queries when Mary did not. At length she heaved herself to her feet and took her leave.

"Cheery-bye, pet, and thanks for the cuppa tea. If you don't have anything he'd fancy in yer fridge, send him across to me and I'll feed him."

Mary nodded absently. Her visitor disappeared down the steps, while she returned to her contemplation of Tim. Glancing at her watch she saw the time was creeping on toward nine, and remembered that these outdoor workmen liked their morning tea around nine. She went inside and made a fresh pot, thawed a frozen chocolate cake and covered it with freshly whipped cream.

"Tim!" she called, putting down her tray on the table under the vines; the sun was stealing across the ridge of the roof, and the table by the steps was getting too hot for comfort.

He looked up, waved to her and stopped the tractor immediately to hear what she was saying.

"Tim, come and have a cup of tea!"

His face lit up with puppyish eagerness; he bounded off the tractor and up the yard, dived into the little fern-house, reappeared with a brown paper bag, and took the back steps two at a time.

"Gee, thanks for calling me, Miss Horton, I wasn't caught up with the time," he said happily, sitting down in the chair she indicated and waiting docilely until she told him he might begin.

"Can you tell the time, Tim?" she asked gently, amazed that she could ask gently.

"Oh, no, not really. I sort of know when it's time to go home, that's when the big hand's at the top and the little hand is three thingies behind it. Three o'clock. But I don't have a watch of my own, because Pop says I'd lose it. I don't worry. Someone always tells me the time, like when it's time to make the tea for smoke-oh or break for lunch or go home. I'm not the full quid, but everyone knows I'm not, so it doesn't matter."

"No, I suppose it doesn't," she answered sadly. "Eat up, Tim, the cake's all for you."

"Oh, goody! I love choccy cake, especially with lots of cream on it like this one! Thanks, Miss Horton!"

"How do you like your tea, Tim?"

"No milk and lots of sugar."

"Lots of sugar? How much is that?"

He looked up at her, frowning, cream all over his face. "Gosh, I can't remember. I just sort of fill it up until it spills into the saucer, then I know it's all right."

"Did you ever go to school, Tim?" she probed, beginning to be interested in him again.

"For a little while. But I couldn't learn, so they didn't make me keep on going. I stayed home and looked after Mum."

"But you do grasp what's said to you, and you did cope with the tractor all by yourself."

"Some things are real easy, but reading and writing's awful hard, Miss Horton."

Much surprised at herself, she patted his head as she stood

stirring his tea. "Well, Tim, it doesn't matter."

"That's what Mum says."

He finished all the cake, then remembered he had a sandwich from home and ate that as well, washing the repast down with three big cups of tea.

"Struth, Miss Horton, that was super!" he sighed, smiling at her blissfully.

"My name is Mary, and it's much easier to say Mary than Miss Horton, don't you think? Why don't you call me Mary?"

He looked at her doubtfully. "Are you sure it's all right? Pop says I mustn't call old people anything but Mister or Missus or Miss."

"Sometimes it's permissible, as between friends."

"Eh?"

She tried again, mentally expunging all polysyllables from her vocabulary. "I'm not really all that old, Tim, it's just this white hair of mine that makes me seem so old. I don't think your Pop would mind if you called me Mary."

"Doesn't your hair mean you're old, Mary? I always thought it did! Pop's hair is white and so is Mum's, and I know they're old."

"He's twenty-five," she thought, "so his Pop and Mum are probably only slightly older than I am," but she said, "Well, I'm younger than they are, so I'm not quite old yet."

He got to his feet. "It's time for me to go back to work. You've got an awful lot of lawn, Mary. I hope I finish it in time."

"Well, if you don't, there are plenty of other days. You can come some other time and finish it, if you'd like to."

He considered the problem gravely. "I think I'd like to come back, as long as Pop says I can." He smiled at her. "I like you, Mary, I like you better than Mick and Harry and Jim and Bill and Curly and Dave. I like you better than anyone except Pop and Mum and my Dawnie. You're pretty, you've got such lovely white hair."

Mary struggled with a hundred indefinable emotions rushing in on her from all sides, and managed to smile. "Why, thank you, Tim, that's very nice of you."

"Oh, think nothing of it," he said nonchalantly, and hopped down the stairs with his hands flapping at each side of his head and his behind poking out. "That was my special imitation of a rabbit!" he called from the lawn.

"It was very good, Tim, I knew you were a rabbit the minute you started hopping," she replied. She gathered up the tea things and carried them inside.

She found it terribly hard to alter her conversation to a toddler level, for Mary Horton had never had anything to do with children since she ceased being a child herself, and she had never really been young anyway. But she was perceptive enough to sense that Tim could be easily hurt, that she had to mind what she said to him, control her temper and her exasperation, that if she let him feel the sting of her tongue he would divine the tenor of the statement if not the actual words. Remembering how she had snapped at him the previous day when he had been, as she thought at the time, deliberately obtuse, she was mortified. Poor Tim, so utterly unaware of the nuances and undercurrents of adult conversation, and so completely vulnerable. He liked her; he thought she was pretty because she had white hair, as did his mother and father.

How could his mouth be so sad, when he knew so little and functioned on such a limited scale?

She got her car out and went down to the supermarket to shop before lunch, since she had nothing in the house that would appeal to him. The chocolate cake was her emergency entertaining fund, the cream a fortuitous mistake on her milkman's part. Tim had brought his lunch with him, she knew, but perhaps he hadn't enough, or could be charmed by the production of something like hamburgers or hot dogs, children's party fare.

"Have you ever been fishing, Tim?" she asked him over lunch.

"Oh, yes, I love fishing," he replied, beginning on his third hot dog. "Pop takes me fishing sometimes, when he isn't too busy."

"How often is he busy?"

"Well, he goes to the races and the cricket and the football and things like that. I don't go with him because I get sick in crowds, the noise and all the people make my head ache and my tummy go all queer."

"I must take you fishing sometime, then," she said, and left it at that.

By the middle of the afternoon he had finished the backyard and came to ask about the front. She looked at her watch.

"I don't think we'll bother about the front today, Tim, it's nearly time for you to go home. Why don't you come back next Saturday and do the front for me then, if your Pop will let you?"

He nodded happily. "All right, Mary."

"Go and fetch your bag from the fern-house, Tim. You can change in my bathroom, then you'll be able to see if you have everything on properly."

The interior of her house, so chaste and austere, fascinated him. He roamed about the gray-toned living room in his bare feet, digging his toes into the deep wool carpet with an expression of near-ecstasy on his face, and stroking the pearl-gray crushed velvet upholstery.

"Gosh, Mary, I love your house!" he enthused. "It all feels so soft and sort of cool!"

"Come and see my library," she said, wanting to show him her pride and joy so badly that she took him by the hand.

But the library did not impress him in the least; it made him frightened and inclined to be tearful. "All those books!" he shuddered, and would not stay even when he saw that his reaction had disappointed her.

It took her several minutes to coax him out of his odd dread of the library, and she took care not to repeat the mistake by showing him anything else intellectual.

Once recovered from his initial delight and confusion, he evinced a critical faculty, and took her to task for not having any color in the house.

"It feels so lovely, Mary, but it's all the same color!" he protested. "Why isn't there any red? I love red!"

"Can you tell me which color this is?" she asked, holding up a red silk bookmark.

"It's red, of course," he answered scornfully.

"Then I'll see what I can do," she promised.

She gave him an envelope with thirty dollars in it, a much higher wage than any laborer could command in Sydney. "My address and telephone number are written on a piece of paper inside," she instructed him, "and I want you to give it to your father when you get home, so that he'll know where I am and how to get in touch with me. Now don't forget to give it to him, will you?"

He gazed at her, hurt. "I never forget anything when I'm told properly," he said.

"I'm sorry, Tim, I didn't mean to hurt you," said Mary Horton, who had never cared whether what she said hurt anyone. Not that she habitually said hurtful things; but Mary Horton avoided saying hurtful things from motives of tact, diplomacy, and good manners, not because she wanted to avoid giving another being pain.

She waved him goodbye from her front stoop, after he had refused to let her drive him to the railway station. Once he had gone a few yards down the street she walked to the front gate and leaned over it to watch him until he disappeared around the corner.

To anyone else in the street watching, he would have seemed

an amazingly handsome young man striding along the road at the height of his health and looks, the world his to command. It was like some divine jest, she thought, the kind of joke the Greek immortals had loved to play on their creation, man, when he got conceited or forgot what was owed to them. The gargantuan laughter Tim Melville must provoke!

Seven

R on was at the Seaside as usual, but early for a Saturday. He had loaded up his portable ice chest with beer and gone off to the cricket match clad in shorts, thong sandals, and a shirt left open all the way down to let in the breeze. But Curly and Dave had not shown up, and somehow the pleasure of lying on the grassy hill in the Sydney cricket ground sleeping in the sun was not the same alone. He stuck it for a couple of hours, but the cricket proceeded at its normal snaily pace and the horses he had backed at Warwick Farm had both come in last, so at about three he had packed up his beer chest and radio, and headed for the Seaside with the unerring instinct of a bloodhound. It would never have occurred to him to go home; Es played tennis with the girls on Saturday afternoons, their local Hit and Giggle Club as he called it, and the house would be deserted with Tim working; Dawnie was off somewhere with one of her Quiz Kid boyfriends.

When Tim turned up a little after four Ron was very pleased to see him, and bought him a schooner of Old.

"How'd it go, mate?" he asked his son as they leaned their backs up against a pillar and stared across the sea.

"The grouse, Pop! Mary's a real nice lady."

"Mary?" Ron peered into Tim's face, startled and concerned.

"Miss Horton. She told me to call her Mary. I was a bit worried, but she said it was all right. It's all right, isn't it, Pop?" he queried anxiously, sensing something unusual in his father's reaction.

"I dunno, mate. What's this Miss Mary Horton like?"

"She's lovely, Pop. She gave me a whole heap of beaut things to eat and showed me all over her house. It's air conditioned, Pop! Her furniture's real nice, so's her carpet, but everything's gray, so I asked her why she didn't have anything red around, and she said she'd see what she could do about it."

"Did she touch you, mate?"

Tim stared at Ron blankly. "Touch me? Gee, I dunno! I suppose she did. She took me by the hand when she was showing me her books." He pulled a face. "I didn't like her books, there were too many of them."

"Is she pretty, mate?"

"Oh, gee, yes! She's got the most lovely white hair, Pop, just like yours and Mum's, only whiter. That's why I didn't know whether it was all right for me to call her Mary, because you and Mum always tell me it isn't polite to call old people by their first name."

Ron relaxed. "Oh!" He slapped his son playfully on the arm. "Struth, you had me worried for a minute there, I tell you. She's an old girl, right?"

"Yes."

"Did she pay you like she promised?"

"Yes, it's here in an envelope. Her name and address is inside. She said I was to give it to you in case you wanted to talk to her. Why would you want to talk to her, Pop? I don't see why you'd want to talk to her."

Ron took the proffered envelope. "I don't want to talk to her, mate. Did youse finish the job?"

"No, she had too much lawn. If it's all right with you, she wants me to do the front garden next Saturday."

There were three crisp, new ten-dollar bills in the envelope; Ron stared at them and at the clear, heavy overtones of authority and education in Mary Horton's handwriting. Silly young girls or lonely housewives didn't have handwriting like that, he decided. Thirty quid for a day's gardening! He put the notes in his own wallet and patted Tim on the back.

"You done good, mate, and you can go back next Saturday and finish her lawn if you want to. In fact, for what she pays you can work for her any time she wants."

"Gee, Pop, thanks!" He wiggled his empty glass from side to side suggestively. "Can I have another beer?"

"Why can't you ever learn to drink it slowly, Tim?"

Tim's face fell into misery. "Oh, gee, I forgot again! I really did mean to drink it slowly, Pop, but it tasted so good I went and forgot."

Ron regretted his momentary exasperation immediately. "No matter, mate, don't let it worry you. Go and ask Florrie for a schooner of Old."

The beer, extremely potent as Australian beer was, seemed to have no effect on Tim. Some dimwits went crazy if they even smelled grog, Ron puzzled, but Tim could drink his old man under the table and then carry him all the way home, he felt it so little.

"Who is this Mary Horton?" Es asked that night, after Tim had been packed off to bed.

"Some old geezer out at Artarmon."

"Tim's very taken with her, isn't he?"

Ron thought of the thirty quid in his wallet and stared at his wife blandly. "I suppose so. She's nice to him, and doing her garden on a Saturday will keep him out of mischief."

"Free you to skip around the pubs and racetracks with the blokes, you mean," Es interpreted with the skill of many years.

"Jesus bloody Christ, Es, what a rotten thing to say to a man!"

"Hah!" she snorted, putting down her knitting. "The truth

hurts, don't it? Did she pay him, eh?"

"A few quid."

"Which you pocketed, of course."

"Well, it wasn't that much. What do you expect for mowing a bloody lawn by machine, you suspicious old twit? No fortune, and that's for bloody sure!"

"As long as I get me housekeeping, I don't give a sweet bugger how much she paid him, mate!" She got up, stretching. "Want a cuppa tea, love?"

"Oh, ta, that'd be real nice. Where's Dawnie?"

"How the hell should I know? She's twenty-four and her own flaming mistress."

"As long as she's not someone else's flaming mistress!"

Es shrugged. "Kids don't think the way we did, love, and there's no getting around it. Besides, are you game to ask Dawnie where she's been and if she's shagging with some bloke?"

Ron followed Es into the kitchen, fondly patting her on the bottom. "Cripes, no! She'd look down that long bloody nose of hers and come out with a string of words I didn't understand, and a man would end up feeling pretty flaming silly."

"I wish God had rationed out the brains a bit more fairly between our kids, Ron, love," Es sighed as she put the kettle on to boil. "If He'd split them down the middle they'd both be all right."

"No use crying over spilt milk, old girl. Got any cake?"

"Fruit or seed?"

"Seed, love."

They sat down on either side of the kitchen table and polished off half a seed cake and six cups of tea between them.

Eight

Self-discipline carried Mary Horton through the week at Constable Steel & Mining as if Tim Melville had not even entered her life. She doffed her clothes before using the lavatory as usual, ran Archie Johnson as well as ever and chewed out a total of seventeen typists, office boys, and clerks. But at home each night she found her books unenticing and spent the time in the kitchen instead, reading recipe books and experimenting with cakes, sauces, and puddings. Judicious pumping of Emily Parker had given her a better idea of Tim's taste in goodies; she wanted to have a varied selection for him when Saturday came.

During one lunch hour she went to a north Sydney interior decorator and bought a very expensive ruby glass coffee table, then found an ottoman in matching ruby crushed velvet. The touch of deep, vibrant color disturbed her at first, but after she got used to it she had to admit that it improved her glacial living room. The bare, pearl-gray walls suddenly looked warmer, and she found herself wondering if Tim, like so many naturals, had an instinctive eye for art. Perhaps one day she could take him around the galleries with her, and see what his eye discovered.

She went to bed very late on Friday night, expecting a phone call any minute from Tim's father to say he didn't want his son hiring himself out as a gardener on precious weekends. But the call never came, and promptly at seven the next morning she was roused from a deep sleep by the sound of Tim's knock. This time she brought him inside immediately, and asked him if he wanted a cup of tea while she dressed.

"No thanks, I'm all right," he replied, blue eyes shining.

"Then you can use the little toilet off the laundry to change in while I get dressed. I want to show you how to do the front garden."

She returned to the kitchen a short time later, cat-footed as always. He did not hear her come in, so she stood silently in the doorway watching him, struck anew by the absoluteness of his beauty. How terrible, how unjust it was, she thought, that such a wonderful shell should house such an unworthy occupant; then she was ashamed. Perhaps that was the *raison d'être* of his beauty, that his progress toward sin and dishonor had been arrested in the innocence of early childhood. Had he matured normally he might have looked quite different, truly a Botticelli then, smugly smiling, with a knowing look lurking behind those clear blue eyes. Tim was not a member of the adult human race at all, except on the sketchiest of premises.

"Come along, Tim, let me show you what's to be done out front," she said at last, breaking the spell.

The cicadas were shrieking and screaming from every bush and tree; Mary put her hands over her ears, grimaced at Tim and then went to her only weapon, the hose.

"This is the worst year for cicadas I can ever remember," she said when the din had subsided somewhat and the heavy oleanders dripped steadily onto the path.

"Breeeek!" gurgled the basso profundo choirmaster, after all the others had ceased.

"There he goes, the old twirp!" Mary went over to the oleander nearest her front door, parting its soggy branches and peering futilely into the cathedral-like recesses of its interior. "I can never find him," she explained, squatting on her haunches and turning her head to smile at Tim, who stood behind her.

"Do you want him?" Tim asked seriously.

"I most certainly do! He starts the whole lot of them off; without him they seem to be dumb."

"I'll get him for you."

He slipped his bare torso in among the leaves and branches easily, disappearing from sight above the waist. He was not wearing boots or socks this morning, since there was no concrete to blister and crack his skin, and wet humus from the grass clung to his legs.

"Breeeeek!" boomed the cicada, drying off enough to begin testing.

"Gotcha!" shouted Tim, scrambling out again with his right hand closed around something.

Mary had never actually seen more of a cicada than its cast-off brown armor in the grass and thus edged up a little fearfully, for like most women she was frightened of spiders and beetles and crawly, cold-blooded things.

"There he is, look at him!" Tim said proudly, opening his fingers gingerly until the cicada was fully exposed, tethered only by Tim's left index finger and thumb on his wing tips.

"Ugh!" Mary shuddered, backing away without really looking.

"Oh, don't be afraid of him, Mary," Tim begged, smiling up at her and stroking the cicada softly. "Look, isn't he lovely, all green and pretty like a butterfly?"

The golden head was bent over the cicada; Mary stared down at them both in sudden, blinding pity. Tim seemed to have some kind of rapport with the creature, for it lay on his palm without panic or fear, and it was indeed beautiful, once one forgot its Martian antennae and lobsterish carapace. It had a fat, bright green body about two inches long, tinted with a powdering of real gold, and its eyes glittered and sparkled like two big

48

topazes. Over its back the delicate, transparent wings were folded still, veined like a leaf with bright yellow gold and shimmering with every color of the rainbow. And above it crouched Tim, just as alien and just as beautiful, as alive and gleaming.

"You don't really want me to kill him, do you?" Tim pleaded, gazing up at her in sudden sadness.

"No," she replied, turning away. "Put him back in his bush, Tim."

By lunchtime he had finished the front lawn. Mary gave him two hamburgers and a heaping pile of chips, then filled his empty corners with a hot steamed jam pudding smothered in hot banana custard.

"I think I'm finished, Mary," Tim said as he drank his third cup of tea. "Gee, but I'm sorry it wasn't a longer job, though." The wide eyes surveyed her mistily. "I like you, Mary," he began. "I like you better than Mick or Harry or Jim or Bill or Curly or Dave, I like you better than anyone except Pop and Mum and my Dawnie."

She patted his hand and smiled at him lovingly. "It's very sweet of you to say that, Tim, but I don't really think it's true, you haven't known me long enough."

"There's no more grass to mow," he sighed, ignoring her refusal to accept the compliment.

"Grass grows again, Tim."

"Eh?" That little interrogative sound was his signal to go slow, that something had been done or said beyond his understanding.

"Can you weed garden beds as well as you can mow a lawn?"

"I reckon I can. I do it for Pop all the time."

"Then would you like to come every Saturday and look after my garden altogether, mow the grass when it needs it, plant seedlings and weed the flower beds, spray the bushes and trim the pathways and put down fertilizer?"

He grasped her hand and shook it, smiling broadly. "Oh,

Mary, I do like you! I'll come every Saturday and I'll look after your garden, I promise I'll look after your garden!"

There were thirty dollars in his envelope when he left that afternoon.

Nine

Tim had been coming for five weeks before Mary Horton phoned his father late on Thursday night. Ron answered the phone himself. "Yeah?" he asked it.

"Good evening, Mr. Melville. This is Mary Horton, Tim's Saturday friend."

Ron pricked up his ears immediately, beckoning Es to join him for a listen. "Oh, nice to hear from you, Miss Horton. How's Tim doing, all right?"

"He's a pleasure to have around, Mr. Melville. I do enjoy his company."

Ron chuckled self-consciously. "From the tales he brings home, I gather he's eating youse out of house and home, Miss Horton."

"No, not at all. It's a pleasure to see him eat, Mr. Melville."

There was an awkward pause, until Ron broke it to say, "What's the matter, Miss Horton? Tim not wanted this week?"

"Well, he is and he isn't, Mr. Melville. The fact of the matter is, I have to go up to Gosford this weekend to see how my summer cottage is getting on. I've neglected it sadly so far, concentrated on the garden at home. Anyway, I was wondering if you'd object to my taking Tim with me, to help me? I could do with some help, and Tim is terrific. It's very quiet out where

I am, and I give you my word he wouldn't be subjected to strangers or undue stress or anything like that. He told me he loved to fish, and the cottage is situated right in the middle of the best fishing for miles around, so I thought perhaps—perhaps he might enjoy it. He seems to like coming to me, and I certainly like his company."

Ron squiggled his eyebrows at Es, who nodded vigorously and took the receiver.

"Hullo, Miss Horton, this is Tim's mother here . . . Yes, I'm very well, thank you, how are you? . . . Oh, that's nice to hear . . . Miss Horton, it's very thoughtful of you to think of inviting Tim to go with you this weekend . . . Yes, he is a bit lonely, it's hard for a poor chap like him, you know . . . I really can't see any reason why Tim couldn't go with you, I think the change would do him good . . . Yes, he does like you an awful lot . . . Let me hand you back to my husband, Miss Horton, and thank you very, very much."

"Miss Horton?" Ron asked, snatching the receiver from his wife. "Well, you heard the Old Woman, it's all right with her, and if it's all right with her it had better be all right with me, ha-ha-ha! Yeah, right you are! Okay, I'll see he packs a bag and gets to your place by seven on this Satiddy morning . . . Right, Miss Horton, thank you very, very much . . . Bye bye now, and ta again."

Mary had planned the sixty-mile trip as a picnic, and had jammed the back of the car with provisions, diversions, and comforts she thought the summer cottage might lack. Tim arrived promptly at seven on Saturday morning. The day was fine and clear, the second weekend in a row that it had not threatened rain, and Mary shepherded Tim out to the garage immediately.

"Hop in, Tim, and make yourself comfortable. Are you all right?"

"All right," he answered.

"My house is not in Gosford itself," she said as the car headed

52

out along the Pacific highway in the direction of Newcastle. "Living and working in the city, I didn't want to have a holiday cottage right in the middle of another crowd of people, so I bought a property quite a way out, on the Hawkesbury near Broken Bay. We have to go into Gosford because the only road to my place starts there, you see.

"My word, how Gosford has grown! I remember it when it used to consist of a pub, a garage, two men, and a dog; now it's jammed with commuters and vacationers, there must be sixty thousand of them at least, it seems. . . ."

She trailed off nervously, glancing sidelong at him in sudden embarrassment. There she was, trying to make conversation with him as though he was somewhat like the person she imagined his mother might be. In his turn he was trying to be an interested auditor, snatching his fascinated glance away from the passing landscape every so often to fix his bright, loving eyes on her profile.

"Poor Tim," she sighed. "Don't take any notice of me, just relax and look out the window."

For a long time after that there was silence. Tim was obviously enjoying the journey, turned side on with his nose almost against the window, not missing a thing, and it made her wonder just how much variety there was in his life, how often he was lifted out of what must be a very humdrum existence.

"Does your father have a car, Tim?"

He didn't bother to turn and face her this time, but continued to look out the window. "No, he says it's a waste of time and money in the city. He says it's much healthier to walk, and much less trouble to catch the bus when you need to ride in something."

"Does anyone ever take you out for a drive?"

"Not very often. I get carsick."

She turned her head to stare at him, alarmed. "How do you feel now? Do you feel sick?"

"No, I feel good. This car doesn't bump me up and down like

53

most cars, and anyway, I'm in the front not the back, so it doesn't bump as much, does it?"

"Very good, Tim! That's quite right. If you should feel sick you'll tell me in plenty of time, though, won't you? It isn't very nice if you make a mess in the car."

"I promise I'll tell you, Mary, because you never yell at me or get cranky."

She laughed. "Now, Tim! Don't be martyrish! I'm quite sure no one yells at you or gets cranky with you very often, and only then if you deserve it."

"Well, yes," he grinned. "But Mum gets real mad if I'm sick all over everything."

"I don't blame her in the least. I'd get real mad too, so you must be sure to tell me if you ever feel sick, and then hang on until you get outside. All right?"

"All right, Mary."

After a little while Mary cleared her throat and spoke again. "Have you ever been out of the city, Tim?"

He shook his head.

"Why not?"

"I dunno. I don't think there was anything Mum and Pop wanted to see outside the city."

"And Dawnie?"

"My Dawnie goes all over the place, she's even been to England." He made it sound as though England were just around the corner.

"What about holidays, when you were a little boy?"

"We always stayed at home. Mum and Pop don't like the bush, they only like the city."

"Well, Tim, I come down to my cottage very often, and you can always come too. Perhaps later on I can take you to the desert or the Great Barrier Reef for a real holiday."

But he wasn't paying any attention to her, for they were coming down to the Hawkesbury River, and the view was magnificent.

"Oh, isn't it *lovely?*" he exclaimed, wriggling on the seat and gripping his hands together convulsively the way he always did when he was moved or upset.

Mary was oblivious of everything except a sudden pain, a pain so new and alien that she had no real idea why she should feel it. The poor, sad fellow! Somehow events had conspired to stunt his every avenue of expansion and mental growth. His parents cared for him very much, but their lives were narrow and their horizons restricted to the Sydney skyline. In all justice she could not find it in her heart to blame them for not realizing that Tim could never hope to get as much out of their kind of life as they did themselves. It had simply never occurred to them to wonder whether he was truly happy or not, because he *was* happy. But could he perhaps be happier still? What would he be like if he were freed from the chain of their routine, permitted to stretch his legs a little?

It was so difficult to draw all the threads of her feeling for him together: one moment she thought of him as a small child, the next moment his physical magnificence would remind her that he was a man grown. And it was so hard for her to feel at all, when it was so long since she had done more than merely exist. She possessed no built-in emotional gauge whereby she could distinguish pity from love, anger from protectiveness. She and Tim were like a weirdly juxtaposed Svengali and Trilby: the mindless it was that mesmerized the mind.

Since first seeing Tim all those weeks ago she had confined herself to action, had kept herself mentally out and about, doing things. She had never allowed herself to sit in the quiet withdrawal of private contemplation, for by nature she was not given to probing how and why and what she felt. Even now she would not do it, would not pull herself far enough away from the center of her pain to come to grips with the cause of it.

The cottage had no neighbors closer than two miles, for the area was not yet "developed." The only road was atrocious, no more than an earthen track through the eucalyptus forest;

55

when it rained mud made it impassable and when it didn't rain the dust rose in vast, billowing clouds that settled on the vegetation nearest to the road, petrifying it into spindling brown skeletons. The ruts, ridges, and potholes in the road itself imperiled the stoutest car so severely that there were few people willing to risk the inconvenience and discomfort for the sake of isolation.

Mary's property was quite large for the area, some twenty acres; she had bought it with an eye toward the future, knowing that the cancerous encroachment of the city would eventually lead to development and fantastic profits. Until such time, it suited her love of solitude very well.

A track diving into the trees indicated the beginning of Mary's land; she swung the car off the road and put it over the track, which continued for about a half a mile through the beautiful, aromatic bush, virgin and unspoiled. At the end of the track lay a big clearing which opened on its far side into a tiny beach; beyond it, still salty and tidal here, the Hawkesbury River twisted and turned its wide way through the towering sandstone landscape. Mary's beach was no more than a hundred yards long, and was flanked at each end by soaring yellow cliffs.

The cottage was unpretentious, a square little frame structure with a corrugated iron roof and a wide, open veranda running all the way around it. Mary kept it painted because she could not abide disorder or neglect, but the drab brownish color she had chosen did not improve the appearance of the house. Two huge galvanized iron water tanks stood on high towers at one end of the rear of the house, which faced the track. Trees had been planted at intervals in the clearing, and were at last growing large enough to take some of the bareness away. She had made no attempt at a garden and the grass grew long, but in spite of everything the place had a certain indefinable charm about it.

Mary had spent a considerable amount of money on the cottage since buying the property fifteen years before. The massive water tanks, to have enough fresh water for modern plumbing; electricity, to avoid lanterns and fuel fires. Mary saw no allure in open fires, candlelight, or outhouses; they meant extra work and inconvenience.

From the approaching car the house showed to worst advantage, but Tim was enthralled. Mary pried him out of his seat with some difficulty, and coaxed him through the back door.

"This is your room, Tim," she said, showing him a plain but big bedroom with white walls and furniture; it looked rather like a nun's cell. "I thought perhaps if you like coming here you might think about what color you'd like your room painted, and what kind of furniture you'd like in it. We could shop for it one day in the city."

He could not reply, too excited and overcome with the whole experience to assimilate this fresh delight. She helped him unpack his suitcase and put his few things in the empty drawers and cupboards, then she took him by the hand and led him out to the living room.

Only here had she made major changes in the actual construction of the house, which had once possessed a dark, poorly lit living room extending the entire length of the front veranda. She had pulled the outer wall away piecemeal and replaced it with floor-to-ceiling sliding glass doors all the way along, so that when the weather was good there was nothing between the living room and the open air.

The view from this room was breath-taking. The grass sloped downward to the bright yellow sand of the sunny, immaculate little beach, the blue water of the Hawkesbury lapped gently along its border, and on the far side of the wide river wonderful cliffs, splendidly crowned with forest, rose to meet the clear, high sky. The only sounds of man to intrude were those coming from the river; the put-put of outboard motors, the chug of excursion ferries, the roar of speedboats towing water skiers.

But the birds screeched and caroled from every tree, the cicadas deafened, the wind moaned softly as it filtered through the sighing branches.

Mary had never shared her retreat with anyone before, but on many occasions she had rehearsed the imaginary conversation she and her first guests would have. They would exclaim and marvel over the view, pass endless comments on everything. But Tim said nothing; she had no idea how much assessment and comparison he could make. That he thought it "lovely" was apparent, but he thought everything was "lovely" that didn't make him unhappy. Was Tim capable of gradations of happiness? Did he enjoy some things more than others?

When she had done her own unpacking and stocked the kitchen, she got him his lunch. He said very little as the meal progressed, chewing steadily through all the food she put in front of him. Unless he was starving or upset, his table manners were impeccable.

"Do you swim?" she asked him after he had helped her wash the dirty dishes.

His face lit up. "Yes, oh, yes!"

"Then why don't you change into your swimming trunks while I finish up here, then we'll go down onto the beach. All right?"

He disappeared immediately, returning so quickly that she had to make him wait while she tidied up the last few odds and ends around the kitchen. Carrying two canvas deck chairs, an umbrella, towels, and various other bits of beach paraphernalia, they staggered laden down to the sand.

She had settled herself into her deck chair and opened her book before she realized that he was still standing looking at her, puzzled and apparently distressed.

She closed her book. "What's the matter, Tim? What is it?"

He fluttered his hands helplessly. "I thought you said we were going swimming!"

"Not we, Tim," she corrected gently. "I want you to swim to your heart's content, but I never go into the water myself."

He kneeled beside her chair and put both his hands on her arm, very upset. "But then it isn't the same, Mary! I don't want to go swimming all by myself!" Tears sparkled on his long fair lashes, like water beading on crystal. "Please, oh, *please* don't make me go in all by myself!"

She reached out to touch him, then drew her hand away quickly. "But I don't have a swimsuit with me, Tim! I couldn't go in even if I wanted to."

He shook his head back and forth, growing more and more agitated. "I don't think you like being with me, I don't think you like me! You're always dressed up as if you're going into town, you never wear shorts or slacks or no stockings the way Mum does!"

"Oh, Tim, what am I going to do with you? Just because I'm always dressed up doesn't mean I don't like being with you! I don't feel comfortable unless I'm all dressed up, it's as simple as that. I just don't like wearing shorts or slacks or no stockings."

But he didn't believe her, and turned his head away. "If you were having fun you'd wear the sort of clothes Mum does when she's having fun," he persisted stubbornly.

There was a long silence, incorporating, though Mary didn't realize it, their first duel of wills. In the end she sighed and put her book down. "Well, I'll go inside and see what I can find, only you must promise me faithfully that you won't play tricks on me in the water, duck me under or disappear on me. I can't swim, which means you'll have to look after me all the time I'm in the water. Do you promise?"

He was all smiles again. "I promise, I promise! But don't be long, Mary, please don't be long!"

Though it galled her tidy soul to do so, Mary eventually put on a fresh set of her customary white cotton underwear, and over it one of her gray linen button-down-the-front weekend dresses which she hacked into briefer form with a pair of scissors. She cut the skirt off at mid-thigh, ripped the sleeves out and lopped the neck away until her collar bones were exposed. The cutting was naturally neat, but there was no time to turn a hem or put on facings, which irritated her and put her out of humor.

Walking down to the beach she felt horribly naked, with her fish-belly white legs and arms and the support of girdle and stockings absent. The feeling had little to do with Tim; even when she was totally alone for days, she always put on every layer of clothes.

Tim, an uncritical audience now that he had got his own way, danced up and down gleefully. "Oh, that's much better, Mary! Now we can both go in swimming! Come on, come on!"

Mary waded into the water with shuddering distaste. As fastidious as the most disdainful of cats, it was all she could do to make herself continue wading out deeper, when what she wanted to do was turn tail and run back to her comfortable, dry deck chair. Displaying the important maturity of a very young male placed in sole charge of a treasure, Tim would not let her go out beyond the point where the water reached her waist. He hovered all around her like a sticky little fly, anxious and confused. It was no use; he could sense that she hated it, and she knew she was spoiling his day. So she suppressed a strong shudder of revulsion and dunked herself down to the neck with a gasp of shock at the coldness, and an involuntary laugh.

The laugh was all he was waiting to hear; he began to frolic around her like a porpoise, as at ease and at home in the water as any fish. Forcing herself to smile and slapping the palms of her hands on the surface of the water in what she hoped was a good imitation of someone thoroughly enjoying a dip, Mary blundered about after him.

The water was exquisitely clear and clean, her disarticulated feet wobbled like sickly white blancmange on the sandy bottom whenever she looked down, and the sun rested on the back of her neck like a warm and friendly hand. After a while she began to enjoy the feel of the mildly stinging saltiness; it stimulated and exhilarated, and to submerge to the shoulders in delicious, weightless coolness with the full strength of the sun rendered suddenly impotent was truly marvelous. The vulnerability of her lack of clothes faded, and she began to luxuriate in feeling her body so free of restriction.

She did not lose quite all her good sense, however, and after twenty minutes or so she called Tim to her side. "I must go out now, Tim, because I'm not used to the sun. See how white I am, and how brown you are? Well, one of these days I'll be as brown as you, but I have to do it very slowly, because the sun burns white skins like mine and it could make me very sick. Please don't think I'm not having fun, because I am, but I really must get into the shade now."

He accepted this calmly. "I know, because when I was a little boy I got so sunburned one day I had to go to the hospital. It hurt so much that I cried all day and all night and all day and all night. I don't want you to cry all day and all night, Mary."

"I tell you what I'll do, Tim, I'll sit under the shade of my umbrella and watch you. I promise I won't read, I'll just watch you. Is that all right?"

"All right, all right, all right!" he sang, playing at being a submarine but nobly refraining from torpedoing her.

Making sure she was entirely shielded by the umbrella, Mary spread her dripping body along the deck chair and mopped her face. The bun at the back of her neck was trickling water down her spine in a most annoying way, so she took the pins out and shook her hair over the back of the chair to dry. She had to admit that she felt wonderful, almost as if the salt water possessed medicinal value. Her skin tingled, her muscles were slack and her limbs heavy. . . .

. . . She was paying one of her infrequent visits to the beauty parlor, and the hairdresser was rhythmically brushing her hair, one-two-three, one-two-three, tugging at her scalp each time the brush engaged and drawing the tug out deliciously as the brush traveled down the length of her hair. Smiling with pleasure, she opened her eyes to find she was not in a beauty parlor at all, but lying in a deck chair on the beach, and that the sun was slipping down so low behind the trees that shadows had blanketed the sand completely.

Tim was standing behind her with his head bent over her face, playing with her hair. Panic overwhelmed her; she sprang away from his touch in inexplicable terror, snatching at her loose hair and scrabbling frantically in the pocket of her cut-down dress for the pins. A safe distance away and more fully awake, she turned to look at him, eyes dilated in fright and heart thumping.

He still stood in the same spot, gazing at her out of those incredible eyes with the peculiarly helpless, agonized expression she only saw when he knew he had done wrong but did not understand what it was he had done wrong. He wanted to atone, he wanted so badly to understand what sort of sin he had unknowingly committed; at such times he seemed to feel his exclusion most acutely, she thought, like the dog which does not know why its master kicked it. Utterly at a loss, he stood wringing his hands together, mouth slack.

Her arms went out to him in a gesture of remorse and pity. "Oh, my dear! My dear, I didn't mean it! I was asleep and you frightened me, that's all! Don't look at me so! I wouldn't hurt you for all the world, Tim, truly! Oh, please don't look at me like that!"

He avoided her hands, holding himself just out of her reach because he wasn't sure if she meant it or not, if she wasn't just trying to soothe him.

"It was so beautiful," he explained timidly. "I just wanted to touch it, Mary."

She stared at him, astonished. Had he said "beautiful"? Yes, he had! And said it as if he really knew what the word meant, as if he understood that it was different from "lovely" or "nice" or "super" or "grouse" or "beaut" in degree, these being the only adjectives of praise she had heard him use. Tim was learning! He was picking up a little of what she said, and interpreting it correctly.

She laughed at him tenderly and went right up to him, taking his reluctant hands and gripping them strongly. "Bless you, Tim, I like you better than anyone else I know! Don't be annoyed with me, I didn't mean to hurt you, really I didn't."

His smile came out like the sun, the pain faded from his eyes. "I like you too, Mary, I like you better than anyone except Pop and Mum and my Dawnie." He paused thoughtfully. "I think I like you better than my Dawnie, actually."

There he went again! He had said "actually," just the way she did herself! Of course, to a large extent it was simply parroting, but not entirely; there was a suggestion of sureness about his usage.

"Come on, Tim, let's go inside before it gets chilly. When the evening breeze comes up the river it cools things down awfully fast, even at the height of summer. What would you like for your supper?"

After the supper had been eaten and the dishes washed and put away, Mary made Tim sit in her one comfortable armchair, then looked through her records.

"Do you like music, Tim?"

"Sometimes," he answered cautiously, craning his neck to see her as she stood behind him.

What would appeal to him? The cottage was actually better equipped with the kind of music he might like than the house in Artarmon, for she had brought all her old, outgrown tastes here. Ravel's *Bolero*, Gounod's *Ave Maria*, Handel's *Largo*, the march from *Aïda*, Sullivan's *Lost Chord*, the *Swedish Rhap-*

63

sody, Sibelius' *Finlandia,* melodies from Gilbert and Sullivan, Elgar's *Pomp and Circumstance* march: they were all there with dozens of other selections equally rich in mood and melody. Try him on stuff like this, she thought; he doesn't care if it's hackneyed, so see how it goes.

Overwhelmed, he sat entranced and all but physically inserted himself into the music. Mary had been doing some reading on mental retardation, and remembered as she sat watching him that many retarded people had a passion for music of a fairly high order and complexity. Seeing that vivid, eager face reflecting every mood change, her heart ached for him. How beautiful he was, how very beautiful!

Toward midnight the wind coming up the river from the sea grew cooler still, gusting in through the open glass doors so vigorously that Mary closed them. Tim had gone to bed about ten, worn out with all the excitement and the long afternoon of swimming. It occurred to her that he might be cold, so she rummaged in the hall closet and unearthed an eiderdown to put over him. A tiny kerosene lantern was burning dimly beside his bed; he had confided to her, rather hesitantly, that he was afraid of the dark, and did she have a little light he could keep near him? Treading noiselessly across the bare white floor with the eiderdown hugged close in her arms in case it brushed against something and made a sound, Mary approached the narrow bed.

He was lying all curled up, probably because he had grown cold, his arms wrapped across his chest, knees almost touching his chest. The blankets had half slipped off the bed, baring his back to the open window.

Mary looked down at him, hands twisting within the cuddly folds of the eiderdown, mouth open. The sleeping face was so much at peace, the crystal lashes fanned down across the lean planes of his cheeks, the wonderful golden mass of his hair curling around his perfectly shaped skull. His lips were slightly turned up, the sad little crease to their left side lending the smile a Pierrot quality, and his chest rose and fell so quietly that for a moment she fancied him dead.

How long she remained staring down at him she never knew, but at length she shivered and drew away, unfolding the eiderdown. She did not attempt to pull the blankets up around him, contenting herself with straightening them on the bed and tucking them in, then dropping the eiderdown over his shoulders and twitching it into place. He sighed and moved, nuzzling into the warmth, but in a moment he had slipped back again into the world of his dreams. What did a mentally retarded young man dream about, she wondered: did he venture forth as limited in his nocturnal wanderings as he was during his waking life, or did the miracle happen which freed him from all his chains? There was no way to know.

After she left his room Mary found the house unbearable. Shutting the glass doors silently, she crossed the veranda and descended the steps to the path which led down to the beach. The trees were tossing restlessly in the grip of the wind, a mopoke was calling, "more pork! more pork!," sitting with his round owl's eyes blinking from the blurred darkness of a low branch that drooped over the path. Mary glanced at the bird without really seeing him, and the next moment ran into something soft and clinging. As it stuck to her face she gasped in fright, then realized it was a spider's web. She felt all over herself cautiously, dreading the thought that the web's owner might be roaming on her somewhere, but her hand encountered nothing more than her dress.

The beach fringes were littered with dead branches; Mary gathered them in her arms until she had enough to build a fire, then she stacked them in the middle of the sand near a convenient rock and put a match to the twigs at their base. The cold sea breeze at night was the East Coast's saving grace, but it was hard on the human body, sweltering all day and then chilling

65

to the bone at night. She could have gone back to the house for a sweater, but there was something very friendly about a fire, and Mary needed comfort desperately. When the flames were spitting and spurting she sat herself on the rock and spread her hands out to warm.

Rocking leisurely back and forth upside down by its tail from a nearby tree, a possum stared at her intently from wise round eyes, its sweet face apprehensive. What an odd creature she was, squatting before the glaring thing he knew only as a danger, with the light throwing bizarre shadows in ever-changing patterns across her. Then he yawned, plucked a loquat from the branch above him and munched it loudly. She was nothing to fear, just a hunched-up woman with a face drawn in pain, not young or pretty or enticing.

It had been a long time since pain had been a part of her life, Mary reflected, chin in hand; she had to go all the way back to a little girl in an orphanage dormitory, sniffling herself to sleep. How lonely it had been then, so lonely there had been times when she had wished for the friendly ignorance of death. People said a child's mind could not comprehend or long for death, but Mary Horton knew differently. There was no memory of a home, of loving arms, of being wanted; her desolation had been one of pure, unrecognized loss, for she could not hunger after something she did not know existed. She had thought her unhappiness was rooted in her unattractiveness, the hurt that came when her adored Sister Thomas passed her by, as usual, for a child who was prettier and more appealing.

But if her genes had not endowed her with personal allure, they had carried the codes of strength; Mary had disciplined herself as she grew up, until by the time she was fourteen and the moment came to leave the orphanage, she had learned to subjugate and crush unhappiness. After that she had ceased to feel on a human, emotional level, contenting herself with the pleasure she got out of doing her job well and watching her savings grow. It had not been an empty pleasure exactly, but it had not softened or warmed her either. No, life had not been empty or lacking in stimuli, but it had been utterly devoid of love.

Never experiencing the stirrings of a maternal drive or the urge to seek a mate, Mary was not capable of gauging the quality of her love for Tim. Indeed, she did not even know whether what she felt for Tim could rightly be called love. He had simply become the pivot of her life. In every waking moment she was conscious of Tim's existence, he sprang to her mind a thousand times a day, and if she thought, "Tim," she found herself smiling or she felt something that could only be called pain. It was almost as if he lived within her mind as an entity quite distinct from his real being.

When she sat in her dimly lit living room listening to the haunting searching of some violin she mentally reached for an unknown, still withholding some reserves of feeling, but when she sat in her dimly lit living room looking at Tim there was nothing left to seek, everything she had ever yearned after was embodied in him. If she had expected anything of him in the few hours between first seeing him and coming to realize that he was mentally undeveloped, once she had discovered the truth she had ceased to expect anything more from him than the mere fact of his existence. He enthralled her; that was the only word she could think of which halfway fitted.

All the hungers and yearnings of her woman's years had been ruthlessly suppressed; they had never gained a hold on her, for she had always been careful to avoid any situation which might encourage them to flower. If she found a man attractive she studiously ignored him, if a child began to laugh its way into her heart she made sure she never saw the child again. She avoided the physical side of her nature as she would the plague, shut it up in some dark and sleeping corner of her mind and refused to admit it existed. *Keep out of trouble,* the orphanage nuns had told her, and Mary Horton had kept out of trouble.

In the very beginning Tim's beauty and helplessness had disarmed her: Mary found herself impaled on the pin of twenty-nine solitary years. It was as if he genuinely needed her, as if he could see something in her to which even she herself was blinded. No one had ever preferred her above all others, until Tim. What was it about her dry, matter-of-fact personality that Tim found so fascinating? The responsibility was a terrible thing, so hard to deal with for one quite unversed in the emotions. He had a mother, so it was not that which he sought; and he was too much the child and she too much an old maid for it to be a sexual thing. There must have been many, many people in his life who had been cruel to him, but there must also have been many, many people who were kind, even loving. No one with Tim's appearance and nature would ever go short of love. Why, then, did he prefer her?

The fire was dying. Mary went to seek more wood, then decided not to build it up again. She sat awhile longer, staring at the twinkling lights among the coals, her eyes unfocused. A worm popped its head out of the sand and looked at her; the heat of the fire was seeping slowly through the ground and forcing hundreds of its minute denizens to flee or fry. Unaware of the havoc her source of warmth was causing, Mary doused the embers with sand instead of water; safe enough as a fire hazard precaution, but no cooler for the sand and its inhabitants.

Ten

Mary continued to take Tim to Gosford with her all through the summer. By the time April was coming in and autumn with it, Tim's mother and father were well acquainted with her, but only over the phone. She had never invited Ron and Es Melville to Artarmon, and they had not liked to ask her to visit them. It did not occur to any of the four to wonder if each held the same impression of Mary Horton.

"I intend taking a holiday on the Great Barrier Reef this winter, perhaps in July or August, and I would very much like to take Tim with me, if it's all right with you," she said to Ron Melville one Sunday evening.

"Cripes, Miss Horton, you're too good to Tim now! He can go with you, yes, but only on condition that he pays his own way."

"If you'd rather it was that way, Mr. Melville, then certainly, but I assure you I'd be only too delighted to have Tim along simply as my guest."

"That's very, very nice of you, Miss Horton, but I do think Tim would be best off paying his own way. We can afford it. We could have taken him ourselves any time if we'd thought of it, but somehow Es and I never seem to get any further from Sydney than Avalon or Wattamolla."

"I quite understand, Mr. Melville. Goodbye."

Ron hung up the receiver, shoved his thumbs through his trouser belt and sauntered into the living room, whistling.

"Hey, Es, Miss Horton wants to take Tim to the Great Barrier Reef with her in July or August," Ron announced as he stretched himself comfortably on the sofa with his feet higher than his head.

"Very nice of her," Es said.

A few minutes later the clip-clop of high heels sounded under the window, followed by the snap of the back door closing. A young woman walked into the room, nodded to them and sat down with a sigh, kicking her shoes off. She was both like Tim and not like him; the height and the fair hair were there, but she lacked the absolute perfection of his bone structure and her eyes were brown.

"I think I just saw the elusive Miss Horton," she mumbled through a yawn, pulling an ottoman close enough to put her feet on.

Es put down her knitting. "What's the old girl like?"

"I couldn't see much detail, but she's sort of stubby and has a head of silver hair with a bun on the back of her neck, typical old maid. Sixty-five-ish, I'd say, though I couldn't really see her face. What a car, mates! A big black Bentley something like the sort of car old Queen Lizzie rides in. Phew! Wall to wall money, I'd reckon."

"I don't know about that, love, but I suppose she must be quite well off to own all that property."

"Rather! I wonder what she sees in Tim? Sometimes it worries me. . . . He's so awfully taken with her."

"Oh, Dawnie, I think it's nice," Es said. "You're getting too clucky about Tim and Miss Horton."

"What do you mean, I'm getting too clucky?" Dawnie demanded sharply. "Darn it all, he's my brother! I don't like this new friendship of his, and that's that. What do we really know about Miss Mary Horton?"

70

"We know all we really have to know, Dawnie," Es said gently. "She's good for Tim."

"But he's so wrapped in her, Mum! It's Mary this and Mary that until sometimes I could strangle him!"

"Oh, come on, Dawnie, don't be such a nark! You sound like green eyes to me!" Es snorted.

Ron frowned at Dawnie. "Who were you out with tonight, sport?" he asked, changing the subject.

Her mood dropped away as her lively, extremely intelligent eyes laughed at him. "The managing director of some big international drug firm. I'm thinking of going into industry."

"My bloody foot! I reckon industry's thinking of going into you! How can you keep so many blokes on a string, Dawnie? What on earth do they see in youse?"

"How should I know?" She yawned, then listened. "And here comes Tim."

A moment later he entered, tired and happy.

"G'day there, mate!" his father said cheerfully. "Have a good weekend?"

"Extra good, Pop. We're making a flower garden all around the house, and we're building a brick barbecue on the beach for cookouts."

"Sounds like you're making a real picture-book place out of it, don't it, Es?"

But Es did not reply; she sat up straight suddenly, clutching Ron's arm. "Hey, Ron, how could Miss Horton talk to you on the phone one minute and be outside dropping Tim off the next?"

"Stone the flaming crows! Tim, did Miss Horton phone us a few minutes ago, just before she dropped you?"

"Yes, Pop. She's got a phone in her car."

"Blimey Charlie! That sounds a bit like putting on the dog to me, mate."

"She has to have a phone in her car!" Tim answered indignantly. "She told me her boss Mr. Johnson needs to talk to her in a hurry sometimes."

"And why couldn't she have come inside for a minute to talk to us in person if she was almost outside the house?" Dawnie sneered.

Tim's brow wrinkled. "I dunno, Dawnie. I think she must be a little bit shy, just like you say I am."

Ron stared at him, puzzled, but said nothing until after Tim had gone to bed. Then he swung his feet off the sofa and sat where he could see his wife and daughter comfortably.

"Is it my imagination, girls, or is Tim improving a bit? It struck me the other day that he's using fancier words than he used to, less down to earth, like."

Es nodded. "Yes, I've noticed it."

"So have I, Pop. Apparently Miss Horton spends some of her time with Tim teaching."

"Hooray and good luck to her!" Es said. "I never had the patience and nor did the teachers at school, but I always reckoned Tim has it in him to learn."

"Oh, come off it, Mum!" Dawnie snapped. "Next thing you'll be expecting us to call her Saint Mary!" She got up abruptly. "Since you can't find anything better to talk about than that woman's influence over Tim, I'm going to bed!"

Ron and Es were left staring after her, startled and perturbed.

"You know, Ron, I think Dawnie's a wee bit jealous of Miss Horton," Es said at last.

"But why on earth should she be jealous?"

"Oh, I dunno, love. Women are real possessive sometimes. I have a feeling Dawnie's peeved because Tim don't hang around her so much these days."

"But she oughta be glad! She always used to moan about Tim getting under her feet, and besides, the older she gets the more she leads her own life."

"But she's human, pet, she don't see it like that. You know, dog in the manger."

"Well, she's going to have to let go a bit, that's all. I'm real glad Tim's got Miss Horton instead of mooning around here waiting for Dawnie to come home."

The following day Ron met his son at the Seaside as usual and walked home with him through the closing darkness, for the days were getting short.

When they came in the back door Es was waiting for them, a peculiar expression on her face. She had a flat, colorful little book in her hand, and waved it at Tim wildly.

"Tim, love, is this yours?" she squeaked, eyes alight.

Tim glanced at the book and smiled, as if at a pleasure remembered. "Yes, Mum. Mary gave it to me."

Ron took the book, turned it over and looked at the title. *"The Kitten Who Thought He Was a Mouse,"* he read out slowly.

"Mary's teaching me to read," Tim explained, wondering what all the fuss was about.

"And can you read any of it yet?"

"A bit. It's awfully hard, but not as hard as writing. But Mary doesn't mind when I forget."

"She's teaching youse to write, mate?" Ron asked, hardly able to believe it.

"Yes. She writes a word for me, and I copy it down so it looks just like hers. I can't write a word of my own yet." He sighed. "It's much harder than reading."

Dawnie came home just then, seething with suppressed excitement, words bubbling on her lips, but for the first time in her life she found herself taking an intellectual back seat to Tim; her parents did not even bother to ask her what she was so excited about, they simply went "Ssssh!" and drew her into the semicircle around Tim.

He read a page in the middle of the book without having to search around too much for a word or a letter, and when he was done they shouted and cheered, clapped him on the back and ruffled his hair. Sticking his chest out like a pouter pigeon, he strutted through to his room holding the little book reverently between his hands, and smiling; in all his life he had never known a moment more supreme. He had pleased them, really pleased them, made them proud of him the way they were proud of Dawnie.

Just after Tim had gone to bed Es raised her head from her endless knitting. "How about a cuppa tea, pet?" she asked Ron.

"That sounds like a real good idea, old girl. Come on, Dawnie, come out to the kitchen with us like a good kid, eh? You've been awful quiet all night."

"There's a bit of nice dark fruitcake with orange juice icing on it, or a cream sponge I bought at the Jungo this arvo," Es announced, putting cups and saucers on the kitchen table.

"Cream sponge," Ron and Dawnie chorused.

There was a delicious nip in the air, for it was the end of April and the worst of the heat was over. Ron got up and closed the back door, then chased an enormous moth with a rolled-up newspaper until he caught it thudding vainly against the light fixture. It fell to the ground amid a faint shower of gold powder from its wings; he picked it up, still fluttering madly, carried it into the bathroom and flushed it down the lavatory.

"Thanks, Pop," Dawnie said, relaxing again. "Jeez, I hate those bloody things, flipping and flopping in my face. I'm always scared they'll get into my hairdo or something."

He grinned. "You women! Frightened of anything that flies, creeps, or crawls." He picked up a huge wedge of cake and jammed most of it into his mouth. "What's the matter, Dawnie love?" he mumbled indistinctly, licking the cream from around his nose.

"Nothing, nothing!" she parried brightly, sectioning her cake and delicately conveying a small piece to her mouth on the tines of a baby fork.

74

"Come on, sport, you can't fool your old man!" he said more clearly. "Spit it out, now! What's moping you, eh?"

Dawnie put her fork down, frowning, then lifted her large, light-filled eyes to his face. They softened, looking at him, for she was genuinely attached to him. "If you must know the gory details, I'm ashamed of myself. I had a piece of news of my own to tell you when I came in tonight, and when I found Tim the center of attention I got a bit peeved. You know, that's disgusting. The poor little bloke! He's taken a back seat to me all his life, and tonight, when he had something to show us that made us proud of him, I got shirty because he'd stolen my thunder."

Es reached out and patted her arm. "Don't fret about it, love. Tim didn't realize anything was wrong and that's the main thing, isn't it, eh? You're a good girl, Dawnie, your heart's in the right place."

Dawnie smiled; suddenly she was very like Tim and it was easy to see why she had so many boyfriends. "Ta, old girl! What a comfort you are, love. You can always find something nice to say, or something to take the sting out."

Ron grinned. "Except when she's lacing into me. Nasty old bat you are, Es!"

"What else can a drunken old sod like you expect?"

They all laughed. Es poured the tea, milk in the bottom of each cup and then a brew of tea on top of it that was as black and strong as coffee dregs. The resulting drink was dark brown in color and opaque because of the milk; they all sugared their cups liberally and drank the steaming liquid straight down. Only when seconds were poured did they resume their talk.

"What was it you wanted to tell us, Dawnie?" her mother asked.

"I'm going to get married."

There was a startled silence, broken by Ron's cup landing noisily in its saucer.

"That's a bombshell!" he said. "Gord struth and little apples,

75

what a bombshell! I never thought you'd go and get married, Dawnie. Cripes, the house'll be empty without youse!"

Es looked at her daughter gently. "Well, love, I knew you'd up and tie the knot one of these days, and if it's what you want, I'm glad for you, real glad. Who's the bloke?"

"Mick Harrington-Smythe, my boss."

They stared at her blankly.

"But isn't he the bloke you never got on with because he reckoned women belonged in the kitchen, not in the research lab?"

"That's him, that's my Mick!" Dawnie replied cheerfully, and grinned. "I suppose he decided marrying me was the only way he'd get me out of the research lab and back into the kitchen where I belong."

"A bit hard to get on with, isn't he?" Ron queried.

"Sometimes, but not if you know how to handle him. His worst fault is that he's a snob. You know the sort I mean—school at King's, home in Point Piper, ancestors who came out with the First Fleet—only they weren't convicts, of course, or if they were the family's not owning up to it now. But I'll wean him away from all that after a while."

"How come he's marrying the likes of you, then?" Es asked acidly. "We dunno what our ancestors were, except most likely they were thieves and cutthroats, and Surf Street Coogee isn't exactly the poshest address in Sydney, nor is Randwick High the poshest girls' school."

Dawnie sighed. "Oh, Mum, don't worry about it! The important thing is that he wants to marry me, and he knows exactly where, what, and who I come from."

"We can't afford a big expensive wedding for you, love," Es said sadly.

"I have a bit of money saved myself, so I can pay for whatever sort of wedding his parents want. Personally I hope they'll decide on a quiet one, but if they want a big, splashy affair they'll get a big, splashy affair."

"Youse'll be ashamed of us," Es quavered, tears in her eyes.

Dawnie laughed, stretching her hands out until the slender muscles rippled under her beautiful brown skin. "Not on your life, mates! Why on earth should I be ashamed of you? You gave me the best and happiest life a girl could ever have asked for, you brought me up free of all the hangups, neuroses, and problems everyone else my age seems to have. In fact, you did a darned sight better job bringing me up than Mick's parents did him, let me tell you! He likes me and my family or he lumps us, that's all there is to it. It must be the attraction of opposites," she went on more thoughtfully, "because we really don't have a thing in common except brains. Anyway, he's thirty-five and he's had his pick of all the blue-bloods Sydney's had to offer in the last fifteen years, but he ended up picking good old common, garden-alley Dawnie Melville."

"A point in his favor, I reckon," Ron said heavily. He sighed. "I don't suppose he'll ever want to meet Tim and me for a beer or two at the Seaside. A scotch and water in some pansy lounge is more the style of that sort of bloke."

"At the moment it is, but he doesn't know what he's missing. You just wait! At the end of a year I'll have him meeting you at the Seaside."

Es got up abruptly. "Leave everything, I'll clear it up in the morning. I'm going to bed, I'm tired."

"Poor old Dawnie, she's in for a miserable time being married to a prawn like that," Es said to Ron as they climbed into their comfortable old bed.

"It don't pay to step out of your class, Es," Ron replied sternly. "I wish she'd had less brains, then she would have married some ordinary bloke from around the next corner and settled down in a fibro Housing Commission house in Blacktown. But Dawnie don't like ordinary blokes."

"Well, I hope it turns out all right, but I can't see that happening unless she breaks her ties with us, Ron. She's not going to like it, but I think we must gradually edge our way out of her

77

life after she's married. Let her carve a spot for herself in their world, because that's the world she'll have to raise his kids in, ain't it?"

"You're dead right, old girl." He stared at the ceiling, blinking hard. "Tim's the one will miss her. Poor old bloke, he won't understand."

"No, but he's like a little kid, Ron, his memory's short. You know how he is, poor little coot. He'll miss her the way a little kid does at first, but then he'll sort of forget her. Just as well he's got Miss Horton, I reckon. I daresay she won't be around forever either, but I hope she'll be around long enough to tide him over Dawnie's marrying." She patted his arm. "Life never works out the way you hope, does it? I'd sort of thought at one time that Dawnie wouldn't marry at all, that she and Tim would end up their days sharing this old house together after we're gone. She's so terribly fond of him. But I'm glad she's taking the plunge, Ron. Like I told her lots of times, we don't expect her to sacrifice her life for Tim. It wouldn't be right. And yet . . . I still think she's a wee bit jealous of Miss Horton. This engagement's so sudden. Tim finds himself a friend, Dawnie's nose is pushed out of joint a bit because Miss Horton's taken the time to teach him how to read and Dawnie never did, and the next thing, boomp! she goes and gets engaged."

Ron reached over and switched out the light. "But why this one, Es? I never even thought she liked him."

"Oh, but he's a lot older than she is, and she's real flattered because he picked her after all those Lady Mucks he could have had. Probably she's a bit scared of him too, a bit bluffed by his background and the fact that he's her boss. You can have all the brains in the world and still not be any wiser than the silliest coot in Callan Park."

Ron wriggled down until his head found its natural dent in the pillow. "Well, love, there's nothing we can do about it, is there? She's over twenty-one, and she never took much notice

78

of us, anyway. The only reason she's stayed out of trouble is that she's so bloody smart, horse-sense smart, like." He kissed her on the mouth. "Night-night, love. I'm tired, aren't you? All this flaming excitement."

"Too right," she yawned. "Night-night, love."

Eleven

When Tim arrived at Mary's house in Artarmon the following Saturday he was quiet and a little with-drawn. Mary did not question his mood, but put him in the Bentley and got on the road immediately. They had to stop at a nursery in Hornsby to pick up a lot of plants and shrubs Mary had ordered during the week, and the business of getting them all in the car occupied Tim so much that she told him to stay in the back seat when they started out again, so he could watch the plants and make sure none of them fell over or stained the leather upholstery.

At the cottage she left him to unload the plants and went through to his room with his case to unpack it, though these days he kept a small wardrobe there permanently. The room was changed; no longer bare and white, it sported a thick orange carpet, pale yellow walls, crome yellow drapes, and Danish modern furniture. His suitcase disposed of, she moved on to her own room and tidied herself up before returning to the car to see how Tim was doing.

Something was wrong with him, he was not himself at all. Frowning, she watched him closely as he finished taking the last of the plants out of the trunk. She did not think his problem was a physical one, for his skin was its usual healthy gold and his eyes were clear and bright. Apparently whatever plagued him was a happening in his personal sphere, though she doubted that it had anything to do with her, unless of course his parents had said something about her which had upset or puzzled him. But surely not! Only the other night she had spoken at length with Ron Melville, and he had been brimming over with enthusiasm about Tim's progress in reading and calculating.

"You're so bloody good for him, Miss Horton," Ron had told her. "Whatever you do, don't give him up as a bad job. I wish he'd known you years ago, I really do."

They had a silent lunch and went out to the garden with Tim's problem, whatever it was, still unmentioned. He would tell her in his own good time; perhaps it was better if she acted as though nothing was the matter, if she went ahead and made him help her plant all the new acquisitions. Last weekend they had had such fun over the garden, wrangling about whether they should have a bed entirely of stocks, or whether they ought to mix larkspurs and snapdragons in with them. He had not known the names of any of the flowers, so she had taken out her books and shown him pictures of them; he had learned about them with delight, and walked around muttering their names over and over to himself.

They worked silently all afternoon, until the shadows lengthened and the sea breeze came gusting up the lofty river canyon to warn of the coming night.

"Let's build a fire in the barbecue and cook on the beach," Mary suggested desperately. "We can go for a swim while the fire's getting itself to the right stage for cooking, and then we can build another fire on the sand to get dry over and warm us while we eat. How does that sound, Tim?"

He tried to smile. "It sounds lovely, Mary."

By this time Mary had learned to love the water and could even swim a few strokes, enough at least to be able to venture out where Tim liked to frolic. She had bought a black grosgrain swimsuit with a fairly long, full skirt on it for modesty's sake; Tim thought it was gorgeous. Her skin had darkened now that she exposed herself to the sun, and she looked better for it, younger and healthier.

Tim was not his usual high-spirited self in the water; he swam about quietly, forgetting to divebomb and torpedo her, and when she suggested they should go out onto the beach he followed her at once. Normally getting him out of the water was a battle royal, for he would stay in until midnight if she let him.

She had tiny baby lamb chops and big fat sausages to toast over the fire, two of his favorites, but he picked half-heartedly at a chop for a while without reducing its size very much, then pushed the plate away with a sigh, shaking his head wearily.

"I'm not hungry, Mary," he said sadly.

They sat side by side on a towel in front of the second fire, warming themselves comfortably in the teeth of the wintry wind. The sun had set, and the world was in that half-dark stage when everything was bled of its vividness but was not yet dimmed to black or white or gray. Above them in the clear vast sky the evening star glittered against an apple-green horizon, and a few more high magnitude stars struggled to overcome the light, appearing for a moment and then disappearing. Birds twittered and screamed everywhere, bedding down for the night in querulous fussiness, and the bush was full of mysterious squeaks and rustles.

Mary never used to notice such things, had been quite indifferent to the world around her except when it intruded itself, but now she found that she was intensely aware of the surrounding sphere, the sky and the land and the water, its animals and plants, all so wonderful and beautiful. Tim had taught her that, from the moment when he had shown her the cicada choirmaster in her oleander tree. He was always coming to display some little natural treasure he had found, a spider or a wild orchid or some tiny furry animal, and she had learned not to jump away

82

in revulsion but to see them as he did for what they were, perfect, as much a functional part of the planet earth as she was herself if not more so, for sometimes what he brought her was rare.

Worried and upset, Mary wriggled around on the towel until she sat looking at his profile, etched against the pearly rim of the sky. The cheek toward her was faintly outlined, the eye sunk invisible into a darkened socket, the mouth at its saddest. Then he moved slightly, and what light there was left collected itself into a sparkling row of tiny droplets on his lashes, glistening all the way down his cheek.

"Oh, Tim!" she cried, her hands going out to him. "Don't weep, my darling boy, don't weep! What is it, what's the matter? Can't you tell me, when we're such very good friends?"

She remembered Ron telling her that he used to cry a lot, and like a small child in noisy, hiccoughing bellows, but that of late he had stopped crying so. On the rare occasions these days when he was moved to tears, he cried more like an adult, Ron said, quietly and into himself. Just the way he was weeping now, she thought, wondering how often he had wept today without her noticing, when she had not been there or when she had been too busy to see.

Too upset to question the wisdom of her own conduct, she put her hand on his arm and stroked it softly, trying to soothe him as best she could. He turned toward her at once, and before she could jerk away he put his head down against her chest, drawing himself in against her like a small animal in need of a place to hide, his hands clutching at her sides. Her arms seemed to find a natural resting place across his back, and she dropped her head until her cheek rested on his hair.

"Don't cry, Tim," she whispered, smoothing his hair back and kissing his brow.

She sat back on her heels cradling him, all else forgotten save the reality of being able to give him comfort. He needed her, he had turned to her and hidden his face as if he thought her empowered to shield him from the world. Nothing could ever have prepared her for this; she had not dreamed life could give her a moment so infinitely sweet, so bounded with pain. His back under her hand was cool and slippery, like satin; the unshaven cheek resting just above her breasts scratched her skin like fine sandpaper.

Awkwardly and hesitantly at first, she gathered him closer, hugging one arm gently but strongly around his back, her other arm protectively about his head, its fingers buried in his thick, faintly salty hair. The forty-three empty, loveless years of her life were canceled out of existence, payment extracted in this one small flake of time. With this at their end they did not matter, and if there were forty-three more just as empty still to be endured, they could never matter either. Not now.

After a while he ceased weeping and lay absolutely motionless within her arms, only the slight rise and fall of his breathing under her hand telling her that he lived. Nor did she move; the thought of moving terrified her, for instinct told her that once either of them shifted even the smallest bit, he would withdraw or she would have to draw away herself. She pressed her mouth further into his hair and closed her eyes, profoundly happy.

He gave a deep, sobbing sigh and moved a little to get more comfortable, but to Mary it was the signal that her moment was over; gently she eased herself slightly away from him, so that he still lay within her arms but could lift his head to look at her. Her hand in his hair tugged at it until he was forced to raise his face, and the breath caught in her throat. In the faint light his beauty had a fey quality about it, he was an Oberon or a Morpheus, unreal, other-worldly. The moon had got into his eyes and sheeted them with a glaze of blued silver; they stared at her blindly, as though he saw her from the other side of a filmy curtain. Perhaps indeed he did, for what he saw in her no one else ever had, she reflected.

"Tim, won't you tell me what's making you so unhappy?"

84

"It's my Dawnie, Mary. She's going away soon and we won't see her very often. I don't want my Dawnie to go away, I want her to keep on living with us!"

"I see." She looked down into the unblinking, moonstone eyes. "Is she getting married, Tim? Is that why she's going away?"

"Yes, but I don't want her to get married and go away!" he cried defiantly.

"Tim, as you go on through the years you'll find that life is made up of meetings, knowings, and partings. Sometimes we love the people we meet, sometimes we don't like the people we meet, but knowing them is the most important thing about living, it's what keeps us human beings. You see, for many years I refused to admit this, and I wasn't a very good human being. Then I met you, and knowing you has sort of changed my life, I've become a better human being.

"Ah, but the partings, Tim! They're the hardest, the most bitter to accept, especially if we loved. Parting means it can never be the same afterward; something has gone out of our lives, a bit of us is missing and can never be found or put back again. But there are many partings, Tim, because they're as much a component of living as meeting and knowing. What you have to do is remember knowing your Dawnie, not spend your time grieving because you have to part from her, because the parting can't be avoided, it has to come. If you remember knowing her rather than grieve at losing her, it won't hurt so much.

"And that's far too long and complex and you didn't understand a word of it, did you, love?"

"I think I understood a bit of it, Mary," he answered seriously.

She laughed, dispelling the last of the moment, and thus inched him out of her arms. Standing upright again, she reached down her hands and pulled him to his feet.

"Mary, what you said, does that mean one day I'll have to see you go away, too?"

"Not unless you want me to go away, or unless I die."

The fires were quenched, thin tendrils of steam curling up between the grains of sand, and the beach was suddenly very cold. Mary shivered, hugging herself.

"Come, let's go back to the house, Tim, where it's warm and light."

He detained her, staring into her face with a passionate eagerness normally quite foreign to him. "Mary, I've always wanted to know, but no one will ever tell me! What's die, and dying, and dead? Are they all the same thing?"

"They all relate to the same thing, yes." She took his hand in hers and pressed its palm against his own chest, just over the left nipple. "Can you feel your heart there beating, Tim? Can you feel that thump-thump, thump-thump, thump-thump under your hand, always there, never stopping for a moment?"

He nodded, fascinated. "Yes, I can! I really can!"

"Well, while it beats, thump-thump, thump-thump, you can see and hear, walk around, laugh and cry, eat and drink and wake up in the morning, feel the sun and the wind.

"When I talk about living that's what I mean, the seeing and hearing and walking around, the laughing and crying. But you've seen things get old, wear out, break apart? A wheelbarrow or a concrete mixer, perhaps? Well, we, all of us with beating hearts under our ribs—and that's everyone, Tim, everyone!—we get old and tired, and wear out too. Eventually we begin to break apart and that beating thing you can feel stops, like a clock that's not been wound. It happens to all of us, when our time comes. Some of us wear out faster than others, some of us get accidentally stopped, if we're in a plane crash or something like that. No one of us knows when we'll stop, it isn't something we can control or foretell. It just happens one day, when we're all worn out and too tired to keep going.

"When our hearts stop, Tim, we stop. We don't see or hear ever again, we don't walk around, we don't eat, we can't laugh or cry. We're dead, Tim, we are no more, we've stopped and we have to be put away where we can lie and sleep undisturbed, under the ground forever.

"It happens to us all, and it's nothing to be frightened of, it can't hurt us. It's just like going to sleep and never waking up again, and nothing ever hurts us while we're asleep, does it? It's nice to be asleep, whether it's in a bed or under the ground. What we have to do is enjoy living while we're living, and then not be frightened to die when the time comes for us to stop."

"Then I might die just as easily as you, Mary!" he said intensely, his face close to hers.

"Yes, you might, but I'm old and you're young, so if we go on as people usually do, I should stop before you. I'm more worn out than you are, you see."

He was on the verge of tears again. "No, no, no! I don't want you to die before I do, I don't want it like that!"

She took his hands in hers, chafing them urgently. "There, there, Tim, don't be unhappy! What did I just tell you? Living is to be enjoyed for every moment we're still alive! Dying is in the future, it isn't to be worried about or even thought about!

"Dying is the final parting, Tim, the hardest one of all to bear, because the parting is forever. But all of us come to it, so it's something we can't close our eyes to and pretend it doesn't exist.

"If we're grown-up and sensible, if we're good strong people, we understand dying, we know about it but we don't let it worry us. Now I know you're grown-up and sensible, I know you're a good strong person, so I want you to promise me you won't worry about dying, that you won't be frightened of it happening to me, or to you. And I want you to promise that you'll try to be a man about partings, that you won't make poor Dawnie unhappy by being unhappy yourself. Dawnie is alive too, she has as much right to find her own way of enjoying living as you do, and you mustn't make it hard for her by letting her see how upset you are."

She took his chin in her hand and looked into the clouded eyes. "Now I know you're good and strong and kind, Tim, so I want you to be all of those things about your Dawnie, and about all the things that will happen to make you sad, because you mustn't be sad a minute longer than you can help. Promise?"

He nodded gravely. "I promise, Mary."

"Then let's go back to the house. I'm cold."

Mary turned on the big space-heater in the living room to warm it up, and put on some music she knew would make him light-heartedly happy. The treatment worked, and he was soon laughing and talking as if nothing had ever happened to threaten his world. He demanded a reading lesson, which she gave him gladly, then declined another form of amusement, curling up on the floor at her feet instead and sitting with his head resting against the arm of her chair.

"Mary?" he asked after a long while, and just before she opened her mouth to tell him it was time to go to bed.

"Yes?"

He twisted around so that he could see her face. "When I cried and you hugged me, what's that called?"

She smiled, patting his shoulder. "I don't know that it's called anything very much. Comforting, I suppose. Yes, I think it's called comforting. Why?"

"I liked it. Mum used to do it sometimes a real long time ago when I was just a little shaver, but then she told me I was too big and never did it again. Why didn't you think I was too big?"

One hand went up to shield her eyes and stayed there a moment before she dropped it onto her lap and clenched it tightly around her other hand. "I suppose I didn't think of you as big at all, I thought of you as a little shaver. But I don't think how big you are is very important, I think how big your trouble is is much more important. You might be a big man now, but your trouble was much bigger, wasn't it? Did it help, to be comforted?"

He turned away, satisfied. "Oh, yes, it helped a lot. It was real nice. I'd like to be comforted every day."

She laughed. "You might like to be comforted every day, but it isn't going to happen. When something is done too often it loses its attraction, don't you think? If you were comforted every day whether you needed it or not, you'd soon get a wee bit tired of it. It wouldn't be nearly as nice any more."

"But I need comforting all the time, Mary, I need to be comforted every day!"

"Pooh! Fiddle! You're a conniver, my friend, that's what you are! Now I think it's bedtime, don't you?"

He climbed to his feet. "Night-night, Mary. I like you, I like you better than anyone except Pop and Mum, and I like you the same as I like Pop and Mum."

"Oh, Tim! What about poor Dawnie?"

"Oh, I like my Dawnie too, but I like you better than I like her, I like you better than anyone except Pop and Mum. I'm going to call you my Mary, but I'm not going to call Dawnie my Dawnie any more."

"Tim, don't be unforgiving! Oh, that's so cruel and thoughtless! Please don't make Dawnie feel that I've taken her place in your affections. It would make her very unhappy."

"But I like you, Mary, I like you better than I like Dawnie! I can't help it, I just do!"

"I like you too, Tim, and really better than anyone else in the whole world, because I don't have a Pop and a Mum."

Twelve

It transpired that Dawnie wanted to marry Michael Harrington-Smythe at the end of May, which left little time for preparations. Learning the background of their son's bride-to-be, Mick's parents were just as anxious as Dawnie's to reduce the size of the wedding to a bare minimum.

The two sets of parents plus the engaged pair met on neutral ground to plan the wedding, neutral ground being a private room at the Wentworth Hotel, where the reception was to be held. Everyone was uncomfortable. Distressed in collar and tie and Sunday corsets, Ron and Es sat on the edges of their chairs and refused to be drawn into polite conversation, while Mick's parents, to whom collar and tie and corsets were an everyday occurrence, chatted in bored voices which held a slight suggestion of plum-in-mouth. Mick and Dawnie tried desperately to lessen the stiffness, without much success.

"Dawn will naturally be married in a long white gown and have at least one attendant," Mrs. Harrington-Smythe said challengingly.

Es looked stupid; she had forgotten that Dawnie's real name was Dawn, and found it disagreeable to be reminded that the Melville family had chosen a low-class diminutive. "Um," she answered, which Mrs. Harrington-Smythe took to mean acquiescence.

"The men in the wedding party had better wear dark suits and plain blue satin ties," Mrs. Harrington-Smythe continued. "Since it's a small, private wedding, morning dress or white tie and tails would be most unsuitable."

"Um," said Es, her hand fumbling underneath the table until it found Ron's and clutched thankfully.

"I'll give you a full list of those the groom's side will want invited, Mrs. Melville."

And so it went, until Mrs. Harrington-Smythe remarked, "I believe Dawn has an older brother, Mrs. Melville, but Michael hasn't given me any idea of what part he's to play in the wedding. Naturally you realize he can't be best man, since Michael's own friend Hilary Arbuckle-Heath is filling that role, and I really can't see what other function is available for him in such a small wedding party. Unless, of course, Dawn chooses to change her mind and have a second attendant."

"That's all right, Ma'am," Ron said heavily, squeezing Es's hand. "Tim don't expect to be in the wedding party. In fact, we were thinking of letting him go to Miss Mary Horton's for the day."

Dawnie gasped. "Oh, Pop, you can't do that! Tim's my only brother, I want him to see me married!"

"But Dawnie love, you know Tim don't like crowds!" her father protested. "Think what an uproar there'd be if he vomited all over the place! Sweet balls of Christ, wouldn't that be just lovely? No, I think it would be better all around if Tim just went to Miss Horton's."

Dawnie's eyes glittered with tears. "Anyone would think you were ashamed of him, Pop! I'm not ashamed of him, I want everyone to meet him and love him as much as I do!"

"Dawnie love, I think your old man's right about Tim," Es contributed. "You know how he hates crowds, and even if he wasn't sick everywhere he wouldn't be very happy if he had to sit still all through a wedding ceremony."

The Harrington-Smythes were looking at each other, absolutely bewildered. "I thought he was older than Dawn," Mrs. Harrington-Smythe said. "I'm sorry, I didn't realize he was only a child."

"Well, he isn't a child!" Dawnie flared, red spots staining her cheeks. "He's a year older than me but he's mentally retarded, that's what they're trying to conceal from everyone!"

There was an appalled silence; Mr. Harrington-Smythe drummed his fingers on the table, and Mick looked at Dawnie in surprise.

"You didn't tell me Tim was retarded," he said to her.

"No, I didn't, because it just never occurred to me that it was important! I've had Tim there all my life, and he's a part of my life, a very important part of my life! I never remember that he's retarded when I'm talking about him, that's all!"

"Don't be angry, Dawn," Mick pleaded. "It really isn't important, you're quite right about that. I was simply a little surprised."

"Well, I am angry! I'm not trying to hide the fact that my only sibling is mentally retarded, it's my mother and father who've apparently taken it upon themselves to do that! Pop, how could you?"

Ron looked embarrassed. "Well, Dawnie, it isn't that we was trying to hide it exactly, it's that we thought it would be less of a business for you if he didn't come. Tim don't like crowds, you know that. Everyone always stares at him so much that it makes him go all funny."

"Oh, dear, is he very bad to look at?" Mrs. Harrington-Smythe asked, a slight doubt in her eyes as they rested on Dawnie. Perhaps it ran in the family? What an idiot Michael was, to choose a low-class girl like this after all the perfectly marvelous girls he had ignored! Of course, they said she was extraordinarily brilliant, but brilliance was no substitute for good breeding, it could never outweigh vulgarity, and the whole wretched family was vulgar, vulgar, vulgar! The girl had absolutely no polish, no idea of how to comport herself in decent company.

"Tim is the finest-looking man I've ever seen," Dawnie replied fiercely. "People stare at him in admiration, not in disgust, but he doesn't know the difference! All he knows is that they're looking at him, and he doesn't like the sensation."

"Oh, he is lovely to look at," Es offered. "Like a Greek god, Miss Horton says."

"Miss Horton?" Mick asked, hoping to change the subject.

"Miss Horton is the lady Tim gardens for on weekends."

"Oh, really? Tim is a gardener, then?"

"No, he's not a bloody gardener!" Dawnie snapped, nettled at the tone. "He works as a builder's laborer during the week, and he earns a little extra money on the weekends by gardening for this wealthy old lady."

Dawnie's explanation only made matters worse; the Harrington-Smythes were shifting on their chairs and trying not to look at each other or the Melvilles.

"Tim has an IQ of about 75," Dawnie said, more quietly. "As such he's not supposed to be employable, but my parents were wonderful about him, right from the start. They realized they wouldn't be here to support him all of his life, so they brought him up to be as self-sufficient and independent as possible under the circumstances. From the day he was fifteen Tim's earned his own living as an unskilled laborer, which is the only kind of work he's fit for. I might add that he's still working for the man who took him when he was fifteen, which may help you understand what a valuable and well-liked employee he is.

"Pop has paid on an insurance policy for him since he first knew Tim was retarded, so he'll never have to worry financially, he'll always have enough to live on. Since I started working I've helped increase the size of the premiums, and some of Tim's wages go into it, too. Tim is the richest member of the family, ha-ha!

"Until recently he couldn't read or write or do any sort of arithmetic, but Mum and Pop taught him the really important things, like how to get about the city from job to job and place to place without having to have someone always with him. They taught him to count money though he can't count anything else, which is strange: you'd think he would associate what he can do with money with other kinds of counting, but he can't. One of the weird little jokes the retarded mind plays, that is. But he can buy himself a ticket for the bus or the train, he can buy himself food and clothes. He isn't a burden to us now any more than he ever has been. I'm very fond of my brother and I'm very devoted to him. A kinder, sweeter, more lovable person doesn't exist. And, Mick," she added, turning to her fiancé, "when Tim's all alone and needs a home, I'm taking him in. If it doesn't suit you, then it's too bloody bad! You'd better call the whole thing off right now."

"My dear, dear Dawn," Mick said imperturbably, "I fully intend to marry you, if you have ten mentally retarded and utterly moronic brothers."

The answer did not please her, but she was too upset to analyze why it did not please her, and later on forgot all about it.

"It don't run in the family," Es explained, a little pathetically. "It was me ovaries, the doctors said. I was over forty when I married Ron, and I'd never had any kids before that. So Tim was born not the full quid, you see. Dawnie was fine because me ovaries had got going by then. It was only the first one, Tim, what got affected by them. But it's like Dawnie says, a nicer little bloke than Tim just don't exist."

"I see," said Mr. Harrington-Smythe, not knowing what else to say. "Well, I'm sure it isn't up to anyone but Mr. and Mrs. Melville to decide whether their son should attend the wedding."

"And we decided," Es said firmly. "Tim don't like crowds, so

Tim don't go. Miss Horton will be glad to take him for the weekend."

Dawnie burst into tears and rushed to the powder room, where her mother found her a few minutes later.

"Don't cry, love," Es soothed, patting her shoulders.

"But everything's going wrong, Mum! You and Pop don't like the Harrington-Smythes, they don't like you either, and I don't know what Mick thinks any more! Oh, it's going to be awful!"

"Stuff and fiddle! Ron and me come from a different world to the Harrington-Smythes, that's all. They don't normally mix with the likes of us, so how can you expect them to know what to do when they find themselves having to mix with the likes of us? And the same goes the other way, love. The Harrington-Smythes aren't the sort of people I play tennis with on Tuesdays and Thursdays and Saturdays, or the sort Ron meets at the Seaside and the Leagues Club.

"You're a big girl, Dawnie, and a real brainy girl. You ought to know we couldn't ever be friends. Why, we don't even laugh at the same things! But we aren't enemies either, not with our kids getting married to each other. We just won't meet either side of this wedding, except maybe for christenings and such-like. And that's how it should be. Why should we have to pee in each other's pockets just because our kids got married, eh? Now you're clever enough to understand that, aren't you?"

Dawnie dried her eyes. "Yes, I suppose so. But, oh, Mum, I wanted everything to be so perfect!"

"Of course you did, love, but life ain't like that, not ever. It was you picked Mick and him you, not us or the Harrington-Smythes. If it had been left to us, we'd never have matched you with Mick, and nor would the pewie Harrington-Smythes. Double-barreled name, indeed! Bloody putting on the dog, if you ask me. But we're all making the best of it, love, so don't go creating a big fuss over poor Tim, for heaven's sake. Tim don't enter into this and it ain't right of you to make him enter it.

95

Leave poor Tim to his own life, and don't go pushing him down the Harrington-Smythes' throats. They don't know him the way we do, so how can you expect them to understand?"

"Bless you, Mum, I don't know what I'd do without you! I'm supposed to be the clever Melville, but sometimes I get the funny feeling that it's really you and Pop who are the clever ones. How did you get so wise?"

"I didn't, love, and nor did your old man. Life makes us wise, the longer we live it. When you've got kids as old as you are now, you'll be doing the dazzling, and I'll be shoving up daisies."

In the end Ron telephoned Mary Horton and asked her to resolve the question of whether Tim should be allowed to go to the wedding. Though they had never met and he was aware that Miss Horton belonged more in the Harrington-Smythe circle than the Melville, Ron somehow felt at home with her; she would both understand his dilemma and offer a reasonable solution for it.

"It's a bad business, Miss Horton," he said, breathing noisily into the receiver. "The Harrington-Smythes aren't too pleased with their precious son's choice of a wife, and I can't honestly say I blame them. They're afraid she won't fit in, and if it wasn't that Dawnie's so bloody smart I'd be afraid on that score, too. As it is, I think she'll learn a lot faster than they can teach, and no one will ever have the chance to be embarrassed because of anything she says or does."

"I don't know Dawnie personally, Mr. Melville, but from what I've heard, I'm sure you're right," Mary responded sympathetically. "I wouldn't worry about her."

"Oh, I ain't!" he answered. "Dawnie's got the iron in her, she'll be apples. It's Tim that's getting me down."

"Tim? Why?"

"Well, he's different, like. He's never going to grow up properly, and he don't know when he makes a mistake, he can't learn from making it. What's going to happen to the poor little bugger after we're gone?"

"I think you've done a splendid job with Tim," Mary said, her throat unaccountably tight. "You've brought him up to be remarkably independent and self-sufficient."

"Oh, I know all that already!" Ron replied, a little impatiently. "If it was just a question of him looking after himself I wouldn't be worried, but it ain't, you know. Tim needs his Mum and Pop for love and peace of mind, because he ain't growed up enough to find someone to replace us, a wife and family of his own, I mean, which is what a man normally does."

"But he'll have you for many years to come, Mr. Melville! You're young yet, you and your wife."

"That's where you're wrong, Miss Horton, Es and me ain't young at all. We was born six months apart, and we had our seventieth birthday this year."

"Oh!" There was a blank silence for a moment, then Mary's voice came again, rather uncertainly. "I hadn't realized you and Mrs. Melville were as old as that."

"Well, we are. I tell you, Miss Horton, with Dawnie marrying a bloke who definitely won't want his wife's mentally retarded brother hanging around, Es and me is nearly mental ourselves worrying about Tim. Sometimes at night I hear poor old Es crying, and I know she's crying about Tim. He won't outlive us long, youse know. When he finds out he's all alone, he'll up and die of a broken heart, you wait and see."

"People don't die of broken hearts, Mr. Melville," Mary said gently, out of the ignorance of her emotionally impoverished existence.

"Bullshit they don't!" Ron exploded. "Oh, I beg your pardon, Miss Horton! I know I shouldn't swear like that, but don't you ever believe people don't die of broken hearts! I've seen it happen, and more than once, too. Tim will, he'll just fade away. You need the will to live as much as the health to live, love. And when there's no one to care about him, Tim will die; he'll just sit there crying and forgetting to eat until he dies."

"Well, as long as I'm here I'll see there's someone to care for him," Mary offered tentatively.

"But you're not young either, Miss Horton! It was Dawnie I was hoping for, but not any longer. . . ." He sighed. "Oh, well, no use crying over spilt milk, is there?"

It was on the tip of Mary's tongue to assure him she wasn't seventy, but before she could speak Ron began again.

"What I really rang to ask you was about Tim going to the wedding. I'd like to have him come but I know he'll be miserable, sitting still all through the ceremony and then the reception. Dawnie was very upset when I said I didn't think Tim ought to go, but I still don't think he ought to go. What I was wondering was, would you mind if Tim stayed with you that weekend?"

"Of course not, Mr. Melville! But it seems a great shame that Tim can't be in the house to see Dawnie getting ready, and that he can't see her married. . . . I tell you what, why don't you bring him to the church to see her married, and I'll pick him up outside right afterward, so he doesn't have to go to the reception?"

"Hey, that's a great idea, Miss Horton! Crikey, why didn't I think of that? It would solve all our worries, wouldn't it?"

"Yes, I think it would. Give me a call when you have all the details about time and place and et cetera, and I give you my word I'll look after Tim after the ceremony."

"Miss Horton, you're the grouse, you really are!"

Thirteen

Tim found the wedding preparations exciting. Dawnie was especially considerate and tender during the week preceding what in her heart she termed her desertion, and devoted all her time to her family.

On the morning of the wedding, a Saturday, he was enthralled with the bustle and panic that seemed threatening to overwhelm them any moment, and wandered about getting under everyone's feet, full of helpful suggestions. They had bought him a new, dark blue suit with flared trousers and a waisted, slightly skirted coat, à la Cardin, and he was thrilled with it. He put it on the moment he got up and strutted about in it preening himself and trying to catch glimpses of his reflection in the mirrors.

When he saw Dawnie dressed he was awed.

"Oh, Dawnie, you look just like a fairy princess!" he breathed, staring at her with blue eyes wide.

She caught him to her in a violent hug, winking away tears. "Oh, Tim, if I ever have a son I hope he'll be as nice as you," she whispered, kissing his cheek.

He was delighted, not with the reference to her son, which he didn't understand, but with the hug. "You comforted me!" he caroled gleefully. "You comforted me, Dawnie! I like being comforted, it's the nicest thing I know!"

"Now, Tim, go out to the front gate and watch for the cars like a good boy," Es instructed, wondering whether she would ever think straight again, and trying to ignore the silly little pain in her side she had felt sometimes of late.

Dawnie was handed into the leading limousine with her father, the lone maid of honor got into the second one, and Es herded Tim into the third with her.

"Now sit still, Tim, and try to be a good boy," she admonished, settling herself onto the luxuriously padded back seat with a sigh.

"You look lovely, Mum," Tim said, more used to the feel of an expensive car than his mother, and taking it completely for granted.

"Thanks, love, I wish I felt lovely," Es replied.

She had tried not to overdress, sensing that Dawnie's grand in-laws would not be impressed with the usual garb of mothers of the bride in the Melville circle. So, with a sigh of regret she had abandoned her delicious dream of a mauve guipure lace dress, coat, shoes, and hat with an corsage of lilies dyed to match; she chose instead a dress and coat of subdued pale blue silk shantung with no corsage to speak of, just two modest white roses.

The church was crowded when she and Tim found their pew in the front on the bride's side; all the way down the aisle Es was conscious of the stares people gave Tim from the groom's side, gaping, she told herself, just as if they were low-class nothings. Mrs. and Mr. Harrington-Smythe were looking at him as though they could scarcely believe their eyes, while every female under ninety fell madly in love with him. Es was devoutly glad he was not going to the reception.

He behaved beautifully during the ceremony, which was not a long one. Afterward, while the photographer's camera flashed and the usual congratulations were under way, Es and Ron quietly led Tim out to the wall near the front gate of the church, and made him sit on it.

"Now you wait here for Mary like a good boy, and don't you dare wander away, do you hear?" Es said firmly.

He nodded. "All right, Mum, I'll wait here. Can I turn around and watch Dawnie come down the steps, though?"

"Of course you can. Just don't wander away, and if anyone comes over to try and talk to you, answer them politely and then don't say anything at all. Now Pop and me have to go back to the church, because they want us for the photographs, heaven help them. We'll see you again tomorrow night when Miss Horton brings you home."

The bridal party and the wedding guests had been gone ten minutes when Mary Horton drove down the street. She was vexed with herself, for she had got lost in the maze of small streets around Darling Point, thinking St. Marks was a different church closer to New South Head Road.

Tim was still sitting on the low stone wall in front, with the autumn sun filtering through the leafy trees in soft gold bars that danced with dust. He seemed so lost, so alone and lonely, staring helplessly at the road and obviously wondering what had happened to her. The new suit fitted him perfectly but it made him seem a stranger, very handsome and sophisticated. Only the pose was Tim, obedient and quiet, like a well-behaved small boy. Or like a dog, she thought; like a dog he would sit there until he died of starvation rather than move on in order to survive, because his loved ones had told him to sit there and not move.

Ron's words on the phone about Tim dying of a broken heart still plagued her; obviously Ron believed she was in his own age group, getting on toward seventy, but she had not disillusioned him, curiously reluctant to air her true age. And why did I do that? she asked herself; it was needless and silly.

Could anyone really die of a broken heart? Women did, in

101

those old romantic tales so much out of fashion at the moment; she had always assumed the heroine's demise to be as much a figment of the writer's fevered imagination as the rest of the lurid plot. But perhaps it truly was so; what would she do herself were Tim to depart from her life forever, taken away by irate parents or, God forbid, by death? How gray and empty life would be if it held no Tim, how futile and useless it would be to continue in a world without Tim. He had become the nucleus of her entire existence, a fact which several people had noticed.

Mrs. Emily Parker had invited herself over not long before, as, she explained, "I don't never get to see youse at the weekends no more, do I?"

Mary had muttered something about being very busy.

"Ha ha ha!" Mrs. Parker leered. "Busy is right, eh?" She winked at Mary and poked her in the ribs good-naturedly. "I must say you've taken quite a fancy to young Tim, Miss Horton. Them old busybodies up and down the street have their tongues wagging something scandalous."

"I did take quite a fancy to young Tim," Mary replied calmly, beginning to regain her equilibrium. "He's such a nice fellow, so anxious to please, and so lonely. At first I gave him the gardening because I gathered he could do with the money, then as I got to know him I began to like him for himself, even if he isn't the full quid, as everyone calls it. He's sincere, warm, and utterly lacking in deceit. It's so refreshing to encounter someone with absolutely no ulterior motives, isn't it?" She stared at Mrs. Parker blandly.

Mrs. Parker stared back, outwitted. "Um, ah, I suppose so. And you being on your own the way you are, it's real company for youse, ain't it?"

"Most certainly! Tim and I have a lot of fun together. We garden and listen to music, swim and picnic, lots of things. He has simple tastes, and he's teaching me to appreciate simplicity. I'm not a very easy person to get on with, but somehow Tim just suits me. He brings out the best in me."

For all her nosiness, the Old Girl was kind-hearted and generally uncritical. She patted Mary on the arm encouragingly.
"Well, I'm real glad for you, duckie, I think it's nice you've
found someone to keep you company, you being so alone and
all. I'll soon put you right with them nasty old biddies up and
down the street. I told them you wasn't the sort to buy yourself
a boyfriend.

"Now how about a cuppa tea, eh? I want to hear all about
young Tim, how he's getting along."

But Mary didn't move for a moment, her face curiously expressionless. Then she looked at Mrs. Parker in wonder. "Is that
what they thought?" she asked sadly. "Is that really what they
thought? How absolutely disgusting, how despicable of them! It
isn't myself I care about that much, but Tim! Oh, God, how
sickening!"

Mary's boss Archie Johnson was another one who had noticed
the change in Mary, though he was not aware of the reason for
it. They were eating a hasty lunch together in the staff cafeteria
one day when Archie broached the matter.

"You know, Mary, it's none of my business and I'm quite
prepared to be put in my place, but have you branched out a
bit lately or something?"

She had stared at him, bewildered and caught off her guard.
"I beg your pardon, sir?"

"Oh, come off it, Mary! And don't call me 'sir' or 'Mr. Johnson'! We're on lunch break."

She put her knife and fork down and looked at him calmly.
He and she had worked together for more years than either of
them cared to count, but their relationship had always been
severely restricted to business, and she still had trouble unbend-
ing sufficiently during their infrequent but obligatory social
encounters.

"If you mean have I changed lately, Archie, why don't you say
so? I won't be offended."

"Well, that is what I mean. You've changed. Oh, you're still

103

a terrible old bitch and you still frighten the living daylights out of the junior typists, but you've changed. By God, how you've changed! Even the other inhabitants of our little world have noticed it. For one thing you look better than you used to, as if you've been out in the sun instead of living under a rock like a slug. And I actually heard you laugh the other day, when that idiot Celeste was clowning around."

She smiled faintly. "Well, Archie, I think it can best be summarized by saying that I've finally joined the human race. Isn't that a lovely phrase? As solid and respectable a cliché as one could possibly hope for."

"What on earth made an old maid like you join the human race after all these years? Got a boyfriend?"

"Of sorts, though not what I'm sure everyone is thinking. Sometimes, my dear Archie, there are things which can benefit an old maid much more than mere sexual gratification."

"Oh, I agree! It's being loved that works the miracles. Mary, it's that wonderful feeling of being wanted and needed and esteemed. The sexual business is just the icing on the cake."

"How very perspicacious of you! It's no wonder we've worked together so well for so many years. You've got lots more sense and sensitivity than the average businessman, Archie."

"Great steaming impossibilities, Mary, but you've changed! And for the better, I might add. If you continue improving I might even ask you out to dinner."

"By all means! I'd love to see Tricia again."

"Who said Tricia was invited?" he grinned. "But I might have known you hadn't changed that much! Seriously, I think Tricia would love to see the change in you for herself, so why don't you come to dinner one evening?"

"I'd love to come. Tell Tricia to call me and I'll put it in the book."

"All right, now, enough evasion! What's the source of your new lease on life, dear?"

"I suppose you would have to say, a child, except that he's a very special kind of child."

"A child!" He sat back, immensely pleased. "I might have guessed it would be a child. A sea-green incorruptible like you would soften far faster under a child's influence than a man's."

"It isn't as simple as that," she answered slowly, amazed that she could be so relaxed and free of self-consciousness; she had never felt so comfortable with Archie before. "His name is Tim Melville and he's twenty-five years old, but he's a child for all that. He's mentally retarded."

"Holy man-eating toads!" Archie exclaimed, staring at her; he was addicted to coining unusual, if benign, expletives. "How on earth did you get into that?"

"It just crept up on me, I suppose. It's hard to be defensive with someone who doesn't understand what defensiveness is, and it's even harder to hurt the feelings of someone who doesn't understand why they're being hurt."

"Yes, it is."

"Well, I take him to Gosford with me at weekends, and I hope to take him to the Great Barrier Reef this winter for a holiday. He genuinely seems to prefer my company to anyone else's, except his parents. They're fine people."

"And why shouldn't he prefer your company, you old fire-eater? Swash me buckles, look at the time! I'll tell Tricia to arrange a date for dinner, then I want to hear all about it. In the meantime, old war-horse, back to the grind. Did you hear from McNaughton about the Dindanga exploration concession?"

She had been glad in a way that both Mrs. Parker and Archie had accepted her friendship with Tim so casually, had been so pleased for her. The promised dinner date with Archie and his equally volatile wife had not yet happened, but she found herself looking forward to the meeting for the first time in twenty years.

105

When Tim saw the Bentley cruising down the street his face lit up with joy, and he jumped off the low stone wall immediately.

"Oh, Mary, I'm so glad to see you!" he exclaimed, wriggling into the front seat. "I thought you'd forgotten."

She took his hand and held it to her cheek for a moment, so filled with pity and remorse over being late that she forgot she had resolved never to touch him. "Tim, I wouldn't ever do that to you. I lost my way. I got St. Marks all confused in my mind with another church and lost my way, that's it. Now sit there and be happy, because I've just decided to go to Gosford."

"Oh, goody! I thought we'd have to stay at Artarmon because it's so late."

"No, why shouldn't we go anyway? There's plenty of time for a swim when we get there unless the water's too cold, and we can certainly cook our supper on the beach no matter how chilly it is." She glanced sidelong at him, savoring the contrast between his smiling happiness now and the despairing solitude of a few minutes before. "How did the wedding go?"

"It was beautiful," he answered seriously. "Dawnie looked like a fairy princess, and Mum looked like a fairy godmother. She had a lovely light blue dress on, and Dawnie had a long white dress on with lots of frills and a big bunch of flowers in her hand and a long white veil on her head, like a cloud."

"It sounds marvelous. Was everyone happy?"

"I think so," he said dubiously, "but Mum cried and so did Pop, only he said it was the wind made his eyes water, then he got mad at me when I said there wasn't any wind in the church. Mum said she was crying because she was so happy about Dawnie. I didn't know people cried when they were happy, Mary. I don't cry when I'm happy, I only cry when I'm sad. Why should you cry if you're happy?"

She smiled, suddenly so happy herself that she was close to tears. "I don't know, Tim, except that sometimes it does happen

106

that way. But when you're so happy you cry it feels different, it feels very nice."

"Oh, I wish I could get so happy that I cried, then! Why don't I get so happy that I cry, Mary?"

"Well, you have to be quite old, I think. One of these days it might happen to you too, when you're old and gray enough."

Perfectly satisfied now that he had been reassured, he sat back and watched the passing view, something he never seemed to tire of. He had all the insatiable curiosity of the very young, and the capacity to do the same thing over and over again without becoming bored. Each time they went to Gosford he acted as if it was the first time, as stunned with the scenery and the parade of life, as delighted to see the cottage at the end of the track, agog to discover what might have grown a little bit larger or burst into flower or withered away.

That night when Tim went to bed Mary did something she had never done before; she came into his room and tucked the blankets around him, then kissed his forehead.

"Goodnight, Tim dear, sleep well," she said.

"Night-night, Mary, I will," he answered drowsily; he was always half-asleep the minute his head touched the pillow.

Then, as she was closing his door softly, his voice came again: "Mary?"

"Yes, Tim, what is it?" She turned around and came back to the bed.

"Mary, you won't ever go away and get married like my Dawnie, will you?"

She sighed. "No, Tim, I promise I won't do that. As long as you're happy I'm here, I'll be here. Now go to sleep and don't worry about it."

Fourteen

In the end Mary could not get away from her job to take Tim on the promised vacation. Constable Steel & Mining bought a mineral-laden piece of territory in the far northwest of the continent, and instead of going to the Great Barrier Reef with Tim, Mary found herself accompanying her boss on an inspection tour. The trip was supposed to be for a week, but ended up lasting over a month.

Usually she enjoyed these infrequent jaunts; Archie was good company and his mode of travel tended to be very luxurious. This time, however, they went to an area which lacked roads, townships, and people. The last stage of the journey had to be made by helicopter, since there was no way to get into the area from the ground, and the party camped in an unseasonal rain, perpetually wet, plagued by heat, flies, mud, and an outbreak of dysentery.

Most of all, Mary missed Tim. There was no way to send him a letter, and the radio telephone was restricted to business and emergency calls. Sitting in her dripping tent trying to scrape some of the gluey black mud from her legs and clothes, with a dense cloud of insects flocking around the solitary kerosene lamp and her face swollen from dozens of mosquito bites, Mary longed for home and Tim. Archie's exuberance at the results of the ore assay were hard to bear, and it took all her customary composure to seem even civilly enthusiastic.

"There were twelve of us in the party," Archie told Tricia when they were safely back in Sydney again.

"Only twelve?" Mary asked incredulously, winking at Archie's wife. "There were times when I'd have sworn there were at least fifty!"

"Listen, you bloody awful old bag, shut up and let me tell the story! Here we are just back from the worst month I've ever spent, and you're stealing my thunder already! I didn't have to ask you to spend your first night back in civilization under my roof, but I did, so the least you can do is sit there nice and quiet and prim the way you used to be, while I tell my wife what happened!"

"Give him another whisky, Tricia, before he has an apoplectic seizure. I swear that's the reason he's so crotchety on his first night back. For the last two weeks, ever since he licked the last drop off the last bottle of scotch we had with us, he's been unbearable."

"Well, how would you be, love?" Archie appealed to his wife. "Permanently soaked to the skin, bitten alive by a complete spectrum of the insect world, plastered with mud, and with nothing female closer than a thousand miles except for this awful old bag? And how would you like it having nothing to eat but canned stew and then the booze running out? Sweet Bartlett pears, what a bog of a place! I would have given half the flaming ore content we found for one single big steak and a Glen Grant to wash it down!"

"You don't need to tell me," Mary laughed, turning to Tricia impulsively. "He nearly drove me mad! You know what he's like when he can't have his rich foods and his twelve-year scotch and his Havana cigars."

"No, I don't know what he's like when he can't have his little comforts, dear, but thirty years of being married to him makes

109

me shudder at the very thought of what you must have had to put up with."

"I assure you I didn't put up with it for long," Mary answered, sipping her sherry luxuriously. "I took myself off for a walk after a couple of days of listening to him moaning, and shot some birds I found wallowing in a swamp so we'd at least have a change from that eternal stew."

"What happened to the supplies, Archie?" Tricia asked curiously. "It's most unlike you not to pop in a few little tidbits in case of emergencies."

"Blame our glamorous outback guide. Roughly half of us were from headquarters here in Sydney, but the surveyors I picked up in Wyndham along with said guide, Mr. Jim Bloody Barton. He thought he'd show us what sterling stuff real bushmen are made of, so after assuring me that he'd take care of the supplies, he stocked up with what he usually eats himself—stew, stew, and more stew!"

"Don't be too hard on the poor man, Archie," Mary remonstrated. "After all, we were outsiders and he was in his element. If he came to the city, wouldn't you make it your business to dazzle him with all our urban frivolities?"

"What utter codswallop, Mary! It was you took all the starch out of him, not me!" He turned to his wife. "I just wish you could have seen her walking back into camp, love! There she was, strolling along in that ghastly British old maid uniform of hers, covered up to her belly button in stinking black mud and lumping about a dozen bloody great dead birds behind her. She'd tied their necks together with a bit of string and she was dragging them on the ground behind her, using the string like a tow-rope. I thought our glamorous Jim Barton was going to have a stroke, he was so mad!"

"He was, wasn't he?" Mary agreed complacently.

"Well, he hadn't wanted to bring Mary along in the first place, being a confirmed misogynist; reckoned she'd slow us down, be

110

nothing but a dead weight and a bloody nuisance and a few other things. And there she was bringing us culinary salvation, just when he was sure he'd begun to show us what soft stuff we city slickers were made of. Hah! Leave it to my Mary to put him in his place! What a doughty old bird you are, love!"

"What sort of birds were they?" Tricia asked, trying to keep a straight face.

"Lord, I don't know!" Mary answered. "Just birds, big gangly tropical ones. They were fat, which was all I was interested in."

"But they might have been poisonous!"

Mary burst out laughing. "What rot! To the best of my knowledge, very little out of what we call living matter is actually poisonous, and if you run the odds through a big computer, you'll find chance is on your side most of the time."

"Barton the Bushman tried that one, too, come to think of it," Archie grinned reminiscently. "Mary chopped the birds up with some of the gravy out of a few cans of stew, and some sort of leaves she'd picked off a bush because she thought they smelled good. Barton the Bushman took off straight up in the air, reckoned they could be poisonous, but Mary just looked at him with that nerve-rattling stare of hers and told him that in her opinion our noses were originally designed to tell us whether things were edible or not, and her nose told her the leaves were perfectly all right. Of course they were, that goes without saying. She then proceeded to give him a long lecture on *Clostridium botulinum*, whatever that might be, which apparently grows in canned stew and is ten times as toxic as anything you can pick off a bush. Lord, did I laugh!"

"Were they happy with your cooking, Mary?" Tricia asked.

"It tasted like nectar and ambrosia rolled in one," Archie enthused before Mary could speak. "Holy galloping stingrays, what a meal! We gorged ourselves, while Mary sat there picking daintily at a wing with not a hair out of place and nary a smile. I tell you, Mary, you must be a local legend in Wyndham about now, with all those surveyors talking about you. You sure took the wind out of Barton the Bushman's sails!"

Tricia was helpless with laughter. "Mary, I ought to be madly jealous of you, but thank God I don't have to be! What other wife not only doesn't need to experience the slightest twinge of jealousy because of her husband's secretary, but can also rely on her bringing him safely home from whatever mess he's landed himself in?"

"It's easier to bring him home in the long run, Tricia," Mary said solemnly. "If there's one thing I hate, it's the thought of breaking in a new boss."

Tricia jumped up quickly, reaching for the sherry. "Have another glass, Mary, please do! I never thought I'd hear myself say I was thoroughly enjoying your company, but I don't know when I've had so much fun!" She stopped, her hand going to her mouth ruefully. "Oh, Lord! That sounded awful, didn't it? I didn't mean it that way, I meant that you've changed, come out of yourself, that's all!"

"You're only making things worse, love," Archie said glee-fully. "Poor Mary!"

"Don't 'Poor Mary!' me, Archie Johnson! I know quite well what Tricia means, and I couldn't agree with her more."

Fifteen

When Tim knocked on the back door the first Saturday after Mary arrived back in Sydney, she went
a little reluctantly to let him in. How would it be, seeing him
again after this first separation? She pulled the door open in a
hurry, words springing to her lips, but they never found voice;
a great lump had blocked her throat, and she could not seem
to clear it away to speak. He was standing on the doorstep
smiling at her, love and welcome shining in his beautiful blue
eyes. She reached out and took his hands in hers speechlessly,
her fingers closing around them hard, the tears running down
her face. This time it was he who put his arms around her and
pressed her head against his chest, one hand stroking her hair.

"Don't cry, Mary," he crooned, rubbing his palm clumsily
across her head. "I'm comforting you so you don't have to cry.
There there, there there!"

But in a moment she drew away, groping for her handkerchief. "I'll be all right, Tim, don't be upset," she whispered,
finding it and drying her eyes. She smiled at him and touched
his cheek caressingly, unable to resist the temptation. "I missed
you so much that I cried from happiness at seeing you again,
that's all."

"I'm awfully glad to see you, too, but I didn't cry. Cripes,

Mary, I missed you! Mum says I've been naughty ever since you went away."

"Have you had your breakfast?" she asked, fighting to regain her composure.

"Not yet."

"Then come and sit down while I make you something." She looked at him hungrily, hardly able to believe that he was really there, that he had not forgotten her. "Oh, Tim, it's so good to see you!"

He sat down at the table, his eyes never leaving her for a second as she moved about the kitchen. "I felt sort of sick all the time you were away, Mary. It was real funny! I didn't feel like eating much, and the TV made my head ache. Even the Seaside wasn't much good, the beer didn't taste the same. Pop said I was a bloody nuisance because I wouldn't keep still or stay in one place."

"Well, you're missing Dawnie too, you know. It must have been very lonely for you, not having Dawnie and not having me either."

"Dawnie?" He said the name slowly, as if pondering its significance. "Gee, I dunno! I think I sort of forgot Dawnie. It was you I didn't forget. I thought of you all the time, all the time!"

"Well, I'm back now, so it's all over and done with," she said cheerfully. "What shall we do this weekend? How about going up to the cottage, even though it's too cold to swim?"

His face lit up with joy. "Oh, Mary, that sounds just great! Let's go to Gosford right now!"

She turned to look at him, smiling at him so very tenderly that Archie Johnson would not have known her. "Not until you've had some breakfast, my young friend. You've got thin since I've been away, so we have to feed you up again."

Chewing the last morsel of his second chop, Tim stared at her in frowning wonder.

"What's the matter?" she asked, watching him closely.

114

"I dunno. . . . I felt funny just now, when I was comforting you. . . ." He was finding it difficult to express himself, seeking words beyond his vocabulary. "It was real funny," he concluded lamely, unable to think of another way to put it, and aware that he had not succeeded in transmitting what he meant.

"Perhaps you felt all grown-up like your Pop, do you think? It's really a very grown-up sort of thing to do, comforting."

The frown of frustration cleared away immediately, and he smiled. "That's it, Mary! I felt all grown-up."

"Have you finished? Then let's get our things together and start, because it gets dark very early these days and we want to get as much work done in the garden as we can."

Winter in the area around Sydney hardly deserved the name, except to its thin-blooded residents. The eucalyptus forest retained its leaves, the sun shone warmly all the daylight hours, things continued to bud and blossom, life did not enter into the curiously stilled, sleeping suspension that it did in colder climes.

Mary's cottage garden was a mass of flowers: stocks and dahlias and wallflowers; the perfume saturated the air for a hundred yards around. Her lawn was much improved, and greener in the winter than at any other time. She had had the cottage painted white with a black trim, and the iron roof had been resilvered.

Driving into the little clearing where it lay, she could not help but admire it. Such a difference between how it looked now and how it had looked six months ago! She turned to Tim.

"Do you know, Tim, you're an excellent critic? See how much prettier it is, all because you said you didn't like it brown, and because you made me go to work on the garden? You were quite right, and it all looks so much nicer than it used to. It's a real pleasure to arrive these days. We must think of more things to do to keep the improvement going."

He glowed at the unexpected praise. "I like helping you, Mary, because you always make me feel as though I'm the full quid. You take notice of what I say. It sort of makes me think I'm just like Pop, all grown up into a man."

She turned off the engine and looked at him gently. "But you are all grown up into a man, Tim. I can't think of you any other way. Why shouldn't I take notice of what you say? Your suggestions and criticisms have been quite right, and so very helpful. It doesn't matter what anyone says about you, Tim, I will always think of you as being absolutely the full quid."

He threw back his head and laughed, then twisted to show her eyes sparkling with unshed tears. "Oh, Mary, I'm so happy I almost cried! See? I almost cried!"

She sprang out of the car. "Come on, lazy-bones, get cracking now, no displays of maudlin sentimentality! We've had far too much of that sort of thing this morning! Off with your good clothes and into your gardening gear, we've got a lot of work to do before lunchtime."

Sixteen

One evening not long after she returned from Archie Johnson's expedition, Mary read an article in the *Sydney Morning Herald* entitled "Teacher of the Year." It dealt with the remarkable success of a young schoolteacher in working with mentally retarded children, and it stimulated her to read more widely on the subject than she had. As she had seen things on the local library's shelves about mental retardation she had taken them out and pored over them, but until reading the newspaper article it had not occurred to her to delve more deeply.

The going was hard; she was forced to read with a medical dictionary at her elbow, though to a layman it was singularly unhelpful in elucidating the meaning of long, technical terms like *Porencephaly* and *Lipidosis* and *Phenylketonuria* and *Hepatolenticular Degeneration*. Indeed, many of the terms were so specialized even the medical dictionary did not list them. She waded miserably through a morass of such words, growing less and less sure of her ground, and less and less informed. In the end she went and saw the young teacher of the newspaper article, one John Martinson.

"I was an ordinary primary schoolteacher until I went to England and got accidentally drafted into a school for mentally retarded kids," John Martinson said as he led her into the school. "It fascinated me from the very beginning, but I didn't have any formal training in the techniques and theories, so I just had to teach them the way I would any normal kids. These are the mildly retarded children I'm referring to, of course; there are many who are totally ineducable. Anyway, I was staggered at how much they learned, how much they responded to being treated like ordinary kids. It was terribly hard work, naturally, and I had to develop a massive storehouse of patience, but I persevered with them, I wouldn't give in, and I wouldn't let them give in either. And I began to study. I went back to school myself, I did research and went all over the place looking at other people's methods. It's been a very satisfying career."

The deep-set, dark blue eyes surveyed her keenly all the time he talked, but without curiosity; he seemed to accept her presence as a phenomenon she would explain herself in her own good time.

"So you think mildly retarded people can learn," Mary said thoughtfully.

"There's no doubt of it. Too many uninformed people treat the mildly retarded child as more retarded than he really is, because in the long run it's easier to adopt this line than spend the staggering amount of time necessary to coax a normal response out of him."

"Perhaps a lot of people feel they haven't got the special qualities needed," Mary offered, thinking of Tim's parents.

"Perhaps. These kids long for approval, praise, and inclusion in normal family life, but so often they're left sitting on some outer perimeter, loved but half-ignored. Love isn't the whole answer to anything; it's an integral part of everything, but it has to be joined to patience, understanding, wisdom, and foresight when dealing with someone as complex as the mentally retarded child."

"And you try to fuse love to all these other things?"

"Yes. We have our failures, of course, quite a few of them, but we have a larger proportion of successes than most schools of this kind. Often it's well-nigh impossible to evaluate a child accurately, either neurologically or psychologically. You have to understand that first and foremost this child is organically impaired, no matter what degree of psychological overlay may also be present. Something upstairs in the brain isn't working just as it should."

He shrugged his shoulders and laughed at himself. "I am sorry, Miss Horton! I haven't given you time to get a word in edgeways, have I? It's a bad habit of mine to talk the leg off my visitors without having the vaguest idea why they've come to see me."

Mary cleared her throat. "Well, Mr. Martinson, it isn't a personal problem really, it's more an interested onlooker's curiosity which prompted me to get in touch with you. I'm very well acquainted with a young man of twenty-five who is mildly retarded, and I want to find out more about his situation. I tried reading, but I didn't understand the technical jargon very well."

"I know. Authoritative tomes there are aplenty, but good basic books for the layman are hard to come by."

"The thing is, since I commenced taking an interest in him, which is over the past nine months or so, he's shown signs of improving. It took a long time, but I've even taught him to read a tiny bit, and do very simple sums. His parents have noticed the change, and are quite delighted. However, I don't know how much progress I ought to expect, how hard I ought to push him."

He patted her arm and put his hand beneath her elbow to signal her that it was time they moved on. "I'm going to take you on a tour of our classrooms, and I want you to look at all the children very closely. Try to find one who strikes you as similar to your own young man in behavior and attitude. We don't permit visitors to disturb our classes, so you'll find we do all our observing through one-way windows. Come with me now, and

119

see what you think of our children."

Mary had never really taken much notice of the scant few retarded children she had encountered during her life, for like most people she was acutely uncomfortable when caught staring. It amazed her now to discover how varied they were in physical make-up, let alone mental capacity; they ranged from children who looked quite normal to some so terribly malformed it was an effort not to turn the eyes away.

"I used to teach a class of mental giants once," John Martinson said a little dreamily as he stood beside her. "Not one kid in the class who rated below 150 on the old IQ scale. But do you know, I get more satisfaction out of spending a month teaching one of these kids to tie his own shoelaces? They never jade or grow bored with achieving, I suppose because they have to work so hard to achieve. The harder anything is to attain, the more one prizes it, and why should that be any the less true for a retarded human being?"

After the tour John Martinson conducted her to his little office and offered her coffee.

"Well, did you see anyone who reminded you of Tim?" he asked.

"Several." She described them. "There are times when I want to weep for Tim, I pity him so much," she said. "He's so aware of his shortcomings, you see! It's dreadful to have to listen to the poor fellow apologizing because he's 'not the full quid' as he terms it. 'I know I'm not the full quid, Mary,' he'll say, and just to hear him breaks my heart."

"He sounds educable, though. Does he work?"

"Yes, as a builder's laborer. I suppose his workmates are kind enough to him in their way, but they're also very thoughtlessly cruel. They get a terrific kick out of playing practical jokes on him, like the time they tricked him into eating excrement. He cried that day, not because he'd been victimized but because he couldn't understand the joke. He wanted to be in on the joke!" Her face twisted, and she had to stop.

John Martinson nodded encouragement and sympathy. "Oh, it's a pretty common sort of pattern," he said. "What of his mother and father, how do they treat him?"

"Very well, all considered." She explained the circumstances of Tim's life to him, surprised at her own fluency. "But they worry about him," she ended sadly, "especially about what will happen to him after they pass away. His father says he'll die of a broken heart. I didn't believe it at first, but as time goes on I'm beginning to see that it's very likely."

"Oh, I agree, very likely. There are many such cases, you know. People like your Tim need a loving home a lot more than we normal people, because they can't learn to adjust to life without it if once they've known it. It's a very difficult world for them, this one of ours." He considered her gravely. "I take it, from your choice among our children who remind you of Tim, that he's quite normal to look at?"

"Normal to look at?" She sighed. "If only he was! No, Tim's not normal to look at. Undoubtedly he's the most spectacular young man I've ever seen—like a Greek god, for want of a more original simile."

"Oh!" John Martinson dropped his eyes from her to his folded hands for a moment, then sighed. "Well, Miss Horton, I'll give you the titles of some books I think you'll have no trouble understanding. You'll find they'll help you."

He rose and walked with her to the front hall, bending his head down to her courteously. "I hope you'll bring Tim to see me one of these days. I'd very much like to meet him. Perhaps you'd better call me first, though, because I think it would be better for him if you came to my home rather than the school."

Mary held out her hand. "I'd like that. Goodbye, Mr. Martinson, and thank you so much for your kindness."

She went away thoughtful and saddened, conscious that the most insoluble problems are those which by their very nature can have no space within them for dreams.

Seventeen

Spring in Sydney was not the brilliant, burgeoning explosion of new growth and awakening it was in the Northern Hemisphere. All but a few kinds of imported deciduous trees retained their leaves throughout the brief, balmy winter, and there was always something flowering in Sydney gardens the year round. The greatest change was in the air, a sparkling softness that somehow filled the heart with renewed hope and joy.

Mary's cottage would have been the showplace of the district, could anyone have seen it. She and Tim had worked hard on the garden all through the winter, even going so far as to buy fully grown trees and having them planted by a specialist. So when October came there were flowers everywhere, massed in huge beds alongside the veranda and circling every tree. Iceland poppies, carnations, asters, pansies, phlox, sweet peas, tulips, wistaria, daffodils, hyacinths, azaleas, gladioli; flowers of every color, size, and shape splashed their crowded heads in sheets of beauty everywhere, and the wind carried their perfumes through the wild forest and out across the river.

Four exquisitely sad weeping cherries drooped their loaded pink branches down over pink hyacinths and tulips growing in the grass beneath them, and six flowering almonds creaked under a weight of white blossom, the grass around them smothered with lily of the valley and daffodils.

The first weekend that everything was fully out in flower, Tim went wild with delight. He capered from cherries to almonds, marveling at Mary's shrewdness in choosing only pink bulbs to surround the cherries and white and yellow for the almonds, exclaiming at how they looked as if they grew wild out of the grass. Mary watched him, smiling in spite of all her resolutions to be serious no matter how he reacted. His joy was so transparent, so tender and experimental; Paris wandering the springtime slopes of Mount Ida before returning to the drudgery of an urban Troy. It was indeed a beautiful garden, Mary thought, her eyes following Tim as he danced about, but how did he see it, how different did it appear in his eyes, that it awed and delighted him so? Insects and even some higher animals were supposed to see a different world through differently constructed eyes, see colors and shapes a human being could not; what shade was infrared, what hue was ultraviolet? Perhaps Tim, too, saw things beyond her ken; perhaps among all the other tangled circuits in his brain he saw a different spectrum and heard a different frequency band. Did he hear the music of the spheres, could he see the shape of the spirit and the color of the moon? If there was only some way to tell! But his world was forever barred, she could not enter it and he could not tell her what it was like.

"Tim," she said that night, as they sat in the darkened living room with the glass doors open to the perfume-saturated wind, "Tim, what do you feel now, at this moment? What do the flowers smell like, how do you see my face?"

He withdrew himself reluctantly from the music they were playing, turning his dream-clouded eyes upon her mistily, smiling in the gentle, almost vacant way he had. Her heart seemed to quiver and dissolve under that look, something unidentifiable welled up in her, so surrounded by sadness that she had to wink away tears.

He was frowning as he puzzled over the questions, and when

123

he answered it was slowly, hesitantly. "Feel? Feel? Cripes, I dunno! Sort of happy, good. I feel good, that's it!"

"And what do the flowers smell like?"

He smiled at her, thinking she was joking. "Why, they smell like flowers, of course!"

"And my face?"

"Your face is beautiful, like Mum's and Dawnie's. It looks like Saint Teresa in my holy picture."

She sighed. "That's a lovely thing to say, Tim. I'm sure I never thought of myself as having a face like Saint Teresa."

"Well, it is," he assured her. "She's on the wall at the end of my bed at home, Mum put her up there because I like her, I like her. She looks at me every night and every morning as though she thinks I'm the full quid, and you look at me like that, too, Mary." He shivered, gripped by a kind of painful joy. "I like you, Mary, I like you better than Dawnie, I like you as much as I like Pop and Mum." The beautifully shaped hands moved, and said more in their moving than his poor, limited speech ever could. "But it's sort of different, Mary, different from Pop and Mum. Sometimes I like them better than you, and sometimes I like you better than them."

She got up abruptly and went to the doors. "I'm going outside for a little walk, Tim, but I want you to stay here like a good fellow and listen to the music. I'll be back soon."

He nodded and turned back to the record player, watching it fixedly, as though to do so helped him hear the music.

The scent of the garden was unbearable, and passing through the daffodils like a shadow she made her way down to the beach. There was a rock in the sand at the far end, just tall enough to serve as a back rest, but when Mary dropped to her knees in the sand she turned to face it, put her arms upon it and buried her face against them. Her shoulders drew together and her body twisted in a spasm of devastating grief, so desolate and despairing that for a moment a part of her held back from participat-

124

ing, horrified. But the grief could not be suppressed or denied any longer; she wept and moaned in pain.

They were like a moth and a bright, burning light, she and Tim; she the moth, endowed with senses and the dignity of life, he the light, filling her entire world with a brilliant, searing fire. He did not know how desperately she buffeted herself against the walls of his isolation, he could never comprehend the depth and urgency of her desire to immolate herself on the flame of his fascination. Fighting the uselessness of her hunger and knowing it was beyond him to appease it, she ground her teeth in rage and pain and wept inconsolably.

What must have been hours later she felt his hand on her shoulder.

"Mary, are you all right?" His voice was filled with fear. "Are you sick? Oh, Mary, please say you're all right, please say you're all right!"

She forced her shaking arms down to her sides. "I'm all right, Tim," she answered wearily, lowering her head so that he could not see her face, even though it was very dark. "I just felt a bit sick, and came out for a breath of air. I didn't want to worry you, that's all."

"Do you still feel sick?" He squatted on his haunches beside her and tried to peer into her face, stroking her shoulder clumsily. "Were you sick?"

She shook her head, inching away from his hand. "No, I'm all right now, Tim, really I am. It passed off." One hand on the rock for leverage, she tried to get to her feet but could not, cramped and defeated. "Oh, Tim, I'm so old and tired," she whispered. "I'm so old and tired."

He stood up and stared at her anxiously, fidgeting nervously. "Mum was sick once and I remember Pop made me carry her to bed. I'll carry you to bed, Mary."

He bent and gathered her up effortlessly, shifting her weight within his arms until one was crooked under her knees and the

125

other cradled her back. Too exhausted to protest, she let him carry her up the path, but when he stepped onto the veranda she turned her face into his shoulder, not wanting him to see it. He paused, blinking in the light, and put his cheek against her head lovingly.

"You're so small, Mary," he said, rubbing his face back and forth across her hair. "You're all soft and warm, like a kitten." Then he sighed and crossed the living room.

He could not find the light switch in her bedroom, and when he would have groped for it she stopped him, her hand pressing gently at his throat.

"Don't worry about the light, Tim, you can see to put me on the bed. I just want to lie down in the dark for a while, then I'll be fine."

He laid her on the bed carefully, looming above her in the darkness, and she sensed his worried indecision.

"Tim, you know I wouldn't tell you a lie, don't you?"

He nodded. "Yes, I know that."

"Then you'll believe me when I tell you that there's no need to worry about me, that I'm all right now. Haven't you ever felt a bit sick after you've eaten something that didn't agree with you?"

"Yes, I did once, after I'd eaten some candied fruit," he answered gravely.

"Then you understand how I felt, don't you? Now I want you to stop worrying about me and go to bed, and sleep, sleep! I feel much better and all I need is to sleep, too, but I can't sleep if I think you're upset or worried. Now promise me that you'll go straight to bed and be happy."

"I will, Mary." He sounded relieved.

"Goodnight, Tim, and thank you very much for helping me like that. It's so nice to be looked after, and you look after me

126

very well. I don't ever need to worry about myself while I've got you, do I?"

"I'll always look after you, Mary." He stooped and kissed her forehead, the way she sometimes did with him when he was in bed. "Night-night, Mary."

Eighteen

When Esme Melville let herself in the back door after her Thursday afternoon tennis match it was all she could do to walk the few yards more to the living room and a comfortable chair. Her legs were shaking; it had been a tremendous strain to get home without letting anyone see how distressed she was. She felt so nauseated that after a few moments in the chair she got up and went to the bathroom. Even kneeling with her head over the lavatory bowl didn't relieve the sickness; somehow she could not vomit, the pain under her left shoulder blade made the effort of retching unbearable. She hung there for several minutes panting, then dragged herself by stages to her feet, grasping at the bathroom cupboard and the shower door. It shocked her to realize that the frightened face in the wall mirror was her own, all muddy gray and beaded with sweat. The sight of it terrified her more than anything ever had, and she took her eyes away from the mirror immediately. She managed to stagger back to the living room and flopped into the chair, gasping, her hands flapping about helplessly.

Then the pain took her and tore at her like some huge, maddened beast; she leaned forward, her arms folded across her chest, their fists digging into her armpits. Small, moaning whimpers escaped her each time the knifelike agony worked itself up to a crescendo, and she could think no further than the pain.

After an eternity it lessened; she leaned back in the chair, spent and shaking in every limb. Something seemed to be sitting on her chest, forcing all the air out of her lungs and making it impossible to suck in more. She was wet everywhere; the white tennis dress was soaked with sweat, her face with tears, the chair seat with urine she had voided during the worst of her rigors. Sobbing and choking through purpled lips, she sat there praying that Ron would think to come home before going to the Seaside. The phone in the hall was light-years away, absolutely beyond her.

It was seven that evening before Ron and Tim let themselves in the back door of the house in Surf Street. All was oddly quiet and undisturbed; no places had been laid on the dining room table, and there was no friendly smell of food.

"Hullo, where's Mum?" Ron asked cheerily as he and Tim stepped into the kitchen. "Es, love, where are youse?" he called, then shrugged. "Must have decided on a couple of extra sets at the Hit and Giggle Club," he said.

Tim went on into the living room while Ron switched on the kitchen and dining room lights. There was a terrified scream from the interior of the house; Ron dropped the kettle he was holding and dashed with pounding heart to the living room. Tim was standing wringing his hands together and weeping, staring at Esme as she lay in the chair, curiously still, her arms folded and her hands knotted into fists in her sides.

"Oh, God!"

The tears sprang to Ron's eyes as he went to the chair and bent over his wife, reaching out a shaking hand to touch her skin. It was warm; hardly able to believe it, he discovered that her chest was rising and falling slowly. He got to his feet at once.

"Now, Tim, don't cry," he said through chattering teeth. "I'm going to ring Dr. Perkins and Dawnie, then I'll come right back. You stay here, and if Mum does anything, you yell. All right, mate?"

Dr. Perkins was at home, eating supper; he told Ron that he

would call an ambulance and meet them at Prince of Wales Hospital casualty room. Wiping away the tears with the back of his hand, Ron dialed Dawnie's number.

Mick answered, his voice betraying his impatience; it was their dinner hour, and he hated to be disturbed then.

"Listen, Mick, it's Ron here," Ron said, enunciating carefully. "Now don't go frightening Dawnie, but it's her Mum. I think she's had a heart attack, only I'm not sure. We're getting her to Prince of Wales casualty immediately, so there's no point in coming here. It would be best for you and Dawnie to meet us at the hospital as soon as you possibly can."

"I'm terribly sorry, Ron," Mick mumbled. "Of course Dawn and I will come immediately. Try not to worry."

When Ron came back to the living room, Tim was still standing watching his mother and weeping desolately; she had not moved. Ron put his arm around his son's shoulders and hugged him, not knowing what else to do.

"Jeez, don't cry, Tim me boy," he muttered. "Mum's all right, the ambulance is coming and we're going to get her to the hospital. They'll fix her up in no time. You've got to be a good bloke and be calm, for Mum's sake. She won't like it if she wakes up and sees you standing there howling like a great big booby, will she?"

Snuffling and hiccoughing, Tim tried to stop crying while his father approached Esme's chair and knelt down, taking her doubled fists in his hands and forcing them into her lap.

"Es!" he called, his face old and lined. "Es, love, can you hear me? It's Ron, love, it's Ron!"

She was gray in the face and shrunken, but her eyes opened. They flooded with light as they saw him kneeling there, and she returned his clasp gratefully.

"Ron. . . . Jeez, I'm glad you come home. . . . Where's Tim?"

"He's here, love. Don't worry about Tim, now, and don't go getting all upset. The ambulance is coming and we're going to get you into POW right away. How do you feel?"

"Like something the . . . cat dragged in. . . . Oh, Christ, Ron . . . the pain . . . it's awful. . . . I wet meself. . . . The chair's sopping. . . ."

"Don't worry about the bloody furniture, Es, it'll dry out. What's the odd leak between friends, eh?" He tried to smile, but his face twisted. For all his control, he began to weep. "Oh, Es, don't let nothing happen to youse, love! Oh, God, what will I do without youse? Hang on, Es, hang on until we get you to hospital!"

"I'll . . . hang on. . . . Can't . . . leave Tim . . . all alone now. . . . Can't . . . leave Tim . . . alone. . . ."

Five minutes after Ron called Dr. Perkins the ambulance was outside. Ron directed the ambulance men around to the back door, for there were twenty steps up to the front door and none to the back. They were big, quietly cheerful men, highly trained professionals in the field of emergency medicine; as aware of their skill as other Sydneysiders, Ron felt no qualms over Dr. Perkins' decision to meet them at the hospital. They checked Es's condition swiftly and lifted her onto the stretcher. Ron and Tim followed their navy blue uniforms out the back door, feeling useless and unwanted.

Ron put Tim in the front with one of the ambulance men and rode in the back with the other. They seemed to know immediately that Tim was not the full quid, for the one who was driving settled Tim in the adjoining seat with a cheery word that seemed to have more effect on him than anything Ron could have said.

They did not put the siren on; the one traveling in the back with Ron slipped a plastic airway into Es's mouth and connected her to his oxygen supply, then draped himself along the stretcher with his hand on her pulse.

"Why don't you put the siren on?" Ron asked, looking about wildly, the oxygen and airway frightening him.

131

Wide, reassuringly steady eyes gazed back at him; the ambulance man patted him on the back. "Now take it easy, mate," he said calmly. "We only put the siren on going to an emergency case, very rarely when there's someone inside. It terrifies the patient, does more harm than good, you know. She's okay, and at this time of night we'll get there just as soon without a siren. Only a couple of miles."

The ambulance threaded its way deftly through the thin traffic, drawing in to the brilliantly lit casualty room at the Prince of Wales Hospital five minutes after leaving Surf Street. Just as the sleek big car came to a halt, Es opened her eyes and coughed out the airway. The ambulance man assessed her rapidly, then decided to leave it out unless she went into another spasm. Maybe she wanted to say something, and that was important; it was better to let a patient find her own level, less distressing.

"Ron . . ."

"I'm here, love. You're at the hospital, we'll soon have you fixed up now."

"I dunno . . . Ron . . ."

"Yes, love?" The tears were running down his face again.

"It's Tim. . . . What we . . . always worried about. . . . What's . . . going . . . to happen to . . . Tim . . . when I'm not . . . here? . . . Ron . . ."

"I'm here, love."

"Look after . . . Tim. . . . Do the . . . right . . . thing . . . for . . . Tim. . . . Poor Tim. . . . Poor . . . Tim. . . ."

It was the last thing she ever said. While Ron and Tim were still milling futilely around casualty entrance, the emergency staff had whisked the stretcher away out of sight. The Melville men stood watching the white doors flap to a stop, then were directed firmly but gently to the waiting area. Someone came not long afterward and brought them tea with some sweet biscuits, smilingly refusing to give them any news.

Dawnie and her husband arrived half an hour later. Dawnie was beginning to be very pregnant, her husband plainly anxious for her. She waddled to her father's side and sat between him and Tim on the bench, weeping.

"Now, now, love, don't cry," Ron comforted. "The old girl will be all right, we got her here okay. They've taken her off somewhere, and when there's any news they'll tell us. You just sit down and stop crying. Think of the baby, love, you mustn't get into a taking at this stage."

"What happened?" Mick asked, lighting a cigarette and trying not to stare at Tim.

"I dunno. When Tim and I come home she was lying unconscious in a chair in the living room. I dunno how long she'd been there. Christ, why didn't I go straight home from work, why did I go to the Seaside? I could of gone home for once!"

Dawnie blew her nose. "Pop, don't blame yourself. You know you always come home at the same time during the week, how were you to know today she'd need you? You know she didn't mind your habits! She liked to see you enjoy your little drop after work, and besides, it gave her the chance to lead her own life. Many's the time I've heard her say it was such a break for her knowing you wouldn't be home from the Seaside before seven, because she could play her tennis until six and still have a meal ready for you and Tim when you came in."

"I oughta knowed she was getting on and not too well, I oughta seen it for meself."

"Pop, there's no point in recrimination! What's done is done. Mum wouldn't have wanted her life or yours any other way, and you know it. Don't waste time fretting over things you can't undo, love, think of her and Tim instead."

"Oh, Christ, I am!" His tone was despairing.

They turned to look at Tim, sitting quietly on the seat with his hands clenched together, his shoulders hunched in the withdrawn pose he always assumed when grief-stricken. He had stopped weeping, his eyes fixed on something they could not see. Dawnie wriggled closer to her brother.

"Tim!" she said softly, her small square hand stroking his arm.

He flinched, then seemed to become aware of her. The blue eyes transferred their gaze from infinity to her face, and he stared at her sadly.

"Dawnie!" he said, as if wondering what she was doing there.

"I'm here, Tim. Now don't worry about Mum, she's going to be all right, I promise."

He shook his head. "Mary says you should never make promises you can't keep."

Dawnie's face stiffened dangerously, and she turned her attention back to Ron, ignoring Tim completely.

The night was very old when Dr. Perkins came into the waiting room, his face drawn and fatigued. They all rose at once, like condemned men as the judge pulls on his cap.

"Ron, may I see you outside?" he asked quietly.

The corridor was deserted, the spotlights dotted down the center of the high ceiling flooding the tiled floor crudely. Dr. Perkins put his arm about Ron's shoulders.

"She's gone, mate."

There seemed to be a terrible, dragging weight in Ron's chest; he looked into the elderly doctor's face pitifully.

"You don't mean it!"

"There was nothing we could do. She'd had a massive heart attack, and then she had another one a few minutes after she got here. Her heart stopped. We tried to get it going again, but it was useless, useless. I suspect she must have had trouble before today, and this sudden cold spell of weather plus the tennis didn't help."

"She never told me she was sick, I didn't know. But that's Es, never complains." Ron had good control now, he could manage. "Oh, Doctor, I dunno what to do! There's Tim and Dawnie in there, thinking she's all right!"

134

"Do you want me to tell them, Ron?"

Ron shook his head. "No, I'll do it. Just give me a minute. Can I see her?"

"Yes. But keep Tim and Dawnie away."

"Then take me to her now, Doctor, before I tell them."

They had wheeled Es out of the intensive care unit and put her in a small side room reserved for such occasions. All the evidence of her medical treatment was gone, the tubes and cables; a sheet was drawn up over her head. It struck Ron like a mammoth fist as he stood in the doorway, looking at the utterly quiet form outlined beneath the drape. That was Es there, under the sheet, and she could never move again; it was all over for her, the sun and laughter, the tears and the rain. No more, no more. Her portion of life's feast was ended, here like this in a dimly lit room with a snowy white cloth to cover her. No fanfare, no warning. No chance to prepare, not even the time for a proper goodbye. Just finished, over, done with. He approached the bed, suddenly conscious of a sickly sweet smell of jonquils stealing from a huge vase on a nearby table. Never afterward could he bear the smell of jonquils.

Dr. Perkins stood on the far side of the narrow bed and twitched the sheet back quickly, then turned his head away; could one ever grow used to the grief in another's face, could one ever learn to accept death?

They had closed her eyes and folded her hands across her breast; Ron looked at her for a long moment, then leaned over to kiss her lips. But it was not like kissing Es. Those bleached, cold lips brought nothing to him of Es. Sighing, he turned away.

In the waiting room, three pairs of eyes riveted themselves on his face when he came in. He stood looking at them, squaring his shoulders.

"She's gone," he said.

Dawnie cried out and let herself be taken into Mick's arms; Tim just sat staring at his father like a lost and bewildered child.

135

Ron came over and took his son's hand very tenderly.

"Let's go for a little walk, mate," he said.

They left the waiting room and the corridor behind them, heading for the open air. Outside it was growing light, and the eastern rim of the world was pearly with the first flush of rose and gold. The little dawn wind puffed itself in their faces softly and sighed away again.

"Tim, there's no use letting you think Mum's ever going to come back," Ron said wearily. "Mum died a little while ago. She's gone, mate, gone. She can't never come back no more, she's gone away from us to a better life, no more pain or sadness. We're going to have to learn to get along without her, and it's going to be awful, awful hard. . . . But she wanted us to carry on without her, it was the last thing she said, to carry on and not to miss her too much. We will at first, but after a while, when we're used to it, it won't be quite so bad."

"Can't I see her before she goes, Pop?" Tim asked desolately.

His father shook his head, swallowing painfully. "No, mate. You can't see her ever again. But you mustn't blame her for that, it wasn't the way she wanted it, to go off so suddenly with never a chance to say goodbye. Sometimes things get out of our control, things happen too fast for us to catch up with them, and then it's too late. Mum died like that, too soon, too soon. . . . Her time had come and there was nothing she could do to push it away, you see, mate."

"Is she really and truly dead, Pop?"

"Yes, she's really and truly dead, Tim."

Tim lifted his head to the cloudless sky; a seagull screeched and wheeled far above them, dipping toward the alien earth and then soaring in search of its watery home.

"Mary told me what dead was, Pop. I know what it is. Mum's gone to sleep, she's gone to sleep in the ground under a blanket of grass and she's going to rest there until we all go too, isn't she?"

"That's about the size of it, mate."

When they came back to the casualty room, Dr. Perkins was waiting for them. He sent Tim in to be with Dawnie and Mick, but detained Ron.

"Ron, there are arrangements to be made."

Ron quivered. "Oh, God! Doctor, what do I do? I don't have the faintest idea!"

Dr. Perkins told him about undertakers, and offered to call one particular man for Ron.

"He's good and kind, Ron," the doctor explained. "He won't charge you more than you can afford and he handles it all very quietly, with a minimum of fuss and glorification. She'll have to be buried tomorrow, you know, because the day after is Sunday and they should be buried within forty-eight hours. It's the hot climate. Don't embalm her, what's the point of it? Just let her alone. I'll tell Mortimer you're an old family of mine, and he'll take care of everything. Now why don't you call a taxi and take your family home?"

When they let themselves into the deserted house Dawnie seemed to come to life a little, and busied herself making breakfast. Ron went through to the phone and called Mary Horton. She answered at once, which relieved him; he had dreaded finding her muddled with sleep.

"Miss Horton, it's Ron Melville here. Listen, I know it's an awful lot to ask, but I'm desperate. My wife died this morning, it was very sudden. . . . Yes, thanks very much, Miss Horton. . . . Yes, I am sort of numb. . . . Yes, I'll try to get some rest. . . . What I rang you about was Tim . . . yes, he knows, I couldn't see the sense in keeping it from him, he had to know sometime, and why not now? . . . Thanks, Miss Horton, I'm real glad you think I done the right thing in telling him. I'm awful grateful to you, too, for explaining dying to him. . . . Well, it was a terrific help, it really was. . . . No, it wasn't nearly as hard making him understand as I thought it would be. I thought it would take me

137

all day to get it through to him, but he took it like a regular little trump. . . . Yes, he's all right, he's accepting it very well, no tears or tantrums. He was the one who found her, terrible. Miss Horton, I know you work all week, but I know you're real fond of Tim, so I'm going to get up my courage to ask if you could come out and see me today, real soon, and maybe take Tim off with you until Sunday. She's being buried tomorrow, can't be buried the day after because it's Sunday. I don't want him at the funeral. . . . All right, Miss Horton, I'll be here and so will Tim. . . . Thanks very, very much, I do appreciate it. . . . Yes, I'll try, Miss Horton. See you soon. Bye bye now, and thanks again."

Dawnie took Tim out into the garden while Ron talked to Mr. Mortimer the undertaker, who was indeed all that Dr. Perkins had promised. A death in an Australian working-class family was neither an expensive nor a long-drawn-out affair, and rigid laws made exploitation of the bereaved difficult. Uncomplicated, earthy people, they felt no compulsion to make up a lifetime of real or imagined guilts to a corpse; no opulent coffins, wakes, or putting the body on display. It was all conducted quickly and quietly, so much so that often friends and neighbors would have known little about it except for the gossip grapevine.

Shortly after the undertaker left, Mary Horton parked her Bentley in the street outside the Melville house and mounted the steps to the front door. Word had got around the vicinity during the early morning, and many front windows showed telltale rifts in their curtains as Mary disappeared onto the front veranda to wait for an answer to her knock.

Dawnie's husband, Mick, opened the door, and stared at Mary in bewilderment. For a moment he thought she was someone professionally connected with the undertaker, and said, "Oh, you've just missed Mr. Mortimer, he left about five minutes ago."

Mary looked at him appraisingly. "You must be Dawn's husband. I'm Mary Horton, and I've come to fetch Tim. But please, would you quietly let Mr. Melville know I'm here first, don't mention my arrival to Tim? I'll wait here."

Mick shut the door and trod down the long hallway, his thoughts in confusion. From what the Melvilles said he had gathered Miss Horton was an old lady, but though the woman on the front veranda had white hair, she was far from old. Ron was trying to interest Tim in a television program; Mick wriggled his brows mutely toward the front door, and Ron got up at once, closing the door between the hallway and the living room as he went out.

"Dawn, Miss Horton's here," Mick whispered as he sat down beside her.

She looked at him curiously. "So?"

"She's not old, Dawn! Why do you speak of her as if she's Ron age? I could hardly believe my eyes when I opened the front door! She can't be more than forty-five, if she's that old!"

"What on earth's the matter with you, Mick? Of course she's old! I admit I didn't get a good look at her that night I saw her outside in her car, but it was close enough to tell she was old. And her hair's whiter than Pop's!"

"People can go white at twenty, you know that. I tell you she's a relatively young woman!"

Dawnie sat in silence for a moment, then shook her head, smiling wryly. "The sly old bezom! So that was her game!"

"What was her game?"

"Tim, of course! She's sleeping with him!"

Mick whistled. "Of course! But wouldn't your parents have suspected something like that? They watch him so carefully, Dawn."

"Mum wouldn't hear a word against her precious Miss Horton, and Pop's been like the cat that swallowed the canary ever since Tim began bringing home the extra money Miss Mary Horton pays him for doing her garden. Hah! Doing her garden, indeed!"

Mick shot a quick glance toward Tim. "Keep your voice down, Dawn!"

"Oh, I could kill Pop for turning a blind eye!" Dawnie said through clenched teeth. "All along I've thought there was something suspicious about that woman, but Pop wouldn't hear a word of it. Okay, I can understand Mum not suspecting, but Pop should have listened to me! Too busy thinking of all that extra money coming in!"

Ron in his turn gaped at Mary Horton, shocked out of his numbness for a moment. "Are *you* Miss Horton?" he croaked, voice cracking from the long hours and the strain.

"Yes, I'm Mary Horton. Did you think I was an old lady too, Mr. Melville?"

"Yes, I did." He recollected himself sufficiently to hold the door fully open. "Won't you come in, Miss Horton? I hope you don't mind stepping into the front bedroom for a minute before I take you through to Tim."

"Of course not." She followed Ron into the bedroom, ill at ease; this looked like the master bedroom, and she wondered how Ron would hold up under the stress of talking to her in the place where he and his wife had lain each night for years. But he scarcely seemed to be aware of his surroundings; he could not take his eyes from her face. She was nothing like the person he had imagined, and yet she was exactly like the person he had imagined. Her face was young and unlined, she could not be more than forty-five, if that. But it was not a rapacious, intensely feminine face, it was a kind, slightly stern face with a touch of suffering about it, in the fierce brown eyes and the determined mouth. Her hair was very white, like crystal. In spite of the shock of discovering she was much younger than he had thought, Ron trusted that face and the person who owned it. A severely handsome sort of exterior, he decided, a fitting exterior for Mary Horton, whom he always thought of as one of the kindest, most generous, and understanding people ever to enter his life.

140

"Mr. Melville, I'm at a loss for words. I'm so very sorry for this, for you and Tim and Dawnie. . . ."

"I know, Miss Horton. Please don't try, I understand. It's a terrible blow, but we'll weather it. I'm only sorry Es never met you. We just never seemed to get around to it, did we?"

"No, we didn't, and I'm sorry for that, too. How is poor Tim?"

"A bit dazed, like. He don't quite know what's happening, except that Mum's dead. I'm awful sorry to have to bring youse into this, but I just don't know what else to do. I can't let Tim come to the funeral, and he shouldn't be left on his own while the rest of us go."

"I quite agree. I'm so glad you thought to call me, Mr. Melville, and you can rest assured I'll take good care of Tim for you. I was wondering if this Sunday night coming I could drive you and Tim up to my cottage and have you stay there for a while, to get over it in different surroundings. I'll keep Tim in Sydney today, tomorrow, and Sunday, then on Sunday evening I'll come back here and collect you, then drive you both up to my cottage. Would that be all right?"

Ron's face twisted for a moment, then composed itself. "That's real considerate of you, Miss Horton, and for Tim's sake I'll take youse up on it, too. His boss and my boss won't mind if we take a week off."

"Then it's all settled. Dawnie would be better off with her husband, don't you think? It will take a load off her mind to know that you and Tim aren't sitting here in the house all alone."

"That's right, it will take a load off her mind. She's just about eight months gone with the baby."

"Oh, I didn't know!" Mary wet her lips and tried not to look at the old double bed against the far wall. "Shall we go and say hullo to Tim now?"

It was a curious little group in the living room. Mick and Dawnie sat huddled together on the sofa and Tim sat in his special chair, hunched over and leaning forward, his unseeing

141

eyes fixed on the television set. Mary stood in the hall doorway quietly, watching him; he had his lost look about him, defenseless and bewildered.

"Hullo, Tim," she said.

He leaped to his feet, half overjoyed and half too saddened to feel joy, then stood with his face twitching and his hands going out to her. She went to him and took them, smiling at him tenderly.

"I've come to take you to my house for a little while, Tim," she said softly.

He snatched his hands away sharply, flushing; for the first time since knowing him Mary saw him uncomfortable and quite conscious of his actions. Involuntarily his eyes had gone to Dawnie, seen her outrage and revulsion, and something in him was developed and mature enough to sense that Dawnie thought he had done something unpardonable, that she condemned him for holding this beloved woman's hands. His own hands fluttered to his sides, lonely and empty again, and he stood looking at his sister pleadingly. She compressed her lips and sidled to her feet like a fizzing cat, eyes flashing angrily from Tim to Mary.

Mary walked forward with her hand extended. "Hullo, Dawnie, I'm Mary Horton," she said pleasantly.

Dawnie ignored the hand. "What are you doing here?" she spat.

Mary pretended not to notice her tone. "I've come for Tim," she explained.

"Oh, I'll just bet you have!" Dawnie sneered. "Look at you! My mother not cold and here you are with your tongue hanging out for poor, stupid Tim! What do you mean, tricking us into thinking you were old? A fine lot of fools you've made us out to be, and in front of my husband at that!"

"Oh, for Christ's sake, Dawnie, pipe down!" Ron interrupted desperately.

142

Dawnie turned on him furiously. "I'll pipe down when I've said what I intend to say, you greedy old bastard! Selling your own dill-brained son every weekend for a few measly dollars! Did it feel good, guzzling your extra beer in the Seaside every day? Did you ever stop to think of the disgrace? Look at her, trying to brazen it out as though her interest in Tim was pure and spiritual and completely altruistic! Well, *Miss* Mary Horton," she hissed, whipping round to face Mary again, "I'm a wakeup to your little game! Tricking us all into thinking you were at least ninety! I wonder how many people up and down Surf Street are laughing their heads off right now because they just got a good long daylight look at Tim's weekend hostess? You've made us the laughingstock of the whole district, you frustrated old cow! If you had to have a man, why the hell couldn't you have bought yourself a gigolo instead of preying on a mental weakling like my poor, silly brother? You're a disgusting, loathsome, wicked woman! Why don't you get your ugly carcass out of here and leave us alone?"

Mary stood in the center of the living room with her hands limply by her sides, two bright patches of color flaring in her cheeks. The tears trickled down her face in mute protest at the appalling accusation; she was so shocked and devastated by it that she could do nothing to justify herself; she had neither the energy nor the will to fight back. Ron had begun to shake, clenching his hands together so tightly that his knuckles showed as bloodless splotches. Tim had gone to his chair and collapsed on it, his upturned face swiveling from the accuser to the accused. He was confused, anguished, and strangely ashamed, but the reason for it was quite beyond him; he could not fathom it. It seemed as though Dawnie thought it was wrong for him to be friends with Mary, but why was it wrong, how could it be wrong? What had Mary done? It didn't seem fair for Dawnie to scream at Mary like that, but he didn't know what to do about it because he didn't understand what it was all about. And why did he want to run away and hide himself in some dark corner, as he had the time he stole Mum's tennis club cake?

Ron shivered, trying to control his anger. "Dawnie, I don't never want to hear you saying things like that ever again, do you hear? What in God's name is the matter with you, girl? A real decent woman like Miss Horton! Struth and little apples, she don't have to stand here and listen to scut like this! You've disgraced me, you've disgraced Tim, and you've disgraced your poor dead mother, and at a time like this! Oh, God, Dawnie, what makes you say things like that?"

"I say them because I think they're true," Dawnie retorted, huddling herself on the sofa within Mick's arm. "You've let her filthy money make you blind and deaf!"

Mary passed a trembling hand across her face, wiping away the tears. She looked directly at Dawnie and her husband. "You're very, very wrong, my dear," she managed to say. "I understand how shocked and upset you are by all that's happened in the last few hours, and I'm sure you don't really think any of the things you're saying." She drew a shuddering breath. "I didn't deliberately conceal my age, it just never seemed that important, because I never thought for one moment that anyone would interpret Tim's and my relationship on such a basic plane. I'm very deeply attached to Tim, but not in the way you're implying. It isn't very complimentary to me; I'm old enough to be Tim's and your mother, you know. And you're quite right, too: if I wanted a man I could afford to go out and buy a gold-plated gigolo. Why indeed should I employ Tim on such a project? Can you in all honesty say that you've seen any evidence of sexual awakening in Tim since he's known me? If it had occurred, you would have seen it immediately: Tim's far too transparent a creature to conceal anything as deep-reaching as that. I've enjoyed Tim so much in, if you'll pardon my hackneyed choice of words, such a pure and innocent way. Tim *is* pure and innocent, it's part of his allure. I wouldn't change that

144

in him if I had ten thousand carnal demons gnawing at my flesh incessantly. And now you've spoiled it, spoiled it for us both, because if Tim can't understand, he can at the very least sense change. It was in its way so perfect, and I use the past tense deliberately. It can never be so again. You've made me conscious of something I hadn't considered, and you've made Tim feel uncomfortable when he extends normal affection to me."

Mick cleared his throat. "But surely, Miss Horton, you must have had some inkling of what other people were bound to think. I find it hard to believe that you, a mature and responsible woman, could go on month after month spending all your free time with a young and extremely good-looking man without so much as a passing thought as to what other people must be thinking?"

"So that's it!" Ron roared, dragging Mick off the couch and holding him by his lapels. "I might have known my girl Dawnie didn't think of all that muck-raking bullshit without some help from you! You certainly are a fast worker, mate! Between answering the door to Miss Horton and her coming into this room ten minutes later you managed to plant your filthy suggestions in my daughter's mind so bloody well that she's shamed and disgraced us all! You cocktail drinking shirt-lifter! Christ, why couldn't Dawnie have married a dinkum bloke instead of a simpering, stuck-up pansy like you? I oughta kick your teeth in, you miserable, rotten, fucking *arsehole!*"

"Pop!" Dawnie gasped, grabbing at her waistline. "Oh, Pop!" She burst into tears, drumming her heels on the floor.

Then Tim moved, so suddenly that it took the rest of them several seconds to realize what had happened. Ron and Mick were separated, Mick put back on the sofa and Dawnie and Ron thrust into chairs, all without a word. Tim turned his back on Mick and touched his father lightly on the shoulder.

"Pop, don't let him get your goat," he said earnestly. "I don't like him either, but Mum said we had to treat him real well, even if we don't like him. Dawnie belongs to him now, that's what Mum said."

Mary began to laugh in shivering, gasping gusts; Tim went to her side and put his arm about her.

"Are you laughing or crying, Mary?" he asked, peering into her face. "Don't take any notice of Dawnie or Mick, they're upset. Why can't we go now? Can't I pack my case?"

Ron was staring at his son in amazement and dawning respect. "You go and pack your case, mate, you go and pack it right this minute. Mary will come and help you in half a tick. And you know something, mate? You're the grouse, the real, dinkum good oil!"

Tim's beautiful eyes shone, his smile flashed out for the first time since they had come home to discover Es. "I like you too, Pop," he grinned, and went to pack his case.

After he had gone there was a strained silence; Dawnie sat looking everywhere but at Mary Horton, and Mary continued to stand in the middle of the floor, not knowing what she ought best to do.

"I reckon you owe Miss Horton an apology, Dawnie," Ron said, staring his daughter down.

She stiffened, her fingers curling into claws. "I'm buggered if I'll apologize!" she spat. "After what's been done to us here I reckon Mick and I are the ones owed an apology! Manhandling my husband like that!"

Ron gazed at her sorrowfully. "I'm real glad your Mum's not here," he said. "She always said you'd change, that we'd have to get out of your life, but I know bloody well she never thought you'd go all twitty like this. You're too big for your boots, my girl, and you could take a few lessons in manners from Miss Horton here, not to mention your flaming snotty husband!"

"Oh, please!" Mary exclaimed wretchedly. "I'm terribly sorry I've caused all this unpleasantness. If I'd known what would happen I assure you I would never have come. Please don't quarrel on my account, I'd hate to think I caused a permanent breach in Tim's family. If it wasn't that I think Tim needs me now, I'd willingly get out of all your lives—including his—and I give you my word that as soon as Tim is over his mother's loss I'll do just that. I'll never see him again or cause any of you further pain and embarrassment."

Ron got up from the chair Tim had thrust him into, his hand extended. "Tommyrot! It's just as well this all came out, it would have eventually. As far as me and Mum are concerned, Tim's the only one who matters, and Tim will always needs youse, Miss Horton. The last thing Mum said was poor Tim, do the right thing for Tim, poor Tim, poor Tim. Well, I'm going to do just that, Miss Horton, and if that pair of gits over on the couch can't see it my way, then it's too bloody bad for them. I gotta honor Mum's wishes, because she ain't here any more." His voice broke, but he lifted his chin toward the ceiling, swallowed several times and managed to continue. "Mum and I wasn't always polite to each other, you know, but we thought a lot of each other for all that. We had some bloody good years, and I'm going to remember them with a smile and a lift of me beer glass. He wouldn't understand"—a jerk of his head toward the sofa— "but Mum would be real disappointed if I didn't give her the old toast in beer every day at the Seaside."

It was with difficulty that Mary restrained her impulse to go to the gallant old man and comfort him physically, but she knew how much his control meant to him, so she kept her arms by her sides and tried to tell him with her tear-dimmed eyes and lopsided smile that she understood very well.

Nineteen

Tim sat silently in the car all the way to Artarmon. He had not slept in her Sydney house very often, and the room he always occupied there did not have the same sense of belonging about it as his room at the cottage did. He did not seem to know what to do when she prepared to leave him to change his clothes and rest; he stood in the middle of the floor fiddling with his hands, looking at her pleadingly. Never proof against that particular expression, Mary sighed and came to his side.

"Why don't you change into your pajamas and try to sleep for a little while, Tim?" she asked.

"But it's not night time, it's the middle of the day!" he protested, the pain and fear he was suffering revealing themselves in his voice.

"That's nothing to worry about, love," she replied, her throat aching. "I think you'd manage to sleep if I closed all the blinds and made the room dark."

"I feel sick," he said, gulping ominously

"Oh, poor old Tim!" she responded instantly, remembering how he dreaded being chided for making a mess. "Come on, I'll hold your forehead for you."

He began to vomit just as they reached the bathroom entrance. She held his brow in the palm of her hand, crooning softly and stroking his back while he writhed and gagged wretchedly.

"Finished?" she asked softly, and when he nodded she sat him on her padded bathroom chair and ran warm water into the bath. "You've made rather a mess of yourself, haven't you? I think you ought to just get out of those clothes and hop into a nice bath, don't you? You'll feel much better the minute you're soaking." She wrung out a washcloth and cleaned the worst of it from his face and hands, slipped his shirt off and folded it in on itself carefully, then used it as a rag to wipe the splattered floor. He watched her apathetically, white and trembling.

"I'm soh-soh-sorry, Mary," he gasped. "I made a meh-meh-mess and you'll be mah-mah-mad at me."

She smiled up at him from where she was kneeling on the tiles. "Never, Tim, never! You couldn't help it, and you tried so hard to get to the bathroom in time, didn't you? That's all that matters, dear heart."

His pallor and weakness alarmed her; he did not seem to be recovering as quickly as he should, so she was not surprised when he fell on his knees in front of the lavatory and began to retch again.

"I think that's definitely it," she said when he was quiet once more. "Now how about that bath?"

"I'm so tired, Mary," he whispered, clinging to the sides of the chair seat.

She dared not leave him; the chair was straight-backed and armless, and if he fainted he would never stay on it. The best place for him was the lukewarm bath, where he could stretch out supine and warm himself through to his bones. Shutting Dawnie's bitter words out of her mind and praying that he would never mention it at home, she got him out of his clothes and helped him into the bath with one arm firmly around his waist and his arm about her shoulders. He sank into the water

149

with a grateful sigh; relieved, she saw his color begin to return, and while he relaxed she finished cleaning the floor and the lavatory. The sickish smell was horribly pervasive, so she opened the door and the window to the windy autumn air. Only then did she turn back to the bath and look at him.

He was sitting like a child, hunched forward and smiling faintly as he watched the tendrils of steam smoking off the surface of the water, his thick gold hair curling damply. So beautiful, so beautiful! Treat him like a child, she told herself as she picked up a bar of soap; treat him like the child he is, don't look at him and see him as a man. Yet even as she said it, her eyes fixed on the full length of his body in the clear water, for he had lain back again suddenly with a murmur of almost voluptuous content. Nudity in a book was, after all, a far cry from Tim's reality; in books it had never possessed the power to move or excite her. She forced herself to look away, but involuntarily her gaze crept back, furtively, until she discovered he had closed his eyes, then in a kind of wondering but disciplined greed, not so much a carnal hunger as a tangled and confused one.

Some change in him made her glance toward his face, to find that he watched her wearily but curiously; the blood felt so hot beneath her skin that she half waited for him to comment, but he did not. With a crablike motion she sat on the edge of the bath and rubbed the soap into his chest and back, her slippery fingers sliding over the flawless skin which was like oiled silk, casually straying every so often to his wrist to check his radial pulse. But he did seem better, if still listless, and he actually laughed when she threw water over his head and made him bend far forward to wash his hair. She did not let him linger, but made him stand up the moment he was washed thoroughly, then she let the water out of the tub and turned on the shower. It amused her to see his naïve pleasure in the huge towel she handed him when he stepped on to the floor, but she managed

150

to listen gravely while he assured her he had never seen such an enormous towel before and what fun it was to be completely wrapped up like a baby.

"That was beaut, Mary," he confided, lying in bed with the covers drawn up to his chin. "I think Mum used to bathe me when I was a little shaver, but I don't remember it. I like being bathed, it's much nicer than bathing myself."

"Then I'm glad," she smiled. "Now I want you to roll over on your side and go to sleep for a little while, all right?"

"All right." He laughed. "I can't say night-night, Mary, because it's the middle of the day."

"How do you feel now, Tim?" she asked, drawing the blinds and plunging the room into semi-darkness.

"I feel all right, but I'm awfully tired."

"Then sleep, love. When you wake up you can come and find me, I'll be here."

The weekend passed fairly uneventfully; Tim was quiet, still not himself physically, but Mary saw little to indicate that he was as yet actively missing his mother. On Sunday afternoon she made him sit in the front of the big Bentley, and drove back to Surf Street to pick up Ron. He was waiting on the front veranda, and when he saw the car draw up he ran down the steps two at a time, suitcase in hand. How old he is, Mary thought, twisting around to open the back door. In spite of his neat, wiry physique and his boyish way of moving, not a young man at all. The sight of him worried her; all she could think of was Tim left utterly alone, bereft of both mother and father. After Dawnie's outburst on Friday there seemed little likelihood that she could or would compensate; her husband had gained the ascendancy. A good thing for Dawnie perhaps, but it boded ill for her erstwhile family. And how on earth could she, Mary Horton, possibly take in Tim if anything happened to Ron? It seemed that everyone thought the worst now, so what would they think and

151

do if Tim came to live with her permanently? The very thought appalled her. Only Ron, Archie Johnson, old Emily Parker next door, and Tim himself thought the relationship was a good thing. She shrank from even imagining what Dawnie would say, and what she might do. Certainly there would be a scandal, maybe a lawsuit as well; but whatever happened, Tim must be shielded from harm and ridicule. It didn't really matter what became of her, or Dawnie, or their lives. Tim was the only one who mattered.

In spite of his shock and grief, Ron was amused at Tim's behavior on the trip to Gosford, how he glued his nose to the window and stared raptly at the passing scene, fascinated. Mary caught him looking at his son when her eyes went to the rear-vision mirror, and she smiled.

"It never palls, Mr. Melville. Isn't that a wonderful thing, to know that he enjoys every trip as much as the first one?"

Ron nodded. "Too right, Miss Horton! I never realized that he enjoyed traveling so much. From what I remember of the few times we tried to take him out in a car, he hurked over everything. What a mess! And terribly embarrassing, because the car wasn't ours. If I'd known he would grow out of it, I would have bought a car and taken him round a bit. Makes me mad I didn't try later on, seeing him now."

"Well, Mr. Melville, I wouldn't be upset about it. Tim is always happy if everything is going well. This is just a different sort of happiness for him, that's all."

Ron did not answer; his eyes filled with tears, and he had to turn his head away to gaze out of his own window.

After she settled them into the cottage, Mary prepared to return to Sydney. Ron looked up, dismayed.

"Crikey, Miss Horton, are youse going? I thought you was going to stay here with us."

She shook her head. "Unfortunately, I can't. I have to be at work tomorrow; my boss has a week of very important meetings and I must be there to support him. I think you'll find everything you might need. Tim knows where things are, and he'll help you if you have any problems in the kitchen or around the house. I want you to make yourselves absolutely at home, do exactly what you like when you like. There's all sorts of food, you won't run short. If you find you have to go into Gosford, the number of the local taxi service is in the telephone notepad, and I insist that you charge it to me."

Ron stood up, for she was drawing on her gloves, ready to go. He shook her hand warmly and smiled.

"Why don't youse call me Ron, Miss Horton? Then I can call youse Mary. It seems a bit silly to go on calling each other Mister and Miss."

She laughed, her hand resting on his shoulder caressingly for a moment. "Yes, I agree, Ron. Let's make it Ron and Mary from now on."

"We'll see youse when, Mary?" Ron asked, not knowing whether as a guest he ought to see her off her own premises or just return to his easy chair.

"Friday night sometime, but don't wait supper for me. I may have to stay in town and eat dinner with my boss."

It was Tim who saw her to the car; surprised, Ron watched his son thrust himself between them rather like a dog bristling with annoyance because it has been forgotten. He took the hint and sat down again with his newspaper, while Tim followed Mary outside.

"I wish you didn't have to go back, Mary," he said, staring down at her with a look in his eyes she had never seen there before, and could not identify.

She smiled, patting his arm. "I have to go, Tim, I really do. But that means I have to rely on you to look after your Pop, because he doesn't know his way round the house or grounds, whereas you do. Be good to him, won't you?"

He nodded. His hands, slack by his sides, moved and clenched in on themselves. "I'll look after him, Mary, I promise I'll look after him."

He stood watching the track until the car had gone into the trees, then turned and went back into the house.

Twenty

Mary's week was quite as hard as she had expected. Of the several meetings the Board of Constable Steel & Mining held during the year, this was the most important one. Three representatives of the parent firm in the United States flew in from New York to attend it. There were the usual secretarial problems related to unsatisfactory hotels, unavailable foods, bored wives, lagging schedules, and the like; when Friday night came Mary's sigh of relief was as heartfelt as Archie Johnson's. They sat in his office on the top floor of Constable Tower with their feet up, staring dazedly out at the spinning panorama of lights spreading away in all directions to the starstruck horizon.

"Christ on a bicycle, Mary, am I glad that's over and done with!" Archie exclaimed, pushing away his empty plate. "That was a jolly good idea of yours to have a Chinese meal sent up, it really was."

"I thought you might like it." She wiggled her toes luxuriously. "My feet feel like size fourteens, and I've been dying to take my shoes off all day. I thought Mrs. Hiram P. Schwartz would never find her passport in time for the plane, and I had ghastly visions of having to put up with her for the weekend."

Archie grinned. His impeccable secretary's shoes were lying

higgledy-piggledy on the far side of the room, and she had almost disappeared into the maw of an enormous chair, her stockinged feet propped up on an ottoman.

"You know, Mary, you ought to have adopted a mentally retarded kid years ago. Sacred blue-arsed flies, what a difference it's made in you! I've never been able to do without you, but I confess it's a great deal more fun to work with you these days. I never thought I'd live to see the day when I'd have to admit I actually enjoyed your company, you nasty old twit, but I do, I really do! To think that all through the years it's been there inside you the whole time, and you never let it out once. That, my dear, is a bloody shame."

She sighed, half smiling. "Perhaps. But you know, Archie, nothing ever happens out of its due time. Had I met Tim years ago I would never have become interested in him. Some of us take half our lives to awaken."

He lit a cigar and puffed at it contentedly. "We've been so busy I haven't had a chance to ask you exactly what happened last Friday. His mother died?"

"Yes. It was dreadful." She shivered. "I took Tim and his father Ron up to my cottage last Sunday, and left them there. I'm going up to join them tonight. I do hope they're all right, but I suppose if they'd had any problems I would have heard from them. Tim hasn't realized yet what's happened, I think. Oh, he knows his mother's dead and he knows what that means, but the concrete reality of her going hadn't begun to work on him, he hadn't begun to miss her before I left. Ron says he'll get over it very quickly, and I hope he does. I feel very sorry for Ron. His daughter made quite a scene when I went out to pick up Tim on Friday."

"Oh?"

"Yes." Mary got up and went to the bar. "Would you like a brandy or something?"

156

"After Chinese food? No, thanks. I'll have a cup of tea, please." He watched her move around behind the bar to the little stove and sink. "What sort of a scene?"

Her head was bent over the kettle. "It's a little embarrassing to talk about it. An ugly scene, let's leave it at that. She—oh, it doesn't matter!" The cups rattled.

"She what? Come on, now, Mary, spit it out!"

The eyes looking at him were bright with defiance and wounded pride. "She implied that Tim was my lover."

"Great sausages of shit!" He threw back his head and laughed. "Way off base, way off base! I would have told her that if she'd asked me." He heaved himself out of his chair and came to lean on the bar. "Don't let it upset you, Mary. What a wart the girl must be!"

"No, she isn't a wart. She married a wart, that's all, and he's doing his best to wartify her. I don't honestly think that what she said was anything more than a parroting of what her husband had been whispering in her ear. She's very fond of Tim, and intensely protective." Her head went down below the level of the bar top, and the next words were muffled. "You see, they all thought I was much older than I really am, so when I appeared to collect Tim they all got rather a shock."

"How did they get that impression?"

"Tim told them I had white hair, and because I had white hair Tim assumed I was old, really old. So he told them I was very old."

"But hadn't you ever met them before the mother died? It isn't like you to sneak around back alleys, Mary! Why didn't you correct their misapprehension?"

She flushed painfully. "I honestly don't know why I didn't ever introduce myself personally to Tim's parents. If I did have any fears that they'd stop the friendship if they found out my true age, I assure you those fears were quite unconscious. I

157

knew Tim was perfectly safe with me. I enjoyed hearing about Tim's family from him, and I think I was sort of postponing meeting them because they wouldn't be at all like the people Tim talked of."

He reached over the counter and patted her shoulder. "Well, not to worry. Go on, you were saying Tim's sister is very fond of him?"

"Yes. Tim was as fond of her as she was of him until she got married, when he rather grew away from her a little. He seemed to feel she had deserted him, though I tried to reason with him. From all he said about her, I had gathered she was a sane, sensible, warm-hearted sort of girl. Very brilliant. Isn't that strange?"

"I don't know. Is it? What did you do?"

Down went the head again. "I was devastated. I think I cried. Fancy me crying!" She looked up, trying to smile. "Boggles the imagination, doesn't it?" Then she sighed, her face pensive and sorrowful. "But I've done my share of crying lately, Archie, I've done my share of crying."

"It does rather boggle the imagination, but I believe you. Still, we should all cry occasionally. I've even cried myself," he admitted grandly.

She laughed, relaxing. "You are, in your own language, a bot, Archie."

He watched her pour the tea, something akin to pity in his eyes. It must have been a terrible blow to her pride, he thought, to have this rare, treasured thing reduced to such an elemental level. For to her the very thought of a physical component debased it; she had a monkish outlook on life, and was it any wonder? Such a strange, sequestered, isolated life she had led! We are what we are, he thought, and we can be no more than what circumstances have made us.

"Ta, dear," he said, taking his tea. Sitting in his chair once more staring out the window, he spoke again. "I'd like to meet

Tim some time if I may, Mary."

There was a long silence behind him, then her voice came, very quietly. "One of these days." She made it sound very far away.

Twenty-one

It was after midnight when Mary parked the Bentley outside the cottage. The lights were still on in the living room, and Tim came bounding out to open the car door. He was trembling with joy at sight of her, and almost lifted her off the ground in a suffocating hug. It was the first time his emotions at seeing her had overridden the training of years, and it told her more than anything else could have done how miserable he had been all week, how much he must have missed his mother.

"Oh, Mary, I'm so glad to see you!"

She disengaged herself. "My goodness, Tim, you don't know your own strength! I thought you'd be in bed by now."

"Not before you came. I had to stay up until you came. Oh, Mary, I'm so glad to see you! I like you, I like you!"

"And I like you, and I'm very glad to see you, too. Where's your Pop?"

"Inside. I wouldn't let him come out, I wanted to see you first all by myself." He danced along beside her, but she sensed that somehow a little of his delight was quenched, that she had failed him. If only she knew how! "I don't like it here without you, Mary," he went on, "I only like it when you're here too."

He calmed down by the time they entered the house, and

Mary went to greet Ron, her hand outstretched.

"How are you?" she asked gently.

"I'm all right, Mary. It's good to see youse."

"It's good to be here."

"Did youse eat yet?"

"Yes, I did, but I'm going to make a cup of tea all the same. Would you like some?"

"Ta, I would."

Mary turned back to Tim, who was standing some distance away from them. He was wearing his lost look. How have I failed him? she asked herself again. What have I done to make him look like that, what did I neglect to do?

"What's the matter, Tim?" she asked, going to him.

He shook his head. "Nothing."

"Are you sure?"

"Yes, it's nothing."

"I'm afraid it's bedtime, my friend."

He nodded desolately. "I know." At the door he looked back, a mute appeal in his eyes. "Will you come and tuck me up, please?"

"I wouldn't miss it for the world, so hurry, hurry! I'll be in to see you in five minutes."

When he had gone she looked at Ron. "How has it been?"

"Good and bad. He cried a lot for his mother. It's not easy, because he don't cry the way he used to, all outward. These days he just sits there with the tears rolling down his face, and you can't tempt him out of them by waving something good under his nose."

"Come to the kitchen with me. It must have been very hard for you, and I'm terribly sorry I couldn't manage to be here to take some of the load off your shoulders." She filled the kettle, then looked at her watch anxiously. "I must go and say good-night to Tim. I'll be back soon."

Tim was already in bed, looking toward the door fixedly. She came over to him, fussed with the covers until they were wedged tightly underneath his chin, and tucked them firmly around him. Then she bent and kissed his forehead. He struggled with the blankets until he got his arms free and put them about her neck, pulling her down so that she was forced to sit on the edge of the bed.

"Oh, Mary, I wish you'd been here," he said, the words muffled against the side of her face.

"I wish I'd been here, too. But it's all right now, Tim, I'm here now, and you know I'll always be here with you as much as I can. I like being here with you better than anything else in the whole world. You missed your Mum, didn't you?"

The arms about her neck tightened. "Yes. Oh, Mary, it's awful hard to remember that she isn't ever coming back! I forget and then I remember again, and I want her to come back real bad and I know she can't come back, and it's all muddled up. But I wish she could come back, I do so much wish she could come back!"

"I know, I know. . . . But it will be easier in a little while, dear heart. You won't always feel it so badly, it will fade. She'll get further and further away from you and you'll grow used to it, it won't hurt so much any more."

"But I get a pain when I cry, Mary! It hurts an awful lot, and it won't go away!"

"Yes, I know. I get it too. It's as if they'd cut a whole big chunk out of your chest, isn't it?"

"That's right, that's exactly what it's like!" He passed his hands clumsily across her back. "Oh, Mary, I'm so glad you're here! You always know what everything is like, you can tell me and then I feel better. It was awful without you!"

The muscles of the leg wedged against the side of the bed went into agonizing spasm, and Mary withdrew her head from his clasp. "I'm here now, Tim, and I'll be here all weekend. Then we'll all go back to Sydney together, I won't leave you here alone. Now I want you to roll over on your side and go to sleep for me, because we have a lot to do in the garden tomorrow."

He turned obediently. "Night-night, Mary. I like you, I like you better than anyone except Pop now."

Ron had made the tea, and sliced up a block of seed cake. They sat in the kitchen, one on either side of the table facing each other. Though she had not met Ron until after Esme died, Mary knew instinctively that he had aged and shrunk in upon himself during this last week. The hand holding the cup to his mouth trembled, and all the life was leached out of his face. There was a hint of transparency about him, a spiritual attenuation that had crept into his flesh. She put out a hand and placed it over his.

"How hard it must have been for you, concealing your own grief and yet having to watch Tim's. Oh, Ron, I wish there was something I could do! Why do people have to die?"

He shook his head. "I dunno. That's the hardest question in the world, ain't it? I've never found an answer that satisfied me. Cruel of God to give us loved ones, make us in His image so that we can love them, then take them away. He oughta thought out a better way of doing it, don't you reckon? I know we're none of us angels and we must seem sort of like worms to Him, but most of us do our best, most of us aren't all that bad. Why should we have to suffer like this? It's hard, Mary, it's awful, awful hard."

The hand under hers went up to shield his eyes, and he wept. Mary sat there helplessly, her heart aching for him. If only there was something she could do! How terrible it was, to have to sit and watch another's grief and be so utterly powerless to lighten it. He wept for a long time, in spasms that seemed to eat away at his very soul, so deep and alone they were. When he could weep no more he dried his eyes and blew his nose.

"Could you drink another cup of tea?" Mary asked.

For a ghostly moment it was Tim's smile that hovered on his lips. "Ta, I could." He sighed. "I never thought it would be like this, Mary. Maybe it's that I'm old, I dunno. I never thought her going would leave such a great big empty space. Even Tim don't seem to matter quite so much any more, only her, only losing her. It ain't the same without the old girl there bitching and snarling about me staying too late at the Seaside, guzzling beer, as she used to put it. We had a real good life together, Es and me. That's the trouble, you grow toward each other as the years go on, until you're sort of like a pair of old boots, warm and comfortable. Then all of a sudden it's gone! I feel like half of me was gone too, sort of like a bloke feels after he loses an arm or a leg, youse know what I mean. He still thinks it's there, and he gets a terrible shock when he goes after an itch and finds there's nothing left to scratch. I keep thinking of things I oughta tell her, or have to stop meself saying out loud that she'd enjoy this joke, we'll have a good laugh about it. It's so hard, Mary, and I dunno that it's even worth trying."

"Yes, I think I understand," Mary said slowly. "A spiritual amputee . . ."

He put his cup down. "Mary, if anything should happen to me, will you look after Tim?"

She didn't expostulate with him, she didn't attempt to tell him he was being morbid or silly, she just nodded and said, "Yes, of course I will. Don't worry about Tim."

Twenty-two

In the long, sad winter which followed his mother's death, Tim changed. It was like seeing an animal mourn; he wandered from place to place looking for something that wasn't there, his eyes lighting restlessly on some inanimate object and then flicking away disappointed and bewildered, as if he always expected the impossible to occur, and was beyond understanding why it did not. Even Harry Markham and his crew could get nowhere with him, Ron told Mary despairingly; he went to work every day without fail, but the thoughtlessly malicious practical jokes of other days fell on stony ground: he endured the crew's tormenting brand of humor as patiently as he endured everything else. It was as if he had withdrawn from the real world, Mary thought, gone into a sphere that was his alone, and forever barred against intruders.

She and Ron had endless, unavailing conferences about him, sitting long into the rainy nights with the wind howling in the trees around the cottage, while Tim took himself off somewhere on his own or went to bed. Since Esme's death Mary had insisted Ron come to the cottage every weekend, for it was more than her heart could bear to drive off with Tim on Friday nights and leave the old man sitting beside his empty fireplace all alone.

There was a dull, dragging weight of sadness on them. For Mary it could not be the same, having to share her hours with Tim; for Ron nothing mattered very much except the barrenness of his days; for Tim, no one knew. It was Mary's first close contact with grief, and she had never imagined anything like it. The most frustrating part of it was her helplessness, her inability to put things right; nothing she could say or do made a particle of difference. She had to bear with the long silences, the furtive creeping away to indulge in bouts of fruitless tears, the pain.

She had come to care for Ron, too, because he was Tim's father, because he was so alone, because he never complained, and as time went on he occupied her thoughts more and more. With the coldest season drawing toward its close she noticed an increasing fragility about him; sometimes when they were sitting in the weak but warming sun together and he held his hand to the light, she fancied that the veined, blotchy extremity let the light shine straight through it until she could see the silhouette of his bones. He trembled so, and his once firm footsteps would hesitate when there was no obstacle in their path. No matter how she tried to feed him, he lost weight steadily. He was dissolving in front of her very eyes.

The trouble pulled at her like an invisible force; she seemed to spend her days walking a featureless plain without landmark or direction, and only working with Archie Johnson had any reality. At Constable Steel & Mining she could be herself, lift her mind from Ron and Tim and plunge it into something concrete. It was the only steadying influence in her life. She had come to dread Fridays and welcome Mondays; Ron and Tim had become a nightmarish incubus chained about her neck, for she did not know what to do to avert the disasters she sensed were coming.

One Saturday morning early in spring she was sitting on the front veranda of the cottage looking toward the beach, where Tim was standing just at the water's edge staring out across the

166

wide river. What did he see? Was he looking for his mother, or was he looking for the answers she had failed to give him? It was her failure with Tim which worried Mary more than anything else, for she sensed that she herself was one of the main reasons for his odd withdrawal. Ever since the night she had returned to the cottage after that week Ron and Tim had spent there alone, Mary was aware that Tim thought she had failed him. But talking to him was like talking to a brick wall, he seemed not to want to hear her. She had tried more times than she could count, approached the subject by casting out what used to be infallible lures, but he ignored them, almost spurning her. Yet it was such an intangible thing; he was his normal polite self, he worked willingly in the garden and about the house, he voiced no discontent. He had just gone away.

Ron came out on to the veranda with a tray of morning tea, and set it on a table near her chair. His eyes followed hers to the still, sentry-like figure on the beach, and he sighed.

"Have a cuppa, Mary. You didn't eat anything for brekkie, love. I baked a real nice seed cake yestiddy, so why don't you have a bit now with your tea, eh?"

She dragged her thoughts away from Tim and smiled. "My word, Ron, you've developed into quite a cook these last few months."

He bit his lip to still its sudden quivering. "Es used to love seed cake, it was her favorite. I was reading in the *Herald* that in America they eat bread with seeds in it, but they don't put seeds in cakes. Barmy! I can't think of anything worse than caraway seeds in bread, but in a nice, sweet yellow cake they're the grouse."

"Customs vary, Ron. They'd probably say exactly the opposite if they ever read in their papers that Australians never put caraway seeds in bread but eat them in cake instead. Though, to be honest, if you go to one of the continental bakeries in Sydney you can buy seeded rye bread these days."

167

"I wouldn't put anything past them bloody new Australian wogs," he said with the old Australian's innate contempt for the new European immigrants. "Anyway, it don't matter. Have a bit of the cake, Mary, go on."

Half her slice of cake eaten, Mary put her plate down. "Ron, what's the matter with him?"

"Gord struth and little apples, Mary, we've squeezed the last juice out of that subject weeks ago!" he snapped, then turned to press her arm contritely. "I'm sorry, love, I didn't mean to bite your head off like that. I know you're only worried about him, I know that's the only reason you keep on asking. I dunno, love, I just dunno. I never ever thought he'd take on so after his Mum died, I never thought it'd last half so long. It's enough to break your heart, ain't it?"

"It's breaking mine. I don't know what to do, but I've got to do something, and soon! He's going farther and farther away from us, Ron, and if we can't pull him back we'll lose him forever!"

He came and sat on the arm of her chair, pulling her head against his meager chest and cradling it there. "I wish I knew what to do, Mary love, but I don't. The worst thing is that I can't make meself care the way I used to, it's sort of as if Tim's not me son any more, as if I can't be bothered. That sounds awful, but I've got me reasons. Wait here."

He let her go abruptly and disappeared into the house, emerging a moment later with a flat portfolio of papers under his arm. He threw it on to the table beside the tea tray. Mary looked up at him, puzzled and upset. Ron got another chair and pulled it over until it faced hers, then he sat down and stared directly into her eyes, his own glittering queerly.

"That's all the papers about Tim," he said. "Inside there is me will, all the bank books and insurance policies and annuities. Everything to make sure Tim's financially secure for the rest of his life." He looked behind him toward the beach, and Mary could no longer see his face.

168

"I'm dying, Mary," he went on slowly. "I don't want to live, and I can't seem to make meself live any more. I'm running down like a clockwork monkey—you know the ones, they beat a little drum and march up and down and then it all goes into slow motion and then it all stops, the feet stop marching and the drum stops beating. Well, that's me. Running down, and there's nothing I can do about it.

"And oh, Mary, I'm glad! If I'd been a young man I wouldn't have felt her going like this, but age makes a big difference. She's left a great big hole I can't fill with anything, even Tim. All I want is to be lying there with her, under the ground. I keep thinking she must be awful cold and lonely. She couldn't be anything else, not after sharing her sleep with me all those years." His face was still turned away from her toward the beach. "I can't stand the thought of her so cold and lonely, I can't bear it. There ain't nothing left with her gone, and I can't even make meself care about Tim. That's why I went to me lawyer this week and got him to make everything all right.

"I'm not leaving youse anything but trouble, I suppose, but somehow right from the beginning I always felt that you was terrible fond of Tim, that you wouldn't mind the trouble. It's selfish, but I can't help it. I'm leaving Tim to you, Mary, and there's all his papers. You take them. I've given you a power of attorney in Tim's financial affairs for as long as you live. I don't think Dawnie will make any big trouble for youse, because Mick doesn't want Tim around, but just in case I've left a couple of letters in there, one for Dawnie and one for that shirt-lifting bugger Mick. I gave me notice at work, told the boss I was retiring. I'm just going to stay at home and wait, except that I'd still like to come up with Tim on weekends if you don't mind. It won't be too long now, anyway."

"Oh, Ron, oh, Ron!" Mary found herself weeping; the slender shape on the beach melted in a shimmer of tears, and she reached out her hands to Tim's father.

They rose and clung together hard, each the victim of a

different kind of pain. After a while Mary discovered that he comforted her more than she could ever comfort him, that it was exquisitely peaceful and healing to stand there within his arms and feel his tenderness and compassion, his intensely male protectiveness. She held him more tightly, her face pushing into the sagging folds of his skinny neck, and closed her eyes.

Suddenly something alien intruded: a shiver of dread passed down her spine, and she opened her eyes with a start of fear. Tim was standing several feet away staring at them, and for the first time in all the long months of their friendship, she saw him angry. He was shaking with rage; it flared in his eyes and turned them as dark as sapphires, it spasmed his muscles into tremor after furious tremor. Terrified, she let her arms fall and stepped back from Ron so abruptly that he staggered and had to grasp at the roof post. Turning, he saw Tim; they stared at each other for perhaps a minute without speaking, then Tim twisted away and ran down the path to the beach.

"What's the matter with him?" Ron whispered, aghast. He made a movement to follow his son, but Mary pulled him back, clawing at him.

"No, no!"

"But I gotta see what's the matter with him, Mary! What did he do? What made youse jump like that and look so frightened of him? Let me go!"

"No, Ron, please! Let me go after him, you stay here, please! Oh, Ron, don't ask me why, just let me find him by myself!"

He yielded reluctantly, stepping away from the edge of the veranda. "Well, all right, love. You're good with him, and maybe he needs a woman's touch more than a man's. If Mum was alive I'd send her, so why not you?"

There was no sign of him on the beach as Mary sped down the path; she stopped on the fringe of the sand and shaded her eyes to peer up and down the whole length of the bay, but he was not there. She turned into the trees, heading for a little clearing where she knew of late he liked to go to be alone. And he was there; gasping with relief, Mary sagged against a tree trunk and watched him silently. His terrible misery and grief struck her like a blow from some gargantuan hammer; every long, achingly beautiful line of him spoke of inarticulate suffering, the pure outline of his profile was knotted into pain. It was impossible to stand aloof, but she came up to him so quietly that he was not aware of her presence until she touched him on the arm. He flinched away as if her fingers burned and her hand fell to her side, useless.

"Tim, what is it? What have I done?"

"Nothing, nothing!"

"Don't keep it from me, Tim! What have I done?"

"Nothing!" He almost screamed the word.

"But I have! Oh, Tim, I've known for months that I've failed you somehow, but I don't know what I did wrong! Tell me, tell me!"

"Go away!"

"No, I won't go away! I won't go away until you tell me what's the matter! It's been worrying your Pop and me out of our minds, and back there on the veranda you looked at us both as if you hated us. Hated us, Tim!" She came round to face him and put her hands on his upper arms, her fingers digging into his skin.

"Don't *touch* me!" He wrenched away and turned his back on her.

"Why, Tim? What have I done that I can't touch you?"

"Nothing!"

"I don't believe you! Tim, I never thought you'd lie to me, but you are lying to me! Please tell me what's the matter, oh, please!"

"I can't!" he whispered despairingly.

"But you can, of course you can! You've always been able to tell me everything! Oh, Tim, don't turn away from me and shut

171

me out any more! You're pulling me into little pieces, I'm so beside myself with worry and fear for you that I don't know what to do!" She began to weep, and wiped the tears away with the palm of her hand.

"I can't, I can't! I don't *know!* I feel so many things that I can't think out, I don't know what they mean!"

He spun round to face her, goaded and harried beyond patience, and she backed away; a stranger glared at her, there was nothing familiar in him to reach for.

"I only know you don't like me any more, that's all! You like Pop better than me now, you don't like me any more! You haven't liked me since you met Pop, and I knew it would happen, I knew it would happen! How could you like me more than him when he's the full quid and I'm not? *I* like him better than me!"

She put out her hands. "Oh, Tim! Oh, Tim! How could you think that? It's not true! I like you as much as I always did, I haven't stopped liking you for one little wee minute! How could I ever stop liking you?"

"You did when you met Pop!"

"No, no! It's not true, Tim! Please believe me, it's just not true! I like your Pop, but I could never like him as much as I like you, never! If you must know, most of the reason I like your Pop is because he is your Pop; he made you." She tried to keep her voice calm, hoping it would calm him.

"You're the one who's lying, Mary! I can feel things! I always thought you thought I was all grown up, but now I know you don't, not now, not now I've seen you and Pop! You don't like me any more, it's Pop you like now! You don't mind if *Pop* hugs you! I've seen you, hugging and comforting him all the time! You won't let *me* hug you and you won't comfort *me!* All you do with me is tuck me into bed, and I want you to hug me and comfort me, but you won't! But you do it to Pop!

"What's wrong with me, why don't you like me any more?

172

Why did you change after Pop started coming with us? Why am I always left out? I can tell you don't like me, I can tell it's Pop you like!"

Mary stood absolutely still, yearning to respond to that despairing, lonely plea for love, but too aghast at its suddenness. He was jealous! He was furiously, possessively jealous! He regarded his own father as a rival for her affections, and it was not entirely the jealousy of a child. There was a man in it: primitive, possessive, sexual man. The glib words of reassurance would not come; she could find nothing to say.

They stood staring at each other, stiff and with hackles raised, then Mary found that her legs were trembling so much they scarcely supported her. She groped for a nearby hillock and sat down without taking her eyes from his face.

"Tim," she said hesitantly, trying to choose her words with extreme delicacy, "Tim, you know I've never lied to you. Never! I couldn't lie to you, I like you far too much. What I'm going to tell you now is something I couldn't tell a little child, I could only say it to a man grown. You've assured me that you're all grown up, so now you have to take all the hard, painful things which go along with being a man. I can't properly explain why I let your Pop hug me and won't let you, but it isn't because you're a little child to me, it's because he's an old man. You've got it the wrong way round, don't you see?

"Tim, you have to be ready to take another shock like your Mum's death, and you have to be strong. You have to be grown up enough to keep what I tell you an absolute secret, especially from your Pop. He must never know I told you.

"Do you remember a long time ago I explained to you what happened to people when they died, why they died, that they just got too old and tired to keep going, that they ran down like a forgotten clock until their hearts stopped beating? Well, sometimes a thing happens which makes the wearing out go much faster, and it's happened to your Pop. When your Mum died he began to run down faster and faster, he got more and more tired with each day he had to live without her."

He was still standing over her, trembling as he listened, but she did not know whether this was an aftermath of his rage or a reaction to what she was telling him. She labored on doggedly.

"I know you miss your Mum dreadfully, Tim, but you don't miss her the way he does, because you're young and he's old. Pop wants to die, he wants to lie under the ground next to your Mum sleeping, just the way they did each night when she was alive. He wants to be with her again. They belong together, you see, he can't get along without her. Just now, when you found me comforting him on the veranda, he had just told me that he knew he was going to die. He doesn't want to go on walking and talking any more because he's old and he can't learn to live without her. And that's why I was holding him. I was saddened and I cried for him; actually it was Pop who was comforting me, not the other way around. You mistook it entirely."

An abrupt movement from him made her look up, and she lifted her hand in command.

"No, don't cry, Tim! Come on now, you've got to be very brave and strong, you can't let him see that you've been crying. I know I've given a lot of time to your Pop that you think rightly belonged to you, but he has so little time left, and you have all your life ahead of you! Is it wrong of me to want to give him a wee bit of happiness to lighten what days he has left? Give him those days, Tim, don't be selfish! He's so alone! He misses your Mum terribly, dear heart, he misses her the way I'd miss you if you died. He's walking around in a half-lit world."

Tim had never learned to school his features to impassivity; the emotions chased each other across his face as he stood staring at her, and it was all too plain that he understood enough. Making Tim comprehend was largely a matter of familiarity, and he had known her a long time now, he had little trouble with the words and phrases she used. The nuances were beyond him, but the truth was not.

174

She sighed wearily. "I haven't found it very easy either all these months, with two of you to look after instead of only you. There have been many, many times when I've longed to have you to myself again. But when I've caught myself wishing that I've been ashamed of myself, Tim. You see, we can't always have things the way we want. Life is so seldom ideal, and we just have to learn to put up with it. During this time we have to think of Pop first. You know what a good, kind man Pop is, and if you're fair to him you'll admit he's never treated you like a baby, has he? He's let you go out into the world on your own, make your own mistakes, he loves to share his time at the Seaside with you, he's been the best and truest mate you've ever had; he's taken the place of the mates your own age you've never had the chance to find. And yet he's led his own life, too, but not because he's selfish; he's always had you and Mum and Dawnie there in his mind, all sort of warm and comforting, rounding out his life. You're very lucky, Tim, to have a father like Ron, so don't you think we ought to try and give him back a little bit of what he's given you so ungrudgingly all these years?

"From now on, Tim, I want you to be very good to your father, and very good to me. You mustn't worry him by going off by yourself the way you've been doing, and you mustn't ever let him know I told you what the matter is. Whenever Pop is around I want you to sing and talk and laugh as if you're happy, really happy.

"I know it's hard for you to understand, but I'll sit here and go over it with you until you get it all straight."

Like rain and wind and sun the grief and joy mingled in his eyes, then they dulled and he burrowed his head into her lap. She sat and stroked his hair and talked to him softly, tracing the outline of his neck and ear tenderly with the tip of her finger, round and round and round.

When he lifted his head at last he looked at her, trying to smile and failing. Then his expression changed, the lost look

175

came into his face and the bewildered eyes retreated behind their veil of sad exclusion. Along the left side of his mouth the little crease became very pronounced; he was the tragic clown of every comedy, he was the unwanted lover, he was the cuckoo in the lark's nest.

"Oh, Tim, don't look at me so!" she pleaded.

"At work they call me Dim Tim," he said, "but if I try really hard, I can think a little bit. Ever since Mum went away I've been trying to think of something to show you how much I like you, because I thought you liked Pop better than me. Mary, I don't know what you do to me, I only feel it and I can't tell you because I don't know the words. I never can find the words. . . . But in the movies I see on TV the man hugs the girl and then he kisses her, and then she knows how much he likes her. Oh, Mary, I like you! I liked you even when I thought you didn't like me any more, I like you, I like you!"

He snatched at her shoulders and pulled her to her feet, his hold inexpertly strong as he put his arms about her back; her head came up, seeking air. Not knowing how to find her mouth, he pressed his cheek against hers until he fumbled to her lips. Completely taken off guard, for his last words and his action had been too swift and startling for immediate comprehension, Mary fought frantically to free herself. Then somehow it no longer mattered, there was only the feel of that beautiful young body and anxiously experimenting mouth. As inexperienced as he but intellectually much better prepared, Mary felt his need for help and reassurance. She could not fail him in this too, she could not bring herself to crush his pride, humiliate him by rejecting him. His hold slackened enough for her to free her hands; they went immediately to his head, smoothing his brows and closing his open eyes, exploring the silkiness of his lashes and the hollowed curves of his cheeks. He kissed her the way he imagined it was done, his lips pressed firmly shut, and it dissatisfied him; she pulled away from him for a moment and pushed her thumb against his lower lip caressingly, slightly

176

opening his mouth, then her hands went up to his hair and drew his head down. He was not dissatisfied this time, and his shivering delight transmitted itself to her.

She had held him in her arms before, but as child, never as man, and the shock of discovering the man in him awed her. To lose herself in his arms, to feel his mouth, permit her hands to follow the planes of his neck down to the smooth muscular chest, was to discover in herself a need for this, an agonized pleasure in feeling his hands on her body. He found the cloth-shielded contours of her breasts without guidance, then his hand slipped under the collar of her dress and curved around her bare shoulder.

"Mary! Tim! Mary! Tim! Where are you, can you hear me? It's Ron! Answer me!"

She wrenched away from him and took his hand, dragging him after her into the shelter of the trees. They ran until Ron's voice had long faded behind them, then stopped. Mary's heart was pounding so hard she could scarcely catch her breath, and for a moment she thought she was going to faint. Panting and gasping, she clung to Tim's arm until she felt better, then moved away from him a little self-consciously.

"You're looking at a stupid old fool," she said then, turning to face him.

He was smiling at her in the old, totally loving way, but there was a difference now, an added fascination and wonder, as if in his eyes she had gained an entire dimension. It sobered her as nothing else could have done; she put her hand to her head, trying to think. How had it happened? How was she going to deal with it, how could she put them back on the old footing without hurting him?

"Tim, we shouldn't have done that," she said slowly.

"Why?" His face was alight with happiness. "Oh, Mary, I didn't know that was how it felt! I liked it, I liked it much better than hugging you or being comforted!"

She shook her head vehemently. "It doesn't matter, Tim! We

177

shouldn't have done it. There are some things people aren't allowed to do, and that's one of them. It's too bad we liked it, because it can't happen again, it must never happen again, not because I didn't like it as much as you did, but because it isn't allowed. You've got to believe me, Tim, it just isn't allowed! I'm responsible for you, I have to look after you the way your Mum and Pop would want, and that means we can't kiss, we just can't."

"But why, Mary? What's wrong with it? I liked it!" All the light had died out of his face.

"In itself, Tim, there's nothing wrong. But between you and me it's forbidden, it's a sin. Do you know what a sin is?"

"Of course I do! That's when you do something God doesn't like."

"Well, God doesn't like us to kiss."

"But why should God mind? Oh, Mary, I've never felt like that before! It was the closest I've ever felt to the full quid! Why should God mind it? It isn't fair that God should mind, it just isn't fair!"

She sighed. "No, Tim, it isn't fair. But sometimes it's hard for us to understand God's purposes. There are a lot of rather silly things you have to do without properly understanding why, isn't that so?"

"Yes, I suppose so," he replied sulkily.

"Well, when it comes to understanding God's purposes none of us are the full quid—you're not the full quid and I'm not the full quid and your Pop's not the full quid, the Prime Minister of Australia isn't the full quid, and nor is the Queen. Tim, you've got to believe me!" she pleaded. "You've got to believe me, because if you won't we can't be friends any more; we'll have to stop seeing each other. It isn't possible for us to hug and kiss, it's a sin in the eyes of God. You're only a young man and you're not the full quid, where I'm getting old and I'm absolutely the full quid. I'm old enough to be your mother, Tim!"

"But what does that have to do with it?"

"God doesn't like us to hug and kiss when there's such a big difference in our ages and mentalities, Tim, that's all. I like you, I like you better than anyone else in the whole world, but I can't hug and kiss you. It isn't allowed. If you try to kiss me again, God will make me stop seeing you, and I don't want to stop seeing you."

He pondered on it sadly, then sighed in defeat. "Well, Mary, I did like it an awful lot, but I'd rather keep on seeing you than kiss you and then not see you."

She clapped her hands together delightedly. "Oh, Tim, I'm so proud of you! That was spoken like a man, a real, full-quidded man. I'm so very proud of you."

He laughed shakily. "I still think it isn't fair, but I like it when you're proud of me."

"Are you happier now that you know everything?"

"Much happier!" He sat down under a tree and patted the ground beside him. "Sit down, Mary. I promise I won't kiss you."

She crouched beside him and took his hand, spreading the fingers apart lovingly. "This is as much as we can do when we touch, Tim. I know you won't kiss me, I'm not at all worried that you'll break your promise. You have to promise me something else, too."

"What?" His free hand plucked at the few dusty blades of grass under his thigh.

"What happened, I mean the kiss, it has to be our little secret. We must never tell anyone about it, Tim."

"All right," he answered docilely. He was reverting to the child again, accepting his role with the peculiar sweetness and desire to please that were so much his alone. After a while he turned his head to look at her, and the wide blue eyes were so filled with love that Mary caught her breath, angry and soured. He was so right; it wasn't fair, it just wasn't fair.

"Mary, what you told me about Pop, how he wants to be asleep with Mum under the ground. I know what you mean. If you died I'd want to die too, I wouldn't like to keep walking and talking and laughing and crying, honest. I'd like to be with you, under the ground asleep. I won't like it if Pop isn't here, but I know why he wants to go."

She raised his hand to her cheek and held it there. "It's always easier to understand things when you can put yourself in the same position, isn't it? Listen, I can hear Pop calling us. Do you think you can talk to him without crying?"

He nodded tranquilly. "Oh, yes, I'll be all right. I like Pop an awful lot, next to you I like him best, but he sort of belongs to Mum, doesn't he? I belong to you, so I'm not worried nearly as much now. I belong to you now. Just belonging isn't a sin, is it, Mary?"

She shook her head. "No, Tim, it isn't a sin."

Ron's voice was drawing closer; Mary hallooed to let him know where they were, and got up to wait.

"Mary?"

"Yes?"

He was still sprawled on the ground, looking up at her in dawning comprehension. "I just thought of something! Do you remember the day after Mum died, when you came to our house to fetch me?"

"Yes, I most certainly do."

"Well, Dawnie said some horrible, nasty things to you, and I didn't know what she was so upset about. I tried and tried, but I didn't know what she was so upset about. When she was yelling at you I felt all queer, because I thought she thought we'd done something awful. Now I think I know! Did she think it was us kissing?"

"Something like that, Tim."

"Oh!" He thought about it for a moment. "Then I do believe you, Mary, I do believe we aren't allowed to kiss. I've never seen

180

Dawnie like that before, and ever since then she's been real unfriendly to Pop and me. She had a big fight with Pop about me coming to stay with you a few weeks after that, and now she doesn't come to see us any more. So I do believe it's a sin, it must be a sin for Dawnie to carry on like that. But why did she think you'd let us kiss all the time? She ought to know you better than that, Mary. You'd never let us do anything wrong."

"Yes, she ought to know it, I agree, but sometimes people get too upset to think straight, and after all she doesn't know me nearly as well as you and Pop do."

He stared at her, strangely wise. "But Pop took your side, and he didn't know you at all then either."

Ron came through the trees, puffing. "Everything all right, Mary love?"

She smiled, winking at Tim. "Yes, Ron, perfectly all right. Tim and I had a talk, and straightened it all out. No big problem, I promise you, just a misunderstanding."

Twenty-three

But everything was not all right; the sleeping dogs had been wakened. Mary had good reason to be thankful that Ron was failing, for if he had been in his normal state of health and mind, he would have seen the change in Tim at once. As it was, the cheerful good humor which had come back to the relationship was enough to satisfy him, and he looked no further. Only Mary realized that Tim was suffering. She would look up to find his hungry, angry eyes on her a dozen times a day, and when she caught him looking so he would go out of the room immediately, guilty and confused.

Why must things change? she asked herself; why can't something perfect stay perfect? Because we're all human beings, her reasoning self would answer, because we're so complex and flawed, because once a thing occurs to us it must recur, and in recurring it alters the form and essence of what has gone before. There was no way back to the first phase of their friendship, therefore only two alternatives remained; to go forward, or to stay still. But neither alternative seemed possible or workable. Had Tim been mentally normal she would have tried, but to go into the matter again would only have confused him, made him even unhappier. It's stalemate, she thought, then shook her head in worried exasperation; too explosive to be a stalemate. Impasse, then.

At first she thought of talking to Archie Johnson, but rejected the idea. He was a brilliant and sympathetic man, but he would never understand all the nuances of the situation. Emily Parker? She was a nice old girl, and from its beginning she had followed Mary's relationship with Tim, keenly interested, but something in Mary shrank from exposing her dilemma to that florid embodiment of matriarchal suburbia. In the end she phoned John Martinson, the teacher of retarded children. He remembered her immediately.

"I've often wondered what happened to you," he said. "How is everything, Miss Horton?"

"Not very good, Mr. Martinson. I need to talk to someone desperately, and you're the only person I can think of. I'm terribly sorry to inflict you with my problems, but I just don't know what to do, and I need qualified help. I was wondering if I could bring Tim to see you."

"Of course you can. How about after supper tomorrow night at my house?"

Mary took the address, then rang the Melville residence.

"It's Mary here, Ron."

"Oh, g'day there, love. What's the matter?"

"Nothing, really. I was wondering if I might take Tim out to see someone tomorrow night after supper."

"I don't see why not. Who is it?"

"A teacher of retarded children, a wonderful man. I thought he might be able to assess Tim, give us some idea of what sort of pace we ought to force in his formal learning."

"Anything you like, Mary. See youse tomorrow night."

"Fine. By the way, I'd appreciate it if you didn't tell Tim too much about it, I want him to meet this man quite unprepared."

"Sure thing. Hooroo, love."

John Martinson lived near his school, which was in the satellite town of Penrith, just at the foot of the Blue Mountains. Tim, used to heading north, enjoyed the drive out of Sydney in another direction; the Post Road flavor of the Great Western

Highway kept his nose glued to the window, counting the brilliantly lit car salesrooms, all-night hamburger joints, and drive-in movie lots.

The Martinson house was big but very unpretentious, built of fibrous board painted pale pink, and it rang with the shrill laughter of children.

"Why don't you come through to the back veranda?" John Martinson asked Mary when he answered the door. "I've made it into my study, and we won't be disturbed there."

They were introduced to his wife and three oldest children briefly, and went straight through to the back of the house.

John Martinson's eyes rested on Tim curiously, and with keen admiration. He produced two quart bottles of beer and shared them with Tim while he talked, sitting easily in a big chair to one side of his work table. For half an hour Mary said nothing while the two men conversed comfortably over the beer. Tim liked the teacher and he relaxed at once, chattering about the cottage and its garden and his work with Harry Markham, quite unaware that he was being drawn out by an expert.

"Do you like TV Westerns, Tim?" John Martinson asked him at last.

"Oh, yes, I love them!"

"Well, I have some business to discuss with Miss Horton for a while, and I don't think you'll find it very much fun to stay here and listen to us. Why don't I take you inside to see my kids? There's a real beaut Western starting on TV in a few minutes."

Tim went happily, and as her host came back into the study Mary could hear Tim laughing somewhere inside.

"He'll be all right, Miss Horton. My family is very used to people like Tim."

"I'm not worried."

"What's it all about, Miss Horton? May I call you Mary?"

"Yes, of course."

"Good! Call me John. By the way, I quite see what you meant

when you told me Tim was spectacular. I don't think I've ever seen a better looking man, even in the movies." He laughed, peering down at his own too-thin body. "He makes me feel like a ninety-pound weakling."

"I thought you were going to say what a shame it is that someone so good-looking should be mentally retarded."

He seemed surprised. "Why should I think that? Not one of us is born without something beautiful and something undesirable within us. I admit that Tim's body and features are magnificent, but don't you think that a great deal of that absolutely stunning beauty comes from the soul?"

"Yes," Mary said gratefully; he understood, she had been right to choose him.

"He's a dear fellow, I could tell that immediately. One of the sweet ones. . . . Do you want me to have him assessed by the experts?"

"No, that isn't why I came to see you at all. I came because circumstances have placed me in what seems to be a total quandary, and I really don't know what to do for the best. It's awful, because no matter what I decide, Tim has to get hurt, perhaps badly."

The dark blue eyes never deviated from her face. "It doesn't sound good. What happened?"

"Well, it all started when his mother died nine months ago. I don't know if I told you, but she was seventy years old. Ron, Tim's father, is the same age."

"I see, or at least I think I do. Tim's missing her?"

"No, not really. It's Tim's father who is missing her, so much so that I don't expect him to live much longer. He's a fine old man, but all the light seemed to go out of his life when his wife died. I can see him fading away before my very eyes. He knows; he told me he knew the other day."

"And when he dies Tim's all alone."

"Yes."

185

"Does Tim have any idea of this?"

"Yes, I had to tell him. He took it very well."

"Has he any sort of financial security?"

"Plenty. The family put almost everything they had into making sure Tim would never want for money."

"And where do you come into it, Mary?"

"Ron—Tim's father—asked me if I'd take Tim when he was gone, and I said yes."

"Do you realize what you're in for?"

"Oh, yes. But there are unforeseen complications." She glanced down at her hands. "How can I take him, John?"

"You mean what will people say?"

"Partly, although if it was only that I'd be prepared to take the consequences. I can't adopt him, he's well over the majority age, but Ron has given me a complete power of attorney in Tim's affairs, and anyway, I have plenty of money myself; I don't need Tim's."

"What is it, then?"

"Tim's always been very attached to me, I don't know why. It was strange. . . . Right from the beginning he liked me, as if he saw something in me that I can't even see myself. It's very nearly two years since I met him. . . . In those early days it was simple. We were friends, such good friends. Then when his mother died I went to see the family, and Tim's sister Dawnie, who is a very clever girl and devoted to Tim, leveled some dreadful and quite untrue accusations at me. She implied that I was Tim's mistress, that I was trading on Tim's mental weakness to exploit and corrupt him."

"I see. It was a shock, wasn't it?"

"Yes. I was horrified, because none of it was true. Tim was present when she said all this, but luckily he didn't understand what she meant. However, she spoiled it for me and thus for him. I was shamed. Tim's father was there, too, but he took my side. Isn't that odd? He refused to believe a word of what she said, so it shouldn't have made any overt difference in my friendship with Tim. But it did make a difference, perhaps unconscious, perhaps conscious too, I don't know. I found it harder to relax with Tim, and besides, I felt so sorry for Ron that I brought him along to the cottage with us at weekends.

"This went on for six months, almost, during which time Tim changed. He grew silent and withdrawn, he wouldn't communicate with either of us. We were terribly worried. Then one morning there was a terrific scene between Tim and me, it all came out into the open. Tim was jealous of his father, he thought Ron had replaced him in my affections. That was why I had to tell him his father was dying."

"And?" John Martinson prompted when she hesitated; he was leaning forward, watching her fixedly.

Strangely, the sheer quality of his interest gave her courage to continue.

"Tim was absolutely overjoyed when he realized that my feelings toward him hadn't changed, that I still liked him. Like is his special little word; he'll say he loves cake or TV Westerns or jam pudding, but if he's talking of people he's fond of, he always says like, never love. Odd, isn't it? His mind is so pure and direct that he took the literal interpretation of like and love; he listened to people say they loved food or a good time, but he noticed that when they talked of another human being, they said like. So he says the same thing, sure he's right. Perhaps at that he is."

Her hands were shaking; she stilled them by clasping them together in her lap. "Apparently during this period when he thought I liked Ron better than I liked him, he was so perturbed that he sat down and worked out a way of proving to me that his own liking for me was genuine and undying. Television gave him his answer; he reasoned it out for himself that when a man liked a woman he showed her by kissing her. No doubt he also noticed that in movies such an action usually results in a happy ending." She shivered slightly. "I'm really to blame. Had I been more on the *qui vive* I might have averted it, but I was too obtuse to see it in time. Fool!

"We had a really dreadful scene, during which he accused me of liking Ron more than I liked him, and so on. I had to explain to him why I was paying so much attention to Ron, that Ron was dying. As you can imagine, he was shattered. Neither of us was our emotional self, we were upset and very tense. When the shock of learning about his father wore off a bit, it dawned on him that I still like him better than Ron. He sort of leaped to his feet and grabbed me so fast that I didn't realize what he was doing until it was far too late."

She stared at John Martinson pleadingly. "I didn't know what to do for the best, but somehow I couldn't bring myself to humiliate him by repulsing him."

"I understand that very well, Mary," he said gently. "So you responded, I take it?"

She had flushed in embarrassment, but she managed to speak calmly. "Yes. At the time it seemed the best thing to do, that it was more important to make sure he suffered no rejection than it was to push him away. Besides, I—I was in too deep myself, I couldn't seem to help it. He kissed me, and luckily I didn't have to contend with anything more serious than that, because we heard Ron calling us and it gave me an excellent excuse to break away from him."

"How did Tim react to the kiss?"

"Not quite as I imagined. He liked it too much, it excited him. From then on I could tell he was seeing me differently, that he wanted more of this new sensation. I explained to him that it was bad, that it was forbidden, that although it could happen between lots of people it couldn't happen between us, and superficially he understood. He really did grasp the fact that it was forbidden, and he cooperated splendidly. It's never happened again, nor will it in the future."

A sudden scream of laughter came from the house; Mary jumped in fright, momentarily losing her train of thought. Plucking at the clasp of her handbag, she sat voiceless and white-faced.

"Go on," he said. "It's never happened again, nor will it in the future."

"I suppose for Tim it must be like opening a door into a whole new world and then discovering that you can't enter. Yet all the time you know this, the door is still open and the new world is green and beautiful. I feel so sorry for him, and so helpless to heal him. I'm the cause of his misery. He won't do it again, but neither can he forget the time it happened. Ron had kept him absolutely ignorant about matters of a physical nature, and never having heard of it, let alone known of it, he didn't miss it. Now he's had a small taste, and it's gnawing at him without mercy."

"Of course." He sighed. "That was inevitable, Mary."

She looked past his head and fixed her eyes on a tiny spider crawling down the wall, unable to meet his gaze. "Naturally I couldn't tell Ron what had happened, and yet at the same time everything is changed. How can I take him when Ron dies? If Ron knew he'd never ask it of me, I'm sure. I *can't* take him now, it would drive me mad! At the moment I manage, I can keep Tim occupied and happy two days a week, especially with Ron there. But how can either of us contend with living in the same house together all the time? Oh, John, I just don't know what to do! If I thought there was any chance Tim might forget it would be different, I'd find the strength somehow. But I know he won't forget, and when I catch him looking at me, I . . . Tim isn't one of those unretentive simpletons, you see; he has the ability to absorb and cement memories if they make a big enough impression or he repeats them enough. Every time he looks at me he remembers, and he isn't clever enough to hide it. He's angry and hurt and very resentful, and though he un-

189

derstands it can't happen again, he'll never really understand why."

"Have you thought of a solution, Mary?"

"Not really. Is there some sort of hostel perhaps, where people like Tim who are adults physically but still children in mind could stay when they're all alone and have no family? If he lived in a place like that I could have him on weekends. I could manage that."

"Anything else occur to you?"

"Not seeing him again. But how can I do that, John? It wouldn't help him to hand him over to Dawnie—or is that simply selfishness on my part? Do I really mean as much to him as I think, or is it only self-delusion? I suppose it's possible that he might forget me once he's installed in Dawnie's house, but I keep seeing her and her husband living their lives with Tim as an afterthought. She has more important responsibilities, she can't devote herself to him the way I can!"

"There is another answer, you know."

"There is?" She leaned forward eagerly. "Oh, if you only knew how much I've yearned to hear you say something like that!"

"Why don't you marry Tim?"

Mary gaped at him, so dumbfounded that it took her a few seconds to say "You're joking!" The chair was suddenly too hard and confining; she got up and paced the length of the room once, then came back to face him. "You're joking?" she repeated pitifully, turning it into a question.

A pipe lay on the work table; he picked it up and began to fill it, tamping the tobacco down slowly and very carefully, as though by doing so he could concentrate on remaining calm. "No, I'm not joking, Mary. It's the only logical answer."

"*Logical answer?* Heavens above, John! It's no answer at all! How can I possibly marry a mentally retarded boy young enough to be my son? It's criminal!"

"Utter twaddle!" He sucked on the pipe furiously, teeth bit-

190

ing down on the stem. "Be sensible, woman! What else is there to do but marry him? I can understand why you didn't think of it for yourself, but now that the idea has been put into your mind there's no excuse for throwing it aside! To do so would be criminal, if you like the word. Marry him, Mary Horton, marry him!"

"Under no circumstances!" She was stiff with anger.

"What's the matter, frightened of what other people will say?"

"You know I'm not! I can't possibly marry Tim! The very idea is straight out of cloudcuckooland!"

"Stuff and nonsense! Of course you can marry him."

"No, I can't! I'm old enough to be his mother, I'm a sour, ugly old maid, no fit partner for Tim!"

He got up, went over to her, took her shoulders, and shook her until she was dizzy. "Now you listen to me, Miss Mary Horton! If you're no fit partner for him, he's no fit partner for you, either! What is this, noble self-sacrifice? I can't abide nobility, all it does is make everyone unhappy. I said you ought to marry him, and I mean it! Do you want to know why?"

"Oh, by all means!"

"Because you can't live without each other, that's why! Good lord, woman, it sticks out a mile how besotted you are for him, and he for you! It's no platonic friendship, and it never was! What would happen if you chose the second of your two alternatives and stopped seeing him? Tim wouldn't survive his father more than six months, you know that, and you'd probably live out a full span of years like a shadow of your former self, in a world so gray and full of tears that you'd wish you were dead a thousand times in each and every endless day. As for your first alternative, there isn't any such place because what places there are have waiting lists literally years long. Tim would never live long enough to make it in the door. Is that what you want—to kill Tim?"

"No, no!" She groped for a handkerchief.

"Listen to me! You've got to stop thinking of yourself as a sour, ugly old maid, even if that's what you really are. I defy anyone to explain what one person sees in another, and as for you, you shouldn't even dare to query it. Whatever you think you are, Tim thinks you're something quite different and much more desirable. You said you didn't know what on earth he saw in you, that whatever it was you couldn't even see it yourself. Be grateful for that! Why toss it away in an excess of self-sacrifice and pride? It's such useless, pointless self-sacrifice!

"Do you think he'll change, grow tired of you? Be your age! This isn't an exquisitely beautiful, sophisticated man of the world, this is a poor, silly creature as simple and faithful as a dog! Oh, you don't like my saying things like that, eh? Well, right at this moment there's no room for euphemism or illusion, Mary Horton; there's only room for the truth, as plain and unvarnished as the truth can get. I'm not interested in why Tim should have fixed his affections on you, I'm only interested in the fact that he has. He loves you, it's as simple as that. He loves you! As improbable, impractical, inexplicable as it may be, he loves you. I don't know why any more than you do, but it is a concrete fact. And what on earth is the matter with you, that you can even contemplate throwing his love away?"

"You don't understand!" Mary wept, her head in her hands, her fingers wreaking havoc upon the orderly strands of her hair.

"Oh, I understand better than you think," he said, more gently. "Tim loves you, with every corner of his being he loves you. For some reason, out of all the people he's ever known, he fixed his affection on you, and with you it will stay. He's not going to grow bored or jaded with you, he's not going to throw you over for a younger, prettier woman in ten years' time, he isn't after your money any more than his father is. You're certainly nothing to write home about now, so it's not as though you've got any beauty to lose, is it? Besides, he has more than enough beauty for the two of you."

She lifted her head and tried to smile. "You're nothing if not honest."

"I am because I have to be. But that's only the half of it, isn't it? Don't tell me you've never admitted to yourself that you love him every bit as much as he loves you?"

"Oh, I've admitted it," she answered wryly.

"When? Recently?"

"A long time ago, before his mother died. He told me one night that I looked like his picture of Saint Terese, and for some reason his saying that knocked the wind out of my sails. I'd loved him from the first moment of seeing him, but it was then I admitted it to myself."

"And are you likely to grow tired of him?"

"Grow tired of Tim? No, oh, no!"

"Then why can't you marry him?"

"Because I'm old enough to be his mother, and because he's so beautiful."

"It isn't good enough, Mary. All that appearance business is crap, and I'm not even going to be bothered arguing with you about it. As to the age objection, I think it's worth discussing. You're *not* his mother, Mary! You don't feel like his mother and he doesn't think of you as his mother. This isn't an ordinary situation, you know; this isn't two people fully grown in mind and body but with a disparity in age casting doubt on the genuineness of the emotional ties between them. You and Tim are unique in the annals of man. I don't mean that a spinster in her middle forties has never married a man young enough to be her son before, even perhaps a mentally retarded one, I mean that you're a completely odd couple from every standpoint and you may as well accept your uniqueness. Nothing holds you together except your love for each other, does it? There's the difference in age, in beauty, in brain, in wealth, in status, in background, in temperament—I could go on and on, couldn't I? The emotional ties between you and Tim are genuine, genuine enough to have transcended all of these innate differences. I don't think anyone on earth including you yourself will ever be able to discover the reason why you fit together. You just do. So marry him, Mary Horton, marry him! You'll have to endure an awful lot of sniggers, leveled fingers, and conjecture, but it doesn't really matter, does it? You've had a fair bit of that all along, I'd say. Why not give the old biddies something really worthwhile to talk about? *Marry him!*"

"It's—it's indecent, it's almost obscene!"

"I'm sure that's what everyone will say."

Her chin went up. "I don't care what other people say, I'm only concerned with its effect on Tim, how people will treat him if he marries me."

John Martinson shrugged. "He'll survive speculation a lot better than separation, I assure you."

Her hands lay clenched in her lap, and he put his own over them strongly, eyes glittering.

"Think about this one, Mary. Why shouldn't Tim marry? What's so special about Tim? You can protest all you like that you think of him as a man, but I disagree. The only times you've thought of him as a man, you've almost died of horror, haven't you? That's because you've made the mistake everyone makes with mentally retarded people. In your mind Tim is fixed as a child. But he's *not* a child, Mary! Like normal people, retards are subject to the growth and change which comes with maturation; within the limited scope of their psychic development, they cease to be children. Tim is a grown man, with all the physical attributes of a grown man and a perfectly normal hormonal metabolism. If he'd been injured in the leg he'd walk with a limp, but because his injury is to the brain he limps mentally, and that kind of handicap doesn't prevent him being a man any more than a maimed leg would.

"Why should Tim have to go through life deprived of the opportunity to satisfy one of the most driving needs his body

194

and his spirit know? Why should he be denied his manhood? Why should he be sheltered and shielded from his body? Oh, Mary, he's already deprived of so much! *So much!* Why deprive him of yet more? Isn't he, a man, entitled to his manhood? Honor the man in him, Mary Horton! Marry him!"

"Yes, I see." She sat silently for a while, thinking. Then she lifted her head. "All right, then, if you think it's the best thing under the circumstances, I'll marry him."

"Good girl!" His face softened. "You'll both get more out of it than you think, you know."

She frowned. "But it's so fraught with difficulties!"

"His father?"

"I think not. No, I imagine Ron will be pleased, though he may well be the only one. But Tim and I, we're equally inexperienced in this, and I'm not sure I'm competent to deal with all the problems involved."

"You're worrying unnecessarily. The trouble is you're a thinker, you try to contend with things that have a habit of solving themselves when the time comes. Where Tim's needs are concerned you're very well attuned, I'd say."

Suppressing her urge to squirm, Mary managed to appear composed. "I shouldn't have children, should I?"

"No, you shouldn't. Not that Tim's deficiencies are hereditary, it doesn't seem there's much chance of that. But you're getting into an age group where it's possible that you won't live to see any offspring through to their maturity, and Tim's condition precludes him from fulfilling your role should anything happen to you. Besides which, you're more than old enough to repeat his mother's misfortune, and if you did that it would be life's greatest irony. Statistically speaking, if you start having children past the thirty-five mark your chances of having a normal child go right down, and the farther you are past thirty-five when you begin, the lower your chances get."

"I know."

"Do you think you'll regret not having children? Is it likely to color your life with disappointment?"

"No! How could it? I never expected to get married, or yearned to get married. Tim is more than enough for me."

"It won't be easy."

"I know."

John put down his pipe and sighed. "Well, Mary, I do wish you all the luck and happiness in the world. It's up to you now."

She rose, gathering her bag and gloves together. "And I thank you very much, John. You've put me deeper than ever in your debt, and I give you my word that I'll work to help your cause in whatever way I can."

"You owe me nothing. The pleasure I'll get from just knowing Tim is happy is more than enough reward for me. Just come and see me from time to time."

Instead of simply dropping Tim off in Surf Street, Mary came in with him. Ron was sitting in the living room with the television blaring a late-night sports roundup.

"G'day there, Mary! I didn't expect you'd come in this late."

She sat down on the sofa while Tim busied himself putting her bag and gloves in a safe place. "I wanted to have a talk with you, Ron. It's rather important, and I'd like to get it over and done with while I've still got the courage."

"Right you are, love! How about a cuppa tea and a bit of fresh cream sponge?"

"That sounds nice." She looked up at Tim, smiling. "Do you have to work tomorrow, Tim?"

He nodded.

"I don't want to push you off, then, but I think it's bedtime for you, Charlie. Your Pop and I have something to talk about, but I promise I won't keep it a secret from you, I'll tell you all about it this weekend. All right?"

"All right. Night-night, Mary." He never requested her to tuck him up in Esme's house.

196

Ron spread cups and saucers and plates on the kitchen table while the kettle heated, watching Mary keenly out of the corner of his eye. "You look real done-in, love," he observed.

"I am, rather. It was an exhausting evening."

"What did the teacher bloke say about Tim?"

Her cup was chipped; she sat rubbing her finger tip back and forth across the pitted rim, turning ways to tackle the subject over in her mind. When she looked up at Ron she seemed old and tired.

"Ron, I wasn't exactly truthful about why I took Tim to see John Martinson tonight."

"No?"

"No." Round and round the cup edge her fingertip moved; she lowered her eyes to it, unable to continue speaking while she looked into those wide blue eyes, so like Tim's in form and so unlike Tim's in expression. "This is very difficult for me, because I don't think you have any idea of what I'm going to tell you. Ron, did it ever occur to you that it's going to be hard for me to take Tim if anything happens to you?"

The hand holding the teapot trembled; tea slopped onto the table. "You've changed your mind, right?"

"No. I won't do that, Ron, unless you don't like my solution to our problem." She folded her hands together in front of her cup and managed to look at him steadily. "Tim and I have always had a very special relationship, you know that. Out of all the people he's ever met he likes me best. I don't know why, and I've given up even wondering about it. It isn't far wrong to say he loves me."

"No, it isn't. He does love you, Mary. That's why I want you to be the one to take him after I'm gone."

"I love him, too. I've loved him from the first instant I ever saw him, standing in the sun watching the concrete truck emptying cement all over Emily Parker's oleanders. I didn't know he was retarded then, but when I found out it didn't change

197

anything, in fact it only made me love him more. For a long while I never attached any importance to the difference in our sexes, until first Emily Parker and then your daughter gave me some pretty rude shocks on the subject. You've always kept Tim sheltered from that sort of thing, haven't you?"

"I had to, Mary. With Es and me being so old, I knew there was a pretty good chance we wouldn't be around when Tim grew up, so we talked over what we oughta do while he was still a little bloke. Without us to watch over him, and him being as handsome as he is, it seemed as though he was likely to get himself into a heap of trouble if he ever found out what women were for while he was still young and the urge was strong. It was easy until he got old enough to work, but once he started with Harry Markham I knew it would be hard. So I went and had a talk with Harry, made it clear that I didn't want any of his blokes getting Tim into trouble or trying to wise him up about the birds and the bees. I warned Harry that if they tried anything I'd put the police on to them for contributing to the delinquency of a minor, and a minor who wasn't the full quid into the bargain. It was the only thing I asked, and I suppose they got their fun from tormenting him about other things, but I must say they was good about the sex business, even used to watch out for him and keep the women away. Bill Naismith usually comes most of the way to and from work with Tim, because he lives at the top of Coogee Bay Road. So between one thing and another, it's turned out fine. We been lucky, of course. There was always the chance that something might happen, but it never has."

Mary felt the prickling march of blood suffuse her face. "Why were you so adamant about it, Ron?" she asked, desperate to delay the moment of confession.

"Well, Mary, you've always got to weigh the pleasure agin the pain, ain't that right? And it seemed to Es and me that poor old Tim would end up getting more pain than he would pleasure

198

from playing around with women and sex and all that. Mum and me thought he'd be better off ignorant. It's terrible true that what you never know you don't miss, and with him working so hard laboring it's never been a burden to him. I suppose it might seem cruel to someone on the outside, but we thought we was doing the right thing. What do you reckon, Mary?"

"I'm sure you acted in Tim's best interests, Ron. You always do."

But he seemed to interpret her answer as noncommittal, for he hurried into a further explanation.

"Lucky for us, we had a good example right under our noses while Tim was growing up. There used to be a simple girl down the street from us, and her Mum had awful trouble with her. She was much worse off than Tim, only about fourpence in the quid, I reckon, and ugly too. Some rotten bugger took a fancy to her when she was fifteen, pimples and fat and slobber and all. Some men will hump anything. And she's been pregnant off and on ever since, the poor little dill, had one cock-eyed, hare-lipped ning-nong of a baby after the other, until they put her away in an institution. That's where the law's wrong, Mary, they oughta have some provision for abortion. Even in the state home people kept getting at her, and in the end they tied her tubes. It was her Mum told us whatever we did, not to let Tim get ideas."

Ignoring Mary's soothing murmur, he got up and paced the room restlessly; it was painfully apparent that the decision taken all those years ago continued to worry him.

"There are blokes and sheilas who don't care if a kid is simple. All they're after is a bit of fun, and they sort of like the fact that they don't have to worry about the kid, because it isn't smart enough to chase after them and give them a hard time when they're sick of it. Why should they care? They reckon that the kid's so dill-brained it can't feel anything the way us ordinary people do. They'd kick it the way they'd kick a dog, smirking all over their faces because the silly ding comes back for more, wagging its tail, belly on the ground.

"But dill-brains like Tim and the girl down the street *do* feel, Mary, they ain't that far off the full quid, especially Tim. Good Christ, even an animal can feel! I'll never forget when Tim was a tiny little bloke, about seven or eight. He was just starting to talk as if he knew what the words meant. . . . He come in with this chewed-up kitten, and Es said he could keep it. Well, not long after the kitten turned into a cat, it started to swell up like a balloon, and the next thing we knew, kittens. I was hopping mad, but lucky for me, I thought, she'd had them behind the bricked-up chimney in our bedroom, and I decided I'd get rid of them before Tim knew anything about it. I had to knock out half the bricks to get at her, I dunno how she got in there in the first place. There she was, all covered in soot, kittens too, and I had Es breathing down me neck laughing her head off and saying it was just as well she was a black cat, you'd never notice the soot. Anyway, I grabbed all the kittens, took them into the backyard and drowned them in a bucket of water. And I've never regretted doing anything so much in all me life. The poor little bugger of a cat walked round the house for days, crying and howling and looking for her kittens, turning her head to look up at me with them big green eyes so full of trust, like, as if she thought I could find them for her. And she cried, Mary, she cried real tears, they rolled down her face just like she was a human-being sort of woman. I never thought animals could cry real tears. Jesus! For a while there I wanted to put me head in the gas oven. Es wouldn't talk to me for a week over it, and every time the cat cried, so did Tim."

Pulling his chair closer to the table, he sat down again with hands outstretched. The old house was so quiet, Mary found herself thinking while Ron got himself together. Just the ticking of the old-fashioned kitchen clock and the sound of Ron swallowing. No wonder he hated it when he had known it so different.

"So you see, Mary," Ron continued, "if a cat can have feelings, so can a dill-brain like Tim, and more feelings, because Tim's not all that bad. He mightn't set the world on fire with his ideas, but he's got a heart, Mary, a great big warm heart just full of love. If he started in with a woman he'd love her, but do youse think she could love him, eh? He'd just be a piece on the side to her, that's all, and him just brimming over for her. I couldn't take it.

"Tim's got a real pretty face and a real pretty body, and there's been women—and men!—after him since he was twelve. After he was dumped, what do you think would happen to Tim? He'd look at me the way that poor bloody little cat did, as if he expected me to get his girlfriend back and couldn't understand why I wasn't even trying."

A silence fell. Somewhere inside came the noise of a door slamming; Ron looked up and seemed to remember that Tim was in the house with them.

"Excuse me a minute, Mary."

She sat listening to the loud monotonous clock until he came back, grinning to himself.

"Typical Aussie, that boy. Can't get him into more clothes than necessary, and if he has half a chance he'll wander around mother-naked. He has a bad habit of coming out of the bathroom after his shower and walking all over the place without a stitch on, so I thought I'd better make sure he didn't come out here for something." He looked at her sharply. "I hope he behaves hisself when he stays with youse? No complaints?"

"He behaves himself perfectly," she answered uncomfortably.

Ron sat down again. "You know, it's a real blessing we're just working-class people, Mary. It's been easier to shelter Tim than if we'd belonged with the likes of Dawnie's man Mick. Them stuck-up snobs is harder to spot, more cunning like, men and women, but men especially, I reckon. Instead of drinking with dinkum blokes in the public bar at the Seaside, he'd be sitting in some pansy lounge with all the idle women and all the lisping fairies in the world. Our class has things better organized than that, thank me lucky stars. Black is blacker and white is whiter, and there ain't so much gray in between. I do hope youse understands, Mary, why we did it."

"I understand. I really do. The trouble is that Tim's woken up, courtesy of the television set. He watched the love scenes and decided it was a good way to show me how much he liked me."

"Oh, God!" Ron sat down abruptly. "I thought we'd frightened him off it, I thought we'd scared the living daylights out of him so much he'd never try it."

"You probably did a good job of scaring him off, but you see, he didn't really associate what he was doing with what you scared him away from. It didn't start off in his mind as a carnal thing. He just wanted to show me how much he liked me. In the process, unfortunately, he also found out how much he liked it."

Ron was horrified. "You mean he raped you? I don't believe it!"

"Of course not! He kissed me, that's all. But he liked it, and it's been preying on his mind ever since. I managed to convince him that between us it was forbidden, but he's awake, Ron, he's awake! It only happened once, I wouldn't ever let it happen again, but how can you or I blot it out of his mind? What's done is done! While there was no truth to what Dawnie or Emily Parker or anyone else thought it didn't matter, but ever since Tim kissed me I've nearly gone crazy wondering what on earth I'm going to do with him if anything happens to you."

Ron had relaxed again. "I see what you mean."

"Well, I didn't know where to turn, who to talk to about it. That was why I took Tim to see John Martinson tonight, I wanted him to meet Tim and then to give me his frank opinion on the whole situation."

"Why didn't you talk to me, Mary?" Ron demanded, hurt.

202

"How could I possibly talk to you, Ron? You're Tim's father, you're too close to everything to be detached. If I'd talked to you first I would have nothing to offer you this moment beyond the facts, I'd have no direction to go and no solution. If I'd talked to you first we'd probably have come to the conclusion that there was nothing to be done save separate Tim from me. I went to John Martinson because he's had a great deal of experience with mentally retarded people, and he's genuinely concerned for them. I thought that out of all the people I know he was the only one capable of thinking of Tim first, and that's what I wanted, someone capable of thinking exclusively of Tim."

"Okay, Mary, I see your point. What did he say?"

"He offered me a solution, and the way he presented it made me see that there's no doubt of it being the wisest thing to do. I told him that I thought you'd agree after you heard it, but I confess I'm not so sure in my own mind about that as I sounded when I reassured John Martinson."

"Whatever you say or think about it, I assure you I've already said or thought it, so nothing you can say will surprise or hurt me." She held out her cup for more tea, anxious to have something to do. "I'm forty-five years old, Ron, old enough to be Tim's mother, and I'm a plain, dowdy woman without any sort of physical attraction for men. What Tim sees in me is totally beyond me, but he sees it all the same. John Martinson says I ought to marry Tim."

"Does he?" Ron's face was curiously expressionless.

"Yes, he does."

"Why?"

"Chiefly because Tim loves me, and because Tim's a man, not a child. When he told me what he thought I should do, I was flabbergasted, and believe me I argued against it. It's like mating a thoroughbred with a mongrel, mating Tim's youth and beauty with me, and I told him so. Forgive me for saying this, but he answered that there were two ways of looking at it, that mating my intelligence with Tim's stupidity was just as bad. They weren't his words; he said, 'If you're no fit partner for Tim, he's no fit partner for you.' His point was that neither Tim nor myself is any marital prize, so what was so appalling about it? I still opposed the whole idea, chiefly on the grounds of the big difference in our ages, but he threw that aside too. It's me Tim likes, not the girl next door or the daughter of one of his work-mates.

"What convinced me that John Martinson was right was something that hadn't occurred to me at all, and I'm sure it hasn't occurred to you either. We're both too close to Tim to see it." She shook her head. "Tim's a grown man, Ron, in that respect he's perfectly normal. John was quite brutally frank about it, he took me by the shoulders and shook me until my teeth rattled because he was so angry at my lack of insight and sympathy for Tim. What was the matter with me, he asked me, that I could deny Tim his right to be a man in the only way he can ever be a man? Why shouldn't Tim get as much out of life as possible?

"I'd never looked at it that way before, I'd been so concerned with what other people would think, how they'd laugh at him and tease and torment him because he'd married a rich spinster old enough to be his mother. But I'd completely overlooked the fact that he's entitled to get as much out of life as he can."

Again she fell to exploring the chipped cup with her fingertip; Ron was concealing his reactions well; she had no idea what he thought, and as if to confuse her more he picked up the teapot to refill her cup.

"We've all heard of reverses. I remember once being very angry because one of the girls in our office fell in love with a paraplegic who refused to marry her. Archie knew the girl well enough to be sure she was a one-man woman, that there'd never be anyone for her but this man. He went to see the fellow, told him not to throw their chance of happiness aside because he wasn't a man in that one sense. And we all agreed that Archie had done the right thing, there was no reason why the girl shouldn't have married her man in a wheelchair. There's more to life than that, Archie told him.

"There is more to life than that, Ron, but what about Tim? How much is there to Tim's life, and how much could there be? Now that the opportunity has presented itself, have we any right to deny Tim everything he's entitled to as a human being? That's the crux of John Martinson's argument."

"He really laid it on the line, didn't he?" Ron pushed his hands tiredly through his hair. "I just never thought of it that way."

"Well, I admitted the truth of his argument, I had to. But why me, I asked? Surely Tim could do better than me? But can he? Can he really? Whatever I am, Tim loves me. And whatever Tim is, I love him. With me he'll be safe, Ron, and if in marrying him I can round out his life as much as it can ever be rounded out, then I'll marry him in everyone's teeth, including yours."

Her feeling of teetering on the brink of a precipice had gone entirely as she talked; Ron watched her curiously. Several times he had seen her shaken from habitual calm, but never quite like this, so ringingly alive. One could not call her mousy in any mood, but mostly her plain good face was distinguished only by her strength of character. Now she seemed lit with a fleeting beauty that would disappear the moment her zeal died; he found himself wondering what marriage to Tim would do for her. Older and infinitely more worldly than Mary, he knew there was never an easy answer.

"Women normally live longer than men," she continued eagerly, "so there's every chance that I'll be with him for many years to come. I'm not so much older that my predeceasing him is a major consideration. He's not going to go off looking for some pretty young thing because his own wife is old and faded. I'm old and faded now, Ron, but it doesn't worry him at all.

"I thought about simply living with him, because in the eyes of most people that would be the lesser sin. But John Martinson is right. Marriage is better. If I marry him I have full legal authority over his life; Dawnie can never take him away. You see, Dawnie's been worrying me for some time. I don't think it's occurred to you how easily she could remove Tim from my custody the moment anything happened to you. Why should it occur to you? She's your daughter, and you love her dearly. But she doesn't love me at all, and she would never admit to herself that I'm better for Tim than she is. Your letters to her and Mick, your power of attorney, all those things mean nothing if Dawnie really wanted to make trouble. Upon your death Dawnie would become Tim's legal guardian in the eyes of any court in the land, no matter what sort of directives you left. I'm no relation, I haven't even known Tim very long, and our association is highly suspect.

"When you first asked me to take Tim, I didn't think beyond the fact that you trusted me so magnificently, but I think you're detached enough to see Dawnie in her true light. She loves Tim, but she hates me just that much more, and Tim would become the victim on her altar. John Martinson wasn't aware of the magnitude of Dawnie's enmity, but he hit on the only feasible solution in spite of it. I *must* marry Tim."

Ron laughed wryly. "Ain't life funny? You're right about one thing, Mary. People would understand it if you just lived together much quicker than they will your marrying. It's one of them queer situations where marriage is a crime, ain't it?"

"That's exactly the word I used to John Martinson. Criminal."

Ron got up and walked round the table to put his arm about her shoulders, then he bent his head and kissed her. "You're a fine person, Mary. I'll be real glad to see you marry my son. Me and Es couldn't have wished for a better answer, and I reckon she's cheering youse on.

"But it had better be soon, Mary, real soon. If I'm there to see it and I leave a testament to the fact that I approve, there's very

206

little Dawnie can do. Leave it until after I'm dead and you don't have a leg to stand on. I oughta seen it for myself, but a man's always a bit blind about his kids."

"That's why I had to bring the matter up tonight. I'm going to have to go into hospital for a few days to see to it that it's impossible for me to have children, but I think the marriage ought to take place as soon as possible."

"Right you are! We'll go into town next Monday to get the license, then youse can be married at the end of the week, I think."

She stroked his scratchy cheek lovingly. "I couldn't have asked for a nicer father-in-law than you, Ron. Thank you so much for understanding and consenting."

Twenty-four

In the end they decided not to tell Dawnie anything about the wedding until after the deed was done, but the day after Mary and Ron agreed on it she told Archie Johnson.

"Sweet suffering rock oysters, you're joking!"

It took some time to convince him that she was serious. And after the initial shock wore off he rallied and congratulated her sincerely.

"Mary love, I couldn't be more pleased for you. It's the oddest match since Chopin and George Sand, but if anyone on this old ball of mud knows what they're doing, it's you. I'm not going to make your life a misery by raising all sorts of objections because I'm bloody sure you've already thought of them for yourself. The only thing I'm sorry about is that after all these years of thinking I was safe I'm going to lose you. On that head I could cry."

"Why on earth should you lose me?"

"Well, won't you have your work cut out looking after your Tim?"

"Heavens, no! I do need to take three months off almost immediately, no notice or anything, for which I'm very sorry, but I'm not going to give up work, nor is Tim. I think we'll both be better off getting out into the world among ordinary people.

If we stopped working and saw no one save ourselves we'd both deteriorate."

"I'd like to come to your wedding, Mary. I'm very fond of you, and though I've never met Tim I'm very fond of him, too, because he made such a difference to your life."

"I'd like you and Tricia to come to my wedding."

"When is it?"

"Next Friday afternoon at the Registrar General's offices."

"Then why don't you begin your leave right this moment? If I have to put up with Celeste Murphy for three months I may as well face the music as soon as possible."

"Bless you, but no thanks. I'll take Celeste under my wing until next Wednesday. That will be soon enough."

Emily Parker heard the news gleefully. Mary invited her over after dinner that night, and told her.

"Lord love a duck, dearie, it's just what youse both needs. I'm tickled pink, love, I really am. Here's your very good health, and may youse live happily ever after."

"Will you come to my wedding?"

"Ta, I wouldn't miss it for the world. Good luck to youse, Miss Horton, I'm real proud of youse!"

Mary also went and saw Harry Markham that night, after she managed to push Emily Parker back to the other side of the camphor laurels.

Harry stared at his visitor curiously, sure he had seen her somewhere before, but unable to place her.

"Do you remember renovating Mrs. Emily Parker's house in Artarmon over two years ago, Mr. Markham?"

"Yair, sure."

"I'm Mary Horton, Mrs. Parker's next door neighbor."

His face cleared. "Oh, right, right! I thought I knew youse from somewhere."

"I'm not here on business, Mr. Markham, I'm here to talk about Tim Melville."

"Tim Melville?"

209

"That's right, Tim Melville. It may come as something of a shock to you, Mr. Markham, but next Friday I'm marrying Tim."

Poor Harry gurgled and gulped for a full minute before he found voice enough to squeak, "You're marrying *Dim Tim?*"

"That's correct, next Friday. Under normal circumstances, having heard from Mrs. Parker what sort of pranks you like to play on him, I'd be tempted to persuade him to find another employer, but he liked working with you and your men, so I'm happy to see him remain with you."

Harry's eyes strayed past her to the huge Bentley parked at his curbside. He remembered now that she was accounted the wealthiest woman in Artarmon, and decided she was worth placating. "Well, youse could knock me down with a bullrout, Miss Horton! This is quite a little bit of news, ain't it?"

"I'm sure it is, Mr. Markham. However, I haven't much time and I'd like to be as brief as possible. There are a couple of things we must decide on right now. Firstly, do you wish to keep Tim in your employ if he takes three months' leave starting next Wednesday? Secondly, if you do wish to keep him in your employ, are you willing to keep your men in order on the subject of Tim's marriage?"

Still floundering, Harry shook his head to clear it. "Crikey, Miss Horton, I don't know what to say!"

"Then I suggest you make up your mind, Mr. Markham. I can't stay here all night."

He thought for a moment. "Well, I'll be honest with you, Miss Horton. I like Tim and me crew likes Tim. It's as good a time as any to do without him for three months because it's coming on summer and I can always find the odd university student or two as casual laborers, though it'll take a few of them to fill Tim's shoes, useless lot of snotty bastards they are. Tim's been with me twelve years and he's a bloody good worker. I'd have to look a lot longer than three months to find another laborer as cheerful

210

and willing and reliable as Tim, so if it's all right with youse, I'd like to keep the little bloke."

"Fine. As to my second point, I'm hoping you have the sense to understand that it would be very bad for Tim to be teased about his marriage. By all means go on with your practical jokes and the sort of ribbing Tim seems to accept as a matter of course. He doesn't really mind it. But the subject of his marriage is absolutely taboo, and I give you my word that if I ever discover you've embarrassed or humiliated him because he married a rich old maid, I'll break you and the members of your staff into little pieces morally and financially. I can't stop you discussing it among yourselves and as a matter of fact I wouldn't dream of doing so, since I'm sure it's a very interesting and intriguing morsel of gossip. But when Tim is around it's never to be mentioned, except to offer him the normal congratulations. Is that understood?"

Mary Horton was more than a match for Harry Markham; he gave in without a struggle. "Yes, certainly, Miss Horton, anything you say, Miss Horton."

Mary held out her hand. "Thank you very much, Mr. Markham, I appreciate your cooperation. Goodbye."

Next on Mary's list was the gynecologist. Having made up her mind what to do, Mary tackled the obstacles one by one in sequence, and enjoyed herself more than she had expected. This was her métier, doing things; she had no attacks of self-doubt, no second thoughts now that her mind was made up.

In the gynecologist's office she explained the situation to him calmly.

"I can't possibly run the risk of a pregnancy, sir, I'm sure you see why. I presume you'll have to hospitalize me to tie off my tubes, so I thought while I'm in there and you're fiddling around with me, you might do something about the fact that I'm an intact virgin. I can't possibly endanger this relationship by evincing the slightest sign of pain, and I understand it's very painful for a woman to commence sexual activity at my age."

The gynecologist put up a hand to his face hastily to hide his involuntary smile; more than most men he was acquainted with Mary Horton's breed, for there were plenty of them working in Australian hospitals. Bloody dedicated old maids, he thought, they're all the same. Brisk, practical, disconcertingly level-headed, and yet for all that women underneath, full of pride, sensitivity, and a curious softness. His amusement under control again, he tapped his pen against the desk and hummed and hawed.

"I think I agree with you, Miss Horton. Now would you please step behind the screen there and remove all your clothes? Nurse will be in to give you a robe in a moment."

By Saturday morning Tim was the only one left to tell. She had asked Ron not to mention the subject, but refused to take Tim to the cottage on his own.

"Of course you'll come with us, Ron," she said firmly. "Why should this make any difference? We're not married yet, you know. I can easily manage to get Tim off on his own and tell him."

The opportunity came in the afternoon; Ron went to lie down for a while, winking broadly at Mary as he took himself off to his bedroom.

"Tim, why don't we go down to the beach and sit in the sun?"

He jumped up at once, beaming. "Oh, that sounds nice, Mary. Is it warm enough to swim?"

"I don't think so, but it doesn't matter anyway. I want to talk to you for a while, not swim."

"I like talking to you, Mary," he confided. "It's such a long time since we talked."

She laughed. "Flatterer! We talk all the time."

"Not the way we do when you say, 'Tim, I want to talk to you.' They're the best sort of talks, it means you've got something really good to say."

Her eyes opened wide. "Aren't you shrewd? Come on, then, mate, no dilly-dallying!"

It was hard to rid herself of the intensely practical, energetic mood of the past few days, and for a while she sat on the sand in silence, trying to come down from her plateau of busy briskness. To adopt this attitude had been essential for her mental well-being; without it she could never have managed to say and do all that was required, for any sign of vulnerability in herself would have resulted in disaster. Now the hardiness was not needed, and must be discarded.

"Tim, have you any idea what marriage is?"

"I think so. It's what Mum and Pop are, and what my Dawnie did."

"Can you tell me anything more than that about it?"

"Golly, I dunno!" He ran his hand through his thick gold hair, grimacing. "It means you go and live with someone you didn't always live with, doesn't it?"

"Partly." She turned to face him. "When you're all grown up and you're not a little kid any more, you end up meeting someone you like so much that you think about going to live with them instead of living with your Mum and Pop. And if the person you like so well likes you just as much, then you go to a priest or a minister or a judge and you get married. You both sign a little piece of paper, and signing that little piece of paper means you're married, you can live together for the rest of your lives without offending God."

"It really does mean you can live together for the rest of your life?"

"Yes."

"Then why can't I marry you, Mary? I'd like to marry you, I'd like to see you all dressed up like a fairy princess in a long white dress the way Dawnie was and the way Mum was in her wedding photo on the dressing table in her bedroom."

"Lots of girls do wear long white dresses when they get mar-

213

ried, Tim, but it isn't the long white dress that makes you married, it's the little bit of paper."

"But Mum and Dawnie wore long white dresses!" he maintained stubbornly, enamored of the idea.

"Would you really like to marry me, Tim?" Mary asked, steering him away from the long white dress.

He nodded vigorously, smiling at her. "Oh, yes, I'd really like to marry you, Mary. I could live with you then all the time, I wouldn't have to go home on Sunday night."

The river ran on its way down to the sea, lapping and gurgling contentedly; Mary brushed a persistent fly away from her face. "Would you want to live with me more than you want to live with your Pop?"

"Yes. Pop belongs to Mum, he's only waiting until he can go and sleep with her under the ground, isn't he? I belong to you, Mary."

"Well, your Pop and I were talking about you the other night after I brought you home from Mr. Martinson's, and we decided it would be a good thing if you and I did get married. We worry a lot over what will happen to you, Tim, and there's no one in all the whole world we like more than you."

The blue eyes sparkled with light reflected off the river. "Oh, Mary, do you mean it? Do you really mean it? You will marry me?"

"Yes, Tim, I'm going to marry you."

"And then I can live with you, I can really belong to you?"

"Yes."

"Can we get married today?"

She blinked at the river, suddenly sad. "Not today, my dear, but very soon. Next Friday."

"Does Pop know when it is?"

"Yes, he knows it's next Friday. It's all arranged."

"And you'll wear a long white dress like Mum and my Dawnie?"

She shook her head. "No, Tim, I can't. I'd like to wear a long

214

white dress for you, but it takes a long time to make one and your Pop and I don't want to wait that long."

Disappointment dimmed his smile for a moment, but then it bloomed again. "And I don't have to go home after that?"

"For a little while you will, because I have to go into the hospital."

"Oh, Mary, no! You can't go into hospital! Please, please don't go into hospital!" Tears welled up in his eyes. "You'll die, Mary, you'll go away from me to sleep under the ground and I won't see you ever again!"

She reached out and took his hands in a strong, reassuring clasp. "Now, now, Tim! Going into the hospital doesn't mean I'm going to die! Just because your Mum died when she went to the hospital doesn't mean I'm going to die too, you know. Lots and lots and lots of people go into hospital and come out again without dying. Hospital is a place where you go when you're sick and you want to get better. It's just that sometimes we're so sick we can't get better, but I'm not sick like your Mum, am I? I'm not all weak and in pain, am I? But I went to see the doctor and he wants to make a little bit of me that's all wrong go all right again, and he wants to do it before you come to live with me so that I'm all better for you."

It was hard making him believe her, but after a while he calmed down and seemed to accept the fact that she was not going to the hospital to die.

"You're sure you're not going to die, now?"

"Yes, Tim, I'm sure I'm not going to die. I can't die yet. I won't let myself die yet."

"And we will get married before you go to the hospital?"

"Yes, it's all arranged for next Friday."

He leaned back on his hands and sighed happily, then rolled over and over down the sloping sand until he ended in the bay, laughing. "I'm going to marry Mary, I'm going to marry Mary!" he sang, throwing water all over her when she followed him down to the river's edge.

215

Twenty-five

In honor of the occasion, Mary wore a peach tussore silk suit to her wedding, with a small peach silk hat and a modest corsage of tea roses on her lapel. The wedding party had arranged to meet on the Hyde Park side of Victoria Square, just across from the Registrar General's offices. Mary parked in the underground Domain lot and took the moving sidewalk from her car to the College Street exit, then walked across the park. Archie had wanted to drive her, but she had refused.

"I have to go straight from the wedding to the hospital, so I think I had better drive myself."

"But you ought to let me drive you, dear!" he had protested. "What do you think you're going to do, drive yourself home from the hospital when you're discharged?"

"Of course. It's a large private hospital run like a hotel, and I'm staying in much longer than is actually necessary so that I'm absolutely fit and well when I come home. I don't want to disappoint Tim by going home and not letting him come to stay with me very soon afterward."

He glanced at her, puzzled. "Well, I suppose you know what you're doing, because you always do."

She shook his arm affectionately. "Dear old Archie, your faith in me is touching."

So she went to her wedding alone, and was the first to arrive on the park corner. Archie and Tricia came soon after. Mrs. Parker puffed up in their wake wearing a startling confection of cerise and electric blue chiffon, and then Tim and Ron emerged from the subway entrance a few feet away. Tim was wearing the suit he had worn to Dawnie's wedding, Ron the suit he had worn to Esme's funeral. They stood in the clear bright sun chatting self-consciously, then Tim gave her a small box, thrusting it at her quickly when no one was looking. He was clearly nervous and unsure of himself; hiding the box with her hand, Mary led him a few steps away from the others and stood with her back to them while she undid the clumsy wrapping.

"Pop helped me pick it out, because I wanted to give you something and Pop said it was all right for me to give you something. We went to the bank and I took two thousand dollars out and we went to the big jeweler down in Castlereagh Street near the Hotel Australia."

Inside the box lay a small brooch, with a magnificent black opal center and a diamond surrounding, fashioned like a flower.

"It reminded me of your garden at the cottage, Mary, all the colors of the flowers and the sun shining on everything."

Off came the tea roses, down they fell to the searing asphalt pavement and lay unnoticed; Mary took the brooch out of its velvet bed and held it out to Tim, smiling at him through a haze of tears. "It isn't my garden any more, Tim, it's our garden now. That's one of the things marrying does, it makes everything each of us owns belong to the other, so my house and my car and my cottage and my garden belong to you just as much as they do to me after we're married. Will you pin it on for me?"

He was always quick and deft with his hands, as if they had escaped his psychic halter; he took the edge of her coat lapel between his fingers and slipped the sharp pin through the fabric easily, did up the safety catch and then the safety chain.

"Do you like it, Mary?" he asked anxiously.

"Oh, Tim, I love it so much! I've never had anything so pretty

217

in all my life, and no one has ever given me a brooch before. I'll treasure it all my life. I have a gift for you, too."

It was a very expensive, heavy gold watch, and he was delighted with it.

"Oh, Mary, I promise I'll try not to lose it, I really will! Now that I can tell the time it's beaut to have my very own watch. And it's so lovely!"

"If you lose it we'll just get you another one. You mustn't worry about losing it, Tim."

"I won't lose it, Mary. Every time I look at it I'll remember that you gave it to me."

"Let's go now, Tim, it's time."

Archie took her elbow to guide her across the street. "Mary, you didn't tell me that Tim was such a spectacular young man."

"I know I didn't. It's embarrassing. I feel like one of those raddled old women you see gallivanting round the tourist resorts in the hope of acquiring an expensive but stunning young man." The arm above his hand was trembling. "This is a terrible ordeal for me, Archie. It's the first time I've exposed myself to the curious gaze of the public. Can you imagine what they'll all think in there when they realize who is marrying whom? Ron looks a more appropriate husband for me than Tim."

"Don't let it worry you, Mary. We're here to support you, and support you we will. I like your Old Girl next door, by the way. I must sit next to her at dinner, she has the richest vocabulary I've encountered in many a long day. Look at her and Tricia there, magging away like old cronies!"

Mary glanced at him gratefully. "Thanks, Archie. I'm sorry I won't be able to attend my own wedding dinner, but I want to get this hospital business over and done with as soon as I can, and if I delay until after dinner my doctor won't put me on his operating list for tomorrow, which means a wait of a week, since he only operates there Saturdays."

"That's all right, love, we'll drink your share of the champagne and eat your share of the chateaubriand."

Because there were sufficient witnesses in the wedding party, only one pair of fascinated eyes beheld the queer couple, those belonging to the officiating representative of Her Majesty's Law. It was quickly over, disappointingly shorn of ceremony or solemnity. Tim made his responses eagerly, a credit to his father's coaching; Mary was the one who stumbled. They signed the required documents and left without realizing that the elderly man who married them had no idea Tim was mentally retarded. He did not think the match odd at all in that way; many handsome young men married women old enough to be their mothers. What he found odd was that no kisses were exchanged.

Mary left them on the same corner where she had joined them, plucking Tim's coat sleeve anxiously.

"Now you'll wait for me patiently and you won't worry about me, promise? I'll be all right."

He was so happy that Tricia Johnson and Emily Parker felt like crying just to see his face; the only shadow to mar his day was Mary's abrupt departure, but even that could not depress him for very long. He had signed the little bit of paper and so had Mary, they belonged together now and he could wait for a long time if necessary before coming to live with her.

The operation made Mary sore and uncomfortable for a few days, but she weathered it well; better, in fact, than her gynecologist had expected.

"You're a sturdy old girl," he informed her as he took the stitches out. "I ought to have known you'd take it in your stride. Old girls like you have to be killed with an ax. As far as I'm concerned you can go home tomorrow, but stay in as long as you like. This isn't a hospital, you know, it's a bloody palace. I'll sign your discharge papers on the way out today and then you can leave whenever you want, this week or next week or the week after that. I'll keep stopping in just in case you're here."

Twenty-six

In the end Mary stayed five weeks, rather enjoying the quiet privacy of the old house on the Rose Bay waterfront, and rather dreading the thought of seeing Tim. She had not told anyone where she was going for her surgery except the dry little man who took care of her legal affairs, and the laboriously written postcards she got from Tim every day were all forwarded through the dry little man's office. Ron must have helped him a great deal, but the handwriting was Tim's and so was the phraseology. She tucked them away in a small briefcase carefully as she received them. During the last two weeks of her stay she swam in the hospital pool and played tennis on the hospital courts, deliberately accustoming herself to movement and exertion. When at length she left she felt as if nothing had ever happened, and the drive home was not at all taxing.

The house in Artarmon was ablaze with lights when she put the car in the garage and let herself in through the front door. Emily Parker was as good as her word, Mary thought, pleased; the Old Girl had promised to make the house look as though it was occupied. She put her suitcase down and stripped off her gloves, throwing them on the hall table along with her bag, then she walked into the living room. The phone loomed large as a monster in front of her, but she did not call Ron to tell him she was home; plenty of time for that, tomorrow or the day after or the day after that.

The living room was still predominantly gray, but many pictures hung on the walls now and splotches of rich ruby red glowered like the embers of a scattered fire throughout the room. A ruby glass vase from Sweden stood on the chaste mantel and a ruby-dyed fur rug lay sprawled across the pearl-gray carpet like a lake of blood. But it was pleasant to be home, she thought, looking around at that inanimate testament to her wealth and taste. Soon she would be sharing it with Tim, who had had a hand in its generation; soon, soon. . . . Yet do I want to share it with him? she asked herself, pacing up and down restlessly. How odd it was; the closer she came to his advent the more reluctant she was to have it occur.

The sun had set an hour before and the western sky was as dark as the rest of the world, pulsing redly from the city lights under a layer of low, sodden clouds. But the rain had fallen farther west, and left Artarmon to the summer dust. What a pity, she thought; we could really do with the rain here, my garden is so very thirsty. She went into the unlit kitchen and stood peering out the back window without switching the kitchen or patio lights on, trying to see if Emily Parker's house was lit. But the camphor laurels hid it; she would have to go out onto the patio to see it properly.

Her eyes were quite accustomed to the darkness as she let herself noiselessly out of the back door, softly cat-footed as always, and she stood for a moment inhaling the perfume of the early summer flowers and the far-off earthy smell of rain, filled with delight. It was so nice to be home, or it would have been had the back of her mind not been consumed with the specter of Tim.

Almost as if she could consciously form his image out of her thoughts, the silhouette of his head and body shaped itself against the distant, weeping sky. He was sitting along the railing of her balustrade, still naked and dewed with the water of his nightly shower, his face raised to the starless night as if he were listening raptly to the lilt of music beyond the limitations of her earthbound ears. What light there was had fused itself into his bright hair and clung in faint, pearly lines along the contours of his face and trunk, where the glistening skin was stretched tautly over the still, dormant muscles. Even the curve of his eyelids was visible, fully down to shield his thoughts from the night.

A month and more than a month, she thought; it's been over a month since I last saw him, and here he is like a figment of my imagination, Narcissus leaning over his pool wrapped in dreams. Why does his beauty always strike me so forcibly when I see him again the first time in a long while?

She crossed the sandstone flags silently and stood behind him, watching the column of sinew in the side of his throat gleam like a pillar of ice until the temptation to touch him could not be gainsaid a moment longer. Her fingers closed softly over his bare shoulder and she leaned forward to rest her face against his damp hair, her lips brushing his ear.

"Oh, Tim, it's so good to find you here waiting," she whispered.

Her coming did not startle him and he did not move; it was almost as if he had felt her presence in the stillness, sensed her behind him in the night. After a while he leaned back against her a little; the hand which had rested on his shoulder slid across his chest to the other shoulder, imprisoning his head within the circle of her arm. Her free hand slipped beneath his elbow to his side, its palm pressing down against his belly and pushing him back harder against her. The muscles of his abdomen twitched as her hand passed across them caressingly, then became utterly still, as if he had ceased to breathe; he moved his head until he could look into her face. There was a remote calmness about him and the eyes searching hers so seriously had the veiled, silvery sheen to them that always shut her out while it locked her in, as if he saw her but did not see Mary Horton. As his mouth touched her own he put his two hands up to grip the arm she had linked across his chest, and they closed over it. The kiss was different from their first, it had a languorous sensuality about it that Mary found fey and witching, as if the creature she had surprised dreaming was not Tim at all, but a manifestation of the soft summer night. Rising from the balcony railing without fear or hesitation, he pulled her into his arms and picked her up.

He carried her down the steps and into the garden, the short grass hushing under his bare feet. Half inclined to protest and make him return to the house, Mary buried her face in his neck and stilled her tongue, yielding up her reason to his strange, silent purpose. He made her sit on the grass in the deep shadow of the camphor laurels and knelt beside her, his fingertips delicately touching her face. She was so filled with love for him that she could not seem to see or hear, and she leaned forward like a rag doll toppled by a careless flick of the finger, her hands splayed far apart and her head down against his chest. He held it there, pulling at her hair until it fell loose about her and her hands lay curled helplessly on his thighs. From her hair he passed to her clothes, peeling them away as slowly and surely as a small child undressing a doll, folding each item neatly and laying it on a growing pile to one side of them. Mary crouched there timidly, her eyes closed. Their roles had somehow become reversed; he had inexplicably gained the ascendancy.

Finished, he took her arms and propped them on his shoulders, gathering her against him. Mary gasped, her eyes opening; for the first time in her life she felt a bare body all along the length of her own, and somehow there was nothing to be done save abandon herself to the feel of it, warm and alien and living. Her dreamlike trance merged into a dream sharper and more real than the entire world outside the darkness under the camphor laurels; all at once the silky skin under her hands took on form and substance: Tim's skin sheathing Tim's body. There was no more than that under the sun, nothing more to be offered her on life's plate than the feel of Tim within her arms, pinning her against the ground. It was Tim's chin driving ribbons of pain from the side of her neck, Tim's hands clawed into her shoulders, Tim's sweat running down her sides. She became aware that he was trembling, that the mindless delight which filled him was because of her, that it mattered not whether hers was the skin of a young girl or a middle-aged woman as long as it was Tim there, within her arms and within her body, as long as it was she, Mary, to give him this, so pure and mindless a pleasure that he came to it unfettered, free of the chains which would always bind her, the thinking one.

When the night was old and the dim western rain was gone over the mountains she pushed herself away from him and gathered the little pile of clothes against her chest, kneeling above him.

"We must go inside, dear heart," she whispered, her hair falling across his extended arm where her head had been. "It's the dark before light, we must go in now."

He picked her up and carried her inside immediately. The lights were still on in the living room; trailing her hand over his shoulder, she extinguished them one by one as he crossed to the bedroom. He put her down on the bed and would have left her alone had she not reached out to pull him back.

"Where are you going, Tim?" she asked, and moved over to make room for him. "This is your bed now."

He stretched out beside her, pushing his arm under her back. She put her head on his shoulder and her hand on his chest, caressing it drowsily. Suddenly the small, tender movement ceased, and she lay stiffening against him, her eyes wide and filled with fear. It was too much to be borne; she lifted herself on one elbow and reached across him to get at the lamp on the bedside table.

Since the silent meeting on the patio he had not spoken one word; all at once his voice was the only thing she wanted to hear, if he did not speak she would know that somehow Tim was not with her at all.

He was lying with his eyes wide open, looking up at her without even wincing in the sudden, drenching light. The face was sad and a little stern, and it wore an expression she had never seen before, it had a maturity she had never noticed. Was it her eyes that had been blind, or was it his face that had changed? The body was no longer strange or forbidden to her, and she could look upon it freely, with love and respect, for it housed a creature as live and entire as she was herself. How blue his eyes were, how exquisitely shaped his mouth was, how tragic the tiny crease to the left side of his lips. And how young he was, how young!

He blinked and shifted the focus of his gaze from some private infinity to the nearness of her face; his eyes dwelled on the tired, worried lines in it, then on the straight, strong mouth so sated with his kisses that its lips were swollen. He lifted one leaden hand and brushed his fingers against her firm, rounded breast gently.

She said, "Tim, why won't you speak to me? What have I done? Have I disappointed you?"

His eyes filled with tears; they ran down his face and fell onto the pillow, but his sweet, loving smile dawned and the hand cupped her breast harder.

"You told me that one day I'd be so happy I'd cry, and look! Oh, Mary, I'm crying! I'm so happy I'm crying!"

She collapsed on his chest, weak with relief. "I thought you were angry with me!"

"With *you?*" His hand cradled the back of her head, her hair slipping through his fingers. "I could never be angry with you, Mary. I wasn't even angry with you when I thought you didn't like me."

"Why wouldn't you speak to me tonight?"

He was surprised. "Did I have to speak to you? I didn't think I had to speak to you. When you came I couldn't think of anything to say. All I wanted was to do the things Pop told me about while you were away in hospital, and then I had to do them, I couldn't stop to talk."

"Your Pop told you?"

"Yes. I asked him if it was still a sin to kiss you if we were married, and he said it wasn't a sin at all when we were married. He told me about lots of other things I could do, too. He said I ought to know what to do because if I didn't I'd hurt you and you'd cry. I don't want to hurt you or make you cry, Mary. I didn't hurt you or make you cry, did I?"

She laughed, holding him hard. "No, Tim, you didn't hurt me and I didn't cry. There I was, petrified because I thought it was all up to me and I didn't know whether I was going to be able to deal with it."

"I really didn't hurt you, Mary? I forgot Pop told me not to hurt you."

"You did magnificently, Tim. We were in good hands, your green hands. I love you so much!"

"That's a better word than like, isn't it?"

"When it's used properly it is."

"I'm going to save it just for you, Mary. I'll tell everyone else I like them."

"That's exactly how it should be, Tim."

By the time dawn crept into the room and lit it with the clear, tender newness of day, Mary was fast asleep. It was Tim who lay staring wakefully at the window, careful not to move and disturb her. She was so small and soft, so sweet-smelling and cuddly. Once he used to hold his Teddy bear against his chest the same way, but Mary was alive and could hold him back; it was much nicer. When they took his Teddy bear away, saying he was all grown up and must not sleep with Teddy any more, he had wept for weeks with empty arms hugging his aching chest, mourning the passing of a friend. Somehow he had known Mum didn't want to take Teddy away, but after he came home from work in tears and told her how Mick and Bill had laughed at him for sleeping with a Teddy bear, she had steeled herself to do it, and Teddy had gone into the garbage can that very night. Oh, the night was so big, so dark and full of shadows which moved mysteriously, coiling themselves into claws and beaks and long, sharp teeth. While Teddy had been there to hide his face against they had not dared to come any closer than the opposite wall, but it took a long time to get used to them all around him, pressing down on his defenseless face and snapping at his very nose. After Mum had given him a bigger night light it was better, but he loathed the dark to this very day; it was deadly with menace, full of lurking enemies.

Forgetting he was not going to move in case he wakened her, he turned his head until he could look down on her, then slid up the pillow until he was much higher than she. Fascinated, he stared at her for a long time in the growing light, assimilating her alien appearance. Her breasts devastated him; he could not tear his eyes away from them. Just thinking about them filled him with excitement, and what he felt when they were crushed against him was indescribable. It was as though her differences had been invented just for him, he had no conscious awareness that she was exactly like any other female. She was Mary, and her body belonged to him as utterly as his Teddy had; it was his and his alone to hold against the inroads of the night, warding off terror and loneliness.

Pop had told him no one had ever touched her, that what he brought to her was foreign and strange, and he had understood the magnitude of his responsibility better than a reasoning man, for he had owned so little and been respected by so few. In the savage heat of his body's blind drive he had not managed to remember all Pop told him, but he thought, looking back on it, that he would remember more next time. His devotion to her was purely selfless; it seemed to come from somewhere outside him, compounded of gratitude and love and a deep, restful security. With her he never felt that he was weighed in the balance and found lacking. How beautiful she was, he thought, seeing the lines and the sagging skin but not finding them ugly or undesirable. He saw her through the eyes of total, unbounded love and so assumed that all of her was beautiful.

At first when Pop had told him he must go to the house at Artarmon and wait there alone for Mary to come home, he had not wanted to come. But Pop had made him, and would not let him return to Surf Street. A whole week he had waited, cutting the grass and weeding the flower beds and trimming the shrubs all day, then wandering the empty house at night until he was tired enough to sleep, with every light on to banish the demons of the formless darkness. He did not belong in Surf Street any more, Pop had said, and when he had begged Pop to come with him he had met with an adamant refusal. Thinking about it now as the sun rose, he decided Pop had known exactly what would happen; Pop always did.

That night the thunder had growled in the west and there was a stinging, earthy smell of rain in the air. Storms used to frighten him badly when he was a little boy, until Pop had shown him how quickly the fear went away if he went outside and watched how lovely it was, with the lightning streaking down the inky sky and the thunder bellowing like a mammoth, invisible bull. So he had taken his nightly shower and wandered naked onto the patio to watch the storm, disturbed and restless. In the house the bogies would have rushed gibbering at him from every cranny, but on the patio with the damp wind stroking his bare skin they had no dominion over him. And gradually the melting night had melted him; he had slipped into a senseless oneness with the unthinking creatures of the earth. It was as though he could see every petal on every dim flower, as though all the bird songs in the world flooded his being with a soundless music.

At first he was only dimly aware of her, until that beloved hand had seared his shoulder and filled him with a pain that yet was not a pain. He did not need to be able to reason to divine the change in her, the self-admission that she loved to touch him as much as he had yearned to touch her. He had leaned back to feel her breasts against him; her hand on his belly numbed and electrified him, he could not breathe for fear she would puff away. Their first kiss all those months ago had set him quivering with a hunger he had not known how to sate, but this second kiss filled him with a queer, triumphant power, armed as he was with what Pop had told him. He had wanted to feel her skin and could find only a part of it, frustrated by her clothes, but he had managed to command himself enough to do what had to be done, take them from her gently so as not to frighten her.

His steps had led him down into the garden because he hated the house at Artarmon; it was not his the way the cottage was, and he did not know where to take her. Only in the garden was he at home, so to the garden he went. And in the garden he felt her breasts at last, in the garden where he was simply another of its myriad creatures he could forget he was not the full quid, he could lose himself in the honeyed, piercing warmth of her body. And he had lost himself so for hours, alight with the unbearable pleasures of feeling her and knowing she was with him all the time in every part of her.

The sadness had come when she banished him to the house, and he realized they must part. He had clung to her as long as he could, carrying her small body within his arms and aching at the thought of having to let her go, wondering how long he must wait before it happened again. It had been dreadful, putting her into her bed and turning to go to his own; when she had drawn him back and made him lie beside her he had done so in numb astonishment, for it had not occurred to him to ask his Pop whether they would be exactly like his Mum and Pop and sleep together all through every night.

Then was the moment he knew he really belonged with her, that he could go down to the ground in the last, endless sleep safe and free from fear because she would be there beside him in the darkness forever. Nothing could ever frighten him again: he had conquered the final terror in discovering he would never be alone. For his life had been so very lonely, always shut out of the thinking world, always on some outer perimeter watching, longing to enter that world and never able to. He never could, never. Now it did not matter. Mary had allied herself to him in the last, most comforting way. And he loved her, loved her, loved her. . . .

Sliding down in the bed again he put his face between her breasts just to feel their softness, the fingertips of one hand tracing the outline of a hard, tantalizing nipple. She woke with a kind of purring noise, her arms slipping around him. He wanted to kiss her again, he wanted to kiss her badly, but he found himself laughing instead.

"What's so funny?" she asked drowsily, stretching as she wakened more fully.

"Oh, Mary, you're *much* nicer than my Teddy!" he giggled.

Twenty-seven

When Mary rang Ron to tell him that she was home and that Tim was well and safe, she thought he sounded tired.

"Why don't you come and stay with us for a few days?" she asked.

"No, thanks, love, I'd rather not. Youse'll be better off without me hanging around."

"That's not true, you know. We worry about you, we miss you and we want to see you. Please come out, Ron, or let me pick you up in the car."

"No, I don't want to." He sounded stubborn, determined to have his way.

"Then may we come and see you?"

"When you go back to work you can come over one night, but I don't want to see youse before then, all right?"

"No, it isn't all right, but if that's the way you want it there's nothing I can do. I understand you think you're doing the right thing, that we ought to be left alone, but you're wrong, you know. Tim and I would be very glad to see you."

"When youse go back to work, not before." There was a tiny pause, then his voice came again, fainter and farther away. "How's Tim, love? Is he all right? Is he really happy? Did we do the right thing and make him feel a bit more like the full quid? Was Mr. Martinson right?"

"Yes, Ron, he was right. Tim's very happy. He hasn't changed at all and yet he's changed enormously. He's rounded out and become more sure of himself, more content, less an outsider."

"That's all I wanted to hear." His voice sank to a whisper. "Thanks, Mary. I'll see youse."

Tim was in the garden, repotting maidenhair ferns from the rockery. With a swing and a lilt in her walk that was new, Mary crossed the grass toward him, smiling. He turned his head and gave her back the smile, then bent over the fragile leaves again, snapping off a fine, brittle black stem below the spot where the frond looked pale and sick. Sitting beside him on the grass, she put her cheek against his shoulder with a sigh.

"I just talked to Pop."

"Oh, goody! When is he coming out?"

"He says he won't come until after we've gone back to work. I tried to convince him he ought to make it sooner, but he won't. He thinks we ought to have this time to ourselves, and that's very kind of him."

"I suppose so, but he didn't need to do it, did he? We don't mind visitors. Mrs. Parker is always dropping in and we don't mind her, do we?"

"Oddly enough, Tim, we don't. She's a good old stick."

"I like her." He laid the fern down and slid an arm about her waist. "Why do you look so pretty these days, Mary?"

"Because I have you."

"I think it's because you don't always dress up as if you're going to town. I like you better with no shoes and stockings and your hair all undone."

"Tim, how would you like to go up to the cottage for a couple of weeks? It's nice here, but it's even nicer up at the cottage."

"Oh, yes, I'd like that! I didn't like this house much before, but it turned out to be real nice after you came home from the hospital. I feel as though I belong here now. But the cottage is my favorite house in all the world."

"Yes, I know it is. Let's go right now, Tim, there's nothing to hold us here. I only waited to see what Pop wanted to do, but he's left us to ourselves for the time being, so we can go."

It never occurred to either of them to look further than the cottage; Mary's grandiose schemes of taking Tim to the Great Barrier Reef and the desert evaporated into the distant future.

They moved into the cottage that night and had great fun deciding where they were going to sleep. In the end they moved Mary's big double bed into his room, and closed the door on her stark white cell until they felt like going into Gosford to buy paint for redecoration. There was very little to do in the blooming garden and less inside the house, so they walked in the bush for hours and hours, exploring its bewitching, untouched corridors, lying with heads together over a busy ant hill or sitting absolutely still while a male lyre bird danced the complicated measures of his ceremonious courtship. If they found themselves too far away to get back to the cottage before dark they stayed where they were, spreading a blanket over a bed of bracken fern and sleeping under the stars. Sometimes they slept the daylight hours away and rose with the setting of the sun, then went down to the beach after dark and lit a fire, revelling in the newfound freedom of having the world entirely to themselves and having no constraint between them. They would abandon their clothes, safe in the darkness from eyes out on the river, and swim naked in the still, black water while the fire died away to ash-coated coals. He would make her lie afterward on a blanket in the sand, the urge of his love too strong to resist a moment longer, and she would lift her arms to draw him down beside her, happier than she had ever thought was possible.

One night Mary wakened from a deep sleep in the sand and lay for a moment wondering where she was. As thought came back she knew, for she had had to accustom herself to sleeping clasped in Tim's arms. He never let her go. Any attempt to move away from him woke him at once; he would reach out until he found her and pull her back again with a sigh of mingled fear and relief. It was as if he thought she was going to be snatched away by something out of the darkness, but he would not talk about it and she never insisted, divining that he would tell her in his own good time.

Summer was at its height and the weather had been perfect, the days hot and dry, the nights sweetly cooled by the sea breeze. Mary stared up at the sky, drawing in a breath of awe and wonder. The massive belt of the Milky Way sprawled across the vault from horizon to horizon, so smothered with the light of the stars that there was a faint, powdery glow even in the starless parts of the sky. No haze conspired to blot them out, and the leaching city lights were miles to the south. The Cross spread its four bright arms to the winds, the fifth star clear and sparkling, the Pointers drawing her eyes away from the still, waxy globe of the full moon. Silver light was poured over everything, the river danced and leaped like cold, moving fire, the sand was struck to a sea of minute diamonds.

And it seemed to Mary for a still, small space of time that she heard something, or perhaps she felt it: alien and thin it was, like a cry teetering on the edge of nothing. Whatever it was, there was peace and finality in it. She listened for a long time, but it did not happen again, and she began to think that perhaps on a night like this the soul of the world was liberated to throw itself like a veil over the heads of all living things.

With Tim she always spoke of God, for the concept was simple and he was uncomplicated enough to believe in the intangible, but Mary herself did not believe in God; she had a basic and unphilosophic conviction that there was only one life to live. And wasn't that the important thing, quite independent of the existence of a superior being? What did it matter whether there was a God if the soul was mortal, if life of any kind ceased on the lip of the grave? When Mary thought of God at all it was in terms of Tim and little children, the good and uncorrupted; her own life had driven the supernatural so far away that it seemed there were two separate creeds, one for childhood and one for full growth. Yet the half-heard, half-felt thing coming out of the night disturbed her, there was an other-world suggestion about it, and she remembered suddenly the old legend that when the soul of someone who had just died passed overhead the dogs howled, lifting their muzzles to the moon and shivering as they mourned. She sat up, clasping her arms about her knees.

Tim sensed her going immediately, waking when his gropings did not find her.

"What's the matter, Mary?"

"I don't know. . . . I feel as if something's happened. It's very strange. Did you feel anything?"

"No, only that you went away from me."

He wanted to make love to her and she tried to divorce herself from her sudden preoccupation long enough to satisfy him, but could not. Something stalked in the back of her mind like a prowling beast, something threatening and irrevocable. Her half-hearted cooperation did not disconcert Tim; he gave up trying to rouse her and contented himself with wrapping his arms about her in what she always thought of as his Teddy-bear hug, for he had told her a little about Teddy, though, she suspected, not all there was to know.

"Tim, would you mind very much if we drove back to the city?"

"Not if you want to, Mary. I don't mind anything you want to do."

"Then let's go back now, right this minute. I want to see Pop. I've got a sort of feeling he needs us."

Tim got up at once, shaking the sand out of the blanket and folding it neatly over one arm.

235

By the time the Bentley pulled up in Surf Street it was six o'clock in the morning, and the sun had long been up. The house was silent and seemed curiously deserted, though Tim assured Mary his father was there. The back door was unlocked.

"Tim, why don't you stay out here for a minute while I go inside and check by myself? I don't want to frighten or upset you, but I think it would be better if I went in alone."

"No, Mary, I'll come in with you. I won't be frightened or upset."

Ron was lying in the old double bed he had shared with Es, his eyes closed and his hands folded on his chest, as if he had remembered how Es was lying the last time he saw her. Mary did not need to feel his cold skin or search for a stilled heart; she knew immediately that he was dead.

"Is he asleep, Mary?" Tim came round to the other side of the bed and stared down at his father, then put out his hand and rested it against the sunken cheek. He looked up at Mary sadly. "He's so cold!"

"He's dead, Tim."

"Oh, I wish he could have waited! I was so looking forward to telling him how nice it is to live with you. I wanted to ask him some things and I wanted him to help me pick out a new present for you. I didn't say goodbye to him! I didn't say goodbye to him and now I can't remember what he looked like when his eyes were open and he was all happy and moving."

"I don't think he could bear to wait a moment longer, dear heart. He wanted so badly to go; it was so lonely for him here and there was nothing more to wait for once he knew you were happy. Don't be sad, Tim, because it isn't sad. Now he can sleep with your Mum again."

All at once Mary knew why his voice had seemed so remote over the phone; he had begun his death-fast the moment Tim left the house in Surf Street forever, and by the time Mary came home from hospital he was already weakening badly. Yet could it be called suicide? She did not think so. The drum had stopped beating and the feet had stopped marching, that was all.

Sitting on the edge of the bed, Tim got his arms under his father's back and lifted the stiff, shrunken form into his arms tenderly. "Oh, but I'm going to miss him, Mary! I liked Pop, I liked him better than anyone else in the whole world except for you."

"I know, dear heart. I'll miss him too."

And was that the voice in the night? she wondered. Stranger things than that have happened to more staunchly doubting people without swaying their doubt. . . . Why shouldn't the living cords which laced a being together flick softly against a loved one in the very moment of their unraveling? He was all alone when it happened, and yet he had not been alone; he had called, and she had woken to answer him. Sometimes all the miles between are as nothing, she thought, sometimes they are narrowed to the little silence between the beats of a heart.

Twenty-eight

Mary hated Ron's funeral, and was glad she persuaded Tim not to come. Dawnie and her husband had taken charge, which was only right and proper, but as Tim's representative she had to be there and follow the little cortege to the cemetery. Her presence was clearly unwelcome; Dawnie and Mick ignored her. What had happened when Ron told them she and Tim were married, she wondered? Since the wedding she had only spoken to Ron that once, and he had not mentioned his daughter's name.

After the sod was turned on Ron's coffin and the three of them moved slowly away from the graveside, Mary put her hand on Dawnie's arm.

"My dear, I'm so sorry for you, because I know you loved him very much. I loved him too."

There was a look of Tim about his sister's eyes as she stared at Mary, but the expression in them—bitter and corroded—was one she had never seen in Tim's.

"I don't need your condolences, sister-in-law! Why don't you just go away and leave me alone?"

"Why can't you forgive me for loving Tim, Dawnie? Didn't your father explain the situation to you?"

"Oh, he tried! You're a very clever woman, aren't you? It

didn't take you long to delude him as completely as you did Tim! Are you happy now that you've got your pet moron by your side permanently and legally?"

"Tim's not my pet moron, you know that. And anyway, does it matter as long as he's happy?"

"How do I know he's happy? I've only got your word for that, and your word's not worth two cents!"

"Why don't you come and see him and find out for yourself what the truth is?"

"I wouldn't soil my shoes by entering your house, *Mrs. Tim Melville!* Well, I suppose you've got what you wanted, you've got Tim all to yourself with the conventions nicely taken care of and both his parents out of the way!"

Mary whitened. "What do you mean, Dawn?"

"You drove my mother to her grave, Mrs. Tim Melville, and then you drove my father after her!"

"That's not true!"

"Oh, isn't it? As far as I'm concerned, now that my father and mother are both dead, my brother's dead too. I never want to see or hear from him again! If you and he want to make a public spectacle of yourselves by flaunting your sick fancies under society's nose, I don't even want to know about it!"

Mary turned on her heel and walked away.

By the time she got from Botany Cemetery to her house in Artarmon she felt better, and was able to greet Tim with a fair semblance of serenity.

"Is Pop with Mum now?" he asked her anxiously, twisting his hands together.

"Yes, Tim. I saw him put in the ground right next to her. You needn't worry about either of them ever again, they're together and at peace."

There was something odd about Tim's manner; she sat down and examined him keenly, not alarmed exactly, but puzzled.

"What's the matter, Tim? Aren't you feeling well?"

239

He shook his head apathetically. "I feel all right, Mary. Just a bit funny, that's all. It's sort of funny not having Pop or Mum any more."

"I know, I know. . . . Have you had anything to eat?"

"No. I'm not very hungry."

Mary walked across and pulled him up out of his chair, looking at him in concern. "Come out to the kitchen with me while I make us some sandwiches. Maybe you'll feel like eating when you see how pretty and dainty they are."

"Little wee ones with all the crusts cut off?"

"As thin as tissue paper, little wee triangles with all the crusts cut off, I promise. Come on now."

It had been on the tip of her tongue to add "my love, my darling, my heart," but somehow she could never bring herself to utter the wild endearments which sprang to mind whenever, as now, he seemed upset or lost. Would she ever find it possible to treat him wholly as the lover he was, would she ever manage to lose that rigid, shrinking horror of making a total fool of herself? Why was it she could only relax completely with him when they were secluded at the cottage or in their bed? Dawnie's bitterness rankled, and all the curious, speculative glances she and Tim got as they passed down Walton Street still had the power to humiliate.

Mary's courage was not the unconventional kind; how could it be? Having nothing as her birthright, her entire life up to the moment of meeting Tim had been designed to achieve material success, earn the approbation of those who had started out much better endowed. It could not come easily now to fly in the face of convention, sanctified by the law though her union with Tim was. While she longed passionately to forget herself, smother him with kisses and endearments whenever the impulse came, his inability to encourage her in a mature way made it quite impossible if there was the least chance of their being disturbed. Her dread of amusement or ridicule had even led her to ask Tim not to chatter about his marriage to anyone not already aware of it, a moment of weakness which she had regretted afterward. No, it was not easy.

As usual, Tim wanted to help her actively as she set about making the sandwiches, getting out the bread and butter, rattling the china noisily as he searched for plates.

"Would you find the big butcher's knife for me, Tim? It's the only one that's sharp enough to cut crusts off."

"Where is it, Mary?"

"In the top drawer," she answered absently, spreading a coat of butter on each slice of bread.

"Ohhhhhh! Mary, Mary!"

She turned quickly, something in his cry filling her with heart-stopping fear.

"Oh, my God!"

For an appalled second it seemed as if the whole room was blood; Tim was standing quite still by the counter, staring down at his left arm in unbelieving terror. From biceps to fingertips it ran pulsating rivers of blood, the outflow of a fountain spraying from the crook of his elbow. With the regularity of a timepiece the blood spurted in a vicious jet halfway across the room, tapered off, spurted again; a thin lake of it was gathering about his left foot, and the left side of his body glistened wetly, dripping its share onto the floor.

There was a roll of butcher's twine on a spool near the stove, and a small pair of scissors hanging on a cord near it; almost in the same instant that she had spun round, Mary ran to it and hacked off a piece several feet long, doubling and quadrupling it feverishly to make a thicker cord.

"Don't be afraid, dear heart, don't be afraid! I'm here, I'm coming!" she panted, snatching up a fork.

But he didn't hear; his mouth opened in a thin, high wail and he ran like a blinded animal, bumping into the refrigerator, caroming off the wall, the gushing arm flailing about him as he

241

tried to shake it off, throw it away so that it no longer was a part of him. Her cries blended with his; she lunged at him and missed, pulled up short and tried again. Spinning in fear-crazed circles, he saw the door and made for it, plucking at his arm and screaming shrilly. His bare feet splashed into the pool of blood on the floor and he slipped, crashing full length. Before he could rise Mary was on him, holding him down, beyond any further attempts to calm him in her frenzy to tie off the blood supply to his arm before it was too late. Half sitting, half lying on his chest, she grasped the arm and wrapped her string about it above the elbow, knotted it securely and put the fork underneath to twist the cord until it almost disappeared into his flesh.

"Tim, lie still! Oh, please, please, Tim, lie still! I'm here, I won't let anything happen to you, only *you must lie still!* Do you hear me?"

Between panic and loss of blood he was done; chest heaving, he lay beneath her and sobbed. Her head came down until her cheek was against his, and all she could think of was the times she had prevented herself from calling him all those lovely, loving names, forced herself to sit calmly opposite him when she longed to take him in her arms and kiss him until he gasped.

There was a pounding on the back door, and the Old Girl's voice; lifting her head, Mary screamed.

"I heard the weirdest noises all the way over in me own house," Mrs. Parker babbled as she pushed at the door, then as she saw the blood-washed kitchen she made a sound halfway between a gasp and a retch. "Jesus Christ!"

"Get an ambulance!" Mary panted, afraid to take her weight off Tim in case he panicked again.

Nothing Mrs. Parker could say would persuade Mary to get up; when the ambulance arrived not five minutes later she was still on the floor with Tim, her face pressed to his, and the two ambulance men had to lift her away.

Emily Parker went with her to the hospital, trying to comfort

242

her as they rode in the back with Tim and one ambulance man.

"Don't worry about him, pet, he'll be all right. It looked like an awful lot of blood, but I've heard people say that a pint of it spilled looks like ten gallons."

The district hospital was only a short distance away, on the other side of the brick pits, and the ambulance reached it so quickly that Mary still had not recovered her powers of speech when they wheeled Tim away from her into casualty. After his fall he had seemed to lapse into a kind of stupor, not aware of her or of his surroundings; he did not open his eyes once, almost as if he was afraid of what he might see should he open them, see that horrible thing which had once been his arm.

Mrs. Parker helped Mary to a seat in the elegant waiting room, chattering all the time. "Ain't this nice?" she asked, try-ing to get Mary's mind off Tim. "I remember when this was just a couple of little rooms squeezed between X-ray and medical records. Now they've got this grouse new place, real nice. All them potted plants and everything make you feel like it ain't a hospital at all! I've seen worse hotel lobbies, pet, honest I have. Now you sit there nice and quiet until the doctor comes while I go and find me old mate Sister Kelly, see if I can get a hot cuppa tea and some bikkies for youse."

The admitting registrar came in soon after Mrs. Parker had gone off on her errand of mercy. Mary managed to get to her feet, licking her lips in an effort to speak; she still had not uttered a word.

"Mrs. Melville? I just saw the ambulance man outside for a moment, and he told me your name."

"Tih-Tih-Tim?" Mary managed to say, shaking so badly she had to sink into her chair again.

"Tim's going to be fine, Mrs. Melville, really he is! We've just sent him into the operating room to have the arm repaired, but there's no reason to fear for him, I give you my word. We've started him on intravenous fluids and we'll probably give him a pint or two of blood the minute we've got his type, but he's quite all right, just in shock from loss of blood, that's all. The arm wound isn't going to be too difficult to attend to, I've looked at it myself. A good clean cut. What happened?"

"He must have let the carving knife slip somehow, I don't know. I wasn't looking at him when it happened, I just heard him call for me." She looked up pitifully. "Is he conscious? Please make him understand that I'm here, that I haven't gone away and left him alone. He gets terribly upset when he thinks I've abandoned him, even now."

"He's under light anaesthesia at the moment, Mrs. Melville, but when he comes round I'll make sure he knows you're here. Don't worry about him, he's a grown man."

"That's just it, he's not. A grown man, I mean. Tim's mentally retarded, and I'm the only person he's got in all the world. It's terribly important that he knows I'm here! Just tell him Mary's outside, very close."

"Mary?"

"He always calls me Mary," she said childishly. "He never calls me anything but Mary."

The admitting registrar turned to go. "I'll send one of our junior residents in to take some particulars for the hospital records, Mrs. Melville, but he'll be brief. This is a simple accident case, no need for too many particulars, unless he's got any health problems aside from his mental retardation."

"No, he's in perfect health."

Mrs. Parker came back with Sister Kelly behind her bearing a tea tray.

"Drink this while it's hot, Mrs. Melville," said Sister Kelly. "Then I want you to go along the corridor to the bathroom, take off all your clothes and have a good steaming bath. Mrs. Parker's volunteered to go home and get you some fresh clothes, and in the meantime you can wear a patient's bathrobe. Tim's fine, and you'll feel so much better after you've soaked awhile in a

244

good hot bathtub. I'll send a nurse to show you the way."

Mary looked down at herself, only then realizing that she was as covered in Tim's blood as he had been himself.

"Drink your tea first, while Dr. Fisher takes some particulars for us."

Two hours later Mary was back in the waiting room with Mrs. Parker, clad in fresh clothing and feeling more like herself. Dr. Minster, the emergency surgeon, came to reassure her.

"You can go home, dear, he's fine. Came through the surgery with flying colors, and now he's sleeping like a baby. We'll leave him in intensive care for a little while, then we'll transfer him to one of the wards. Two days just to watch him, then he can go home."

"He must have the best of everything, a private room and anything else he might need!"

"Then we'll transfer him to the private wing," Dr. Minster soothed expertly. "Don't worry about him, Mrs. Melville. He's a beautiful physical specimen, really beautiful."

"Can't I see him before I go?" Mary pleaded.

"If you like, but don't stay. He's under sedation and I'd prefer it if you didn't try to rouse him."

They had put Tim in a huge, trolley-like bed behind a screen, in one corner of a room filled with a bewildering array of equipment that emitted muted clanks, hisses, and beeps. There were seven other patients, ill enough to trigger a momentary panic in Mary's mind. A young nurse was standing beside Tim unwrapping a blood pressure cuff from around his good arm. Her eyes were on her patient's face instead of on what she was doing, and Mary stood for a moment watching her obvious admiration. Then she looked up, saw Mary and smiled at her.

"Hello, Mrs. Melville. He's asleep, that's all, so don't worry about him. His blood pressure's excellent and he's out of shock."

The waxen pallor had gone from his face, leaving it, sleeping and smooth, softly flushed; Mary reached out to push the mat-

245

ted hair away from his forehead.

"I'm just about to take him down to the private wing, Mrs. Melville. Would you like to walk along with me and see him put into bed before you go home?"

They told her not to visit him until the following day late in the afternoon, for he continued to sleep and Mary knew that her presence could be at best a vigil. When she arrived she found him gone from his room, away to undergo tests; she sat and waited for him patiently, refusing all the offers of tea and sandwiches with a polite, strained smile.

"Does he realize where he is and what happened?" she asked the ward Sister. "Did he panic when he woke up and found I wasn't there?"

"No, he was fine, Mrs. Melville. He settled down very quickly and he seems to be happy. In fact, he's such a sunny, bright person that he's become the ward favorite."

When Tim saw her sitting in the chair waiting for him he had to be discouraged from leaping off his trolley to hug her. "Oh, Mary, I'm so glad you're here! I thought I might not see you for a long time."

"Are you all right, Tim?" she asked, kissing his brow quickly because two nurses were standing watching.

"I feel fine again, Mary! The doctor made my arm all better; he sewed it all together where the knife cut it, and there's no more blood or anything."

"Does it hurt?"

"Not much. Not like the time a load of bricks fell on my foot and it got broken."

Early the following morning Mary got a phone call from the hospital, telling her that she could take Tim home. Stopping only to tell Mrs. Parker the good news, she flew to the car with a small case containing Tim's clothes in one hand and her breakfast toast in the other. Sister met her at the ward door and took the case, then ushered her into a sitting room to wait.

She was just beginning to become impatient when Dr. Minster and the admitting registrar walked in.

"Good morning, Mrs. Melville. Sister told me you'd arrived. Tim ought to be ready very soon, so don't worry. They won't let you out of this place without a bath and a fresh dressing and Lord knows what."

"Tim is all right?" Mary queried anxiously.

"Absolutely! He'll have a scar to remind him to be more careful with carving knives in the future, but all the nerves to the hand are intact, so he won't lose power or sensation. Bring him to my rooms in a week's time and I'll see how everything is going. I may take the stitches out then, or leave them awhile longer, depending on how it looks."

"Then he really is all right?"

Dr. Minster threw back his head and laughed. "Oh, you mothers! You're all alike, full of worry and anxiety. Now you've got to promise me that you'll stop flapping over him, because if you let him see you've been reduced to this sort of state you'll give him ideas and he'll begin to favor the arm more than he ought. I know he's your son and your maternal feelings are particularly strong because of his special dependence on you, but you *must* resist your tendency to cluck over him needlessly."

Mary felt the blood welling up under her skin, but she pressed her lips together and lifted her head proudly. "You've misunderstood, Dr. Minster. Funny that it didn't occur to me, but I suppose you've all misunderstood. Tim isn't my son, he's my husband."

Dr. Minster and the admitting registrar looked at each other, mortified. Anything they tried to say would sound wrong, and in the end they said nothing, just got themselves to the door and slipped outside. What could one possibly say after making a gaffe like that? How ghastly, how absolutely ghastly, and how embarrassing! Poor, poor thing, how dreadful for her!

Mary sat in a haze of tears, fighting their tendency to spill

247

over with every ounce of what strength she had left. Whatever she felt, Tim must not see her eyes all red, nor must any of those pretty young nurses. No wonder they had all been so open to her about their admiration for Tim! One said some things to mothers and quite different things to wives, and now that she thought about it they had indeed treated her like a mother, not like a wife.

Well, it was her own stupid fault. If she had been her usual calm, collected self throughout those agonized hours of waiting and wondering, it would never have slipped her attention that they all assumed she was Tim's mother. It was even possible that they had asked her and she had replied in the affirmative. She remembered the young intern coming up to her and asking if she was the legal next of kin, but she could not remember what she had answered. And why shouldn't they have assumed she was his mother? At her best she looked her age, but with the shock and worry of Tim's accident weighing her down she looked sixty at least. Why hadn't she used a personal pronoun which could have offered them some clue? How odd the quirks of fate; she must have said and done everything to reinforce their misapprehension, done nothing to dispel it. Mrs. Parker must have done the same, and Tim, poor, anxious-to-please Tim, had absorbed her lesson too well when she had impressed on him that he must not rave about marrying her. They probably thought his calling her Mary was just his way. And no one had ever asked her if he was single or married; hearing he was not the full quid, they simply took it for granted that he was single. Mentally retarded people did not marry. They lived at home with their parents until they were orphaned and then they went to some sort of institution to die.

Tim was waiting in his room, fully dressed and very eager to be gone. Steeling herself to an outward calmness and composure, she took his hand in hers and smiled at him very tenderly.

"Come on, Tim, let's go home," she said.

AN INDECENT OBSESSION

for

"baby sister"

Mary Nargi Bolk

I am grateful to Colonel R. G. Reeves, Australian Staff Corps (Ret.), Mrs. Alma Critchley, and Sister Nora Spalding for their generous technical help.

CMcC

ONE

1

The young soldier stood looking doubtfully up at the unlabelled entrance to ward X, his kit bag lowered to the ground while he assessed the possibility that this was indeed his ultimate destination. The last ward in the compound, they had said, pointing him gratefully off down a path because they were busy and he had indicated he could find his own way. Everything save the armaments his battalion gunsmith had taken from him only yesterday was disposed about his person, a burden with which he was so familiar he didn't notice it. Well, this was the last building, all right, but if it was a ward it was much smaller than the ones he had passed along his way. Much quieter, too. A troppo ward. What a way to end the war! Not that it mattered how it ended. Only that it did end.

Watching him undetected through her office window, Sister Honour Langtry gazed down neatly divided between irritation and fascination. Irritation because he had been foisted on her at a stage when she had confidently expected no further admissions, and because she knew his advent would upset the delicate balance within ward X, however minutely; fascination because he represented an unknown whom she would have to learn to know. *Wilson, M. E. J.*

He was a sergeant from an illustrious battalion of an illustrious division; above the line of the pocket over his left breast he wore the red-blue-red ribbon of the Distinguished Conduct Medal, most prestigious and infrequently awarded, together with the ribbons of the 1939–1945 Star, the Africa Star without an 8, and the Pacific Star; the almost white-looking puggaree around his hat was a relic of the Middle East and bore a grey-bordered divisional color patch. He was wearing faded greens neatly laundered and pressed, his slouch hat was at the regulation angle, chin strap in place, and the brass of his buckles shone. Not very tall, but hard-looking, the skin of his throat and arms burned dark as teak. He'd had a long war, this one, and looking at him, Sister Langtry couldn't begin to guess why he was scheduled for ward X. There was a subtle aimlessness about him, perhaps, as of a man normally well accustomed to knowing his direction suddenly finding his feet pointing down an utterly unfamiliar path. But that any man coming to any new place might feel. Of the more usual signs—confusion, disorientation, disturbances of comportment or behavior—there were none. In fact, she concluded, he looked absolutely normal, and that in itself was abnormal for ward X.

Suddenly he decided it was time to act, swung his kit bag off the ground and set foot on the long ramp which led up to the front door. At precisely the same moment Sister Langtry walked round her desk and out of her office into the corridor. They met just inside the fly-curtain, almost perfectly synchronized. Some wag long since recovered and gone back to his battalion had made the fly-curtain out of beer bottle caps knotted on endless yards of fishing line, so that instead of tinkling musically like Chinese glass beads, it clashed tinnily. They met therefore amid a discord.

"Hello, Sergeant, I'm Sister Langtry," she said, her smile welcoming him into the world of ward X, which was her world. But the apprehensive irritation still simmered beneath the surface of her smile, and showed in the quick peremptory demanding of her hand for his papers, which she had seen were unsealed. Those fools in admissions! He'd probably stopped somewhere and read them.

Without fuss he had managed to shed sufficient of his gear to salute her, then removed his hat and gave her the envelope containing his papers without demur. "I'm sorry, Sister," he said. "I didn't have to read them to know what's in them."

Turning a little, she flicked the papers expertly through her office door to land on her desk. There; that should inform him she wasn't going to expect him to stand like a block of wood in

254

front of her while she delved into his privacy. Time enough to read the official story later; now was the time to put him at his ease.

"Wilson, M. E. J.?" she asked, liking his calmness.

"Wilson, Michael Edward John," he said, a tiny smile of answered liking in his eyes.

"Are you called Michael?"

"Michael or Mike, it doesn't matter which."

He owned himself, or so it seemed; certainly there was no obvious erosion of self-confidence. Dear God, she thought, let the others accept him easily!

"Where did you spring from?" she asked.

"Oh, further up," he answered vaguely.

"Come on, Sergeant, the war's over! There's no need for secrecy now. Borneo, I presume, but which bit? Brunei? Balikpapan? Tarakan?"

"Balikpapan."

"You couldn't have timed the hour of your arrival better," she said cheerfully, and walked ahead of him down the short corridor which opened into the main ward. "The evening meal's due shortly, and the kai's not bad here."

Ward X had been thrown together from the bits left over, parked like an afterthought down on the perimeter of the compound, never intended as housing for patients requiring complex medical care. When full it could hold ten beds comfortably, twelve or fourteen at a pinch, besides what beds could be fitted on the verandah. Rectangular in shape, it was built of unlined ship-lapped timber painted a shade of pale brown the men called baby-cack, and it had a hardwood plank floor. The windows might more accurately have been termed large apertures, unglazed, with wooden louvers to shut out the weather. The roof was unlined palm thatch.

There were only five beds in the main ward room at the moment, four down one wall in proper hospital rank, the fifth oddly out of place, for it lay on its own against the opposite wall and along it rather than at right angles to it, in contravention of hospital regulations.

They were drab low cots, each neatly made up, no blankets or counterpanes in this steamy latitude, just a bottom and a top sheet of unbleached calico long gone whiter than old bones from hard use in the laundry. Six feet above the head of each bed was a ring rather like a basketball hoop, yards of jungle-green mosquito netting attached to it and draped with a style and a complication worthy of Jacques Fath at his best. Beside each bed sat an old tin locker.

"You can dump your kit on that bed there," said Sister Langtry, pointing to the end bed in the row of four, the one nearest to the far wall, and so with louvered openings along one side of it as well as behind. A good bed for catching the breeze. "Stow everything away later," she added. "There are five other men in X, and I'd like you to meet them before dinner arrives."

Michael placed his hat on the pillow, the various components of his kit on the bed, then turned toward her. Opposite his bed was an area of ward completely fenced off by a series of screens, as if behind it lay some mysterious dying; but calmly beckoning him to follow, Sister Langtry slipped with the ease of long practice between two of the screens. No mystery, no dying. Just a long narrow refectory table with a bench drawn up along either side, and at its head one fairly comfortable-looking chair.

Beyond was a door leading out onto the verandah, which was tacked like a showy petticoat down one side of the ward building, ten feet wide and thirty-six feet long. There were bamboo blinds below the eaves to keep out the weather when it rained, but at the moment they were all rolled up out of the way. A post-and-rail fence formed a balustrade, slightly less than waist high. The floor was hardwood like the ward, and rolled with a hollow drum sound at the beat of Michael's booted steps. Four beds were lined up against the ward wall, rather close together, but the rest of the verandah was furnished with a motley collection of chairs. A longer twin of the refectory table within the ward was standing near the door, benches down either side;

256

quite a few of the chairs were scattered nearby, as if this part of the verandah was a favorite spot to sit. The ward wall consisted mostly of louvered apertures, wooden slats fully opened to permit whatever breeze there was full entry to the interior, for though the verandah was on the monsoon lee of the hut, it also happened to be the side of the southeast trades.

The day was dying, but not yet spent of its last breath; pools of soft gold and indigo shadows dappled the compound beyond the verandah railing. A great black thunderhead swimming in bruised light sat down on the tops of the coconut palms, stiffening and gilding them to the panoply of Balinese dancers. The air glittered and moved with a languid drifting of dust motes, so that it seemed a world sunk to the bottom of a sun-struck sea. The bright banded rib cage of a rainbow soared upward, a crutch for the vault of the sky, but was cruelly smeared out of existence in mid-arch. The butterflies were going, the night moths coming, and met, and passed each other without acknowledgment, no more than silent flickering ghosts. A chiming and a clear joyous trilling of many birds came from the cages of the palm fronds.

Oh, God, here goes, thought Sister Langtry, preceding Sergeant Michael Wilson out onto the verandah. I never know what they're going to be like, because whatever rationale they obey is beyond all save my instincts, and how galling that is. Somewhere inside me is a sense or a gift that understands them, yet my thinking mind can never manage to grasp what it is.

She had informed them half an hour ago there was a new patient coming, and felt their uneasiness. Though she had expected it; they always regarded a newcomer as a threat, and until they got used to him, readjusted the balance of their world, they usually resented him. And this reaction was in direct proportion to the newcomer's state when he arrived; the more of her time he took away from them, the deeper their resentment. Eventually things righted themselves, for he would slide from new hand to old hand, but until he did her life was bound to be hard.

Four men sat around or near the refectory table, all save one

257

shirtless; a fifth man lay full-length on the nearest of the beds, reading a book.

Only one of them rose at the intrusion: a tall, thin fellow in his middle to late thirties, fair and bleached fairer by the sun, blue-eyed, dressed in a faded khaki bush jacket with a cloth belt, long straight trousers and desert boots. His epaulettes carried the three bronze pips of a captain. The courtesy he manifested in rising seemed natural to him, but it extended only to Sister Langtry, at whom he smiled in a way that excluded the man at her side, the newcomer.

The first thing Michael noticed about them was the way in which they looked at Sister Langtry; not lovingly as much as possessively. What he found most fascinating was their refusal to look at him, though Sister Langtry had placed her hand on his arm and drawn him out of the doorway until he stood alongside her, so that not to look at him was difficult. However, they managed it, even the slight sickly lad reclining on the bed.

"Michael, I'd like you to meet Neil Parkinson," said Sister Langtry, blandly ignoring the atmosphere.

Michael's reaction was perfectly instinctive; because of the captain's pips he stiffened to rigid attention, precise as a guardsman.

The effect of his respect was more in keeping with a slap across the face.

"Oh, for Christ's sake, stuff it!" Neil Parkinson hissed. "We're all tarred with the same brush in X—there's no rank to barmy yet!"

Training stood Michael in good stead; his face showed no reaction to this gross rudeness as his pose relaxed from attention to an informal at ease. He could feel Sister Langtry tensing, for though she had dropped her hand from his arm, she stood close enough to him for her sleeve to brush against his; as if she wished in some way to support him, he thought, and deliberately moved a little away from her. This was his initiation, and he had to pass it on his own.

"Speak for yourself, Captain," said another voice. "We are not *all* tarred with the troppo brush. You can call yourself barmy if you like, but there's nothing wrong with me. They shut me in here to shut me up, for no other reason. I'm a danger to them."

Captain Parkinson moved aside to turn on the speaker, a young man lolling half naked in a chair: fluid, insolent, striking.

"And you can get stuffed too, you slimy bastard!" he said, the sudden hatred in his voice unnerving.

Time to take over, before it got out of hand, thought Sister Langtry, more annoyed than she showed. It seemed this was going to be one of their more intolerable welcomes, if any could be called a welcome. They were going to play it in a meanly minor key, the sort of behavior she found hardest to take always, for she loved them and wanted to be proud of them.

So when she spoke her tone was cool, detachedly amused, and threw, she hoped, the small clash into its right perspective for the newcomer. "I do apologize, Michael," she said. "To repeat myself, this is Neil Parkinson. The gentleman in the chair who contributed his mite is Luce Daggett. And on the bench next to Neil is Matt Sawyer. Matt's blind, and prefers me to tell people straight away. It saves embarrassment later. In the far chair is Benedict Maynard, on the bed Nugget Jones. Gentlemen, this is our latest recruit, Michael Wilson."

Well, that was it. He was launched. Frail human ship, frailer than most or he wouldn't be here, setting his sails into the storms and swells and calms of ward X. God help him, she thought. There doesn't look to be a thing the matter with him, but there must be. He's quiet, yes, but that seems natural to him. And there is a strength, a core of resilience quite undamaged. Which in my duration on ward X is unique.

She looked sternly from one man to another. "Don't be so touchy," she said. "Give poor Michael half a chance."

Subsiding onto the bench, Neil Parkinson laughed, and slewed himself sideways so he could keep one eye on Luce while he addressed his remarks to the latest recruit.

"Chance?" he asked. "Oh, Sis, come off it! What sort of chance do you call it to wind up in here? Ward X, this salubrious establishment in which you find yourself, Sergeant Wilson, is really

259

limbo. Milton defined limbo as a paradise of fools, which fits us to a tee. And we wander our limbo about as much use to the world and the war as tits on a bull."

He paused to check the effect of his oratory on Michael, who still stood beside Sister Langtry: a fine young man in his full tropical uniform, his expression interested but undismayed. Normally Neil was kinder than this, and would have served as buffer between the newcomer and the other men. But Michael Wilson didn't fit the X mold. He was not uncertain, emotionally impoverished, dazed, any of the multitude of things he might have been and still fitted. Indeed, Michael Wilson looked like a hard, fit, young but veteran soldier in full possession of his wits and in no need of the concern Sister Langtry was plainly suffering on his behalf.

Ever since the news had come several days ago of the cessation of hostilities with Japan, Neil had felt the anguish of time outstripping him, of decisions not yet satisfactorily made, of strengths returning but untested. What time was left to Base Fifteen and ward X he needed, every second of it, without the disruption a new man was bound to cause.

"You don't look troppo to me," he said to Michael.

"Nor to me," said Luce with a chuckle, and leaned to poke the blind man in the ribs a little too hard and viciously. "Does he look troppo to you, Matt?" he asked.

"Cut that out!" snapped Neil, his attention diverted.

Luce's chuckle became a laugh; he threw back his head and roared, a barrage of sound without amusement.

"That's *enough!*" said Sister Langtry sharply. She looked down at Neil, found nothing to help her, and then looked at each of the others in turn. But their resistance was complete, they were determined to show themselves to the new patient in prickly, squabbling disorder. At such times her impotence tormented her, yet experience had taught her never to push them too hard. Moods like this never lasted, and the worse the mood, the stronger the swing in an opposite direction was likely to be when it was over.

260

She finished her scansion of the group with Michael, and discovered his eyes on her intently, which was a little disquieting too, for unlike most new patients, his eyes had erected no walls to hide behind, held no rudderless plea for help; he was simply staring at her as a man might regard a charming novelty, or a pup, or some other article of great sentimental appeal but little practical value.

"Do sit down," she said to him, smiling, concealing the irritation she felt at being so dismissed. "You're probably weak at the knees by now."

He picked up immediately the fact that her comment about being weak at the knees was more a reprimand to the other men than sympathy directed at himself, which surprised her. But she got him settled in a chair facing Neil and the others, then seated herself where she could see Neil, Michael, Luce and Benedict, and leaned forward, unconsciously smoothing the grey cesarine of her uniform.

Used to focussing her attention on those among them who seemed to warrant it at any particular time, she made a mental note that Ben was beginning to look restless and distraught. Matt and Nugget had the happy knack of ignoring the bickering which was a permanent thing between Neil and Luce, where Ben flinched from the discord, and if it was allowed to go on would become very distressed.

Luce's eyes, half shut, were dwelling on her with the kind of chilling sexual familiarity her whole character, upbringing and training found offensive, though since being in ward X she had learned to suppress her disgust, had become more interested in discovering just what made a man stare at her so. However, Luce was a special case of it; she had never managed to make any headway with him at all, and sometimes felt a little guilty for not trying harder. That she did not try harder she readily admitted was a consequence of the fact that during his first week in ward X he had fooled her gloriously. That she came to her senses quickly and with no harm done either to him or to herself could not mitigate her original lack of judgment. Luce had a power, and he stirred a timorousness in her which she hated to feel but had perforce to endure.

With an effort she turned her gaze away from Luce and back to Ben; what she saw in his long dark drawn face caused her to glance casually down at her watch, which she wore pinned to the breast of her uniform. "Ben, would you mind seeing what's become of the kitchen orderly, please?" she asked. "Dinner's late."

He got jerkily to his feet, nodded to her solemnly, and stalked inside.

As if the movement had triggered some other train of thought in him, Luce sat up straighter, opened his yellowish eyes fully, and let them drift to Michael. From Michael they wandered to Neil, then back to Sister Langtry, where they rested very thoughtfully, no sexuality in them now.

Sister Langtry cleared her throat. "You're wearing a lot of spaghetti, Michael. When did you join up? In the first batch?" she asked.

His hair was cut very short and glittered like pale metal; his skull was beautiful, and he had the sort of face which made an onlooker think of bones rather than flesh, yet it didn't have the death's-head look of Benedict's face. There were fine lines in the skin around the eyes, and two deep lines furrowing between cheeks and nose. A man, not a boy, but the lines were premature. Single-minded sort of chap, probably. His eyes were grey, not the changeful camouflaging color of Luce's eyes, which could turn green or yellow; an ageless and remorseless grey, very still, very self-controlled, very intelligent. Sister Langtry absorbed all that in the fraction of a second it took him to draw breath to reply, unaware that every eye was fixed on her and her interest in the newcomer, even the eyes of blind Matt.

"Yes, I was in the first batch," said Michael.

Nugget completely abandoned the dog-eared nursing dictionary he had been pretending on and off to read, and turned his head sideways to stare fixedly at Michael; Neil's flexible brows rose.

262

"You've had a long war," said Sister Langtry. "Six years of it. How do you feel about it now?"

"I'll be glad to get out," he said, matter-of-fact.

"But you were anxious to go in the beginning."

"Yes."

"When did your feelings about it change?"

He looked at her as if he thought her question incredibly naive, but he answered courteously enough, shrugging. "It's one's duty, isn't it?"

"Oh, duty!" sneered Neil. "That most indecent of all obsessions! Ignorance got us in, and duty kept us in. I would love to see a world that raised its children to believe the first duty is to oneself."

"Well, I'm darned if I'd raise my children to believe that!" said Michael sharply.

"I'm not preaching hedonism nor advocating the total abandonment of ethics!" said Neil impatiently. "I'd just like to see the establishment of a world less prone to slaughter the flower of its manhood, that's all."

"All right, I'll grant you that and agree with you," said Michael, relaxing. "I'm sorry, I misunderstood you."

"I'm not surprised," said Luce, who never missed an opportunity to irritate Neil. "Words, words, words! Is that how you scored all your kills, Neil, by talking them to death?"

"What would you know about kills, you sideshow freak? It's not a duck shoot! They had to drag you into the army squealing like a stuck pig all the way, and then you dug yourself into a nice cushy job well behind the lines, didn't you? You make me sick!"

"Not as sick as you make me, you stuck-up bastard," snarled Luce. "One of these days I'm going to have your balls for breakfast!"

Neil's mood altered magically; his anger fell away, his eyes began to dance. "My dear old chap, it really wouldn't be worth the effort," he drawled. "You see, they're such *little* ones."

Nugget sniggered, Matt whooped, Michael laughed aloud, and

Sister Langtry dipped her head suddenly downward to look desperately at her lap.

Then, composure recovered, she terminated the exchange. "Gentlemen, your language tonight is offensive," she said, cool and crisp. "Five years in the army may have improved my education, but my feelings are as fine as they ever were. When I am within earshot, you will kindly refrain from bad language." She turned to glare fiercely at Michael. "That goes for you too, Sergeant."

Michael looked at her, quite unintimidated. "Yes, Sister," he said obediently, and grinned.

The grin was so infectiously likable, so . . . *sane*, that she sparkled.

Luce got to his feet in a movement which was both naturally and artificially graceful, slid between Neil and Benedict's vacant chair, and leaned over to ruffle Michael's hair impudently. Michael made no attempt to jerk away, nor indeed showed anger, but suddenly there was a quick, guarded watchfulness about him—a hint perhaps that here was someone not to be played with? wondered Sister Langtry, fascinated.

"Oh, you'll get on!" Luce said, and turned to look derisively at Neil. "I do believe you've got yourself a bit of competition, Captain Oxford University! Good! He's a late starter, but the winning post's not in sight yet, is it?"

"Push off!" said Neil violently, hands closing into fists. "Go on, damn you, push off!"

Luce got himself past Michael and Sister Langtry with a boneless sideways twist and headed for the door, where he collided with Benedict and stepped back with a gasp, as if he had been burned. He recovered quickly, lifting his lip contemptuously, but standing to one side with a bow and a flourish.

"How does it feel to be a killer of old men and little children, Ben?" he asked, then disappeared inside.

Benedict stood so starkly alone, so devastated, that for the first time since entering ward X Michael experienced a stirring of deep feeling; the look in those quenched black eyes moved him profoundly. Maybe that's because this is the first honest emotion I've seen, he thought. The poor bastard! He looks the way I feel, as if someone has switched off all the light inside.

As Benedict moved to his chair with a monklike shuffle, hands folded one on top of the other across his midriff, Michael's gaze followed, studying the dark face intently. It was so eaten away, so consumed by what went on behind it, so very pitiable. And though they were not alike, Michael found himself suddenly reminded of Colin, and he wanted so badly to help that he willed the withdrawing eyes to look back at him; when they did, he smiled.

"Don't let Luce get your goat, Ben," said Neil. "He's nothing more than a very lightweight twerp."

"He's *evil*," said Benedict, bringing the word out as if it chewed its way into utterance.

"So are we all, depending how you look at us," said Neil tranquilly.

Sister Langtry got up; Neil was good with Matt and Nugget, but somehow with Ben he never managed to hit the right note. "Did you find out what's happened to dinner, Ben?" she asked.

For a moment the monk became a boy; Benedict's eyes warmed and widened as they looked at Sister Langtry with unshadowed affection. "It's coming, Sis, it's coming!" he said, and grinned, grateful for the consideration which had prompted her to send him on the errand.

Her eyes on Ben were soft; then she turned away. "I'll help you get your stuff sorted out, Michael," she said, stepping inside. However, she wasn't quite finished with the group on the verandah yet. "Gentlemen, since dinner's late, I think you had better have it inside, shirts on and sleeves rolled down. Otherwise you won't beat the mossies."

Though he would rather have remained on the verandah to see what the group was like when she wasn't present, Michael took her request as an order and followed her into the ward.

His webbing, his pack and his kit bag lay on the bed. Arms folded, standing to watch him, Sister Langtry noticed the methodical ease with which he proceeded to dispose of his possessions; he commenced with the small haversack attached to his webbing and unearthed toothbrush, a grimy but precious morsel of soap, tobacco, shaving tackle, all of which he stowed neatly in the drawer of his locker.

"Did you have any idea what you were getting into?" she asked.

"Well, I've seen plenty of blokes go troppo, but it isn't the same thing as this. This is a troppo ward?"

"Yes," she said gently.

He undid the roll of his blanket and groundsheet from the top of his pack, then began to remove socks, underwear, a towel, clean shirts, trousers and shorts from the pack's interior. As he worked he spoke again. "Funny, the desert never sent a tenth as many men around the bend as the jungle. Though it stands to reason, I suppose. The desert doesn't hem you in; it's a lot easier to live with."

"That's why they call it troppo . . . tropical . . . jungle." She continued to watch him. "Fill your locker with what you'll need. There's a cupboard over there the rest can go in. I've got the key, so if you need anything, just yell. . . . They're not as bad as they must seem."

"They're all right." A faint smile turned one corner of his nice mouth up. "I've been in a lot loonier places and predicaments."

"Don't you resent this?"

He straightened, holding his spare pair of boots, and looked directly at her. "The war's over, Sister. I'll be going home soon anyway, and at this stage I'm so fed up I don't much care where I wait it out." He gazed around the room. "It's better housing than camp by a long shot, and the climate's better than Borneo. I haven't slept in a decent bed in ages." One hand went up, flicked the folds of mosquito netting. "All the comforts of home, and a mum too! No, I don't resent it."

The reference to a mum stung; how dared he! Still, time would disabuse him of that impression. She went on probing. "Why don't you resent it? You should, because I'll swear you're not troppo!"

266

He shrugged, turned back to his kit bag, which seemed to contain as many books as items of spare clothing; he was, she had noted, a superb packer. "I suppose I've been acting under pretty senseless orders for a long time, Sister. Believe me, being sent here isn't nearly as senseless as some of the orders I've had to follow."

"Are you declaring *yourself* insane?"

He laughed soundlessly. "No! There's nothing wrong with my mind."

She felt flummoxed; for the first time in a long nursing career she really didn't know what to say next. Then, as he reached into his kit bag again, she found a logical thing to say. "Oh, good, you've got a decent pair of sandshoes! I can't abide the sound of boots on this board floor." Her hand went out, turned over some of the books lying on the bed. Modern Americans mostly: Steinbeck, Faulkner, Hemingway. "No English writers?" she asked.

"I can't get into them," he said, and gathered the books together to stack in his locker.

That faint rebuff again; she fought an annoyance she told herself was quite natural. "Why?" she asked.

"It's a world I don't know. Besides, I haven't met any Poms to trade books with since the Middle East. We've got more in common with the Yanks."

Since her own reading background was thoroughly English and she had never opened a book by a modern American, she let the subject drop, returned to the main theme. "You said you were so fed up it didn't matter where you waited it out. Fed up with what?"

He tied the cords around his kit bag again, and picked up the emptied pack and webbing. "The whole thing," he said. "It's an indecent life."

She unfolded her arms. "You're not frightened of going home?" she asked, leading the way across to the cupboard.

"Why should I be?"

Unlocking the cupboard, she stood back to allow him to place his clobber inside. "One of the things I've noticed increasingly over the last few months in most of my men—and in my nursing colleagues too, for that matter—is a fear of going home. As if it's been so long all sense of familiarity and belonging has been lost," she said.

Finished, he straightened and turned to look at her. "In here, it probably has. This is a home of sorts, it's got some permanence to it. Are you frightened of going home too?"

She blinked. "I don't think so," she said slowly, and smiled. "You're an awkward beggar, aren't you?"

His answering smile was generous and bone deep. "It has been said of me before," he said.

"Let me know if there's anything you want. I go off duty in a few minutes, but I'll be back about seven."

"Thanks, Sister, but I'll be all right."

Her eyes searched his face; she nodded. "Yes, I think you will be all right," she said.

2   The orderly had arrived with dinner and was making a racket in the dayroom; instead of going straight to her office, Sister Langtry entered the dayroom, nodding to the orderly.

"What is it tonight?" she asked, removing plates from a cupboard.

The orderly sighed. "I think it's supposed to be bubble-and-squeak, Sister."

"More squeak than bubble, eh?"

"More flop than either, I'd say. But the pud's not bad, sort of dumplings in golden syrup."

"Any pud's better than none, Private. It's remarkable how much the rations have improved in the last six months."

"My word, Sister!" the orderly agreed fervently.

As she turned toward the Primus stove on which it was her habit to reheat the meal before serving it, a small movement in her office caught Sister Langtry's eye; she put the plates down and stepped soundlessly across the corridor outside the dayroom.

Luce was standing by her desk, head bent, the unsealed envelope containing Michael's papers in his hand.

"Put that down!"

He obeyed quite casually, as if he had simply picked the envelope up in passing; if he had read them, the deed was already done, for she could see that the papers resided safely inside the envelope. But looking at Luce she could not be sure. That was the trouble with Luce: he existed on so many levels he had difficulty himself knowing which end was up; of course, that meant he was always able to assure himself he had done nothing wrong. And to look at, he was the epitome of a man who could have no need to spy or have recourse to un-

269

derhand dealings. But such was not his history.

"What do you want in here, Luce?"

"A late pass," he said promptly.

"Sorry, Sergeant, you've had more than your share of late passes this month," she said coldly. "Did you read those papers?"

"Sister Langtry! As if I'd do such a thing!"

"One of these days you'll slip, and I'll be there to catch you," she said. "For the moment you can help me get the dinner on, since you're down this end of the ward."

But before she left the office she took Michael's papers and locked them away in the top drawer, cursing herself for a degree of carelessness she could not remember ever committing before, not in her entire career. She ought to have made sure the papers were under lock and key before taking Michael into the ward. Perhaps he was right; the war had gone on too long, which was why she was starting to make mistakes.

3 "For the food we are about to receive, may the good Lord make us truly thankful," said Benedict into a partial silence, and then lifted his head.

Only Luce had ignored the call to grace, eating all the way through it as if he were deaf.

The others waited until Benedict finished before picking up knives and forks to dissect the dubious messes on their plates, neither embarrassed by Benedict's prayer nor thrown off balance by Luce's irreverence. The whole ritual had long lost any novelty it might once have had, Michael concluded, finding his palate titillated by an unfamiliar cook, even if the cooking was army yet. Besides, there were luxuries here. Pudding.

To form conclusions about any new group of men had come to be a routine with him, a part of survival—and a game, too. He would bet himself imaginary sums of money on the correctness of his conclusions, preferring to do this than to acknowledge that for the last six years what he was usually actually betting was his life.

The men of ward X were a rum lot, all right, but no rummer than some other men he had known. Just men trying to get on with other men, and succeeding about as well as most. If they were like himself, they were tired past endurance with the war, and with men, men, men.

"Why on earth are you here in X, Mike?" asked Benedict suddenly, eyes bright.

Michael laid his spoon down, for he had finished the pudding anyway, and pulled out his tin of tobacco. "I nearly killed a bloke," he said, working a sheet of rice paper out of its folder. "I would have killed him, too, if there hadn't been enough other blokes around to stop me."

"Not one of the enemy, then, I presume?" asked Neil.

271

"No. The RSM in my own company."

"And that's *all?*" asked Nugget, making the most peculiar faces as he swallowed a mouthful of food.

Michael looked at him, concerned. "Here, are you all right?"

"It's just me hiatus hernia," said Nugget in a tone of fatal acceptance. "Hits me every time I swallow."

This was announced with great solemnity and the same kind of reverence Benedict had given to his little prayer; Michael noticed that the others, even Luce, simply grinned. They were fond of the little ferret-faced lad, then.

His cigarette rolled and lit, Michael leaned back, his arms behind his head because the bench offered no spinal support, and groped after what sort of men they were. It was very pleasant to be in a strange place, surrounded by strange faces; after six years in the same battalion, you knew from the smell which one of your fellow soldiers had farted.

The blind one was probably well into his thirties, didn't say much, didn't demand much. The opposite of Nugget, who was their mascot, he decided. Every company had its good luck talisman; why should ward X be different?

He wasn't going to like Luce, but then probably no one ever did like Luce. As with Nugget, there was nothing about him which suggested he had ever seen battle action. On no one would Michael have wished battle action, but the men who had seen it were different, and not in terms of courage, resolution, strength. Action couldn't manufacture these qualities if they weren't there, couldn't destroy them if they were. Its horror went far deeper than that, was far more complex. Looking death in the eye, weighing up the importance of living. Showing a man the randomness of his own death. Making a man realize how selfish he was, to thank his lucky stars the bullet had every name on it save his own. The dependence on superstition. The anguish and self-torment after each action was over because at the time a man became an animal to himself, a statistic to those in control of his military destiny. . . .

Neil was talking; Michael forced himself to listen, for Neil was

272

a person to respect. He'd had a very long war. His garb was desert, and he bore himself like a real soldier.

"...so as far as I can gather, we've got about eight more weeks," Neil was saying; Michael had been half listening, and understood that Neil was referring to the duration of ward X.

Fascinated, he directed his eyes from one face to another, his mind assimilating the discovery that the news of an imminent return home dismayed them. Blind Matt actually shivered in dread! They're a rum lot, all right, he thought, remembering Sister Langtry's saying they were frightened to go home.

Sister Langtry... It was a very long time since he had had anything to do with women, so he wasn't quite sure how he felt about her. The war had turned things topsy-turvy; he found it hard to conceive of women in authority, women with a kind of confidence he never remembered their owning before the war. For all her kindness and her interest, she was used to being the boss, and she felt no discomfort in exercising her authority over men. Nor, to give her credit, did she appear to relish that authority. No dragon, Langtry, even a young one. But he found it awkward to deal with a woman who calmly assumed they spoke the same language, thought the same thoughts; he couldn't even reassure himself he had seen more of the war than she, for it was likely that she had spent a considerable part of it under fire herself. She wore the silver pips of a captain in the nursing corps, which was a fairly high rank.

The men of ward X adored her; when she had first led him out onto the verandah he was immediately aware of the resentment in them, the wary bristling assessment of committed owners for a potential shareholder. That reaction of theirs, he decided, was the reason for their display of crotchety lunacy. Well, they needn't worry. If Neil was right, it seemed none of them would be here long enough to be obliged to readjust the pecking order on his behalf. All he wanted was to be rid of the war, the army, every last memory of the six years coming to a close.

And though he had welcomed the idea of a transfer to Base Fifteen, he didn't relish the idea of spending the next couple of months lying idle round a ward; too much time to think, too much time to remember. He was well, he had full command of his mental faculties; he knew it, and so did the blokes who had been responsible for sending him here. But as for these poor bastards in ward X, they suffered; he could see it in their faces, hear it in their voices. In time he could come to learn why, how. In the interim it was enough to understand they were all troppo, or had been troppo. The least he could do was to make himself useful.

So when the last man had finished with his pudding, Michael rose to his feet and collected the dirty enamel dishes, then made himself familiar with the lay of the land in the dayroom.

4   At least six times a day Sister Langtry crossed the compound between the nurses' quarters and ward X, the last
two of her trips being after nightfall. During the day
she enjoyed the opportunity to stretch her legs, but she
had never felt at ease in the dark; in childhood she had
actively feared it and refused to sleep in a room without
a night light, though of course she had long since culti-
vated sufficient self-control to be able to cope with such
an idiotic, groundless terror. Still, while she walked the
compound after dark she used the time to think about
some concrete idea, and lit her way with an electric
torch. Otherwise the shadows menaced too tangibly.

On the day of Michael Wilson's admission to X, she
had left the ward when the men sat down to dinner, to
walk back to the mess for her own dinner. Now, the
beam of her torch projecting a steady dot of light onto
the path in front of her, she was returning to X for what
she regarded as the most pleasant tenure of each day,
that slice of time between her own evening meal break
and lights out in the ward. Tonight she particularly
looked forward to it; a new patient always added interest, and sharpened her wits.

She was thinking about different kinds of pain. It
seemed very long ago that she had railed at Matron because of her posting to ward X, protested angrily to that
adamant lady that she had no experience with mental
patients and indeed felt antagonistic toward them. At
the time it had appeared as a punishment, a slap in the
face from the army as all the thanks she got for those
years in casualty clearing stations. That had been another life—tents, earthen floors, dust in the dry and
mud in the wet, trying to keep healthy and fit for nursing duty when the climate and the conditions ground
one down remorselessly. It had been a battering ram of

275

horror and pain, it had lasted for weeks on end and stretched across years. But the pain had been different then. Funny, you could weep your heart out over an armless man, a sticky mass of entrails spilling everywhere, a heart suddenly as cold and still as a piece of meat in an ice chest; yet they were physical *faits accomplis*. Over and done with. You patched up what you could, mourned what you could not, and proceeded to forget while you moved always onward.

Whereas the X pain was a suffering of the spirit and the mind, not understood, often derided or dismissed. She herself had regarded her posting to X as an insult to her nursing ability and her years of loyal service. She knew now why she had felt so insulted. Bodily pain, physical maiming in the course of duty, had a tendency to bring out the best in those who suffered it. It had been the heroism, the downright nobility, which had come close to breaking her during those years in casualty clearing stations. But there was nothing noble about a nervous breakdown; it was a flaw, evidence of a weakness in character.

In that frame of mind had she come to ward X, tight-lipped with resentment, almost wishing she could hate her patients. Only the completeness of her nursing ethic and the scrupulousness of her attention to duty had saved her from closing her mind against any change in her own attitude. A patient was a patient after all, a mind in need as much a reality as a body in need. Determined no one would be able to accuse her of dereliction, she got herself through the first few days on ward X.

But what turned Honour Langtry from a caring custodian into someone who cared far too much to limit her role to mere custodian was the realization that at Base Fifteen no one was interested in the men in ward X. There were never very many X-type patients in a hospital like Base Fifteen, which had started off its existence much too close to the actual fighting to gear itself toward tropponess. Most of the men who wound up in ward X were transferred there from one of the other wards, like Nugget, Matt and Benedict. Severe cases of psychic disturbance were mostly shipped straight back to Australia; those who came to ward X were less disturbed, more stealthy in their symptoms. The army had few psychiatrists, none of whom were attached to places like Base Fifteen, at least in Sister Langtry's experience.

Since there was little or no real nursing for her to do, she began to apply her considerable intelligence and that boundless energy which had made her such a good medical nurse to the problem of what she called the X pain. And told herself that to recognize what the men of X suffered as a genuine pain was the beginning of a whole new nursing experience.

The X pain was travail of the mind as distinct from the brain; amorphous and insidious, it was based in abstractions. But it was no less an entity, no less the ruin of an otherwise sound organism than any physical pain or handicap. It was futile, ominous, uneasy and empty; its malaise was enormous, its effect far longer-lasting than physical hurt. And less was known about it than almost all other branches of medicine.

She discovered in herself a passionate, partisan interest in the patients who passed through ward X, was fascinated by their endless variety, and discovered, too, a talent in herself for actively helping them through the worst of their pain. Of course she had failures; being a good nurse meant one accepted that, provided one knew one had tried everything one could think of. But unschooled and ignorant though she knew herself to be, she also knew that her presence in ward X had made a great deal of difference to the well-being of most of her patients.

She had learned that the expenditure of nervous energy could be more draining by far than the most gruelling of physical work; she had learned to pace herself differently, to cultivate huge reserves of patience. And understanding. Even after she got over her mild prejudices against those "character weaknesses," she had to cope with what seemed a total self-centeredness in her patients. To someone whose adult life to date had been devoted to a busy, happy and largely altruistic selflessness, it came hard to realize that the apparent self-orientation of her patients was only evidence of lack of self. Most of what she learned was through personal experience, for there was no one to teach her, and little to read. But Honour Langtry was truly a born nurse; she battled on, stimulated, absorbed, quite in love with this different kind of nursing.

Often for far longer than she hoped or expected, there was no tangible evidence that she had reached a patient. Often the breakthrough when it came made her wonder if anything she had done personally had actually contributed. Yet she *knew* she helped. Had she doubted that for one moment, she would have wangled herself a transfer months ago.

X is a trap, she thought, and I'm in it. What's more, I enjoy being in it.

When the beam of the torch slid onto the beginning of the ramp, she turned it off and walked up its wooden length as quietly as her booted feet would permit.

Her office was the first door on the left down the corridor, a six-by-six cubbyhole which two louvered exterior walls saved from a submarine-like horror. It barely held the small table she used as a desk, her chair on one side, a visitor's chair on the other, and a small L-shaped area of plank shelving plus two lockable wooden drawers which she referred to as her filing cabinet. In the top drawer resided the paper shells of all the men who had been inmates of ward X since its inception, not very many files altogether; she had kept carbon copies of the men who had been discharged from the ward. In the second drawer she kept the few drugs Matron and Colonel Chinstrap deemed necessary for her to have on hand—oral paraldehyde and paraldehyde for injection, phenobarb, morphine, mist APC, pot cit, milk of magnesia, mist creta et opii, castor oil, chloral hydrate, sterile water, placebos, and a large bottle of Chateau Tanunda three-star hospital brandy.

Sister Langtry took off her slouch hat, her gaiters and her army boots, and stacked them very neatly behind the door, then tucked the little wicker basket in which she carried her few personal requirements while on duty beneath her desk and put on her sandshoes. Since Base Fifteen was in an officially designated malarial zone, all personnel were obliged after dark to clothe themselves from wrists to neck to toes, which in a miserable heat made life just that bit more miserable. In actual fact, copious spraying with DDT for miles around had rendered the anopheles threat almost nonexistent, but the rule about after-dark apparel still held. Some of the more emancipated nurses wore their grey bush jackets and long trousers during the day as well as after nightfall, vowing that skirts had never been so comfortable. But those like Honour Langtry who had spent most of the war in casualty clearing stations where trousers were mandatory preferred amid the relative luxury of Base Fifteen to wear a more feminine uniform when they could.

Besides, Sister Langtry had a theory. That it did her patients good to see a woman in a dress rather than in a uniform akin to their own. She also had a theory about noise, removed her own boots when she entered the ward after dark, and forbade the men to wear boots indoors.

On the wall behind the visitor's chair a collection of pencil portraits was pinned, about fifteen in all: Neil's record of the men who had passed through ward X in his time, or were still residents of ward X. When she looked up from her work she stared straight at that most revealing pictorial record; as a man moved on elsewhere his sketch was removed from the central row and placed more peripherally on the wall. At the moment there were five faces in the central row, but there was more than enough room for a sixth. The trouble was she hadn't counted on a sixth face appearing, not with time for Base Fifteen rapidly dwindling, the war over, the sound of the guns stilled. Yet today Michael had arrived, a fresh subject for Neil's piercing eye. She wondered what Neil would see in Michael, found herself looking forward to the day when the result of that eye would be pinned up opposite her.

She sat down in her chair and put her chin on her hand, staring at the central row of drawings.

They're mine, she caught herself thinking complacently, and pulled herself sharply away from that most dangerous concept.

Self, she had discovered since being in X, was an unwelcome intruder, of no help to the patients. After all, she was, if not the arbiter of their final destinies, at least the fulcrum of their sojourns in X. In that lay considerable power, for the balance of X was a very delicate thing, and she was the one who stood at the point where it could tip either way, ready to shift her weight as needed. She tried always to respect her power by not using it and not dwelling upon it. But just occasionally, as now, awareness that she did possess it popped into consciousness and stared her a little too smugly in the eye. Dangerous! A good nurse should never develop a sense of mission, nor delude herself that she was the direct cause of her patients' recovery. Mental or physical, recovery came from within the patients.

Activity was what she needed. She got up, unearthed the tape which pinned her keys to the inside of her trouser pocket and pulled it through her hands until she came at the key for the top drawer, unlocked it and took out Michael's case history.

5   When Neil Parkinson came in on the echo of his knock she was getting herself settled back in her chair, the papers still unopened on the desk in front of her. He sat down in the visitor's chair and looked at her gravely. She, taking his look for granted, merely smiled and waited.

But the eyes she took for granted never gazed on her with the blinded ease of a friendly liking; they took her apart and put her back together again at each meeting, not in any lascivious sense, but as a delighted small boy might dissect the mystery of his most treasured toy. The novelty in discovering her had never left him, and he took fresh pleasure in it every evening when he came to her office to sit with her and chat in private.

Not that she was any raving beauty, or could substitite sensuality for beauty. She did have youth and the advantage of a particularly lovely skin, so clear the veins showed under it smokily, though atabrine yellow marred it now. Her features were regular, a little on the small side save for her eyes, which were the same soft brown as her hair, large and tranquil unless she was angry, when they snapped fiercely. She had a born nurse's figure, neat but sadly flat-chested, with very good legs, long, slender yet well-muscled, fine in the feet and ankles; all this the result of constant movement and much hard work. During daylight hours when she wore a dress, the white crisp folds of her nurse's veil formed a charming frame for her face; at night when trousered, she wore a slouch hat to and from duty, but went bareheaded within the ward. Her short, wavy hair she kept that way by trading off a part of her generous nurses' liquor allowance in return for a cut, shampoo and set from a QM corporal who had been a hairdresser in civilian life and did the nurses' hair upon request.

281

That was her surface. Underneath she was as tough as an-
nealed metal, intelligent, very well read in a posh girls' school
way, and shrewd. She had decision, she was crisp, and for all her
kindness and understanding she was clinically detached in some
core of her. She belonged to them, she had committed herself to
them, these patients of hers, yet whatever it was that lay at the
center of her being she always held back from them. Maddening,
but probably a part of the secret of her attraction for Neil.

It couldn't have been easy, finding the lightest and deftest
touch in dealing with soldiers to whom she was a restatement of
that almost forgotten race, women. Yet she had managed it beautifully, never given one of them the slightest indication of sexual
interest, romantic interest, call it what you would. Her title was
Sister, they called her Sis, and that was how she always presented herself—as a sister to them, someone who was extremely fond
while not willing to share all of her private self.

However, between Neil Parkinson and Honour Langtry there
existed an understanding. It had never been discussed nor indeed even so much as openly mentioned, but they both knew
that when the war was over and they were back on Civvy Street
he would pursue his relationship with her, and she would welcome that pursuit.

They were both from the very best homes, had been brought
up with an exquisite appreciation of the nuances duty scarcely
began to define, so that to each of them it was inconceivable that
personal matters should claim precedence over what was owed
to duty. At the time they met, the war had dictated a strictly
professional kind of relationship, to which they would adhere
strictly; but after the war circumspection could be abandoned.

To that prospect Neil clung, looking forward to it with something more painful than eagerness; what he dreamed of was virtually the rounding out of his life, for he loved her very much.
He was not as strong as she, or perhaps it was simply that his
passions were more involved than hers, for he found it difficult
to keep their relationship within the bounds she laid down. His
minor infringements were never more than glances or remarks;

the idea of touching her intimately or kissing her appalled him, for he knew were he to do so, she would send him packing on the spot, patient or no. The admission of women to wartime front conditions had been reluctant, and was largely limited to nurses; to Honour Langtry, the army had placed her in a position of trust which could not permit an emotionally draining intimate relationship with a man who was patient as well as soldier.

Yet he never doubted the existence of the unspoken understanding between them; had she not shared it, and acquiesced to it, she would have disabused him immediately, feeling it to be her duty to do so.

The only child of wealthy, socially prominent Melbourne parents, Neil Longland Parkinson had undergone the peculiar genesis of that time in that country, Australia: he had been molded into a young man more English than the English. His accent held no single trace of his Australian lineage, it was as pear-shaped and upper-crust as any accent that ever belonged to an English noble. He had gone straight from Geelong Grammar School to Oxford University in England, taken a double first in history, and since his Oxford days he had spent no more than months back in the land of his birth. It was his ambition to be a painter, so from Oxford he gravitated to Paris, and then to the Greek Peloponnese, where he settled to an interesting but undemanding life enlivened only by stormy visits from the Italian actress who functioned as his mistress but would have preferred to be his wife. Between these exhausting bouts of emotional stress he learned to speak Greek as fluently as he spoke English, French and Italian, painted frantically and thought of himself far more as an expatriate Englishman than as an Australian.

Marriage had not entered his plans, though he was aware that sooner or later it must; just as he was aware that he was postponing all decisions about the future course of his life. But to a young man not yet into his thirties there had seemed all the time in the world.

Then everything changed, suddenly, catastrophically. Even in the Greek Peloponnese murmurs of war had been sounding for some time when a letter had come from his father: a stiff, unsympathetic letter to the effect that his days of sowing wild oats were over, that he owed it to his family and his position to come home immediately, while he still could.

So he had sailed for Australia in the latter part of 1938, arriving back in a country he scarcely knew to greet parents who seemed as remote and devoid of love for him as Victorian gentry, which happened to be exactly what they were—not Queen Victoria, but the State of Victoria.

His return to Australia coincided with his thirtieth birthday, milestones which even now, over seven years later, he found hard to remember without a fresh upsurge of the awful terrors which had plagued him since last May. *His father!* That ruthless, charming, crafty, incredibly energetic old man! Why hadn't he sired a whole quiverful of sons? It didn't seem believable that he had produced only one, and late at that. Such a burden, to be Longland Parkinson's only son. To want to match, even to surpass, Longland Parkinson himself.

It was not possible, of course. Had the old man only realized it, he was himself the cause of Neil's failure to measure up. Deprived of the old man's working-class background with all its attendant bitterness and challenge, saddled with his mother's refined preciousness into the bargain, Neil knew himself defeated from the time when he became old enough to form opinions about his world.

He was into his teens before he realized that he cared for his father a great deal more than he cared for his mother. And that in spite of his father's indifference to him, his mother's cloyingly brainless protectiveness. It had been an enormous relief to go away to boarding school, and set a pattern which he was to follow from that first term at Geelong Grammar until the day of his thirtieth birthday. Why try to struggle with a situation that was manifestly impossible? Avoid it, ignore it. His mother's money had been settled on him at the time of his majority, and was more than enough for his needs. He would live his own life, then, far from Melbourne and parents, carve his own kind of niche.

But the imminence of war had destroyed all that. Some things could not be avoided or ignored, after all.

His birthday dinner had been a splendid affair, very formal, the guest list liberally sprinkled with ladylike young debutantes his mother considered eligible contenders for marriage to her son. There were two archbishops at the board, Church of England and Roman Catholic, one minister from the state legislature and one from the federal, a fashionable medical practitioner, the British High Commissioner and the French ambassador. Naturally his mother had been responsible for all the invitations. During the meal he scarcely noticed young ladies or important personages, indeed was hardly conscious of his mother. All his attention was focussed on his father, sitting at the far end of the table, wicked blue eyes forming irreverent conclusions about most of the guests. How he could divine so accurately what was going on in his father's head Neil didn't know, but it warmed him deliciously and made him long for an opportunity to talk with the little old man who had contributed nothing to his son's appearance save the color and shape of his eyes.

Later Neil had understood the magnitude of his own immaturity at that relatively late stage in his life, but when his father had linked an arm through his as the men finally rose to join the ladies in the drawing room, he was simply absurdly pleased at the gesture.

"They can do without us," said the old man, and snorted derisively. "It'll give your mother something to complain about if we disappear."

In the library full of leather-bound books he had never opened, let alone read, Longland Parkinson settled himself into a wing chair, while his son chose to subside onto an ottoman at his feet. The room was dimly lit, but nothing could disguise the signs of hard living in the old man's seamed face, nor diminish the laceration of a gaze that was fierce, stone hard, predatory. Behind the gaze one could see an intelligence which lived quite

285

independent of people, emotional weakness, moral shibboleths. It was then Neil translated what he felt for his father in terms of love, and wondered at his own contrariness; why choose to love someone who did not need to be loved?

"You haven't been much of a son," the old man said without rancor.

"I know."

"If I'd thought a letter would bring you home, I'd have sent it a long time ago."

Neil spread out his hands and looked at them; long, thin-fingered, smooth as a girl's, having the kind of childishness which only comes from never putting them to work that had soul-deep meaning and importance to the brain controlling them; for his painting had not meant that to him. "It wasn't your letter which brought me home," he said slowly.

"What was it, then? War?"

"No."

The wall sconce shining behind his father's head lit up its pink hairless dome, threw all the shadows forward onto his face, in which the eyes burned but the hard gash of a mouth remained resolutely closed.

"I'm no good," said Neil.

"No good at what?" Typical of his father, to interpret the statement dynamically rather than morally.

"I'm a rotten painter."

"How do you know?"

"I was told so, by someone who does know." The words began to come more easily. "I'd accumulated enough work for a major showing—somehow I always wanted to start with a bang, no single work hanging here, a couple there. Anyway, I wrote to a friend in Paris who owns the gallery I wanted for my debut, and since he rather fancied the idea of a holiday in Greece, he came down to see what I'd done. And he wasn't impressed, that's all. Very pretty, he said. Quite, quite charming, really. But no originality, no strength, no instinctive feeling for the medium. He then suggested I turn my talents to commercial art."

If the old man was moved by his son's pain he didn't show it, just sat there watching intently.

"The army," he said finally, "will do you the world of good."

"Make a man out of me, you mean."

"To do that, it would have to start on the outside and work in. I mean that what's on the inside has to have a chance to work its way out."

Neil shivered. "What if there's nothing there?"

And the old man had shrugged, smiled a small indifferent smile. "Then isn't it better to know that there's nothing there?" he asked.

Not one word had been said about his learning the family businesses; Neil had known any such discussion to be superfluous. In a way he felt his father wasn't worried about the businesses; what happened to them after his own hands relinquished control did not concern him. Longland Parkinson was as detached from generational empire building as he was from wife and son. He didn't demand that his son prove himself, felt no animosity toward a son who didn't measure up; it wasn't necessary for him to fuel his ego by demanding that his son be what he was himself, or achieve what he had achieved. No doubt when he married Neil's mother he had known what sort of progeny she was likely to throw, and not cared; in marrying her he was thumbing his nose at the very society he aspired to enter by marrying her. In this as in everything, Longland Parkinson acted to please himself, fulfill himself.

Yet as he sat watching his father, Neil had seen a fondness there, and a pity which had wounded to the heart. The old man simply didn't think Neil had it in him, and the old man was a very good judge of character.

So Neil had gone into the army, commissioned rank of course. On the outbreak of war he had been posted to an A.I.F. battalion and shipped out to North Africa, which he enjoyed immensely, feeling more at home there than he had in his native country, picking up Arabic with extreme ease and generally making himself useful. He became a very capable and conscientious soldier,

287

and turned out to have a streak of extraordinary braveness; his men liked him, his superiors liked him, and for the first time in his life he began to like himself. There *is* a bit of the old man in me after all, he told himself exultantly, looking forward to the end of the war, seeing himself returned home seasoned, honed by his experiences to a fine sharp ruthlessness which he felt his father would instantly recognize and admire. More than anything else in life, he wanted those bird-of-prey eyes to look on him as an equal.

Then came New Guinea, and after that the Islands, a kind of war far less to his taste than North Africa. It taught him that even while he had assumed his maturing process to be complete, he had really only been playing games. The jungle closed in on his soul the way the desert had freed it, drained him of exhilaration. But it strengthened him too, brought out a stubborn endurance he had not known he owned. He ceased finally to act a part, to care how he looked to others, too busy reaching into himself for the resources which would ensure survival for himself and his men.

In a fruitless, extremely bloody minor campaign early in 1945 it had all come to an end. He made a mistake, and his men paid for it. All the precious hoard of confidence crumbled immediately, disastrously. If they had only held it against him, only reviled him for it, he could have borne it better, he told himself; but everyone from the surviving men in his company to his superior officers *forgave* him! The more they told him it wasn't his fault, that no one was perfect, everyone made a blue sometimes, the more depressed he became. Having nothing to fight against, he faltered, broke down, and stopped.

In May of 1945 he was admitted to ward X. On his arrival he was weeping, so immersed in his despair that he neither knew nor cared where they put him. For several days he had been permitted to do as he pleased, and all he pleased to do was huddle inside himself, shake, weep, grieve. Then the person who had hovered greyly in the background began to intrude upon his misery, make an irritating nuisance of herself. She stuck herself onto him, bullied and even forced him to eat, refused to admit there was anything different or special about his plight, made him sit with the other patients when all he wanted to do was to shut himself inside his cubicle, gave him jobs to do, needled and poked him into talking, first about anything, then about himself, which he infinitely preferred.

Returning awareness stirred sluggishly at first, then seemed to leap. Things not directly concerning himself impinged upon him; he began to see his fellow patients, and to notice his surroundings. He started to be interested in the phenomenon of ward X, and in Sister Honour Langtry.

She had acquired a name and an identity within his mind. Not that he always liked her at first; she was too matter-of-fact and unimpressed by his uniqueness. But just as he had decided she was a typical army nurse, she began to thaw, to reveal a softness and a tenderness so alien to most of the experiences of the last few years that he would have drowned in it had she let him. She never, never did. Only when he deemed himself cured did he begin to understand how subtly she had chivvied him along.

He had not needed to be shipped to Australia for further treatment. But he wasn't shipped back to his unit, either. Apparently his CO preferred that he remain where he was; the division had been laid off active duty for the moment, so he wasn't needed.

In many ways his continued enforced rest in ward X delighted him, since it kept him near Sister Langtry, who these days treated him more as colleague than as patient, and with whom he was establishing the foundations of a relationship having nothing to do with ward X. But from the time when he considered himself cured and ready to resume duty, doubt had begun to gnaw at him. Why didn't they want him back? He found the answer for himself—because he couldn't be trusted any more, because if for some reason the war flared up again, he would not prove equal to command, more men would die.

Though everyone denied it, Neil knew that was the real reason why after almost five months he still remained a prisoner of ward X. What he couldn't yet understand was that his neurosis lingered on, showing itself chiefly as an extreme self-doubt. Had the war flared up again, he would probably have been returned on probation to duty, and would probably have done very well. Neil's tragedy was that the war really had ended, and there was no more active duty.

He leaned across to read the name on the papers lying on Sister Langtry's desk, and grimaced. "A bit of a slap in the eye, isn't it, getting him at this late date?"

"A shock, yes. A slap in the eye remains to be seen. Though he doesn't strike me as the troublesome type."

"There we agree. Very bland. He reminds me a bit of a cliché-ridden parrot."

Startled, she turned from the window to look at him; Neil wasn't usually so obtuse about men, nor so critical.

"I think he's quite a man," she said.

An unexpected and inexplicable irritation rushed up and out, surprising him as much as it did her. "Why, Sister Langtry!" he exclaimed. "Are you attracted, then? I wouldn't have said he was your type at all!"

Her frown became a laugh. "Not on me, Neil! It's unworthy of you, my dear friend. You sound exactly like Luce, and that isn't a compliment. Why be so hard on the poor chap?"

"I'm just jealous," he said flippantly, and drew his cigarette case out of his pocket. It was plain heavy gold, expensive-looking, and bore his initials in one corner. No one else in the ward smoked tailor-mades, but at the moment no one else in the ward was an officer.

He flipped the case open and offered its contents to her, lighter ready in his other hand.

She sighed, but took a cigarette and held it while he lit it. "I should never, never have let you talk me into sneaking a smoke with you while I'm on duty," she said. "Matron would hang, draw and quarter me. Besides, I'm going to have to throw you out in a tick. I've got to plough through Michael's papers before Colonel Chinstrap arrives."

290

"Oh, God! Don't tell me we've got to put up with him to-night!"

She looked amused. "Well, actually it's me has to do any putting up with, not you."

"And what brings our stalwart chief so far down the compound after dark?"

"Michael, of course. I rang and asked him to come, because I have no instructions about Michael. I don't know why he's here in Base Fifteen or why he's been slotted into X. Personally, I'm mystified." She sighed suddenly, and stretched minutely. "Somehow it hasn't been a very nice day today."

"As far as I'm concerned, no day in X is ever a very nice one," Neil said somberly, leaning to tap his cigarette into the spent shell case she used as an ashtray. "I've been moldering in X for nearly five months, Sis. Others seem to come and go, but here I sit like a lily on a dirt tin, a permanent fixture."

And there it was, the X pain, in him and in her. So galling to have to watch them suffer, to know she was incapable of removing the cause of their suffering, since it was rooted in their own inadequacies. She had learned painfully that the good she did them during the more acute stage of illness rarely extended to this long-drawn-out period of almost-recovery.

"You did have a bit of a breakdown, you know," she said gently, understanding how futile a comfort that must sound. And recognizing the beginning of an oft-repeated cycle of conversation, in which he would castigate himself for his weaknesses, and she would try, usually vainly, to point out that they were not necessarily weaknesses.

He snorted. "I got over my breakdown ages ago, and you know it." Extending his arms in front of him, he clenched his fists until the sinews knotted, the muscles shaped themselves into ridges, unaware that it was when she watched a small display of physical power like this that she felt a sharp jerk of attraction to him. Had he known it, he might have nerved himself to make a positive move toward cementing his relationship with her, kissed her, made love to her; but in almost all circumstances

291

Sister Langtry's face never betrayed her thoughts.

"I may not be any good as a soldier any more," he said, "but surely there's *something* useful I could be doing somewhere! Oh, Sis, I am so terribly, terribly tired of ward X! I am not a mental patient!"

The cry moved her; their cries always did, but this man's especially. She had to lower her head and blink. "It can't be too much longer. The war is over, we'll be going home soon. I know home's not the solution you want, and I understand why you rather dread it. But try to believe me when I say you'll find your feet in seconds once the scenery changes, once you've got lots to do."

"How can I go home? There are widows and orphans at home because of me! What if I meet the widow of one of those men? I killed those men! What could I possibly say to her? What could I do?"

"You'd say and do exactly the right thing. Come on, Neil! These are just phantoms you're exploiting to torment yourself because you haven't enough to do with your time in ward X. I hate to say stop pitying yourself, but that is what you're doing."

He wasn't disposed to listen, settling into his mood with a kind of inverted pleasure. "My incompetence was directly responsible for the deaths of over twenty of my men, Sister Langtry! There's nothing phantom about their widows and orphans, I assure you," he said stiffly.

It was many weeks since she had seen him so passionately down; Michael's advent, probably. She knew better than to interpret his behavior tonight as entirely related to herself; the arrival of a new man always upset the old hands. And Michael was a special case—he wasn't leadable, wasn't the sort who would knuckle under to Neil's brand of domination. For Neil did tend to dominate the ward, to dictate its patient policy.

"You have to lose this, Neil," she said curtly. "You're a fine, good man, and you were a fine, good officer. For five years no officer did a better job. Now listen to me! It isn't even established that your mistake was what actually caused the loss of life.

292

You're a soldier, you know how complicated any action is. And it's *done!* Your men are dead. Surely the least you owe them is to live with all your heart. What good are you doing those widows and orphans, sitting here in my office stewing, pitying not them but yourself? There's no written guarantee that life is always going to go the way we want it to. We just have to deal with it, bad as well as good. You know that! Enough's enough."

Mood visibly soaring, he grinned, reached out to take her hand, and leaned his cheek upon it. "All right, Sis, message received. I'll try to be a better boy. I don't know how you manage to do it, but I think it's more your face than what you say. You always manage to take away the pain. And if you only knew how much difference you've made to my sojourn in X. Without you—" He shrugged. "Oh, I can't imagine what X might have been like."

He said she always managed to take away the pain. But how, why? It wasn't enough to do good; her intelligence needed to know what the magic formula was, and it always eluded her.

Frowning, she sat staring across the little desk at his face, wondering whether it was prudent of her to give him the few small encouragements she had. Oh, to be able to divorce personal feelings entirely from duty! Was she in fact doing Neil more harm than good by becoming involved with him? For instance, how much of this performance had been a ploy to gain her attention? Feeling more for the man than for the patient destroyed true perspective; she would find herself running along lines of thought having more to do with the future than the present situation, when the present situation should have had her whole energy bent upon it. Admittedly there were delicious possibilities in a peacetime relationship with Neil, from experiencing his first kiss to making up her mind whether she would actually marry him, but it was wrong to dwell on that now, here. Wrong, wrong!

As a man she found him attractive, exciting, interesting. His world was much like her world, which had made their friendship logical. She liked the way he looked, his manners, his education, his family background. And she more than liked the kind of man he was—except for this perpetual, unfortunate obsession of his. When he persisted in hearkening back to that day of slaughter as if it would permanently color the rest of his life to mourning, she doubted the viability of a peacetime relationship very much. For she didn't want to spend her own emotional coin on an emotional cripple, no matter how understandable that crippling was. She wanted, *needed,* someone able to meet her as an equal, not someone who leaned on her while simultaneously he worshipped her as a goddess.

"That's what I'm here for, to take away the pain," she said lightly, and removed her hand in a way which could not hurt his feelings. Michael's papers still lay under her other hand; she picked them up. "Sorry to have to cut it short, Neil, but I do have work to do."

He got to his feet, looking down at her anxiously. "You will be down to see us later, won't you? This new admission business won't prevent that, will it?"

She glanced up, surprised. "Nothing can prevent that! Have you ever known me to miss my late cuppa in the ward?" she asked, smiling at him, then bent her head back to Michael's papers.

6 Colonel Wallace Donaldson picked his way down to the far end of the compound by the light of a torch, feeling hard done by. It really was disgraceful! In these peacetime days, with the blackout at an end, and yet the super couldn't even arrange for a little exterior lighting! In fact the bulk of the hospital lay in utter darkness, for it was uninhabited, and did not give off so much as a reflection from inside lights.

Over the last six months Base Fifteen military general hospital had shrunk pitifully in people, though not in area; like a fat man gone thin yet doomed still to go on wearing his fat man's clothes. The Americans had built it a little more than twelve months previously, but had moved on immediately, leaving it, partially unfinished and only partially furnished, to the Australians who were driving in a more westerly direction through the East Indies.

During its heyday it had managed to squeeze five hundred patients within its compound, and had kept thirty MOs plus one hundred and fifty nurses so busy that off duty was a distant dream. Now there were only half a dozen inhabited wards left. And ward X, of course, right down on the margin of the palm forest that had once yielded a small fortune in copra for its Dutch owner. Of those thirty MOs, only five general or specialist surgeons and five general or specialist physicians were left, along with a single pathologist. Barely thirty nurses flitted through the huge nurses' quarters.

As the neurologist, Colonel Donaldson had been assigned ward X when Base Fifteen passed into Australian hands; he always did inherit the handful of emotionally disturbed men who came bobbing to the top of the brew, there to be skimmed off, placed in a ward X.

Before the war Colonel Donaldson had been busy set-

295

ting himself up in a Macquarie Street practice, struggling to become one of the entrenched on that most prestigious but capricious of Sydney specialist medical scenes. A lucky share speculation in 1937 as the world tried to haul itself out of the Depression had given him the money to buy into a Macquarie Street address, and the big honorariums at the major hospitals were just beginning to come his way when Hitler invaded Poland. At which point everything changed; sometimes he caught himself wondering fearfully whether things could ever go back to what they were before 1939. From the vantage point of this hellhole called Base Fifteen, the last in a succession of hellholes, it didn't seem possible that anything could ever be the same again. Even he himself.

Socially his background was excellent, though during the Depression the family money reserves had dwindled alarmingly. Fortunately he had a stockbroker brother who was largely responsible for the family's recovery. Like Neil Parkinson, he spoke without a trace of an Australian accent; his school was Newington, his university Sydney, but all his postgraduate medical qualifications had been secured in England and Scotland, and he liked to think of himself as more English than Australian. Not that he was precisely *ashamed* of being Australian; more that it was better to be English.

If he had a pet hate, the woman he was on his way to see now was most certainly that pet hate. Sister Honour Langtry. A snippet, barely thirty years old if that, a professional nurse but not army trained, though he was aware she had been in the army since early 1940. The woman was an enigma; she spoke very well, was obviously very well educated and finished, and had trained as a nurse at P.A., a very good training hospital indeed. Yet she had no spit and polish, no exquisite deference, no awareness of her basically servant status. Could he have been so honest with himself, he would have admitted that she frightened him to death. He had to gird himself up mentally and spiritually to all his encounters with her, for what good it did him. She always ended in wringing his balls so brutally it would be hours before he felt himself again.

Even the fly-curtain made of beer bottle caps irritated him. Nowhere but ward X would have been permitted to keep it, but Matron, foul underbred besom though she was, trod always very carefully in X. During its early days a patient had grown tired of listening to Matron harangue Sister Langtry, and had dealt with her in a stunningly simple and effective way; he just reached out and ripped her uniform apart from collar to hem. Mad as a March hare, of course, and shipped off forthwith to Australia, but after that incident Matron made sure she did nothing to offend the men of ward X.

The light in the corridor revealed Colonel Wallace Donaldson to be tall, a dapper man of about fifty, with the high petechial complexion of a spirits-lover. He had a carefully tended iron-grey moustache of military proportions, though the rest of his face was perfectly shaven. His hair now that his cap was off displayed a deep groove in its oiled greyness where the edge of his cap had rested and cut into the scalp, for it was not thick hair, not springy hair. His eyes were pale blue and a little protuberant, but he still showed the lingering vestiges of a youthful handsomeness, and his figure was good, broad-shouldered, almost flat-bellied. In an impeccably tailored conservative suit he had been an imposing man; in an equally impeccably tailored uniform he looked more like a field marshal than any of the real ones did.

Sister Langtry came to receive him at once, ushered him into her office and saw him comfortably seated in the visitor's chair, though she did not sit down herself—one of her little tricks, he thought resentfully. It was the only way she could tower over him.

"I apologize for having to drag you all the way down here, sir, but this chap"—she lifted the papers she was holding slightly—"came in today, and not having heard from you, I presumed you were unaware of his arrival."

"Sit, Sister, *sit!*" he said to her in exactly the same tone he would have used to a disobedient dog.

She dipped down into her chair without demur or change of

expression, looking like a schoolboy cadet officer in her grey trousers and jacket. Round one to Sister Langtry; she had provoked him into being rude first.

She extended the papers to him silently.

"No, I don't want to look at his papers now!" he said testily. "Just tell me briefly what it's all about."

Sister Langtry gazed at him without resentment. After his first meeting with the colonel, Luce had given him a nickname—Colonel Chinstrap—and because it suited him so perfectly, it had stuck. She wondered if he knew that the entire human complement of Base Fifteen now called him Colonel Chinstrap behind his back, and decided he did not. He couldn't have ignored a derogatory nickname.

"Sergeant Michael Edward John Wilson," she said levelly, "whom I will call Michael from now on. Aged twenty-nine, in the army since the very beginning of the war, North Africa, Syria, New Guinea, the Islands. He's seen a great deal of action, but there's no evidence of mental instability due to seeing action. In fact, he's an excellent and a very brave soldier, and has been awarded the DCM. Three months ago his only close friend was killed in a rather nasty engagement with the enemy, after which he kept very much to himself."

Colonel Chinstrap heaved a huge, long-suffering sigh. "Oh, do get on with it, Sister!"

She continued without a tremor. "Michael is suspected of unsound mind following an unsavory incident in camp one week ago. A fight broke out between him and a noncommissioned officer, highly unusual behavior for both of them. Had others not been present to drag Michael away from the RSM, it appears the RSM would now be dead. Michael's only comment since the incident was that he wanted to kill the man, and would have killed him. He has repeated this often, though he won't enlarge upon it.

"When the CO tried to find out what was at the bottom of it, Michael refused to answer. However, the RSM was very vociferous. He accused Michael of making homosexual advances to him, and insisted there be a court-martial. It appears Michael's dead friend had definite homosexual leanings, but as to whether Michael himself was actively involved, opinion was strongly divided. The RSM and his followers maintained the two had been lovers, where the vast majority of men in the company maintained just as firmly that Michael's attitude toward his dead friend was that of protector and friend only.

"The battalion CO knew all three men very well, as they'd all been with the battalion a long time—Michael and the dead man since its inception, the RSM since New Guinea. And it was the CO's opinion that under no circumstances should Michael come to court-martial. He preferred to believe that Michael had suffered a temporary derangement, and ordered Michael to submit to a medical examination, the results of which indicated he was definitely of unsound mind, whatever that might mean." Her voice was noticeably sadder, sterner. "So they bunged him on a plane and sent him here. The admitting officer automatically slotted him into X."

Colonel Chinstrap pursed his lips together and watched Sister Langtry carefully. She was choosing sides again, a most regrettable habit of hers. "I'll see Sergeant Wilson in my clinic in the morning. You can walk him down there yourself, Sister." He glanced up at the meager wattage of the light bulb in a naked socket over the desk. "I'll look at his papers then. I don't know how you can read anything in this light—I certainly could not." The chair became too hard, too uncomfortable; he rolled his buttocks on it, hemmed a little, frowned fiercely. "I loathe cases with a sexual connotation!" he said suddenly.

Sister Langtry was idly holding a pencil, and her hands closed around it convulsively.

"My heart bleeds for you, sir," she said without any attempt to disguise the sarcasm. "Sergeant Wilson does not belong in X—in fact, he does not belong in any hospital ward of any kind." Her voice shook, she shoved an impatient hand into the front of her hair and slightly dislocated the set of its neat brown waves. "I think it's a pretty poor show when a fight and a highly suspect

299

accusation can break up a young man's life, already greyed because his friend had died. I keep thinking of how he must feel at this moment. As if, I'm sure, he's groping through some appalling fog he's never going to manage to find his way out of. I've talked to him, you haven't. And there is absolutely nothing wrong with him, mentally or sexually or any other way you care to think of. The medical officer responsible for his being sent here ought to be the one facing a court-martial! To deny Sergeant Wilson the opportunity to clear himself by whisking him off instead to a place like ward X is a disgrace to the army!"

As always, the colonel found himself unable to deal with this kind of adamant insolence, for normally men in hospital positions as high as his did not encounter it. Dammit, she talked to him as if she regarded herself as his educated and intellectual equal! Perhaps their officer status was what was wrong with these army nurses, that and the high degree of autonomy they enjoyed in places like Base Fifteen. And those stupid bloody veils nurses wore didn't help, either. Only nuns ought to wear veils, only nuns ought to be addressed as sister.

"Oh, come now, Sister!" he said, holding onto his temper and trying to be reasonable. "I do agree that the circumstances are somewhat unusual, but the war's over. The young man's stay here cannot possibly be any longer than a few weeks. And he could be in worse predicaments than ward X, you know."

The pencil flipped through the air, bounced onto the corner of the desk and fell with a hollow clatter just to one side of the colonel, who sat wondering whether her aim was good or bad. Strictly speaking, she ought to be reported to Matron; as head of nursing, Matron was the only officer permitted to discipline the nursing staff. But the trouble was that since the incident of the ravished uniform, Matron held Sister Langtry in considerable awe. Lord, what a fuss there would be if he complained!

"Ward X is a limbo!" cried Sister Langtry, more angry than he had ever seen her. His curiosity began to stir; Sergeant Michael Wilson's plight had certainly had an extraordinary effect on her. It might be interesting to see him in the morning after all.

She continued, fuelling her anger on her own words. "Ward X is a limbo! The patients no one knows what else to do with are just filed under X and forgotten! You're a neurologist. I'm a general-trained nurse. Not a whisker of experience or qualification between us. Do *you* know what to do with these men? I don't, sir! I grope! I try my best, but I'm miserably aware that it's nowhere near good enough. I come on duty every single morning praying—praying that I'll manage to get through the day without crushing one of these frail and difficult people. My men in ward X deserve better than you or I can give, sir."

"That is quite enough, Sister!" he said, a purplish tinge creeping under his skin.

"Oh, but I'm not finished yet," she said, unimpressed, unswerving. "Shall we leave Sergeant Wilson entirely out of it, for example? Let's look at the other five current inmates of ward X. Matt Sawyer was transferred here from neuro when they couldn't find an organic lesion to account for his blindness. Diagnosis hysteria. You cosigned that one yourself. Nugget Jones was transferred from abdominothoracic after two NAD laparotomies and a history of driving the entire ward mad with his complaining. Diagnosis hypochondria. Neil—Captain Parkinson, that is—had a simple breakdown which one might better call grief. But his CO thinks he's protecting him, so here Neil continues to sit, month after month. Diagnosis involutional melancholia. Benedict Maynard went quite mad after his company opened fire on a village in which it turned out there were no Japanese at all, just a lot of native women and children and old men. Because he sustained a mild scalp wound at the time his mental problems began, he was admitted to neuro as a concussion, and then transferred here. Diagnosis dementia praecox. I agree with that diagnosis, as a matter of fact. But it means Ben ought to be among the experts in Australia, receiving proper care and attention. And Luce Daggett, why exactly is he here? There's no diagnosis of any kind on his papers! But we both know why he's here. Because he was living the life of Riley, blackmailing his commanding officer into letting him do precisely whatever he wanted. But they couldn't make the charge stick, and they didn't know what else to do with him except to send him to a place like X until the shooting was all over."

The colonel stumbled to his feet, crimson with suppressed rage. "You are impertinent, Sister!"

"Do I sound impertinent? I beg your pardon, sir," she said, reverting to that unruffled calm which was usually her trademark.

His hand on the door, Colonel Chinstrap paused to look at her. "Ten in the morning in my clinic for Sergeant Wilson, and don't forget to bring him yourself." His eyes glittered, he searched for something hurtful to say, a mot capable of penetrating that impregnable facade. "I do find it peculiar that Sergeant Wilson, an apparently exemplary soldier, highly decorated, consistently in the front line for six years, has managed to rise no higher in rank than sergeant."

Sister Langtry smiled sweetly. "But, sir, we can't *all* be great white chiefs! Someone has to do the dirty work."

7   After the colonel had gone, Sister Langtry sat at her desk without moving, the slightly nauseating aftermath of her anger filming her brow and upper lip with a chill perspiration. Stupid, to rail at the man like that. It did no good, it simply revealed her inner feelings to him, when she preferred he remain ignorant of them. And where was the self-control which usually carried her victorious through her encounters with Colonel Chinstrap? A waste of time to talk to that man about ward X and its victims. She couldn't ever remember being quite so angry with him. That pathetic history had started it, of course. If he had arrived a little later, given her time to get her emotions under control, she would not have lost her temper. But he had arrived scant seconds after she put Michael's papers down.

Whoever the MO was who had written up Michael's case—and she didn't connect the signature with a face in memory—was no mean stylist. As she read his notes, the people involved had come alive. Especially Michael, alive for her already. That brief encounter in the ward had triggered lots of speculations, but none had rivalled the real story. How awful for the poor chap, and how unfair! How unhappy he must be. Without realizing what she was doing, as she read the history she wove her own emotions into the story it unfolded; she grieved so for Michael in the loss of his friend that she could hardly swallow for the lump in her throat, the pain in her chest. And then enter Colonel Chinstrap, who got the lot.

Ward X is getting to me, she thought; I've committed every sin in the nursing book these last few minutes, from unwarranted emotional involvement to gross insubordination.

But it was the memory of Michael's face. He could

303

cope, he was coping, even with the fact of his admission to ward X. Usually her griefs were for the inadequacies in her patients, yet here she was, quite overcome by the plight of a man who patently had no need of her support. There was a warning in that. One of her chief defenses against personal involvement with her patients was always to think of them as unwell, sad, frail, any condition which paled them as men. Not that she was frightened of men, or of personal involvement. Only that to give of her best, a good nurse had to remain detached. Not steeled against feeling emotion; steeled against an all-out woman-with-man relationship. It was bad enough when that happened in medical nursing, but with mentally disturbed patients it was disastrous. Neil had cost her much thought, and she still wasn't sure she had done the right thing in allowing herself to contemplate seeing him when they returned home. She had told herself it was all right because he was so very nearly well now, because the existence of ward X was finite now, and because she could still command enough control of the situation to be able to think of him as poor, sad, frail, when it became necessary.

I am only human, she thought. I have never forgotten that, never! And it is so hard.

She sighed, stretched, pushed her thoughts away from Neil, and away from Michael. It was too soon to appear in the ward; her respiration and her color hadn't returned to normal. The pencil—where had the pencil gone when she threw it at the colonel? How unbelievably dense that man could be! He didn't know how close he came to bombardment by the rear end of a six-pounder shell when he came out with that remark about Michael's lack of promotion. Where had the man been hiding for the last six years? Sister Langtry's knowledge of other armies was sketchy, but after six years of nursing Australians, she was well aware that her country at least produced quite a few very special men—men who had intelligence, the gift of command, and all the other qualities associated with army officers, but who steadfastly refused promotion above the rank of sergeant. It probably

304

had something to do with class consciousness, though by no means in a negative sense. As if they were content where they were, couldn't see any point in acquiring additional rank. And if Michael Wilson didn't belong to that special group of men, then her experience with soldiers had led to many more than this wrong conclusion.

Hadn't anyone ever told the colonel about men like Michael? Hadn't he managed to see it for himself? Very obviously not, unless he had simply seized at a straw in order to get under her skin. Colonel bloody Chinstrap. Those vowels of his were unbelievable, even more plummily rounded than Neil's. Stupid to be so angry with him. Pity him instead. Base Fifteen was a long way from Macquarie Street after all, and he was nowhere near his dotage. He wasn't bad-looking, and presumably under his pukka uniform he suffered from the same urgencies and importunities as other men. Rumor had it that he had been having an affair with Sister Heather Connolly from theatres for months. Well, most of the MOs had their little flutters, and who else was there to flutter with except the nurses? Good luck to him.

The pencil was under the far edge of the desk; she crawled under to retrieve it, put it where it belonged, and sat down again. What on earth would Heather Connolly talk to him about? Presumably they did talk. No one spent every moment with a lover in loving. As a peacetime practicing neurologist, Wallace Donaldson's great interest had been an obscure set of spinal diseases with utterly unpronounceable hyphenated names; perhaps they talked about these, and mourned the lack of obscure spinal diseases in a hospital where when spines were treated it was for the gross, final, ghastly indignities inflicted by a bullet or shrapnel. Perhaps they talked about his wife, keeping the home fires burning in Vaucluse or Bellevue Hill. Men did tend to talk about their wives to their mistresses, like discussing the merits of one friend with another while simultaneously mourning the lack of opportunity to make them known to each other. Men were always so positive their wives and mistresses would be great friends could the social rules permit it. Well, that stood to reason. To think otherwise might reflect badly on their judgment and choice of women.

Her man had done that, she remembered all too painfully. Talked to her incessantly about his wife, deplored the fact that the conventions did not permit their meeting, sure they would adore each other. After his first three descriptive sentences about his wife, Honour Langtry had known she would loathe the woman. But she had far too much good sense to say so, naturally.

What a long, long time ago that was! Time, which could not be measured in the ticking away of hours and minutes and seconds, but grew in fits and starts like a gargantuan insect shrugging itself free of successive shells, always emerging looking and feeling different into a different-looking and different-feeling world.

He had been a consulting specialist, too, at her first hospital in Sydney. Her only hospital in Sydney. A skin specialist—a very new breed of doctor. Tall, dark and handsome, in his middle thirties. Married, of course. If you didn't manage to catch a doctor while he still wore the full whites of a resident, you never caught one at all. And she had never appealed to the residents, who preferred something prettier, more vivacious, fluffier, more empty-headed. It was only in their middle thirties that they got bored with the choice of their twenties.

Honour Langtry had been a serious young woman, at the top of her nursing class. The sort there was always a bit of speculation about as to why she chose nursing instead of medicine, even if medicine was notoriously hard going for a woman. Her background was a wealthy farming one, and her education had been acquired at one of Sydney's very best girls' boarding schools. The truth was she chose to nurse because she wanted to nurse, not understanding entirely why before she began, but understanding enough to know it was physical and emotional closeness to people that she wanted, and that in nursing she would find this. Since nursing happened to be the most admirable and ladylike of all female occupations, her parents had been pleased and re-

306

lieved when she declined their offer to put her through medicine if she really wanted it.

Even as a new trainee nurse—probationers they were called—she didn't wear spectacles and she wasn't gawky or aggressive about her intelligence. Both at boarding school and at home she had pursued an active social life without any real attachment to any one young man, and during the four years of her nursing training she did much the same kind of thing—went to all the dances, was never a wallflower, met various young men for coffee in Repins or an evening at the pictures. But never with a view to serious involvement. Nursing fascinated her more.

After she graduated she was appointed to one of the female medical wards at P.A., and there she met her skin specialist, newly appointed to his honorarium. They hit it off together from the beginning, and he liked the quick way she came back at him; she realized that early on. It took her much longer to realize that she attracted him deeply as a woman. By the time she did, she was in love with him.

He borrowed the flat belonging to a bachelor lawyer friend of his in one of the tall buildings down toward the end of Elizabeth Street, and asked her to meet him there. And she had agreed knowing exactly what she was getting herself into. For he had gone to great pains to tell her, with a directness and frankness she thought wonderful. There was no possibility he would ever divorce his wife to marry her, he said, but he loved her, and he wanted an affair with her desperately.

Founded honestly, the affair foundered honestly about twelve months later. They met whenever he could manufacture an excuse, which sometimes wasn't easy; skin specialists didn't have important emergencies like general surgeons or obstetricians. As he had put it humorously, whoever heard of a skin specialist being pulled out of bed at three in the morning to minister to a critical case of acne? It was not easy for her to find the time either, for she was a mere junior sister, still in an apron, and not able to demand any preferential treatment in the rostering of time off. During the course of the affair they managed to meet as often as once a week, sometimes as little as once every three or four weeks.

It had rather tickled Honour Langtry to think of herself, not as a wife, but as a mistress. Wifehood was tame and safe. But to all mistresses clung an indefinable aura of glamour and mystery. The reality just didn't measure up, however. Their meetings were furtive and too short; it was disconcerting to discover that too much of them had to be given over to lovemaking rather than to a more intelligent form of communication. Not that she disliked the lovemaking, or deemed it an activity beneath her dignity. She learned from him quickly, was intelligent enough to modify and adapt her new knowledge so that she could continue to please him sexually, and thereby also please herself. But the little clues he offered her to the central core of himself could never be followed up satisfactorily, for there just wasn't sufficient time.

And then one day he got tired of her. He told her immediately, offering no excuses for his conduct. With quiet good manners she accepted her congé in the same spirit, put on her hat and gloves and walked out of his life. Someone who looked and felt different.

It had hurt; it had hurt very badly. And the worst hurt of all was in not really knowing why. Why it had begun for him, why he felt compelled to terminate it. In her more optimistic moments she told herself it ended because he was getting out of his depth, caring for her too deeply to be able to bear the transience of their relationship. In her more honest moments she knew that the real reason was a combination of inconvenience and the hideously trapped feeling of sameness the affair had begun to assume. In all likelihood the identical reason why he had originally embarked on the affair. And she knew there was one more reason: her own changing attitude toward him, the resentment she found it harder and harder to hide, that she meant very little more to him than someone different in his bed. To hold him enthralled forever she would have had to devote all her time and energy to him alone, as very possibly his wife did.

Well, that degree of feminine acrobatics just wasn't worth it. She had more to do with her life than devote it exclusively to pleasing a rather egotistical and selfish man. Though the great majority of women seemed to want to live that way, Honour Langtry knew it never would be her way. She didn't dislike men; she just felt it would be a mistake for her to marry one.

So she had continued to nurse, and found in it a pleasure and a satisfaction she had not genuinely found in love. In fact, she adored to nurse. She loved the fussing, the busyness, the constantly changing parade of faces, the really absorbing problems life on the ward threw at her constantly. Her good friends, and she had several, looked at each other and shook their heads. Poor Honour was badly bitten with the nursing bug, no doubt about it.

There would probably have been other love affairs, and perhaps one profound enough to cause her to change her mind about marriage. But the war intervened. Twenty-five years old, she was one of the first nurses to volunteer, and from that moment of entering army life there had been no time for thinking of herself. She had served in a succession of casualty clearing stations in North Africa, New Guinea and the Islands, which had effectively destroyed all vestiges of normality. Oh, what a life that had been! A treadmill so demanding, so fascinating, so alien that in many respects she knew nothing thereafter would ever measure up to it. They were a pretty exclusive band, the nurses on active service, and Honour Langtry belonged heart and soul to that band.

However, those years had taken their toll. Physically she had survived better than most, for she was both tough and sensible. Mentally she had also survived better than most, but when Base Fifteen appeared in her life she greeted it with a sigh of relief. They had wanted to send her back to Australia, but she had fought that successfully, feeling that her experience and her basically sound health would be of more service to her country in a place like Base Fifteen than back in Sydney or Melbourne.

When the pressure had begun to ease about six months ago,

she had time to think a little, to reassess her feelings about what she wanted to do with the remainder of her life. And began to wonder if indeed nursing back in some civilian hospital would ever satisfy her again. She also found herself thinking of a more personal, concentrated, intimate emotional life than nursing offered.

Had it not been for Luce Daggett, she might not have been in a state of readiness to respond to Neil Parkinson. When Luce was admitted, Neil was still in the worst throes of his breakdown; she thought of him in no other way than as a patient. Luce did something to her, she was still not quite sure what. But when he strolled into ward X looking so *complete*, so in command of himself and the situation in which he found himself, he took her breath away. For two days he fascinated her, attracted her, made her feel as she had not felt in years. Womanly, desirable, lovely. Being Luce, he destroyed her feeling himself, by tormenting a pathetic little private they had had at the time following a suicide attempt in camp. The discovery that he was lead rather than gold had almost caused her to resign from her nursing commission, which was a foolish overreaction, she told herself later. At the time it had seemed that big. Luckily Luce had never realized the effect he had on her; one of the few times in his life, no doubt, when he had failed to follow up an advantage. But ward X was new to him, all the faces were new, and he left his move to cement a relationship with Sister Langtry just one day too late. When he turned the full power of his charm upon her, she rebuffed him stingingly, and without caring about frailty.

However, that very minor aberration in her conduct marked the commencement of a change. It may have been awareness that the war was all but won, and this bizarre life she had led for so long was going to come to an end; it may have been that Luce performed the office of a Prince Charming, and wakened Honour Langtry from a self-imposed personal sleep. But ever since, she had been unconsciously moving herself and her thoughts away from utter dedication to her duty.

So when Neil Parkinson popped out of his depression and

310

manifested interest in her, and she saw how attractive a person he was, how attractive a man, that hitherto sturdy adherence to proper nursing detachment began to erode. She had begun in liking Neil enormously, and only now was starting to love him. He wasn't selfish, he wasn't egotistical, he admired and trusted her. And he loved her. To look forward to a life with him after the war was bliss, and the faster that life approached, the more eagerly she welcomed it.

With iron self-discipline she had never permitted herself to dwell upon Neil as a man, to look constantly at his mouth or his hands, to imagine kissing him, making love with him. She couldn't, or it would already have happened. And that would have been disastrous. Base Fifteen was no place to commence an affair one hoped would last a whole lifetime. She knew he felt the same way, or it would already have happened. And it was rather fun to walk an emotional tightrope above the rigidly suppressed wants, desires, appetites; to pretend she didn't see the passion in him at all. . . .

Startled, she saw that her watch said a quarter past nine. If she didn't get into the ward soon they would all be thinking she wasn't coming.

8   As Sister Langtry walked out of her office, down the short corridor and into the ward, she had no presentiment that the subtly poised balance of ward X was already beginning to wobble.

There was a quiet drone of conversation from behind the screens arranged opposite Michael's bed; she slipped between two of them and emerged at the refectory table. Neil was sitting on one bench at the end nearest to her chair, with Matt beside him. Benedict and Nugget sat on the opposite bench, but had left the section next to her chair vacant. She assumed her usual position at the head of the table unobtrusively, and looked at the four men.

"Where's Michael?" she asked, a tiny spurt of panic bubbling into her chest—fool, was her judgment already so distorted that she could have decided he lay in no mental peril? The war wasn't over yet, nor was ward X defunct. Normally she would never have left a new admission unobserved for so long during his first few hours in X. Was Michael going to mean bad luck? To leave his papers lying around while she talked to him—now she couldn't even guard the man himself.

She must have lost color; all four men were looking at her curiously, which meant her voice had betrayed her concern, too. Otherwise Matt could not have noticed.

"Mike's in the dayroom making tea," said Neil, producing his cigarette case and offering it to each of the other men. He would not, she knew, commit the indiscretion of offering her a cigarette outside the four walls of her office.

"It seems our latest recruit likes to make himself useful," he went on, lighting all the cigarettes from his lighter. "Cleared away the dirty plates after dinner, and helped the orderly wash them. Now he's making tea."

312

Her mouth felt dry, but she didn't dare add to the oddity of her reaction by trying to moisten it. "And where is Luce?" she asked.

Matt laughed silently. "He's on the prowl, just like a tomcat."

"I hope he stays out all night," said Benedict, lips twisting.

"I hope he doesn't, or he's in trouble," said Sister Langtry, and dared to swallow.

Michael brought the tea in a big old pot that had seen better days, rusting where the enamel had chipped off, and badly dented. He put it down in front of Sister Langtry, then returned to the dayroom to fetch a piece of board which functioned as a tray. On it were six chipped enamel mugs, a single bent teaspoon, an old powdered milk tin containing sugar, and a battered tin jug containing condensed milk in solution. Also on the board was a beautiful Aynsley china cup and saucer, hand-painted and gold-washed, with a chased silver spoon beside it.

It amused her to note that Michael sat himself down opposite Neil at her end of the table, as if it never occurred to him that perhaps the place was being saved for Luce. Good! It would do Luce good to discover he wasn't going to have an easy mark in the new patient. But then why should Michael be bluffed or intimidated by Luce? There was nothing the matter with Michael, he didn't have the apprehensions and distorted perceptions the men of X were usually suffering on admission. No doubt to him Luce was more ridiculous than terrifying. In which case, she thought, if I am as it seems using Michael as my standard of normality, I too am a little queer, for Luce bothers me. He's bothered me ever since I came out of that early daze to discover he's some sort of moral imbecile, a psychopath. I'm frightened of him because he fooled me; I almost fell in love with him. I welcomed what seemed his normality. As I'm welcoming what seems to be Michael's normality. Am I wrong, too, in my first judgment of Michael?

"I imagine the mugs are ours and the cup and saucer belong to you, Sister," said Michael, looking at her.

She smiled. "They do indeed belong to me. They were my birthday present."

313

"When's your birthday?" he asked immediately.

"November."

"Then you'll be at home to celebrate the next one. How old will you be?"

Neil stiffened dangerously, so did Matt; Nugget merely looked awed, Benedict disinterested. Sister Langtry looked more caught off guard than offended, but Neil got in first, before she could answer.

"It's none of your business how old she is!" he said.

Michael blinked. "Isn't that for her to say, mate? She doesn't look old enough to make it a state secret."

"*She* is the cat's mother," said Matt. "*This* is Sister Langtry." His voice trembled with anger.

"How old will you be in November, Sister Langtry?" Michael asked, not in a spirit of defiance, but as if he thought everyone was far too touchy, and he intended to demonstrate his independence.

"I'll be thirty-one," she said easily.

"And you're not married? Not widowed?"

"No. I'm an old maid."

He laughed, shaking his head emphatically. "No, you don't have the old-maidy look," he said.

The atmosphere was darkening; they were very angry at his presumption, and at her tolerance of it. "There's a tin of bikkies in my office," she said without haste. "Any volunteers to get it?"

Michael rose immediately. "If you tell me where it is, Sister, I'd be glad to."

"Look on the shelf below the books. It's a glucose tin, but it has a label on the lid marked Biscuits. How do you take your tea?"

"Black, two sugars, thank you."

While he was gone there was absolute silence at the table, Sister Langtry pouring the tea placidly, the men producing smoke from their cigarettes as if it were an organic offshoot of fury.

He came back bearing the tin, but instead of sitting down went around the table, offering the biscuits to each man. Four

314

seemed to be the number each man picked out, so when he came to Matt he took four from the tin himself and placed them gently beneath one of the loose unseeking hands folded quietly on the table. Then he moved the mug of tea close enough to them for Matt to be able to locate it by the warmth it gave off. After which he sat down again next to Sister Langtry, smiling at her with an unshadowed liking and confidence she found very touching and not at all a reminder of Luce.

The other men were still silent, watchful and withdrawn, but for once she didn't notice; she was too busy smiling back at Michael and thinking how nice he was, how refreshingly devoid of the usual rich assortment of self-inflicted horrors and insecurities. She couldn't imagine he would ever use her to further his own emotional ends the way the others did.

Nugget emitted a loud groan and clutched at his belly, pushing his tea away pettishly. "Oh, God, I'm crook again! Ohhhhhhhhh, Sis, it feels like me intussusception or me diverticulitis!"

"All the more for us," said Neil unsympathetically, grabbing Nugget's tea and emptying it into his own drained mug. Then he nipped Nugget's four biscuits away and dealt them out deftly, as if he handled playing cards.

"But, Sis, I do feel crook!" Nugget mewed piteously.

"If you didn't lie on a bed all day reading medical dictionaries you'd feel a lot better," said Benedict with dour disapproval. "It's unhealthy." He grimaced, gazed around the table as if something present at it offended him deeply. "The air in here is unhealthy," he said, then got to his feet and stalked out onto the verandah.

Nugget began to groan again, doubling up.

"Poor old Nugget!" said Sister Langtry soothingly. "Look, why don't you pop down to my office and wait there for me? I'll be with you as soon as I can. If you like, you can take your pulse and count your respirations while you wait, all right?"

He got up with alacrity, clutching his belly as if its contents were about to fall out, and beaming triumphantly at the others. "See? Sis knows! She knows I'm not having you all on! It's me

315

ulcerative colitis playing up again, I reckon." And he sped away down the ward.

"I hope it isn't serious, Sister," said Michael, concerned. "He does look sick."

"Huh!" said Neil.

"He's all right," said Sister Langtry, apparently unperturbed.

"It's only his soul that's sick," said Matt unexpectedly. "The poor little coot misses his mother. He's here because here is the only place that can put up with him, and we put up with him because of Sis. If they had any sense, they would have packed him off home to Mum two years ago. Instead, he gets backaches, headaches, gutsaches and heartaches. And rots like the rest of us."

"Rot is right," said Neil moodily.

There was a tempest blowing up; they were like the winds and the clouds at this same latitude, thought Sister Langtry, eyes travelling from one face to another. All set for fair weather one moment, swirling and seething the next. What had provoked it this time? A reference to rotting?

"Well, at least we've got Sister Langtry, so it can't be all bad," said Michael cheerfully.

Neil's laughter sounded more spontaneous; maybe the storm would abort. "Bravo!" he said. "A gallant soul has arrived in our midst at last! Over to you, Sis. Refute the compliment if you can."

"Why should I want to refute it? I don't get too many compliments."

That cut Neil, but he leaned back on the bench as if perfectly relaxed. "What a plumping lie!" he said gently. "You know very well we shower you with compliments. But for that plumper, you can tell us why you're rotting in X. You must have done something."

"Yes, as a matter of fact I have. I've committed the terrible sin of liking ward X. If I didn't, nothing compels me to stay, you know."

Matt got up abruptly, as if he found something at the table

316

suddenly unbearable, moved to its head as surely as if he could see, and rested his hand lightly on Sister Langtry's shoulder. "I'm tired, Sis, so I'll say good night. Isn't it funny? Tonight's one of those nights I almost believe that when I wake tomorrow, I'm going to be able to see again."

Michael half rose to help him through the barrier of the screens, but Neil put out a hand across the table to restrain him.

"He knows the way, lad. None better."

"More tea, Michael?" asked Sister Langtry.

He nodded, was about to say something when the screens jiggled afresh. Luce slid onto the bench beside Neil, in the place where Matt had been sitting.

"Beaut-oh! I'm in time for some tea."

"Speak of the devil," sighed Neil.

"In person," Luce agreed. He put his hands behind his head and leaned back a little, looking at the three of them through half-shut eyes. "Well, what a cozy little group this is! I see we've lost the riffraff, only the big guns are left. It's not ten o'clock yet, Sis, so there's no need to look at your watch. Are you sorry I'm not back late?"

"Not at all," said Sister Langtry calmly. "I knew you'd be back. I've never yet known you to stay out one minute past ten without a pass, or commit any other breach of regulations, for that matter."

"Well, don't sound so sad about it! It makes me think nothing would give you greater pleasure than to be able to report me to Colonel Chinstrap."

"It wouldn't give me any pleasure at all, Luce. *That* is your whole trouble, my friend. You work so darned hard at making people believe the worst of you that you literally force them to believe the worst, just to have a little peace and quiet."

Luce sighed, leaned forward to put his elbows on the table and prop his chin on his hands. Thick and waving and a little too long to meet the strict definition of short-back-and-sides, his reddish-gold hair fell forward across his brow. How absolutely perfect he is, thought Sister Langtry with a shiver of real repulsion.

Perhaps he's too perfect, or the coloring is impossible to absorb. She suspected he darkened his brows and lashes, maybe plucked the one and encouraged the growth of the other, but not because of sexual inversion; purely out of overweening vanity. His eyes had a golden sheen, were very large and set well apart below the arch of those too-dark-to-be-true brows. Nose like a blade, straight, thin, flaring proudly at the nostrils. The kind of cheekbones which looked like high, purely structural supports, the flesh beneath them hollowed. Though it was far too determined to be called generous, his mouth was not thin, and had the exquisitely defined edges one usually saw only on statues.

Little wonder that he knocked me sideways when I first saw him. . . . Yet I'm no longer attracted by that face, or the height of the man, or his splendid body. Not the way I am to Neil—or to Michael, come to think of it. There's something wrong with Luce, inside; not a weakness, nor merely a flaw, but something that is *all* of him, innate and therefore ineradicable.

She turned her head slightly to look at Neil, who in any company save Luce's would pass for a handsome man. Much the same sort of features as Luce's, though far less spectacular coloring. Most handsome men looked better with the sort of lines graven into the flesh of the face Neil had; yet when those lines appeared on Luce he would change from beauty to beast. They would be the wrong lines, perhaps. Would indicate dissipation rather than experience, petulance rather than suffering. And Luce would run to fat, which Neil never would. She particularly liked Neil's eyes, a vivid blue and fringed with fairish lashes. He had the sort of brows a woman might like to stroke with one fingertip, over and over and over again, just for the sheer pleasure of it. . . .

Now Michael was quite different. He might pass for the very best kind of ancient Roman. Character rather than beauty, strength rather than self-indulgence. Caesarish. There was a contained singularity about him which said, I've been looking after others as well as myself for a long time now, I've been through heaven and hell, but I'm still a whole man, I still own myself.

Yes, she decided; Michael was enormously attractive.

Luce was watching her. She felt it, and brought her eyes back to him, making their expression cool and aloof. She defeated him, and she knew it. Luce had never been able to discover why his charm hadn't worked on her, and she was not about to enlighten him, either about his initial impact on her, or the reasons why it had been shattered.

Tonight for a change his guard was down a bit; not that he was vulnerable, exactly, more that perhaps he would have liked to be vulnerable.

"I met a girl from home tonight," Luce announced, his chin still propped on his hands. "All the way from Woop-Woop to Base Fifteen, no less! She remembers me, too. Just as well. I didn't remember her at all. She'd changed too much." His hands fell; he assumed a high and breathlessly girlish voice, conjuring for them an image so strong Sister Langtry felt physically thrust into the middle of that encounter. "My mother did her mother's washing, she said, and I used to have to carry the basket, she said. Her father was the bank manager, she said." His voice changed, dropped to become Luce at his most superior, most sophisticated. "That must have won him a lot of friends with the Depression on, I said. Foreclosing right, left and center, I said. Just as well my mother didn't have anything worth foreclosing on, I said. You're cruel, she said, and looked as if she was going to cry. Not at all, I said, just being truthful. Don't hold it against me, she said, big black eyes all wet with tears. How could I ever hold anything against anyone as pretty as you, I said." He grinned, quick and wicked as a razor slash. "Though that wasn't being at all truthful. I've got one thing I'd *love* to hold against her!"

Sister Langtry had adopted his earlier pose, elbows on table, chin on hands, watching fascinated as he mimicked and postured his way through the story.

"So much bitterness, Luce," she said gently. "It must have hurt a great deal to have to carry the bank manager's laundry."

Luce shrugged, tried unsuccessfully to assume his normal

319

devil-may-care insouciance. "Yah! Everything hurts, doesn't it?" His eyes widened, glittered. "Though in actual fact carrying the bank manager's laundry—and the doctor's, and the headmaster's, and the Church of England minister's, and the dentist's—didn't hurt half so much as having no shoes to wear to school. *She* used to be in the same school; I remembered her when she said who she was, and I even remember the kind of shoes she used to wear. Little black patent-leather Shirley Temples with straps and black silk bows. My sisters were much prettier than any of the other girls, and prettier than her, too, but they had no shoes of any kind."

"Didn't it occur to you that those with shoes probably envied you your freedom?" asked Sister Langtry tenderly, trying to find something to say which would help him see his childhood in better perspective. "I know I always did, when I went to the local public school before I was old enough to be sent away to boarding school. I had shoes a bit like the bank manager's daughter. And every day I'd have to watch some wonderfully carefree little urchin dance his way across a paddock full of bindy-eye burrs without so much as a wince. Oh, I used to long to throw my shoes away!"

"Bindy-eyes!" exclaimed Luce, smiling. "Funny, I'd forgotten all about them! In Woop-Woop the bindy-eyes had spines half an inch long. I could pull them out of my feet without feeling a thing." He sat up straighter, glaring at her fiercely. "But in the winter, dear well-educated and well-fed and well-clothed Sister Langtry, the backs of my heels and all around the edges of my feet and up my shins used to *crack!*"—the word came out like a rifle shot—"and bleeeeeed"—the word oozed out of him—"with the cold. Cold, Sister Langtry! Have you ever been cold?"

"Yes," she said, mortified, but a little angry too at being so rebuffed. "In the desert I was cold. I was hungry and I thirsted. In the jungle I've been hot. And sick, too sick to keep down food or drink. But I did my duty. I am not an ornament! Nor am I insensitive to your plight when you were a child. If my words were wrong, I apologize. But the spirit in which they were intended was *right!*"

320

"You're pitying me, and I don't want your pity!" cried Luce painfully, hating her.

"You haven't got it. I don't pity you. Why on earth should I? Whatever you came from doesn't matter. It's where you're going that does."

But he abandoned the mood of wistfulness and self-revelation, turned bright, metallic, chatty. "Well, anyway, before the army grabbed me I was wearing the best shoes money could buy. That was after I went off to Sydney and became an actor. Laurence Olivier, stand aside!"

"What was your stage name, Luce?"

"Lucius Sherringham." He rolled it out impressively. "Until I realized it was too long for the marquees, that is. Then I changed it to Lucius Ingham. Lucius is a good name for the stage, not bad for radio, either. But when I get to Hollywood I'll change the Lucius to something more swashbuckling. Rhett or Tony. Or if my image turns out more Colman than Flynn, plain John would sound good."

"Why not Luce? That has a swashbuckling air to it."

"It doesn't fit with Ingham," he said positively. "If I stay Luce, the Ingham has to go. But it's an idea. Luce, eh? Luce Diablo would thrill the girls, wouldn't it?"

"Daggett wouldn't do?"

"*Daggett!* What a name! It sounds like a sheep's bum." His face twisted as if at some half-remembered pain the years since had dulled. "Oh, Sis, but I was so good! Too young, though. I didn't have enough time to make a big enough dent before King and Country called me up. And when I get back, I'll be too old. . . . Some smarmy little bastard with high blood pressure or a rich father to buy him a discharge will be out there in *my* lights. It just isn't fair!"

"If you were good, it can't make any difference," she said. "You'll get there. Someone will see how good you are. Why didn't you try for one of the entertainment units after they were formed?"

He looked revolted. "I'm a serious actor, not an old music-hall comedian! The men in charge of recruiting for those units were

321

old vaudeville types themselves; they only wanted jugglers and tappers. Young men need not apply."

"Never mind, Luce, you will get there. I know you will. Anything anyone wants as badly as you want to be a famous actor has to happen."

Sister Langtry became aware that someone in the far distance was groaning; she came reluctantly out of the insidious spell Luce had woven, almost loving him.

Nugget was making a terrific racket somewhere up near her office, and probably waking up Matt.

"Sis, I feel so crook!" came the wail of his voice.

She got to her feet, looking down at Luce with genuine regret. "I'm terribly sorry, Luce, I really am, but if I don't go, you'll all pay for it later tonight."

She was already halfway down the ward when Luce said, "It's not important. After all, *I* don't feel crook!"

His face was twisted again, bitter and frustrated, the glorious little moment of approbation and limelight snatched away by a child's peevish howl for Mummy. And Mummy, as all mummies must, had gone immediately to minister where ministry was really needed. Luce looked down at his mug of tea, which had cooled off enough to smear a thick ugly scum of congealing milk across its surface. Disgusted, he lifted the mug in his hand, and very slowly and deliberately he turned it upside down on the table.

The tea went everywhere. Neil leaped to his feet away from the main stream of it, dabbing at his trousers. Michael moved just as quickly the other way. Luce remained where he was sitting, indifferent to the fate of his clothes, watching the slimy liquid course over the edge of the board and drip steadily onto the floor.

"Clean it up, you ignorant bastard!" said Neil through his teeth.

Luce looked up, laughed. "Make me!" he said, biting off each of the two words and giving them an intolerable edge of insult.

Neil was shaking. He drew himself up stiffly and curled his

lip, face white. "If I were not your superior in rank, Sergeant, it would give me the greatest of pleasure to make you—and to rub your nose in it." He turned on his heel and found the opening between the screens as if more by chance than design, not floundering, but blinded.

"Sez you!" Luce called after him, shrill and mocking. "Go on, *Captain*, run away and hide behind your pips! You don't have the guts!"

The muscles in Luce's hands unlocked, went limp. Slowly he turned his face back to the table and discovered Michael busy with a rag, mopping up the mess. Luce stared in pure amazement.

"You stupid drongo!" he said.

Michael didn't reply. He picked up the dripping rag and the empty mug, piled them among the other things on the makeshift tray, lifted it easily and carried it away toward the dayroom. Alone at the table, Luce sat with the light and the fire in him dying, willing himself fiercely and successfully not to weep.

9 Of her own choice entirely, Sister Langtry worked a split shift. When ward X was founded shortly after Base Fifteen, about a year earlier, there were two sisters on Matron's roster to care for its patients. A frail and antipathetic woman, the second sister was not the right temperament to cope with the kind of patients ward X contained. She lasted a month, and was replaced by a big, bouncingly brisk sister whose mentality was still in the jolly-hockey-stick schoolgirl stage. She lasted a week, and demanded a transfer not because of anything done to her personally, but after watching Sister Langtry deal with a terrifying episode of patient violence. The third sister was hot-tempered and unforgiving. She lasted a week and a half, and was removed at Sister Langtry's heated request. Full of apologies, Matron promised to send someone else as soon as she could find someone suitable. But she never did send anyone, whether because she couldn't or just forgot, Sister Langtry had no way of knowing.

It suited Sister Langtry beautifully to work ward X on her own, in spite of the toll it took in strength and sleep, so she had never agitated for a second sister. After all, what could one do with days off in a place like Base Fifteen? There was absolutely nowhere to go. Since she was not the partying or the sunbathing type, the only two diversions Base Fifteen had to offer were less enticing to Sister Langtry than the company of her men. So she worked alone, tranquilly convinced after three samples that it was better for the well-being of her men to have to cope with one female only, one set of orders and one routine rather than two. Her duty seemed clear: she wasn't a part of the war effort to serve her own interests, or to pamper herself unduly; as the servant of her country with her country in peril, she had to give of her very best, do her job as well as it could possibly be done.

It never occurred to her that in electing to run ward X on her own she cemented her power; not the shadow of a doubt ever crossed her mind that she might be perpetrating a wrong upon her patients. Just as her own very comfortable upbringing made it impossible for her to understand with heart as well as mind what poverty could do to a man like Luce Daggett, so a lack of experience prevented her from seeing all the ramifications of ward X, her tenure in it, and her true relationship with her patients. Conscious that she was freeing up a trained nurse for service in some other area than ward X, Sister Langtry merely carried on. When she was ordered away on a month's leave, she handed the ward over to her substitute without too much heartache; but when she returned to find mostly new faces, she simply picked up where she had left off.

Her normal day began at dawn, or shortly before it; at this latitude the length of the days varied little between winter and summer, which was nice. By sunup she was in the ward, well ahead of the kitchen orderly who would attend to breakfast. When a kitchen orderly turned up at all, that is. If none of her men were up, she made them a pot of early morning tea accompanied by a plate of bread and butter, and roused them. She partook of this early morning tea herself, then attended to the sluice room and the dayroom while the men went off to the bathhouse to shower and shave. Should an orderly still not have turned up, she also prepared the breakfast. About eight o'clock she ate breakfast with her men, after which she set them firmly on the road of the day: made beds with them, supervised one of the taller ones like Neil or Luce in the task of producing that complicated Jacques Fath drape to the mosquito nets. Matron had invented the style of daytime disposal of the nets herself, and it was a well-known fact that provided when she arrived to inspect a ward she found its nets properly arranged, she noticed little else.

In a ward full of ambulant men, housekeeping presented no

problem, and did not require the services of an orderly. They managed cleanliness for themselves, under Sister Langtry's trained and meticulous eye. Let the orderlies go where they were most needed, they were a nuisance anyway.

The minor irritations of ward X's afterthought construction had long since been ironed out satisfactorily. Neil, an officer, had been given as his private quarters the old treatment room, a cubicle six feet wide and eight feet long, adjoining Sister Langtry's tiny office. No one in X needed medical treatment, and there was no psychiatrist to administer a more metaphysical kind of treatment. So the treatment room had always been available to house the rare officer patients. When Sister Langtry needed to attend to minor but ever-present ailments like tinea, boils, skin ulcers and dermatitis, she used her office. Malarial recurrences and the gamut of tropical enteric fevers were treated from the patient's bed, though occasionally if the illness was severe enough, the patient would be transferred to a ward more geared to physical illness.

There was no indoor toilet for the men, or for the staff. In the interests of hygiene, Base Fifteen's ambulant patients and all its staff used deep-trench latrines built at intervals through the compound; these were disinfected once a day and periodically fired with petrol or kerosene to prevent bacterial proliferation. Ambulant patients performed their ablutions in concrete structures called bathhouses; the bathhouse for ward X lay behind it and about two hundred feet away, and had once been patronized by six other wards as well. The other wards had been closed for six months now, so the bathhouse belonged solely to the men of X, as did the nearby latrine. The sluice room inside ward X, which held urine bottles, bedpans and bowls, covers for same, a meager supply of linen and a disinfectant-reeking can for bodily wastes, was rarely if ever needed. Water for the ward was stored in a corrugated iron tank on a stand which raised it to roof level and permitted a gravity feed of water to dayroom, sluice room and treatment room.

After the ward was straight, Sister Langtry retired to her office to deal with the paper work, everything from forms, requisitions

326

and laundry lists to daily entries in the case histories. If it was X's morning for visiting the stores hut, an iron structure under lock and key and ruled from the quartermaster's office, she and one of her men walked across to fetch back whatever they managed to get. She had found Nugget to be her best escort to stores; he always looked so insignificant and shrunken, yet when they got back to X he would blithely produce from around his scraggy person everything from bars of chocolate to tinned puddings or cakes, saline powder, talcum powder, tobacco and cigarette papers and matches.

Visits from the brass—Matron, Colonel Chinstrap and the red-hat colonel who was the superintendent, and others—always occurred during the later part of the morning. But if it was a quiet morning undisturbed by brass, as most were, she would sit on the verandah with her men and talk, or perhaps even just be silent in their company.

After the men's lunch arrived somewhere around half-past twelve, depending upon the kitchen, she left the ward and headed for her own mess to eat her own lunch. The afternoon she spent quietly, usually in her room; she might read a book, darn a pile of her men's socks, shirts and underwear, or sometimes if it was cool and dry enough she might nap on her bed. Around four she would head for the sisters' sitting room to drink a cup of tea and chat for an hour with whoever might appear; this represented her only truly social contact with her fellow nurses, for meals in the mess were always snatched, hurried affairs.

At five she went back to ward X to supervise her men's dinner, then returned to the sisters' mess for her own dinner about six-fifteen. By seven she was on her way back to X for the segment of the day she enjoyed the most. A visit and a smoke with Neil in her office, visits and talks with the other men if they felt the need or she felt they needed it. After which she made the last and most major entry of the day in the case histories. And a little after nine someone made a final cup of tea, which she drank with her patients at the refectory table behind its screens inside the ward. By ten her patients were readying themselves for bed,

327

and by half past she would have left the ward for the night.

Of course, these days things were quiet, it was an easy life for her. During ward X's heyday she had spent far more time in the ward, and would dole out sedation before she left. If she had a patient prone to violence, an orderly or a relief sister would have remained on duty all night, but those so ill did not stay long unless a definite improvement was noted. By and large ward X was a team effort, with the patients a most valuable part of the team; she had never known the ward not to contain at least one patient who could be relied upon to hold a watching brief in her absence, and she had found such patients more of a help than additional staff would have been.

This ward team effort she deemed vital, for the chief worry she had about the men of X was the emptiness of their days. Once through the acute phase of his illness, a man faced weeks of inertia before discharge was possible. There was nothing to do! Men like Neil Parkinson fared better because they possessed a talent which was easy to cater to, but painters were rare. Unfortunately Sister Langtry herself had no gift for handicraft teaching, even had it been possible to obtain the materials. Occasionally a man evinced a desire to whittle, or to knit, or to sew, and this she did what she could to encourage. But whichever way one looked at it, ward X was a dull place to be. So the more the men could be persuaded to participate in the everyday routine of the ward, the better.

On that night of Michael's arrival in X, as on every other night, Sister Langtry came out of her office at a quarter past ten, a torch in her right hand. The lights in the ward were all extinguished save for one still burning at the far end above the refectory table. That she put out herself by flicking a switch at the junction of the short corridor and the main ward. At the same time she switched on her torch and directed its beam toward the floor.

Everything was quiet, except for a slight susurration of breathing around her in the semidarkness. Curiously, none of this pre-

328

sent group of men snored; she sometimes wondered if this was one of the chief reasons why they had managed to put up with each other in spite of the rawnesses and the oddities. At least in sleep they did not encroach upon each other's privacy, could get away from each other. Did Michael snore? For his sake, she hoped not. If he did, they would probably end in disliking him.

The ward was never fully dark since the lifting of the black-out. The light in the corridor behind her remained on all night, as did a light at the top of the steps which led eventually to the bathhouse and the latrine; its wan rays penetrated through the windows in the wall alongside Michael's bed, for the door to the steps stood just beyond the foot of the bed.

All the mosquito nets were pulled down, draped in easy curves across and over each bed like ambitious catafalques. Indeed, there was something tomblike about the effect, a series of unknown warriors sleeping that longest and most perfect of sleeps lapped in dark clouds like smoke from funeral pyres.

Automatically after so many years as a nurse, Sister Langtry changed her hold on the torch; her hand slid across its front to mask the brightness, reduce it to a ruby glow and small white sparkles between the black bars of her embracing fingers.

She walked first to Nugget's bed and directed the dimmed light through the mosquito netting. Such a baby! Asleep of course, though in the morning he would inform her he had not so much as closed his eyes. His pajamas were neatly buttoned up to his neck in spite of the heat, the sheet drawn tidily up under his arms. If he wasn't constipated he had diarrhoea; if his head let him alone, his back played up; if his dermo wasn't flared to weeping bloody patches like raw meat, his boils had risen like beehives on his backside. Never happy unless tortured by some pain, real or imagined. His constant companion was a battered, dog-eared nursing dictionary he had filched from somewhere before arriving in X, and he knew it by heart, understood it too. Tonight she had dealt with him as she always did, kindly, full of commiseration, willing to engage in an interested discussion of whatever set of symptoms was currently uppermost, willing to purgate, analgize, anoint, follow obediently down the path of treatment he selected for himself. If he ever did suspect that most of the pills, mixtures and injections she fed him were placebotic, he never said so. Such a baby!

Matt's bed was next. He too was asleep. The gentle reddened glow from the torch probed at his lowered eyelids, softly illuminated the spare dignity of his man's features. He saddened her, for there was nothing she could do for him or with him. The shutter between his brain and his eyes remained fast closed and permitted no communication between. She had tried to persuade him to badger Colonel Chinstrap into weekly neurological examinations, but Matt refused; if it was real, he said, it would kill him anyway, and if as they thought it was imagined, why bother? A picture sat on top of his locker, of a woman in her early thirties, hair carefully rolled over wadding in best Hollywood style, a neat little white Peter Pan collar over the dark stuff of her dress. Three small girls wearing the same white Peter Pan collars were arranged around her like ornaments, and on her lap sat a fourth child, also a girl, half infant, half toddler. How strange, that he who could not or would not see was the only one who kept and treasured a picture of his loved ones. Though during her service in X she had noticed that a lack either of loved ones or of pictures of loved ones was commoner in X than in other kinds of ward.

Benedict asleep was not like Benedict awake. Awake he was still, quiet, contained, withdrawn. Asleep he thrashed and rolled and whimpered without true rest. Of all of them, he worried her the most: that eating away inside she could not seem to arrest or control. She couldn't reach him, not because he was hostile, for he never was, but because he didn't seem to listen, or if he listened, he didn't seem to understand. That his sexual instincts were a great torment to him she had suspected strongly enough to tax him with it one day. When she had asked him if he had ever had a girl friend, he had said a curt no. Why not? she had inquired, explaining she didn't mean a girl to sleep with, only someone to know and to be friends with, perhaps think of marrying. Benedict had simply looked at her, his face screwed up into an expression of complete revulsion. "Girls are dirty," he said, and would not say more. Yes, he worried her, for that and many other reasons.

Before she went to check on Michael she attended to the screens around the refectory table, for they came a little too close to the end of Michael's bed if he should need to get up during the night. Pleating them up into the economy of a closed fan, she pushed them away against the wall. It had been some time since anyone slept in that bed; it was not popular because of the light shining in the windows alongside it.

But she was pleased to see that Michael slept without a pajama jacket. So sensible in this climate! She worried far more for the welfare of those like Matt and Nugget who persisted in wearing confining nightclothes. Nothing she had managed to find to say could persuade Matt or Nugget to give up properly buttoned pajama jackets. She wondered if that was because both men lay enthralled by women who represented the decencies and modesties of the civilized world, a world far from ward X: wife, mother.

Michael was turned away from the ward, apparently not disturbed by the light shining on his face. That was good; he mustn't mind the bed, then. Unless she walked around to the other side his features were hidden from her, but she was loath to look upon his sleeping face, so stayed where she was. The soft light played upon the skin of back and shoulder, caught a glitter of silver from the chain on which he wore his meat-tickets, two dull-colored pieces of some pressed board material which sprawled one below, the other across the pillow behind him. That was how they would identify him if they found enough of him still intact enough to wear meat-tickets; they would chop off the lower one to send home with his effects, bury him with the other still around his neck. . . . That can't happen now, she told herself. The war's over. That can't possibly happen.

He had looked at her as if he found it difficult to take her seriously, as if she had somehow stepped out of a natural role

331

and into an inappropriate one. Not exactly Run away and play, little girl; more Run away and deal with the poor coots who do need you, because I don't, and I never will. He was like suddenly running into a brick wall. Or encountering an alien force. The men felt it too, recognizing that Michael did not belong in ward X.

She continued standing beside him for longer than she realized, the torch fixed without deviation on the back of his head, her left hand extended, unconsciously smoothing and stroking the mosquito net.

A soft movement from the other side of the ward intruded. She looked up, able to see Luce's bed where it lay along the far wall because she had moved the screens back from the refectory table. Luce was sitting on the edge of his bed, naked, one leg propped up, both arms around it, watching her watch Michael. She felt suddenly as if she had been caught in the middle of some undignified and furtively sexual act, and was glad the ward was too dark to betray her blush.

For a long moment she and Luce stared at each other across the distance, like duelists coolly measuring the quality of the opposition. Then Luce broke his pose, lowering the leg as his arms fell away, and raised one hand to her in a mocking little wave. He twisted sideways under the edge of the net and disappeared. Moving quite naturally, she crossed the ward softly and bent to tuck in his net securely. But she made sure she didn't look anywhere near his face.

It was not her habit to check on Neil; unless he called for her, which he never did, once he was inside his own sanctum his life was absolutely his own. It was as much as she could do for him, poor Neil.

All was well; Sister Langtry paused at her office to change from sandshoes back into boots and gaiters, and clapped her hat on her head. She bent to pick up her basket, dropped two pairs of socks into it which she had culled from Michael's kit because they needed darning badly. At the front door she slipped absolutely without a sound through the fly-curtain, and let herself

out. Her torch beam unshielded now, she set off across the compound toward her quarters. Half-past ten. By eleven she would
have bathed and prepared herself for bed; by half past she would
be enjoying the beginning of six uninterrupted hours of sleep.

The men of ward X were not entirely unprotected during her
absence; if the inner alarm bell which was intrinsic to every
good nurse sounded in her, she would visit the ward during the
night herself, and tip off Night Sister to keep a special eye on X
as she patrolled from ward to ward. Even without prior warning
from Sister Langtry, the Night Sister would always look in once
as a matter of course. And if the worst came to the worst, there
was a telephone. It was three months since any sort of crisis had
occurred during the night, so her dreams were easy.

TWO

1 The visit to Colonel Chinstrap's clinic accomplished nothing, as Sister Langtry had expected. The colonel concentrated fiercely upon Michael's body, preferring to ignore soul and mind. He palpated, auscultated, poked, prodded, pinched, tapped, pricked, tickled, struck, all of which Michael bore with unruffled patience. On command Michael closed his eyes and touched the tip of his nose with the tip of his finger, used his eyes without moving his head to follow the erratic course of a pencil back and forth and up and down. He stood with feet together and eyes closed, walked a straight line, hopped first on one leg and then on the other, read off all the letters on a chart, had his visual fields plotted, played a little word association game. Even when the colonel's bloodshot eye loomed down on his own, ophthalmoscope at the ready, he endured that most intense and oppressive of close-quarters scrutiny with equanimity; Sister Langtry, sitting on a chair watching, was amused to see that he didn't even flinch at first contact with the colonel's halitosis.

After all this Michael was dismissed to wait outside, while Sister Langtry sat observing the colonel prodding at the inside of his own upper lip with the ball of his thumb; it always reminded her of nose-picking, though it was only the technique whereby the colonel stimulated his thinking processes.

"I'll do a lumbar puncture first thing this afternoon," he said at last, slowly.

"What on earth for?" asked Sister Langtry before she could restrain herself.

"I beg your pardon, Sister!"

"I said, what on earth for?" Well, in for a penny, in for a pound. She had started and she owed it to her patient to finish. "There's absolutely nothing neurologi-

337

cally wrong with Sergeant Wilson, and you know it, sir. Why subject the poor chap to a rotten headache and bed rest when he's in the pink of health considering the sort of life and climate he's been enduring?"

It was too early in the morning to fight with her. Last night's tiny excess with the whisky bottle and Sister Connolly had largely been due to his run-in with Langtry yesterday evening, and made the very idea of renewing battle insupportable. One of these days there would be a final reckoning, he promised himself dourly, but today was not going to be the day.

"Very well, Sister," he said stiffly, putting down his fountain pen and closing Sergeant Wilson's file. "I will not perform a lumbar puncture this afternoon." He handed her the notes as if they were contaminated. "Good morning to you."

She rose at once. "Good morning, sir," she said, then turned and walked out.

Michael was waiting, and fell in beside her as she strode a little too quickly from the clinic hut into the welcome fresh air.

"Is that that?" he asked.

"That is most definitely that! Unless you develop an obscure disease of the spinal cord with an unpronounceable name, I can safely predict that you have seen the last of Colonel Chinstrap except on ward inspections and his weekly general round."

"Colonel who?"

She laughed. "Chinstrap. Luce nicknamed him that, and it's stuck. His real name is Donaldson. I only hope that Chinstrap doesn't follow him all the way back to Macquarie Street."

"I must say this place and the people in it are full of surprises, Sister."

"No more than camp and your own battalion, surely?"

"The trouble with camp and my own battalion," said Michael, "was that I knew all the faces far too well, some of them for years and years. Not all of us who originally belonged were killed or invalided out. On the move or going into action, you don't notice the monotony. But I've spent almost all of the last six years in some sort of camp. Camps in desert dust storms,

338

camps in monsoon rains, even camp in the Showground. Always hot camps. I keep thinking of the Russian front, wondering what a really cold camp would be like, and I find myself actually dreaming about it. Isn't it queer that a man's life can become so monotonous he dreams of a different camp rather than of home or women? Camp is just about all I know."

"Yes, I agree, the chief trouble with war is the monotony. It's the chief trouble with ward X, too. For me and for the men. I prefer to work long hours and run X on my own because if I didn't, I'd be troppo myself. As for the men, they're physically well, quite capable of doing a hard day's work at something. But they can't. There isn't any work to do. If there were, they'd be the better for it mentally." She smiled. "Still, it can't be for too much longer now. We'll all be going home soon."

Going home didn't appeal to them, Michael knew, but he said nothing, just marched shoulder to shoulder with her across the compound.

It occurred to her that he was nice to walk with. He didn't bend his head down to her deferentially as Neil did, nor posture like Luce, nor skulk like Nugget. In fact, he took it quite naturally and companionably, almost one man to another. Which sounded odd, perhaps, but felt *right*.

"Do you have a civilian occupation, Michael?" she asked, turning away from the direction of ward X to take a path which led between two deserted wards.

"Yes. Dairy farmer. I've got three hundred acres of river flat on the Hunter near Maitland. My sister and her husband are working it for the duration, but they'd rather be back in Sydney, so when I get home I'll take over. My brother-in-law's a real city bloke, but when it came to the pinch he decided he'd rather milk cows and get woken up by roosters than wear a uniform and get shot at." Michael's face was faintly contemptuous.

"Another bush bunny for X! We're in the majority, then. Neil, Matt and Nugget are city, but now you're here, that makes four bush bunnies."

"Where are you from?"

339

"My father's got a property near Yass."

"Yet you ended up in Sydney, like Luce."

"In Sydney, yes. But not like Luce."

He grinned, gave her a quick sideways glance. "I beg your pardon, Sister."

"You'd better start calling me Sis the way the rest of them do. Sooner or later you will anyway."

"All right, Sis, I will."

They climbed a small undulating rise, sandy yet spidered with long rhizomes of coarse grass, dotted with the slim neat boles of coconut palms, and arrived at the edge of a beach. There they stopped, the breeze tugging at Sister Langtry's veil.

Michael pulled out his tobacco makings and squatted down on his heels the way all country men do, so Sister Langtry knelt beside him, careful not to get her duty shoes full of sand.

"It's when I see something like this I don't mind the Islands so much," he said, rolling a cigarette. "Isn't it amazing? Just when you think you can't take another day of mossies, mud, sweat, dysentery and triple dye, you wake up and it's the most perfect day God ever put upon the earth, or you see something like this, or something else happens that makes you think it isn't really so bad after all."

It was lovely, a short straight stretch of salt-and-peppery sand darkened near the water where it was wet from the retreating tide, and absolutely deserted. It seemed to be one side of a long promontory, for it ended against sky and water to the left, and to the right petered out in a mangrove flat reeking of decay. The water was like a thin wash of color laid on top of white: glassy, palest green, profoundly still. Far out was a reef, and the sea's horizon was hidden by the white spume fans of surf breaking.

"This is the patients' beach," she said, sitting back on her heels. "In the morning it's out of bounds, which is why there's no one here. But between one and five each afternoon it's all yours. I couldn't have brought you here then, because between one and five it's out of bounds to all females. Saves the army having to issue you with swimming costumes. The orderlies and the other noncom staff use it too, the same hours. For me it's been a godsend. Without the beach to divert them, my men would never get well."

"Do you have a beach, Sis?"

"The other side of the point is ours, though we're not as lucky as you. Matron's down on nude bathing."

"Old killjoy."

"The MOs and officers have their own beach too, on our side of the point, but cut off from us by a little headland. The officer patients can swim there or here."

"Do the MOs wear costumes?"

She smiled. "I really haven't thought to inquire." Her position was uncomfortable, so she used a glance to her watch as an excuse to get to her feet. "We'd better head back. It's not Matron's morning for rounds, but I haven't taught you yet how to drape your mosquito net. We've got time for an hour's practice before your lunch comes."

"It won't take an hour. I'm a quick learner," he said, reluctant to move, reluctant to break the pleasantness of this truly social contact with a woman.

But she shook her head and turned away from the beach, obliging him to follow. "Believe me, it's going to take you much longer than an hour. You haven't tried anything until you've tried to drape your net the right way. If I knew exactly what it portends, I'd suggest to Colonel Chinstrap that he use the Matron Drape as a test of mental aptitude."

"How do you mean?" He caught up with her, brushing a little sand from his trousers.

"Certain X patients can't do it. Benedict can't, for instance. We've all tried to teach him, and he's very willing to learn, but he just can't get the hang of it, though he's intelligent enough. He produces the most weird and wonderful variations on Matron's theme, but do it her way he can't."

"You're very honest about everyone, aren't you?"

She stopped to look at him seriously. "There's no point in being anything else, Michael. Whether you like it or not, whether

341

you think you fit in or not, whether you belong or not, you're a part of X now until we all go home. And you'll find that in X we can't afford the luxury of euphemisms."

He nodded, but said nothing, simply stared at her as if her novelty value was increasing, yet with more respect than he had admitted yesterday.

After a moment she dropped her eyes and continued to walk, but strolling along rather than striding out at her customary brisk pace. She was enjoying the break from routine, and enjoying his rather unforthcoming company. With him she didn't have to worry about how he was feeling; she could relax and pretend he was just someone she had met socially somewhere.

However, all too soon ward X came into sight around the corner of a deserted building. Neil was standing outside waiting for them. Which vaguely irritated Sister Langtry; he looked like an overanxious parent who had allowed his child to come home alone from school for the first time.

2 In the afternoon Michael went back to the beach with Neil, Matt and Benedict. Nugget had refused to come, and Luce was nowhere to be found.

The sureness with which Matt moved had Michael quite fascinated, discovering that a small touch on elbow or arm or hand from Neil was all Matt needed to navigate; Michael watched and learned, so that in Neil's absence he could substitute competently. Nugget had informed him in the bathhouse with much technical detail that Matt was not really blind, that there was nothing at all wrong with his eyes, but to Michael his inability to see seemed absolutely genuine. A man feigning blindness would surely have groped, stumbled, playacted the part. Where Matt did it with dignity and understatement, his inner self uncorrupted by it.

There were about fifty men scattered up and down the sand, which could have absorbed a thousand men without seeming crowded. All were naked; some were maimed, some scarred. Since there were noncom staff admixed with systemic convalescents after malaria or some other tropical disorder, the three whole healthy-looking men from ward X were not entirely out of place. However, Michael noticed that conviviality tended to confine itself within ward groups: neuros, plastics, bones, skins, abdominothoracics, general medicals; the staff element congregated together too.

The troppos from X shed their clothes far enough away from any other group not to be accused of deliberate eavesdropping, and swam for an hour, the water as warm and unstimulating as a tepid baby's bath. Then they spread themselves on the sand to dry off, skins powdered with rutile-bearing grains like tiny elegant sequins. Michael sat up to roll a cigarette, lit it and handed it to Matt. Neil smiled faintly but said nothing, merely

343

watched the sure hands as Michael embarked upon making one for himself.

A nice change from camp, Michael was thinking, staring out across the water with eyes narrowed against the glare, watching the thin blue streaks of his smoke hover for a moment before being taken by a breath of wind and swirled into nothing. Nice to witness a different family than the battalion, though this was a much closer-knit family, gently ruled by a woman, as all families ought to be. Nice to have a woman around, too. Sister Langtry represented his first more than transient contact with a woman in six years. One forgot: how they walked, how they smelled, how different they were. The sensation of family he felt in X stemmed directly from her, the figurehead of whom no one in X, not even Luce, spoke lewdly or with disrespect. Well, she was a lady, that was true, but she was more than a lady. Ladies with nothing to back up a set of manners and attitudes than more of the same had never interested him; Sister Langtry, he was beginning to see, had qualities he felt he shared, most men shared. Not afraid to speak her mind, not afraid of men because they were men.

At first she had put his back up a little, but he was fair enough to admit the fault lay in him rather than in her; why shouldn't women have authority and rank if they could cope with it? She could, yet she was a womanly woman, and very, very nice. Without seeming to exert any obvious wiles, she held this motley collection of men together, no doubt about that. They loved her, really loved her. Which meant they all saw sex in her somewhere. At first he hadn't seen sex, but after only one day and two private talks with her, he was beginning to. Oh, not throwing her down and having her; something more pleasant and subtle than that, a slow and delicious discovery of her mouth, her neck and shoulders, her legs ... A man switched off when he was unable to avail himself of anything save the guilty misery of masturbation, but having a woman around all day started the juices flowing again; his thoughts began to stir beyond the level

344

of an unattainable dream. Sister Langtry wasn't a pinup poster, she was *real*. Though for Michael she did have a dreamlike quality—nothing to do with the war, or its scarcity of women. She was upper crust, a squatter's daughter, the kind of woman he would never have met in the ordinary sequence of civilian life.

Poor Colin, he would have hated her. Not the way Luce hated her, because Luce wanted her at the same time, and loved her to boot. Luce could pretend to himself that what he felt for her was hate because she didn't want him back, and he couldn't understand it. But Colin had been different. Which had always been Colin's trouble. They had been in it together since the beginning. He had gravitated toward Colin very soon after enlisting, for Colin was the sort of bloke other blokes picked on, not really understanding why he irritated them, just lashing out because the irritation was perpetually there; like horses pestered by flies. And Michael had a strong protective streak which had plagued him since early childhood, so that he had always accumulated lame ducks.

Colin had been girlishly skinny and a little too pretty and a demon soldier, as handicapped by the way he looked and how he felt as Benedict probably was. Burying the butt of his cigarette in the sand, Michael rested his eyes thoughtfully on Benedict. There was a lot of trouble packed down inside Ben's narrow frame, torment and soul-searching and a fierce rebellion, just as there had been inside Colin. He would have bet any sum an onlooker cared to name that Ben had been a demon soldier too, one of those unlikely men who were the picture of mildness until battle euphoria got into them, when they went mad and behaved like ancient heroes. Men with much to prove to themselves usually were demon soldiers, especially when spiritual conflicts gingered up the mixture of troubles.

Michael had started in pitying Colin, that protective instinct very much to the fore, but as the months went on and one country succeeded another, a curious affection and friendship had grown between them. They fought well together, they camped well together, and they discovered neither had a taste for whoring or getting blind drunk when on leave, so that to stick together at all times became natural, welcome.

However, proximity can blind, and it blinded Michael. It was not until they reached New Guinea that he fully came to understand the extent of Colin's troubles. The company had been saddled with a new noncommissioned officer, a big, confident, rather blustering regimental sergeant major who soon displayed a tendency to use Colin as his butt. It hadn't worried Michael too much; he knew things could only go so far while he was there to draw a line over which no one stepped. The RSM had got Michael's measure too, and wasn't about to step over the line. So the pinpricks directed at Colin were minor, confined to comments and looks. Michael waited placidly, knowing that as soon as they went into action again the RSM would see a different side to the flimsy, girlish Colin.

Therefore it came as a complete shock to Michael one day to discover Colin weeping bitterly, and it had taken much patient probing to learn what the problem was: a homosexual overture from the RSM which tormented Colin on many levels. His inclinations lay that way, he confessed. He knew it was wrong, he knew it was unnatural, he despised himself for it, but he couldn't help himself, either. Only it wasn't the RSM he wanted; he wanted Michael.

There had been no revulsion, no outraged propriety on Michael's part; only an enormous sorrow, the tenderness and pity long friendship and genuine love permitted. How could a man turn away from his best mate when they'd been through so very much together? They talked for a long time, and in the end Colin's confession had made no difference to their relationship, save perhaps to strengthen it. Michael's preferences didn't lie in that direction, but he could feel no differently toward Colin because his did. That was life, that was men, that was a fact. The war and the existence it had forced upon him had meant Michael had learned to live with many things he would have rejected outright when a civilian, for the alternative to living with them was literally to die. Choosing to live simply meant learning tolerance;

346

so long as a man was let alone, he didn't inquire too closely into the private activities of his fellows.

But it was a burden to be loved as a lover; Michael's responsibilities toward Colin had suddenly multiplied. His very inability to return Colin's love the way Colin wanted it returned laid additional care upon Michael, increased his urge to protect. Together they had seen death, battle, hardship, hunger, loneliness, homesickness, illness; too much by far to abandon. Yet to be unable to return love fully was a burden of guilt only to be expiated in what help and service he could permit within the bounds of his own nature. And Colin, though the ultimate joy of a sexual relationship was always unattainable, bloomed and brightened immeasurably after that day in New Guinea.

When Colin died Michael hadn't been able to believe what his eyes were showing him, one of those fluke kills from a tiny splinter of metal driven faster than sound through the close-cropped hair between neck and skull, so that he just lay down and died, so very quietly, without any blood, without disgust. Michael had sat beside him for a long time, sure that his clasp on the stiff cold hand would eventually be returned; in the end they had had to prise the two hands apart, living one and dead one, and persuade Michael to come away, that there was absolutely no hope of ever seeing life in that calmly sleeping face. It looked noble, at rest, sacred, inviolate. Death would have changed it in some way. It always did, for death was slack and emptied. He still found himself wondering whether in truth Colin's dead face had seemed to sleep, or whether his eyes had wrought a change in it that made it seem simply to sleep. Grief he had often known, but not grief like this.

Then after the first shock of Colin's death had evaporated Michael was horrified to discover in himself, living it appeared right alongside that intolerable grief, a wonderful sense of release. He was free! The incubus of duty toward one more helpless and less capable than himself was gone. As long as Colin had lived he would have been tied by that duty. Perhaps it would not have prevented his seeking love elsewhere, but it would certainly have hampered him, and Colin would not have been strong enough to resist trying to retain exclusive possession of him, he knew. So death after all came as a reprieve, and that tormented him.

For months afterward he kept to himself as much as he could given his peculiar status in the battalion; there were demon soldiers aplenty in a unit as illustrious as his, but Michael was more than a demon soldier. His CO called him the quintessential soldier, meaning by that a degree of military professionalism rarely found in any man. To Michael it was a job, and he never failed in it because he believed not only in himself but in the ultimate goodness of the cause. He conducted himself without passion, no matter what the provocation, which meant that he could be relied upon at all times to keep his head, do what had to be done without dwelling upon the consequences even in terms of his own life. He would dig a trench, a road, a dugout or a grave; he would take an untakable position or take it upon himself to retreat if he so judged; he never complained, he never made trouble, he never questioned an order even if he was already making up his mind to circumvent it. His effect on his fellow soldiers was calming, steadying, encouraging. They thought he bore a charmed life, and saw in him their luck.

After the landing on Borneo settled down, he was sent on a mission which appeared quite routine; since the battalion was short of officers, the RSM who had badgered Colin was put in charge of the sortie. It consisted of three barges of men. Their instructions were to proceed to such-and-such a beach, take possession of it, and infiltrate. Earlier reconnaissance had revealed no Japanese within the area. But when the exercise began the Japanese were there all right, and more than half the company died or was wounded. One barge had got clean away, its men not yet landed; one barge was sunk under fire; Michael, another sergeant and the RSM among them had managed to rally and collect the unwounded or lightly wounded men, and all together they had carried the seriously wounded on board the third barge, still afloat. Halfway home they were met by a relief party

348

bearing medics, plasma, morphine; the unharmed barge had got home and sent them timely aid.

The RSM had taken the loss of so many good men hard, blamed it upon himself, for it had been his first independent command. And Michael, remembering New Guinea days and Colin, felt obliged to do what he could to comfort the man. It backfired spectacularly; the RSM had literally welcomed his attentions with open arms. For five hideous minutes Michael went mad; the quintessential soldier who never allowed his passions to become involved was consumed by passion. He saw the whole hideous cycle beginning again—an unwanted love, a painful servitude, himself the victim and the cause at one and the same time—and he suddenly hated the RSM as he had never in his entire life hated anyone. If this man had not made advances to Colin in the first place, none of it would ever have happened, for Colin would not have found the courage to unburden himself.

Luckily Michael's hands were all he had, but training, rage, and the advantage of surprise would have proven more than enough had the RSM not managed to scream for help, and had that help not been very near.

Once the madness lifted, Michael found himself destroyed. In all the years of his service in the army he had never hungered to kill, never got any satisfaction from it, never actually hated his adversaries. But with his hands around the RSM's throat he felt a pleasure akin only to sexual heights, and with his thumbs pressing down on the hyoid cartilage he had gloried in the sheer feeling of it, was driven on by the same sort of mindless carnality he had always despised in others.

Only he could know how he felt during those brief and violent seconds; and knowing, he elected not to fight the consequences. He refused to justify his actions, refused to say anything except that he had intended to kill.

The CO of the battalion, one of the best commanding officers men were ever lucky enough to have, collared Michael in a private interview. The only other man present was the RMO, an excellent doctor and a strong humanitarian. Together they in-

349

formed Michael that the matter had been taken over their heads to divisional HQ; the RSM was determined on a court-martial, and was not prepared to be blocked at battalion level.

"The stupid bloody bugger," said the battalion CO dispassionately.

"He's not himself these days," said Michael, who was still occasionally shaken by a fit of something perilously close to tears.

"If you go on like this they'll convict you," said the RMO. "You'll lose everything you should come out of the war wearing proudly."

"Let them convict me," said Michael wearily.

"Oh, come off it, Mike!" said the CO. "You're worth ten of him, and you know it!"

"I just want to be out of this," said Michael, closing his eyes. "Oh, Johnno, I'm so bloody fed up with the war, men, the whole bloody lot!"

The two officers exchanged glances.

"What you obviously need is a good rest," said the RMO then, briskly. "It's all over bar the shouting anyway. How about a nice comfortable bed in a nice comfortable base hospital with a nice comfortable nurse to look after you?"

Michael had opened his eyes. "It sounds like heaven," he said. "What do I have to do to get there?"

"Just go on acting like a dill," said the RMO, grinning. "I'm sending you to Base Fifteen as suspected of unsound mind. It won't appear on your discharge papers, you have our word on that. But it will force our noncom friend to pull his horns in."

So the pact was sealed. Michael handed in his Owen gun and his ammunition, was loaded into a field ambulance and taken to the airfield, and thence to Base Fifteen.

A nice comfortable bed in a nice comfortable hospital with a nice comfortable nurse to look after him. But did Sister Langtry fit the definition of a nice comfortable nurse? He had rather imagined someone fortyish, stout, motherly in a no-nonsense sort of way. Not a whippy, fine-boned little thing scarcely older than he himself, with more aplomb than a brigadier and more brains than a field marshal. . . .

He came out of his reverie to find Benedict staring at him unwinkingly, and he had smiled back with unshadowed affection before the alarm bells could prevent him. No, never again! Not even for this poor, miserable bastard with the half-starved wistful look of a homeless mongrel cur. Never, never again. Still, forewarned was forearmed, and he could make sure this time that what friendship he offered remained limited. Not that Michael took Benedict for a homosexual. Ben just needed a friend badly, and none of the others were the slightest bit interested in him. No wonder. He had that disconcerting stoniness Michael had seen in other men from time to time, and it always rendered them friendless. They didn't so much rebuff overtures as react peculiarly, would start spouting religion or talk about things most men preferred to ignore. He probably frightened girls to death, and they probably frightened him to death, too. Ben struck him as the sort of man whose life had been an emotional desert, with the juicelessness starting inside. No wonder he loved Sister Langtry; she treated him so normally, where the rest of the men regarded him as a kind of freak. What they sensed without understanding it, though maybe Neil had had enough experience to see it, was the violence. God, what a soldier he must have been!

At which moment Benedict stirred; his face began to squeeze in on itself, nostrils pinched, eyes glassy. It turned to stone under Michael's eyes. Curious, Michael turned his head to see what Benedict had seen. And there was Luce in the distance, parading up the beach from its far end toward them, and parade he did. Stepping high in a mincing parody of a lifesaver's strut, superbly aware of his own superbness, the sun lighting up his golden body, the length and the thickness of his penis mocking every other man on the beach into sullen inadequacy and secret loathing envy.

351

"The bastard!" said Neil, long cobbled toes digging into the sand as if this were but the commencement of a mole process which would end in burying him. "God, if only I had the guts to take a Bengal razor to that load he's carrying!"

"Just once I wish I could see him," said Matt wistfully.

"A sight to behold," said Michael, looking amused.

Luce reached them and swung round gracefully to stand above them, one hand absently caressing his hairless chest. "Tennis, anyone?" he asked, the other hand swishing an imaginary racquet.

"Oh, is there a court here?" asked Michael, ingenuously surprised. "I'll have a game with you, then."

Luce stared at him suspiciously, the realization that the offer wasn't meant seriously dawning slowly. "You're pulling my leg, you sarcastic bastard!" he said, astonished.

"Why not?" asked Michael, grinning. "You've got three."

Matt and Neil laughed uproariously, and Benedict succumbed to a self-conscious titter, which the group nearest to them on the beach echoed, ears tuned guiltily. Luce stood for a moment flabbergasted, uncertain how to act. It was an infinitesimal pause; he shrugged and moved away toward the water as if such had been his intention all along.

"Very good, Mike," he said over his shoulder. "Very good indeed! I'm glad to see you noticed."

"How could a bloke not notice a donger like that? I thought at first it was a bit left over from the Sydney Harbor Bridge!" Michael called after him.

The next group down the beach abandoned all pretense at disinterest and burst out laughing; Luce's grand moment had become a farce. Neil picked up a handful of sand and threw it at Michael joyously. "Full marks, old son," he said, wiping his eyes. "God, how I wish I'd said that!"

When Sister Langtry came on duty a little after five, to discover that the rest of her charges had resoundingly decided to like Michael, she felt like cheering and waving flags. It mattered tremendously to her that they should like him, wished on them at the very last moment as he had been. Just why it should matter so much she had not quite worked out, but she suspected it was more on his behalf than for the sake of the others.

At first he had stirred her curiosity, then her sense of justice and fair play, then her frank interest. If she had doubted how he would settle into ward X, her doubt lay not so much with him as with Neil, the ringleader of X. For Neil had not been warm in his welcome; he might mock himself, but he was a leader, a naturally autocratic personality. The other men looked to him, even Luce, so it lay within his power to make ward X as much heaven or hell as limbo.

To discover Neil treating Michael as a full equal made her profoundly thankful. Michael would be all right from now on, therefore the rest of them would be too.

Then Benedict appeared and was delighted to learn that Michael played chess. Chess was apparently Ben's one fleshly weakness, but it bored Neil and frightened Nugget; Matt had liked to play when he could see the board and the pieces, but said he found keeping a visual image in his mind all the time too much of a strain. Luce played well, but couldn't resist turning black against white into a metaphorical struggle between good and evil, which upset Ben more than Sister Langtry felt was good for him, so she had forbidden him to play with Luce.

Watching Benedict settle pleasurably on the bench opposite Michael after dinner, the chess set out, made Sister Langtry feel as if the ward was finally complete within itself. How nice to have an ally! she thought contentedly, too generous to resent the fact that apparently Michael was succeeding with a patient she had always known was not amenable to her own brand of help.

3 Luce had more than one quality in common with a cat: not only did he move like one, he could see in the dark like one. Thus he carried no torch as he moved surefooted through the spaces between deserted huts, making for a spot at the end of the nurses' beach where it was brought up short by a tall outcrop of rocks Sister Langtry had described erroneously to Michael as a headland.

The MPs were lax these days, as Luce well knew; the war was over, Base Fifteen was as quiet as the corpse it was soon to become, and there was no feeling of discord in the air. Sensitive to such things, MP antennae registered zero.

Tonight he was on his way to an important assignation, feeling powerful and light and almost painfully alive. Oh, yes, little Miss Woop-Woop, the bank manager's precious daughter! It hadn't been easy persuading her to meet him like this, and she had consented only when she realized there were no other ways of seeing him than illicitly or in the full public gaze of the verandah outside the nurses' mess. She was a nurse officer, he was a man from the ranks, and while innocent intercourse between old school chums was quite permissible, any intercourse more intimate would bring a sharp reprimand and disciplinary action from Matron, a real stickler for military conventions. But he had succeeded in persuading her to meet him on the beach after dark, and he had no doubts as to how matters would proceed from now on; the biggest hurdle was already behind him.

There was no moon to betray them, but in this place of dark peacefulness the sky shone with an unearthly brilliance, and the matted clouds of nebulae and star clusters along the axis of the galaxy breathed a still, cold light upon the world, faintly silvering it. Thus he had

354

no trouble in picking out her form among the denser shadows around it, and moved very quietly until he stood alongside her.

She drew in her breath sharply. "I didn't hear you!" she said, shuddering a little.

"You can't possibly be cold on a night like this," he said, rubbing the goose bumps on the back of her hand with a friendly impersonal touch.

"It's nerves. I'm not used to sneaking out like this up here—it's different from sneaking out of a nice safe nurses' home in Sydney."

"Calm down, it's all right! We'll just sit ourselves over here where it's comfortable, and have a cigarette." With a hand under her elbow, he helped her down onto the sand, and sat far enough away from her to reassure her. "I hate to be a bludger, but do you happen to have any tailor-mades?" he said, teeth flashing in the dimness. "I can roll you one, but you mightn't like the taste."

She fumbled in one of the pockets of her bush jacket and produced a packet of Craven As, which he took without permitting his fingers to touch hers. Then he gave the act a certain intimacy by lighting the cigarette in his own mouth and passing it to her. For himself, he produced his makings and rolled one leisurely.

"Won't someone see our cigarettes?" she asked.

"Well, I suppose they might, but it isn't very likely," he said easily. "The nurses here are a pretty tame lot, so the MPs don't usually bother with places like this." He turned his head to watch her profile. "How's the old town these days?"

"A bit empty."

It came hard to say it, but he managed. "How's my mother? My sisters?"

"When did you hear from them last?"

"A couple of years ago."

"What? Don't they write?"

"Oh, all the time! I just don't read their letters."

"Then why feign interest in them by asking?"

The flash of spirit surprised him. "We have to talk about something, don't we?" he asked gently, and reached out to touch her hand. "You're nervous."

"You're just the way you were at school!"

"No, not a bit. There's been too much water under the bridge since then."

"Has it been very awful?" she asked, pitying him.

"The war, you mean? Sometimes." He thought of the office he had occupied, the pleasant safe job with the quivering jellyfish of a major who had been his titular boss, though in actual fact it had been the other way around. Luce sighed. "A man has to do his duty, you know."

"Oh, I know!"

"It's good to see a friendly face here," he said, after a slight silence.

"For me, too. I was so happy when Manpower released me to go into the army, but it hasn't been at all what I expected. Of course it would have been different if the war had still been on. But Base Fifteen's rather a dead place, isn't it?"

He laughed softly. "That's a good description of it."

The question she was burning to ask came out all of a sudden, before she could bite it back, or phrase it more tactfully. "What are you doing in ward X, Luce?"

His answer had been ready since the moment when he realized what he had in mind for little Miss Woop-Woop. "Battle fatigue, plain, pure and simple," he said, and heaved a huge sigh. "It happens to the best of us."

"Oh, Luce!"

This is the worst dialogue ever written, he thought to himself, but life's like that. No point in wasting Shakespeare where Daggett would do.

"Feeling warmer?" he asked.

"Much! It's hot up here, isn't it?"

"How about coming for a swim?"

"Now? I don't have my swimming costume!"

And pause to count four, then say: "It's dark, I can't see you. Even if I could, I wouldn't look."

356

Of course she knew as well as he that in consenting to meet him here she was also consenting to whatever liberties he planned to take; but the ritual moves had to be made, the ritual responses elicited. Otherwise conscience would not be satisfied, nor parents' ghosts propitiated. She was panting for him, and she meant to have him, but he mustn't ever think her cheap or easy.

"Well, all right then, but only if you go in first and promise to stay in until I'm out and dressed again," she said hesitantly.

"Done!" he exclaimed, and he sprang to his feet and twisted free of his clothes with the speedy dispatch of one who had been trained in quick-change techniques.

She didn't want to lose him in the water, so she followed him as quickly as she could, but things like boots and gaiters were new to her, slowed her down.

"Luce! Where are you?" she whispered, wading in until her knees were submerged, and frightened that he would grab her in a kind of sport she considered juvenile.

"I'm here," he said reassuringly, from somewhere fairly close at hand, and without attempting to grab her.

Breathing a sigh of relief, she waded further in and bobbed down until her shoulders were covered.

"It's nice, isn't it?" he asked. "Come on, swim out for a little bit with me."

She followed in the phosphorescent glitter of his wake, swimming strongly, and feeling for the first time in her life the voluptuous freedom of her unclothed body supported by the water. It excited her too much; she turned and began to swim in again, not looking to see whether he still swam out, or was accompanying her.

It was like some magic, enchanted dream, and her mind winged ahead of her flying body, already skin-deep in loving him. No tremulous virgin, she knew what was going to happen, and knew because it was *him* that it was going to be better than it ever had been in her life.

Her conviction that she was caught up in a spell was height-

357

ened when out of the corner of her eye she saw him alongside her; she stopped, trod water, found her feet on the bottom and stood up, waiting for his kiss. But instead he lifted her bodily into his arms and walked from the water, up to the place where he had strewn his clothes, and laid her on them. She held up her hands to him, he sank down beside her and buried his face in her neck. When she first felt his teeth she arched her back and whimpered with pleasure, but the sound quickly became a suppressed groan of pain, for these were no gentle, nuzzling nips. He was biting her, really biting her, with a silent, savage, crushing ferocity that at first she bore, thinking it would stop, that he was starved for her. But the agony went on, became unbearable; she began to fight to get away, could not from his heavy, incredibly strong hold. Mercifully he moved from her neck, began biting less painfully at one breast, but when the pressure of his teeth increased again she could no longer keep the cry of terror in, for suddenly she was sure he intended to kill her where she lay.

"Oh, Luce, don't! Please, please, I beg of you! You're hurting me!"

The thin, wailing words seemed to penetrate, for he did stop, began to kiss the breast he had mauled so cruelly a moment before; but the kisses were perfunctory and soon ceased.

It was going to be all right. Her childhood love and her want came back, she sighed and murmured. He propped himself on his hands above her, nudged her knees apart imperatively, and fitted his legs between hers. Feeling the blind thing pushing at her, she reached down to guide it, found the right place with a shiver and took her fingers away to clasp his shoulders, draw him down onto her, welcome him, feel the weight of him and the skin of him, his hands across her back. But he refused to lower himself, remaining propped away from her by the full length of his arms, supporting himself on his hands, touching her only where apparently he thought it mattered; as if to touch her elsewhere would channel precious energy away from the task at hand. The first great thrust made her gasp with pain, but she was young, wet, relaxed and desperately anxious for this; she let her legs rest fully on the ground to lessen the depth to which he could penetrate, and began to pick up his rhythm until she moved with him, not back when he moved forward, but forward to meet each thrust.

And it became beautiful, though she longed to feel him embrace her instead of holding himself aloof. His exasperating posture diminished the friction she found necessary, so it was a full ten minutes before she came to orgasm, which she did more hugely and wildly than ever in her life, feeling the spasms from her jaw to her feet like the clonic jerks of some ecstatic epilepsy.

Enormously grateful to him for controlling himself so long to please her, she expected him to follow immediately with his own orgasm; but he did not. That grim, steady, obsessive pounding continued and continued and continued. Exhaustion began to suffocate her; she went limp, dried up, endured it until she could endure no more.

"For God's sake, Luce! Enough! That's enough!"

He withdrew himself at once, still erect, not having achieved a climax. And it crushed her utterly. Never before had she felt so joyless, so devoid of any sweet victory. No use to whisper to him the timeless, inevitable "Was it all right?" It had clearly not been all right.

But it was not in her nature to remain cast down by the actions of others; if he wasn't satisfied, it was his problem, not hers. For a moment she lay where she was, hoping he would kiss her, hug her, but he did not; from the time when he picked her up until the end of it there had been no kiss; as if to touch her lips with his own would have destroyed his pleasure. Pleasure? Did he get any pleasure out of it at all? Surely he must! He had been as hard as a rock throughout.

She drew her legs to one side, rolled over on her elbow and began to grope for her cigarettes. The moment she found them Luce held out his hand for one for himself; she passed it over, and leaned to light it for him. The match revealed his face, expressionless, long dark lashes down to hide the eyes. He drew deeply on the cigarette, and the match went out, snuffed by the strength of his exhalation.

Well, that ought to keep the silly bitch happy, he thought, lying back with his hands behind his head, the cigarette held between lightly clenched lips. Thump them until they yelled for mercy, then they had no right to complain or criticize. How long that took didn't matter to him. He could keep it up all night if he had to. He despised the act, he despised them, he despised himself. The act was a tool, the tool of the tool between his legs, but he had vowed long ago never to be the tool of either. Always the operator. He was master, they were servants, and the only people he couldn't bend to his will were those like Langtry who felt no tug toward servants or master. God, what he wouldn't give to see Langtry down on her knees, begging and pleading for any and all of them, servants and master . . .

He glanced at his watch, saw that it was after half-past nine. Time to go or he would be late in, and he was not about to give Langtry the satisfaction of reporting him to Colonel Chinstrap. Reaching out, he gave the reclining figure near him a neat slap on her bottom.

"Come on, love, I've got to go. It's late."

He assisted her into her clothes with the scrupulous attention to detail of a ladies' maid, kneeling to lace up her boots, buckle her gaiters. He dusted her down, twitched the grey bush jacket into place, did up its belt and adjusted the set of her slouch hat to his satisfaction. His own clothes were wet in places from the sea, but he slid into them indifferently.

Then he walked with her to the boundary of the sisters' blocks, his hand beneath her elbow to guide her through the darkness with an impersonal care she found infuriating.

"Will I see you again?" she asked when he stopped.

He smiled. "You certainly will, my love."

"When?"

"In a few days. We can't make the pace too fierce or we'll be nobbled. I'll come to pay my respects to you on the verandah outside your mess, and we'll arrange something then. All right?"

She stood on tiptoe to kiss his cheek self-consciously, then commenced the last lap home on her own.

He changed immediately into a cat, went slipping off into the gloom, skirting the patches of light, keeping well alongside buildings when he came to them.

And he thought about what he had been thinking about through most of the lovemaking: Sergeant Wilson, hero and shirt-lifting poofter. Shipped off to X by an embarrassed CO to escape the disgrace of a court-martial, he was willing to bet. Well, well! The admissions to X were certainly getting queerer and queerer all the time.

It had not escaped him that Langtry thought the new admission was a bit of all right. Perked her up no end, he had! Of course she didn't believe what she'd read in his papers, no woman ever did—especially when the bloke was as manly and strong as Sergeant Wilson, a proper answer to an old maid's prayers. The question: Was Sergeant Wilson the answer to Langtry's prayers? Luce had thought for a long time that privilege was going to be Neil's, but at the moment he was not so sure. He'd better do a bit of praying himself, that Langtry preferred a sergeant to a captain, a Wilson to a Parkinson. If she did, it would be a lot easier to do what he was planning to do. Make Langtry grovel.

He became aware that his balls ached all the way through to his teeth, and stopped in the lee of a deserted ward to urinate. But as usual the wretched stuff wouldn't come; it always took him ages to manage to pee. He dallied as long as he dared, willing the stream to start, holding his despised prize tool between his fingers, wrinkling its skin back and forth in a quiet frenzy of desperation. No use. Another look at his watch told him there wasn't any more time; he would have to endure the ache a few minutes more.

THREE

1 Michael had been a patient in ward X for about two
weeks when Sister Langtry first began to experience an
odd feeling of premonition. Not a pleasant anticipation
of pleasantness, but a morbid, crawling dread which
had absolutely no basis in reality. The reality was the
converse, a smooth new completeness. There were no
undercurrents; everyone liked Michael, and Michael
liked everyone. The men were relaxed, and certainly
more comfortable, for Michael waited on them hand
and foot, fetched and carried cheerfully. After all, he explained to her, he couldn't read endlessly, he had his
indolent periods on the beach, and he needed to move
around with some purpose. So he mended the plumbing such as it was, hammered in nails, fixed things.
There was a cushion sewn to the back of her office
chair, courtesy of Michael; the floors almost gleamed;
the dayroom was tidier.

Yet still her disquiet persisted. He is a catalyst of some
kind, she thought; in his own nature and essence harmless, but in ward X, who knows? Yes, everyone liked
him and he liked everyone. And there were no undercurrents. But ward X was different since his advent,
though she could not discover what the difference was.
Just an atmosphere.

The heat became oppressive, very still, and the air
brooded; the slowest, most leisurely of movements produced rivers of sweat, and the waters of the ocean beyond the reef turned a sullen green, horizon smudged.
With the full moon came the rain, two days of awesome
steady downpour which laid the dust but brought mud
instead. Mildew popped out on everything: mosquito
nets, sheets, screens, books, boots, clothes, woodwork,
bread. But with the beach unavailable, it saved the men
from complete idleness, for Sister Langtry kept them all

365

hard at it cleaning off the mildew with spirit-dampened rags. She issued an order that all boots and shoes must come off just inside the front or back door, yet still by some osmotic process the mud infiltrated everywhere into the ward, and that kept the men busy too, with buckets and mops and floor cloths.

Luckily there was nothing depressing about the rain itself, as it didn't mourn the passing of the sun the way the tender, colder rains of higher latitudes did. As long as it didn't set in, such rain as this almost had the power to exalt, filling the human mind with a vast impression of might. If it set in, as it would when the real monsoons came, its effect was worse than any other rain, for the power became remorseless and overwhelming, human beings mere scurrying impotent ants.

But this rain was too early to be the beginning of the monsoon, and when the rain cleared, even that drab unlovely collection of buildings called Base Fifteen looked unexpectedly beautiful: scrubbed, rinsed, swept.

Well, that's that, thought Sister Langtry, feeling an enormous relief. All I was worrying about was rain! It always affects them this way. Affects me, too.

"How silly," she said to Michael, handing him a bucket of muddy water.

He was putting the finishing touches on the sluice room after the swabbing party had downed tools and was taking a well-earned rest on the verandah.

"What's silly?" he asked, tipping the water down the drain and wiping off the galvanized iron with a rag.

"I've had a feeling there was trouble brewing, but I think all it was was rain brewing. After all this time in the tropics you'd think I'd know better." She leaned her back against the doorjamb and watched him, the intent thoroughness with which every single task was done, the smooth roundedness of the whole.

After the rag was draped to dry over the edge of the bucket he straightened and turned, eyeing her with amusement. "I agree, you'd think so." He reached past her to pluck his shirt off a nail behind the door, and put it on. "It gets you down after a while, doesn't it? Never anything by halves up here. I never remember getting in a tizzy about a couple of days of rain back home, but up here I've seen it lead almost to murder."

"Did it in your own case?"

The smiling eyes looked arrested for a moment, then continued to smile. "No."

"If not rain, why?"

"That's my business," he said, quite pleasantly.

Her cheeks reddened. "It's also mine, considering the circumstances! Oh, why won't you see that it's better to talk about things? You're as standoffish as Ben!"

The shirt was buttoned and tucked in, all without any self-consciousness. "Don't get upset, Sis. And don't worry about me."

"I'm not worried about you in the least. But I've been in charge of X long enough to know that it's better for my patients to talk things out."

"I'm not your patient," he said, poised as if he expected to see her move out of his way.

She didn't. She continued to stand where she was, more exasperated than angry. "Michael, of course you're my patient! A pretty stable patient, admittedly, but you can't have been admitted to X for no good reason!"

"There was a very good reason. I tried to kill a bloke," he said dispassionately.

"Why?"

"The reason's there in my papers."

"It's not a good enough reason for me." Her mouth straightened, set hard. "I don't understand your papers. You're not a homosexual."

"How do you know?" he asked coolly.

She drew a breath, but met his eyes very directly. "I know," she said.

Whereupon he laughed, head thrown back. "Well, Sis, it doesn't matter to me why I'm here, so why should it matter to you? I'm just glad I am here, that's all."

She moved away from the door, into the room. "You're fenc-

367

ing with me," she said slowly. "What are you trying to hide? What's so secret you can't bear to tell me?"

For a moment he was startled into dropping his ever-present guard, and she caught a glimpse of someone who was very tired, a little bewildered, and troubled within himself. And seeing these things, she was quite disarmed.

"No, don't even bother to answer that," she said, smiling at him in genuine friendship.

He responded by softening his expression into an affection purely for her, and said, "I'm just not a talker, Sis, when it comes to myself. I *can't* talk."

"Are you frightened I might sit in judgment?"

"No. But to talk, you have to find the right words, and I never seem to manage to find them. Or at least not at the right time. About three o'clock this morning they'll all be there, right where I want them."

"That's true of everyone. But all you have to do is start! I'll help you go on, because I want to help you."

His eyes closed, he sighed. "Sis, I do not need help!"

She gave up—for the moment. "Then tell me what you think of Benedict," she said.

"Why ask me about Ben?"

"Because you're succeeding with him, where I never have. Please don't think I'm resentful. I'm too glad to see it happen. But I am interested."

"Benedict." His head lowered while he thought. "I told you, I'm not good with words. What do I think of him? I like him. I pity him. He's not well."

"Dating only back to that incident in the village?"

Michael shook his head positively. "Oh, no! It goes back a long way further than that."

"Is it because he lost his parents at an early age? Or because of the grandmother who brought him up?"

"Maybe. It's hard to tell. Ben's not sure who he is, I think. Or if he is sure, then he doesn't know how to deal with what he is. I don't know. I'm not a mental specialist."

"Nor am I," she said ruefully.

"You do all right."

"If I'm honest with myself, Ben's the only one I fret about after Base Fifteen."

"When he gets out of the army, you mean?"

"Yes." She searched for the right words, not wanting to wound Michael's feelings; he was trying so hard with Ben. "You see, I'm not sure Ben's going to be capable of living independently of some kind of enclosed unit. Yet I don't feel it's fair to him to suggest that he be placed under detention."

"A mental asylum?" he asked incredulously.

"I suppose that's what I mean. They're all we've got for people like Ben. But I hesitate to do that."

"You're wrong!" he cried.

"I may well be. That's why I hesitate."

"It would kill him."

"Yes." Her face was sad. "As you see, my job's not all beer and skittles."

His hand came out to grip her shoulder hard, shake her. "Just don't do anything in a hurry, please! And don't do it without talking to me first!"

It was a heavy hand; she turned her head to look at it. "Ben's improving," she said. "Thanks to you. That's why I'm talking to you now. Don't worry!"

Neil spoke from the doorway. "We thought the pair of you must have gone down the drain," he said lightly.

Sister Langtry stepped back from Michael, whose hand had fallen away the moment he became aware of Neil. "Not quite down the drain," she said, and smiled at Neil a little apologetically; then she was annoyed with herself for feeling apology. And annoyed with Neil, for more obscure reasons.

Michael remained where he was, watching the slightly proprietary manner in which Neil ushered Sister Langtry from the sluice room. Then he sighed, shrugged, and followed them out onto the verandah. Ward X was about as private a place to conduct a private conversation as the middle of a parade ground.

Everyone kept tabs on everyone else; and that was particularly true of Sister Langtry. If they didn't know where she was, who she was with, they couldn't rest until they found her. And sometimes they did a little mental arithmetic to make sure she was apportioning her time correctly among all of them. All of them? The ones who mattered. Neil was a master at mental arithmetic.

2 By dawn of the next day the weather had settled to an intoxicating balminess which caused everyone's mood to soar. The cleaning chores done, the men gathered on the verandah while Sister Langtry went into her office to catch up on her paper work. The beach would be open in the afternoon, and would be relatively crowded; only when it was closed did the patients of ward X realize how much it meant to be able to shrug off clothes and cares, switch off thought, swim and sun and doze themselves into pleasant stupor.

With half the morning still to get through, the usual fretting apathy was missing, everyone was so looking forward to the beach. Luce disposed himself to sleep on one of the verandah beds, Neil persuaded Nugget and Benedict to play cards at the table, and Michael took Matt up to the far end of the verandah, where some chairs sat beneath the back window of Sister Langtry's office, isolated enough to command peace.

Matt wanted to dictate a letter to his wife, and Michael had volunteered to act as his amanuensis. So far Mrs. Sawyer didn't know about Matt's blindness; he had insisted that it be kept from her, that he wanted to tell her himself, that no one had the right to deprive him of his request. Pitying him, Sister Langtry agreed to comply, knowing his real reason to be a despairing hope that before he met his wife again some miracle would have happened, and the blindness would have passed away.

When it was finished, Michael read the letter back to him slowly.

". . . and so because my hand has not yet healed properly, my friend Michael Wilson has volunteered to write this to you for me. However, you must not worry. All is going well. I think you are sensible enough to know

371

that if the injury was a serious one they would have sent me back to Sydney a long time ago. Please do not worry about me. Give Margaret, Mary, Joan and little Pam a hug and a kiss from Daddy, and tell them it won't be long now. I miss you very much. Look after yourself and the girls. Your loving husband, Matthew."

All the letters home were stilted, the efforts mostly of men who had never expected to be far enough away from home and their loved ones to have to put pen to paper. And besides, the censors read everything, and you never knew who the censors were. So most men kept themselves polite and aloof, successfully resisting the temptation to pour out their miseries and their frustrations. And most men wrote home regularly, the way children do who are sentenced to a boarding school they loathe; where happiness and busyness are, the urge to communicate with loved ones far away diminishes very quickly.

"Will that do?" asked Matt anxiously.

"I think so. I'll put it straight into an envelope now and give it to Sis before lunch . . . Mrs. Ursula Sawyer . . . What's the address, Matt?"

"Ninety-seven Fingleton Street, Drummoyne."

Luce came strolling down the verandah and flopped into a nearby cane chair. "Well, if it isn't little Lord Fauntleroy about his good deeds!" he said provocatively.

"If you sit in that chair wearing nothing but shorts you'll be striped like a convict," said Michael, slipping Matt's letter into his pocket.

"Oh, bugger the stripes!"

"Keep it clean and keep it down, Luce," said Matt, gesturing accurately toward the open louvers of Sister Langtry's office.

"Hold on a tick, Mike! I've got a letter for Matt's wife you can post along with that one," Luce said, too softly for any but the three of them to hear. "Like me to read it? Dear madam, did you know your husband's as blind as a bat?"

Matt was out of the chair too quickly for restraint, but Michael placed himself between the frantic blind man and his tormentor,

372

and held Matt firmly. "It's all right, mate! He's just being nasty. Calm down, now! It's all right, I tell you! He couldn't do that even if he wanted to. The censors would catch it."

Luce watched, enjoying the spectacle, and made no attempt to draw up his legs when he realized Michael had decided to put Matt with the others at the table. But rather than make an issue of it, Michael chose to guide Matt around the outflung legs, and so departed in peace.

After they were gone, Matt to the table and Michael into the ward, Luce got up and went to the verandah railing, leaning on it, his head cocked to hear the murmur of Michael's and Sister Langtry's voices through the open window; though his position and pose indicated that he was not listening should the inhabitants of the office look his way, he was still within earshot. Then the office door closed, all was silent again. Luce slipped past the cardplayers and went into the ward.

He found Michael in the dayroom buttering bread. Fresh crusty bread was the only culinary thrill, and a recent one at that, which Base Fifteen had to offer its inmates. Patients and staff alike consumed vast quantities of the bread at every opportunity, for it was excellent. By nine o'clock in the evening and the last cup of tea of the day, there was never any of the fairly generous daily ration left.

The dayroom was not a kitchen, simply a food repository and utensil cleaning/storing area. It had a rough counter and cupboard unit running under one louvered opening and along the wall between it and the sluice room next door. There was a sink beneath the window, and a spirit stove on the counter some distance away from the sink. It lacked any sort of device to keep food cold, but there was a wire-mesh meat safe hanging on a rope from the roof joists and dangling in lazy turns like a Chinese lantern.

Tucked in the far corner of the bench was a small spirit-fired sterilizer in which Sister Langtry boiled up her hypodermic equipment and what few instruments she was ever likely to need, in the unlikely event of ever needing them at all. As a matter of good practice she kept two syringes, hypodermic needles, suture needles, a pair of suture needle holders, mosquito forceps and straight forceps permanently sterile in case a patient injured himself, required sedation by injection in a hurry, or was attacked, or attempted suicide. When ward X had first been opened there was heated debate as to whether its patients might be permitted to keep their razors, belts and other potential instruments of destruction, and whether kitchen knives should be kept under lock and key. But in the end it was admitted to be impractical, and only once had a patient availed himself of a suicide tool, luckily unsuccessfully. Violence of one patient toward others had never been sufficiently premeditated to review the decision, for patients who could not be managed under Base Fifteen's conditions did not remain there.

After dark the dayroom was alive with cockroaches; not all the hygiene in the world could eliminate them, for they flew in from outside, crawled up through the drain, dropped from the thatched roof, almost popped into existence out of nothing. If a man saw one he killed it, but there were always others to take its place. Neil was in the habit of organizing a full-scale hunt once a week, in which every man except Matt was expected to bag at least twenty cockroaches, and that probably kept the cockroach population down to something tolerable. However, the dreary little room was always very clean and tidy, so the pickings for scavengers of any kind were scant.

Luce stood in the doorway watching Michael for a few moments, then reached into the pocket of his shorts, withdrew his makings, and began rolling a cigarette. Though Michael was five inches shorter than Luce's six feet two, they looked well matched, each shirtless, broad in chest, wide in shoulders, and flat-bellied.

Turning his head toward the left, Luce saw that the door to Sister Langtry's office opposite the dayroom was firmly closed.

"I never manage to get under your skin, do I?" he asked Michael, tobacco tin back in his pocket and both hands lazily rolling a cylinder out of the shreds he had plucked from it; a little sheet of rice paper dangled from his bottom lip, and fluttered as he talked.

When Michael didn't bother to answer, he repeated it in a tone calculated to make anyone jump: *"I never manage to get under your skin, do I?"*

Michael didn't jump, but he did answer. "Why should you want to?" he asked.

"Because I like getting under people's skins! I like making people squirm. It breaks the God-awful monotony."

"You'd do better to occupy yourself being pleasant and useful." The way Michael said it, there was a vicious bite to it; he still felt Matt's distress.

The half-made cigarette fell unheeded to the floor, the rice paper flew away as he spat it out; Luce crossed the dayroom in one bound and grasped Michael hard about the upper arm, swinging him roughly around.

"Who do you think you are? Don't you *dare* patronize me!"

"That sounds like something you had to spout in a play," said Michael, looking steadily up into Luce's face.

For perhaps a minute they didn't move, simply stared at each other.

Then Luce's hand relaxed, but instead of falling away it cupped itself around Michael's biceps, its fingers caressing the angry marks which were beginning to flare up under the skin he had gripped so hard.

"There's something in you, our Michael, isn't there?" Luce whispered. "Sister's darling little blue-eyed boy and all, there's something in you she wouldn't like one bit. But I know what it is, *and* I know what to do about it."

The voice was insidious, almost hypnotic, and the hand slipped down Michael's forearm, over his fist, gently forcing him to drop the butter knife. Neither man so much as took breath. Then as Luce's head came closer, Michael's lips parted, he hissed an intake of air between clenched teeth, and his eyes blazed into life.

375

They heard the noise simultaneously, and turned. Sister Langtry was standing in the doorway.

Luce's hand dropped from Michael's casually, not too quickly or guiltily, then with the action completed he moved naturally one pace away.

"Aren't you finished yet, Michael?" asked Sister Langtry, voice not quite normal, though the rest of her seemed so, even her eyes.

Michael picked up the butter knife. "Nearly, Sis."

Luce left his side, gave Sister Langtry a wickedly gleeful look as he passed her, and went out. The forgotten cigarette lay on the floor, tendrils and paper moving in a little wind.

Taking a deep breath, Sister Langtry walked into the room, not aware that she was wiping the palms of her hands against her dress, up and down, up and down. She stood where she could see Michael in profile as he began to cut the buttered bread into small segments and pile them on a plate.

"What was all that about?" she asked.

"Nothing." He sounded unconcerned.

"Are you sure?"

"Quite sure, Sis!"

"He wasn't . . . trying to get at you, was he?"

Michael turned away to make the tea; the kettle on the spirit stove was boiling fiercely, adding its steam to an atmosphere already laden. Oh, God, why wouldn't people leave him alone? "Trying to get at me?" he repeated, hoping simple obtuseness would deflect her.

She tried desperately to marshal her thoughts and her emotions into some sort of disciplined order, aware that she had rarely been so upset, so thrown off balance. "Look, Michael," she said, speaking without a tremor, "I'm a big girl now, and I don't like being made to feel like a little girl again. Why do you persist in treating me as if whatever you've got on your mind is too much for me to cope with? I'll ask you again—was Luce making some sort of advance to you? *Was he?*"

Michael tipped a great bubbling stream of water between the kettle and the waiting empty teapot. "No, Sis, honestly he wasn't. He was just doing a Luce." A faint smile turned up the corner of his mouth; he put the kettle down on the stove, turned out the flame, and swung round to face her fully. "It's very simple. Luce was just trying to find a way to get under my skin. That's how he put it himself. But he can't. I've met men like Luce before. No matter how I'm provoked, I'm never going to lose control of myself again." One hand closed into a fist. "I can't! I'm afraid of what I might do."

There was something about him; funny, Luce had used those words, too. Her gaze fixed on his bare shoulder to one side of the fair hair on his chest, not sure if the skin was pearled with sweat or steam. Suddenly she was terrified to meet his eyes, felt light-headed and empty-bellied, as helpless and inadequate as a girl in the grip of her first crush on some remote adult figure.

The color drained from her face, and she swayed. He moved quickly, sure she was going to faint, and put his arm about her waist, supporting her with sufficient strength to remove all sensation of weight from her feet. Nothing else could she feel save his arm and side and shoulder, until, horrified, she felt something surge within herself that squeezed the flesh of her nipples into tight hard tingling ridges and swelled her breasts painfully.

"Oh, God, no!" she cried, wrenching herself away, and turning it like lightning into a protest against Luce by pounding her fist softly on the counter. "He's a menace!" she said through clenched teeth. "He would destroy anything just to watch it twitch."

She was not the only one so affected; Michael's hand when he lifted it to brush the sweat from his face shook, and he half turned away from her, forcing himself to take easy breaths, not trusting himself to look at her.

"There's only one way to deal with Luce," he said, "and that's not to let him get under your skin."

"What he needs is six months on a pick and shovel!"

"I could do with that myself. All of us in X could," he said gently, and found the strength to pick up the tray. "Come on, Sis. You'll feel better after a cuppa."

She managed a travesty of a smile and looked at him, not knowing whether to be ashamed or exalted, and searching his face for something to reassure her. But save for the eyes it was quite impersonal, and the eyes gave nothing away except a high degree of emotional excitement, for the pupils were dilated. Which could as well have been because of Luce.

There was no sign of Luce in the ward, nor on the verandah. The cardplayers abandoned their game somewhat thankfully at sight of the teapot, for its advent had been expected for some time.

"The more I sweat, the more tea I drink," said Neil, draining his mug at a gulp, then holding it out for more.

"Salt tablet time for you, my friend," said Sister Langtry, trying to get the correct degree of cheerfulness and detachment back into her voice.

Neil glanced at her quickly; so did the others.

"Is anything wrong, Sis?" asked Nugget anxiously.

She smiled, shook her head. "A slight attack of the Luces. Where is he?"

"I have a feeling he took himself off in the direction of the beach."

"Before one o'clock? That doesn't sound like Luce."

Nugget grinned, his likeness to a small rodent enhanced by the appearance of two prominent upper incisors. "Did I say he was going swimming? And did I say which beach? He just went for a walk, and if he happens to meet a nice young lady—well, they stop and talk, that's all."

Michael sighed audibly, smiling at Sister Langtry as if to say, See, I told you there was nothing to worry about, and stretched back on the seat as he lifted his arms to put his hands behind his head, the heavily developed pectorals tightening, the hair in his armpits flattened and glistening darkly with sweat.

She felt her color going again, and managed with a huge effort to put her cup down in its saucer without spilling tea. This is ridiculous! she thought, fighting back stubbornly. I am not a schoolgirl! I'm a grown and an experienced woman!

Neil stiffened, reached out his hand to close it over hers reassuringly. "Here, steady on! What's the matter, Sis? A touch of fever?"

She stood up perfectly. "I think it must be. Can you manage if I go off early? Or would you rather I asked Matron for a relief until after lunch?"

Neil accompanied her into the ward while the others sat on at the table looking worried, Michael included.

"For God's sake don't inflict a relief on us!" Neil begged. "We'll go right round the bend if you do. Will you be all right by yourself? It might be better if I walk you to your quarters."

"No, Neil, truly. I doubt if it's anything more than that I just don't feel myself today. The weather, perhaps. It promised to be so cool and dry earlier, but now it feels like a soup tureen. An afternoon's rest should put me right." She parted the fly-curtain and smiled at him over her shoulder. "I'll see you this evening."

"Only if you feel better, Sis. If you don't, don't worry, and no relief, please. The place is as quiet as the grave."

3 Sister Langtry's room was one of a bank of ten similar rooms constructed in typical Base Fifteen style, side by side in a row and fronted by a wide verandah, the whole rickety structure standing ten feet above the ground on piles. For four months she had been the block's only inhabitant, an indication not of antisociality on her part, but of a mature woman's starvation for privacy. Since joining the army in 1940 she had shared accommodation, four to a small tent during her casualty clearing station days. When she had first come to Base Fifteen it had seemed like a paradise, though she had been obliged to share her room, the same she still occupied, and the block had vibrated shrilly with the sounds of women living far too close to each other. Little wonder then that as the nursing staff shrank those left on it put as much space between each other as they could, and wallowed in the luxury of being alone.

Sister Langtry let herself into her room and crossed immediately to the bureau, opened its top drawer and withdrew a bottle of Nembutal grains one and a half. There was a carafe of boiled water lidded with a cheap glass tumbler on top of the bureau; taking the glass off, she poured a little water into it, and swallowed the tablet before she could change her mind. The eyes looking back at her from the corroded depths of the little mirror on the wall above the bureau were dark-ringed and blank; she willed them to remain that way until the Nembutal took effect.

With practiced ease she found and removed the two long grips that fixed her veil in place and lifted the entire edifice off her sweat-lank hair, placing it empty and stiff on a hard chair, where it sat mutely mocking her. She subsided onto the edge of her bed to unlace her daytime duty shoes, put them neatly together far

380

enough away to ensure that she wouldn't kick them getting in and out of bed, then stood up to remove her uniform and underclothes.

A cotton robe of vaguely Oriental design hung on a nail behind the door; she shrugged it on and went to take a shower in the clammy cheerless bathhouse. And finally, skin clean, decently clothed in limp cotton pajamas, she lay down on her bed and closed her eyes. The Nembutal was working, giving her a sensation not unlike that following too much gin, vertiginous and faintly nauseating. But at least it was working. She sighed and struggled to abandon her grasp on consciousness, thinking, Am I in love with him, or does it have a far different name than love? Have I simply been away too long from a normal life, been subjugating my physical feelings too harshly? It could be that. I hope it's that. Not love. Not here. Not with him. To me he doesn't seem the kind of man to esteem love. . . .

The images blurred, rocked, fused; she fell asleep so thankfully that she was able to tell herself it would be paradise never to have to wake up from sleep again, never, never. . . .

4 When she walked up the ramp of X about seven that evening she met Luce just outside the door; he would have nipped by her smartly, but she stepped across his path, looking grim.

"I'd like to see you for a moment, please."

He rolled his eyes. "Oh, Sis, fair go! I've got an appointment!"

"Then break it. Inside, Sergeant."

Luce stood watching her while she removed her slouch hat with its red-striped grey band, hung it where her red cape hung during the day; he liked her better in her night gear, a small soldier all in grey.

Settled behind her desk, she looked up at him to find he was lounging against the wall by the open door, arms folded, ready for a quick getaway.

"Come in, shut the door, and stand to attention, Sergeant," she said curtly, and waited until he complied. Then she continued. "I'd like you to explain to me exactly what was going on in the dayroom this morning between you and Sergeant Wilson."

He shrugged, shook his head. "Nothing, Sis."

"Nothing, *Sister*. It didn't look like nothing to me."

"Then what did it look like?" he asked, still smiling, still, it seemed, more amused at her than perturbed.

"As if you were making some sort of homosexual advance to Sergeant Wilson."

"I was," he said simply.

Taken aback, she had to pause for a moment to search for the next thing to say, which was, "Why?"

"Oh, it was just an experiment, that's all. He's a fairy. I wanted to see what he'd do."

"That's slander, Luce."

He laughed. "Then he can sue me! I tell you he's a great big fairy."

"Which doesn't explain why you were the one making the advance, does it? Leaving Sergeant Wilson out of it, you're not the slightest bit homosexual."

So suddenly the movement made her draw back involuntarily, he slid his hip onto the desk and sat side-on, leaning his face so close to hers that she could see the extraordinary structure of his irises, the multitude of differently colored streaks and flecks which gave them such a chameleon quality; his pupils were slightly enlarged and lustrous with reflections. And her heart took off at a gallop, remembering his effect on her during those first two days in the ward; she felt drowsy, hypnotized, almost bewitched. But what he said next jerked her out of the spell, away from the power.

"Sweetie, I'm *anything*," he said softly. "Anything you like to name! Young, old, male, female—it's all meat to me."

She couldn't prevent the gasp of revulsion. "Stop it! Don't say such things! You're damned!"

His face came even nearer, his clean and healthy smell curled around her. "Come on, Sis, try me! Do you know what your trouble is? You haven't tried anyone. Why don't you start with the best? I'm the best there is, I really am—oh, woman, I can make you shiver and yell your head off and beg for more! You couldn't imagine what I can do to you. Come on, Sis, try me! Just try me! Don't throw yourself away on a queen or a fake Pom who's too tired to get it up any more! Try *me!* I'm the best there is."

"Please go," she said, nostrils pinched.

"I don't usually like kissing people, but I am going to kiss you. Come on, Sis, kiss me!"

There was nowhere to go; the back of her chair was so close to the wall that it barely permitted her room to seat herself. But she pushed the chair back so sharply it whacked against the windowsill behind her, her body reared back in a convulsion of outrage even Luce could not mistake for anything but what it really was.

"Out, Luce! *Immediately!*" She clapped her hand across her

383

mouth as if she was going to be sick, eyes fixed on that fascinating face as if she looked on the devil himself.

"All right, then, throw yourself away," he said, and stood up, plucking and rubbing at his trousers to ease his erection. "What a fool you are! You won't get any joy out of either of them. They're not men. I'm the only man here."

After he had gone she stared at the closed door with rigid attention to its construction until she felt the horror and the fright begin to ebb, and wanted so badly to weep that only a continued inspection of the door prevented the tears from coming. For she had felt the power in him, the will to have what he wanted at any cost. And wondered if that was how Michael had felt in the dayroom, impaled on those staring goatish eyes.

Neil knocked, entered and closed the door, one hand behind his back concealing something. Before he sat down in the visitor's chair he produced his cigarette case and offered it across the desk. It was a part of the ritual that she should make a token demur, but tonight she snatched the cigarette and leaned to have it lit as if she needed it far too badly to remember to demur.

Her boots scraped on the floor as she moved her feet; Neil raised one eyebrow.

"I've never known you to sit down without taking off your boots first, Sis. Are you sure you're fit to be here? Any fever? Headache?"

"No fever or headache, doctor, and I'm quite all right. The boots haven't come off because I caught Luce going out just as I was coming in, and I wanted a word with him. So the boots were rather forgotten."

He got up, came round the desk and knelt in the tiny space to one side of her chair, patting his thigh. "Come on, foot up."

The buckles on her webbing gaiter were stiff; he had to work at them before they came undone, after which he peeled the gaiter off, loosened the laces of her boot enough to lever it off, and rolled her sock up over the trouser bottom. Then he performed the same service for her other foot, sat back on his heels

384

and twisted to look for the pair of rubber-soled canvas shoes she wore in the ward after dark.

"Bottom shelf," she said.

"That's better," he said, the sandshoes laced to his satisfaction. "Comfortable?"

"Yes, thank you."

He returned to his chair. "You still look a bit washed out to me."

She glanced down at her hands, which trembled. "I've got the Joe Blakes!" she said, seeming surprised.

"Why don't you go on sick parade?"

"It's only nerves, Neil."

They smoked in silence, she looking purposely out the window, he looking intently at her. Then, as she turned to stub out her cigarette, he put the piece of paper he had been concealing down on the desk in front of her.

Michael! Just the way she herself saw him, fine and strong, eyes staring up at her so honestly and directly it seemed impossible to believe anything unmanly could ever lurk behind them.

"It's the best one you've done yet; even better than Luce, I think," she said, gazing down greedily at the drawing, and hoping she had not visibly jumped when she saw what he had brought her. Handling it carefully, she gave it back to him. "Would you pin it up for me, please?"

He obliged, fixing it at each corner with a thumbtack, positioning it at the right-hand end of the central row, next to himself. It outshone him, for in trying to depict himself his detachment had failed, and the face on the wall was weak, strained, attenuated.

"We're complete," he said, and sat down again. "Here, have another cigarette."

She took it almost as hastily as she had the first one, drew a deep breath on the smoke, and while exhaling said to him rapidly and artificially, "Michael represents to me the enigma of men," pointing to the new drawing.

"You've got your signals crossed, Sis," Neil said easily, not betraying that he understood how difficult it was for her to broach

385

the subject of Michael, nor betraying his own obsessive preoccupation with the subject of her and Michael. "It's women who are the enigma. Ask anyone from Shakespeare to Shaw."

"Only to men. Shakespeare and Shaw were men. It cuts both ways, you know. The opposite sex is the terra incognita. So every time I think I have men solved, you give some sort of complicated wriggle and you're off again. Swimming in the opposite direction from me." She tapped ash off her cigarette and smiled at him. "I suppose the chief reason why I like running this ward on my own is because it's such an excellent opportunity to study a group of men without other women interfering."

He laughed. "How very clinical! Say it to me, by all means, but don't ever say it to Nugget or he'll come down with a combined case of bubonic plague and anthrax." The expression in her eyes was a little indignant, as if she was about to protest that he misjudged her, but he continued smoothly before she could actually interrupt, wondering if she might yet be deflected by a mildly facetious response. "Men are basically the simplest of creatures. Not quite down to protozoa, perhaps, but certainly not up in the angels-on-a-pinhead class of conundrum."

"Rot! You're a bigger mystery than any number of angels on a pinhead, and far more important! Take Michael—"

No, she couldn't do it. Couldn't bring herself to talk about what had happened between Michael and Luce in the dayroom, though walking from her quarters back to X she had decided Neil might be the only person who could help her. But she suddenly saw how telling him about them would expose herself, and she couldn't do that. And then there was her awful scene with Luce; she'd end in telling him about that as well, and there would be murder done. She closed her mouth, didn't finish the sentence.

"All right, then, let's take Mike," Neil said, as if she had produced a finished statement. "What's so special about our ministering angel Michael? How many of him could we fit on a pinhead?"

"Neil, if you say things that sound like Luce Daggett, I swear I will never speak to you again!"

He was so startled he dropped his cigarette, bent to pick it up and then sat staring at her with suspicion and consternation. "What on earth provoked that?" he asked.

"Oh, drat the wretched man! He rubs off," was all she would say.

"Sis, do you count me your friend? I mean someone really on your side, with you all the way?"

"Of course I do! You don't have to ask me that."

"Is it really Luce who's troubling you, or is it Mike? I've known and suffered Luce for over three months without feeling the way I do at the moment—ever since Michael arrived, as a matter of fact. In just two weeks this place seems to have turned into an unstable boiler. I keep waiting from minute to minute for it to explode, but so far it keeps seething up into the danger zone and flopping again. To wait for something to explode that you know must explode is a most unsettling feeling. Like being back under fire."

"I knew you were a bit down on Michael, but I didn't realize it went so deep," she said, tight-lipped.

"I am not down on Michael! He's a splendid chap. But Michael is the difference. Not Luce. Michael."

"That's ridiculous! How could Michael make everything different? He's so—so quiet!"

Well, here goes nothing, he thought, watching her carefully. Did she know what was happening to her, to him, to all of them?

"Perhaps because *you're* different. Since Michael came," he said steadily. "You must surely realize that we tend to take our moods and attitudes from you, even Luce. And since Michael came you are a very different person—different moods, different attitudes."

Oh, God. Keep your face straight, Sister Langtry, don't let it give away a thing. It didn't; it looked at him with an almost polite interest, smooth and calm and impassive. Behind it her brain raced to cope with all the implications of this interview, and to formulate a behavior pattern which would if not pacify Neil, at least seem logical to him. Given what he knew of her, and he had just made her realize that he knew her better than she suspected. Everything he said was true, but she couldn't admit as much to him; she was too aware of his frailty, his dependence upon her. And damn him for trying to force an issue with her that she hadn't managed to sort out yet in her own mind!

"I'm tired, Neil," she said, her face suddenly showing all the strain of the long, difficult day. "It's just gone on too long. Or I'm proving too weak. I don't know. I wish I did know." She wet her lips. "Don't blame it all on Michael, please. It's far too complicated to deserve a simplification like that. If I'm different, it's because of things inside me. We're coming to an end, something else is about to begin. I think I'm preparing for that, and I think all of you are, too. And I'm so tired. Don't make it any harder, please. Just support me."

Something extraordinary was happening to Neil; he could actually physically feel it while he sat listening to an Honour Langtry who almost admitted defeat. As if in seeing her brought low his own inner resources were growing. As if he fed on her. And that was it, he thought exultantly; she was suddenly as human as he, a person with limits to her energies and endurance, and therefore fallible. To see her thus was to understand his own strengths instead of being forever paled by hers.

"When I first met you," he said slowly, "I thought you were made of solid iron. Everything I didn't have, you had. Lose a few men in a fight? You'd grieve for that, yes, but it wouldn't put you in a place like X. Nothing in the whole wide world could put you in a place like X. And I suppose at the time you were what I needed. If I hadn't needed that, you couldn't have helped, and you did help. Enormously. I don't want you to crack now. I'll do everything in my power to stop you cracking. But it's so nice to feel the balance tip a little bit my way for a change!"

"I understand that," she said, smiling. But then she sighed.

"Oh, Neil . . . I am sorry. I really do feel a bit under the weather, you know. Not that I'm pleading it as an excuse. I'm not. You're quite right about my moods and attitudes. But I can deal with them."

"Just why is Michael in X?" he asked.

"You know better than to ask me that!" she said, astonished. "I can't discuss one patient with another!"

"Unless he's named Benedict or Luce." He shrugged. "Oh, well, it was worth a try. I didn't ask from idle curiosity. He's a dangerous man. He's got so much integrity!" The moment it was out he regretted saying it, not wishing to see her draw away when she had suddenly come so close to him.

However, she didn't recoil or become defensive, though she did get to her feet. "It's high time I put in an appearance on the ward. Which is not a dismissal, Neil. I have too much to thank you for." At the door she stopped to wait for him. "I agree with you, Michael is a dangerous man. But so are you, and so is Luce—and Ben, for that matter. In different ways, perhaps, but yes—you're all dangerous."

5 She left the ward a little earlier than usual that night, declining Neil's offer of an escort, and walked to her room slowly. Awful, not to have anyone to turn to. If she tried to talk to Colonel Chinstrap he'd mark her down for a mental examination herself, while as for Matron . . . There was no one she felt she could turn to, even among her nursing friends, for the dearest of them had gone when Base Fifteen partially closed down.

This had been the most disastrous day of her entire life, a shattering series of encounters which tormented, confused, worried and wearied her. Michael, Luce, Neil and herself, twisting and turning and popping in and out of focus like the images in those fun-parlor mirrors which reduced familiar forms to grotesqueries.

Probably there was a logical explanation for most of what she saw—or thought she saw—in the dayroom. Her instincts about Michael pointed her one way, his conduct in the dayroom and some of his statements to her another. Why hadn't he just shoved Luce away, even knocked him down? Why stand there like a ninny for what seemed like hours, letting that horrible physical presence dominate him? Because the last time he shoved someone away a lethal fight ensued and he wound up in X? That could very possibly be, though she didn't know for sure if that was the way the lethal fight had ensued. His papers weren't specific, and he said nothing. Why did he stand there letting Luce paw him? Surely he could simply have walked out! When he saw her standing watching there had been shame and disgust in his eyes, and after that he closed himself away from her completely. None of it made any sense at all.

The sound of Luce whispering. I'm anything, anything you like to name. . . . Young, old, male, female—

it's all meat to me. . . . I'm the best there is. . . . I'm even a little bit of God. . . . Despite her personal and her nursing experience, it had never occurred to her that people like Luce existed, people who could gear themselves to permit sexual functioning on any level, purely as an expedient. *How* had Luce become what he was? Just to imagine the amount of pain necessary to create a Luce frightened her. He had so much, looks and brains and health and youth. And yet he had nothing, nothing at all. He was an emptiness.

Neil in the driver's seat, wringing admissions out of her she hadn't had time to understand fully herself. In her quite long and close acquaintance with Neil she had never thought of him as an innately strong man, but clearly he was. A hard man. Heaven help you if he didn't love you, or you did something to turn that love back in upon itself. Those gentle blue eyes had gleamed like two chips of lapis.

The shock of her own enormous, involuntary response to Michael, a weakness and a leaping that were there before she even knew. She had never felt like that in her life before, not in the wildest throes of what she had thought a complete love. If Michael had kissed her, she would have dragged him down onto the floor and had him then and there like a bitch on heat. . . .

Once in her room, she looked at the top drawer of the bureau longingly, but made herself leave the bottle of Nembutal untouched. Earlier in the day its employment had been absolutely necessary; she knew that if she spent the afternoon awake, nothing on earth would ever have forced her to go back to X. Shock treatment. But she was over the shock now, even if there had been plenty of fresh ones since. She had done her duty and gone back to X, back to the nightmare X had become.

Neil was right, of course. The change was in her, it was due to Michael, and it was affecting all of them badly. Fool, not to have realized that her presentiment of trouble had nothing to do with the ward or her patients per se; it started and it ended within herself. Therefore it had to stop. It *had* to stop! It had to, it had to, it had to, it had to. . . . Oh, God, I'm mad, I'm as insane as any man who ever passed through X, and where do I go from here? Where, God, where?

There was a stain on the floorboards in the corner where she had once spilled the only container of lighter fluid she owned. At the time it had upset her, she remembered. Now the stain sat there, an unsightly memento of clumsiness.

Sister Langtry fetched a bucket and a brush, got down on her hands and knees and scrubbed the patch until the wood began to look white. Then the rest of the floor seemed dirty by comparison, so she moved on, piece by piece, until all of the floor was wet, clean, bleached. But it had made her feel better. Better than the Nembutal. And she was tired enough to sleep.

6   "I tell you there is something wrong with her!" Nugget insisted, and shivered. "Christ, I feel crook!" He coughed from the bottom of his lungs, hawked, spat with stunning accuracy at a palm trunk over Matt's shoulder.

All six of them were squatting on the beach, naked, formed into a circle; from far enough away they looked like a ring of small standing stones, brown and quiet and put there intentionally at the bidding of some oracle or ritual. It was a perfect day, hovering between warmth and heat, and free from humidity. But in spite of the alluring weather their backs were turned on sea, sand and palms. They were looking inward at themselves.

Sister Langtry was the subject under discussion. Neil had called a council, and they were hard at it. Matt, Benedict and Luce felt that she was physically a bit under the weather but otherwise all right; Nugget and Neil thought something was radically wrong; and Michael, to Neil's fury, kept abstaining every time his opinion was asked.

How many of us are being honest? wondered Neil. We toss our theories back and forth about everything from dermo to malaria to women's troubles as if we really do believe it's only her body ailing. And I for one am not game to suggest a different cause than body. I wish I could crack Michael, but so far I haven't even opened up a cranny. He doesn't love her! I love her, he doesn't. Is that right or fair when she can't see me for him? Why doesn't he love her? I could kill him for what he's doing to her.

The discussion didn't rage, it jerked along punctuated by lengthy silences, for they were all afraid. She mattered so much, and they had never before had occasion

393

to worry about her for any reason. The one unshakable rock in their uncertain sea, to which they had tethered themselves and ridden out their storms to eventual calm. The metaphors were endless: their beacon, their madonna, their rock, their hearth, their succor. For each of them had special memories and concepts of her, special only to himself, an absolutely individual reason for loving her.

To Nugget she was the only person other than his mother who had ever cared enough for him to worry about his precarious health. Transferred from abdominothoracic to ward X amid grateful cheers from the whole crew he was leaving, he was carried out of a busy, smelly, noisy world wherein no one ever had time to listen to him, and so had forced him to keep his voice insistently raised, demanding attention. He was sick, but they just wouldn't believe it. When he arrived in X he had a headache, admittedly not one of his migraines, but a thumping protest against muscular tension which at the time he had felt was just as bad as a migraine in a different way. And she had sat on the side of his bed and listened raptly while he described the exact nature of his pain, interested and concerned for him. The more lyrical he waxed about his pain, the more impressed and sympathetic she became. Cold towels were produced, a battery of little pills of different kinds displayed—and the *bliss* of being able to discuss sensibly with her the problems involved in choosing the most suitable medication for this particular headache as distinct from all the other headaches he had ever had. . . . Of course he knew it was her technique; no fool, Nugget. The diagnosis on his history didn't change, either. But she really did care about him, for she devoted her precious time to him, and that to Nugget was the only criterion for caring. She was so pretty, so complete a person; and yet she always looked at him as if he mattered to her.

Benedict saw her as infinitely superior to all other women, distinguishing as always between women and girls. Females

394

were born one or the other, they didn't change. Girls he found disgusting; they laughed at how he looked, they teased as cruelly and deliberately as cats. Women on the other hand were calm creatures, the guardians of the race, beloved of God. Men might kill and maim and fornicate, girls might tear the world apart, but women were life and light. And Sister Langtry was the most perfect of all women; he never saw her without wanting to wash her feet, die for her if necessary. And he tried never to think of her dirtily, feeling this as a betrayal, but sometimes in his unruly dreams she walked unbidden amid breasts and hairy places, and that alone was more than enough to convince him that he was unworthy to look upon her. He could atone only if he found the answer, and somehow he always felt that God had put Sister Langtry into his life to show him the answer. It still eluded him, but with her he lost his differences, he felt as if he belonged. Michael gave him the same sort of feeling; since Michael's arrival he had come to think of Sister Langtry and Michael as one person, indivisible, surpassingly good and kind.

Whereas the rest of ward X was like the rest of the world, a series of things. Nugget was a weasel, a stoat, a ferret, a rat. He knew it was silly to imagine that were Nugget to grow a beard he would grow rodent whiskers, but he did imagine it, and whenever he saw Nugget in the bathhouse shaving he worried, longed to urge him to borrow a Bengal and shave even closer, because those whiskers were lurking just beneath his skin. Matt was a lump, worry bead, a dull stone, an eyeball, a currant, an octopus turned inside out with all its tentacles chopped off, a single tear, all those round smooth opaque things, for tears were opaque too, they led from nowhere to nowhere. Neil was an old mountainside gouged deep by rain, a fluted column, two boards that fitted tongue in groove, the marks of anguished fingers down a pillar of clay, a sleeping seed pod that could not open, because God had stuck its edges together with celestial glue and was laughing at Neil, laughing! Luce was Benedict, the Benedict God would have fashioned had Benedict been more pleasing to Him; light and life and song. And yet Luce was evil, a treason to

God, an insult to God, an inversion of intent. Luce being so, what did that make Benedict?

Neil was very worried. She was slipping away, and that could not be borne. Not at any price. Not now that he was finally beginning to understand himself, to see how like he was after all to the old man in Melbourne. He was growing in his power and enjoying the process. How odd, that it had taken a Michael to hold up the mirror in which he saw himself properly for the first time. Life could be cruel. To come to know himself through the offices of one who simultaneously was removing the reason why he was so anxious to know all about himself.... Honour Langtry belonged to Neil Parkinson, and he was not going to let her go. There had to be a way to bring her back. There had to be!

To Matt she was a link with home, a voice in the darkness more dear to him than all other voices. He knew he would never physically see his home again, and at night he lay trying to remember what his wife's voice sounded like, the thin bells of his daughters' voices, but he could not. Where Sister Langtry's voice was cemented within the cells of the brain he knew was dying, the only echo which came to him of other times and other places, as if in her they had crystallized. Though his love for her was quite devoid of desire for her body. To him who had never seen her, she had no body. Somehow he didn't have the strength for bodies any longer, not even in his imagination. Meeting Ursula again was a terrifying thought, for he knew she would expect him to summon up a desire he did not have any more. The very idea of groping across and through and down his wife revolted him; like a snail or a python or a drift of seaweed, wrapping himself aimlessly around a chance obstacle. For Ursula belonged to a world he had seen, where Sister Langtry was the light in his darkness. No face, no body. Just the purity of pure light.

Luce was trying not to think of her at all. He could not bear to think of her, because every time she popped into his brain she had that look of nauseated rejection on her face. What on earth was the matter with the woman? Couldn't she just take one look at him and see what he would be like? All he wanted from her was the chance to prove to her what she was missing in ignoring him, and for once he just didn't know how to go about persuading a woman to try. It was usually so easy! He didn't understand. But he hated her. He wanted to pay her back for that look, that disgust, that adamant rejection. So instead of thinking about Langtry he thought about the details of the exquisite revenge he was going to take; and somehow every idea ended in a vision of Langtry kneeling at his feet, admitting she was wrong, begging for another chance with him.

Michael didn't know her yet, but the beginnings of a pleasure in learning to know her were stirring in him, which brought him no pleasure at all. Sex apart, his knowledge of women was extremely limited; the only one he had ever really known well was his mother, and she had died when he was sixteen. Died because apparently she had suddenly decided there was nothing worth living for, and it had been a great blow. He and his father somehow had both felt responsible, yet they genuinely didn't know what they had done to tire her of life. His sister was twelve years older than he, so he didn't know her at all. While he had still been at school it had awed and fascinated him to learn that girls thought him interesting and attractive, but his explorations as a result of discovering this had never been very satisfactory. His girls were always jealous of his lame ducks, and of his tendency to think of his lame ducks first. There had been one fairly long affair with a girl from Maitland, a bodily affair which had consisted only of constant and varied sex. It had pleased him to have it so, for she limited her demands to this, and he felt free of her. The war had broken it up, and very soon after he went to the Middle East she married someone else. When he found out it had not hurt much; he was too busy keeping alive to have time to dwell upon it. The oddest thing was that he didn't seem to miss the sex, felt stronger and more whole without it. Or perhaps he was just lucky enough to be one of those people who could turn sex off. He didn't know, wasn't concerned about, the reason.

His chief feeling for Sister Langtry was liking, nor was he sure just when something more personal and intimate had begun to color his liking. But that morning in the dayroom had come as a shock. Luce playing silly buggers, himself riding an absolute control on anger until the right moment to vent it, a moment in which he knew it could not proceed to that awful hunger to kill. And the moment had come; his mouth was literally open to tell Luce what he could do with himself when she made some sort of noise from the doorway. At first his shame had almost over-whelmed him—what must he and Luce have looked like? How could he possibly explain? So he hadn't even tried to explain. And then he touched her, and something had happened to both of them, something deeper than body yet all wrapped up in body. He knew it had affected her as strongly as it had himself; there were some things which didn't need words or even glances. Oh, God, why couldn't the sister in charge of ward X have been that comfortable middle-aged dragon he imagined be-fore his admission? There was no point to a personal relationship with Sister Langtry, for where could it go? And yet . . . Oh, yes, the thought of it was wonderful. It carried a promise of excite-ment that had little to do with bodies; he had never, he realized, been enchanted by a woman before.

"Look," said Neil, "I think we've got to face one thing. Sis has been on X for a year now, and it seems logical to me that she's tired of Base Fifteen, tired of X, and tired of us. We're all she ever sees. Mike, you're the newest, what do you think?"

"That of all of you, I'm the least qualified to judge, so instead I'll ask Nugget. What do you think?"

"I won't have it!" said Nugget vehemently. "If Sis was fed up with us, I'd be the first to know."

"Not fed up, just tired! There's a difference," said Neil patient-ly. "Aren't we all tired? Why should it be any different for her? Do you really think when she wakes up in the mornings she

398

jumps out of her bed singing a song of joy because in a few minutes she's going to be back in X, back with us? Come on, Mike, I want an opinion from you, not from Nugget or any of the others. You're the newcomer, you're not in so deep you can't see straight any more. Do you reckon she wants to be with us?"

"I don't know, I tell you! Ask Ben," said Michael, and stared at Neil very directly. "You're barking up the wrong tree, mate."

"Sister Langtry is far too good a woman to grow tired of us," said Benedict.

"She's frustrated," said Luce.

Matt chuckled. "Well, X is a frustrating place," he said.

"Not that way, you blinkered dill! I mean she's a woman, and she's not getting any, is she?"

The revulsion stabbed at Luce from all sides, but he endured it as if he enjoyed it, grinning.

"You know, Luce, you're so low you'd have to climb a ladder to reach a snake's belly," said Nugget. "You make me want to puke!"

"Name something that doesn't make you want to puke," said Luce scornfully.

"Be humble, Luce," said Benedict softly. "Be very humble. All men should learn humility before they die, and none of us know when we'll die. It could as easily be tomorrow as fifty years from now."

"Don't you preach at me, spindleshanks!" snarled Luce. "If you go on the way you're going, you'll be in Callan Park a week after you're on Civvy Street."

"You'll never see that," said Benedict.

"My oath I won't! I'll be too busy being famous."

"Not on my money you won't," said Matt. "I wouldn't pay a farthing to watch you pee."

Luce guffawed. "If you can watch me pee, Matt, I'll *give* you the bloody farthing!"

"Neil is right!" said Michael suddenly, very loudly.

The bickering stopped; they all turned their heads to look at

399

him curiously, for the tone of his voice was one they had never heard from him before—full of passion, full of anger, full of authority.

"Of course she's tired, and can you blame her? The same sort of thing day after day, Luce picking on everyone, and everyone picking on Luce. Why the hell can't you lay off each other, and lay off her? Whatever's wrong with her is her business, not yours! If she wanted to make it yours, she'd talk to you about it. Lay off her! You're enough to drive a man to drink!" He got to his feet. "Come on, Ben, into the water. Wash yourself clean. I'm going to try to, but with the amount of crap that's been flying around here, it may take a week."

A tiny chink in his armor at last, thought Neil, but with no exultation, watching Michael and Benedict walk toward the sea. Michael's back was very straight. Dammit, he does care for her! But the thing is, does she know it? I don't think she does, and if I can, I'm going to keep it that way.

"That's the first time I've ever seen you lose your temper," said Benedict to Michael, wading into the water.

Michael stopped, waist deep, and looked at the thin dark worried face with worry written on his own face. "It was a stupid thing to do," he said. "It always is stupid to go off half-cocked. I don't have a hot temper, so I hate it when people drive me to that sort of behavior. It's so useless! That's why I left them. If I'd stayed, I would have made a worse fool of myself."

"You're strong enough to resist temptation," said Benedict wistfully. "I wish I was!"

"Go on, mate, you're the best of the lot of us," said Michael affectionately.

"Do you really think so, Mike? I try so hard, but there's no easy way. I've lost too much."

"You've lost yourself, Ben, nothing else. It's all there, waiting for you to find your way back."

"It's the war. It's made me a murderer. But then I know that's only an excuse. It's not really the war, it's me. I just wasn't strong enough to pass the test God set me."

"No, it's the war," said Michael, hands floating on the water. "It does something to all of us, Ben, not only to you. We're all in X because of what the war's done to us. If it hadn't happened along we'd be all right. They say war's a natural thing, but I can't see it. Maybe it's natural for the race, natural for the old men to start it, but for the men who have to fight it—no, it's the most unnatural life a man can live."

"But God's in there," said Benedict, sinking down until his shoulders were submerged, then bobbing up again. "It must be natural. God sent me to the war. I didn't volunteer to go, because I prayed about it and God told me to wait. If He felt I needed testing, He'd send me. And He did. So it must be natural."

"As natural as birth and marriage," said Michael wryly.

"Are you going to get married?" asked Benedict, his head cocked as if he didn't want to miss the reply.

Michael thought about it; thought of Sister Langtry, well educated, well born, an officer and a gentlewoman. A member of a class he'd had little to do with before the war, and had elected not to join during the war. "No," he said soberly, "I don't think I've got enough to offer any more. I'm just not the way I used to be. Maybe I know too much about myself. To live with a woman and raise children I think you've got to have some illusions about yourself, and I don't have any these days. I've been there and I've come all the way back again, but where I am now isn't where I would have been if there'd been no war. Does that make sense?"

"Oh, yes!" agreed Benedict fervently, to please his friend; for he didn't understand at all.

"I've killed men. I've even tried to kill a compatriot. The old Shalt Nots don't apply the way they did before the war. How could they? I've hosed chunks of men out of bomber turrets because there wasn't enough of them left to pick up for decent burial. I've hunted for meat tickets in blood and offal inches deep, worse messes than any civilian slaughterhouse. I've been so afraid I thought I'd never again be able to move. I've cried a lot. And I think to myself, raise a son of mine to go through that? Not if I was the last man left to repopulate the earth."

"It's the guilt," said Benedict.

"No, it's the grief," said Michael.

7 Since it was well after four o'clock, the sisters' sitting room was very nearly deserted when Sister Langtry walked in. It was a large and airy room, for it had great French doors on either side opening out onto verandahs, and it was screened with mesh, an unbelievable luxury, as was the mess next door. Whatever obscure military planner was responsible for its furnishing must have loved nurses; there were cushions on the cane settees and a brave attempt at cheerfulness through chintz. If the mildew had long since marred the patterns on the chintz and the laundry had managed to reduce color to noncolor, it really didn't matter. In spirit it was a big, cheerful room, and had a corresponding effect on the nurses who used it.

When Sister Langtry came in she saw that its only occupant was Sister Sally Dawkin from neuro, a crusty middle-aged major who was no more a professional army nurse than Sister Langtry was, fat and jolly and chronically overworked, poor soul; neuro was a notoriously hard ward for any nurse to run. In fact, Sister Langtry could think of no more depressing branch of medicine to be in than wartime neuro, with its dismal prognoses and the incredible way its cases sometimes lingered in defiance of all the natural laws governing survival. An arm didn't grow back, but the organism did function without it, mourned its loss yet coped with life in much the same way. Brains and spines never grew back either, but what was missing was not the tool; it was the operator of the tool. Neuro was a place where no matter how religious you might be, you sometimes yearned to be able to reconcile euthanasia with humanitarian ethics.

Sister Langtry knew that she could survive the very worst ward X could ever offer her, where she would never have survived neuro. Sister Dawkin felt the opposite. Which was just as well. Their values and skills were alike excellent, but their preferences were quite different.

"Tea's fresh—well, not bad," said Sister Dawkin, looking up and beaming. "Good to see you, Honour."

Sister Langtry sat down at the small cane table and reached for a clean cup and saucer. She added milk to the cup first, poured in a dark and aromatic stream of tea not quite to the revoltingly stewed stage, then sat back and lit a cigarette.

"You're late, Sally," she said.

Sister Dawkin grunted. "I'm like Moses, always late. You know what the Lord said: Come forth, and Moses came fifth and lost his job."

"You'd have to have half a brain missing to appreciate that joke fully," said Sister Langtry, smiling.

"I know. What can you expect? It's the company I keep." Sister Dawkin bent to unlace her shoes, then hauled her uniform dress up and unhitched her suspenders from her stocking tops. Sister Langtry got a good glimpse of the army-issue bloomers everyone called "passion-killers" before the stockings were peeled off and thrown onto a vacant chair.

"Most of the time, Honour my pet, when I think of you stuck right down at the end of the compound with half a dozen loonies for company and no help, I don't envy you one bit. I much prefer my thirty-odd neuros and a few female cohorts. But today is one of the days when I'd gladly change places with you."

There was an ugly galvanized iron bucket full of water on the floor between Sister Dawkin's feet, which were bare now and revealed as being short, broad, bunioned and minus anything in the way of an instep arch. While Sister Langtry watched, amused and touched, Sister Dawkin plonked both feet into the bucket and slopped and splashed luxuriously.

"Ohhhhhhhhhh, that's so beeeeeee-yew-tiful! Truly, I could not have gone another flipping step on them."

"You've got heat oedema, Sally. Better take some pot cit before it gets any worse," observed Sister Langtry.

"What I need is about eighteen hours flat out in bed with my legs elevated," said the sufferer, and chuckled. "Sounds good when you put it that way, doesn't it?" She withdrew a foot from the bucket and probed with merciless fingers at the puffy red ankle above it. "You're right, they're up like a bishop at a girlie show. I'm not getting any younger, that's my real trouble." The chuckle came again. "Oh, well, it was the bishop's trouble, too."

A solid, well-known tread sounded at the door; in sailed Matron, her starched white veil perfectly formed into a lozenge down her back, her impossibly starched uniform not showing a crease, the glitter from her shoes quite blinding. When she saw the two at the table she smiled frostily and decided to come over.

"Sisters, good afternoon," she boomed.

"Good afternoon, Matron!" they chorused like obedient schoolgirls, Sister Langtry not rising to her feet out of consideration for Sister Dawkin, who could not.

Matron spotted the bucket, and recoiled. "Do you think, Sister Dawkin, that soaking your feet in a public room is quite seemly?"

"I think it all depends on the room and the feet, ma'am. You'll have to forgive me, I came from Moresby to Base Fifteen, and we didn't have many niceties at Moresby." Sister Dawkin hauled one foot out of the bucket and regarded it clinically. "I must agree, it's not a very *seemly* foot. Got bent out of shape in the service of good old Florence Nightingale. But then again," Sister Dawkin went on in exactly the same tone of voice, foot back in the water and splashing merrily, "nor is a grossly understaffed neuro ward quite *seemly*."

Matron stiffened alarmingly, thought better of what she had been about to say because Sister Langtry was there as a witness; she turned sharply on her heel and marched out of the room.

"Old bitch!" said Sister Dawkin. "I'll give her *seemly!* She's been down on me like a ton of bricks all week because I had the temerity to ask her for extra staff in front of a visiting American surgeon general. Well, I'd been asking her in private for days without getting anywhere, so what did I have to lose? I've got

405

four quads, six paras, nine hemis and three comas as well as the rest of the rabble. I tell you, Honour, if it wasn't for the three or four blokes who are compos enough and fit enough to lend us a hand, my ship would have sunk to the bottom a fortnight ago." She blew a very rude-sounding raspberry. "Flipping mosquito nets! I'm just waiting for her to tell me D ward's nets aren't quite *seemly*, because the minute she does, I'm going to wrap one of her precious nets around her neck and strangle her with it!"

"I agree she deserves a lot of things, but strangling? Really, Sally!" said Sister Langtry, enjoying the sparks.

"The old cow! She couldn't hit a bull on the bum with a handful of wheat!"

But the very promising display of Dawkin fireworks fizzled damply the moment Sister Sue Pedder walked through the door. Any further eruptions became impossible. It was one thing to blow one's top comfortably to Honour Langtry, who was if not in the same age group at least a topflight nurse of many years' experience; to Sister Dawkin they were peers. Besides, they had served together from New Guinea to Morotai, and they were friends. Where Sister Pedder was a kid, no older than the AAMWAs who had worked for something like forty-eight hours at a stretch in Moresby. And that was the rub, perhaps. No one could imagine Sister Pedder working for forty-eight hours at a stretch anywhere.

Barely twenty-two, extremely pretty and extremely vivacious, she was in theatres, and had not been on the Base Fifteen staff for very long. It was a current joke that even old Carstairs the urinary surgeon had whinnied and pawed the ground when Sister Pedder waltzed through his theatre door. Several nurses and patients had lost money at that moment, having laid bets that Major Carstairs was really dead but didn't have the grace to lie down.

The nurses left to man Base Fifteen until its extinction were all senior in age and experience, all veterans of jungle warfare and jungle nursing. Except for Sister Pedder, who was not generally regarded as part of the group, and was eyed by some with a great deal of resentment.

"Hello, girls!" said Sister Pedder brightly, coming over. "I must say I don't see much of the ward stars these days. How is life on the wards?"

"A darned sight harder than life in theatres making goo-goo eyes at the surgeons," said Sister Dawkin. "But enjoy it while you can. If I have anything to say about it, you'll be off theatres and on neuro."

"Oh, no!" squeaked Sister Pedder, looking utterly terrified. "I can't stand neuro!"

"Too bloody bad," said Sister Dawkin unsympathetically.

"I can't stand neuro either," said Sister Langtry, trying to make the poor girl feel more at ease. "It takes a strong back, a strong stomach, and a strong mind. I dip out on all three counts myself."

"So do I!" agreed Sister Pedder fervently. She gulped a mouthful of tea, discovered it was tepid and horribly stewed, but swallowed it because there was nothing else to do save swallow it. A rather awkward silence fell, which frightened her almost as much as the thought of being transferred from theatres to neuro.

In desperation she turned to Sister Langtry, who was always very pleasant but standoffish, she thought. "By the way, Honour, I met a patient of yours from X a couple of weeks ago, and discovered I went to school with him. Isn't that amazing?"

Sister Langtry sat up straight and bent a far more searching gaze on Sister Pedder than Sister Pedder considered her statement warranted.

"The bank manager's daughter from Woop-Woop!" she said slowly. "Saints be praised! I've been wondering for days which one of us he could possibly mean, but I forgot all about you."

"*Woop-Woop?*" asked Sister Pedder, affronted. "Well! I know it's not Sydney, but it's not quite Woop-Woop either, you know!"

"Don't get shirty, young Sue; Woop-Woop is just Luce's nickname for his home town," soothed Sister Langtry.

"Oh, Luce Daggett!" said Sister Dawkin, comprehending. She bent a fierce eye on Sister Pedder. "If you're seeing him on the sly, ducky, you'd better wear your tin pants—and don't let him reach for his tin-cutters."

Sister Pedder reddened and bridled; fancy being stuck on neuro with this old dragon! "I assure you that there's no need to be concerned about me," she said haughtily. "I knew Luce when we were both children."

"What was he like, Sue?" asked Sister Langtry.

"Oh, not much different." Sister Pedder began to lose her defensiveness, liking the fact that Sister Langtry was interested in her. "All the girls were crazy about him, he was so handsome. But his mother took in washing, which made it a bit difficult. My parents would have killed me if I'd looked sideways at him, but luckily I was a couple of years younger than Luce, so by the time I got out of the primary school he had already gone to Sydney. We all followed his career, though. I never missed one play he did on radio because our local station used to rebroadcast them. But I missed seeing him when he was in that play at the Royal. Some of the girls went down to Sydney, but my father wouldn't let me."

"What was *his* father like?"

"I really don't remember. He was the stationmaster, but he died not long after the start of the Depression. Luce's mother was very proud, she wouldn't go on the dole. That's why she took in washing."

"Does he have any brothers? Any sisters?"

"No brothers. Two older sisters, very pretty girls. They were the handsomest family in the district, but the girls came to no good. One drinks and the less said about her morals the better, and the other got herself in the family way and still lives with her mother. She kept her baby, a little girl."

"Was he good at school?"

"Awfully clever. They all were."

"Did he get on with his teachers?"

Sister Pedder laughed a little shrilly. "Good lord, no! The teachers all detested him. He was so sarcastic, and yet so slippery they could never manage to pin him down hard enough to have much excuse to punish him. Besides, he had a habit of always getting back at the teachers who did punish him."

"Well, he hasn't changed much," said Sister Langtry.

"He's much handsomer now! I don't think in all my life I've ever seen anyone so handsome," said Sister Pedder, lapsing into a reverie and smiling.

"Oooops! Someone's riding for a fall!" Sister Dawkin chuckled, eyes twinkling, but not unkindly.

"Don't take any notice of her, Sue," Sister Langtry said, trying to keep her source of information in a receptive frame of mind. "Matron's on her back and she's got heat oedema."

Sister Dawkin removed her feet from the bucket and rubbed them sketchily with a towel, then picked up her shoes and stockings.

"There's no need to talk about me as if I wasn't even here," she said. "I am here, all thirteen and a half stone of me. Oh, my feet do feel better! Don't drink the water in the bucket, girls, it's full of Epsom salts. I'm off; I've got time for a quick nap." She pulled a face. "It's those darned boots we have to wear after dark do my feet in."

"Have you elevated the foot of your bed?" called Sister Langtry after her.

"Years ago, love!" came the faint reply. "It's a lot easier to look for the pair of boots that are never there, and I don't mean my own, either!"

This raised a laugh, of course, but after their spurt of amusement died the two sisters left at the table could do no better than an uncomfortable silence.

Sister Langtry sat wondering whether it was advisable to warn Sister Pedder about Luce, or at least make the attempt. In the end she decided that was where her duty lay, and reflected how unpalatable duty often was. She was well aware of the special difficulties young Sister Pedder faced at Base Fifteen, how friendless and isolated she must feel in this nest of senior sisters. There weren't even any AAMWAs for her to mix with. Still, Luce was a definite menace, and Sister Pedder looked ripe, nubile and ready for mischief. And since Luce represented childhood and home town, her guard would be down.

409

"I do hope Luce isn't giving you any trouble, Sue," she said at last. "He can be difficult."

"No!" said Sister Pedder, coming out of her daze with a start.

Sister Langtry picked up her cigarettes and matches and dropped them into the basket at her feet. "Well, I'm sure you've been a nurse long enough to be able to look after yourself. Just remember that Luce is a patient in X because he's a little disturbed. We can handle that, but we can't handle you if it rubs off."

"You make him sound as if he was a leper!" said Sister Pedder indignantly. "After all, there's no disgrace in battle fatigue; it happens to a lot of fine men!"

"Is that what he told you?" asked Sister Langtry.

"Well, it's the truth," said Sister Pedder, with just enough doubt in her voice to make Sister Langtry think something had happened which had given Sister Pedder pause to wonder already. Which was interesting.

"No, it is not the truth. Luce has never been any closer to the front lines than the orderly room of a base ordnance unit."

"Then why is he in X?"

"I don't think I'm at liberty to tell you more than that he displayed some rather disagreeable characteristics which made his COs feel he might be better off in a place like X."

"He *is* strange sometimes," said Sister Pedder, thinking of that hideously passionless, automatic, merciless ramming, and of those savage bites. Her neck had been so deeply bruised, the skin broken in places, that she had thanked her lucky stars for the precious little container of pancake makeup she had bought at the American PX in Port Moresby on her way up here.

"Then take my advice, and don't see Luce any more," said Sister Langtry, picking up her basket and rising to her feet. "Truly, Sue, I'm not coming a matron act at you, and I'm not preaching. I have absolutely no wish to pry into your personal business, but Luce happens to be my business in every way. Steer clear of him."

But that was too much for Sister Pedder to take; she puffed up

410

with indignation, feeling chastised and belittled. "Is that an order?" she asked, white-faced.

Sister Langtry looked surprised, even a little amused. "No. Orders come from Matron."

"Then you can stick your damned advice up your jumper!" said Sister Pedder recklessly, then gasped. The precepts and disciplines of her training were too fresh still for her to be able to say things like that without immediately becoming devastated by her own temerity.

However, her retort fell sadly flat, for Sister Langtry had gone from the room without appearing to hear it.

She sat on for a few moments longer, chewing at her lip until the skin shredded, torn between the huge attraction she had for Luce and the feeling that Luce didn't really care two hoots about her.

FOUR

1   It took almost a week for Sister Langtry's rigidly suppressed feelings of confusion and embarrassment over her weakness in the dayroom to evaporate. Thank God Michael didn't seem to suspect anything, for he was his normal courteous, friendly self at all times. A great salve for her pride, perhaps, but not much help with the pain she suffered in other areas of her being. Still, every day she continued to survive was one day less ward X had to go, one day closer to freedom.

When she walked into the ward one late afternoon about two weeks after the incident in the dayroom, she almost collided with Michael coming out of the sluice room in a hurry, a worn and dented metal bowl in one hand.

"Put a cover over that, please, Michael," she said automatically.

He stopped, torn between the urgency of his mission and her seniority.

"It's for Nugget," he explained. "He's got a terrible headache and he feels sick."

Sister Langtry stepped around him and reached one hand into the sluice room, where some drab but clean cloths sat on the shelf just inside the door. She took the bowl from Michael and draped a cloth over it.

"Then Nugget's got a migraine," she said calmly. "He doesn't get them very often, but when he does he's quite prostrated, the poor little chap."

She walked into the ward, took one look at Nugget lying very still on his bed, a cool damp cloth over his eyes, and drew up a hard chair noiselessly to the side of his bed.

"Is there anything I can do, Nugget?" she asked him softly, putting the bowl down very quietly on his locker.

415

His lips barely moved. "No, Sis."

"How long to go?"

"Hours yet," he whispered, two tears trickling from under the cloth. "It's just come on."

She didn't touch him. "Don't worry, just lie quiet. I'll be here to keep an eye on you."

She remained sitting beside him for perhaps another minute, then got up and went into her office.

Michael was waiting there, looking anxious. "Are you sure he's all right, Sis? I've never seen Nugget lie so still! He hasn't even squeaked."

She laughed. "He's all right! It's just an honest-to-goodness migraine, that's all. The pain is so acute he doesn't dare move or make a noise."

"Isn't there something you could give him?" Michael demanded, impatient at her callousness. "How about some morphine? That always does the trick."

"Not for migraine," she said positively.

"So there's nothing you're prepared to do."

His tone annoyed her. "Nugget is in no danger whatsoever. He's simply feeling ghastly. In about six hours he'll vomit, and that will relieve the worst of his pain immediately. Believe me, I'm very sorry for what he's going through, but I do not intend to run the risk of making him dependent upon drugs like morphine! You've been here quite long enough to understand what Nugget's real trouble is, so why are you making me out to be the villain of the piece? I'm not infallible by any means, but I do not appreciate being told my business by patients!"

He laughed heartily, putting his hand out to grip her arm and giving it a friendly little shake. "Good for you, Sis!" he said, grey eyes alight with more than warmth.

Her own eyes lit up; she was consumed by an enormous rush of gratitude. There could be no mistaking the way he was now looking at her. In that moment all her doubts were resolved; she knew she loved him. No more misery, no more self-examination.

She loved him, and it felt like the end of a journey she had not wanted to make.

He searched her face, then his lips parted to speak; dumb with longing, she waited. But he didn't speak. She could literally see his mind working, watched the love driven out by . . . fright? Caution? The grip on her arm changed its quality, from a caress to a merely friendly touch again.

"I'll see you later," he said, and walked out the door.

Luce didn't even give her the time to think about it; she was still standing numbed when he walked in.

"I want a word with you, Sis, and I want it now," he said, white-faced.

She moistened her lips. "Certainly," she managed to say, and put Michael out of her mind.

Luce advanced until he stood before her desk; she went to her chair and sat down.

"I've got a bone to pick with you."

"Sit down, then," she said calmly.

"It's not going to take long enough, pet," he said, lips lifted back from his teeth. "Why did you queer my pitch with little Miss Woop-Woop?"

Sister Langtry's eyes opened wide. *"Did I?"*

"You know bloody well you did! Everything was coming along beautifully, and now suddenly out of the blue she starts telling me that it isn't proper for her to associate with the likes of Sergeant Luce Daggett, because your talk with her made her see a lot of things she didn't see before."

"Nor is it proper for the two of you to associate in a clandestine manner," said Sister Langtry. "Officers do not engage in intimate relationships with men from the ranks."

"Oh, come off it, Sis! You know as well as I do that those rules are broken every night in this bloody place! Who else is there except men from the ranks? The MOs? There's not an MO in Base Fifteen who could get it up for Betty Grable! The officer patients?

417

The only ones left are crocks who couldn't get it up for the Virgin Mary!"

"If you must be cheap and vulgar, Luce, you might at least refrain from blasphemy!" she snapped, her face set, her eyes hard.

"But it's a cheap and vulgar subject, sweetie, and I feel like doing a lot worse than blaspheming. What a prissy old maid you are! No gossip in the mess about Sister Langtry, is there?"

He leaned forward across the desk, hands on its edge, his face looming within inches of her own, as it had loomed once before, but with a far different expression now.

"Let me tell you something! Don't you ever dare to interfere with me, or I'll make you wish you'd never been born! Do you hear? I was enjoying little Miss Woop-Woop in more ways than you'll ever know, you dried-up scrubber!"

The epithet penetrated where he could not be sure that anything else he said did; he saw her flare of pain and outrage, and pressed home this unexpected advantage with all the venom he could summon.

"You really are dried up, aren't you?" he drawled. "You're not a woman, you're just an apology for one. There you are, dying to go to bed with Mike, yet you can't even treat the poor coot like a man! Anyone would think he was your pet dog. Here, Mike, heel, Mike! Do you really think you'll get him to sit and beg for it? He's not interested enough, sweetie."

"You can't make me lose my temper, Luce," she said, coldly and slowly. "I prefer to treat your personal aspersions as not made at all. No exercise in the world is as futile as a post-mortem, and that's what this is, a post-mortem. If Sister Pedder has thought better of her association with you, I'm glad for both your sakes, but especially for hers. Ranting at me is not going to change how Sister Pedder feels."

"You're not an iceberg, Sister Langtry, because ice melts. You're stone! But I'm going to find a way to pay you back. Oh, yes I am! *I* am going to make you weep tears of blood!"

"What idiotic melodrama!" she said contemptuously. "I'm not

418

frightened of you, Luce. Disgusted and sickened by you, yes. But not frightened. Nor can you bluff me the way you do the others. I see through you; I always have seen through you. You're nothing but a petty little confidence trickster!"

"But I'm not bluffing," he said airily, straightening. "You'll see! I've found something you think belongs to you, and I'm going to take great pleasure in destroying it."

Michael. Her and Michael. But Luce couldn't even begin to destroy that. Only Michael could. Or she could.

"Oh, go away, Luce!" she said. "Just go away! You're wasting my time."

"The dirty bitch!" Luce said, looking at his curled hands as if they astonished him, looking at the bed where Benedict sat hunched apathetically, looking at the ward crowding in around him. "The dirty bitch!" he said again more loudly, straight at Ben. "Do you know who I'm talking about, you barmy fucker— do you? Your precious Langtry, the dirty bitch!" He was beside himself, too obsessed by his own hatred to remember that Ben was not a man he usually provoked. He just wanted to lash out at anyone, and Ben was the only one around. "You think she cares about you, don't you?" he asked. "Well, she doesn't! She doesn't care about anyone except Sergeant bloody hero Wilson! Isn't that a laugh? Langtry in love with a shirt-lifting pansy!"

Ben came slowly to his feet. "Don't say it, Luce. Keep your filthy tongue off her and Mike." His tone was gentle.

"Oh, come off it, you stupid drongo! What do I need to do to show you? Langtry's nothing but a silly old maid in love with the biggest queen in the A.I.F.!" He moved across the space between his own bed and Benedict's with a slow, sideways gait that made him look immense and powerful. "A queen, Ben! That's Mike I'm talking about!"

The rage was gathering in Benedict, and in rage he grew too, his dark dour face sloughing its layers of dejection and apology off until something deeper and more appalling began to show like bones at the bottom of a wound. "Lay off them, Luce,"

419

he said calmly. "You don't even know what you're talking about."

"Oh, but I do, Ben! I do! I read it in his papers! Your darling Mike's a queen!"

Two small bubbles puffed out at the corners of Ben's mouth, thick and glistening. He began to tremble, a quick, minute shaking. "You're a liar."

"Why should I lie? It's all there in his papers—he buggered the arses off half his battalion!" Luce stepped back a pace hastily, deciding that he didn't want to be too close to Ben. "If Mike's a queen," he taunted, unable to stop himself, "what does that make you?"

A thin, wailing scream came ripping out of Benedict, a very quiet scream, but before his tensed muscles could react in the violence that leaped ahead of his body like a great shadow, Luce began to emit a staccato series of noises which sounded eerily like the chattering of a submachine gun. Benedict jerked and recoiled, his whole body jumping in time to the volley.

"Ah-ah-ah-ah-ah-ah-ah-ah-ah! Remember that, old son? Of course you do! That's the sound of your gun killing all those innocent people! Think of them, Ben! Dozens of them, women and children and old men, all dead! You murdered them in cold blood just so you could come to X and crawl to scum like Mike Wilson!"

His rage drowned in another, greater torment, Benedict subsided onto the bed, head back, eyes closed, tears flooding down his face, a human vacuum of despair.

"Get out of here, Luce!" said Matt's voice from behind Luce's shoulder.

Luce jumped, but as he remembered that Matt couldn't see, he turned, wiping the sweat from his face. "Go to hell!" he said, as he pushed roughly past Matt and plucked his hat off his bed. He put the hat on his head with a nonchalant air and walked away down the ward to the front door.

Matt had heard most of it, but until he judged the imminence of physical violence to be past he hadn't had the courage to interfere, thinking that he could well make matters worse by floundering between them, and knowing Ben would be more than a match for Luce—hoping for it, too.

He groped for the end of Benedict's bed, found it, sat down and slid up until his questing hands encountered an arm. He sighed. "It's all right, Ben," he said gently, feeling the tears and through them the face. "Come on now, it's all right. The bastard's gone, and he won't worry you again. Poor old bloke!"

But Benedict didn't seem to hear; his tears were drying, his arms were wrapped about his body, and he rocked back and forth on the bed.

The scene in the ward had gone undetected by all save Matt because Nugget was beyond caring, Michael had slipped across to the nearest inhabited ward to borrow some powdered milk, and Neil had invaded Sister Langtry's office almost as Luce slammed out of it. He discovered Sister Langtry sitting with her face buried in her hands.

"What is it? What's the bastard done to you?"

She removed her hands immediately, to reveal neither tears nor ravages. Just a very calm, composed countenance.

"He didn't do anything," she said.

"He must have! I could hear him all the way down into the ward."

"Histrionics, that's all. He is an actor. No, he was letting off steam because I put the kybosh on a little romance he was having with one of the sisters. The girl from Woop-Woop, the bank manager's daughter, remember?"

"I remember vividly," he said, sitting down and breathing easier. "That remains the only occasion on which I have ever found myself in danger of liking Luce."

Out came his cigarettes; she took one greedily, drew in the smoke greedily.

"His interest in the girl is vindictive, of course," she said, exhaling. "I realized that the moment I found out what was going on. I don't suppose she ever figured personally in his fantasies, but when she popped up here in the flesh, he soon saw how he could use her."

"Oh, yes," said Neil, shutting his eyes. "Lucius Ingham the famous stage actor and Rhett Ingham the famous Hollywood film star, thumbing his nose at the inhabitants of Woop-Woop."

"I gather Sister Woop-Woop fancied Luce when they were children, but I'll bet she was far too stuck-up to let the washer-woman's son know she fancied him. And a bit too young to take his fancy then. So to compromise her now is doing wonderful things for him."

"Naturally." Neil opened his eyes to look at her intently. "I take it he wasn't pleased at being foiled?"

She laughed shortly. "That's a fair assessment."

"I thought it might be. I couldn't hear what he was saying, but I did hear the tone of his voice." He studied the tip of his cigarette. "I would venture to say that our Luce is pretty angry about it. Did he threaten you?"

"Not specifically. He was far more concerned with telling me all about my shortcomings as a woman." Her face screwed up in disgust. "Pah! Anyway, I simply let him see that I thought he was talking nonsense."

"No threats, though?" Neil persisted.

She sounded tired of being quizzed as she said impatiently, "What could Luce do to me, Neil? Assault me? Kill me? Come off it! That sort of thing happens in fiction, not in life. There's no sort of opportunity. Besides, you know nothing's more important to Luce than the safety of his own skin. He won't do anything he might be punished for. He just spreads those dark wings of his over our heads and lets our own imaginations do his dirty work for him. Only I don't fall for his tricks."

"I hope you're right, Sis."

"Neil, while ever I sit in this chair I *cannot* let any patient frighten me," she said very seriously.

He shrugged, prepared to let it go. "I shall now change the subject with typical Parkinsonian lightness, and inform you that I heard a rumor today. Well, more fact than a rumor, I suppose."

"Thank you so much," she said sincerely. "What rumor?"

"The place is on the skids at last."

"Now where did you hear that? It hasn't reached any of the nurses yet."

"From dear old Colonel Chinstrap himself." He grinned. "I happened to be passing his quarters this afternoon, and there he was on his balcony like Juliet after a visit from Romeo, ecstatic at the thought of going back to Macquarie Street. He invited me up for a drink, and told me, one officer and gentleman to another, that we have probably less than a month to go. The CO heard from Div HQ this morning."

Her face showed a dismay Luce had not been able to bring to it. "Oh, God! Only a month?"

"Give or take a week. We'll just squeak out ahead of the Wet as it is." He frowned at her, perplexed. "You stump me, you really do. The last time we had a serious heart-to-heart, you sat there looking like death warmed up wondering how you were going to get through to the end. Now you look like death warmed up because the end's definitely in sight."

"I wasn't well then," she said stiffly.

"If you ask me, I don't think you're well now."

"You don't understand. I shall miss ward X."

"Even Luce?"

"Even Luce. If it were not for Luce, I wouldn't know the rest of you half so well." She smiled wryly. "Or know myself for that matter."

Michael knocked on the door and poked his head around it. "I hope I'm not interrupting, Sis—tea's made."

"Did you manage to get milk?"

"No trouble."

She got to her feet immediately, relieved to be able to break off her conversation with Neil so naturally. "Come on, then, Neil. Grab the bikkies, would you? You're closer to them than I am."

Waiting until Neil found the biscuit tin, she stood back to let him precede her out the door, then followed the two men into the ward.

2   By Nugget's bed she signalled Neil and Michael to go on without her, and slipped behind the screen someone had put around his bed. He lay without moving and did not acknowledge her presence, so she merely changed the cloth over his eyes for a fresh one before leaving him in peace.

At the refectory table she discovered Luce was missing, looked at her watch and was surprised to find it much later than she had thought.

"If Luce isn't careful he's going to blot his copybook at last. Does anyone know where he is?" she asked.

"He went out," said Matt brusquely.

"He lied," said Benedict, rocking back and forth.

Sister Langtry looked at him closely; he seemed odder, more enclosed, and the rocking was something new.

"Are you all right, Ben?"

"All right. No, all wrong. It's all wrong. He lied. There's an adder in his tongue."

Sister Langtry's eyes met Michael's; she lifted one eyebrow in a mute query, but he, as puzzled as she, shook his head quickly. Neil was frowning, mystified too.

"What's all wrong, Ben?" she asked.

"All of it. Lies. He sold his soul a long time ago."

Neil leaned across to pat the thin bowed shoulder near him reassuringly. "Don't let Luce worry you, Ben!"

"He's *evil!*"

"Have you been crying, Ben?" asked Michael, sitting down next to him.

"He was talking about you, Mike. Dirty talk."

"There's nothing dirty about me, Ben, so why let it bother you?" Michael got up to fetch the chess set, and began to lay it out on the table.

"I'll be black tonight," he said.

424

"*I* am black."

"All right, then, I'll be white and you can be black. My advantage," said Michael cheerfully.

Benedict's face twisted, his eyes closed, his head reared back and tears began to catch the light between his lashes. "Oh, Mike, I didn't know there were any children there!" he cried.

Michael paid no attention. Instead, he moved his king's pawn two squares forward, and simply sat waiting. After a moment Benedict's eyes opened, saw the move through a wall of tears; he duplicated it quickly, snuffling like a child, wiping his nose on the side of his hand. Michael advanced his queen's pawn to stand alongside the king's pawn, and again Benedict duplicated the move, his tears beginning to dry. And when Michael lifted his king's knight over the pawn in front of it and set it down ahead of his king's bishop, Benedict chuckled, shaking his head.

"You never learn, do you?" he asked, toying tenderly with a bishop.

Sister Langtry heaved an enormous sigh of relief and got up, smiling a good night to everyone before leaving. Neil also got up, but walked around the table to where Matt was sitting, quite forgotten in the little crisis.

"Come and have a talk with me in my room," Neil said, touching him lightly on the arm. "Colonel Chinstrap gave me something this afternoon I'd like to share with you. It's got a black label, just like Luce, but inside—ah! It's pure, unadulterated gold."

Matt looked bewildered. "Isn't it lights out?"

"Officially I suppose it is, but we all seem to be a bit wound up tonight, which is probably why Sis has gone off duty without tucking us up. Besides, Ben and Mike look settled to chess. And don't forget Nugget—if we do get to sleep before he heaves up his guts, he'll only wake us."

Matt's movements as he got up seemed a little fumbling, but he was smiling with keen pleasure. "I'd love to come and talk. And solve your riddle. What's labelled black yet inside is pure gold?"

Neil's cubicle was just that, a space six feet wide by eight feet long, into which he had managed to jam a bed, a table and one hard chair, besides several shelves nailed rather precariously to the walls where he wasn't likely to stand up and hit his head on them. It was littered with painter's impedimenta, though someone in the know would have seen immediately that he had limited his techniques to less permanent and messy media than oil. Pencils, papers, charcoal, brushes, jars of dirty water, tins of children's watercolors, tubes of poster color, crayons and pastels. There was absolutely no order in the chaos; Sister Langtry had given up long ago trying to make him keep the cubicle tidy, and merely bore with fatalistic calm Matron's endless strictures about the state of Captain Parkinson's room. Luckily he could when he wanted charm the birds out of the trees, even, as he said most disrespectfully, a silly old chook like Matron.

The perfect host, he got Matt settled comfortably on the bed and swept various bits and pieces off the hard chair onto the floor before seating himself on it. There were two small tooth tumblers and two bottles of Johnnie Walker black label Scotch whisky sitting on the end of the table. Neil slit the seal and prized the cork carefully out of one bottle, then poured a generous measure into each glass.

"Cheers!" he said, and drank deeply.

"Mud in your eye," said Matt, and did the same.

They gasped rather like two swimmers coming up after a dive into unexpectedly frigid water.

"I've been a sober man too long," Neil said, his eyes watering. "God, this stuff packs a punch, doesn't it?"

"It tastes like heaven," said Matt, and drank again.

They paused to breathe deeply and savor the effect.

"Something must have happened tonight to push Ben off the deep end," said Neil. "Do you know anything?"

"It was Luce, chattering like a machine gun and taunting Ben with killing civilians. Poor old Ben burst out crying. Bloody Luce! He told me to go to hell and pushed off out somewhere. I think that man's possessed."

"Or else he really is the devil," said Neil.

"Oh, he's flesh and blood, all right."

"He wants to be mighty careful, then. Otherwise, one of us might put his mortality to the test."

Matt laughed, holding out his glass. "I'll volunteer."

Neil refilled the glass, then refilled his own. "God, how I needed this! Colonel Chinstrap must be a mind reader."

"Did he really give it to you? I thought you were joking."

"No, it came from him in person."

"What on earth for?"

"Oh, I expect it's a part of his ill-gotten hoard, and he worked out how much he can get through himself before Base Fifteen folds up. Then he decided to be Father Christmas and give the surplus away."

Matt's hand trembled. "We're going home?"

Cursing the loosening effect of the whisky on his tongue, Neil looked at Matt gently, but of course all the gentle looks in the world couldn't penetrate blindness, real or imagined. "About a month to go, old son."

"So soon? She'll know!"

"Sooner or later she has to know."

"I thought I'd have a bit more time than that."

"Oh, Matt . . . She'll understand."

"Will she? Neil, I don't want her any more! I can't even think of that any more! She's been waiting to have her husband back, and what's she going to get? Not a husband."

"You can't say that from where you're sitting now. Try not to cross your bridges—you don't know what's going to happen. But the more you stew about it, the worse it will be."

Matt sighed, tipped up his glass. "I'm glad you had this stuff on hand. It's like an anaesthetic."

Neil changed the subject. "Luce must have been in the foul mood to end all foul moods tonight. He had a go at Sis before he had a go at Ben," he said.

"I know."

"Did you hear it too?"

"I heard what he said to Ben."

427

"You mean there was more to it than the machine gun?"

"A lot more. He came raving out of Sis's office and went for Ben because Ben objected to the things he was calling Sis. But what got Ben so upset was what he said about Mike."

Neil's head turned; he looked at Matt as if at something precious. "What exactly did he say about Mike?"

"Oh, that he was a queen. Did you ever hear anything so silly? He kept telling Ben he'd read it in Mike's papers."

"The bastard!" Oh, sometimes fate was kind! Handed all this, and by a blind man, a man who couldn't see how he looked, what effect the news had.... "Here, Matt, have some more."

The whisky went very quickly to Matt's head, or at least so Neil thought until he looked at his watch and saw it was well past eleven. He got up, draped Matt's arm about his shoulders and hoisted him to his feet, feeling none too steady on his own.

"Come on, old son, time you were in bed."

Benedict and Michael were putting the chess set away; Michael came quickly to help Neil, and together they stripped Matt of his trousers, shirt, singlet and underpants, then tipped him into bed, for once without his pajamas.

"Out to it," said Michael, smiling.

And looking at that calm, immensely strong face, knowing what he was going to do to blight it, Neil suddenly loved it clear through to his whisky-maudlined soul; he put his arms around Michael's neck and his head on Michael's shoulder, close to tears.

"Come and have a drink," he said sadly. "You and Ben come and have a drink with an old man. If you don't I'm going to cry, because I'm my old man's son. If I start thinking about you and him and her I'm going to cry. Come and have a drink."

"We can't have you crying," said Michael, disentangling himself. "Here, Ben, we've got an invitation."

Benedict had finished stowing the chess set in the ward cupboard, and came across. Neil reached out an arm and hung onto him.

"Come and have a drink," he said. "There's a bottle and a half left. I'm going to stop, but I can't leave all that lovely grog there undrunk, can I?"

Benedict drew back. "I don't drink," he said.

"It'll do you good tonight," said Michael firmly. "Come on now, none of that holier than thou crap."

So all together they walked across the ward, Michael and Benedict supporting Neil between them. At the corridor junction Michael reached up to switch off the light above the refectory table. There was a discordant rattle from the fly-curtain inside the front door as Luce came in, not stealthily but defiantly, as if he expected Sister Langtry to be lying in wait for him.

The three men stood looking at him, and he at them. Michael cursed Neil's dead weight between him and Benedict, worried that Luce's sudden appearance would start Ben off again. But at that moment Nugget managed to terminate his headache by vomiting.

"Oh, God, what a revolting noise!" said Neil, coming to life immediately.

He pushed Benedict and Michael through into his cubicle, went in after them, and shut the door firmly.

3 Luce continued toward his bed without another glance in the direction of the cubicle; he was alone in the ward in the soft dimness, with only a hideous retching sound for company.

So tired he could hardly move, he sat down on the edge of his bed; he had walked for hours up and down the paths of Base Fifteen, along the beaches, through the pallid groves of coconut palms. Thinking, thinking. . . . Wanting with a blind ferocity to lash out at Langtry until her head went rolling away as free as a football. The stuck-up bitch! Luce Daggett wasn't good enough, and then she'd had the hide to compound the insult by throwing herself away on a shirt-lifting pansy. She was mad. If she'd picked him she could have led the life of a princess, for he knew he was going to be rich and famous, a bigger star than Clark Gable and Gary Cooper combined. You couldn't want something as much as he wanted that and not get it. She'd said that, too. Every single minute of every single hour of every single day since before he left Woop-Woop had been directed toward hitting the big time as an actor.

On the day he arrived in Sydney, a half-grown lad of almost fifteen, he already knew that acting was his ticket to the big time. And he already hungered for the big time. He had never seen a play nor been to the moving pictures, but he had been listening for most of his school days to the adoring chatter of the girls about this actor and that actor, and fended off their suggestions that he should try to get into pictures when he grew up. Let them mind their own business; he'd do it his way and not have any idiot female walking around boasting that she'd pushed him into it, that it was all her brilliant idea.

He went to work as a storeman in a dry goods warehouse down on Day Street, filching the job right out from under the noses of several hundred men who had also applied. The manager had not been able to resist the lad with the beautiful hair and the amazing bright face, the quick mind to back them up. And the lad turned out to be a very good worker, too.

It hadn't taken Luce long to discover where and how to break into the acting profession, and he was working, therefore he was eating, so he grew quickly, filled out and soon looked older than his age. He sat around in Repins drinking innumerable cups of coffee, hung around Doris Fitton at the Independent Theatre, made his face known to the Genesians, and finally began to get small parts in radio plays at 2GB and the ABC, even a few one-liners at 2CH. He had a wonderful voice for radio, nonsibilant, the right timbre, and a quick ear for accents, so that by the time he had been six months moving in the right circles he had polished the Australian from his voice unless it was required.

Envying the people who could afford to finish high school and go on to university, he educated himself as best he could by reading everything people recommended, though his pride would not permit him to ask outright what he should read; he would winkle the information out of his friends very cleverly, then go to the library.

By the time he was eighteen he was earning enough from small radio jobs to be able to quit his warehouse employment. He found a little room for rent on Hunter Street, and did it up as artfully as he could by lining the walls with solid books, only he didn't tell anyone that the books were job lots purchased at Paddy's Markets for as little as threepence the dozen, as much as two and eightpence for a leather-bound set of Dickens.

As an escort he was a notorious nipfarthing—the girls soon learned that if Luce took them out, they paid. And after thinking it over, most of them decided to continue to pay quite cheerfully for the privilege of being seen out with a man who could literally turn all heads in a room. It was not long, of course, before he discovered the world of older women, women who liked nothing better than to foot his bills in return for the pleasure of his company in public, his penis in private.

At this time he began to train himself sexually, so that no matter how uninspiring, offputting or downright ugly the lady was who took him into her bed, he could rise to the occasion most satisfactorily. Simultaneously he developed a line of lover's small talk which charmed them into overestimating their desirability. And the presents flowed in, suits and shoes, hats and coats, cuff links and watches, ties and shirts and hand-made underwear. It worried him not at all to be the recipient of such largesse, for he knew he paid in full.

Nor did it worry him when he learned there were plenty of older men willing to indulge him financially in return for his sexual favors, and in time he came to prefer older men to older women; they were more honest about their needs and their monetary obligations, nor did he have to weary himself to distraction perpetually reassuring them that they were still beautiful, still desirable. Older men had better taste, too; from them he discovered how to dress superlatively well, how to conduct himself like an aristocrat at everything from a cocktail party to a ministerial banquet, and how to sniff out the best people.

After several small parts in small plays put on at small theatres, he auditioned for the Royal, and almost got the part. The second time he auditioned for the Royal he did get the part, a significant role in a straight drama. The critics treated him kindly, and he knew as he read the notices that he was really on his way at last.

But the year was 1942, he was twenty-one, and he was conscripted into the army. His life from then until now he regarded as useless, an utterly wasteful blank. Oh, it had been easy enough; it hadn't taken him long to learn how to get comfortable, nor to find the perfect fool to fool, an elderly career army officer who was more a spiritual than a practicing homosexual— until he met Luce, his new assistant. This man had fallen violently, pathetically in love, and Luce had used his love with total calculation. The affair lasted until the middle of 1945, when Luce, bored and restless because he knew the war was ending, ended the relationship in a diatribe of scathing, contemptuous repudiation. There was a suicide attempt, a scandal, and serious discrepancies in the accounting of moneys and equipment which had passed through their office. The investigation panel soon got Luce's measure, in particular his capacity for wreaking havoc, and dealt with him very simply. They sent him to ward X. And in ward X he remained.

But not for much longer, he told himself.

"Not for much longer!" he said to the darkness of the ward.

A friendly MP had stopped him on his peregrinations around Base Fifteen, and told him that the hospital would soon be no more. He had retired to the MP's doghouse and split a bottle of beer with him, toasting the news with light heart. But now that he was back inside ward X he knew postwar dreams could wait. First things first. And the first thing was fixing Langtry.

4 True to his word, Neil poured no more whisky for himself, but filled the two tumblers and gave one to Benedict, one to Michael.

"God, I'm turpsed to the eyeballs," he said, blinking. "My head's going round like a top. Stupid bloody thing to do. It's going to take me hours to get myself together."

Michael rolled his first sip around his tongue. "It is strong, all right. Funny, I never did like whisky."

Benedict seemed to have overcome his initial reluctance very well, for he polished off his first glass fairly quickly, and held it out for more. Neil obliged, feeling it would do the poor coot good.

Luce was a proper bastard. But wasn't it odd the way desired information arrived after one had despaired of ever getting it? In a roundabout way, what he needed to know about Michael had come from Luce. He forced his eyes to focus on Michael's face, trying to see in it any trace of what Luce had maintained. Well, anything was possible, of course. For himself, that particular answer to the riddle would never have come. He didn't really believe it, no matter what Michael's papers said. They always, always gave themselves away; they had to give themselves away or they'd never get any, and Michael he was sure had nothing to give away. But Sis knew what was in those papers, and she wasn't nearly as experienced as men who had spent most of six long years almost exclusively in the company of other men. Did Sis have her doubts about Michael? Of course she did! She wouldn't be human if she didn't and of late she hadn't been very sure of anything within herself. Nothing had happened between her and Michael—yet. So he still had time.

"Do you think," he said, speaking laboriously but

quite distinctly, "that Sis knows we're all in love with her?"

Benedict looked up, glassy-eyed. "Not *in* love, Neil! Just love. Love and love and more love. . . ."

"Well, she's the first woman any of us have known as a part of our lives for a long time," said Michael. "It would be strange if we didn't all love her. She's very lovable."

"Do you think she's lovable, Mike? Really?"

"Yes."

"I don't know. Lovable seems the wrong word. I always think of lovable as . . . cuddly. Snub noses and freckles and a charming giggle. The sort of thing you see right off. But she's not like that at all. When you meet her she's all starch and steel, and she's got a tongue like an upper-crust fishwife. She's not pretty. Fantastically attractive, but not pretty. No, I wouldn't have said lovable was the right word at all."

Michael put his glass down and thought about it, then smiled and shook his head. "If that's how you saw her, Neil, you must have been a very sick man. I thought she was dinky. She made me want to laugh—not at her, because of her. No, I didn't see the starch and the steel at all, not at first. I do now. To me she was lovable."

"Is she still lovable?"

"I said so, didn't I?"

"Do you think she knows we're all in love with her?"

"Not the way you mean," Michael said steadily. "She's a dedicated person who hasn't lived her life dreaming about love. She hasn't got a schoolgirl mentality. I have a funny feeling about her, that when the chips are down she'll always love her nursing best."

"There's not a woman born who wouldn't opt for marriage given the right circumstances," said Neil.

"Why?"

"They all live for love."

Michael's expression was actually pitying. "Oh, come on, Neil, grow up! Do you mean men can't live for love? But love comes in all shapes and sizes—and both sexes!"

435

"What would you know about it?" Neil asked bitterly, feeling chastised, a little the way he sometimes felt in the presence of his father, and that wasn't right. Michael Wilson was no Longland Parkinson.

"I don't know how I know about it," said Michael. "It's an instinct. It can't be anything else, can it? I certainly can't claim to be an expert. But there are some things I know without ever remembering learning. People find their own levels, and every person is different." He stood up, stretched. "I'll be back in a tick. I'm just going to see how Nugget is."

When Michael returned a few minutes later Neil looked up at him rather derisively; he had created a third glass by the simple expedient of emptying the dirty water out of a watercolor jar, and had filled it with whisky for himself.

"Drink up, Mike," he said. "I decided I felt like another one after all. I'm celebrating."

5 Sister Langtry's alarm went off at one o'clock in the morning; she had set it because of Nugget, wanting to check on him at an hour when his headache should have eased off. And something about the men tonight had triggered a sharp attack of premonitory disquiet; it would not be a bad idea to check on everyone.

Since probationer days she had trained herself to rouse rapidly, so she got out of bed immediately, and took off her pajamas. She climbed into trousers and bush jacket without bothering to don underwear first, then pulled on thin socks and tied up her daytime duty shoes. At this time of night no one would be interested in whether she was in proper uniform or not. Her watch and keys were on the bureau along with her torch; she put them into one of the jacket's four patch pockets and belted it securely. Right. Ready. Just pray everything in X was nice and quiet.

When she slid around the fly-curtain and tiptoed into the corridor everything did seem to be quiet; too quiet, perhaps, as if the place brooded. There was something missing and something added which together gave the ward an alien lack of welcome. After a few seconds she realized what the differences were: no sounds of sleeping breathing, but a thin beam of light and a soft murmur of voices from under Neil's door. Only Matt's and Nugget's mosquito nets were tucked in.

At Nugget's bed she moved around the screen so softly he could not have heard her, but his eyes she saw were open, gleaming faintly.

"Have you managed to be sick yet?" she asked, after a check of the bowl's interior beneath its cloth showed nothing.

"Yes, Sis. A while ago. Mike gave me a new bowl." He sounded thin and lost and distant.

437

"Feeling better?"

"Much."

She was busy for a while taking pulse and temperature and blood pressure, entering them with the aid of her torch on the chart clipped to the bottom of his cot.

"Could you drink a cup of tea if I made you one?"

"Could I ever!" A little strength began to creep into his voice at the very thought. "Me mouth's like the bottom of a cocky's cage."

She smiled at him and went away, into the dayroom. No one prepared tea as she did, with the enormous ease and economy of an endless practice which stretched back through innumerable dayrooms to her weepy probationer days. If one of the men did it there was always some sort of tiny accident, tea leaves spilled or the freshness boiled out of the water or the pot insufficiently warmed, but when she did it, it was perfect. In less time than seemed possible she was back beside Nugget's bed with a steaming mug in her hand. She put it down on the locker and helped him to sit up, then drew a chair alongside and remained with him while he drank thirstily, blowing on the surface of the liquid impatiently to cool it, and taking quick, minute sips like a bird.

"You know, Sis," he said, pausing, "while the pain is there I think that as long as I live I'm never going to forget what it's like—you know, I could describe it with lots of words the way I can my ordinary headaches. Then the minute it goes away I can't for the life of me remember what it was like, and the only word I can find to describe it is 'awful.'"

She smiled. "That's a characteristic of our brains, Nugget. The more painful a memory is, the quicker we lose the key to unlock it. It's healthy and right to forget something so shattering. No matter how hard we try, we can never conjure up any kind of experience with its original sharpness. We ought not even want to try, though that's human nature. Just don't try too hard and too often—that's how you get yourself into a muddle. Forget the pain. It's gone! Isn't that the most important thing?"

438

"My oath it is!" said Nugget fervently.

"More tea?"

"No, thanks, Sis. That was the grouse."

"Then slide your legs off the bed and I'll help you up. You'll sleep like a baby if I change you and the bed."

While he sat shivering on the chair she stripped and remade his bed, then helped him clothe his skinny shanks in fresh pajamas. After which she tucked him in securely, gave him a last smile and shut him inside his mosquito net.

A quick check of Matt revealed him lying in a most unusual abandon, mouth slackly open and something suspiciously like a snore issuing from it. His chest was bare. But he slept she thought so deeply that there didn't seem to be any point in disturbing him. Her nose wrinkled, she stiffened in shock; there was a definite smell of liquor about him!

For a moment she stood regarding the empty beds with a frown between her brows, then in sudden decision turned and walked quickly to Neil's door. She didn't bother to tap on it, and she was speaking even as she entered.

"Look, chaps, I hate to have to act like Matron, but fair's fair, you know!"

Neil was sitting on the bed, Benedict on the chair, both slack-shouldered. Two bottles of Johnnie Walker, one empty and one just about full, stood on the table.

"You *idiots!*" she snapped. "Do you want to get us all court-martialled? Where did that come from?"

"The good colonel," said Neil, working hard at speaking distinctly.

Her lips thinned. "If he had no more sense than to give it to you, Neil, you ought to have had more sense than to take it! Where are Luce and Michael?"

Neil thought about that deeply, and finally said, with many pauses, "Mike went for a shower. No fun at a party. Luce wasn't in here—went to bed. Huffy."

"Luce is not in bed, and he's not in the ward."

"Then I'll find him for you, Sis," Neil said, struggling to get

439

off the bed. "I won't be long, Ben, I've got to find Luce for Sis. Sis wants Luce. I don't want Luce, but Sis does. Beats me why. I think I'm going to puke first, though."

"If you puke in here I'll rub your nose in it!" she said fiercely. "And stay where you are! The state you're in you couldn't even find yourself! Oh, I could murder the lot of you!" Her temper began to die, a trace of fondness crept into her exasperation. "Now will you be good chaps and clear the evidence of debauchery away? It's past one in the morning!"

6   After a thorough check of the verandah failed to locate either Luce or Michael, Sister Langtry marched across to the bathhouse like a soldier, chin up, shoulders back, still simmering. What on earth had possessed them to carry on like that? There wasn't even a full moon! Just as well X was down at the other end of the compound, right away from any of the other inhabited wards. She was so busy fuming that she ran into the clothesline the men had rigged up so they could do their own washing, and floundered amid towels, shirts, trousers, shorts. Damn them! It was a measure of the degree of her annoyance that she didn't even see the funny side of her collision with the clothesline, simply got it together again and marched on.

The squat bulk of the bathhouse loomed straight ahead. It had a wooden door which opened into one very large room, a barnlike place with showers along one wall and basins along the opposite wall, and a few laundry tubs at the back. There were no partitions or stalls, nowhere for a man to hide. The floor sloped to a drain in its middle, and was perpetually wet on the shower side of the room.

During the night a low-watt light bulb in the ceiling burned continually, but these days the bathhouse rarely saw visitors after dark, since the men of X showered and shaved in the morning and the latrine was in a separate, far less substantial building.

Coming in from the moonless night outside, Sister Langtry had no difficulty in seeing. The whole incredible scene was lit up for her like players on the stage for their audience. A shower, forgotten, still trickling its small curtain of water; Michael in the far corner, naked and wet, staring mesmerized at Luce; and Luce, naked, smiling, erect, standing some five feet away from Michael.

441

Neither of them noticed her in the doorway; she had a panicked sensation of déjà vu, and saw the scene as some sort of bizarre variation on that other scene in the dayroom. For a moment she stood paralyzed, then suddenly knew that this was something she couldn't handle on her own, didn't have the knowledge or the understanding to handle. So she turned and ran for the ward, running as she had never run in her life before, up the steps, in through the door near Michael's bed, up the ward.

When she burst into Neil's cubicle he and Benedict still seemed to be exactly as she had left them; had so little time passed? No, something had changed. The whisky bottles and the glasses had gone. God *damn* them, they were drunk! Everyone must be drunk!

"The bathhouse!" she managed to say. "Oh, quick!"

Neil seemed to sober, or at least he got to his feet and moving more quickly than she would have believed possible, and Benedict didn't seem too bad either. She herded them out like sheep and got them through the ward, down the steps, across the compound toward the bathhouse. Neil tangled himself in the clothesline and fell, but she didn't wait, just grabbed the hapless Benedict by the arm and hustled him along.

The scene in the bathhouse had changed. Luce and Michael were now crouched like wrestlers in a ring, arms half extended, circling each other; but Luce was still laughing.

"Come on, lover! You know you want it! What's the matter, afraid? Can't you take it that big? Oh, come on! It's no use playing hard to get, I know all about you!"

At first glance Michael's face looked very still, almost remote, but beneath that burned something vast and awful and terrifying, though Luce seemed not to be affected by it. Michael didn't speak, didn't evince a flicker of change as the flow of Luce's words went on; it was as if he hardly saw the real Luce, so intent was he upon the turmoil within himself.

"Break it up!" said Neil sharply.

The scene dissolved immediately. Luce swung round to face

the three in the doorway, but for a moment Michael maintained his pose of defensive readiness. Then he collapsed back against the wall, leaning on it and drawing great gasping breaths as if his lungs were bellows. And suddenly he began to shake uncontrollably, his teeth chattering audibly, diaphragm still pumping beneath the skin of his upper abdomen.

Sister Langtry stepped past Luce, and Michael saw her for the first time, his face running sweat, his mouth open on the agony it was to breathe. At first he had to assimilate the simple fact of her presence, after which he looked at her with a passionate appeal that slowly faded into hopelessness; he turned his head away and closed his eyes as if it didn't matter, sagging but not falling, supported still by the wall behind him, something draining out of him so fast he seemed visibly to shrink. Sister Langtry turned away.

"We're none of us in a fit state to make this public tonight," she said, addressing Neil.

Then she turned to Luce, her eyes filled with a sick contempt. "Sergeant Daggett, I will see you in the morning. Kindly return to the ward immediately and don't leave it under any circumstances whatsoever."

Luce appeared triumphant, unrepentant, jubilant; he shrugged, bent to pick up his clothes where he had strewn them just inside the door, opened it and went out, the set of his naked shoulders indicating that he fully intended to make things as difficult as possible in the morning.

"Captain Parkinson, I am making you responsible for Sergeant Daggett's good conduct. When I come on duty I expect to see everything shipshape and normal, and heaven help the man who has a hangover. I am very, very angry! You've abused every trust I've put in you. Sergeant Wilson will not return to X tonight, nor will he return until after I have interviewed Sergeant Daggett. Now do you understand? Are you fit enough to cope?" This last was said with less stringency, and the look in her eyes had softened.

"I'm not as drunk as you appear to think I am," said Neil,

gazing down at her with eyes that seemed nearly as dark as Benedict's. "You're the boss. Everything shall be exactly as you wish."

Benedict had neither moved nor spoken since coming into the bathhouse, but as Neil turned stiffly to leave he jumped convulsively, and his eyes flew from their unwinking contemplation of Sister Langtry's face to Michael, still leaning exhausted against the wall. "Is he all right?" he asked anxiously.

She nodded, managed a small, twisted smile. "Don't worry, Ben, I'll look after him. Just go back to the ward with Neil and try to get some sleep."

Alone in the bathhouse with Michael, Sister Langtry looked around for his clothes, but all she could find was a towel; he must have walked across to have his shower already stripped, the towel perhaps wound about his waist. Not allowed in the rules, of course, which stipulated that all personnel abroad at night be covered from neck to feet; still, he had probably never counted on being discovered.

She took the towel from its peg and walked across to him, pausing to turn the shower off.

"Come on," she said, sounding very tired. "Put this around you, please."

He opened his eyes but didn't look at her, took the towel and wrapped it about himself clumsily, his hands still shaking, then he moved away from the wall as if he doubted whether he could stand up unsupported; but he did.

"And how much have *you* had to drink?" she asked bitterly, grasping him ungently by the arm, urging him to walk.

"About four tablespoons," he said in a stiff, small, weary voice. "Where are you taking me?" And suddenly he shook himself free of her hand as if the peremptory and authoritative quality in it stung his pride.

"We're going to my quarters," she said curtly. "I'll put you in one of the vacant rooms there until the morning. You can't go

444

back to the ward unless I call in the MPs, and I don't want to do that."

He followed her then without further protest, defeated. What could he possibly say to this woman that could make her refuse to believe the evidence of her own eyes? It must have looked like the dayroom all over again, only so much worse. And he was utterly exhausted, he didn't have an ounce of reserve strength left after that brief but superhuman struggle with himself. For he had known its outcome the moment Luce appeared; if he swung for it, he was going to have the deep and gloriously satisfying pleasure of killing the stupid, ignorant bastard.

Two things had prevented his leaping for Luce's throat immediately: the memory of the RSM and of the pain that had followed every day since, of the culminating pain which was ward X and Sister Langtry; and the drawn-out savoring of a moment which was going to be exquisite. So when Luce made his move, Michael hung grimly on and on to his shredding self-control.

Luce looked big and masculine and capable, but Michael knew he didn't have the hardness, the experience or the lust for killing. And he had always known that behind Luce's brash confidence, behind the insatiable appetite the man had to torment, there crouched a coward. Luce always thought he could get away with his antics forever, that men took one look at his size, felt his malice and lost their own courage. But Michael knew the moment his bluff was called he would crumble. And as he dropped into an attack position the whole of his future life was there, but it couldn't make any difference any more. He was going to call Luce's bluff, but when the big cocky bastard fell apart he was still going to kill him. Kill him just for the sheer pleasure of it.

Twice destroyed. Twice brought to face the knowledge that he was no better than anyone else exposed to killing; that he too could come to throw everything away for the gratification of a lust. It was a lust, he had always known that. There were many things he had learned about himself which he had also learned to live with; but this? Was having this inside him what closed his mouth on love in Sister Langtry's office? It had welled up, would have spilled out. And then he felt a shadow, something nameless and fearful. This. It had to be this. He had thought of it as his own unworthiness, but now for all time unworthiness had a name.

Thank God she had come! Only how could he ever explain?

7 As they mounted the steps outside her quarters, Sister Langtry realized the other rooms in the block were locked and barred. Not that it meant she was defeated; there were ways of getting into any locked room, and trained nurses who had undergone the convent-like incarceration of a nurses' home were always experts at getting in and out of supposedly secured premises. But it would take time. So she opened the door to her own room, flicked the light switch and stood back for Michael to enter in front of her.

How odd. Except for Matron on inspection rounds, he was the only person ever to see her private domain, for all the sisters preferred to congregate in the recreation area when they sought social contact; it was such a hike to go to a colleague's room. In spite of her weariness she looked at the place with new eyes, noting its drab bare impersonal quality. A cell rather than a lived-in space, though it was larger than a cell. It contained a narrow cot similar to the ones in X, a hard chair, a bureau, a screened-off area to hang her clothes, and two shelves nailed to the wall on which resided her books.

"You can wait in here," she said. "I'm going to find you something to wear, and open up one of the other rooms."

Scarcely waiting to see him seat himself on the hard chair by the bed, she closed the door and moved off, her torch beam going on before her. It was easier to raid one of the nearby wards for something for him to wear than to trek all the way back to X and disturb the men. Besides, she didn't feel up to seeing Luce before morning; she needed time to think first. A visit to B ward produced pajamas and a robe, upon solemn promise that tomorrow she would replace them.

The room right next door to her own was the obvious

447

one in which to deposit Michael, so she set to work levering the wooden slats out of its louvered window. The locks were mortice and too strong to pick with a hairpin. There. Four panels ought to be plenty. She shone the torch through the gap to make sure there was still a bed inside, and discovered it in much the same position as her own, its mattress rolled up. He would have to make do without any sheets, that was all, and she couldn't summon up much pity for his plight anyway.

By the time she let herself back into her own room she had been absent for perhaps three-quarters of an hour. The night was close and humid, and she was soaked with sweat. There was a pain in her side; she stood for a moment massaging it with one hand, then looked toward the chair. He wasn't on it. He was on the bed, curled up on his side with his back to her, and he looked as if he was fast asleep. Asleep! How could he sleep after what he'd just been through?

But it softened her as nothing else could have. After all, what was she so angry about? Why did she feel like turning and rending the nearest object limb from limb? Because they'd all got drunk? Because Luce had merely acted true to form? Or because she wasn't sure any more about Michael, had not been since he turned away from her in the office? Yes, a little over the whisky, perhaps, but the poor beggars were only human, and none too strong at that. Luce? He didn't matter one iota. By far the largest part of her anger was rooted in her grief and uncertainty over Michael.

Quite suddenly she realized she was near to exhaustion herself. Her clothes were stuck to her, mottled with dark patches of sweat, and chafing because she had thought it would be a brief visit and so had not donned underwear. Well, as soon as she got him settled next door she could have a shower. She went across to the bed, not making a sound.

It was after half-past two by the clock on the bureau, and he was so absolutely relaxed that in the end she didn't have the heart to rouse him. Even when she tugged the upper sheet out from under him and spread it up over him, he didn't stir. Out to it.

Poor Michael, the victim of Luce's determination to pay her back for little Miss Woop-Woop. Tonight must have seemed like manna from heaven to Luce, all of them stupid with drink, Nugget incapacitated with a headache, the field clear when Michael went to the bathhouse. She wanted to believe that Michael had done nothing to invite Luce's advances, but surely if that was so he would simply have told Luce to get stuffed and walked out. He wasn't physically afraid of Luce, he never had been physically afraid of Luce. But had all that power made him afraid in a different way? If only she knew men better!

It looked as if she was going to have to be the one to sleep without sheets next door, unless she found the resolution to wake him. In the meantime, she could postpone that decision by going to have a shower. So she pulled her cotton robe off its hook behind the door and went to the bathhouse, shed her trousers and jacket and stood beneath the trickle of tepid water almost ecstatically. To be washed clean was a feeling that sometimes went far deeper than skin. The robe was a large, loose kimono-like affair which belted around the middle; rather than wait for a complete drying, which was debatable anyway on such a humid night, she dabbed herself with a towel and then pulled the robe on, folded it overlapping across the front, and belted it.

And, she thought, picking up her clothes, I'm darned if I see why it has to be me to sleep on a mattress full of crawlies. He can jolly well get himself together and transfer right now!

The clock said five past three. Sister Langtry dropped her sweat-soaked clothes onto the floor, moved to the bed and put the palm of her hand on Michael's shoulder. It was a hesitant, delicate touch, for she hated to have to wake him, and it remained delicate, for she decided after all not to wake him. Too tired even to be amused by her own lack of decision, she sank down onto the hard chair beside the bed and rested her whole

449

hand on his bare skin, unable to resist the fulfillment of an impulse she had known all too often: to *feel* him. A sensation not to be resisted. She tried to remember what it had been like to feel the bare skin of a beloved man, but could not, perhaps because between him and that other man so long ago there stretched a life so different it obliterated sensuous memory; more than six years of burying her own needs beneath the more urgent needs of others. And, she realized with a shock, she hadn't really missed it! Not intolerably, not yearningly.

But Michael was real, and her feeling for him was real. For how long had she wanted to do this, touch the life in him as if she had every right to do so. This is the man I love, she thought; I don't care who he is, what he is. I love him.

Her hand moved on his shoulder, at first experimentally, then in small circles, the touch more and more like a caress. It was her moment, she didn't feel any sense of shame in knowing he had done nothing to indicate he wanted this; she touched him with love to please herself, for a memory. And utterly absorbed now in the perfect delight of feeling him, she leaned to put her cheek against his back, held it there, then turned it to taste his skin through her lips.

Yet when he moved toward her she stiffened in shock, her private paradise exposed; mortified, furious at her own weakness, she jumped away. He caught both her forearms, lifting her up from the chair so quickly and lightly that she had no sensation of force, moving himself at the same time. There was no aggression, no roughness; he seemed to shift himself and her so deftly she was scarcely aware of how he did it. She found herself sitting on the bed, one leg folded under her, his arms about her back, his head against her breast, and felt him trembling. Her own arms curved about him possessively, and the two of them remained thus, almost still, until whatever it was that had made him tremble ceased to plague him.

The grip on her back relaxed, his hands fell away, passed lightly around her waist and began to tug at the knot in her belt. He undid it, then moved the material of the robe aside so that he could turn his face against her skin. One slight breast was curved within his hand, an almost reverent taking of it that moved her unbearably. His head came up, his body lifted away from hers, and her face turned of its own volition to seek his. She moved her shoulders to help him slide the robe off, then fitted her breasts against him, her hands around his shoulders, her mouth fascinated and entranced in his.

Only then did she permit the whole of her love to well up in her, closing her eyes which had been open and shining, feeling in every part of her surely some kind of love in him. He couldn't not love her yet be so much a joy in her, waking her to sensations now long forgotten, even unimportant, yet so familiar still, of a poignant sharpness quite new and wonderfully strange.

They rose to kneel; his hands drifted down her sides with hesitant slowness, as if he wanted to prolong everything to an agony point, and she didn't have the strength to help him or resist him any more, she was too intent on being one with a miracle.

FIVE

1   A little before seven the next morning Sister Langtry let herself quietly out of her room, clad in full daylight uniform—grey dress, white veil, red cape, celluloid cuffs and collar, the silver rising sun at her throat as polished as if it were new. She had taken special care in dressing, wanting to look how she felt, someone with the mark of love on her. And smiling, she lifted her face to greet the new day, and stretched her tired muscles luxuriously.

The way across to the ward had never been so long nor yet so short, but she wasn't sorry to be leaving him asleep behind her, wasn't sorry to be going to ward X. She had not slept herself at all, nor really had he until about six o'clock, when she left the bed and went outside. Before showering she did remember to replace the slats in the window of the next-door room, and so was away for half an hour, a little more. When she returned to her room he was sound asleep; she had left him with a kiss on unknowing lips. There would be time, years of it. They were going home soon, and she was a bush girl anyway; it wouldn't come to her as any shock to have to do without the conveniences of city living. Besides, Maitland wasn't so very far from Sydney, nor was dairy farming in the Hunter Valley anything like as harsh an existence as sheep and wheat out west.

Normally someone was up by half-past six, but then normally she would already have been in the ward for half an hour by that time, would have made the early morning tea and got them stirring. This morning everything was still and quiet, all the mosquito nets save Michael's fastened down.

She put her cape and basket in her office, then went to the dayroom, where an orderly had already deposited the day's ration of fresh bread, a tin of butter and a new tin of jam—plum again. The spirit stove didn't want to go, and by the time she had managed to persuade it that its only function was the production of hot water she had lost all the advantages of her early shower; the warmth of the day and the ferocious blaze of the spirit stove combined to produce an outpouring of sweat. The wet season was coming soon; humidity had increased twenty percent in the last week.

When the tea was made and the bread buttered she loaded everything except the teapot onto the board which served as a tray and carried it down the ward, out onto the verandah. A quick return for the teapot, and everything was ready for them. No, not quite! Though last night she had been so annoyed with them she had never thought to pity them in the morning, the later part of the night and Michael melted her resolve to be hard on them for once. After consuming so much of the colonel's whisky, they would be dreadfully hung over.

She went back to her office and unlocked the drug drawer, took out the bottle of mist APC. The aspirin and the phenacetin had sunk in coarse white granules to the bottom, the caffeine floated as a straw-colored syrup on top. It was an easy matter to decant off some of the liquid caffeine into a medicine glass. When she had them all assembled outside she would give each man a tablespoon of the caffeine; it was the oldest hospital trick in the world for treating a hangover, and it had saved many a young doctor's and young nurse's reputation.

At Neil's door she did no more than poke her head around it. "Neil, the tea's made! Rise and shine!" The air in the cubicle smelled foul; she withdrew her head quickly and went into the ward.

Nugget was awake, and gave her a sickly grin as she yanked the netting away from around him, twisted it swiftly into a bundle and threw it upward with an expert flick to rest higgledy-piggledy on the ring; time later to do battle with the Matron Drape.

"How's the headache?"

"All right, Sis."

"Good morning, Matt!" she said cheerfully, repeating her act with the mosquito net.

"Good morning, Ben!"

Of course Michael's bed was empty. She turned to go across to Luce, and something of her happiness died. What was she going to say to him? How would he behave during the interview she couldn't very well postpone much beyond breakfast? But Luce wasn't in his bed; the net was torn away from under the mattress, and the bed when she unveiled it had been slept in, but was quite cold.

She turned back toward Benedict and Matt, to find both of them sitting on the edges of their beds, their heads in their hands, shoulders hunched, looking as if every small movement provoked pain.

"Damn the Johnnie Walker!" she said under her breath as she caught sight of Neil weaving gagging from his cubicle to the sluice room opposite, his face grey-green.

Well, it seemed as usual as if she was the only one capable of locating Luce. So she opened the door next to Michael's bed, stepped onto the little landing outside, then headed down the plank steps toward the bathhouse.

But it was a beautiful, beautiful day, humidity and all, she thought, half blind with the dizziness of too little sleep and the glitter of the early sun on the grove of palms just beyond the compound perimeter. The light had never seemed so clear, so sparkling, so soft. When she found the clothesline in ruins she simply smiled and stepped over the tangled heaps of shorts, shirts, trousers and underclothes and socks, trying to picture her dear dignified Neil drunk and fighting free of laundry.

The bathhouse was very quiet. Too quiet. Luce was very quiet. Too quiet. He lay sprawled half against the wall, half on the rough concrete floor, a razor in his spasmed hand. His glistening golden skin was strewn with stiffened, cracking rivers of blood, a congealing pool lay stagnant in the hollow of his belly amid other more hideous things, and the floor around him was awash with blood.

She came only as close to him as she needed to see properly what he had done to himself: the mutilated genitals, the hara-kiri

457

slash which had opened up his abdomen from side to side. It was his own razor, the ebony-handled Bengal he preferred to a safety razor because of the closeness of its shave, and his fingers around it were unquestionably the only fingers which had ever been around it: there was nothing artificial about his grip on the handle, nor about the blood sticking razor and fingers inextricably together—thank God, thank God! His head was tilted unnaturally far back, and almost she fancied his eyes moved derisively at her beneath half-lowered lids; then she saw that it was the golden sheen of death in them, not the gold they had been in the gold of his so vital life.

Sister Langtry didn't scream. Once she had looked, her reaction was instinctive; she stepped quickly back through the door and slammed it shut, scrabbling frantically at the padlock which hung by its unsnapped handle through an eyelet on the doorjamb. With controlled desperation she managed to fling the hinge nailed to the door itself over the eyelet, to thread the padlock back through and press its handle home. Then she leaned against the door limply, her mouth opening and closing, yammering up and down with the nightmarish automatism of a shiny wooden ventriloquist's dummy.

It was perhaps as many as five minutes before the yammering stopped, before she could unglue her hands from their flattened stance against the door.

The insides of her thighs felt sticky, and for a horrid humiliating moment she thought she must have wet herself, then realized it was only sweat and the aftermath of Michael.

Michael, oh, Michael! She beat one fist against the door in a sudden frenzy of rage, of despair. God damn Luce to eternal hell for doing this! Oh, why hadn't those drunken fools in there kept better custody of him? Did she have to do everything herself? Luce, you bastard, you've won after all! You utter, foul, insane, maggoty bastard, to have carried your notions of revenge so far. . . .

Oh, Michael! There were tears on her face, tears of a terrible grief at a snatched imperfect brutally brief joy, with all the dear bright morning in ruins at her feet, drowned in blood. Oh, Michael! My Michael . . . It wasn't fair. They hadn't even talked yet. They hadn't begun to get together the unravelled knots of what had been their previous relationship, hadn't had the time to knit them into a common thread. And, straightening, moving away from the door, she knew then, knew irrevocably, that there could be no hope of happiness for her and Michael. No relationship of any kind. Luce had won after all.

The walk across the compound she did like a robot, moving quickly and jerkily and mechanically, heading at first she knew not where, then heading in the only possible direction. Remembering the feel of tears on her face, she lifted one hand to wipe her eyelids with its palm, tinkered with the set of her veil, smoothed down her brows. There. There, Sister Langtry, *Sister Langtry*, you're in charge of this mess, it's your damned duty! Duty, remember duty. Not only your duty to yourself, but to your patients. There are five of them who have to be protected at any cost from the consequences of Luce Daggett.

2 Colonel Chinstrap was sitting out on his little private verandah attached to his little private hut, stirring his tea reflectively and not thinking anything very much at all. It was that sort of a day, somehow. A nothing very much at all sort of day. After a night with Sister Heather Connolly it usually was, but last night had been hard in a different way; they had spent most of it talking about the coming disintegration of Base Fifteen and the possibility of continuing their affair when they returned to civilian life.

As it was his habit to overstir his tea, he was still turning his spoon over and over in his cup when Sister Langtry, looking neat and precise as a pin, marched around the corner of his hut and stood on the grass below him, looking up.

"Sir, I have a suicide!" she announced loudly.

He half leaped off his chair, subsided onto it again, then slowly managed to lay the spoon down in the saucer and find his feet. He tottered across to the flimsy balustrade and leaned on it gingerly, looking down at her.

"Suicide? But this is dreadful! Dreadful!"

"Yes, sir," she said woodenly.

"Who?"

"Sergeant Daggett, sir. In the bathhouse. Very messy. Cut himself to ribbons with his razor."

"Oh, dear! Oh, dear!" he said feebly.

"Do you want to have a look for yourself first, sir, or do you want me to go straight for the MPs?" she asked, dragging him inexorably on to decisions he felt he didn't have the energy to make.

He mopped his face with his handkerchief, the color so died out of his skin that the grog blossoms on his nose stood out in blue and crimson glory. His hand twitched, a betrayal; he thrust it defensively into his pocket and turned away from her toward the interior of his hut.

"I suppose I had better have a look for myself first," he said, and raised his voice peevishly. "My hat, where the devil is my damned hat?"

They looked quite normal as they moved together across the compound, but Sister Langtry set the pace and it kept the colonel puffing.

"Any . . . idea . . . why . . . Sister?" he panted, slowing down experimentally, but discovering that she continued to forge ahead without any sort of regard for his wind.

"Yes, sir, I do know why. I caught Sergeant Daggett last night in the bathhouse attempting to molest Sergeant Wilson. I imagine that at some time during the night Sergeant Daggett was seized by some sort of fit of guilt or remorse, and decided to end his life where the attack had occurred, in the bathhouse. There's a definite sexual motif—his genitals have been slashed about rather badly."

How could she speak so effortlessly when she was walking so damned quickly? "God spare me days, Sister, will you bloody slow down?" he shouted. Then what she had said about genitals penetrated, and the dismay crept over him as lankly as a jellyfish. "Oh, dear! Oh, dear!"

The colonel took but one brief look inside the bathhouse, which Sister Langtry had unlocked for him with rock-firm hands. He dodged out again barely hanging onto his gorge, but also determined that he was not going to lose it in front of this woman above all people in the world. After a period of deep breathing which he disguised by strutting about with his hands behind his back, looking as important and thoughtful as his gorge would let him, he harumphed and stopped in front of Sister Langtry, who had waited patiently, and now eyed him with faint derision. Damn the woman!

461

"Does anyone know about this?" he asked, bringing out his handkerchief and mopping his face, which was gradually returning to its normal high color.

"The suicide, I don't think so," she said, voice coolly considering. "Unfortunately the attempt to molest Sergeant Wilson was witnessed by Captain Parkinson and Sergeant Maynard as well as by me personally, sir."

He clicked his tongue. "Most regrettable! At what time did the attempt to molest Sergeant Wilson occur?"

"Approximately half-past one in the morning, sir."

He stared at her in mingled suspicion and exasperation. "What on earth were you all doing buzzing round the bathhouse at that hour? And how did you permit any of this to happen, Sister? Why didn't you put an orderly in the ward overnight, if not a relief nurse?"

She stared back expressionlessly. "If you're referring to the attack on Sergeant Wilson, sir, I had no basis to suppose Sergeant Daggett's intentions lay in that direction. If you're referring to the suicide, I had absolutely no indication that such were Sergeant Daggett's intentions regarding himself."

"Then you have no doubt that it's suicide, Sister?"

"None at all. The razor was in his own hand when the injuries were inflicted. Didn't you see that for yourself? Holding a Bengal to cut down deeply instead of to scrape the surface of the skin is the same hold reinforced by strength."

He resented the inference that his gorge had not permitted his staying long enough to inspect the corpse as thoroughly as apparently she had done, so he switched tactics. "I repeat, why did you not have someone stand guard in the ward during the night, Sister? And why did you not report Sergeant Daggett's attack on Sergeant Wilson to me immediately?"

Her eyes opened guilelessly wide. "Sir! At two in the morning? I really didn't think you'd thank me for rousing you at such an hour for something which was not a true medical emergency. We broke it up before Sergeant Wilson sustained any physical harm, and when I left Sergeant Daggett he was in full possession of his wits and his self-control. Captain Parkinson and Sergeant Maynard agreed to keep an eye on Sergeant Daggett during the night, but provided Sergeant Wilson was removed from the ward, I did not see any necessity to restrain Sergeant Daggett forcibly, nor to have him placed under arrest and taken into custody, nor to start yelling for staff assistance. In fact, sir," she concluded calmly, "I was hoping not to have to draw your attention to the incident at all. I felt that after talking to Sergeant Daggett and to Sergeant Wilson when both of them had recovered somewhat, everything might be resolved without an official fuss. At the time I left the ward I was optimistic such would prove to be the case."

He seized upon a new item of information. "You say you removed Sergeant Wilson from the ward, Sister. Just what do you mean by that?"

"Sergeant Wilson was in severe emotional shock, sir, and considering the circumstances I thought it advisable to treat him in my own quarters rather than in the ward right under Sergeant Daggett's nose."

"So Sergeant Wilson was with you all night."

She looked at him fearlessly. "Yes, sir. All night."

"All night? You're sure it was all night?"

"Yes, sir. He's still in my quarters, as a matter of fact. I didn't want to bring him back to the ward until after I had talked to Sergeant Daggett."

"And were you with him all night, Sister?"

A tiny horror crept into her mind. The colonel was not busy thinking salacious thoughts about her and Michael; he probably didn't consider her the least capable of salacious activity. He was contemplating something far different than love—he was contemplating murder.

"I did not leave Sergeant Wilson's side until I came on duty half an hour ago, sir, and I discovered Sergeant Daggett only minutes after coming on duty. He had then been dead for several hours," she said, her tone brooking no argument.

"I see," said Colonel Chinstrap, tight-lipped. "This is a pretty mess, isn't it?"

"I disagree, sir. It isn't pretty at all."

He returned to the main theme like a worrisome dog. "And you're absolutely sure that Sergeant Daggett did or said nothing to indicate a suicidal state of mind?"

"Absolutely nothing, sir," she said firmly. "In fact, that he did commit suicide staggers me. Not that it's so inconceivable he'd take his own life. Only that he chose to do so with so much blood, so much . . . *ugliness.* As for the assault on his own masculinity—I can't even begin to grasp why. But then, that's the trouble with people. They never do what you expect them to do. I'm being quite open and honest with you, Colonel Donaldson. I could lie and say Sergeant Daggett's state of mind was definitely suicidal. But I choose to speak the truth. My incredulity over Sergeant Daggett's suicide doesn't alter my conviction that it is suicide. It can't be anything else."

He turned and began to walk toward X, setting a sober pace which she seemed content to follow at last. By the collapsed clothesline he paused to poke about in the heaps of laundry with his swagger stick, reminding Sister Langtry of the matron of a mixed-sex teenage camp looking for suspicious stains. "There seems to have been a bit of a fight here," he said, straightening.

Her lips twitched. "There was, sir. Between Captain Parkinson and some shirts."

He moved on. "I think I had better see Captain Parkinson and Sergeant Maynard before I send for the authorities, Sister."

"Of course, sir. I haven't been back to the ward since I discovered the body, so I imagine none of them know what's happened. Even if any of them have tried to get into the bathhouse, I locked it before I went to find you."

"That at least is something to be grateful for," he said austerely, and suddenly realized life was offering him the perfect opportunity to slap Sister Langtry down for good. A man in her quarters all night, an absolutely sordid sexual mess culminating in a

464

killing—by the time he was finished with her, she'd be pilloried and out of the army in disgrace. Oh, God, the bliss! "Permit me to say, Sister, that I consider you have botched this entire affair from start to finish, and that I shall make it my personal business to see that you receive the censure you so richly deserve."

"Thank you, sir!" she exclaimed, apparently without irony. "However, I consider that the direct cause of this entire affair was two bottles of Johnnie Walker whisky which were consumed in full last night by the patients of ward X. And if I only knew the identity of the brainless fool who was responsible for giving Captain Parkinson, an emotionally unstable patient, those two bottles yesterday, I would take great pleasure in making it *my* personal business to see that *he* receives the censure *he* so richly deserves!"

He tripped going up the steps and had to grab at the rickety banister to save himself. Brainless fool? Blithering idiot! He had forgotten all about the whisky. And she knew. Oh, she knew, all right! He would have to forget revenge. He would have to back-pedal very quickly indeed. Damn the woman! That smooth and oh, so fearless insolence was bone deep; if her nursing training had not eradicated it, bloody nothing ever would.

Matt, Nugget, Benedict and Neil were sitting at the table on the verandah, looking ghastly. Poor souls, she hadn't even given them the caffeine she had skimmed off the top of the mist APC, and she couldn't very well dole it out to them now, with Colonel Chinstrap looking on.

At sight of the colonel they all rose to attention; he sat down heavily on one end of a bench and was obliged to make a flying leap for its middle when it tipped dangerously.

"As you were, gentlemen," he said. "Captain Parkinson, I would greatly appreciate a cup of tea, please."

The teapot had already gone through several refills and one remake, so the tea Neil poured with a none-too-steady hand was fairly fresh. Colonel Chinstrap took the mug without seeming to notice its ugliness, and buried his nose in it gratefully. But eventually he had to put the mug down, at which time he glared sourly at the four men and Sister Langtry.

"I understand that Sergeants Wilson and Daggett were involved in an incident early this morning in the bathhouse?" he asked, his manner indicating that this was what had brought him all the way down the compound to ward X so early in the day.

"Yes, sir," said Neil easily. "Sergeant Daggett made an attempt to molest Sergeant Wilson sexually. Sister Langtry fetched us— Sergeant Maynard and myself, that is—to the bathhouse, and we broke it up."

"Having seen the actual incident with your own eyes, or only having heard of it from Sister Langtry?"

Neil eyed the colonel with a contempt he didn't even bother to conceal. "Why, having seen it with our own eyes, of course!" He packed his voice with the nuances of someone forced to pander to an inexplicably prurient interest. "Sergeant Wilson must have been surprised in the shower. He was naked, and quite wet. Sergeant Daggett was also naked, but not at all wet. He was, however, in a state of extreme sexual arousal. When Sister Langtry, Sergeant Maynard and myself entered the bathhouse, he was attempting to grapple with Sergeant Wilson, who had dropped into a defensive position to ward him off."

Neil cleared his throat, looked carefully past the colonel's shoulder. "Luckily Sergeant Wilson had not imbibed very freely of the whisky we just happened to have in our possession last night, otherwise things might have gone a lot harder for him."

"All right, all right, that's quite enough!" said the colonel sharply, feeling every nuance like a rapier, and the mention of the whisky like a club. "Sergeant Maynard, do you agree with Captain Parkinson's description?"

Benedict looked up for the first time. His face had the strung and drawn weariness of someone who had reached a point of no return, and his eyes were red-rimmed from the whisky. "Yes, sir, that's the way it happened," he said, dragging the words out as if he had been sitting there for days concentrating on nothing but

466

those words. "Luce Daggett was a blot on the face of the earth. Dirty. Disgusting—"

Matt got up quickly and put his hand unerringly on Benedict's arm, the grip pulling Benedict to his feet. "Come on, Ben," he said urgently. "Hurry! Take me for a walk. After all that grog last night I don't feel well."

Colonel Chinstrap didn't argue, for a fresh reference to the whisky terrified him. He sat as quietly as a mouse while Benedict led Matt rapidly from the verandah, then turned to Neil again. "What happened after your arrival put an end to the incident, Captain?"

"Sergeant Wilson had a bit of a reaction, sir. You know, the sort of thing that can happen after you've been keyed up to fight. He got the shakes, couldn't breathe properly. It seemed to me better that he go with Sister Langtry, so I suggested to her that she remove Sergeant Wilson from the ward, somewhere like her quarters, right away from Sergeant Daggett. That left Sergeant Daggett without—ah—further temptation during the remainder of the night. It also left him in a state of considerable apprehension, which I freely confess I did rather encourage him to feel. Sergeant Daggett, sir, is not my favorite person."

At the beginning of this speech Sister Langtry merely watched Neil courteously, but when she heard him tell the colonel it had been his idea to remove Michael from the ward, her eyes widened in surprise, then softened in gratitude. The silly, noble, wonderful man! It would never occur to the colonel to doubt that it had been Neil's doing; he expected men to take charge and make the decisions. But it also seemed Neil knew very well where she had intended to put Michael for the night, and that gave her pause; had the latter part of the night been written even then on her face, or was it just an inspired guess?

"How was Sergeant Daggett after you returned to the ward, Captain?" asked the colonel.

"How was Sergeant Daggett?" Neil closed his eyes. "Oh, much the same as always. An acid-tongued bastard. Not a bit sorry, except for being caught. Full of his usual spite. And carrying on about getting even with us all, but especially with Sister Langtry. Luce detests her."

So much undisguised dislike of someone dead offended the colonel, until he remembered they didn't know Luce was dead. He pressed on toward his denouement.

"Where is Sergeant Daggett now?" he asked casually.

"I neither know nor care, sir," said Neil. "As far as I'm concerned, I would be delirious with joy if he were never to set foot in ward X again."

"I see. Well, Captain, you're honest."

Everyone could see the colonel trying to make allowances for the precarious emotional balance of the men of X, but when he turned to Nugget his exasperation was beginning to show. "Private Jones, you're sitting there very quietly. Have you anything to add?"

"Who, sir, me, sir? *I* had a migraine," said Nugget importantly. "The classical pattern, sir, it really was—you would have been fascinated! A two-day prodroma of lethargy and some dysphasia, followed by an hour-long aura of scotomata in the right visual field, and then a left hemicranial headache. I was as flat as a tack, sir." He thought for a moment. "Well, flatter, really."

"Flashing lights are not called scotomata, Private," said the colonel.

"*Mine* were scotomata," said Nugget decisively. "They were fascinating, sir! I told you, it wasn't your minimal migraine by a long shot. If I looked at something big, I saw it all, no trouble. But if I looked at a small bit of the big thing, like a knob on a door or a knothole in the wall, I only saw the left half of the knob or knothole. The right half was—I don't know! Just not there! Scotomata, sir."

"Private Jones," said the colonel tiredly, "if your knowledge of military matters even remotely equalled your knowledge of your own symptomatology, you'd be a field marshal, and we would have been marching through Tokyo in 1943. When you go back to civilian life, I strongly suggest that you consider studying medicine."

"Can't, sir," said Nugget regretfully. "I've only got me Intermediate. But I am thinking about training as a male nurse, sir. At the Repat."

"Well, the world will have lost a Pasteur, perhaps, but it may gain Mister Nightingale instead. You'll do splendidly, Private Jones."

Out of the corner of his eye the colonel noticed that Matt had returned without Benedict, and was standing in the doorway listening intently.

"Corporal Sawyer, what have you to offer?'

"Never saw a thing, sir," said Matt blandly.

The colonel's lips disappeared; he was obliged to draw a deep breath. "Have any of you gentlemen visited the bathhouse since Sergeant Daggett's attack on Sergeant Wilson?"

"Afraid not, sir," said Neil, looking apologetic. "Sorry you've caught us unwashed and unshaved, but after our little lapse with the whisky last night what we all seemed to need first this morning was gallons of tea."

"I do think you might have issued them the top off the APC, Sister!" snapped the colonel, glaring at her.

Her brows lifted; she smiled slightly. "I have it all ready to go, sir."

The colonel finally reached his denouement. "I suppose none of you are aware that Sergeant Daggett has been found dead in the bathhouse, then," he said curtly.

As a climax it was dismally ineffective; no one evinced surprise, shock, sorrow or even interest. They just sat or stood looking much as if the colonel had made a particularly banal remark about the weather.

"Now why on earth would Luce do a thing like that?" asked Neil, apparently feeling the colonel was waiting for some sort of comment. "I didn't think he'd be so considerate."

"Good riddance to bad rubbish," said Matt.

"All me Christmases have come at once," said Nugget.

"Why do you assume it is suicide, Captain?"

Neil looked astonished. "Well, isn't it? He's a bit on the young

469

side to be popping off from natural causes, surely?"

"True, he did not die from natural causes. But why do you assume it was suicide?" the colonel persisted.

"If he didn't have a heart attack or a stroke or whatever, then he put the kybosh on himself. I'm not trying to say that we wouldn't have been delighted to assist him, but last night was not a night for murder, sir. It was a night for a wee drop of whisky."

"How did he die, sir?" asked Nugget eagerly. "Cut his throat? Stab himself? Hang himself, maybe?"

"You would be the one to want to know that, wouldn't you, you little ghoul?" exclaimed the colonel, looking fed up. "He committed what the Japanese call hara-kiri, I believe."

"Who found him, sir?" asked Matt, still in the doorway.

"Sister Langtry."

This time their reaction was all he might have hoped for when he had announced Luce's death; there was an appalled silence as every eye turned toward Sister Langtry. Nugget looked as if he were about to weep, Matt stunned, Neil despairing.

"My dear, I am so sorry," Neil said eventually.

She shook her head, smiled at them lovingly. "It's all right, truly. As you can see, I've survived. Don't look so upset, please."

Colonel Chinstrap sighed and slapped his hands on his thighs in defeat; what could one do with men who felt no regret at the death of a fellow man, then flew into small pieces because their darling Sister Langtry had had a nasty experience? He rose to his feet. "Thank you for your time and the tea, gentlemen. Good morning to you."

"They knew," he said, walking down the ward with Sister Langtry. "Those smug devils *knew* he was dead!"

"Do you think so?" she asked coolly. "You're quite wrong, you know. They were just trying to get on your nerves, sir. You shouldn't let them succeed the way you do; it only makes them worse."

"When I need your advice, madam, I shall ask for it!" he

470

snapped, fizzing with rage. Then recollection of his own very delicate position and the dictatory position of Sister Langtry occurred simultaneously, but he couldn't resist saying, rather maliciously, "There will have to be an inquiry. "

"Naturally, sir," she said calmly.

It was all far too much, especially after the kind of night he had passed. "It would seem there was no foul play," he said wearily. "Luckily for him, perhaps, Sergeant Wilson has an ironclad alibi furnished by no less a person than your good self. However, I shall reserve my decision until after the military police have inspected the corpse. If they concur that there is no suspicion of foul play, I imagine the inquiry will be a mere matter of form. However, that's up to Colonel Seth. I shall notify him immediately." He sighed, cast her a quick sidelong glance. "Yes, indeed, how fortunate for young Sergeant Wilson! It would be wonderful if all the sisters on all my wards were so solicitous of patient welfare."

She stopped just inside the fly-curtain, wondering why there were some people one felt compelled to hurt, yet why one was amazed when they in their turn lashed back. That was she and Colonel Chinstrap; from their first moment of meeting and sizing each other up, it had been a competition to see who could strike hardest. And, by now dedicated to that course, she didn't feel charitable enough to let him get away with his taunts about Michael.

So she said like silk, "I shall request the men to refrain from this running on at the mouth about their alcoholic indiscretions, sir, don't you think? I really can't see why it has to be mentioned at all, provided the military police feel there is no doubt Sergeant Daggett committed suicide."

He writhed, would have given anything he owned to fling it back in her smiling face, shout at her to tell the whole bloody world he had given troppo patients whisky, but he knew he couldn't. So he merely nodded stiffly. "As you see fit, Sister. Certainly *I* shall not mention it."

"You haven't seen Sergeant Wilson yet, sir. I left him asleep,

471

but he's quite all right. Fit for an interview, of that I'm sure. I'll walk over to my quarters with you now. I would have put him in one of the vacant rooms around my own if I could, but they're all locked up. Which as it turns out was just as well, wasn't it? I had to keep him in my own room, right under my eye. Very uncomfortable, as there's only one small bed."

The bitch, the *bloody* bitch! If Private Nugget Jones was a potential Pasteur, she was a potential Hitler. And, he was forced to admit, even on his best days he was never equal to Sister Langtry. He was so tired, and the affair had been a considerable shock.

"I'll see the sergeant later, Sister. Good morning."

3 Sister Langtry watched without moving until the colonel was well on his way back in the direction of his own hut, then she walked down the ramp and began the journey to her room.

If only when things happened there was time to think! It never seemed to turn out that way, unfortunately. The best she could do was to keep on the move and one jump ahead. She didn't trust Colonel Chinstrap an inch. It would be just like him to scuttle like a cockroach back to his hut and then to dispatch Matron to do his dirty work by having Matron descend on her room. Michael had to be moved, and at once. But she would have liked more time before seeing him, a few precious hours in which to find the perfect way to say what had to be said. A few precious hours; days would not have been long enough for this.

There was ruin in the air. The cynics might have put it down to a gathering monsoon, but Sister Langtry knew better. Things built themselves up and then tumbled back to nothing again so fast one knew immediately there had been no proper foundations laid. Which was certainly true of Michael and herself. How could she ever have hoped for something enduring to come out of an utterly artificial situation? Hadn't she resolutely refused to develop her relationship with Neil Parkinson because of that? Usually a man went to bed, if not with someone he knew, at least with someone he thought he knew. But to Michael there could have been nothing real about Honour Langtry; she was a figment, a phantasm. The only Langtry he knew was Sister Langtry. With Neil she had preserved enough sanity to understand this, to suppress her hopes until both of them were back in a more normal environment, until he had a chance to meet Honour Langtry rather than Sister

473

Langtry. But with Michael there had been no thought, no sanity, nothing save a drive to find love with him here and now and hang the consequences. As if in some utterly unconscious part of her she had known how tenuous it was, how unviable.

Years ago a sister in the preliminary training school at P.A. had taken the probationers for a special lecture on the emotional hazards involved in nursing. Honour Langtry had been one of those probationers. Among the hazards, said the sister tutor, was that of falling in love with a patient. And if a nurse should insist upon falling in love with a patient, she said, let him be an acute patient. Never, never a chronic one. Love might grow and prove durable with an acute abdomen or a fractured femur. But love with spastic or paraplegic or tuberculotic was not, in the measured words of that measured voice, a viable proposition. A viable proposition. It was a phrase Honour Langtry never forgot.

Not that Michael was ill, and certainly he was not chronically ill. But she had met him in a long-term nursing situation, colored by all the darknesses of ward X. Even supposing he was not infected, she definitely was. Her first and her only duty should have been to see Michael as an inmate of ward X. With Neil Parkinson she had succeeded; but she didn't love Neil Parkinson, so duty had proceeded on its serene way.

Now here she was, trying to wear two hats at once, love and duty, both donned for the same man. The same patient. The job *said* he was a patient. It didn't matter that he didn't fit that description at all. For there was duty. There was always duty. It came first; not all the love in the world could change the ingrained habits of so very many years.

Which hat do I wear, love or duty? she asked herself, treading more heavily than usual up the steps onto the verandah outside her room. Shall I be his lover or his nurse-custodian? What is he? My lover or my patient? A sudden puff of wind caught under the edge of her veil and lifted it away from her neck. Questions all answered, she thought. I am wearing my duty hat.

When she opened the door she saw Michael dressed in the pajamas and robe she had borrowed from B ward, sitting waiting patiently on the hard chair. The chair he had relocated half the room away from the bed, now neatly made up and looking as if under no stretch of the wildest imagination could it ever have been the site of more pleasure and pain, more gloriously hard work than any oversized, pillow-strewn voluptuary's couch. In an odd way the bed's spartan chasteness came as a shock; she had already enacted the scene to come as she crossed the verandah, and in that scene she had pictured him still lying naked in her bed.

Had he been so she might have been able to be soft, might have sunk onto the mattress beside him, might in spite of her duty hat have summoned up the courage from somewhere to do what she most longed to do: put her arms about him, offer her mouth for one of those powerful and ardent kisses, reinforce with fresh experiences the memories of the night so horribly overshadowed by the dead thing still sprawled in the bathhouse.

She stood in the doorway, unsmiling, stripped of the capacity to move or speak, quite without resources. But the look on her face must have told him more than she realized, for he got up immediately and came across to her, standing close, but not close enough to touch her.

"What's happened?" he asked. "What is it? What's the matter?"

"Luce committed suicide," she said baldly, and stopped, run down again.

"*Suicide?*" At first he gaped, but the astonishment and revulsion faded more rapidly than they should have, and were replaced by a curious, horrified consternation, as if at some action of his own. "Oh, my God, my God!" he said slowly, and looked as if he was beginning to die. The guilt and distress on his face grew whitely; then he said, "What have I done?" and repeated it, "What have I done?" in the voice of an old, enfeebled man.

Her heart came uppermost at once, and she moved close enough to him to clasp his arm in both her hands, looking into his face imploringly. "You've done nothing, Michael, nothing at all! Luce destroyed *himself*, do you hear? He was just using you to

475

get back at me. You cannot blame yourself! It's not as if you led him on, encouraged him!"

"Isn't it?" he asked harshly.

"Stop it!" she cried, terrified.

"I should have been there with him, not here with you. I had no right to leave him."

Appalled, she stared at him as if she hardly knew him, but then somehow she managed to find a small mocking smile from somewhere in her grab bag of emergency expressions, and smeared it across her mouth. "My word!" she exclaimed. "That's quite a compliment to me!"

"Oh, Sis, I didn't mean it that way!" he cried wretchedly. "I wouldn't hurt you for the world!"

"Can't you remember to call me Honour even now?"

"I wish I could. It suits you—oh yes, it does suit you. Yet I always think of you as Sis, even now. I wouldn't hurt you for the world, Sis. But if I had stayed where I belonged, this could never have happened. He'd be safe, and I—I'd be free. It is my fault!"

His agony could mean nothing to her, for she didn't know its source. Who was he? What was he? A nauseated revulsion and a huge nameless sorrow welled up from some central part of her, spread insidiously through her from fingertips to wide incredulous eyes. Who was he, that after spending hours making the most passionate and loving of love to her, he could stand now bewailing it, dismissing it in favor of *Luce?* Horror, grief, pain, she might have dealt with those, but not when he was experiencing all of them for Luce. She had never in her life felt less a woman, less a human being. He had thrown her love right back in her face in favor of Luce Daggett.

"I see," she said tautly. "I've been terribly mistaken about a lot of things, haven't I? Oh, how stupid of me!" The bitter laugh came unbidden, and was so successful he flinched. "Hang on for a minute, would you?" she asked, turning away. "I must have a quick wash. Then I'll take you back to X. Colonel Chinstrap wants to ask you a few questions, and I'd much rather he didn't find you still here."

There was a tin dish on a little shelf below the back window, and it contained a small quantity of water. With face averted she hurried to it, the tears pouring down, and made a great show of splashing in the water, then stood with a towel pressed against her eyes and cheeks and nose, willing with will of iron those senseless, shaming tears to stop.

He was what he was; should that therefore automatically mean her love for him was worthless? Should that mean there was nothing in him worth loving, that he could prefer Luce to her? Oh, Michael, Michael! In all her life she had never felt so betrayed, so dishonored, Honour without honor indeed, and yet why should she feel so? He was what he was and it had to be beautiful or she would never have loved him. But the void between reason and her own feminine feelings was unbridgeable. No rival woman could ever have hurt like that. Luce. Weighed and found wanting in favor of *Luce*.

What an idiot Colonel Chinstrap was, to suspect Michael of killing Luce! A pity he couldn't have witnessed this little scene. It would have scotched his suspicions on the spot. If any man was ever sorry another man was dead, that man was Sergeant Michael Wilson. He could have done it, she supposed; during the night she had been absent from her room long enough for him to have made the journey, done the deed and returned. But he hadn't. Nothing would ever convince her he had. Poor Michael. He was probably right. If he had remained in ward X, Luce would not have needed to kill himself. His victory over her would have been complete—no, more complete.

Oh, God, the mess! What a tangle of desires, a confusion of motives. Why had she removed Michael from the ward? At the time it had seemed the right thing to do, the only thing to do. But had she planned all along to seize any opportunity to have Michael to herself? Ward X gave one no chance of that; they were all so jealous of time spent alone with any of them. And men, she supposed, were men. Since she had virtually thrown herself at a Michael suffering some sort of withdrawal from his encounter in the bathhouse, why should she blame him for picking her up and using her?

The tears dried. She put the towel down and walked to the

mirror. Good, the tears hadn't lasted long enough to mar. Her veil was crooked, her duty hat that never, never betrayed her. Love might; duty never did. You knew where you stood with duty—what you gave to it, you got back. She slid open some deep dark drawer in her mind and dropped the love into it, straightening her veil in the mirror above eyes as cool and detached as that sister tutor so many years ago. Not a viable proposition. She turned away from herself.

"Come on," she said kindly. "I'll take you back where you belong now."

Stumbling occasionally, Michael plodded along beside her, so wrapped in his own misery he scarcely knew she was there. It was not merely beginning again; it had already begun, and it was a life sentence this time, a whole eternity of living. Why did it have to happen to him? What had he ever done? People kept dying. And all because of him, of something in him. A Jonah.

The temptation to lie on her bed, smell her sheets, press his body flat where hers had lain . . . She was regretting it now, but she hadn't then. All that love he had never known, and it was there. Like a dream. And it had come at the end of something hideous, was born in his shame at being caught naked and compromised by Luce Daggett. It was born in the destruction of his self-esteem, the total realization that he too hungered to kill.

Visions of Luce danced in his brain, Luce laughing, Luce mocking, Luce staring at him in amazement because he had been willing to clean up the mess Luce had made, Luce in the bathhouse unable to believe his overtures were unwelcome, Luce sublimely unaware that murder hung above him like a sword. *You stupid drongo!* As Luce had once said it to him, so now he said it to the ghost of Luce. You stupid, stupid drongo! Didn't you realize how you were asking for it? Didn't you realize that war blunts a man's objections to killing, accustoms him to it? Of course you didn't. You never got closer to war than a base ordnance unit.

There was no future left. No future for him. Perhaps there

never had been. Ben would say a man always brought it upon himself. It wasn't fair. Oh, God, how angry he was! And she, whom he didn't know, he would never know now. She had looked at him just now as at a murderer. And he was a murderer; he had murdered hope.

4　The moment they arrived in the ward Michael hurried away; the one glance into his face that he permitted her tore afresh at her own ribboned feelings, for the grey eyes had gone beyond tears, so deeply troubled she would have been willing to put herself aside and offer him what comfort she could. But no; he hurried away as if he couldn't escape from her quickly enough. And yet the moment he saw Benedict sitting disconsolate on the side of his bed he swerved, and sat down.

Sister Langtry could bear it no longer, and turned to go into her office, as much angry now as anguished. Clearly everyone was more important to Michael than she was.

When Neil came in with a cup of tea and a small plate of bread and butter she was tempted to order him out, but something in his face prevented her. Not a vulnerability, exactly, more a simple anxiety to serve and to help that could not thus be so lightly dismissed.

"Drink and eat," he said. "You'll feel better."

She was very grateful for the tea, but didn't think she would be able to get any of the bread down; however, once her first cup was succeeded by her second she managed to eat about half of what was on the plate, and did indeed feel better.

Neil sat down in the visitor's chair and watched her intently, fretting at her grief, frustrated by his own impotence, chafing at the restrictions she had imposed upon his conduct toward her. What she was prepared to do and give for Michael did not apply to himself, and that was galling, for he knew he was the better man. Better for her in every way. He had more than an inkling that Michael knew it too, this morning if not yesterday. But how to convince her? She wouldn't even want to hear.

As she pushed the plate away he spoke. "I am so desperately sorry that you of all people had to be the one to find Luce. It can't have been pretty."

"No, it wasn't. But I can cope with that sort of thing. You mustn't let it worry you." She smiled at him, unaware that she looked as if she waded through the depths of a private hell. "I must thank you for taking the blame for my decision to remove Michael from X."

He shrugged. "Well, it helped, didn't it? Let the colonel cling to his stronger-sex convictions. If I had told him I was drunk and incapable where you were well in command, he would have found me far less believable."

She pulled a face. "That's true."

"Are you sure you're all right, Sis?"

"Yes, perfectly all right. If I feel anything, it's rather as if I've been cheated."

His brows twitched. "Cheated? That's an odd word!"

"Not to me. Did you know I had taken Michael to my quarters, or was it purely a shot in the dark?"

"Logic. Where else would you take him? I knew last night that when it came to the morning you wouldn't want to haul Luce up before the MOs or the MPs. So that meant you couldn't create speculation by putting Mike in another ward, for instance."

"You're very acute, Neil."

"I don't think you realize how acute I actually am."

Not being able to answer, she turned slightly away and looked out the window.

"Here, have a cigarette," he said, pitying her, but bitter too, because he knew there were some things of which she would not permit him to speak.

She turned back. "I daren't, Neil. Matron is bound to be along any tick of the clock. By now the colonel will have told her and the super and the MPs, and she at least will be champing at the bit. The seedier the sensation the better, as far as she's concerned, provided she's not an active part of the seediness. She's going to lap this little chapter of disasters up."

481

"How about if I light a cigarette for myself, and you sneak the odd puff from it? You need something more than tea."

"If you dare mention whisky to me, Neil Parkinson, I'll order you to stay in your room for a month! And I can do without the cigarette, truly. I have to salvage what respectability I can or Matron will drum me out of the corps. She'd smell the smoke on my breath."

"Well, at least as the donor of the grog the colonel's well and truly hoist with his own petard."

"Which reminds me of two things. First, I'd be grateful if none of you mentions the whisky to a soul. Second, take this glass to the ward with you and give yourself and the others a tablespoon each. It'll cure your hangovers."

He grinned. "For that I could kiss your hands and feet!"

At which point Matron bustled through the door, nostrils quivering like a bloodhound's. Neil disappeared with a sketchy obeisance to Matron en route, leaving Sister Langtry to face her superior officer alone.

5 Matron was the start of a different kind of wearing day. She was followed by the super, a mild little red-hat colonel who really only cared about hospitals in the abstract, and felt quite helpless when faced with patients in the flesh. As commanding officer of Base Fifteen, he bore the responsibility of determining the style of the inquiry. After a brief inspection of the bathhouse, he rang the DAPM at divisional headquarters, and requested the services of a Special Investigations sergeant. A busy man, the super had scant interest in what his eyes clearly told him was an open and shut case of suicide, albeit suicide of a particularly unpleasant kind. So he handed the physical execution of the inquiry over to Base Fifteen's quartermaster, a tall, amiable and most intelligent young man named John Penniquick; then with mind relieved of a burden having considerable nuisance value, he went back to the complicated business of closing a whole hospital down.

Captain Penniquick was if anything even busier than the super, but he was also a very efficient and hard-working officer, so when the SI sergeant arrived from HQ he briefed him thoroughly.

"I'll see any of them myself whom you think I ought," he said, peering over his glasses at Sergeant Watkin, whom he found perceptive, sensible and likable. "However, it's your pigeon entirely, unless the pigeon turns out to be a hawk, in which case, yell your head off and I'll come running."

After ten minutes in the bathhouse with the major who was Base Fifteen's pathologist, Sergeant Watkin walked carefully across the distance between the bathhouse and the back steps of ward X, then skirted the ward and came in up the ramp at its front. Though Sis-

483

ter Langtry was not in her office, the telltale rattle of the fly-curtain alerted her, and she came speeding up the ward. A neat little thing, thought the sergeant with approval; real officer material, too. It cost him no pangs to salute her.

"Hello, Sergeant," she said, smiling.

"Sister Langtry?" he asked, removing his hat.

"Yes."

"I'm from the DAPM's office at divisional HQ, and I'm here to look into the death of Sergeant Lucius Daggett. My name's Watkin," he said, his voice slow, almost sleepy.

But he wasn't a bit sleepy. He declined her offer of tea once they were established in her office, and got straight down to business. "I'll need to see your patients, Sister, but I'd like to ask you a few questions first, if you don't mind."

"Please do," she said tranquilly.

"The razor. Was it his own?"

"Yes, I'm sure it was. Several of the men use Bengals, but I fancy Luce's was the only one with an ebony handle." She decided to be quite open, and thus establish the fact that she was in charge of things, too. "Though there's surely no doubt in your mind as to suicide, Sergeant? I saw the way Luce was holding the razor. The fingers had spasmed on it exactly the way the living hand would have held it, and the hand and arm were caked with an enormous amount of blood, as they would be while he made incisions like those I saw. How many cuts were there?"

"Three only, as a matter of fact. But they were two more than he needed to finish himself fast."

"What does the pathologist say? Have you brought in someone from outside, or are you using Major Menzies?"

He laughed. "How about I just take a little snooze on one of your spare beds and let you handle the inquiry?"

She looked mortified, demure, and somehow oddly girlish. "Oh, dear, I do sound bossy, don't I? I'm so sorry, Sergeant! It's just that I'm fascinated."

"It's all right, Sister, ask away. You tickle me to death. Seriously, there's very little doubt that it was suicide, and you're quite right about the way the razor was held. Major Menzies says there's no doubt in his mind that Sergeant Daggett inflicted the wounds on himself. I'll just ask around among the men about the razor, and if it all tallies I reckon the whole thing can be wound up pretty quickly."

She heaved a huge sigh of relief and smiled at him enchantingly. "Oh, I'm so glad! I know everyone thinks mentally unstable patients are capable of anything, but truly my men are a gentle lot. Sergeant Daggett was the only violent one."

He looked at her curiously. "They're all soldiers, aren't they, Sister?"

"Of course."

"And mostly front line, I'll bet, or they wouldn't be troppo. Sorry to contradict you, Sister, but your men can't be a gentle lot."

Which told her that the investigations he carried out would be as thorough as he felt necessary. So it all devolved upon whether he had spoken the truth when he said he believed Luce had committed suicide.

His inquiries about the razor revealed that indeed the only ebony-handled Bengal had belonged to Luce. Matt owned an ivory-handled Bengal, and Neil a set of three with mother-of-pearl handles which had been custom made for his father before the First World War. Michael used a safety razor; so did Benedict and Nugget.

The men of X made no attempt to hide their dislike of the dead man, nor did they hinder Sergeant Watkin's investigations by any of the means they had at their disposal, from assumed lunacy to assumed withdrawal. At first Sister Langtry had feared they would be recalcitrant, for loneliness, segregation and idleness sometimes did lead them to play childish games, as they had on the afternoon of Michael's admission. But they rallied to the call of good sense and cooperated splendidly. As to whether Sergeant Watkin found talking at length to them a pleasant task, he didn't say, though he paid rapt attention to everything, including Nugget's lyrical description of the scotomata which had prevented his seeing more than mere knobs and knotholes, and then only the left halves.

Michael was the only member of ward X the quartermaster asked to see personally, but it was a friendly talk rather than an interrogation. He held it in his own office simply because ward X was a difficult place in which to obtain any real privacy.

Though Michael didn't realize it, his own appearance was his best defense. He reported in full uniform save for his hat, and so did not salute when he came in, only stood to attention until bidden to sit down.

"There's no need to worry, Sergeant," said Captain John Penniquick, his desk clear except for the various papers pertaining to the death of Sergeant Lucius Daggett. The pathologist's report covered two handwritten pages, and indicated besides a detailed description of the wounds which had caused death that there had been no foreign substances in stomach or bloodstream such as barbiturates or opiates. Sergeant Watkin's report was longer, also handwritten, and included synopses of all the conversations he had had with the men of X and with Sister Langtry. Forensic investigations were extremely limited in a wartime army, and did not run to fingerprinting; had Sergeant Watkin seen anything suspicious he would heroically have done his duty in this respect, but a wartime army SI sergeant was not very conversant with fingerprints. As it was, he had seen nothing suspicious, and the pathologist had concurred.

"I really only wanted to ask you about the circumstances which led up to Sergeant Daggett's death," the quartermaster said, a little uncomfortably. "Had you any suspicion that Sergeant Daggett intended to proposition you? Had he made any sort of advance to you before?"

"Once," said Michael. "It didn't go anywhere, though. In all honesty I don't think Sergeant Daggett was a proper homosexual, sir. He was a mischief-maker, that's all."

"Are your own leanings homosexual, Sergeant?"

"No, sir."

486

"Do you dislike homosexuals?"

"No, sir."

"Why not?"

"I've fought alongside and under the command of them, sir. I've had friends who were inclined that way, one very good friend especially, and they were decent blokes. That's the only thing I ask of anyone, that he be a decent bloke. I reckon homosexuals are like any other group of men, some good, some bad, and some indifferent."

The QM smiled faintly. "Have you any idea why Sergeant Daggett had his eye on you?"

Michael sighed. "I think he got at my papers and read them, sir. I can't think why else he would have looked at me twice." He stared very directly at the QM. "If you've read my papers, sir, you'll know this isn't the first time I've been involved in trouble about homosexuals."

"Yes, I know. It's very unfortunate for you, Sergeant. Did you leave Sister Langtry's room at any time during the night?"

"No, sir."

"So after the incident in the bathhouse you never saw Sergeant Daggett again?"

"No, sir, I never did."

The QM nodded, looked brisk. "Thank you, Sergeant. That will be all."

"Thank you, sir."

After Michael had gone Captain Penniquick gathered all the papers concerning the death of Sergeant Lucius Daggett into one sheaf, pulled a fresh piece of paper into the middle of his desk, and began to write his report to the super.

6 Though Base Fifteen was still three or four weeks away from its appointment with extinction, for the five patients and one nursing sister of ward X all sense of belonging to any kind of community ceased upon the death of Sergeant Lucius Daggett. Until the result of the inquiry they walked on eggshells around each other, each so conscious of the huge unspoken undercurrents which sucked and thundered through the ward that anything more than a bland contact with the others could not be borne. The general misery was a palpable thing, the individual miseries touchy and secret and shaming. To speak of it was impossible, to generate a false gaiety equally so. Everyone simply prayed for an innocuous finding at the end of the inquiry.

Not so immersed in her own troubles as to lose sight of how fragile these her men were, Sister Langtry watched for the slightest sign of breakdown in any and all of them, including Michael. Strangely, it didn't appear. Withdrawn they were, but not from reality; they had withdrawn from her, flung her into a chilly outer orbit where she was merely called upon to do unimportant things, like get their early morning tea, get them out of bed, get them through the cleaning, get them down to the beach, get them into bed. Courteous and deferential they always were; truly warmly friendly, never.

She wanted to beat her fists against the wall, cry out that she didn't need punishing like this, that she too suffered, that she wanted, needed desperately, to be drawn into the circle of their regard, that they were killing her. Of course she couldn't do that, didn't do that. And since she could only interpret their reaction in the light of her own guilts, the path her own thoughts trod, she understood very well what they were too basically kind to tell her in so many words. That she had failed in her duty, and so failed them. Madness, it must have been madness! To have so lost all regard for what was the right thing to do for all her patients that she had spiritually abandoned them for the sake of her own physical gratification. The balance and insight which would normally have assured her this was far too simple an assumption had entirely deserted her.

Honour Langtry had known many different kinds of pain, but never a pain like this, all-pervasive, self-perpetuating, asphyxiating. It wasn't even that she dreaded walking into ward X; it was the bitter knowledge that there was no longer a ward X to walk into. The family unit was broken.

"Well, the verdict's in," she said to Neil on the evening three days after Luce's death.

"When did you hear?" he asked, but as if it didn't really interest him very much.

He still came for those private little chats with her, but a chat was all it could be. Banal observations about this and that and the other thing.

"This afternoon, from Colonel Chinstrap, who stole a march on Matron. Since she told me later, I got it twice. Suicide. The result of an acute depressive state following an acute burst of mania—claptrap, but convenient claptrap. They have to put something impressive down."

"Did they say anything else?" he asked, leaning forward to ash his cigarette.

"Oh, we're none of us too popular, as you can imagine, but no blame is attached to us officially."

He kept his voice light as he asked, "Did you get your knuckles rapped, Sis?"

"Not officially. However, Matron had a few words of her own to say on the subject of my taking Michael to my quarters. But luckily my blameless reputation stood me in good stead. When it came right down to it she just couldn't imagine *me* hauling poor Michael off with any but the purest of motives. As she said, it

489

merely looked bad, and because it looked bad, I let the whole side down. I seem to have been letting whole sides down all over the place lately."

During the past three days his imagination had played indescribable tricks, visualizing her with Michael in any one of a thousand different ways, by no means all to do with sex. Her betrayal ate at him, try as he would to be dispassionate, and so understand. There wasn't the room for understanding when he had also to accommodate his own torment and jealousy, his own unshakable determination to have what he wanted, what he *needed*, in spite of her obvious preference for Michael. She had turned to Michael without thinking of any of the rest of them, and he couldn't seem to forgive her. Yet his feelings for her were as strong, as intense as ever. I am going to have her, he thought; I will not give her up! And I am my father's son. It has taken this to make me see how much I am my father's son. It's a strange sensation. But it's a good sensation.

She, poor lost soul, suffered so. He couldn't take any pleasure in witnessing that, nor did he wish it upon her, but he did feel hers was a case where to suffer would eventually lead her back to the place where she had once been, where he, Neil, belonged rather than Michael.

He said, "Don't take it so hard."

She thought he was referring to her rapped knuckles, and smiled wryly. "Well, it's over and done with now, thank God. It's a pity that life with Luce wasn't more pleasant. I never wished him dead, but I did wish we didn't have to put up with his living presence. Only now it's some kind of hell."

"Is that really to be laid at Luce's door?" he asked; perhaps now that the verdict was in they could both relax enough to begin communicating again.

"No," she said sadly. "It has to be laid at my door. At no one else's."

Michael tapped. "Tea's made, Sis."

She forgot where the conversation with Neil might have been

leading, and looked straight past Neil to Michael. "Come in for a moment, would you? I'd like to talk to you. Neil, will you hold the fort? I'll be down shortly, but you might like to pass on the news to the others."

Michael shut the door behind Neil's back, his face a mixture of unhappiness and dread. And discomfort. And fear. As if he would rather be any place on earth than standing in front of her desk, *her* desk.

In that she was correct; he would rather have been anywhere else than there. But what she saw in his face was on his own behalf, not anything to do with her. And yet everything to do with her. He was terrified of breaking down in front of her, aching to spill all the reasons for his pain to her; but that would be to lift a floodgate which must remain closed. It was all gone, and perhaps it had never been, and certainly it could never be. A chaos. A confusion more desperate than any he had ever known, while he stood there and longed for things to be different, and knew things could not be different. Sorrowing for her because she didn't know, agreeing that she couldn't be permitted to know, fighting himself and what he wanted. Knowing that what she wanted could not make her happy. And continuing to learn as he watched her face that he had hurt her very cruelly.

Some of this showed on his face, too, while he stood in front of her desk, waiting.

And suddenly it literally blazed in her, that look of his, set fire to a store of wounded pride and pain she had scarcely known she possessed.

"Oh, for God's sake will you get that bloody look off your face?" she cried, her voice a quiet scream. "What on earth do you think I'm going to do to you, get down on my bended knees and beg for a repeat performance? Well, I'd rather be dead! Do you hear me? Dead!"

He flinched, whitened, set his mouth, said nothing.

"I can assure you, Sergeant Wilson, that the thought of any personal relationship with you is the farthest thing from my mind!" she went on feverishly, like a lemming to the killing sea.

491

"I simply called you in here privately to inform you that the verdict on Luce's death is in, and it's suicide. Along with the rest of us, you've been completely exonerated. And now perhaps you'll be able to stop this nauseating display of self-recrimination. That's all."

It had never occurred to him that the largest part by far of the hurt he had inflicted upon her was due to what she saw as his rejection of her. Horrified, he tried to put himself in her place, to feel that rejection as she was feeling it, a purely personal thing all tied in with her womanhood. Had he valued himself more, he might have understood sooner, better. But to him, her reaction was almost inconceivable; she was interpreting the whole thing in a way he could not. Not because he wasn't sensitive, or perceptive, or involved with her. But because where his mind had been dwelling since Luce's death was so divorced from the personal aspects of what had happened in her room. There had been so many other considerations to torment him—and so much to do—that he hadn't stopped to think how his behavior looked to her. And it was too late now.

He seemed ill, grief-stricken, curiously defenseless. And yet, Michael as always, still his own man. "Thank you," he said, without irony.

"Don't *look* at me like that!"

"I'm sorry," he said. "I won't look at all."

She transferred her gaze to the papers on her desk. "So am I sorry, Sergeant, believe me," she said with cold finality. The papers might have been written in Japanese for all the sense she could make of them. And suddenly it was just too much to bear; she looked up, her heart in her eyes, and cried, "Oh, Michael!" in a very different tone of voice.

But he had already gone.

It took her five minutes to get moving, the reaction was so devastating. She sat and shook, her teeth chattered, she wondered for a moment if she might truly be going mad. So much shame, so little self-control. It had not occurred to her that she could possess such a huge blind urge to hurt anyone she loved, or that the knowledge she had succeeded in hurting could be so comfortless and intolerable. Oh, God, dear God, she prayed, if this is love, heal me! Heal me or let me die, for I cannot live with this kind of agony one minute more. . . .

She went to the door of her office, reaching to unhook her hat, then remembered she had to change back into boots. Her hands were still trembling; it took time to lace the boots, do up the gaiters.

Neil appeared as she bent over in her chair to pick up her basket.

"You're going off now?" he asked, surprised and disappointed. After that promising final remark of hers before Michael had appeared he had been hoping to resume where they had been cut off. But as usual Michael took precedence over him.

"I'm awfully tired," she said. "Do you think you can manage without me for the rest of the evening?"

It was gallantly said, but he only had to look at her eyes to see that there was very little between gallantry and despair. In spite of himself he reached out, took her hand and held it between both his own, chafing the skin to instill in it a little warmth.

"No, my very dear Sister Langtry, we can't possibly do without you," he said, smiling. "But we will, just this once. Go to bed and sleep."

She smiled back at him, her comrade of so many months in X, and wondered where her burgeoning love for him had gone, why Michael's coming had so abruptly snuffed it out. The trouble was she had no key to the logic behind love, if key there was, if logic there was.

"You always take away the pain," she said.

It was his phrase he used of her; her saying it affected him so powerfully he had to remove his hands quickly. Now was not the time for him to say what he longed to.

Taking her basket from her, he ushered her out of the ward as if he were the host and she a visitor, refusing to give the basket back until they reached the bottom of the ramp. And then he stood until long after her grey shape flickered and vanished into

493

the darkness, looking up at the darkness, listening to the soft dripping of condensation on cooling eaves, the vast chorus of the frogs and the endless murmur of the surf far out on the reef. There was a downpour in the air; it would rain before very long. If Sis didn't hurry she'd be wet.

"Where's Sis?" asked Nugget when Neil sat down in her chair and reached for the teapot.

"She's got a headache," said Neil briefly, avoiding eye contact with Michael, who sat looking as if he too had a headache. Neil pulled a face. "God, I loathe being mother! Who is it has milk again?"

"Me," said Nugget. "Good news, eh? Luce is properly dead and buried at last. Phew! It's a relief, I must say."

"May God have mercy on his soul," said Benedict.

"On all our souls," said Matt.

Neil finished his chore with the teapot, and began pushing the various mugs down the table. Without Sis there was little joy in late tea, he reflected, staring at Michael because Michael's attention was on Matt and Benedict.

With a great show of importance, Nugget produced a very large book, spread it out where there was no danger of spilling tea on it, and began on page one.

Michael glanced at him, amused and touched. "What's that in aid of?" he asked.

"I've been thinking about what the colonel said," Nugget explained, one hand extended across the open book with the reverence of a holy man for his bible. "There's no reason why I can't go to night school to get me matriculation, is there? Then I could go to university and do medicine."

"And do something with your life," Michael said. "Good on you and good luck to you, Nugget."

I wish I didn't like him through every moment of hating him, thought Neil; but that's the real lesson the old man wanted me to learn out of the war—not to let my heart stand in the way of what has to be done, and to learn to live with my heart after it's done. So Neil was able to say very calmly, "We've all got to do something with our lives when we're out of the jungle greens. I wonder how I'll look in a business suit. I've never worn one in my life." Then he sat back and waited for Matt to respond to the deliberate stimulus.

Matt did, quivering. "How am I going to earn a living?" he asked, the question bursting from him as if he had never meant to say it, yet had been thinking of nothing else. "I'm an accountant, I've got to see! The army won't give me a pension; they reckon there's nothing wrong with my eyes! Oh, God, Neil, what am I going to do?"

The others were very still, everyone looking at Neil. Well, here goes, he thought, as deeply moved by Matt's cry as the others, yet filled with a purpose that overruled his pity. Now isn't the right time and place to go into specifics, but there's been enough groundwork laid for me to see if Mike gets the message.

"That's my share, Matt," Neil said positively, his hand on Matt's arm firmly. "Don't worry about anything. I'll see you're all right."

"I've never taken charity in my life, and I'm not about to start now," said Matt, sitting straight and proud.

"It is not charity!" Neil insisted. "It is *my share*. You know what I mean. We made a pact, the lot of us, but I have yet to contribute my full share." And he said this looking not at Matt but at Michael.

"Yes, all right," said Michael, who knew immediately what was going to be demanded of him. In a way it came as an exquisite relief to have it asked of him rather than to have to offer it. He had known the only solution for some time, but he didn't want it, and so had not found the strength to offer it. "I agree with that, Neil. Your share." His eyes left Neil's stern unyielding face, rested on Matt with great affection. "It's not charity, Matt. It's a fair share," he said.

495

7   Sister Langtry beat the rain. It came cascading down just as she let herself in her door, and within minutes every kind of living small creature seemed to materialize out of it: mosquitoes, leeches, frogs, spiders reluctant to wet their feet, ants in syrupy black rivers, bedraggled moths, cockroaches. Because her two windows were screened she usually did not need to pull the net down around her bed, but the first thing she did tonight was to tug it free of its ring and drape it down.

She went to take a shower in the bathhouse, then wrapped herself in her robe, packed her two pathetically thin pillows against the wall at the head of her bed, and lay back against them with a book she hadn't even the strength to open, though sleep felt far away. So she put her head back and listened instead to the ceaseless hollow roar of rain on an iron roof. Once it had been the most thrilling and wonderful sound in the world, during her childhood days in country where rain was the harbinger of prosperity and life; but here, in this profligate climate of perpetual growth and decay, it meant only an external deadening to everything save what went on in her mind. You couldn't have heard anyone speak unless he shouted in your ear; the only voices you really heard were those which chattered on inside your head.

The sick horror of discovering she could lash out at someone beloved as she had lashed out at Michael had faded to an almost apathetic self-disgust. And right alongside it had crept a hunger for self-justification. Hadn't he done to her what no man should ever do to any woman? Hadn't he indicated a perverse preference for Luce Daggett? Of all the men in the world, Luce Daggett!

This was fruitless. Round and round and round in

ever-diminishing circles, getting nowhere, achieving nothing. She was so tired of herself! How could she have allowed this to happen? And who was Michael Wilson? There were no answers, so why bother to ask the questions?

Mosquito nets suffocated. She threw hers back impatiently, not having heard the tiny dive-bomber sound of a mosquito, and forgetting that the rain would have drowned the noise of a real dive-bomber. There was never enough light within the confines of the net to read, and she felt better; she would read for a while and hope sleep came.

A leech dropped with a soundless plop from some crevice in the unlined roof, and landed wriggling obscenely on her bare leg. She tore at it in a frenzy, gagging at the feel of it, but could not dislodge it. So she leaped to light a cigarette, and without caring whether she burned herself, she applied the red-hot tip to the leech's slimy black stringlike body. It was a big tropical leech, four or five inches long, and she could not have borne to wait the process out, invaded by it, watch it grow bloated and congested on her blood, then finally roll off replete like a selfish man from a woman after sex.

When the thing was fried enough to shrivel away from her skin she ground it to smeared pulp beneath a boot, shivering uncontrollably, feeling as violated and besmirched as any Victorian heroine. Loathsome, repulsive, horrible thing! Oh, God, this climate! This rain! This awful, eternal dilemma. . . .

And then of course the place where the leech had fastened its blind seeking mouth kept bleeding, bleeding, the tissue impregnated with an anticlotting factor from its saliva, and it had to be attended to immediately or in this climate the wound would ulcerate. . . .

It was not very often that she found herself reminded so physically of Base Fifteen, its difficulties, isolation, introspection. Of all the places she had ever been, she thought, dealing with iodine and sterile swabs, Base Fifteen had made less impression than any. In fact, almost no impression at all. As if it were a stage set, without substance or real meaning of its own, simply a claus-

497

trophobic backdrop for a complicated interplay of human emotions, wills, desires. Which was logical. Base Fifteen as anything more than an insubstantial backdrop didn't make sense. A more sterile, dreary institution had never been erected; even the wet canvas world of a casualty clearing station had more personality. Base Fifteen was there to serve a war, it had been dumped where the convenience of war dictated, without respect to the ideal site, staff contentment, or patient welfare. No wonder it was a painted cardboard world.

And, leg propped up on the wooden chair, the walls oozing sweat and speckled with great patches of mildew, the cockroaches waving their antennae from every dark cranny, itching for the light to go off, Sister Langtry looked around her like someone doubting the reality of a dream.

I shall be so glad to go home, she thought for the very first time. Oh, yes, I shall be so glad to go back to my home!

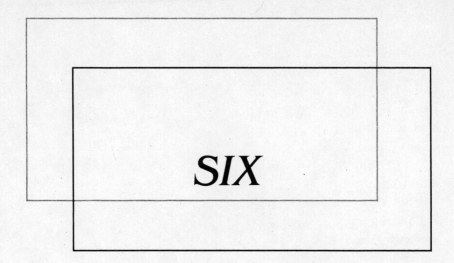

SIX

1 Sister Langtry came into the sisters' sitting room about four the next afternoon feeling more like herself, and looking forward to a cup of tea. There were five sisters scattered in two groups about the room, and Sister Dawkin on her own, sitting in one chair with her feet propped up on another, her head nodding toward her ample chest in a series of jerks which culminated in one large enough to startle her into waking. Eyes about to close again, she saw who was standing in the doorway, waved and beckoned.

As Sister Langtry walked across to join her friend a strong wave of dizziness provoked a sudden panic; she wasn't sleeping and she wasn't eating properly, and if she wasn't careful she would become ill. Contact with the men of X and their problems had educated her sufficiently to understand that her present symptoms were escapist, a means whereby to manufacture an end demanding her removal from ward X without the humiliation of having to request Matron for a transfer. Therefore pride dictated that she sleep and eat. Tonight she would take a Nembutal, something she had not done since the day of the incident in the dayroom.

"Sit down, love, you look knocked up," said Sister Dawkin, tugging at a chair without getting up herself.

"You must be pretty knocked up yourself to snatch forty winks in here," said Sister Langtry, seating herself.

"I had to stay on the ward last night, that's all," said Sister Dawkin, disposing her feet in a new position. "We must look like Abbott and Costello to the rest of the room, me like the wreck of the *Hesperus* and you like a poster to recruit army nurses. That tomfool of a woman, even daring to suggest there was any ulterior motive! As if you'd ever stoop to anything vulgar or underhand!"

501

Sister Langtry winced, wishing that Matron had had the good sense to hold her tongue. But the stupid woman had blabbed to her best friend, who had blabbed to her best friend, and so on, and so on. The whole nursing staff (which meant the MOs as well) knew that Sister Langtry—of all people!—had kept a soldier in her quarters all night. And of course the place was buzzing about the hara-kiri suicide; it was no use hoping such drama would not be talked about. Though luckily her own reputation was so good that few indeed believed there was anything more in her conduct with the soldier than an urgent and understandable desire to keep him out of harm's way. If they only knew, thought Sister Langtry, feeling the eyes on her from the two other tenanted tables, if they only knew what my real troubles are! Inversion, murder, rejection. Though murder has gone, thank God. I don't have to worry about that one.

The kind fading eyes that forthrightness saved from being commonplace were looking at her shrewdly; Sister Langtry sighed and moved a little, but did not say anything.

Sister Dawkin tried another gambit. "As of next week, me dear, it's back to dear old Aussie and Civvy Street," she said.

Sister Langtry's cup just missed making contact with its saucer, and slopped tea all over the table. "Oh, bother! Now look what I've done!" she exclaimed, reaching into her basket for a handkerchief.

"Are you sorry, Honour?" Sister Dawkin demanded.

"Just taken by surprise," Sister Langtry said, mopping up tea with her handkerchief and wringing it out into her cup. "When did you hear, Sally?"

"Matey told me herself a few minutes ago. Came sweeping into D ward like a battleship in full sail and let it drop with her mouth all pursed up as if she'd been eating alum for a week. She's devastated, of course. She'll have to go back to that poky little convalescent home she ran before the war. None of the big hospitals or even the district hospitals would touch her with a barge pole. It beats me how she ever got so high up in the army."

502

"It beats me too," said Sister Langtry, spreading her handkerchief out to dry on a corner of the table, then dispensing more tea into a fresh cup and saucer. "And you're right, none of the decent hospitals would touch her with a barge pole. Somehow she always reminds me of a night-shift forewoman in a big food factory. Still, if the army will keep her on she might remain in the army. She'd be better off. Better pension when she retires, too, and she can't be all that far off retirement."

"Hah! If the army keeps her it will be better luck than she deserves." Sister Dawkin reached for the teapot and replenished her own cup. "Well, I know I'm going to be sorry to go home," she said abruptly. "I hate this place, I've hated every place the army has sent me, but I've loved the work, and God, how I've loved the freedom!"

"Yes, freedom is the right word, isn't it? That's what I've loved too. . . . Do you remember that time in New Guinea when there was no one else fit to operate but you and me? I'll never forget that as long as I live."

"We did all right, too, didn't we?" Sister Dawkin smiled, swelling visibly with pride. "Patched those boys up as if we'd got our FRCSs, and the boss recommended us for decoration. Ah! I'll never wear any ribbon with more pride than my MBE."

"I am sorry it's over," said Sister Langtry. "I'm going to loathe Civvy Street. Bedpan alley again, women patients again. Bitch bitch, moan moan. . . . It would be just my luck to land on gynae or obstets. Men are so easy!"

"Aren't they? Catch women patients lending you a hand if the staff situation's desperate! They'd rather be dead. When women hit a hospital they expect to be waited on hand and foot. But men pop on their halos and do their best to convince you that their wives never treated them the way nurses do."

"What are you going to do on Civvy Street, Sally?"

"Oh, have a bit of a holiday first, I suppose," said Sister Dawkin unenthusiastically. "Look up a few friends, that sort of thing. Then back to North Shore. I did my general at Royal Newcastle and my midder at Crown Street, but I've spent most of my nurs-

503

ing career at North Shore, so it's more or less home by now. Matron ought to be glad to see me if no one else is. As a matter of fact, I'm in line for a deputy matronship, and that's about the only thing I am looking forward to."

"My matron will be glad to see me, too," said Sister Langtry thoughtfully.

"P.A., right?" asked Sister Dawkin, using the universal nursing slang for the Royal Prince Alfred Hospital.

"P.A. it is."

"Never fancied a hospital quite that big myself."

"Actually, though, I'm not sure I want to go back to P.A.," Sister Langtry remarked. "I'm toying with the idea of going to Callan Park."

Since Callan Park was a mental hospital, Sister Dawkin sat up very straight and subjected Sister Langtry to a hard stare. "Seriously, Honour?"

"Deadly earnest."

"There's no status to mental nursing! I don't even think there's a certificate to collect. I mean you must know that mental nurses are regarded as the dregs."

"I've got my general certificate and my midder, so I can always go back to proper nursing. But after X, I'd like to try a mental hospital."

"They're not the same as X, though, Honour! Troppo is a temporary thing, most men get over it. But when a patient walks through the gates of a mental hospital he's facing a life sentence."

"I know all that. But maybe it's going to change. I like to hope it will, anyway. If the war helps it as much as it's helped things like plastic surgery, lots of things are going to happen in psychiatry. And I'd like to be in on the ground floor of the changes."

Sister Dawkin patted Sister Langtry's hand. "Well, ducky, you know your own mind best, and I never was one to preach. Just remember what they always say about mental nurses—they wind up dottier than their patients."

Sister Pedder walked into the room, looking around to see

504

which group would welcome her most cheerfully. On seeing Sister Dawkin and Sister Langtry she gave Sister Dawkin a wide smile and Sister Langtry a frosty nod.

"Have you heard the news, young Sue?" called Sister Dawkin, nettled by the girl's rudeness.

Common courtesy therefore compelled Sister Pedder to approach the table, looking as if there was a bad smell in the vicinity.

"No, what news?" she asked.

"We're almost a thing of the past, dearie."

The girl's face came alive. "You mean we're going home?" she squeaked.

"Jiggety-jig," said Sister Dawkin.

Tears sprang to Sister Pedder's eyes, and her mouth hovered between the twisted tremble of weeping and the softer curve of smiling. "Oh, thank God for that!"

"Well, well! A proper reaction at last! Easy to tell the old warhorses among us, isn't it?" asked Sister Dawkin of no one in particular.

The tears began to fall; Sister Pedder saw how she could rub it in. "How am I ever going to be able to face his poor mother?" she managed to articulate between sobs, so distinctly that all the heads in the room turned.

"Oh, dry up!" said Sister Dawkin, disgusted. "And grow up, for pity's sake! If there's one thing I can't stand, it's crocodile tears! What gives you the right to judge your seniors?"

Sister Langtry sprang to her feet, appalled. "Sally, please!" she cried. "It's all right, truly it's all right!"

Neither of the other two groups of nurses was making any pretense at disinterest any more; those with their backs to the Langtry table had frankly swung their chairs around so they could watch comfortably. It was not a malicious interest at all. They just wanted to see how Sally Dawkin handled that presumptuous young monster Pedder.

"In your quarters all night with Sergeant Wilson, t-t-t-t-t-treating him for shock!" said Sister Pedder, and brought out her handkerchief to cry in good earnest. "What luck for you there's

505

no one else in your block these days! But I know what's been going on between you and Sergeant Wilson, because Luce told me!"

"Shut up, you silly little bitch!" shouted Sister Dawkin, too angry now to remember discretion.

"It's all right, Sally!" begged Sister Langtry, trying desperately to get away.

"No, dammit, it's not all right!" roared Sister Dawkin in the voice which made probationers shiver. "I won't have such talk! Don't you dare make insinuations like that, young woman! You ought to be ashamed of yourself! It wasn't Sister Langtry in over her head with a man from the ranks, it was you!"

"How dare you!" gasped Sister Pedder.

"I dare pretty bloody easy," said Sister Dawkin, who somehow still managed in spite of posture and stockinged misshapen feet to gather the awesome power of a senior sister about her. "Just you remember, my girl, that in a few weeks it's all going to be mighty different. You'll be just another pebble on that big civilian beach. And I'm warning you now, don't ever come looking for a job anywhere I am! I wouldn't have you on my staff as a wardsmaid! The trouble with all you young girls is that you climb into a smart officer's uniform and you think you're Lady Muck—"

The tirade came to a sudden halt, for Sister Langtry gave such a horrifyingly despairing cry that Sister Dawkin and Sister Pedder forgot their quarrel. Then she collapsed onto a settee and began to weep; not soft, fluttering sobs like Sister Pedder's, but great grinding tearless heaves which seemed to the worried eyes of Sister Dawkin almost like convulsions.

Oh, it was such a *relief!* Out of the angry atmosphere, out of the misguided affection of Sister Dawkin and the dislike of Sister Pedder, Honour Langtry finally managed to give birth to the terrible lump of suffering which had grown and chewed inside her for days.

"Now see what you've done!" snarled Sister Dawkin, lumbering out of her chair and sitting down beside Sister Langtry. "Go

506

away!" she said to Sister Pedder. "Go on, skedaddle!"

Sister Pedder fled, terrified, as the other sisters began to gather around; for Sister Langtry was well liked.

Sister Dawkin looked up at the others, shaking her head, and began with infinite kindness to stroke the jerking, shuddering back. "There there, it's all right," she crooned. "Have a good cry then, it's more than time you did. My poor old girl! My poor old girl, so much trouble and pain. . . . I know, I know, I know. . . ."

Only vaguely conscious of Sister Dawkin beside her, talking so kindly, of the other sisters still gathered around and concerned for her too, Sister Langtry wept and wept.

2 A kitchen orderly brought the news of Base Fifteen's imminent demise to ward X, transmitting it to Michael in the dayroom, and grinning from ear to ear as he babbled incoherently about seeing home again, home for good.

Michael didn't move back to the verandah at once after the orderly had gone; he stood in the middle of the dayroom with one hand plucking at his face and the other pressed against his side, kneading it. So soon, he thought dully. So soon! I'm not ready because I'm frightened. Not depressed, and not unwilling, either. Just so frightened of what my future holds, what it's going to do to me, what it's going to make me. But it has to be done, and I am strong enough. It's the best way for all concerned. Including me. Including her.

"This time next week we're all going to be on our way back to Australia," he said when he returned to the verandah.

A leaden silence greeted his news. Reclining on the nearest bed with a Best & Taylor he had wheedled out of Colonel Chinstrap held up in front of him, no mean feat of strength, Nugget lowered the enormous book and stared. Matt's long hands closed into fists, and his face became still. Busy with a pencil and a piece of paper, Neil dropped the pencil onto the drawing, which happened to be of Matt's hands, and looked ten years older than his age. Only Benedict, rocking back and forth in a chair that had never been designed to rock, seemed uninterested.

A slow smile began to dawn on Nugget's mouth. "Home!" he said experimentally. "Home? I'm going to see Mum!"

But Matt's tension didn't lessen, and Michael knew he was thinking of that first encounter with his wife.

508

"What a pisser!" said Neil, picking up his pencil again, and discovering that the repose of the beautiful hands was quite destroyed. He put the pencil down, got up, strolled to the edge of the verandah and stood with his back to everyone. "What a bloody pisser!" he said to the palms, voice bitter.

"Ben!" said Michael sharply. "Ben, do you hear that? It's time to go home; we're going back to Australia!"

But Benedict rocked on, back and forth, back and forth, the chair creaking dangerously, face and eyes shut away.

"I'm going to tell her about it," said Michael suddenly, strongly. He spoke to any and all of them, but it was at Neil he looked sternly.

Neil didn't turn, but his long slim neat back subtly altered; all at once it didn't appear slack or weary or without resource. The back looked as if it was the property of a powerful and an aggressive man.

"No, Mike, you're not going to tell her," he said.

"I have to," said Michael, not pleading, not looking at Matt or Nugget or Benedict, though both Matt and Nugget had tensed warily.

"You can't say one thing to her, Mike. Not one thing! You can't without all our consents, and we don't give them."

"I can tell her, and I will tell her. What does it matter now? If she knows, it can't change anything; we've all decided what to do in that situation." He reached out to put his hand on Benedict's shoulder, as if the rocking irritated him, and Benedict stopped rocking immediately. "I've taken the biggest share because I'm the only one who can, and because it was more my fault than anyone else's. But I'm not willing to suffer in silence! I'm just not that much of a hero. Yes, I know I'm not the only sufferer. But I *am* going to tell her."

"You can't tell her," said Neil, voice steely. "If you do, so help me I'll kill you. It's too dangerous."

Michael didn't mock, as Luce might have done, but the set of his face was unafraid. "There'd be no point in killing me, Neil, and you know it. There's been enough killing."

509

Sister Langtry's soft step sounded; the group froze. When she walked out onto the verandah she stood taking stock of them, a little puzzled, wondering just what she had interrupted. If someone had got ahead of her with the news about Base Fifteen, why should that provoke a quarrel? But they knew about Base Fifteen, and they had been quarreling.

"That footstep!" said Matt suddenly, breaking the silence. "That wonderful footstep! It's the only woman's step I know. When I had eyes I didn't listen. If my wife were to walk in now, I wouldn't be able to pick up the sound of her."

"No, mine is not the only woman's step you know. There's one other," said Sister Langtry, walking over to Matt and standing behind him, her hands on his shoulders.

He closed the eyes that couldn't see and leaned back a little against her, not enough to offend her.

"You hear Matron's step at least once a week," said Sister Langtry.

"Oh, her!" he exclaimed, smiling. "But Matron clomps like a GOPWO, Sis. There's no woman's sound to her feet."

"A GOPWO?" she asked, stumped.

"A Grossly Over-Promoted Warrant Officer," he said.

She burst out laughing, gripping his shoulders hard, laughing at some joke that was entirely her own, and laughing with real, happy abandon. "Oh, Matt, that's a truer description than you'll ever know!" she said when she could. "Wait until I tell Sally Dawkin that one! She'll love you forever."

"Sis! Sis! Isn't it good news, eh?" called Nugget from his bed, Best & Taylor forgotten. "I'm going home, I'm going to see my mum soon!"

"It certainly is good news, Nugget."

Neil remained standing with his back turned. Sister Langtry leaned over to study the drawing of Matt's hands, then she straightened and released Matt's shoulders, moving slightly away. And managed then finally to look at Michael, whose hand still rested on Benedict's shoulder, a parody of her own touching of Matt. Their eyes met, both armored against pain, both stern

510

with some purpose; met like the eyes of strangers, politely, without personal interest.

She swung away and went back inside.

Neil appeared not long afterward, shutting the office door behind him with an air that said he wished he had a Do Not Disturb sign to hang outside it. When he saw her face, eyes swollen down to the cheekbones, he studied it grimly.

"You've been crying."

"Like a waterfall," she admitted readily. "I made an utter fool of myself right in the middle of the sisters' sitting room, as a matter of fact, and not while I had the place to myself, either. I had quite an audience. A delayed reaction, I suppose. The young sister from Woop-Woop—you know, the bank manager's daughter—came in at the wrong moment and accused me of victimizing Luce. That annoyed my friend Sister Dawkin from D ward, they began to squabble, and suddenly there I was, in floods of tears. Ridiculous, isn't it?"

"That's what really happened?"

"Now could I make up a story like that?" She sounded more like her old self, placid and calm.

"Do you feel better for it?" he asked, offering her one of his cigarettes.

She smiled slightly. "Deep down, yes. On the surface, quite the opposite. I feel ghastly. Like something the cat dragged in. My mainspring's all unwound."

"That's a very mixed metaphor," he said gently.

She considered it. "I'd say it all depended what the cat dragged in, wouldn't you? Perhaps it was a mechanical mouse. I feel mechanical."

He sighed. "Oh, Sis! Have it your own way, then. I'll leave the subject—and you—severely alone."

"Thank you, I'd appreciate that," she said.

"And in a week it comes to an end," he said conversationally.

"Yes. I suspected they'd try to have us all out before the monsoons really begin."

511

"Going home to Australia—I mean when you're discharged?"

"Yes."

"To do what, may I ask?"

Even with the swollen relic of tears on her face, she looked very remote. "I'm going to nurse at Callan Park. Since you're from Melbourne, you may not know that Callan Park is a big mental hospital in Sydney."

He was shocked, then saw that she really meant it. "God, what a waste!"

"Not at all," she said crisply. "It's useful and necessary work. I badly need to continue doing something useful and necessary. I'm lucky, you see. My family has sufficient means to ensure that when I'm old and unable to work, I won't be on the breadline. So I can please myself what I do with my life." Her congested eyelids lifted, the cool eyes looked him over. "But you? What are you going to do, Neil?"

That was that, then. Exit Neil Parkinson. Her voice, her look, her manner all said that he would not be welcomed into her life after the war.

"Oh, I'll be off to Melbourne," he said easily. "What I would really like to do is return to the Greek Peloponnese—I have a cottage near Pylos. But my parents, particularly my father, aren't getting any younger—nor am I getting younger, for that matter. So I fancy it will be Melbourne rather than Greece for me. Besides, Greece would have meant painting, and I'm only a competent painter, nothing more. That used to hurt, oddly enough. But it doesn't now. It seems a minor consideration. I've learned so much during the last six years, and ward X has rounded off my education beautifully. I've got my priorities right these days, and I know now that I can be an active help to the old man—to my father. If I'm to follow in his steps, I'd better start finding out how the family businesses are run."

"You'll be busy."

"Yes, I will." He rose to his feet. "Will you excuse me? If we're really moving out of here soon I have a great deal of packing to do."

She watched the door shut behind him, and sighed. If Michael had done nothing else for her, he had at least shown her that there was a vast difference between affection and love. She was fond of Neil, but she certainly didn't love him. Steady, reliable, upright, courteous, well-bred Neil, willing to yield up everything he was to her. A very good marriage prospect. Handsome, too. Stuffed with all the social graces. To prefer Michael to him was not sensible. But what she prized in Michael was his self-containment, that air which said no one could ever turn him from his elected path. An enigma he might be, but not knowing him had not prevented her loving him. She loved his strength. She didn't love Neil's willingness to subjugate his own wishes before hers.

Odd that Neil should seem so much better in himself these days, though he must know she had decided there was no future in a relationship with him after the war. And it was a relief to find him not upset by that decision, not sounding as if he felt rejected. The knowledge that she was hurting him had been there ever since the incident in the dayroom, but so much else had happened she hadn't thought very much about how Neil must be feeling. Now was about the time her guilt would have turned in on itself to plague her, and it seemed not necessary after all. His fondness for her showed again today, but there was no sign of bitterness, of hurt. And that was such a relief! To have given expression to her grief at last, and now to find Neil was whole in spite of her conduct; today was the first good day in weeks.

3

It was an odd week which followed. Normally when the occupants of one place for months or years prepare to leave it, there is a distracted flurry of activity, worries about everything from pets to vehicles. The quick disintegration of Base Fifteen was not like that. Its inhabitants had been steadily whittled down for months anyway; all that remained was a nucleus which would be shelled out swiftly and competently. No one was encumbered by the kind of baggage which usually clutters up a life, for in essence Base Fifteen was minus clutter. The country around it did not abound in desirable handcrafts, handmade furniture or any of the other impedimenta collectors had accumulated in the war theatres of Europe, India, the Middle East, North Africa. A lot of the sisters found themselves the recipients of shy gifts from their men, mostly small things made in the ward, but on the whole the inmates of Base Fifteen would depart with no more to ship than what they had brought with them when they arrived.

A target time to be ready was posted, and adhered to with the easy discipline of trained personnel; it came and it went, but Base Fifteen remained. No one had expected it to be any different. The target date was actually a warning bell, at the sound of which everyone had to be prepared to evacuate at once.

Matron fussed and clucked, mosquito nets less important than the schedules and timetables she carried everywhere with her to consult during interminable briefings of her nurses, all of whom could cheerfully have strangled her. Now that Base Fifteen was ending, what the nurses really wanted to do was spend the maximum amount of time with their patients.

Ward X lay fairly much outside the main area of activity, down in its little afterthought building far away

514

from the other inhabited wards, with its tiny complement of five patients and one lone nurse. And among its tiny complement there was more awkwardness than joy, sudden silences which were hard to break, forced cheerfulness when things became too unbearable, and a rather chilling loss of rapport. Sister Langtry was absent quite a lot, unwillingly pressed into service on various Matron-inspired subcommittees to handle the evacuation. And the five patients took to haunting the beach all day, for the old official times governing its use had gone by the board.

Sorrowfully Sister Langtry realized her patients had decided to do without her where possible, even had she more time to spend with them. Neil seemed to have forgiven her, the others had not. And she noticed that a certain polarization had come into being among them. Nugget had shifted himself away from the rest, filled with a new purpose and a happy optimism which seemed to be a combination of rejoining his mother and reorganizing his civilian life to encompass a career as a doctor. His aches and pains had quite vanished. Neil and Matt were inseparable; she knew Matt leaned on Neil heavily, unburdening himself about the many problems he would have to face. Which left Michael to concentrate on Benedict, as indeed he always had. They too were inseparable.

Benedict, she thought, was not well, but what she could do about it she didn't know. A talk to Colonel Chinstrap had got her predictably nowhere, yet he had been willing, even eager, to do what he could to procure a military pension for Matt in spite of the hysterical tag on his history. When she begged the colonel to consider shipping Ben straight into a proper psychiatric unit for further investigation, his attitude was unyielding. If she had no more to base her suspicions on than a vague disquiet, he said, what did she expect him to do? His examination of Sergeant Maynard had revealed no deterioration. How to explain to a man who was a competent enough neurologist but had no interest in mental disorders without organic foundation that she wanted to call a man back who was slipping away? And how did one call him back? That was what nobody in the world knew how to do.

Ben had never been an easy patient to contend with because of that very tendency to shut himself away; what worried her was that without the security of ward X about him, Benedict would accomplish the ultimate in disappearing acts, and swallow himself up. So Michael's attachment to him she viewed as a godsend, for he did have more success with Ben than anyone else, including herself.

Watching them all more or less doing without her, she began to understand better what was happening to them, and to herself. The overemotional interpretation she had put on everyone's conduct including her own since Luce's death was fading; that outburst in the sisters' sitting room, she realized, must have done her a great deal of good. Without consciously knowing it, the inhabitants of ward X were all relinquishing their ties to each other; the family unit that had been ward X was falling apart right along with Base Fifteen. And she, as its mother figure, was probably more sensitive and more hurt by what she saw than her men, her children. Odd, that as her strength waned theirs appeared to be growing. Was that what mothers did? Tried to hold a family unit together when the natural reasons for its existence had ceased?

They are going back to a different world, she thought, and I'm sending most of them back equipped to deal with it. Or I'm trying. So I mustn't cling, I mustn't let them cling. I must let them go with as much grace and dignity as I can possibly muster.

4   And then it began, with a roaring of trucks and a huge windlike stirring. Luckily the monsoon had not yet arrived in force, and it looked as if evacuation would be completed in plenty of time to avoid being rained out.

Apathy changed to euphoria, as if now that it was actually here, people could bring themselves to believe in it; suddenly home was not a dream, it was a coming reality. Cries rose and fell on the air, shrill whistles, cooees, snatches of song.

Iron-disciplined sisters found themselves caught up in a mood they could not control, were subjected to hugs, kisses, fabulously exotic Hollywoodish embraces, sometimes tears, and turned one and all into adorably confused women. For them it was a parting of great moment, the end of the high point in their lives; they were all unmarried women, most of them halfway at least toward retirement, and in this most difficult, isolated place they had put forth their very best, a vital part of a great cause. Life would never again hold quite so much of everything; these boys were the sons they never had, and they knew themselves worthy mothers of such sons. But now it was all over, and while they had to thank God for that, they knew nothing ever again could equal the pleasure and the pain and the heights of these last few years.

Down in X the men waited that final morning clad in full uniform instead of what was clean and came first to hand; their tin trunks, kit bags, packs and haversacks lay in mounds on the floor, and that same floor was assaulted for the first time in its memory by the heavy pounding of many pairs of boots. A warrant officer came, gave Sister Langtry last-minute instructions as to

517

where she was to bring her enlisted men for embarkation, and supervised the removal of extra kit which the men would not normally be expected to carry.

As she turned away from the front door after the warrant officer left, Sister Langtry saw Michael alone in the dayroom, making tea. A quick glance down the ward assured her no one was watching; the rest of them apparently were out on the verandah waiting to be waited on.

"Michael," she said, standing in the dayroom doorway, "come for a walk with me, please. There's only half an hour left. I should very much like to spend ten minutes of it with you."

He considered her thoughtfully, looking much as he had that afternoon he had arrived, jungle-green trousers and shirt, American gaiters, webbing, tan boots polished until they shone, brass glittering, everything neat, pressed, and worn so well.

"I'd like that too," he said seriously. "Just let me drop this out on the verandah first. I'll meet you at the bottom of the ramp."

I wonder if he'll appear with Benedict in tow? she asked herself as she stood in the watery sun at the bottom of the ramp. See one and you saw the other.

But Michael was alone, and fell into step alongside her. They paced down the path which led to the beach, stopping just short of the sand.

"It came too quickly. I'm not ready after all," she said, looking at him a little guardedly.

"Nor am I," he said.

She began to babble. "This is the first opportunity I've had to see you alone since—since Luce died. No, since the verdict came in. That was awful. I said so many awful things to you. I want you to know I didn't mean them. Michael, I'm so sorry!"

He listened to her quietly, his face sad. "There's nothing to be sorry for. I'm the one who ought to be doing all the apologizing." Seeming to deliberate within himself, he went on slowly. "The others don't think so, but I feel I owe you some sort of explanation, now that it doesn't matter much any more."

All she heard was the last little bit. "Nothing matters much any more," she said. "I'd like to change the subject, ask you about home. Are you going back to your dairy farm right away? What about your sister and your brother-in-law? I'd like to know, and we don't have much time."

"We never did have much time," he said. "Well, I have to get my discharge first. Then Ben and I are going to head for my farm. I've just had a letter from my sister and they're counting the days until I can take over again. Harold—my brother-in-law—wants to get his old job back before too many soldiers are demobbed."

She gaped. "Ben and you? Together?"

"Yes."

"Ben and you."

"That's right."

"In God's name, *why?*"

"I owe it to him," said Michael.

Her face twisted. "Oh, come off it!" she snapped, rebuffed.

He set his shoulders. "Benedict is alone, Sis. He doesn't have anyone at all waiting for him. And he needs someone with him all the time. Me. It's my fault, I wish I could make you see that! I have to make sure it never happens again."

Her torment became bewilderment; she stared at him and wondered if she would ever begin to get to the bottom of the mystery that surrounded Michael. "What are you talking about? What never happens again?"

"I said it before," he said patiently. "I think I owe you an explanation. The others don't agree. They think you ought to be kept right out of it forever, but I want to tell you. I understand why Neil's so set against your knowing, but I still believe I owe you an explanation. Neil wasn't with you that night, I was. And it entitles you to an explanation."

"What explanation? What is all this?"

There was a big petrol drum lying on its side just where the path petered out; he turned, put one foot up on it, gazed down at his boot. "It's not easy to find the right words. But I don't want you to look at me the way you've been looking at me ever since

519

that morning, not understanding. I agree with Neil, telling you isn't going to change anything, but it might mean that the last time I ever see you, you won't be looking at me as if half of you hated me and the other half was wishing it could hate me too." He straightened, faced her. "This is hard," he said.

"I don't hate you, Michael. I couldn't ever hate you. What's done is done. I'm not fond of post-mortems. So tell me, please. I want to know. I have a right to know. But I don't hate you. I never have, I never could."

"Luce didn't kill himself," he said. "Benedict did the killing."

She was back in the midst of all that blood, all that ruined magnificence, Luce sprawled without consideration of grace, fluidity of line, theatrical effect—unless sheer horror was the effect he had aimed for, and Luce was not like that. Luce loved himself too much, visually anyway.

Her face went so pale the light striking down through the palms gave it a greenish hue; for the second time in their acquaintance Michael moved close to her, slipped an arm around her waist and supported her so strongly all she could feel was the feel of him.

"Here, love, don't pass out on me! Come on now, take a few deep breaths, that's the good girl!" He spoke tenderly, he held her tenderly.

"I knew it all the time," she said slowly, when at last she was able to speak. "There was something wrong. It just wasn't typical of Luce. But it's typical Benedict, all right." The color stole back beneath her skin, she clenched her fists in an impotent anger directed entirely against herself. "Oh, what a *fool* I am!"

Michael released her and stepped back a pace, looking more at ease with himself. "If I didn't think so much of you I wouldn't have told you, but I couldn't bear to see you hate me. It's been killing me. Neil knows that, too." Then, seeming to decide he was drifting from the subject, he turned back to it. "Benedict won't ever do anything like it again, Sis, you have my word. As long as I'm there to look after him, he can't do it again. You do understand that, don't you? I have to look after him. He's my responsibility. He did it for me, or he thought he did it for me, which amounts to the same thing. I told you in the morning, remember? I told you it was wrong of me to stay with you all night. I should have gone back to the ward to keep an eye on Ben. If I had been there where I belonged, it would never have happened. Funny, I've killed men, and for all I know they were better men by far than Luce. But Luce's death is my responsibility. The death of the others I've killed is the responsibility of the King; the King has to answer to God for them, not me. I could have stopped Ben. No one else could have, because no one else had any idea what was going on in Ben's mind." He closed his eyes. "I was weak, I gave in to myself. But oh, Honour, I wanted to stay with you! I couldn't believe it! A little bit of heaven, and I'd been in hell so long. . . . I loved you, but I never dreamed you loved me until then."

Huge reserves of strength, she had huge reserves of strength; she plundered them with the carelessness of a freebooter. "I should have known that," she said. "Of course you loved me."

"I was thinking of myself first," he said, apparently happy he could talk to her at last. "If you knew how much I blame myself! There was *no need* for Luce to die! All I had to do was be there in the ward to show Ben I was all right, that it wasn't in Luce's power to harm me." His chest heaved, more a shudder than a sigh. "While I was with you in your room, Ben was all alone, thinking Luce had somehow managed to destroy me. And once Ben came to that conclusion, the rest followed naturally. If Neil had known, it might have been different. But Neil had no idea. He had other things on his mind. And I wasn't even there to tidy up the mess, the rest had to do that too." His hand went out to her, fell back to his side. "I have a lot to answer for, Honour. The way I hurt you—there are no excuses for that, either. I can't make any, even to myself. But I'd like you to know that I . . . feel it, that I do understand what I've done to you. And that of everything I have to answer for, hurting you is the hardest to bear."

The tears were coursing down her face, more for his pain than her own. "Don't you love me now at all?" she asked. "Oh, Michael, I can stand anything but losing your love!"

"Yes, I love you. But there's no future in it—there couldn't be, there never was, Luce and Ben aside. If it hadn't been for the war, I would never have met anyone like you. You would have met men like Neil, not men like me. My friends, the sort of life I like to lead, even the house I live in—they don't fit with you."

"You don't love a life," she said, wiping the tears away. "You love a man, and then you *make* a life."

"You would never have made your life with a man like me," he said. "I'm just a dairy farmer."

"That's a ridiculous thing to say! I'm not a snob! And tell me the difference between one kind of cocky and another—my father's a cocky too. The scale's bigger, that's all. Nor am I dependent upon having money for my happiness."

"I know. But you are from a different class than me, and we don't have the same outlook on life."

She stared at him strangely. "Don't we, Michael? Now I find that an odd thing for you of all people to say! I think we do have the same outlook on life. We both like to look after those less capable than ourselves, and we both aim at the exact same thing—encouraging them to become self-sufficient."

"That's true. . . . Yes, that's very true," he said slowly, and then: "Honour, what does love mean to you?"

The apparent non sequitur took her aback. "Mean?" she asked, hedging for more time to think.

"Mean. What does love mean to you?"

"My love for you, Michael? Or for others?"

"Your love for me." He seemed to enjoy saying it.

"Why—why, it means sharing my life with you!"

"Doing what?"

"Living with you! Keeping your home, having your babies, growing old together," she said.

He looked remote; her words affected him, she could see, but had no power to penetrate deeply enough to reach that calm determination which possessed no image of self.

"But you haven't served any sort of apprenticeship for that," he said. "You're thirty now, and your apprenticeship has been for something quite different. A different sort of life. Hasn't it?" He paused, not taking his eyes off her face, raised to his in a fearful bewilderment that yet showed the germ of a comprehension she was unwilling to acknowledge. "I think neither of us is suited for the life you're describing. When I started to talk to you I didn't think I'd mention this, but you're a good fighter, you won't be palmed off with anything but the real root of the matter."

"No, I won't," she said.

"The real root of the matter is just what I said—neither of us is suited for the sort of life you describe. It's too late to wonder what or why now. I'm the sort of man who mistrusts the wants that come out of a part of me I'm normally able to control. I don't want to cheapen it by calling it my bodily desires, and I don't want you to think I'm belittling my feelings for you." He gripped her arms near the shoulder. "Honour, listen to me! I'm the sort of bloke who mightn't come home one night because on a trip into town I found someone who in my mind needed me more than you do—I don't mean I'd desert you, and I don't necessarily mean another woman; I mean that I'd know you could get along without me until I could come home again. But I might be two days helping that person, or I might be two years. I'm like that. The war gave me a chance to see what I am. It's given you a chance to see what you are, too. I don't know how much you're willing to admit to yourself about yourself, but I've learned that when I'm moved to pity, I'll always be moved to help. You are a complete person. You don't need my help. And not needing my help, I know you can get along without me. You see, love is beside the point."

"You're approaching a paradox," she said, throat aching from the effort to quell fresh tears.

"I suppose I am." He paused, searching for the next thing to say. "I don't think I have a very high opinion of myself. If I did, I wouldn't need to be needed. But I do need to be needed, Honour! I've got to be needed!"

523

"I need you!" she said. "My soul, my heart, my body—every bit of me needs you; it always will! Oh, Michael, there are all kinds of need, all kinds of loneliness! Don't confuse my strength with a lack of need! *Please* don't! I need you to fulfill my very life!"

But he shook his head, obdurate. "You don't. You never will. You're already fulfilled! If you weren't, you couldn't be the person I know you to be—warm, loving, interested, happy doing a job few women can do. Almost all women can make a home, have babies. But you're too different to be content in that sort of cage. Your apprenticeship's wrong for it. Because after a while that's how you'd see the life you described with me, devoted exclusively to me. As a cage! You're a stronger bird than that, Honour. You've got to stretch your wings in wider territory than a cage."

"I'm prepared to risk that happening," she said, white-faced, desolate, but still fighting.

"I'm not. If it was just you I was describing, maybe I would risk it. But I'm describing me as well."

"You're chaining yourself to Ben far more rigidly than you would to me."

"But I can't hurt Ben the way I'd end in hurting you."

"Looking after Ben is a full-time job. You won't be able to take off to help anyone else on a trip to town."

"Ben needs me," he said. "I'll live for that."

"What if I offered to share your charge of Ben?" she asked. "Would you agree to a life with me that shared our need of being needed?"

"Are you offering that?" he asked, uncertain.

"No," she said. "I can't share you with the likes of Benedict Maynard."

"Then there's no more to be said."

"About us, no." She still stood between his hands, and made no move to escape them. "Do the others agree that you should look after Ben?"

"We made a pact," he said. "We all agreed. No lunatic asylum for Ben, no matter what happens. Nor will Matt's wife and children go hungry. We all agreed."

"*All* of you? Or you and Neil?"

He acknowledged the accuracy of this with a rueful twist of lips and head. "I'll say goodbye now," he said, hands sliding up across her shoulders to cradle the sides of her neck, thumbs moving against her skin.

He kissed her, a kiss of deep love and pain, a kiss of acceptance for what must be and hunger for what might have been. And a voluptuous, erotic kiss filled with the memories of that one night. But he took his mouth away abruptly, too soon; a lifetime would scarcely have been long enough.

Then he came stiffly to attention, a smile in his eyes, turned on his heel and walked away.

The petrol drum was there; she sank down onto it so that she wouldn't have to watch him until he disappeared, looking at her shoes, at the weak brown tendrils of grass, at the infinity of grains which made up the sand.

So that was that. How could she compete with the kind of need a Benedict had for a Michael? He was right thus far. And how lonely he must be, how driven. Wasn't that always the way it was? The strong abandoned in favor of the weak. The compulsion—or was it the guilt?—the strong felt to serve the weak. Who battened first? Did the weak demand, or did the strong offer themselves unsolicited? Did strength beget weakness, or reinforce it, or negate it? What was strength, what weakness, for that matter? He was right, she could get along without him. Was that therefore a lack of need for him? He loved her for her strength, yet he couldn't live with what he loved. In loving, he turned away from loving. Because it didn't, or it couldn't, satisfy him.

She had wanted to cry out to him, Forget the world, Michael, curl yourself up in me! With me you'll know a happiness you've never dreamed of! Only to cry that would have been to cry for the moon. Had she done it deliberately? Chosen to love a man who preferred to minister than to love? Since the day of his arrival in X she had admired him, and her love had grown out of that admiration, out of valuing what he was. Each of them had loved the other's strength, self-reliance, capacity to give. Yet it seemed these very qualities pushed them apart, not together. Two positives. My dearest, my most beloved Michael ... I shall think of you, and pray for you, that you continue always to find the strength.

She looked out over the beach, a little battered after the wind and rain of a few days before. There were two beautiful white terns soaring, soaring, wingtip to wingtip as if tied; they wheeled suddenly, still tied, dipped, and were gone. That's what I wanted, Michael! No cage! Only to fly with you against a great blue sky.

Time to get going. Time to walk Matt, Benedict, Nugget and Michael to the assembly point. It was her duty to do so. Neil as an officer would leave separately, she didn't yet know when. They'd tell her in due time.

As she walked, other thoughts than Michael began to intrude. There had been a conspiracy among the patients of ward X. A conspiracy in which Michael had been a willing party. And Neil was its ringleader. It didn't make any sense. Oh, it made sense to keep her in ignorance of what had really happened in the bathhouse until the cause of death was officially established and any inquiry closed. But why was Neil so against Michael's wish to tell her now, when it couldn't possibly matter? Neil knew her well enough to understand it was not in her nature to go running off to Colonel Chinstrap with the true story. What use would there be in that? What could it change? It could ensure Benedict's permanent commitment to some civilian institution, perhaps, but it would also result in dishonorable discharges for the rest of them, if not prison. Probably too they had agreed to close ranks against her, and would have denied all she might have told Colonel Chinstrap. *Why* had Neil fought to retain her ignorance? Not only Neil. Matt and Nugget were in it too.

What had Michael said, right at the last? They made a pact. Matt's wife and children would not go hungry. No doubt Nugget would get through medicine without starving, either. Benedict would not go to a mental asylum. Michael and Neil . . . They had split up the responsibilities between them, Michael and Neil. But what did Neil get out of it, if he was furnishing the money for Matt's family and Nugget's education? Two weeks ago she would have said, nothing; but today she wasn't so sure.

That hurt Neil didn't seem to have, his apparent acceptance of her rejection with sufficient tranquillity and lack of concern to make her feel he couldn't possibly be hurt. And who had been talking to Michael, that he came out with all those antiquated class differences between them? She clutched at this prideful straw eagerly. Someone had been working on Michael, trying to convince him he had to give her up. Someone? Neil!

5   The evacuation was very well organized. When she reached the assembly point with her four men they were snatched from her very quickly, barely time for a hug and a pecking kiss from each. And afterward she couldn't even remember how Michael looked at her, or how she looked at him. It seemed futile to linger hoping for another sight of them, so she slipped through the knots of waiting men and shepherding sisters, and walked back to X.

Second nature to tidy and straighten up; she went down the length of the ward smoothing the sheets, adjusting the nets for the last time in the Matron Drape, opening lockers, folding up the screens which hid the refectory table.

Then she went into her office, kicked her shoes off without unlacing them and sat down in her chair with her feet tucked under her, something she had never done before in that official seat. It didn't matter. There was no one to see, ever again. Neil was gone too. A harassed sergeant with a clipboard informed her of Neil's departure. She didn't understand what or who had slipped up, but it was too late to do anything about it anyway. And perhaps it was better not to be obliged to confront the ringleader of the conspiracy. There would be too many uncomfortable questions to ask him.

Her head drooped, propped on her hand; she dozed, and dreamed not unpleasantly of Michael.

It was about two hours later that Neil came swinging across the compound behind ward X, whistling jauntily, looking neat and at home in his captain's uniform, swagger stick tucked into the crook of his arm. He leaped lightly up the steps at the back of X and came into the dim and lifeless interior. Shocked, he pulled up sharply. X was empty; its emptiness shouted at him

528

from everywhere. After a moment he began to move again, but less surely, less lightheartedly; he opened the door to his cubicle and received another shock, for all his baggage was gone. There was not a trace of Neil Parkinson, troppo patient, left.

"Hello?" came Sister Langtry's voice through the thin wall. "Hello; who's there, please?"

She was sitting in a pose he had never seen before, not dignified, not professional, side-on to her desk, with her legs curled up under her on the chair, and her shoes empty on the floor. The room was full of smoke; her own cigarettes and matches lay in full view on the desk. And she looked as if she had been sitting so for a very long time.

"Neil!" she said, staring. "I thought you were gone! They told me you went hours ago."

"Tomorrow for me. What about you?"

"I'll be detailed to special one of the serious stretcher cases all the way to wherever we're going—Brisbane or Sydney, I suppose. Tomorrow or the day after." She stirred. "I'll find you something to eat."

"Don't bother, honestly. I'm not hungry. I'm just glad I didn't have to go today." He sighed luxuriously. "I've got you all to myself at last."

Her eyes gleamed. "Have you really?"

The way she said that gave him pause, but he sat back easily in the visitor's chair, and smiled. "Indeed I have. And not before time, too. It took some wangling, but the colonel's still a little sensitive about the whisky, so he managed to get my departure postponed. And he gave me a clean bill of health while he was about it. Which means I am no longer a patient in ward X. For tonight I'm merely a tenant."

She answered obliquely. "Do you know, Neil, I loathe the war and what it's done to us? I feel so personally responsible."

"Assuming the guilt of the whole world, Sis? Come now!" he chided gently.

"No, not the whole world, Neil. Only that share of the guilt which you and the rest withheld from me," she said harshly, and looked at him.

529

He drew a long, hissing breath. "So Michael couldn't keep his damned mouth shut after all."

"Michael was in the right of it. I was entitled to know. And I want to know. All of it, Neil. What *did* happen that night?"

Shrugging, mouth screwed up, he settled himself as if to embark upon a rather boring anecdote he secretly felt was not worth the telling. She watched him closely, thinking that the wall behind him, stripped now of its drawings because they resided in her baggage, threw his face into an intense relief it had always needed.

"Well, I had to have another drink, so I went back to the whisky," he said, lighting a cigarette and forgetting to offer her one. "The racket Luce was making woke up Matt and Nugget, so they decided to help me finish the second bottle. That only left Benedict to look after Luce, who had gone to bed. I'm afraid we did rather forget Luce. Or maybe we just didn't want to have to remember him."

As he talked the memory of that night began to move in him, to regenerate something of its original horror, and his face reflected this vividly. "Ben dug into his kit and found one of those illicit souvenirs we all have tucked away somewhere—a Japanese officer's pistol. He made Luce take his own razor, and he marched Luce to the bathhouse with the pistol right against his ribs."

"Was it Ben who told you about marching Luce to the bathhouse?" she asked.

"Yes. That much we got out of him, but as to what actually happened inside, I have only the sketchiest of ideas. Ben gets confused about it himself." He lapsed into silence.

"And?" she prompted.

"We heard Luce screaming like one damned, all the way from the bathhouse, screaming, screaming. . . ." He grimaced. "But by the time we got there it was far too late for Luce. It's a miracle no one else heard, except that the wind was blowing toward the palm grove, and we are a long way from civilization. We were too late—I said that, didn't I?"

"Yes. Can you give me any idea of how Ben did it?"

"I would guess Luce didn't have the guts to fight his way out, and maybe didn't even believe what was going to happen until it was too late. Those damned razors are so sharp.... Having forced Luce at gunpoint to hold the razor properly, I think Ben just reached out, grabbed Luce's hand, and it was all over. I can see Luce screaming and gibbering in fear, not even realizing what Ben was doing to him until it was done. You don't realize it, with something as sharp as a Bengal razor."

Frowning, she thought about it. "But his hand wasn't bruised, Neil," she objected. "If it had been, Major Menzies would have seen it. And Ben must have had to grip Luce very hard indeed."

"Hands don't bruise all that easily, Sis. Not like arms. The major wouldn't have been looking for anything more than external bruising—this isn't Scotland Yard, thank God. And it was done, knowing Ben, so quickly. He must have thought and thought about how he was going to kill Luce. It wasn't spur of the moment. And yet he could never have carried it through without being found out, because the minute it began to happen he went slightly mad—or mad in a different way; I don't know. Besides, he wasn't worried about getting caught. He just wanted to dispatch Luce in a way he knew would ensure Luce retained consciousness until the end. Because I think what he really wanted Luce to see was the maiming of his own genitalia."

"Was Luce dead when you got there?"

"Not quite. That was what saved our bacon. We got Ben away from him just before Luce went into some sort of death convulsion, still hanging onto the razor, and bleeding like a fountain. There were vital arteries severed. So while Matt took Ben outside and kept watch, Nugget and I tidied up. It only took a few minutes. What took the time was waiting until we were absolutely sure Luce had breathed his last, because we didn't dare touch him."

"It *must* have occurred to you to fetch help, to try to save him," she said, tight-lipped.

"Oh, my dear, there was not the slightest chance of saving

531

him! Give me more credit than that! Had we been able to save him, Ben wouldn't have been in such jeopardy. I'm not medically trained, no, but I am a soldier. I admit I never liked Luce, but it was hell to have to stand there and watch the man die!"

Grey-faced, he leaned to ash his cigarette, watching her absolutely absorbed, pain-filled eyes.

"Nugget was remarkably calm and competent, would you believe that? It just goes to show that you can live with a man for months without ever knowing what's inside him. And in all the days afterward, not once did I see him look as if he was going to lose his nerve."

His hand shook as he decided to stub the cigarette out. "The worst part was being sure we had done everything possible to make it look like a suicide, that we hadn't overlooked anything which might lead to a suspicion of murder.... Anyway, when we finished, we took Ben down to the next bathhouse, and while Matt kept watch—he's an excellent night watchman, he hears everything—Nugget and I hosed Ben down. He was covered in blood, but luckily he hadn't got his feet in it. I don't think we could have obliterated footprints. We burned his pajama pants. You were a pair short on your laundry count, do you remember?"

"How was Ben?" she asked.

"Very calm, and quite unrepentant. I think he still feels he was only doing his Christian duty. To him Luce wasn't a man, he was a demon from hell."

"So you shielded Benedict," she said coldly. "All of you shielded him."

"Yes, all of us. Even Michael. The minute you told him Luce was dead, he realized what must really have happened. I felt very sorry for Mike. You would have thought his own hand had done the deed, he was so upset, so choked with remorse. Kept saying he ought not to have been so self-centered, ought not to have stayed with you, that his duty was to stay with Benedict."

She didn't flinch; this too was a part of her share of the guilt.

"He said that to me, too. That he ought not to have stayed with me, that he ought to have been with *him*. He . . . him! He never used a *name!* I thought he meant Luce." Her voice broke, she had to pause to compose herself before going on. "It never, never occurred to me that he meant Benedict! I assumed he meant Luce, and I assumed he was homosexually involved with Luce. All the things I said, all the things I did! How much I hurt him! And what a mess I made of it! I'm ill even remembering."

"If he didn't use a name, you made a natural mistake," Neil said. "His papers implied homosexuality."

"How do you know that?"

"From Luce, via Ben and Matt."

"You're a very clever man, Neil. You knew or guessed it all, didn't you? And you set out to compound the confusion, deliberately. How could you do that?"

"What else did you expect us to do?" he asked, using the collective rather than the singular. "We couldn't just hand Ben over to the authorities! Luce was no loss to the world, and Ben certainly doesn't deserve to be shut up in some civilian mental asylum for the rest of his life because he killed Luce! You forget! We're all inmates of ward X! We've had a tiny taste of what life must be like for mental patients."

"Yes, I understand all that," she said patiently. "But it doesn't negate the fact that you took the law into your own hands, that you deliberately elected to cover up a murder, and that you also elected to deprive me of any opportunity to rectify the matter. I would have had him committed on the spot had I known! He's dangerous, don't any of you understand that? Benedict belongs in a mental asylum! You were wrong, all of you, but you especially, Neil. You're an officer, you know the rules and you're supposed to abide by them. If you plead your own illness as an excuse, then you belong in an institution, too! Without obtaining my consent, you've made me a party to it, and had it not been for Michael, I would never have known. I have a lot to be grateful to Michael for, but above all, I'm grateful to him for telling

533

me how Luce really died. Michael's thinking isn't the straightest, either, but he's one up on the rest of you! Thank God he told me!"

He threw his cigarette case down on the desk so violently that it bounced into the air and fell to the floor with a clatter, the catch springing open, cigarettes flying. Neither of them noticed; they were too intent upon each other.

"Michael, Michael, Michael!" he shouted, face convulsed, tears starting to his eyes. "Always, always Michael! For God's sake will you snap out of this—this *obsession* you have for Michael? Michael this, Michael that, Michael, Michael, Michael! I am so sick to death of that bloody name! Since the moment you set eyes on him you've had no time for anyone else! *What about the rest of us?*"

As in that scene with Luce, there was nowhere to go, nowhere to hide; she sat there filled with a dawning understanding of what Neil was crying from the heart about, her anger at him suddenly vanquished.

Rubbing his hand angrily across his eyes, he fought visibly for self-control, and when he spoke again he tried to make his voice sound calmer, more reasonable. Oh, Neil, she thought, how you've changed! You've grown. Two months ago you could never have managed that kind of self-discipline in the midst of such torment.

"Look," he said, "I know you love him. Even Matt, blind as he is, saw that a long time ago. So let's take it as read, and put it to one side as the prime consideration. Before Mike came you belonged to all of us, and we belonged to you. You *cared* about us! Everything you had, everything you were, was channeled to us—toward healing us, if you like. But when you're sick you can't see it as objectively as that, it's completely, exclusively personal. You—you wrapped us in you! And it never occurred to any of us that you spent your heart anywhere but inside X, and on us. When Michael came, it stuck out like a sore thumb that there was nothing the matter with him. To us, that meant you shouldn't need to bother with him at all. Instead—you turned right away from us, you went toward him. You abandoned us! You betrayed us! And that's why Luce died. Luce *died* because you looked at what Michael was, all that sanity and—and strength of being, and you loved it. You loved him! How do you think that made the rest of us feel?"

She wanted to shriek, But I didn't stop caring about you! I didn't, I didn't! All I wanted was something for myself for a change! There's only so much you can go on giving without taking something for yourself, Neil! It didn't seem a very large something at the time. My tenure in X was ending. And I loved him. Oh, God, I'm so tired of giving, giving! Why couldn't you be generous enough to let me have something too?

But she couldn't say any of it. Instead, she leaped to her feet and headed for the door, anywhere to get away from him. He grasped at her wrist in passing, swung her round and held her hard, grinding the bones of both her hands cruelly until she ceased to struggle.

"You see?" he asked softly, his grip slackening, his fingers sliding up her arms. "I've just held you a lot harder than Ben probably had to hold Luce, and I don't think you'll have any bruises."

She looked up into his face, a long way further than Michael's would have been, for Neil was very tall. His expression was both serious and aloof, as if he knew well all that she was feeling, and didn't blame her. But as if, like a priest-king of old, he was fully prepared to endure anything in order to achieve the ultimate end.

Until this interview she had not even begun to understand what sort of man Neil was; how much passion and determination lay in him. Nor the depth of his feelings for her. Perhaps he had hidden his hurt too skillfully, perhaps, as he charged, her absorption in Michael had made it all too easy for her to assure herself Neil was not devastated by her defection. He had been devastated. Yet it had not prevented him from moving to contain the threat Michael presented. It had not stopped his functioning. Bravo, Neil'

"I'm very sorry," she said, sounding quite matter-of-fact. "I don't seem to have the strength left to wring my hands as I say it, or weep, or go down on my knees to you. But I *am* sorry. More than you'll ever know. I'm too sorry to try to justify myself. All I can say is that we, those who care for you, our patients, can be as blind and misguided as any patient who ever walked through the door of a ward X. You mustn't think of me as a goddess, some kind of infallible being. I'm not. None of us are!" Her eyes filled with tears. "But oh, Neil, you have no idea how I wish we were!"

He gave her a light hug, kissed her brow, and let her go. "Well, it's done, and you know the old saying—even the gods can't unscramble eggs. I feel better for speaking my piece. But I'm sorry too. It's no joy for me to find that I can hurt you, even though you don't love me."

"I wish I could love you," she said.

"But you can't. I know. It's inescapable. You saw me the way I was when I first came to X, and it put me under a liability to you I don't suppose I'd ever cancel, even if there had been no Michael. You fell for him because he started out as a man for you—a whole man. He never hid himself away, or blubbered with self-pity, or completely unmanned himself. You never had to change his pants or clean up his messes or listen for long boring hours at a time to a litany of his woes—the same woes you must have heard from two dozen men just like me."

"Oh, please!" she cried. "I have never, never thought of it—or you—like that!"

"It's how I think of myself, looking back. I *am* able to look back now. So it's probably a more accurate picture of me than you're prepared to admit. But I'm cured, you know. From where I'm standing now I can't even see why it ever happened to me in the first place."

"That's good," she said, walking to the door. "Neil, please, can we make this goodbye? Right now, I mean. And can you manage to take it for what it is, not a sign of dislike or neglect or lack of love? It's just been the sort of day I want desperately to see end. And I find I can't end it with you. I'd rather not see you again.

Not for any other reason than it would be like holding a wake. Ward X is no more."

He accompanied her out into the corridor. "Then I shall hold my own wake. If you ever feel you'd like to see me, you'll find me in Melbourne. The address is in the phone book. Toorak. Parkinson, N.L.G. It took me a long time to find the right woman. I'm thirty-seven years old, so I'm not likely to change my mind in a hurry." He laughed. "How could I ever forget you? I've never kissed you."

"Then kiss me now," she said, almost loving him. Almost.

"No. You're right. Ward X is no more, but I'm still standing in its uncooled corpse. What you're offering is a favor, and I want no favors. Never any favors."

She held out her hand. "Goodbye, Neil. All the best of luck. But I'm sure you'll have it."

He took the offered hand, shook it warmly, then lifted it and kissed it lightly. "Goodbye, Honour. Don't ever forget—I'm in the Melbourne phone book."

The last trek from X across the compound; one never really thought it would come to that, even after one began to long for it. As if Base Fifteen represented a segment of life as huge as life itself. Now it was over. And it had ended with Neil, which was only fitting. That was quite a man. Yet she could see the truth in his saying he had started out with a big disadvantage. She *had* thought of him chiefly as a patient. And lumped him in with the rest. Poor, sad, frail . . . Now to find him none of those things was exhilarating. He implied his cure had come out of the situation in X during the last few weeks of its duration, but that wasn't true. His cure had come out of himself. The cure always did. So, in spite of the grief, the horror, and the pain, she commenced this last trek feeling as if ward X had existed for a purpose, a good purpose.

Neil hadn't even bothered to ask her whether she was going to try to exact the justice he felt was already done and she felt had been miscarried. Too late by far. Thank God Michael had told

537

her! Knowing what they had done had freed her from a large measure of the guilt she might otherwise have preserved over her conduct toward them. If they thought she had betrayed them in turning to Michael, she knew they had betrayed her. For the rest of their lives they would have to live with Luce Daggett. So would she. Neil hadn't wanted her told because he feared her brand of intervention would liberate Michael, and because he genuinely wished to spare her a share of the guilt. Half good, half bad. Half self, half nonself. About normal, that was.

SEVEN

1   When Honour Langtry got off the train in Yass there
     was no one to meet her, which didn't dismay her; she
     hadn't let her family know she was coming. Loving
     them was one thing, facing them quite another, and she
     preferred to face them in private. This was childhood
     she was coming back to, and it seemed so very far away.
     How would they see her now? What would they think?
     So she had put the moment of reunion off. Her father's
     property wasn't far out of town; someone would give
     her a lift.

     Someone did, but he was no one she knew, which
meant she could sit back and enjoy the fifteen-mile
drive in peace. By the time she arrived home the family
would know she was back, of course; the stationmaster
had welcomed her with open arms, found her the lift,
and undoubtedly telephoned ahead that she was on her
way.

     They were all gathered on the front verandah, waiting:
her father growing stouter and balder; her mother looking exactly the same; her brother Ian a younger, slimmer
edition of her father. There were hugs, kisses, much
standing back to look, exclamations and sentences that
never got finished because someone else interrupted.

     It was only after a fatted-calf sort of dinner that some
semblance of normality returned; Charlie Langtry and
his son went to bed, for their days began at dawn, while
Faith Langtry followed her daughter to her bedroom,
there to sit and watch her unpack. And talk.

     Honour's room was pleasant and unpretentious; how-
ever, it was large and had had money spent on it. No
particular skill with color or line had been applied
when the money had been spent, but the big bed
looked comfortable, so did the chintz-covered easy chair
in which Faith Langtry sat. There was a highly polished

541

old table with a wooden carver chair to serve as a work area, a vast wardrobe, a full-length mirror on a stand, a small dressing table, and one more easy chair.

While Honour moved around between wardrobe, dressing table drawers and her suitcases on the bed, her mother sat fully absorbing her daughter's appearance for the first time since her arrival home. Of course there had been periods of leave during the years in the army, but their lack of permanence, their atmosphere of urgency, had permitted no real and lasting impressions. This was different; Faith Langtry could look her fill without applying half her mind to what had to be fitted in tomorrow, or how they were all going to get through the next period of duty for Honour when it was bound to be dangerous. Ian hadn't been able to go into the army, he was needed on the land. But when she was born, thought Faith Langtry, I never realized it would be my daughter I sent to a war. My firstborn. Sex isn't as different or as important as it used to be.

Each time she had come home they had noticed changes, from the atabrine yellow in her skin to the little tics and habits which branded her an adult, her own woman. Six years. God knows exactly what those six years had contained, for Honour had never wanted to talk about the war when she came home, and if asked, parried the questions lightly. But whatever they might have contained, as Faith Langtry looked at Honour now she understood that her daughter had forever moved farther than the moon from the place which had been her home.

She was thin; that was to be expected, of course. There were lines in the face, though there was no sign of grey in her hair, thank God. She was stern without being hard, extraordinarily decisive in the way she moved, locked away without being withdrawn. And though she could never be a stranger, she was someone different.

How glad they had been when she chose to do nursing rather than medicine! Thinking of the suffering that decision would spare their daughter. But had she done medicine she would have stayed at home, and looking at Honour now, Faith wondered if

542

that might not have meant less suffering in the long run.

Her service medals came out, and her decorations—how bizarre to have a *daughter* who was a Member of the British Empire! And how proud Charlie and Ian would be!

"You never told me of your MBE," Faith said, a little reproachfully.

Honour looked up, surprised. "Didn't I? I must have just forgotten. Things were pretty busy around that time; I had to hurry through my letters. Anyway, it's only recently been confirmed."

"Have you any photos, darling?"

"Somewhere." Honour fished in the pocket of a case, and produced two envelopes, one much larger than the other. "Here we are." She came across to the second easy chair and sat down, reaching for her cigarettes.

"That's Sally and Teddy and Willa and me. . . . That's the Boss at Lae. . . . Me in Darwin, about to take off for I can't remember where. . . . Moresby. . . . The nursing staff on Morotai. . . . The outside of ward X. . . ."

"You look wonderful in a slouch hat, I must say."

"They're more comfortable than veils, probably because they have to come off the minute you walk inside."

"What's in the other envelope? More photos?"

Honour's hand hovered as if not sure whether to take both envelopes away without revealing the contents of the second, bigger one; after a slight hesitation she opened it. "No, not photos. Some drawings of some of my patients from ward X—my last command, if I can put it that way."

"They're marvelously well done," said Faith, looking at each face closely, but, Honour was relieved to see, passing over Michael as if he held no more significance for her than any of the others—but how could he? And how strange, that she had fully expected her mother to see what she had seen that first meeting in the corridor of ward X.

"Who did them?" asked Faith, putting them down.

"This chap," said Honour, riffling through them and putting Neil on top of the sheaf. "Neil Parkinson. It's not very good; he

543

failed miserably when it came to drawing himself."

"It's good enough for his face to remind me of someone, or else I've actually seen him somewhere. Where does he come from?"

"Melbourne. I gather his father's quite a tycoon."

"Longland Parkinson!" said Faith triumphantly. "I've met this chap, then. The Melbourne Cup in 1939. He was with his mother and father that year, in uniform. I've met Frances—his mother—several times in Melbourne at one do or another."

What had Michael said? That in her world she met men like Neil, not men like himself. How odd. She might indeed in the course of time have met Neil socially. Had there not been a war.

Faith leafed through the pile again, found the sketch she was looking for and laid it down on top of Neil. "Who *is* this, Honour? That face! The expression in his eyes!" She sounded almost spellbound. "I don't know whether I like him, but it's a fascinating face."

"Sergeant Lucius Daggett. Luce. He was—he committed suicide not long before Base Fifteen folded up." Oh, God! She had nearly said he was murdered.

"Poor chap. I wonder what could have led him to do that? He looks so—well, above that sort of thing." Faith gave her back the drawings. "I must say I like them much better than photos. Arms and legs don't tell you nearly as much about people as faces do, and I always find myself squinting at photos to try to see the faces, and all I ever do manage to see is blobs. Who was your personal favorite among that lot?"

The temptation was too great to resist; Honour found Michael and held the drawing out to her mother. "That one. Sergeant Michael Wilson."

"Really?" asked Faith, looking at her daughter doubtfully. "Well, you knew them all in the flesh, of course. A fine chap, I can see that. . . . He looks like a station hand."

Bravo, Michael! thought Honour. There speaks the wealthy grazier's wife who meets Neil Parkinson at the races and knows her social strata instinctively, about as well as anyone can without being a snob. Because Mummy's not a snob.

"He's a dairy farmer," she said.

"Oh, that accounts for the look of the land." Faith sighed, stretched. "Are you tired, darling?"

"No, Mummy, not a bit." Honour put the drawings on the floor beside her chair and lit a cigarette.

"Still no sign of marriage?" Faith asked.

"No," said Honour, smiling.

"Oh, well, it's better to stay a spinster than to marry for the wrong reasons." This was said with a tongue-in-cheek demureness that made her daughter splutter into laughter.

"I quite agree, Mummy."

"I suppose that means you'll be going back to nursing?"

"Yes."

"Prince Alfred again?" Faith knew better than to ask if it was likely her daughter's choice would fall on little Yass—Honour had always liked high-powered places of work.

"No," said Honour, and paused, unwilling to go on.

"Well, where then?"

"I'm going to a place called Morisset to train as a mental nurse."

Faith Langtry gaped. "You're joking!"

"No, I'm not."

"But—but that's ridiculous! You're a senior sister! You can go anywhere after the sort of experience you've had! *Mental nursing?* Good God, Honour, you might as well have applied to become a prison wardress! The pay's better!"

Honour's mouth set; her mother suddenly saw the best display yet of the power and determination which were so alien to her concepts of her daughter.

"That's one of the reasons why I'm doing mental nursing," she said. "For the last year and a half I've nursed men who were emotionally disturbed, and I found I liked that sort of work better than any other branch of nursing. People like me are *needed*—because people like you become horrified at the thought of it, among other reasons! Mental nurses have so little status it's almost a stigma to be one, so if people like me don't get into it, it will never move with the times. When I rang up the Department of Public Health to get some information about training as a mental nurse and said who and what I was, they thought I was some sort of crank! It took two trips in person to convince them that I, a senior nursing sister, was genuinely interested in becoming a mental nurse. Even the Department of Public Health, which administers all mental hospitals, thinks of it as becoming a madmen's keeper!"

"That's exactly what you will be," said Faith.

"When a patient enters a mental hospital he enters a world he will probably never leave," Honour tried to explain, her voice full of feeling. "The men I nursed weren't as badly off as that, but there were still enough direct comparisons to make me see that people like me are needed."

"Honour, you sound as if you're doing penance, or preaching conversion to some religion! Surely whatever happened to you during the war can't have warped your judgment that much!"

"I suppose I do sound as if I'm all fired up with a sense of mission," Honour said thoughtfully, lighting another cigarette. "But it isn't so. Nor am I atoning for anything. But I *won't* concede that to want passionately to do my bit to help lessen the plight of mental patients is an indication of mental instability on my part!"

"All right, darling, all right," Faith soothed. "I was wrong to suggest anything of the kind. Now don't get hot under the collar if I ask you whether you're going to get anything concrete out of it, like another certificate?"

Honour laughed, her indignation dead. "I'm very much afraid I don't get a thing out of it, Mummy. There's no proper course of instruction, no certificate, no nothing. Even when I'm finished my training I won't be a sister again, I'll still be plain Nurse Langtry. However, when I'm put in charge of a ward I understand my title becomes Charge Nurse Langtry—'Charge' for short."

"How did you find all this out?"

"I went to see the Matron of Callan Park. That was where originally I thought I'd go, but after we'd talked for a while she said she strongly advised me to go to Morisset instead. The teaching's just as adequate, it seems, and the atmosphere's a lot better."

Faith got up and began to pace. "Morisset. That's near Newcastle, isn't it?"

"Yes, the Sydney side of Newcastle. About sixty miles from Sydney, which means I'll be able to pop off to Sydney when I need diversion, and I think I'm going to need all the diversion I can get. I'm not looking at this through rose-colored spectacles, you know. It's going to be very hard, especially being a probationer again. But do you know, Mummy, I'd rather be a probationer and learning something new than stuck at P.A. as a senior sister, bowing and scraping to everyone from Matron to the HMOs to the Super, and having to leap some sort of rules and regulations hurdle every five minutes. I just couldn't take the formality and the drivel after the sort of life I've led in the army."

Faith reached out for Honour's packet of cigarettes, took one and lit it.

"Mummy! You're smoking!" said Honour, shocked.

Faith laughed until the tears came. "Oh, well, it's comforting to know you still have some prejudices! I was starting to think I'd produced some sort of latter-day Sylvia Pankhurst. You smoke like a chimney. Why shouldn't I?"

Honour got up, went to hug her. "You're quite right. But do sit down and be comfortable about it! No matter how enlightened one thinks one is, one's parents are always godlike. No human failings, no human appetites. I apologize."

"Accepted. Charlie smokes, Ian smokes, you smoke. I just decided I was being left out in the cold. I've taken to drink as well. I join Charlie in a whisky every night before dinner, and it's very nice."

"Very civilized, too," said Honour, smiling.

"Well, I just hope it all turns out as you hope, darling," Faith

547

said, puffing away. "Though I confess I do rather wish you had never been posted to a troppo ward."

Honour thought before she spoke, wanting her words to be telling. "Mummy, even to you I find I can't talk about the things that happened to me while I was nursing troppo men, and I don't think I ever will be able to talk about them. Not your fault, mine. But some things go too deep. They hurt too much. I'm not bottling them up, exactly. Just that no one could ever understand unless they knew the kind of world ward X was. And to try to explain with all the details I'd need to make you understand—I don't have that kind of strength. It would kill me. And yet, this much I can tell you. I don't know why I think so, but I do know that I'm not finished with ward X. There's more of it to come. And if I'm a mental nurse, I'll be better equipped to cope with what's still to come."

"What could possibly come?"

"I don't know. I have some ideas, perhaps, but I don't have any facts."

Faith stubbed out her cigarette, got to her feet, and bent to kiss her daughter tenderly. "I'll say good night, darling. It's so good to have you home! We worried a lot when we didn't know where you were exactly, or how close you were to the lines. After that sort of worry, mental nursing's a sinecure."

She went from Honour's bedroom to her own, ruthlessly switched on the bedside lamp and flooded her sleeping husband's face with light. He grimaced, grunted, and turned away from it. Leaving it on, she climbed into the bed and leaned heavily on Charlie's shoulder, patting his cheek with one hand and shaking him with the other.

"Charlie, if you don't wake up, I'll murder you!" she said.

Opening his eyes, he sat up, running his fingers through his almost nonexistent hair and yawning. "What's the matter?" he asked, knowing her too well to be annoyed. Faith didn't wake a man up for the fun of it.

"It's Honour," she said, her face crumpling. "Oh, Charlie, I

548

didn't realize it until just now, when I was talking to her in her room!"

"Realize what?" His voice sounded wide awake.

But she couldn't tell him then, for the grief and the fear overcame her; she wept instead, long and bitterly.

"She's gone and she can never come back again," she said when she was able.

He stiffened. "She's gone? Where?"

"Not bodily. That's still in her room. I'm sorry, I didn't mean to frighten you. It's her soul I'm talking about, whatever it is keeps her going. Oh, God, Charlie, we're such *babies* compared to her! It's worse than having a nun for a daughter—at least if your daughter's a nun you know she's safe, the world hasn't touched her. But Honour's got the footprints of the world all over her. And yet she's somehow bigger than the world. I don't know what I'm saying, it isn't right, you'll have to talk to her and watch her for yourself to see what I mean. I took up smoking and drinking, but I think Honour took up all the cares of the world, and that's unbearable. You don't want your children to have to suffer like that."

"It's the war," said Charlie Langtry. "We oughtn't to have let her go."

"She never even asked us for permission, Charlie. Why should she? She was twenty-five when she joined up. A grown woman, I thought then, old enough to survive it. Yes, it's the war."

2   So Sister Langtry doffed her veil, donned a cap and became Nurse Langtry at the Morisset mental hospital. A huge rambling place of many buildings scattered over many acres, it lay in some of the loveliest country to be found anywhere: sea lakes to form a part of its boundaries, wild mountains behind it smothered in rain forest, fertile placid flatlands, and the coastal surfing beaches not far away.

At first her situation was a little awkward, for no one at Morisset had ever heard of a general-trained sister giving up all that her career had gained for her to become a mental-nursing trainee. Many of her fellow trainees were at least as old as she was, some had been in the armed services during the war even, since mental nursing tended to attract women rather than girls, but her peculiar status set her apart. Everyone knew that Matron had told her she would be permitted to sit the charge nurses' examination at the end of two years instead of three, and everyone knew that Matron not only respected but esteemed her. Gossip said she had done arduous nursing during the war, for which she had been made an MBE, and gossip it remained, for Nurse Langtry made no reference to those years whatsoever.

It took her six months to show everyone she was not doing penance, was not snooping on behalf of some mysterious agency in Sydney, or was not a little mental herself. And at the end of those six months she knew she was very well liked by the charge nurses, for she worked hard and with superb efficiency, was never sick, and proved on countless occasions that her general nursing training could be a godsend in a place like Morisset, where the handful of doctors could not possibly keep an eye on every patient to detect the physical maladies which tended to compound the mental state.

550

Nurse Langtry could spot an incipient pneumonia, knew how to treat it, and had a knack for transmitting her knowledge to others. She could spot herpes, tuberculosis, acute abdomens, inner and middle ear infections, tonsillitis and most of the other complaints which occasionally struck at the patients. She could also tell a sprain from a break, a cold from hay fever, a migraine from a tension headache. It made her very valuable.

The work was gruelling. There were two shifts only, day duty from 6:30 A.M. to 6:30 P.M., and night duty, which covered the other twelve hours. Most wards contained between sixty and a hundred and twenty patients, had no domestic staff whatsoever, and only three or four nurses including the charge nurse. Every patient had to be bathed daily, though most wards owned only one plunge bath and one shower. All cleaning duties from the washing of walls and light fixtures to the polishing of floors were the sole responsibility of the nursing staff. The hot water was supplied to each ward by a coke-fired boiler which the nurses had to stoke. The nurses cared for the patients' clothes, from laundering to mending. Though the food was cooked in a central kitchen, it was delivered to each ward in bulk, which meant it had to be reheated, then portioned or carved by the nurses, who often had to cook the dessert and the vegetables in the ward as well. All the dishes, cutlery, pots and pans were washed in the ward. Patients on special diets had their food prepared by the nurses on the ward, for there was no such thing as a diet kitchen, no dieticians either.

No matter how hard or how long they were prepared to work, three or four nurses without domestic help looking after a minimum of sixty patients, often double that number, could never have hoped to complete all that had to be done. So, as at Base Fifteen, the patients worked too. Jobs were highly prized, and the first thing a new nurse learned was not to interfere in any way with any patient's job. When trouble broke out it was usually because one patient had stolen another's job, or made the execution of a job intolerable. The jobs were done well, and there was a strict patient hierarchy which depended upon patient use-

551

fulness, and patient pride. The floors always shone like glass, the wards were spotless, the bathing facilities and kitchens sparkled.

Contrary to popular opinion about mental hospitals, and perhaps fairly peculiar to Morisset, there was a lot of love. Everything possible to create a homelike atmosphere was done, and the vast majority of nurses cared about their patients. The staff was a part of the same community as the patients; indeed, there were whole families—mother, father, grownup children—all employed and living at Morisset, so that to many of the staff the hospital was a genuine home, and meant what any genuine home means.

Social life was quite active, and of great interest to patients and staff alike. Pictures were screened in the hall every Monday night for patients and staff together; there were frequent concerts in which patients and staff participated as well as formed the enthusiastic audience; once a month a dance was held, followed by a lavish and delicious supper. At the dances the male patients sat along one wall, the female along the opposite wall, and when a dance was announced the males would dart across the floor to grab their favorite partners. The staff were expected to dance too, but only with patients.

All the wards were locked, and male patients were kept in separate buildings from females; before and after the social functions where the two sexes were permitted to mix, a careful count of patients was always performed. Female patients were nursed by female staff, male patients by males only.

Very few of the patients ever had visitors, very few had private incomes; some received a small remuneration for doing special jobs about the hospital or grounds. To all intents and purposes the inmates regarded the hospital as a permanent home; some remembered no other, some had forgotten any other, some died from pining after a remembered real home with loving parents or spouses. It was not uncommon to see an aged demented patient keeping company during the hours permitted with a spouse who though quite sane had committed himself or herself rather than part completely.

552

It was no paradise, but the attitude was a caring one, and most of the staff realized there was nothing to be gained but much to be lost by making it an unhappy place; the lot of the patients was unhappy enough to begin with. Of course there were bad wards, bad charges, bad nurses, but not in the large proportions myth and legend contended. Overly sadistic staff, at least in the female wards where Nurse Langtry worked, were not tolerated, nor were charges permitted to run their wards like independent empires.

At times it could be an unconsciously humorous, old-fashioned place. Some of the wards were so far removed by distance from the nurses' home that the nurses staffing them were fetched on and off duty and to and from meals by a male patient driving a horse-drawn covered buggy. Matron and the superintendent did daily rounds, commencing at nine o'clock in the morning. They travelled from ward to ward in a horse and sulky driven by a male patient, Matron sitting up regally in all the splendor of her full whites, a parasol held above her head in strong sunlight, an umbrella when it rained. At the height of summer the horse always wore a big straw hat with his ears poking out of two holes cut in it.

Nurse Langtry knew that the things which troubled her most were to be expected. It was difficult to go back to probationer status, not so much in the taking of orders as in the lack of privileges and comforts, though she suspected it would have gone far harder with her had she not gone through and survived the grind of wartime nursing. However, for a woman turned thirty who had already been a sister-in-charge, who had helped man a field ambulance under fire in battle conditions, who had worked in casualty clearing stations and a military general hospital, it came hard to have to turn out her room for Matron to inspect every Tuesday morning. Her mattress had to be rolled up so Matron could examine beneath her bed, her blankets and sheets folded in a stipulated manner and neatly arranged on top of the mattress. She tried not to mind, for at least she had not been asked to share a room with another nurse, a small concession to her age and professional status.

As her first year at Morisset drew to a close she began to get into stride, and her personality popped to the surface again at full strength. There had been no struggle to subdue it, for it had sunk to the bottom of its own accord, a protective mechanism engineered to cope with probationer status and a job which was not yet at her fingertips.

But truth will out, and the tartar in Honour Langtry was still very much present, considerably refreshed too from its enforced rest. Its reappearance did her no harm, for it had only ever lashed out at stupidity, incompetence or negligence, as it did again now.

She caught a nurse abusing a patient physically, and reported the incident to the charge nurse, who tended to think that Nurse Langtry was being hysterical in her interpretation of what had happened.

"Su-Su's an epileptic," said the charge, "and they can't be trusted."

"What rot!" said Nurse Langtry scornfully.

"Don't you try to tell me my job just because you've got your general!" snapped the charge. "If you doubt me, read your Red Book, it's there in black and white. Epileptics are not to be trusted. They're sly, deceitful and malicious."

"The Red Book is wrong," said Nurse Langtry. "I know Su-Su well, so do you, and she's completely trustworthy. Which is beside the point anyway. Even the Red Book doesn't advocate the beating of a patient."

The charge looked at her as if she had blasphemed, as in truth she had; the Red Book was a red-covered manual of notes for mental nurses, and represented the only written source of authority the nurses possessed. But it was out of date, hopelessly inaccurate and designed for students of degradingly low mentality. No matter what the illness, it seemed chiefly to recommend an enema as treatment. Nurse Langtry had given it one perusal which showed her so many glaring errors she largely abandoned it, preferring to go on her own abilities to learn about mental disorders, and to buy textbooks in psychiatry every time she visited Sydney. She was convinced that the reform in nursing techniques, when it came, would reflect what the latest textbooks of psychiatry were already saying.

The battle over Su-Su went all the way to Matron, but nothing could quieten Nurse Langtry, or make her back down. In the end the guilty nurse was disciplined and transferred to another ward, where she was watched carefully; the charge nurse was not disciplined, but got the message where Nurse Langtry was concerned: have your facts absolutely straight when you dealt with Langtry or you'd live to rue the day you crossed swords with her. She was not only intelligent, she was quite unawed by titular authority, and she had an extremely persuasive tongue.

When she went to Morisset, Honour Langtry was well aware that Michael's dairy farm was only about eighty miles away to the northwest, though its proximity was not the reason she chose to nurse there. In that she had allowed herself to be guided by the Matron of Callan Park, and knew after a year on the Morisset staff that she had been excellently advised.

During the times when she wasn't so physically spent that she simply slept and ate when she was off duty, she thought often about Michael. And about Benedict. One day she would venture over to Maitland instead of heading down to Sydney, she knew, but not yet. The wound still hurt, yes, but that was not the reason why she kept postponing the day of her visitation. She had to give Michael time to understand that what he was attempting to do with Ben couldn't succeed. If her first year at Morisset had taught her anything, it was that people like Benedict must not be thrust into the isolation of a farm, for instance, couldn't be allowed to limit themselves even further by limiting the company they kept to one other human soul, no matter how gentle and loving a keeper that one human soul was. In a situation like Michael's farm, Benedict could only grow worse. Which worried

555

her, though she felt there would be no point in her interfering until enough time had elapsed to show Michael he was wrong and she was right.

Within the grounds of Morisset Hospital was a prison hospital for the criminally insane; the sight of it above the trees, tall red brick blocks barred and walled and under the rigid supervision of a separate staff, always had the power to chill her. In there would Benedict now be living, had events in the bathhouse taken a different turn. And it was not a good place to be. So how could she blame Michael for trying? All she could do was to hold herself ready for the day when he might appeal to her for help, or she gauged she could offer it.

3   When she was notified one evening that someone was
waiting to see her in the visitors' room, Nurse Langtry
thought immediately of Michael. If he had had the patience to trace her, he must have need of her indeed—
though it could also be Neil waiting, Neil who had the
sophistication and the money to know how to go about
tracing anyone. It would be like Neil too, the new and
tempered Neil from whom she had parted eighteen
long months ago, to grow tired of waiting for her to
come to him, to decide it was time he insinuated himself
into her life again. Also, she was aware that her mother
and his could cross paths at any time, though nothing in
a recent letter from her mother indicated it.

She walked to the visitors' room as sedately as she
could, enacting the scene to come with every possible
variation, and for two different men. For there was no
doubt in her mind that she was going to be very glad to
see either of them.

But the person in the chair, feet stretched out and
shoeless, was Sister Sally Dawkin.

Nurse Langtry stopped as if she had been shot, both
hands over her heart. Oh, God, *why* are women such
fools? she wondered, finding a smile and sticking it in
place for this first-ever visitor to find her at Morisset.
We all live like this, focussed on some man. We can convince ourselves for months on end that it isn't so, but
give us half a chance and there's the man again, right
back in the middle of everything.

Sister Dawkin smiled broadly, but didn't get up. "I
was here earlier, but I didn't like to drag you off your
ward, so I had a bit of tea at the fish-and-chippery in
Wyong, and came back again. How are you, Honour?"

Nurse Langtry sat down in the chair facing her, still
smiling fixedly. "I'm very well. How are you?"

557

"Oh, a bit like one of those balls tied to a racquet with a long piece of elastic. I don't know which is going to give out first, me or the elastic."

"It won't ever be you," said Nurse Langtry. "You are the great imperishable."

"You tell that to my feet; I've given up trying. They might believe you," said Sister Dawkin, scowling down at them ferociously.

"You and your feet! Some things never change."

Sister Dawkin was wearing rather drab and badly put together mufti, as was the tendency of so many long-term nurses, used only to appearing awesome in all the starched severity of a uniform and veil.

"You look so different, Honour," said Sister Dawkin, staring. "Much younger and happier!"

And indeed she didn't look any older than the average trainee nurse anywhere, clad in the same sort of uniform she had worn while training at P.A. The variations were minor. At Morisset she wore a dress pinstriped in white and lilac, long-sleeved and high to the neck, with detachable celluloid cuffs and collar. And the apron was the same, a voluminous affair in white, stiff with starch, wrapping completely around the skirt of the dress, up over the chest in a bib, securing across the back with broad straps. Her waist looked neat and very tiny, confined by a wide stiff white belt. Both dress and apron were mid-calf in length. She wore black lace-up shoes with flat heels, and opaque black cotton stockings, just as she had at P.A. The Morisset cap was less attractive than the P.A. one, being a pudding-cloth design, white, secured at the nape of the neck with a drawstring and with a broad stiff band across its front, notched twice in Nurse Langtry's case to indicate that she was a second-year trainee.

"It's just the uniform," said Nurse Langtry. "You're used to seeing me without an apron and with a veil."

"Well, whatever you wear, you still look like a new pin."

"Did you get your deputy matronship at North Shore?"

Sister Dawkin looked suddenly very sad. "No. I couldn't stay in Sydney after all, worse luck. I'm back at Royal Newcastle because it's close enough to home to live at home. How's mental nursing?"

"I love it," said Nurse Langtry, her face glowing. "It's not like general nursing in the least, of course, though we do have our medical crises. I've never seen so many status epilepticus cases in all my life! We don't save them all, poor things. But as a mental nurse I feel more important, somehow, more wanted and needed. As a senior sister I'd lost all touch with real nursing, but here, no matter what, you *nurse*. The patients are like relatives, almost. You know they're going to be here as long as you are and longer, unless they die in status or of pneumonia—they're frailer than people whose brains are intact, I've found. And I'll tell you this much, Sally—if you think general nursing involves a commitment, you ought to try mental nursing." She sighed. "I wish I'd done a couple of years here before I had charge of X. I made a lot of mistakes on X through sheer ignorance. Still, better late than never, as the bishop said to the dancing girl."

Sister Dawkin grinned. "Now, now, that's my style of remark, not yours! If you don't watch out you'll end up just like me, a cross between a dragon and a court jester."

"I can think of worse fates," said Nurse Langtry, smiling in a sudden genuine rush of pleasure. "Oh, Sally dear, it's so nice to see you! I didn't know who might be waiting for me. This place is so far out in the sticks that I've never had a visitor before."

"It's nice to see you, too. You've been conspicuous by your absence at reunions and suchlike. Don't you even try to keep up with the old gang from Base Fifteen?"

"No. Funny, I always did loathe post-mortems," said Nurse Langtry uneasily. "I think it's the way they take the face, grab it round the edges and yank it down—one should never have to see what's on the inside of a face."

"But that's mental nursing you're describing."

Nurse Langtry folded her arms across her stomach and leaned forward. "I never thought of it quite like that. But I still hate post-mortems."

"You're going dotty, is your trouble," said Sister Dawkin comfortably. "I knew you would, living and working in a place like this, pretty gardens and all."

"What made you ask about Base Fifteen, Sally?"

"Oh, nothing, really, except that before I left North Shore to go to Newcastle I had one of your men from X as a patient."

Nurse Langtry's skin prickled and shivered and twitched like a horse's. "Which one?" she asked, dry-mouthed.

"Matt Sawyer. His blindness was no hysteria."

"I knew that. What was it?"

"Walloping great tumor impinging on the optic tract. An olfactory groove meningioma. Sitting getting bigger all the time. Only it didn't cause his admission to North Shore. He had a subarachnoid bleed."

Nurse Langtry sighed. "So he's dead, of course."

"Came in comatose and passed away a week later in no pain. Shame about his family. Lovely little girls, nice little wife."

"Yes, it is a shame," said Nurse Langtry colorlessly.

A small silence fell, not unlike the silence of respect which is accorded to those of sufficiently worldly note who go to meet their Maker. Nurse Langtry occupied it by wondering how his wife had coped with Matt's blindness when she finally learned of it. What effect had it had on his children? And did his wife understand the magnitude of the stigma they had attached to him, the diagnosis of hysteria? Had his wife perhaps railed at a mind which obstinately refused to permit its eyes to see any more? Or had she been convinced something more malignant than mere mind was causing the blindness? Surely the last, if the photographer had truly captured the eyes of the real Mrs. Sawyer in that picture he used to keep on his locker. Well. Sleep easy, my dearest Matt, she thought tenderly. The long battle's over.

"What made you leave North Shore to go to Newcastle, Sally?" she asked, puzzled as to why when Sister Dawkin had dreamed so of that deputy matronship she had been willing to let it go.

560

"It's my old father, actually," said Sister Dawkin miserably. "Atherosclerosis, senile dementia, cortical atrophy—same difference. I had to commit him this morning."

"Oh, Sally! I am so sorry! Where is he? Here?"

"Yes, he's here. I just hated to have to do it, and I did try not to, believe me. I came home to Newcastle hoping I'd be able to manage, but Mum's well into her seventies, and she can't cope with Dad piddling his pants and taking it into his head to trot down to the grocer's without a stitch on. The only way I might have managed was to give up work entirely, but I'm the only one, there isn't that sort of money, and I'm an old maid into the bargain. No husband to bring home the Dawkin bacon, worse luck."

"Don't worry, he'll be all right," said Nurse Langtry, her voice strong with reassurance. "We're good to our oldies here, and we've got lots of them. I'll look in on him regularly. Is that how you found out I was here?"

"No. I thought you were at Callan Park, so I tried desperately to get Dad in there rather than here. I even went to see Matron at Callan Park—thank God I'm on the inside of the profession, it makes such a difference!—and I found out from her that you were here. She remembered your interview with her at once. It isn't often nurses with your kind of background front up to apply to train as mental nurses, I suppose. Well, as you can imagine, it was manna from heaven to find out you were here. I've been paddling around this place all day. Matron offered to call you off your ward to see me, but I didn't like to do that, and anyway, I'm an awful coward. Lord, I don't want to have to walk in tonight and face poor old Mum—" She stopped for a moment to compose herself. "So I put the nasty deed off for a few hours, and here I am to cry on your shoulder."

"Always, Sally, you know that. I've cried on yours."

Sister Dawkin brightened. "Yes, you certainly did, didn't you? That bloody little bitch Pedder!"

"I don't suppose you know what's happened to her?"

"No, and what's more, I don't care. Oh, by now she'll be married, I'd bet a year's pay on it. Pedder wasn't cut out to work for a living."

"Then let's hope whoever her husband is, he's comfortably off and sanguine by nature."

"Yes," said Sister Dawkin, but a little absently. She hesitated, drew a breath as if to embark upon something she found unpalatable, and spoke awkwardly. "Actually, Honour, there's another reason besides Dad why I wanted to see you. When Matron at Callan Park told me where you were, a few pennies dropped. Do you by any chance read the Newcastle papers?"

Nurse Langtry looked blank but wary. "No."

Sister Dawkin nodded. "Well, I knew you weren't a Hunter Valley girl, and I just had an idea when I found out where you were that you couldn't be reading anything out of Newcastle. Because if you did, I don't think you'd still be here."

Nurse Langtry flushed, but sat looking so proud and unapproachable that Sister Dawkin found it difficult to go on.

"Your fondness for Michael Wilson was fairly obvious to me in Base Fifteen days, and I must confess I rather expected you and him to make a go of it after the War. But when I read the story in the Newcastle paper I knew you hadn't made a go of it. Then when I found out you were here at Morisset, it looked to me as if you'd put yourself down somewhere close but not too close, maybe hoping to run into him, or planning to see him after the dust settled. . . . Honour, you don't have the foggiest idea what I'm talking about, do you?"

"No," whispered Nurse Langtry numbly.

Sister Dawkin didn't flinch; she had been dealing with situations akin to this for too many years to flinch, but she performed her duty with great kindness, understanding and directness. "My dear, Michael Wilson died over four months ago."

Nurse Langtry's face looked empty, featureless, lifeless.

"I'm not a gossip-monger, and I'm not telling you all this just to watch you suffer. But I thought if you didn't know, you ought to know. I was your age once, and I understand exactly what

562

you're going through. Hope can be the cruelest thing in the world, and there are times when the very best thing one can do for someone is to kill a hopeless hope. I decided if I told you now, you might want to do something different with your life before it's too late, and you find yourself ingrained. Like me. And it's better that it should come from me than from some Maitland shopkeeper one nice sunny day."

"Benedict killed him," said Nurse Langtry tonelessly.

"No. He killed Benedict, and then he killed himself. It was all over a fool dog they owned that got in and played merry hell with another farmer bloke's chooks. The farmer bloke drove over to Michael's place hopping mad, and went for Michael. Then Benedict went for the farmer bloke, and if Michael hadn't managed to hold Benedict off, the farmer bloke might have died too. He went to the police instead, but by the time the police got out to Michael's place, it was all over. They were both dead. Michael had given Benedict an overdose of barbiturates, and then he shot himself. He didn't suffer at all. He knew too much about where to aim."

Nurse Langtry literally heaved her whole body away from Sister Dawkin, flopping, sagging limply, an old rag doll.

Oh, Michael, my Michael! All the buried love and need and hunger leaped fully armed into consciousness. She ran with pain, she rocked with it, she smothered in it. *Oh, Michael!* Never, never, never to see him again, and she had missed him so unbearably. All these months close enough to call in on him any off-duty day, and she had not. He was dead and she hadn't even known it, hadn't even felt it in the bones which missed him so much, so terribly.

The thing with Benedict had gone to its inevitable end. There was, she saw now, no other possible end for it. While he was there Benedict was safe; that was what he had to believe, for he had willingly shouldered the burden of caring for Benedict, and every duty must have its reward, in the knowledge of a job well done. So when he could no longer be sure, he had put Benedict down, quietly and kindly. After which he had no choice save to put himself down as well. No prison could hold Michael, even ward X, even Morisset. He was a bird, but the cage had to be one of his own making.

Oh, Michael, my Michael! A man is no more than he can be. Cut down like the grass.

She turned on Sister Dawkin fiercely. "Why didn't he come to me?" she demanded. "Why *didn't* he come to me?"

Was there a way to deliver the truth without hurting? Sister Dawkin doubted it, but she tried. "Maybe he just forgot you. They do forget us, you know," she said gently.

That was unbearable. "They have no right to forget us!" Nurse Langtry cried.

"But they do forget. It's their nature, Honour. It isn't that they don't love us. They move on! And we move on. None of us can afford to live in the past." Her hand swept, encompassing Morisset mental hospital. "If we did, we'd end up in here."

One by one Nurse Langtry picked up the pieces, old and cold and lonely. "Yes, I suppose we would," she said slowly. "Still, I'm already in here."

Sister Dawkin rose to her feet, slid into her shoes, held out her hand and pulled Nurse Langtry up out of the chair. "That's right, you are in here. But you're on the caring side of the fence. You've got to stay on the caring side, never forget that, no matter what you decide to do." She sighed. "I have to go. Mum's still waiting."

Oh, Sally, you're the one with real troubles! thought Nurse Langtry, walking with her friend through the foyer of the nurses' home. It was no way to end a life, too little money and aged parents and no hope of help. And eventual aloneness. All duty had bought for Sally Dawkin was more duty. Well, decided Nurse Langtry, I for one am fed up with duty. It has ruled my whole life. And it killed Michael.

They walked to where Sister Dawkin had left the car she had borrowed to move her father to Morisset; before she climbed into it Nurse Langtry reached out and hugged her briefly, tightly.

"Do take care of yourself, Sally, and don't worry about your father. In here he'll always be all right."

"I'll take care, don't worry. Today I'm down, but tomorrow, who knows? I might win the lottery. And Royal Newcastle's not such a pipsqueak of a place. I might get to be matron instead of just one of her deputies." She clambered into the car. "If you ever decide to head north to Newcastle, give me a ring, and we'll meet for a bite and a natter. It isn't good to lose all contact with people, Honour. Besides, every time I come to see Dad I'm going to force my company on you."

"I'd love that, but I don't think I'm going to be here very many days longer. There's someone in Melbourne I intend to remind that I still exist before it's too late," said Nurse Langtry.

Sister Dawkin beamed. "Good girl! You get on with your life the way you feel it ought to be lived." She let in the clutch, waved cheerfully, and kangaroo-hopped away.

Nurse Langtry stood watching for a moment, waving back, then turned to walk to the nurses' home, head bent to let her eyes follow the alternating black blurs of her feet in the night.

Neil had said he would wait for her. It wasn't very far to Melbourne if she flew. She could fly down on her next four days off. And if indeed he was still waiting, she need never come back to Morisset again. She was thirty-two years old, and what did she have to show for it? A few scraps of official paper, a few ribbons, a couple of medals. No husband, no babies, no life of her own. Just service to others, a memory, and a dead man. Nowhere near enough.

Her head lifted; she stared at the yellow squares of light all around her in this vast dumping ground for the hopeless and the destitute. When was she next due for four days off? She was on for three more days, had three days off, on for four days, then off for four days. About ten days away.

Oh, that worked out well! She wouldn't have to go to Melbourne until after the big concert. It was going to be their best effort yet, if only poor old Marg could manage to remember the two words she had to say. But she had wanted so badly to be in it no one had the heart to say no. Everyone prayed a lot, that was all. What luck charge had found out Annie could sing! She was quite a pretty little soul when she was all done up, and some of the male patients in basketry were going to make a great big wicker cage, and paint it gold, and Annie would sing "I'm Only a Bird in a Gilded Cage." The sketch about the cat and the mouse would bring the hugely uncritical house down, if only Su-Su could get through her part without falling over in a fit. . . .

Nurse Langtry halted as if a giant hand had suddenly chopped down to bar her way. What on earth am I thinking of? I can't abandon them! Who else have they got, if people like me go rushing off blindly chasing a dream? For it is a dream! A silly, immature girl's dream. This is what my life is all about. This is what I served my apprenticeship for. Michael knew. And Sally Dawkin is right. The truth is cruel, yet there's no escaping the truth forever, and if it hurts, one must simply bear the hurt. They forget us. Eighteen months without so much as a word from him. Neil too has quite forgotten. When I was the center of his universe he loved me and he needed me. What does he need me for now? And why should he love me now? I sent him on his way back to a different sort of life, bigger, more exciting, oh, yes, more exciting by far, and dewed with women. Why on earth should he remember a part of his life that gave him so much pain? More importantly, why do I expect him to remember? Michael was right. Michael knew. A strong bird needs lots of room to fly.

She had a duty here. How many people were equipped to do what she could do effortlessly? How many had the training, the knowledge, the inborn skill? For every mental nurse who had the stamina to last the three-year training period, ten didn't last. She had the stamina. And she had the *love*. This wasn't just a job—her heart was in it, fathoms deep in it! This was what she truly wanted. Her duty lay here among those the world had forgotten, or couldn't use, or sometimes just plain couldn't bear to look at.

Nurse Langtry began to walk again, briskly and without any fear, understanding herself at last. And understanding that duty, the most indecent of all obsessions, was only another name for love.

THE LADIES OF MISSALONGHI

For Mother,

who has finally attained her dream of

living in the Blue Mountains

Author's Note:

For the information of readers who notice that Missalonghi is spelled with an *a* rather than the *o* now commonly accepted as correct, in Australia at the time this story takes place, the old-fashioned *a* was more usual.

CAN YOU TELL ME, Octavia, why our luck never seems to change for the better?" asked Mrs. Drusilla Wright of her sister, adding with a sigh, "We need a new roof."

Miss Octavia Hurlingford dropped her hands into her lap, shook her head dolefully and echoed the sigh. "Oh, dear! Are you sure?"

"Denys is."

Since their nephew Denys Hurlingford ran the local ironmongery and had a thriving plumbing business as well, his word was law in such matters.

"How much will a new roof cost? Must it be a whole one? Couldn't we have the worst sheets replaced?"

"There isn't one sheet of iron worth keeping, Denys says, so we're looking at about fifty pounds, I'm afraid."

A gloomy silence fell, each sister cudgelling her brain in search of a source for the necessary funds. They were sitting side by side on a horsehair-stuffed sofa whose better days were so far in the past that no one remembered them. Mrs. Drusilla Wright was hemstitching pulled threads around the border of a linen cloth with microscopically fine, meticulous skill, and Miss Octavia Hurlingford was occupied with a crochet hook, the work dangling from it as exquisitely done as the hemstitching.

"We could use the fifty pounds Father put in the bank for me when I was born," offered the third occupant of the

571

room, anxious to make amends for the fact that she saved not a penny of her egg and butter money. She was also working, sitting on a low stool producing lace from a tatting shuttle and a ball of ecru thread, her fingers moving with the complete efficiency of a task known so well it was sightless, mindless.

"Thank you, but no," said Drusilla.

And that was the end of the only conversation occurring during the two-hour work period of Friday afternoon, for not long afterwards the hall clock began to chime four. While the last vibrations still lingered in the air, all three ladies proceeded with the automatism of long custom to put away their handicrafts, Drusilla her sewing, Octavia her crocheting, and Missy her tatting. Each lady disposed of her work inside an identical grey flannel drawstring bag, after which each lady disposed of her bag inside a battered mahogany sideboard sitting beneath the window.

The routine never, never varied. At four o'clock the two-hour handwork session in the second-best parlour came to an end, and another two-hour session began, but of a different kind. Drusilla moved to the organ which was her only treasure and only pleasure, while Octavia and Missy moved to the kitchen, there to prepare the evening meal and finish off the outside chores.

As they clustered in the doorway like three hens unsure of the pecking order, it was easy to see that Drusilla and Octavia were sisters. Each was extremely tall and each had a long, bony, anaemically fair face; but where Drusilla was sturdily large and muscular, Octavia was crabbed and diminished by a longstanding bone disease. Missy shared the height, though not so much of it, being a mere five feet seven to her aunt's five feet ten and her mother's six feet. Nothing else did she have in common, for she was as dark

as they were fair, as flat-chested as they were fulsome, and owned features as small as theirs were large.

The kitchen was a big bare room at the back of the dim central hall, its brown-painted wooden walls contributing their mite to the general atmosphere of gloominess.

"Peel the potatoes before you go out to pick the beans, Missy," said Octavia as she strapped on the voluminous brown pinny which protected her brown dress from the perils of cooking. While Missy peeled the three potatoes considered sufficient, Octavia shook up the coals smouldering in the firebox of the black iron range which occupied the whole frontage of the kitchen chimney; she then added fresh wood, adjusted the damper to cull more draught, and put a huge iron kettle on to boil. This done, she turned to the pantry to get out the raw materials for next morning's porridge.

"Oh, bother!" she exclaimed, emerging a moment later to display a brown paper bag whose bottom corners bled a flurry of oats that floated to the floor like turgid snowflakes. "Look at this! Mice!"

"Don't worry, I'll set some traps tonight," said Missy without much interest, putting her potatoes into a small pot of water, and adding a pinch of salt.

"Traps tonight doesn't get our breakfast on the table, so you'll have to ask your mother if you can run to Uncle Maxwell's to buy more oats."

"Couldn't we do without for once?" Missy hated oats.

"In *winter?*" Octavia stared at her as if she had gone mad. "A good big bowl of porridge is cheap, my girl, and sets you up for the whole day. Now hurry, for goodness sake!"

On the hall side of the kitchen door the organ music was deafening. Drusilla was an appallingly bad player who had never been told other than that she was very

575

good, but to play with such consistent ineptitude required remorseless practice, so between four and six every weekday afternoon, Drusilla practised. There was some point to it, as she inflicted her lack of talent on the largely Hurlingford congregation at the Byron Church of England each Sunday; luckily no Hurlingford had an ear for music, so all the Hurlingfords thought they were very well served during service.

Missy crept into the parlour, not the room where they did their handwork, but the one reserved for important occasions, and where the organ lived; there, Drusilla was assaulting Bach with all the clangor and thunder of a jousting knight his rival in the lists, seated with her back straight, her eyes closed, her head tilted, and her mouth twitching.

"Mother?" It was the smallest whisper, a filament of sound in competition against whole hawsers.

However, it was enough. Drusilla opened her eyes and turned her head, more in a spirit of resignation than anger.

"Well?"

"I'm sorry to interrupt, but we need more oats before Uncle Maxwell shuts. The mice got at the bag."

Drusilla sighed. "Bring me my purse, then."

The purse was fetched, and sixpence fished from its flaccid recesses. *"Bulk* oats, mind! All you pay for with a proprietary brand of oats is the fancy box."

"No, Mother! Proprietary oats taste much better, and you don't have to boil them all night to cook them, either." A faint hope entered Missy's breast. "In fact, if you and Aunt Octavia would rather eat proprietary oats, I'll gladly go without to make up the difference in expense."

Drusilla was always telling herself and her sister that she lived for the day her timid daughter showed signs of defiance, but this present humble bid for independence only ran up against an authoritarian wall the mother didn't know she had erected. So she said, shocked, "Go without? Most definitely not! Porridge is our winter staple, and it's a lot cheaper than coal fires." Then the tone of her voice became friendlier, more equal-women. "What's the temperature?"

Missy consulted the thermometer in the hall. "Forty-two!" she called.

"Then we'll eat in the kitchen and spend the evening there!" shouted Drusilla, beginning to give Bach another belting.

Wrapped up in her brown serge overcoat, a brown fleecy scarf and a brown knitted bonnet, with the sixpence from her mother's purse tucked down into the finger of one brown woollen glove, Missy let herself out of the house and hurried down the neat brick path to the front gate. In a small shopping bag was her library book; opportunities to sneak in an extra trip to the library were few and far between, and if she really scampered, no one need ever know she had done more than go to Uncle Maxwell's in search of oats. Tonight her Aunt Livilla would be manning the library herself, so it would have to be an improving sort of book instead of a novel, but in Missy's eyes any sort of book was better than no book at all. And next Monday Una would be there, so she could have a novel.

The air was full of a soft, fine Scotch mist that dithered between fog and rain and covered the privet hedge along the boundary of the house named Missalonghi with fat round drops of water. The moment Missy stepped out into Gordon Road she began to run, only slowing to a rapid walk at the corner because that wretchedly painful stitch was back in her left side, and it really did hurt.

Slowing down definitely eased her discomfort, however, so she trotted along more sedately and began to experience the glow of happiness which always came when she was offered this rarest of treats, a chance to escape on her own from the confines of Missalonghi. Picking up her pace again the minute the stitch disappeared, she commenced to look around her at the familiar sights Byron had to offer on a misty late afternoon of a short winter's day.

Everything in the town of Byron was named after some aspect of the poet, including her mother's house, Missalonghi, christened after the place where Lord Byron had expired untimely. This bizarre urban nomenclature was the fault of Missy's great-grandfather, the first Sir William Hurlingford, who had founded his town hard on the heels of reading *Childe Harold,* and was so pleased that he had actually discovered a great work of literature he could understand that ever after he had rammed indigestible amounts of Byron down the throats of everyone he knew. Thus Missalonghi was situated in Gordon Road, and Gordon Road ran into Noel Street, and Noel Street ran into Byron Street, which was the main thoroughfare; on the better side of town George Street meandered for several miles before plunging over the edge of the mighty Jamieson Valley. There was even a tiny cul-de-sac called Caroline Lamb Place, situated of course on the wrong side of the railway line (as was the house named Missalonghi); here dwelled a dozen very brassy women divided between three houses, and here came many masculine visitors from the fettlers' camp just up the line, as well as from the huge bottling plant that marred the town's southern outskirts.

It was one of the more puzzling and interesting facets of the first Sir William's intriguing character that on his deathbed he had firmly enjoined his surviving progeny not to interfere with the course of Nature by changing the function of Caroline Lamb Place, which in consequence had remained distinctly shady ever since, and not just due to its chestnut trees. In fact, the first Sir William had been addicted to what he always described as "an orderly system of naming things", and had called all his daughters by Latin names because they were popular in the higher ranks of society. His descendants kept the custom up, so there were Julias, Aurelias, Antonias, Augustas; only one branch of the family had tried to improve upon this policy by starting, with the arrival of their fifth son, to call their boys by Latin numbers, thereby glorifying the Hurlingford family tree with a Quintus, a Sextus, a Septimus, an Octavius and a Nonius. Decius died at birth, and no one wondered at it.

Oh, how beautiful! Missy stopped to marvel at a huge spider's web beaded by the soft feelers of mist that trailed pulsating up out of the invisible valley on the far side of Gordon Road. There was a very large sleek spider at the web's middle, apologetically escorted by her tiny mate-of-the-moment, but Missy felt neither fear nor revulsion, only envy. Not merely did this lucky creature own her world intrepidly and securely, but she flew the original suffragette banner not only by dominating and using her husband, but also by eating him once his purpose was scattered over her eggs. Oh, lucky, lucky spider-lady! Demolish her world, and she would serenely remake it to inborn specifications so lovely, so ethereal, that impermanence could never matter; and when the new web was finished, she would arrange the next series of consorts upon it like a movable feast, the modestly robust husband of today just off-centre, and his successors getting littler and littler the farther they were from Mother at the hub.

The time! Missy began to run again, turning into Byron

Street and heading for the row of shops which marched down either side of one block in the centre of the town, just before Byron Street became grandiose and produced the park and the railway station and the marble-fronted hotel and the imposing Egyptian facade of the Byron Waters Baths.

There was the grocery and produce store, owned by Maxwell Hurlingford; the ironmongery, owned by Denys Hurlingford; the millinery shop, owned by Aurelia Marshall, née Hurlingford; the smithy and petrol pump, owned by Thomas Hurlingford; the bakery, owned by Walter Hurlingford; the clothing emporium, owned by Herbert Hurlingford; the news agency and stationery shop, owned by Septimus Hurlingford; the Weeping Willow Tea Room, owned by Julia Hurlingford; the lending library, owned by Livilla Hurlingford; the butchery, owned by Roger Hurlingford Witherspoon; the sweet shop and tobacconist, owned by Percival Hurlingford; and the Olympus Café and Milk Bar, owned by Nikos Theodoropoulos.

As befitted its importance, Byron Street was sealed with tarmacadam as far as its junctions with Noel Street and Caroline Lamb Place, provided with an ornate polished granite horse-trough donated by the first Sir William, and possessed of proper hitching-posts right along its awninged section of shops. It was lined with very beautiful old gum trees, and contrived to look both peaceful and prosperous.

There were very few private dwellings in the central part of Byron. The town made its living from summer visitors anxious to escape the heat and humidity of the coastal plain, and year-round visitors who aspired to ease their rheumatic aches and pains by soaking in the hot mineral waters some geological freak had placed beneath

Byron ground. Therefore all along Byron Street were many guest-houses and boarding-houses — mostly owned and run by Hurlingfords, of course. The Byron Waters Baths provided a most agreeable standard of comfort for those not precisely penny-pinched, the vast and prestigious Hurlingford Hotel boasted private baths for the exclusive use of its own guests, while for those whose pecuniary resources just stretched to bed and breakfast in one of the cheaper boarding-houses, there existed the clean if spartan pools of the Byron Spa, just around the corner on Noel Street.

Even those too poor to come to the town of Byron at all were catered for. The second Sir William had invented the Byron Bottle (as it was known throughout Australia and the South Pacific): a one-pint, artistically slender, crystal-clear bottle of Byron's best spring water, gently effervescent, mildly but never disastrously aperient, distinctly tasty. Vichy water be damned! said those fortunate enough to have travelled to France. The good old Byron Bottle was not only better, it was also a great deal cheaper. And there was a penny refund on the empty too. Judicious buying of shares in the glassworks had put the final polish on this extremely inexpensive to run but remarkably lucrative local industry; it continued to thrive and to make enormous sums of money for all the male descendants of the second Sir William. The third Sir William, grandson of the first and son of the second, currently presided over the Byron Bottle Company empire with all the ruthlessness and rapaciousness of his earlier namesakes.

Maxwell Hurlingford, in direct line from the first Sir William and therefore a hugely wealthy man in his own right, did not need to run a grocery and produce store. However, commercial instinct and acumen in the Hurlingfords died hard, and the Calvinistic precepts which governed the clan dictated that a man must work to have grace in the eyes of the Lord. Rigid adherence to this rule should have made Maxwell Hurlingford a saint on earth, but instead had only managed to create a street-angel cum house-devil.

When Missy entered the shop a bell tinkled raucously, that being a perfect description of the sound Maxwell Hurlingford had devised in order to gratify his ascetics as well as his prudence. He emerged immediately the bell summoned him from the nether regions out the back, where resided the bran and chaff and wheat and barley and pollard and oats in towering stacks of hempen bags; not only did Maxwell Hurlingford cater to the gastronomic needs of the human population of Byron, he also victualled its horses, cows, pigs, sheep and chooks. As one local wit said when his grass failed, Maxwell Hurlingford got you going and coming.

His face bore its normal expression, sour, and his right hand a big scoop whiskered with webby strands of fodder.

"Look at this!" he snarled, waving the scoop at Missy in an uncanny imitation of his sister Octavia bearing her mouse-pillaged bags of oats. "Weevils all over the place."

"Oh, dear! The bulk oats too?"

"The lot."

"Then you'd better give me a box of proper breakfast oats, please, Uncle Maxwell."

"Just as well horses aren't fussy," he grumbled, putting the scoop down and squeezing behind the grocery counter.

The bell erupted into agitated life again as a man came through the door with a huge swirl of cold misty air and a dazzling briskness of purpose.

"Bloody hell, it's colder than a stepmother's tits out there!" gasped the newcomer, slapping his hands together.

"Sir! There are *ladies* present!"

"Oops!" said the newcomer, neglecting to follow this sop with an apology proper. Instead, he bellied up to the counter and grinned wickedly down at the gaping Missy. "Ladies in the plural, man? I can only see half a one!"

Neither Missy nor Uncle Maxwell could work out whether this was merely an insulting reference to her lack of height in a town of giants, or whether he was grossly insulting her by implying she was not really a lady. So by the time Uncle Maxwell had collected the use of his famously acid wits and tongue, the stranger was already well embarked upon his list of requirements.

"I want six bags of bran and pollard, a bag of flour, a bag of sugar, a box of twelve-gauge cartridges, a side of bacon, six tins of baking powder, ten pounds of tinned butter, ten pounds of raisins, a dozen tins of golden syrup, six tins of plum jam, and a ten-pound tin of Arnott's mixed biscuits."

"It is five minutes to five, and I close at five on the dot," said Uncle Maxwell stiffly.

"Then you'd better hop to it, hadn't you?" asked the stranger unsympathetically.

The box of proprietary oats was sitting on the counter; Missy milked her sixpence out of the finger of her glove and tendered it, waiting in vain for Uncle Maxwell to give her any change and quite lacking the courage to ask him whether a small quantity of a basic commodity could cost so much, even dolled up in a fancy box. In the end she picked up the oats and left, but not before stealing another glance at the stranger.

He had a cart drawn by two horses, for such was tethered outside the store, and had not been there when Missy entered. A good-looking equipage too; the horses were trim and sleek with a sensible dash of draft in them, and the cart seemed new, the spokes of its wheels picked out in yellow on a rich brown background.

Four minutes to five. If she reversed the order of their arrival in Uncle Maxwell's shop, she could plead the stranger's rudeness and vast order as an excuse for being late, and thereby manage to fit in a dash to the library.

The town of Byron possessed no public library; few towns in Australia did in those days. But there was a privately owned lending library to fill the gap. Livilla Hurlingford was a widow with a very expensive son; economic need allied to the need always to appear respectable had driven her to open a well-stocked book room, and its popularity and profitability had led her to ignore the general blue laws which closed the shops of Byron at five on weekday afternoons, for the bulk of her patrons preferred to exchange their books in the evenings.

Books were Missy's only solace and sole luxury. She was permitted to keep the money she made from selling Missalonghi's excess eggs and butter, and she spent all of this pittance borrowing books from her Aunt Livilla's library. Both her mother and aunt disapproved strongly, but having announced some years earlier that Missy should have an opportunity to put something by above and beyond the fifty pounds her father had bestowed upon her at her birth, Drusilla and Octavia were too fair to rescind their decree simply because Missy turned out a spendthrift.

Provided she did her allotted share of the work—and did it properly, without skimping by a whisker—no one objected if Missy read books, where they objected strenuously if she voiced a desire to go walking through the bush. To walk through the bush was to place her debatably desirable person smack in the path of murder or rapine, and was not going to be permitted under any circumstances. Drusilla therefore ordered her cousin Livilla to supply Missy only with *good* books; no novels whatsoever, no scurrilous or scandalous biographies, no sort of reading matter aimed at the masculine gender. This dictum Aunt Livilla policed rigorously, having the same ideas as Drusilla about what unmarried ladies should read.

But for the last month Missy had harboured a guilty secret; she was being supplied with novels galore. Aunt Livilla had found herself an assistant to run the library on Monday and Tuesday and Saturday, thus enabling Aunt Livilla to enjoy a four-day respite from the grizzling importunities of locals who had read everything on her shelves and visitors whose tastes her shelves did not cater for. Of course the new assistant was a Hurlingford, though not a Hurlingford from Byron; she hailed from the fleshpots of Sydney.

People rarely took any notice of the tongue-tied and sadly inhibited Missy Wright, but Una, as the new assistant was named, had seemed instantly to detect in Missy the stuff of a good friend. So from the beginning of her tenure, Una had drawn Missy out to an amazing degree; she knew Missy's habits, circumstances, prospects, troubles and dreams. She had also worked out a foolproof system whereby Missy might borrow forbidden fruit without Aunt Livilla's finding out, and she plied Missy with novels of all kinds, from the most adventurous to the most wildly romantic.

Of course tonight it would be Aunt Livilla on duty, so her book would have to be of the old kind. Yet when Missy opened the glass door and came into the cheery warmth of the book room, there sat Una behind the desk, and of the dreaded Aunt Livilla there was no sign.

More than Una's undeniable liveliness, understanding and kindness had endeared her to Missy; she was a truly remarkable-looking woman as well. Her figure was excellent, her height sufficient to mark her out as a true Hurlingford, and her clothes reminded Missy of her cousin Alicia's clothes, always in good taste, always in the latest fashion, always verging on the glamorous. Arctically fair of skin and hair and eye, still Una contrived not to appear half bald and wholly washed out, which was the fate of every Hurlingford female except Alicia (who was so ravishingly beautiful that God had given her dark brows and lashes when she grew up) and Missy (who was entirely dark). Even more intriguing than Una's positive brand of fairness was a curious, luminous quality she owned, a delicious bloom that lay not so much upon her skin as inside it; her nails, oval and long, radiated this light-filled essence, as did her hair, piled in the latest puffs all around her head and culminating in a glittering topknot so blond it was almost white. The air around her took on a sheen that was there and yet was not there. Fascinating! Lifelong exposure to none save Hurlingfords had left Missy unprepared for the phenomenon of the person with an aura; now within the space of a single little month she had met two of them, Una with her luminescence, and today the stranger in Uncle Maxwell's with his fizzy blue cloud of energy crackling around him.

"Goody!" cried Una at sight of Missy. "Darling, I have a novel you're going to adore! All about a young noblewoman of indigent means who is obliged to go governessing in the house of a duke. She falls in love with the duke and he gets her into trouble, then refuses to have anything to do with her because it's his wife has all the money. So he ships her to India, where her baby dies of cholera just after it's born. Then this terrifically handsome maharajah sees her and falls in love with her on the spot because her hair is red-gold and her eyes are lime-green where of course all his dozens of wives and concubines are dark. He kidnaps her, intending to make her his plaything, but when he gets her into his clutches he finds out he respects her too much. So instead, he marries her and casts off all his other women because he says she is a jewel of such rarity she must have no rival. She becomes a maharanee, and very powerful. Then the duke arrives in India with his regiment of hussars to quell a native uprising in the hills, which he does, only he's fatally wounded in the battle. She takes the duke into her alabaster palace, where he finally dies in her arms, but only after she forgives him for so cruelly wronging her. And the maharajah understands at last that she really does love him more than she ever loved the duke. Isn't that a wonderful story? You'll just adore it, I promise!"

Being told the entire plot never put Missy off a book, so she accepted *Dark Love* at once and tucked it down on the bottom of her shopping bag, feeling as she did so for her own little money-purse. But it wasn't there.

"I'm afraid I've left my purse at home," she said to Una, as mortified as only someone very poor and very proud can be. "Oh, dear! I was sure I put it in! Well, you'd better have the book back until Monday."

"Lord, darling, it's not the end of the world to forget your money! Take the book now, otherwise someone else will grab it, and it's so good it'll be out for months. You can pay me next time you're in."

"Thank you," said Missy, knowing she ought not embark upon a course of action utterly against the precepts of Missalonghi, but helpless in the face of her lust for books. Smiling awkwardly, she began to back out of the shop as fast as she could.

"Don't go yet, darling," pleaded Una. "Stay and talk to me, do!"

"I'm sorry, I really can't."

"Go on, just a wee minute! Between now and seven it's as quiet as the grave, everyone's home eating tea."

"Honestly, Una, I can't," said Missy wretchedly.

Una looked mulish. "Yes, you can."

So, discovering that to refuse favours to those who held one in debt was quite impossible, Missy capitulated. "Well, all right then, but only for a minute."

"What I want to know is if you've set eyes on John Smith yet," said Una, her sparkling nails fluttering about her sparkling topknot, her blue-white eyes glowing.

"John Smith? Who's John Smith?"

"The chap who bought your valley last week."

Missy's valley was not actually her valley, of course, it simply lay along the far side of Gordon Road, but she always thought of it as hers, and had told Una more than once about her longing to walk through it. Her face fell.

"Oh, what a shame!"

"Pooh! It's a jolly good thing, if you ask me. Time someone got his foot in the Hurlingford door."

"Well, I've never heard of this John Smith, and I'm sure I've never seen him," Missy said, turning to go.

"How do you know you've never seen him when you won't even stay to hear what he looks like?"

A vision of the stranger in Uncle Maxwell's shop rose in front of Missy's eyes; she closed them and said, more positively than usual, "He's very tall and solidly built, he has curly auburn hair, an auburn beard with two streaks of white in it, his clothes are rough and he swears like a trooper. His face is nice, but his eyes are even nicer."

"That's him, that's him!" squeaked Una. "So you have seen him! Where? Tell me all!"

"He came into Uncle Maxwell's shop a few minutes ago and bought a great many supplies."

"Really? Then he must be moving into his valley."

Una grinned at Missy wickedly. "I think you liked what you saw, didn't you, little Missy Sly-Boots?"

"Yes, I did," said Missy, blushing.

"So did I when I first saw him," said Una idly.

"When was that?"

"Ages ago. Years ago, in fact, darling. In Sydney."

"You *know* him?"

"Very well indeed," said Una, sighing.

The last month's spate of novels had vastly expanded Missy's emotional education; she felt confident enough to ask, "Did you love him?"

But Una laughed. "No, darling. One thing you can be absolutely sure of, I never loved him."

"Does he come from Sydney?" asked Missy, relieved.

"Among other places."

"Was he a friend of yours?"

"No. He was a friend of my husband's."

This was news indeed to Missy. "Oh, I am sorry, Una! I had no idea you were widowed."

Una laughed again. "Darling, I am not a widow! The saints preserve me from wearing black! Wallace—my husband—is still very much alive. The best way to describe my late marriage is to say that my husband divorced himself from it—and me."

In all her life Missy had never before met a divorcée; Hurlingfords did not sunder marriages, be they made in heaven or hell or limbo. "It must have been very difficult for you," she said quietly, on her mettle not to appear prim or shocked.

"Darling, only I know how difficult it was." Una's light disappeared. "It was a marriage of convenience, actually. He found my social standing convenient—or rather his father did—and I found his pots and pots of money convenient."

"Didn't you love him?"

"My whole trouble, darling—and it has wound me up in a lot of trouble—is that I have never loved anybody half so well as myself." She pulled a face and down went her inner light again, having just regained its normal intensity. "Mind you, Wallace was very well schooled in all the proper things, and very presentable to look at. But his father—ugh! His father was a dreadful little man who smelled of cheap pomade and even cheaper tobacco, and didn't know the first thing about manners. However, he had a burning ambition to see his son sitting right on top of the Australian heap, so he'd poured a great deal of his time and money into producing the kind of son a Hurlingford wouldn't baulk at. Where the truth was that his son liked the simple life, didn't want to sit on top of the heap, and only tried because he loved that awful old man quite desperately."

"What happened?" asked Missy.

"Wallace's father died not long after the marriage came crashing down. A lot of people reckoned the cause was a broken heart, including Wallace. As for him—I made him hate me as no man should hate any woman."

"I can't believe that," said Missy loyally.

"I daresay you genuinely can't. But it's true, all the same. Over the years since it happened, I've been forced to admit that I was a greedy selfish bitch who should have been drowned at birth."

"Oh, Una, don't!"

"Darling, don't weep for me, I'm not worth it," said Una, hard and brilliant again. "Truth's truth, that's all. So here I am, washed ashore for the very last time in a backwater like Byron, doing penance for my sins."

"And your husband?"

"He's come good. He's finally found a chance to do everything he always wanted to do."

There were at least a hundred other questions Missy was dying to ask, about Una's obvious change of heart, about the possibility she and her lost Wallace might patch things up, about John Smith, the mysterious John Smith; but the small pause which ensued after Una finished speaking brought time back with a jolt. A hasty goodbye, and she fled before Una could detain her further.

She ran almost all the five miles home, stitch or no stitch in her side, and her feet must have grown wings, for when she came breathless through the kitchen door she discovered mother and aunt perfectly ready to accept the story of John Smith's huge order as sufficient excuse for tardiness. Drusilla had milked the cow, Octavia's bones being unequal to the task, the beans were picked and simmering on the back of the range, and three lamb chops sizzled in a frying pan. The ladies of Missalonghi sat down on time to eat their dinner. And afterwards came the final chore of the day, the darning of much-laundered and much-worn stockings and underwear and linens.

Her mind half on Una's painful story and half on John Smith, Missy listened rather sleepily to Drusilla and Octavia as they indulged in their nightly dissection of whatever news might have come their news-starved way. To-night, after an initial period of mystified discussion about the stranger in Maxwell Hurlingford's shop (Missy had not passed on what she had gleaned from Una), they proceeded to the most interesting event looming on the Byron social calendar—Alicia's wedding.

"It will have to be my brown silk, Drusilla," said Octavia, winking away a tear of wholehearted grief.

"And it will have to be my brown grosgrain, and it will have to be Missy's brown linen. Dear God, I am so tired of brown, brown, brown!" cried Drusilla.

"But in our straitened circumstances, sister, brown is

the most sensible colour for us," comforted Octavia, not very successfully.

"Just once," said Drusilla savagely, jamming her needle into her reel of thread and folding the invisibly mended pillowcase with more passion than it had known in its entire long life, "I would so much like to be silly rather than sensible! As tomorrow is Saturday, I shall have to listen to Aurelia endlessly vacillating between ruby satin and sapphire velvet for her own wedding outfit, asking my opinion at least a dozen times, and I would— I would dearly love to *kill* her!"

Missy had her own room, timber-panelled and as brown as the rest of the house. The floor was covered in a mottled brown linoleum, the bed in a brown candlewick spread, the window in a brown Holland blind; there was an ugly old bureau and an even older, uglier wardrobe. No mirror, no chair, no rug. But the walls did bear three pictures. One was a faded and foxed daguerreotype of an incredibly shrivelled, ancient first Sir William, taken about the time of the American Civil War; one was an embroidered sampler (Missy's earliest effort, and very well done) which announced that THE DEVIL MAKES WORK FOR IDLE HANDS; and the last was a passe-partouted Queen Alexandra, stiff and unsmiling, but still to Missy's uncritical eyes a very beautiful woman.

In the summer the room was a furnace, for it faced south of west, and in the winter it was an ice-box, taking the full brunt of the prevailing winds. No deliberate cruelty had been responsible for Missy's occupying this particular chamber; simply, she was the youngest and had drawn the shortest straw. No room in Missalonghi was truly comfortable, anyway.

Blue with cold, she shed her brown dress, her flannel petticoat, her woollen stockings and spencer and bloomers, folding them neatly before placing the underwear in a drawer and the dress on a hook in the wardrobe ceiling. Only her Sunday-best brown linen was hung up properly, for coat-hangers were very precious commodities. Missalonghi's tank held only 500 gallons, which made water the most precious commodity of all; bodies were bathed daily, the three ladies sharing the same scant bath-water, but underwear had to last two days.

Her nightgown was of prickly grey flannel, high to the neck, long-sleeved, trailing on the floor because it was one of Drusilla's hand-me-downs. But the bed was *warm.* On Missy's thirtieth birthday her mother had announced that she might have a hot brick during cold weather, since she was no longer in the first flush of youth. And when that happened, welcome though it had been, Missy abandoned forever any hope she might have cherished that she might one day find a life for herself outside the confines of Missalonghi.

Sleep came quickly, for she led a physically active life, however emotionally sterile it was. But the few moments between lying down in this blessed warmth and the onset of unconsciousness represented her only period of utter freedom, so Missy always fought sleep as long as she could.

She would begin by wondering what she really looked like. The house owned only one mirror, in the bathroom, and it was forbidden to stand and gaze at one's reflection. Thus Missy's impressions of herself were hedged with guilt that she might have stayed too long gazing. Oh, she knew she was quite tall, she knew she was far too thin, she knew her hair was straight and dark, that her eyes were black-brown, and her nose sadly out of kilter due to a fall as a child. She knew her mouth drooped down at its left corner and twisted up at its right, but she didn't know how this made her rare smiles fascinating and her normal solemn expression a clownlike tragicomedy. Life had taught her to think of herself as a very homely person, yet something in her refused to believe that entirely, would not be convinced by any amount of logical evidence. So each night she would wonder what she looked like.

She would think about owning a kitten. Uncle Percival, who ran the combined sweet shop and tobacconist and was by far the nicest Hurlingford of all, had bestowed a cheeky black kitten upon her for her eleventh birthday. But her mother had taken it from her immediately and found a man to drown it, explaining to Missy with undeniable truth that they could not afford another mouth to feed, even one so small; it was not done without compassion for her daughter's feelings, nor without regret, but nevertheless it had to be done. Missy had not protested. She had not cried, either, even in her bed. Somehow the kitten had never been real enough to trigger desperate grief. But her hands could still, all these long and vacant years later, could still remember the feel of its downy fur and the vibrating thrum of its pleasure at being held. Only her hands remembered. Every other part of her had managed to forget.

She would dream of being allowed to walk through the bush in the valley opposite Missalonghi, and this was always the waking dream that passed tranquilly into sleeping dreams she could never recall. If she wore clothes they did not hamper her, nor did they get wet when she waded cascading streams, nor did they become soiled when she brushed against mossy boulders; and they were never, never brown. Bellbirds flew chiming round her head, butterflies flickered gorgeously coloured amid canopies of giant tree-ferns that made the sky seem satin under lace; everywhere was peace, nowhere did another human soul intrude.

Lately she had begun to contemplate death, who appeared to her more and more a consummation devoutly to be wished. Death was everywhere, and visited young and in-between as often as old. Consumption, fits, croup, diphtheria, growths, pneumonia, blood-poisoning, apoplexy, heart trouble, strokes. Why then should she be exclusively preserved from his hand? Death was not an unwelcome prospect at all; he never is, to those who exist rather than live.

But this night she remained wakeful through the gamut of looks, kitten, bush walks and death, in spite of an extreme weariness resulting from that scamper home and the painful stitch in her left side she seemed to be suffering more and more. For Missy had made herself save some time to devote to the big wild stranger named John Smith who had bought her valley, or so Una said. A wind of change, a new force in Byron. She believed Una was right about him, that he did intend to take up residence down in the valley. Not her valley any more; his valley now. Eyelids nearly closed, she conjured up an image of him, tall and heavy-set and strong, that lovely luxuriant dark red hair all over scalp and jaws, and two startling white ribbons in his beard. Impossible to tell his age accurately because of his weather-beaten face, though she guessed him to be somewhere on the wrong side of forty. His eyes were the colour of water that had passed over decaying leaves, crystal-clear yet amber-brown. Oh, such a *nice* man!

And when to round out this nocturnal pilgrimage she went once more upon her bush walk, he walked with her all the way into sleep.

The poverty which ruled Missalonghi with such cruel inflexibility was the fault of the first Sir William, who had sired seven sons and nine daughters, most of whom had survived to produce further progeny. It had been Sir William's policy to distribute his worldly goods among his sons only, leaving his daughters possessed of a dowry consisting of a house on five good acres of land. On the surface it seemed a good policy, discouraging fortune-hunters whilst ensuring the girls the status of land-owners as well as a measure of independence. Nothing loath (since it meant more money for them), his sons had continued the policy, and so in their turn had their sons. Only as the decades passed, the houses became steadily less commodious, less well built, and the five good acres of land tended to become five not-so-good acres of land.

The result two generations later was that the Hurlingford connection was sharply divided into several camps; uniformly wealthy males, females who were well off due to fortunate marriages, and a group of females who had either been tricked out of their land, or forced to sell it for less than its real value, or struggled still to subsist upon it, like Drusilla Hurlingford Wright.

She had married one Eustace Wright, the consumptive heir to a large Sydney accounting firm with good interests in some manufacturing concerns as well; naturally enough, at the time of her marriage she had not suspected the consumption any more indeed than had Eustace himself. But after his death only two years later, Eustace's father, surviving him, had elected to leave his property entirely to his second son rather than divert part of it to a widow with no better heir than a sickly girl-child. So what had started as an excellent essay into matrimony ended dismally in every way. Old man Wright had taken into consideration the fact that Drusilla had her house and five acres and came from a very wealthy clan who would be obliged to look after her, if only for appearance's sake.

What old man Wright failed to take into account was the indifference of the Hurlingford clan to those of its members who were female, alone, and without power.

So Drusilla eked out an existence. She had taken in her spinster sister Octavia, who sold her own house and five acres to their brother Herbert in order to contribute cash to Drusilla's household. Therein lay the rub; it was inconceivable to sell to an outsider, yet the male Hurlingfords took gross advantage of this. The ungenerous sum Herbert gave Octavia for her property was immediately invested by him on her behalf, and, as investments masterminded by Herbert had a habit of doing, this particular one yielded absolutely nothing. The few timid enquiries Octavia had made of her brother were brushed aside at first, then treated with outraged anger and indignation.

Of course, just as it was inconceivable that any female Hurlingford should dispose of her property to an outsider, so also was it inconceivable that she should disgrace the clan by going out to work, unless work could be found for her safely within the bosom of the immediate family. Thus Drusilla, Octavia and Missy stayed at home, their utter lack of capital preventing their sanctifying work through the medium of owning a business, their utter lack of useful talents meaning the immediate family regarded them as unemployable.

Any pipe-dreams Drusilla might have harboured about Missy's growing up to snatch the ladies of Missalonghi out of penury via a spectacular marriage died before Missy turned ten; she was always homely and unprepossessing. By the time she turned twenty, her mother and her aunt had reconciled themselves to the same remorselessly straitened circumstances all the way to their respective graves. Missy in time would inherit her mother's house and five acres, but there would be none of her own to swell that, as she was a Hurlingford only on the distaff side, and therefore ineligible.

Of course they did manage to live. They had a Jersey cow which produced wonderfully rich and creamy milk as well as splendid calves, a Jersey heifer they had kept because she was superlative, half a dozen sheep, three dozen Rhode Island Red fowls, a dozen assorted ducks and geese, and two pampered white sows which farrowed the best eating-piglets in the district, as they were allowed to graze instead of being penned up, and ate the scraps from Julia's tea room besides the scraps from Missalonghi's table and vegetable garden. The vegetable garden, which was Missy's province, produced something all year round; Missy had a green thumb. There was a modest orchard too —ten apples of various kinds, a peach, a cherry, a plum, an apricot, and four pear trees. Of citrus they had none, Byron being too cold in winter. They sold their fruit and butter and eggs to Maxwell Hurlingford for a lot less than they could have got elsewhere, but it was inconceivable that they should sell their produce to any but a Hurlingford.

Food they did not lack; money was what beggared them. Prevented from earning a wage and cheated by those who by rights should have been their greatest support, they depended for the cash which meant clothing and utensils and medicines and new roofs upon sale of a sheep or a calf or a litter of piglets, and could permit of no relaxation in their eternal financial vigilance. That Missy was dearly loved by the two older women showed visibly in only one way; they let her squander her egg and butter money upon the borrowing of books.

To fill in their empty days the ladies of Missalonghi knitted and tatted and crocheted and sewed endlessly, grateful for the gifts of wools and threads and linens that came their way each Christmas and birthday, giving back some of the end results as their gifts in their turn, and stockpiling a great deal more in the spare room.

That they acquiesced so tamely to a regimen and a code inflicted upon them by people who had no idea of the loneliness, the bitter suffering of genteel poverty, was no evidence of lack of spirit or lack of courage. Simply, they were born and lived in a time before the great wars completed the industrial revolution, when paid work and its train of comforts were a treason to their concepts of life, of family, of femininity.

Her genteel poverty was never more galling to Drusilla Wright than each Saturday morning, when she came on foot into Byron and through it and out to where the most prosperous of the Hurlingford residences hunched across the flanks of the magnificent hills between the town and an arm of the Jamieson Valley. She went to have morning tea with her sister Aurelia, never forgetting as she trudged that when they were girls and engaged to be married, she, Drusilla, was considered to have made by far the better bargain in the matrimonial marketplace. And she made the pilgrimage alone, Octavia being too crippled to walk the seven miles, and the contrast between Missy and Aurelia's daughter Alicia too painful to be endured. Keeping a horse was out of the question, as horses were destructive grazers and Missalonghi's five acres had to be safeguarded against drought at all times. If they couldn't walk, the ladies of Missalonghi stayed home.

Aurelia had also married out of the family, but far more judiciously, as things turned out. Edmund Marshall was the general manager of the bottling plant, having a talent for practical administration every Hurlingford lacked. So Aurelia lived in a twenty-roomed imitation Tudor mansion set within four acres of parkland planted

599

with prunus and rhododendron and azalea and ornamental cherry that transformed the place into a fairyland each late September and lasted for a month. Aurelia had servants, horses, carriages, even a motorcar. Her sons Ted and Randolph were apprenticed to their father in the bottling plant and showed great promise, Ted on the accounting side and Randolph as a supervisor.

Aurelia also had a daughter, a daughter who was everything Drusilla's daughter was not. The two possessed only one fact in common; they were both thirty-three-year-old spinsters. But where Missy was as she was because no one had ever dreamed of asking her to change her single status, Alicia was still single for the most glamorous and heartrending of reasons. The fiancé she had accepted in her nineteenth year was gored to death by a maddened work elephant only weeks before their wedding, and Alicia had taken her time about recovering from the blow. Montgomery Massey had been the only child of a famous family of Ceylon tea planters, and very, very rich. Alicia had mourned him in full accordance with his social significance.

For a whole year she had worn black, then for two more years she wore only dove-grey or pale lilac, these being the colours referred to as "half-mourning"; then at twenty-two she announced the period of retirement was over by opening a millinery boutique. Her father purchased the old haberdashery shop that time and Herbert Hurlingford's clothing emporium had made redundant, and Alicia put her one genuine talent to good stead. Convention demanded that the business be placed in her mother's name, but no one, least of all her mother, was under any illusion as to whose business it was. The hat shop, called Chez Chapeau Alicia, was a resounding success from the moment it opened its doors, and drew customers from as far afield as Sydney, so delightfully attractive and flattering and fashionable were Alicia's confections in straw and tulle and silk. She employed two landless, dowerless female relations in her work room and her spinster Aunt Cornelia as her aristocratic sales dame, confining her own share of the enterprise to design and banking the profits.

Then, just when everyone had assumed that Alicia was going to wear the willow for Montgomery Massey until she too died, she announced her engagement to William Hurlingford, son and heir of the third Sir William. She was thirty-two, and her prospective bridegroom was only just nineteen. Their wedding was set for the first day of this coming October, when the spring flowers would make a garden reception *de rigueur;* the long wait would finally be over. That there had been a long wait was the fault of the third Sir William's wife, Lady Billy, who on hearing the news had attempted to flog Alicia with a horse whip. The third Sir William had been forced to forbid the couple to marry until the groom turned twenty-one.

So it was with no joy in her at all that Drusilla Wright marched up the well-raked gravel drive of Mon Repos and applied the knocker to her sister's front door with a vigour born of mingled frustration and envy. The butler answered, informed Drusilla loftily that Mrs. Marshall was in the small drawing room, and conducted her there imperturbably.

The interior of Mon Repos was as charmingly right as its facade and gardens; pale imported wood panellings, silk and velvet wallpapers, brocade hangings, Axminster carpets, Regency furniture, all perfectly arranged to show off the lovely proportions of the rooms to best advantage. No need to use brown paint here, where economy and prudence so patently did not reign.

The sisters kissed cheeks, more alike in every way than either of them to Octavia or Julia or Cornelia or Augusta or Antonia, for both of them possessed a certain brand of haughty frostiness, and their smiles were identical. In spite of their contrasting social circumstances they were also more fond of each other than of any of the rest; and only Drusilla's implacable pride prevented Aurelia from assisting her financially.

After the greetings were over they settled on either side of a small marquetry table in velvet-covered chairs, and waited until the maid had served them from a tray of China tea and two dozen fairy cakes before getting down to business.

"Now it's not a scrap of use being proud, Drusilla, I do know how desperately you need the money, and can you give me one good reason why all those lovely things should pile up in your spare room instead of in Alicia's glory box? You can't plead that you're saving them for Missy's glory box when we both know Missy said her last prayers years ago. Alicia wants to buy her household linens from you, and I am in full accord," said Aurelia firmly.

"I am of course flattered," said Drusilla stiffly, "but I cannot *sell* them to you, Aurelia. Alicia may have whatever she wants as our gift."

"Nonsense!" countered the lady of the manor. "One hundred pounds, and let her take her pick."

"She may have her pick gladly, but only as our gift."

"One hundred pounds, or she will have to spend several times that buying her linens from Mark Foy's, for I will not permit her to take anything like as much as she needs from you as a gift."

The argument went on for some time, but in the end poor Drusilla was obliged to give in, her outraged pride warring with a secret relief so great it finally vanquished pride. And after she had drunk three cups of fragrant Lapsang Souchong and eaten her confection-starved way through almost the entire plate of perfectly iced pink and white fairy cakes, she and her sister had passed from the awkwardness of their social disparity to the cosiness of their social consanguinity.

"Billy says he's a jailbird," said Aurelia.

"In *Byron?* Good God, how did Billy let this happen?"

"He couldn't do a thing to prevent it, sister. You know as well as I do that it is a myth, the Hurlingfords owning every acre of land between Leura and Lawson. If the man could buy the valley, which apparently he has done, and if he has paid his debt to society, which apparently he has also done, then there is nothing Billy or anyone else can do to drive him out."

"When did all this take place?"

"Last week, according to Billy. The valley has never been Hurlingford land, of course. Billy assumed it was Crown land—a mistaken impression dating back to the first Sir William, it seems, so no one within the family has ever thought to verify the fact, more's the pity. Had we only known, a Hurlingford would have bought it long since. Actually it has been a Master of Lunacy estate for donkey's years, and then this chap bought it at auction in Sydney last week without our even learning it was for sale. The whole valley, if you please, and *dirt* cheap! Wouldn't it? Billy is livid."

"How did you find out about it?" asked Drusilla.

"The fellow arrived in Maxwell's shop yesterday just on closing time—Missy was there too, apparently."

Drusilla's face cleared. "So that's who he was!"

"Yes."

"Maxwell found out, I take it? He could prise information out of a deaf mute."

603

"Yes. Oh, the fellow wasn't at all backward, he talked about it very frankly—too frankly, in Maxwell's judgement. But you know Maxwell, he thinks any man a fool who advertises his business."

"What I fail to understand is why anyone other than a Hurlingford would *want* to buy the valley! I mean, to own it would have significance for a Hurlingford, because it's in Byron. But he can't farm it. It would take him ten years to clear enough to put to the plough, and it's so wet down there that he couldn't keep it cleared. He can't log it because the road out is too dangerous. So why?"

"According to Maxwell, he said he just wants to live alone in the bush and listen to the silence. Well, if he isn't actually a jailbird, you must admit he's certainly a bit of an eccentric!"

"What exactly makes Billy think he's a jailbird?"

"Maxwell phoned Billy as soon as the fellow had loaded up his cart and gone. And Billy set enquiries going at once. The fellow calls himself John Smith, if you please!" Aurelia snorted derisively. "Now I ask you, Drusilla, would anyone call himself John Smith unless there was real dirty work at the crossroads?"

"It might be his proper name," said Drusilla fairly.

"Pooh! One is forever reading about John Smiths, but have you ever actually *met* one? Billy thinks the John Smith is an—an—what do the Americans call it?"

"I haven't the faintest idea."

"Well, not that it matters, this isn't America. A false name, anyway. Billy's investigations have revealed that the man has no records with any official body. He paid in gold for the valley, and that's as much as can be found out."

"Perhaps he's a lucky strike miner from Sofala or Bendigo?"

"No. Every gold field in Australia has been in company hands for years, and there have been no big finds by a private individual, Billy says."

"How extraordinary!" said Drusilla as she absently reached for the second-last fairy cake. "Did Maxwell or Billy have anything else to add?"

"Well, John Smith bought a very large quantity of food, and he paid in gold. Out of a big money-belt under his shirt, and he not wearing an under-garment, either! Luckily by then Missy had gone, for Maxwell swears the fellow would have pulled up his shirt just the same. He *cursed* in front of Missy, *and* he said something or other that implied Missy was no lady! With *no* provocation, I assure you!"

"I believe that," said Drusilla dryly, taking the last fairy cake from the plate.

At which point Alicia Marshall came into the room. Her mother beamed at her proudly and her aunt gave her a wry little smile. Why oh why couldn't Missy have been like Alicia?

A truly exquisite creature, Alicia Marshall. Very tall and built on voluptuous yet disciplined lines, she was angelically fair of skin and hair and eyes, with beautiful hands and feet, and a swanlike neck. As always, she was dressed in perfect taste, and wore her ice-blue silk gown (eyelet embroidered, its shorter overskirt fashionably pointed) with incomparable flair and grace. One of her own hats, a tumbled mass of ice-blue tulle and ice-green silk roses, adorned her profusion of palest gold hair. Miraculous, that her brows and lashes were a definite, visible brown! For naturally Alicia did not tell the world that she darkened brows and lashes any more than Una did.

"Your Aunt Drusilla would be happy to provide your

605

household linens, Alicia," announced Aurelia triumphantly.

Alicia removed her hat and stripped off her long ice-blue kid gloves carefully, unable to answer while she concentrated on these enormously important tasks. Only when she had placed the shed articles on a table well out of harm's way and seated herself nearby did she activate her disappointingly flat and unmusical voice.

"How very kind of you, Aunt," she said.

"Kindness does not enter into it, my dear niece, since your mother is determined to pay me," said Drusilla stiffly. "You had better come to Missalonghi next Saturday morning and pick out whatever you want. I shall host morning tea."

"Thank you, Aunt."

"Shall I order some fresh tea for you?" Aurelia asked Alicia anxiously; she was just a little bit afraid of her big, capable, ambitious and driving daughter.

"No, thank you, Mother. I really came in to see what if anything you've discovered about the stranger in our midst, as Willie insists upon calling him." Her lovely lip curled.

So the news was given again and discussed again, after which Drusilla rose to go.

"Next Saturday morning at Missalonghi," she adjured her relatives, giving herself into the butler's custody.

All the way home she mentally catalogued the contents of the spare room and various cupboards, terrified that the amount and variety were not going to prove sufficient for the honest sale of one hundred pounds. One hundred pounds! What a lovely windfall! Of course it must not be *spent.* It must go into the bank and begin to accrue its minuscule interest, there to reside until disaster struck. Just what disaster, Drusilla did not know; but every blind corner on life's road concealed a disaster—illnesses, property damages and repairs, increased rates and taxes, deaths. Part of it would have to pay for the new roof, certainly, but at least they would not have to sell the Jersey heifer now to pay for that; stretched into the future with numerous as yet unconceived offspring to her credit, the Jersey heifer was worth a lot more than fifty pounds to the ladies of Missalonghi. Percival Hurlingford, a kind man with a kind wife, had always allowed them the services of his very valuable Jersey bull without charge, and had besides been responsible for the gift of their original Jersey cow.

Yes, it was most satisfactory! Perhaps Alicia, a notable trend-setter, would start a fashion among the girls of the Hurlingford connection; perhaps in future other brides-to-be would come to the ladies of Missalonghi to buy their household linens. This would be condoned as an acceptably ladylike form of business venture, where simple dressmaking would never be condoned, for that would have exposed them to the whims of anyone and everyone rather than the whims of the family.

"So, Octavia," said Drusilla to her crippled sister that night in the kitchen after they had settled to their hand-work while Missy buried her head in a book, "we had better spend next week really going through everything we have, to make sure it's fit for Aurelia and Alicia to see. Missy, you will have to cope with the house and garden and animals on your own, and since you have the lightest hand with flour, you will have to make the refreshments for morning tea. We'll have pikelets with jam and cream, a sponge, some little butterfly cakes, and a sour-apple tart cooked with cloves."

This sorted out to Drusilla's satisfaction, she then passed to a spicier topic, the advent of John Smith. For

607

once the conversation attracted Missy more than her book did, though she pretended to continue reading, and when she went to bed she carried this additional information with her to integrate and correlate among what Una had told her.

Why shouldn't his real name be John Smith? Of course the real basis for so much Hurlingford mistrust and suspicion was his acquisition of the valley. Well, John Smith, good for you! thought Missy. It's high time someone shook up the Hurlingfords. She fell asleep smiling.

The fuss of preparation which preceded the visit of the two Marshall ladies was largely futile, a fact of which all three Missalonghi ladies were well aware. However, none of them minded the change of pace, for it had the virtues of novelty and misrule. Only the housebound Missy felt any pangs of regret, and her pangs were due to a combination of booklessness and fear that Una would think she had defected upon payment for the novel taken out last Friday.

The delicacies Missy had taken such pains to prepare were not eaten by the ladies for whom they were intended; Alicia "watched her figure", as she phrased it, and so too these days did her mother, who wanted to cut a figure of high fashion at her daughter's wedding. However, the goodies were not wasted upon the pigs, for later on Drusilla and Octavia gobbled them up. Though they both adored sweet things, they rarely ate them because of the additional expense.

The amount of linen displayed for Aurelia and Alicia staggered them, and after a pleasant hour spent discussing the final choices, Aurelia pressed not one but two hundred pounds into Drusilla's reluctant hand.

"No arguments, if you please!" she said, at her most imperious. "Alicia is getting a bargain."

608

"I think, Octavia," said Drusilla later, after the visitors had driven off in their chauffeured motorcar, "that now we can all afford new dresses for Alicia's wedding. A lilac crêpe for me, with a beaded bodice and beaded tassels around the overskirt—I have just the right beads put by! Do you remember the ones our dear mother bought to sew onto her new best half-mourning gown just before she passed away? Ideal! And I think you might purchase that powder-blue silk you so admired in Herbert's material department, don't you? Missy could tat up some lace insertions for the neck and sleeves—very smart!" Drusilla stopped to ponder, brow furrowed, looking at her dusky daughter. "You're the really difficult one, Missy. You're too dark for pale colours, so I think it will have to be . . ."

Oh, let it not be brown! prayed Missy. I want a *scarlet* dress! A lace dress in the sort of red that makes your eyes swim when you look at it, that's what I want!

". . . brown," Drusilla finished at last, and sighed. "I understand how disappointing this must be, but the truth of the matter is, Missy, that no other colour *becomes* you half so well as brown! In pastels you look sick, in black you look jaundiced, in navy you are at death's door, and the autumn tones turn you into a Red Indian."

Missy said not a word, the logic of this being inarguable, and not knowing how much her docility pained Drusilla, who would have welcomed a suggestion at least—though of course scarlet would not have been countenanced under any circumstances. It was the colour of tarts and trollops, fully as much as brown was the colour of the respectable poor.

However, nothing could keep Drusilla's spirits oppressed for long tonight, so she cheered up again rapidly. "In fact," she said happily, "I think we can all have new

609

boots as well. Oh, what a dash we're going to cut at the wedding!"

"Shoes," said Missy suddenly.

Drusilla looked blank. *"Shoes?"*

"Not boots, Mother, please! Let us have shoes, pretty dainty shoes with Louis heels and bows on the front."

It is possible that Drusilla may have considered the idea, but Missy's cry from the heart was smothered immediately by Octavia, who, in her invalidish way, did quite a lot of the ruling at the house called Missalonghi.

"Living all the way out at the end of Gordon Road?" Octavia snorted. "You're not right in the head, girl! Just how long do you think shoes would last in the dust and the mud? Boots are what we must have, good sturdy boots with good sturdy laces and good sturdy thick heels on them. Boots *last!* Shoes are not for those who must go on Shank's pony."

And that was that.

❧

By the Monday following the visit of Aurelia and Alicia Marshall, life had returned to normal at Missalonghi, so Missy was allowed to take her habitual walk to the lending library in Byron. Of course it wasn't all selfish pleasure; she went armed with two large shopping bags, one for either hand to balance the load, and she did the week's marketing as well.

Quiescent for the week she had stayed at home, the stitch in Missy's side came back in full force. Odd, that it only seemed to bother her on long walks. And it was painful, so wretchedly painful!

Today her own purse had joined company with her mother's, and her mother's purse was unusually fat, for Missy had been commissioned to buy the lilac crêpe and the powder-blue silk and her own brown satin at Herbert Hurlingford's clothing emporium.

Of all the shops in Byron, Missy hated Uncle Herbert's the most, for he staffed it exclusively with young men, sons or grandsons naturally; even if one were purchasing stays or under-drawers, one had to suffer the attentions of a sniggering cad who found his task exquisitely funny and his customer the embarrassed butt of his jokes. However, this sort of treatment was not meted out to everyone, only to those whose means were sufficiently pinched to make shopping in Katoomba or—God forbid!—Sydney an impossibility; it was also chiefly reserved for Hurlingford women who had no men to exact retribution. Old maids and indigent widows of the clan were uniformly regarded as fair game.

As she stood watching James Hurlingford bring down the bolts she indicated, Missy wondered what he would have done had her own brown satin been a request for scarlet lace. Not that the clothing emporium stocked such a fabric; the only reds it offered were cheap and vulgar artificial silks kept for the denizens of Caroline Lamb Place. So along with the lilac crêpe and the powder-blue silk, Missy bought a length of very beautiful delustred satin in the shade known as snuff. Had the material been any other colour she would have loved it, but since it was brown, it may as well have been jute sacking. Every dress Missy had ever owned had been brown; it was such a serviceable colour. Never showed the dirt, never went in or out of fashion, never faded, never looked cheap or common or trollopy.

"New dresses for the wedding?" asked James archly.

"Yes," said Missy, wondering why it was that James always succeeded in making her feel so uncomfortable; perhaps it was his exaggeratedly womanish manner?

611

"Let's see, now," burbled James, "how about a weeny game of guessies? The crêpe is for Auntie Drusie, and the silk is for Auntie Octie, and the satin—the *brown* satin—must therefore be for little brown Cousin Missy!"

Her brain must still have been filled with the image of that impossible scarlet lace dress, for quite suddenly Missy saw nothing but scarlet, and out of the recesses of her memory she dredged the only insulting phrase she knew.

"Oh, go bite your bum, James!" she snapped.

He would not have been so shocked had his wooden dress dummy come to life and kissed him, and he measured and he cut with a hitherto unknown alacrity, thereby unintentionally giving each lady an extra yard of fabric, and he couldn't get Missy out of the shop fast enough. The pity was that he knew he couldn't confide his dreadful experience to any of his brothers or nephews, because they would probably echo Missy's words, the bastards.

The library was only two doors down, so when Missy went in she was still flying the flags of her anger in her cheeks, and she banged the door after her.

Una looked up, startled, and began to laugh. "Darling, you look absolutely splendid! In a paddy, are we?"

Missy took a couple of deep breaths to calm down. "Oh, just my cousin James Hurlingford. I told him to go bite his bum."

"Good for you! Time someone told him." Una giggled. "Though I imagine he'd much rather someone else bit it for him—preferably someone masculine."

This sailed straight over Missy's head, but Una's burst of merriment did the trick, and Missy found herself able to laugh too. "Dear oh dear, it wasn't very ladylike of me, was it?" she asked, sounding more surprised than horrified. "I don't know what came over me!"

The radiant face turned up to her looked suddenly sly, not the slyness of dishonesty but the slyness of someone fey, away with the fairies. "Straws and camels," intoned Una in a singsong voice, "eyes of needles and days of dogs, revolving worms and well reaped whirlwinds. There's a lot in you, Missy Wright, that you don't even know is there." She sat back and hummed like a gleeful naughty child. "But it's started now, and it can't be stopped."

Out came the story of the scarlet lace dress, the terrible longing to wear something other than brown, the defeat of having to admit no other colour than brown suited her, so that on this glorious day when she might actually have attained a dress in some other colour, still she must wear brown. Her feyness quite vanished, Una listened sympathetically, and when Missy had got it all out of her system, she looked her up and down deliberately.

"Scarlet *would* suit you beautifully," she said. "Oh, what a pity! Still, never mind, never mind." And she changed the subject. "I've saved another new novel for you—two pages into it, and I promise you won't even remember your red dress. It's all about a drab young woman who is utterly downtrodden by her family until the day she finds out she's dying of heart trouble. There's this chap she's been in love with for years, only of course he's engaged to someone else. So she takes the letter from the heart specialist telling her she's going to die to this young man, and she begs him to marry her rather than the other girl, because she's only got six months to live and after she's dead he can marry the other girl anyway. He's a bit of a wastrel, but he's just waiting for someone to reform him, only he doesn't know that, naturally. Anyway, he agrees to marry her. And they have six heavenly months together. He finds out that under her drab exterior she's an entrancing person, and her love for him reforms him completely. Then one day when the sun is shining and the birds are singing, she dies in his arms—I love books where people die in each other's arms, don't you? —and his old fiancée comes round to see him after the funeral because she got a letter from his dead wife explaining why he jilted her. And his old fiancée says she forgives him and she'll marry him the minute he's out of mourning. But he jumps up, wild with grief, rushes to the river and throws himself in, calling out his dead wife's name. And then his old fiancée throws herself in the river, calling out his name. Oh, Missy, it's so sad! I cried for days."

"I'll take it," said Missy instantly, paid up all her debts, which made her feel a lot better, and tucked *The Troubled Heart* into the bottom of one of her shopping bags.

"I'll see you next Monday," said Una, and went to the door to wave at her until she disappeared from sight.

As long as she walked it on her own, the five miles from Byron's shops to Missalonghi never seemed half so much. For as she walked, she dreamed, fantasising herself into roles and events and characters far beyond her real ken. Until Una had come to the library these characters had all looked exactly like Alicia, and the antics they got up to revolved around hat shops or dress shops or tea rooms of awesome gentility, and the men in their lives were a composite Hurlingford beau ideal, Siegfrieds in boots, bowlers, and three-piece suits. Nowadays her imagination had better grist to work on, and whatever character she played through whatever adventure it might be bore far more resemblance to the latest novel Una had smuggled her than to any aspect of Byron life.

614

So for the first half of her walk home that Monday, Missy metamorphosised herself into a divinely beautiful strawberry blonde with amazing lime-green eyes; she had two men in love with her, a duke (fair and handsome) and an Indian prince (dark and handsome). In this guise she shot tigers down from the howdahs of richly caparisoned elephants without assistance, she led an army of her husband's subjects against Muslim marauders without assistance, she built schools and hospitals and mothers' institutes without assistance, while her two lovers drifted vaguely in the background rather like the little male spider consorts not permitted into the wife's parlour.

But halfway home, where Gordon Road branched off from the long straggle of Noel Street, began her valley. At this point Missy always stopped daydreaming and looked about her instead. It was a beautiful day, as late winter days on the Blue Mountains can be when the wind takes time off to rest. Answering the lure of the valley, she crossed to the far side of Gordon Road and lifted her face to the kindly sky and swelled her nostrils to take in the heady tang of the bush.

No one had ever produced a name for the valley, though from now on it would in the way of Byron folk come to be known as John Smith's Valley, no doubt. Compared to the Jamieson Valley or the Grose Valley or even the Megalong Valley it was not very big, but it was perfect, a bowl some fifteen hundred feet lower than the three-thousand-foot ridge upon which Byron and all the other towns of the Blue Mountains were built. In shape it was a symmetrical oval, one narrow curving end lying just beyond the place where Gordon Road petered out and the far end some five miles away to the east, where its otherwise uninterrupted wall was dramatically broken by a chasm through which flowed its nameless river on its

615

way to join the Nepean-Hawkesbury system of the coastal plain. All the way round the margin was a stunning drop of dull orange sandstone cliff a thousand feet high, and below this sheer precipice a tree-covered skirt of fallen rock curved down to the course of the river which had made the valley aeons before. And the valley was, looking across it, stuffed with lush native forest, a blue ocean of gums that sighed and whispered ceaselessly.

On winter mornings the valley was filled with brilliant white cloud that sat like turning milk below the level of the cliff tops, and suddenly as the sun increased in warmth it would lift up in a moment and vanish. Sometimes the cloud would come down from above, fingers seeking out the tree tops far below until it succeeded in covering them from sight under a spectral blanket. And as sunset approached, winter and summer, the cliffs began to take on deeper, richer colour, glowering rose-red, then crimson, and finally the purple that faded into night's mysterious indigo. Most wonderful of all was the rare snow, when all the crags and outcrops of the cliffs were picked out in white, and the moving leafy trees shook off their powdering of icy moisture as fast as it fell upon them, unwilling to accept a touch so alien.

The only way down to the valley's floor was a terrifyingly steep track just wide enough for a large wagon, a track that emerged onto the top of the rim just beyond the end of Gordon Road. Fifty years earlier, someone had made the track in order to plunder the rainforest below of its massive cedars and turpentines, but after a whole team of eighty oxen, their driver, two loggers and a dray bearing a mighty tree trunk had gone over the edge, the plundering had ceased abruptly. There were easier forests to log. And gradually the track had been forgotten, as indeed had the valley; visitors preferred to go south to the Jamie-

son rather than north to this less awesome cousin, bereft as it was of kiosks and properly landscaped lookouts.

That wretched stitch came back just as Missy rounded the corner not far from Missalonghi, and ten seconds later the pain struck at her chest like a blow from an axe. She faltered and dropped her loaded shopping bags, her arms flying up to pluck at this terrifying agony; then she saw the neat hedge of Missalonghi through her terror, and ran for home. At precisely the same moment John Smith rounded the corner from its other side, striding along with his head down in thought.

Only ten yards short of the gate in the hedge, she pitched headlong. No one inside Missalonghi saw, for it was about five o'clock, and the rolling chords of Drusilla's organ were erupting into the outside air like a suffocating fall of hot volcanic ash.

But John Smith saw, and came running. His first thought was that the odd little soul had tripped after bolting to escape meeting him, but when he knelt and turned her face upwards, one look at her grey skin and sweat-soaked hair told him differently. He half-sat her against his thigh, rubbing her back helplessly, wishing he knew of some way to force air into her lungs. That much knowledge he had, not to lie her flat on the ground, yet farther than that his knowledge did not extend. She put up her hands to clutch at his arm where it lay lightly across the front of her shoulders, supporting her; the whole of her body was heaving with the fight to breathe, and her eyes were turned up to his, silently beseeching him for an aid he was incapable of giving. Caught mesmerised, watching the extraordinary cavalcade of an inner horror and bewilderment and pain pass through those eyes, he began to think she was going to die.

Then with startling swiftness the grey colour faded, a

warmer and healthier tinge crept into her skin, and her hands relaxed on his arm.

"Please!" she gasped, struggling to rise.

He got to his feet at once, slipped one arm under her legs and scooped her up. Though he had no idea where she lived, there must surely be some assistance in the dingy house behind the hedge, so he carried her through the gate and down the path, calling for help at the top of his voice and praying he would be heard above the bellowing of the organ.

Apparently he was heard, for two ladies came out of the house immediately, both unknown to him. There was no nonsense about them, which he appreciated deeply; one pointed wordlessly to the front door, while the other slipped around ahead of him and ushered him into the parlour with his burden.

"Brandy," said Drusilla curtly, bending to loosen her daughter's clothes. She wore no stays, having no need of them, but her dress was tightly belted and high to the neck.

"Do you have a telephone?" asked John Smith.

"I'm afraid not."

"Then if you give me directions, I'll go for the doctor right now."

"The corner of Byron and Noel, Dr. Neville Hurlingford," said Drusilla. "Tell him it's Missy—she's my daughter."

He went immediately, leaving Drusilla and Octavia to administer the brandy every prudent household kept in the sauce cupboard in case of heart trouble.

By the time Dr. Neville Hurlingford arrived some sixty minutes later, Missy had almost fully recovered. John Smith did not return with him.

"Very puzzling," said Dr. Hurlingford to Drusilla in the kitchen; Octavia was helping Missy into bed.

The experience had shaken Drusilla badly, as she was used to assuming that everyone she knew enjoyed the same rude health she did herself; Octavia's bones were such old friends they didn't really count. So soberly and quietly she made a pot of tea, and drank from her own cup more gratefully than Dr. Hurlingford did from his.

"Did Mr. Smith tell you what happened?" she asked.

"I must say, Drusilla, that in spite of the tall stories going around at the moment, Mr. Smith seems to me to be a good fellow—a sensible and practical man. According to him, she grabbed at her chest, ran across the road in a panic, and collapsed. She was grey and sweating and having great trouble breathing. The attack lasted about two minutes, and her recovery was quite sudden. Her colour came back, so did her breath. That was when Mr. Smith brought her inside, I gather. I could find nothing wrong with her a minute ago, but I may find more when I do a proper examination once she's in bed."

"There's no heart trouble in our branch of the family, as you know," said Drusilla, feeling betrayed.

"She takes after her father's family in the rest of her bodily makeup, Drusilla, so she may have inherited a bad heart from that side too. She has had no other attack like it?"

"Not that we know of," said Drusilla, properly rebuked. "*Is* it her heart?"

"I honestly don't know. It's possible." But he sounded doubtful. "I'll go in and see her again now, I think."

Missy was lying in her narrow little bed with her eyes closed, but the moment she heard Dr. Hurlingford's unfamiliar step she opened them and looked at him, then unaccountably seemed disappointed.

621

"Well now, Missy," he said, sitting gingerly alongside her. "What happened, eh?"

Drusilla and Octavia hovered in the background; he would dearly have liked to dismiss them, sensing that their presence inhibited Missy, but decency and convention forbade it. In all of Missy's life he had only seen her two or three times, so he knew only the little about her that everyone knew; she was the sole dark Hurlingford in history, and she had been doomed to spinsterhood before she was into her teens.

"I don't know what happened," lied Missy.

"Come now, you must remember something."

"I got short of breath and fainted, I suppose."

"That's not what Mr. Smith says."

"Then Mr. Smith is wrong—where is he? Is he here?"

"Did you experience any pain?" pressed Dr. Hurlingford, not satisfied, and not bothering to answer Missy's question.

A ghastly vision of herself reduced to the status of a chronic invalid at Missalonghi rose up in front of Missy's mind; the awful additional monetary burden she would become, the guilt she would in consequence feel every day of her bed-bound life, the impossibility of ever getting away on her own to walk past her valley into Byron and the library—no, it could not be borne!

"I had no pain at all," she insisted.

Dr. Hurlingford looked as if he didn't believe her, but for a Hurlingford he was fairly perceptive, and he too knew what sort of life Missy would lead from the moment she was diagnosed a case of heart trouble. So he forebore to press the poor girl further, merely got out his old-fashioned funnel-shaped stethoscope and listened to her heart, which was beating quite normally, and to her lungs, which were clear.

"Today is Monday. You had better come and see me on Friday," he said as he rose. He patted Missy reassuringly on top of her head and then walked into the hall, where Drusilla lurked in wait. "I can't find anything wrong," he said to her. "Lord knows what happened, I don't! But mind she sees me on Friday, now, and if anything else happens in the meantime, send for me at once."

"No medicine?"

"My dear Drusilla, how can I prescribe medicine for a mystery illness? She's as skinny as a wormy cow, but she seems healthy enough. Just leave her alone, let her sleep, and give her plenty of good nourishing food."

"Should she stay in bed until Friday?"

"I don't think so. Let her stay in bed tonight, but let her get up tomorrow. Provided she only does light duties, I can see no harm in her leading a normal and active life."

With that Drusilla had to be satisfied. She ushered her uncle the doctor out, tiptoed across the hall to the door of Missy's room and peeped in, saw that Missy was asleep, and so retreated to the kitchen, where Octavia was sitting at the table polishing off the last of the doctor's pot of tea.

Actually Octavia looked very shaken; the hands that both were needed to lift her cup to her lips trembled badly.

"Uncle Neville doesn't seem to think it's serious," said Drusilla, sitting down heavily. "Missy is to stay in bed for what's left of this evening, but she can get up tomorrow and move around, though only light duties until Uncle sees her again on Friday."

"Oh, dear!" A large pale tear rolled down Octavia's large pale cheek as she looked down at her gnarled fingers. "I will try in the garden, Drusilla, but I really cannot milk the cow!"

"I'll milk," said Drusilla. She put her hand to her head

and sighed. "Don't worry, sister, we'll manage somehow."

The disaster! Drusilla saw her precious two hundred pounds frittering itself away on a series of doctors and hospitals and treatments, none of which would she grudge for a moment; what depressed her was the disappearance of her tail just when she thought she had caught up with it at last. If she had not already cut out the lilac crêpe and the powder-blue silk and the snuff-brown satin, back they would have gone to Herbert's emporium on the morrow. *Wouldn't* it?

At dinner time Drusilla brought Missy a huge bowl of beef-and-barley broth and sat by the bed until Missy managed to struggle through it; but after that she was left mercifully alone. The long sleep of the earlier part of the evening had left her wakeful, though, so she settled to think. About the pain and what it might mean. About John Smith. About the future. Between the pain and the future, two deserts of appalling dreariness, John Smith stood lit up and glorious. So she abandoned all thought of pain or future, and concentrated upon John Smith.

Such a nice man! Interesting too. How easily he had lifted her off the ground and carried her inside. The recent avalanche of second-hand knowledge Una's smuggled novels had tipped on top of her was suddenly of genuine benefit; Missy understood that she was in love at last. But hope was not present at all in the sweet and smiling train of thought this realisation of love triggered. The Alicias of this world might scheme and plot to attain their ends, but the Missys could not. The Missys didn't know enough about men, and the smidgin they did know lay in the realm of generality. All men were untouchables, even jailbirds. All men had choices. All men had power. All men were free. All men were privileged. And presumably jailbirds had more of everything than men like poor Little

Willie Hurlingford, sheltered as he had been from every adverse wind that might have blown a little stiffening into him. Not that she believed John Smith was really a jail-bird; Una had known him during her years in Sydney, and presumably that meant he had moved at least on the fringes of the highest society—unless of course despite his friendship with Una's husband he had delivered the ice, or the bread, or the coal.

Oh, but he had been nice to her! Nice to a nonentity like Missy Wright. Even through that hideous and fright-ening pain she had been conscious of his presence, felt too some strange passage of strength from him to her that had, she fancied, tossed death aside like so much chaff.

John Smith, she thought, if I were only young and pretty, you would stand no more chance of escaping me than poor Little Willie did Alicia! I would chase you re-morselessly until I caught you. Wherever you went, there I would be, with my best foot forward to trip you up. And once I had you in my toils, I would love you so much and so well that you would never, never want to get away from me.

John Smith came in person the next day to enquire after Missy, but Drusilla dealt with him at the front door and did not permit him sight or sound of Missy. It was merely a courtesy call, as Drusilla perfectly understood, so she thanked him nicely but not profusely and then stood watching as he strode off down the path to the gate with his hands swinging loosely and his lips whistling a saucy tune.

"Fancy that!" said Octavia, coming out of the parlour, where she had been hiding to watch John Smith through a lifted curtain edge. "Are you going to tell Missy he called?"

"Why?" asked Drusilla, surprised.

625

"Oh, well . . ."

"My dear Octavia, you sound as if you've been reading those penny dreadful romances Missy's been bringing home from the library recently!"

"Has she?"

Drusilla laughed. "You know, until I realised what a dither she was in trying to hide the covers of her books, I'd forgotten all about our original rule as to the kind of books she might read. After all, it was fifteen years ago! And I thought, why should the poor little wretch not read romances if she wants? What has she to enjoy the way I enjoy my music?"

Nobly Drusilla refrained from adding that Octavia had her rheumatics to enjoy, and Octavia, who might under different circumstances have implied aloud how bereft she herself was of things to enjoy, wisely decided to leave the subject of enjoyment alone.

"Aren't you going to tell her she may read romances?" Octavia asked instead.

"Certainly not! If I did that, it would remove most of her pleasure, you know. Pure freedom to read them would only give her sufficient detachment to see how dreadful they are." Drusilla frowned. "What intrigues me is how Missy managed to persuade Livilla of all people to let her borrow them. But I can't ask Livilla without letting the cat out of the bag, and I wouldn't spoil Missy's fun for the world. I see it as a wee bit of defiance, and that gives me hope that there's some starch in Missy's backbone after all."

Octavia sniffed. "I can't see anything laudable about a sort of defiance that necessitates her becoming *underhanded!*"

A small sound halfway between a growl and a mew escaped Drusilla's lips, but then she smiled, shrugged, and led the way into the kitchen.

Drusilla accompanied Missy to the doctor the following Friday morning. They went off on foot in good time, warmly clad—naturally—in brown.

The surgery waiting room, dim and fusty, was empty. Mrs. Neville Hurlingford, who did service as her husband's nurse, ushered them into it with a cheery word for Drusilla and a rather blank stare for Missy. A moment later, the doctor poked his head round his consulting room door.

"Come in, Missy. No, Drusilla, you can stay there and talk to your aunt."

Missy went in, sat down, and waited warily, her guard up.

He commenced with a frontal attack. "I do not believe you were merely short of breath," he said. "There had to be pain, and I want to hear all about it, and no nonsense."

Missy gave in, told him about the stitch in her left side, the way it only bothered her on long walks if she hurried, and the way it had ushered in that sudden, terrifying onslaught of severe pain and breathlessness.

So he examined her again, and afterwards sighed. "I can find absolutely nothing the matter with you," he said. "When I examined you last Monday there were no residual signs to indicate heart trouble, and today is the same. However, from what Mr. Smith told me, you certainly did have some sort of genuine turn. So, just to make sure, I'm going to send you to a specialist in Sydney. If I can arrange an appointment, would you like to go down with Alicia on her weekly Tuesday trip to the city? It would save your mother having to go."

Was there an understanding twinkle in his eyes? Missy wasn't sure, but she looked at him gratefully all the same. "Thank you, I'd like to go with Alicia."

In fact, Friday was a very good day, for in the afternoon Una drove up to Missalonghi in Livilla's horse and sulky, and she had half a dozen novels with her, discreetly wrapped in plain brown paper.

"I didn't even know you were ill until Mrs. Neville Hurlingford told me this morning in the library," she said, sitting down in the best parlour, to which Octavia had ushered her, dazzled by her elegance and composure.

Neither Drusilla nor Octavia offered to let the two young women talk alone, not because they were consciously spoilsporting, but because they were always starved for company, especially when the company took the form of a brand new face. Such a lovely face too! Not beautiful like Alicia, yet—disloyal though the thought was, they fancied Una was perhaps the more alluring of the two. Her arrival pleased Drusilla particularly, since it answered the vexed question as to how Missy was suddenly managing to borrow novels.

"Thank you for the books," said Missy, smiling at her friend. "The one I brought home last Monday is nearly worn out."

"Did you enjoy it?" asked Una.

"Oh, very much!" As indeed she had; its dying heroine with her dicky heart could not have come at a more appropriate moment. Admittedly the heroine actually had managed to die in her beloved's arms, but she, Missy, had had the good fortune merely *almost* to die in her beloved's arms.

Una's manners were perfect. By the time she had partaken of a cup of tea and some plain home-made biscuits, she had won Drusilla and Octavia over completely. To have no better fare to offer was humiliating, but Una's appreciation turned the despised biscuits into an inspired guess as to what the visitor really liked and wanted.

"Oh, I get so tired of cream cakes and asparagus rolls!" she exclaimed, smiling with dazzling effect at her hostesses. "How clever of you, and how considerate! These little biscuits are delicious, and *so* much better for my digestion! Most Byron ladies swamp one in oceans of jam and cream, and as a guest it is of course impossible to refuse refreshments without offending."

"What a lovely person," said Drusilla after Una had gone.

"Delightful," agreed Octavia.

"She may come again," said Drusilla to Missy.

"Any time," said Octavia, who had made the biscuits.

On Sunday afternoon Missy announced that she didn't care to read, she was going for a walk in the bush instead. So calm and decided was her tone that for a moment her mother just stared at her, at a loss.

"A walk?" she asked at last. "In the *bush?* Most definitely not! You don't know who you might meet."

"I won't meet anyone," said Missy patiently. "There has never been any kind of prowler or molester of women in Byron."

Octavia pounced. "How do you know there's never been a prowler, madam? It's that ounce of prevention, and never do you forget it! If a prowler is prowling hereabouts, he never finds anyone to molest, because we Hurlingfords keep our girls safe at home, which is where you ought to be."

"If you are set on the idea, then I suppose I must come with you," said Drusilla in the tones of a martyr.

Missy laughed. "Oh, Mother! Come with me when you're so engrossed in your beading? No, I'm going on my own, and that's final."

She walked out of the house wearing neither overcoat nor scarf to protect her from the wind.

Drusilla and Octavia looked at each other.

"I hope her brain's not affected," said Octavia dolefully.

So secretly did Drusilla, but aloud she said stoutly, "At least you can't call this bit of defiance *underhanded!*"

In the meantime Missy had let herself out of the front gate and turned left instead of right, down to where Gordon Road dwindled to two faint wheelmarks meandering into the heart of the bush. A glance behind her revealed that no one was following; Missalonghi's squat ugliness sat with front door firmly closed.

It was a still clear day and the sun was very warm, even filtering through the trees. Up here on top of the ridge the bush was not thick, for the soil was scanty and whatever did grow mostly had to scrabble for an unloving hold on the sandstone substrate. So the eucalypts and angophoras were short, stunted, and the undergrowth sparse. Spring had arrived; even high up in the Blue Mountains it came early, and two or three warmish days were sufficient to bring the first wattle popping out into a drift of tiny fluffy yellow balls.

The valley went on to her right, glimpsed through the trees; where was John Smith's house, if house he had? Her mother's Saturday morning visit to Aunt Aurelia's yesterday had elicited no further information about John Smith, save a wild rumour that he had engaged a firm of Sydney builders to erect him a huge mansion at the bottom of the cliffs, made out of sandstone quarried on the spot. But Missalonghi could offer no evidence to support this, and Missalonghi sat plump on the only route such builders would have to use. Besides which, Aunt Aurelia apparently had more important worries than John Smith; it seemed the upper echelons of the Byron Bottle Company

630

were becoming extremely alarmed about some mysterious movements in shares.

Missy had no expectation of meeting John Smith on top of the ridge, as it was Sunday, so she decided to find out where his road went over the edge of the valley. When at last she stumbled upon the spot she could see the logic behind the site, for a gargantuan landslide had strewn boulders and rocks in a kind of ramp from top to bottom of the cliff, thus decreasing the sheerness of the drop. Standing at the commencement of the track, she could just glimpse it twisting back and forth across the landslide in a series of zigzags; a perilous descent, yes, but not an impossible one for a cart like John Smith's.

However, she was far too timid to venture down, not from fear of falling but from fear of walking into John Smith's lair. Instead, she struck off into the bush on top of the ridge along a narrow path that might have been made by animals going to water. And sure enough, as time went by a sound of running water gradually overpowered the omnipresent sound of the trees talking in that faint, plaintive, fatigued speech gum trees produce on calm days. Louder and louder was the water, until it became a bewildering roar; then when she came upon the stream, it offered her no answer, for though it was quite deep and wide, it was sliding along between its ferny banks without a flurry. Yet the roar of rushing water persisted.

She turned to the right and followed the river, inside her dream of enchantment at last. The sun glanced off the surface of the water in a thousand thousand sparks of light, and the ferns dripped tiny droplets, and dragonflies hovered with rainbow-mica wings, and brilliant parrots wheeled from the trees of one bank to the trees of the other.

Suddenly the river vanished. It just fell away into

nothing, a smoothly curving edge. Gasping, Missy drew back quickly, understanding the roar. She had come to the very head of the valley, and the stream which had cut it was entering it in the only way possible, by going down, down, down. Working cautiously along the brink for a good quarter of a mile, she came to a place where a great rock jutted far out over the cliff. And there, right on its end, legs dangling into nothingness, she sat to watch the waterfall in awe. Its bottom she could not discover, only the beautiful untidy tangle of its flight through the windy air, and a rainbow against a mossy place on the cliff behind it, and a chilly moistness that it exhaled as it fell, like a cry for help.

Several hours slipped away as easily as the water. The sun left that part of the ridge. She began to shiver; time to go home to Missalonghi.

And then where her path joined the road leading down into John Smith's valley, Missy met John Smith himself. He was driving his cart from the direction of Byron, and she saw with surprise that the cart was laden with tools and crates and sacks and iron machinery. Somewhere was a shop open on Sunday!

He pulled up at once and jumped down, smiling broadly. "Hello!" he said. "Feeling better?"

"Yes, thank you."

"I'm glad to catch you like this, because I was beginning to wonder if you were still in the land of the living. Your mother assured me you were when I called, but she wouldn't let me see for myself."

"You came to see how I was?"

"Yes, last Tuesday."

"Oh, thank you for that!" she said with fervour.

His brows rose, but he didn't attempt to quiz her. Instead, he left his conveyance where it was, and turned to walk back with her towards Missalonghi.

632

"I take it there was nothing serious wrong?" he asked after some minutes during which they just paced along together without speaking.

"I don't know," said Missy, recognising the emanations of pity and sympathy his obviously healthy being was giving off. "I have to see a doctor in Sydney quite urgently. A *heart* specialist, I believe." Now why did she say it like that?

"Oh," he said, at a loss.

"Whereabouts exactly do you live, Mr. Smith?" she asked, to change the subject.

"Well, further around in the direction you've just come from is a waterfall," he said, not at all reticently, and in a tone of voice which told Missy that, whether because of her sickly condition or because maybe she was so manifestly harmless, he had decided she could be counted a friend. "There's an old logger's hut near the bottom of the waterfall, and I'm camping in that for the time being. But I'm starting to build a house a bit closer to the waterfall itself—out of sandstone blocks I'm quarrying on the site. I've just been down to Sydney to pick up an engine to drive a big saw. That way I can cut my blocks a lot faster and better, and mill my own timber too."

She closed her eyes and heaved a big unconscious sigh. "Oh, how I envy you!"

He stared down at her curiously. "That's an odd thing for a woman to say."

Missy opened her eyes. "Is it?"

"Women usually don't like being cut off from shops and houses and other women." His tone was hard.

"You're probably right for the most part," she said thoughtfully, "but in that sense I don't really count as a woman, so I envy you. The peace, the freedom, the isolation—I dream of them!"

633

The end of the track came into sight, and so did the faded red corrugated iron roof of Missalonghi.

"Do you do all your shopping in Sydney?" she asked, for something to say, then chastised herself for asking a silly question; hadn't she met him first in Uncle Maxwell's?

"I do when I can," he said, obviously not connecting her with Uncle Maxwell's, "but it's a long haul up the mountains with a full load, and I've got only this one team of horses. Still, Sydney's definitely preferable to shopping in Byron—I've never encountered a place so full of Nosey Parkers."

Missy grinned. "Try not to blame them too much, Mr. Smith. Not only are you a novelty, but you've also stolen what they have always regarded as their exclusive property, even if they never thought about it, or wanted it."

He burst out laughing, evidently tickled that she should bring the matter up. "My valley, you mean? They could have bought it, the sale wasn't secret—it was advertised in the Sydney papers and in the Katoomba paper. But they're just not as smart as they think they are, that's all."

"You must feel like a king down there."

"I do, Miss Wright." And he smiled at her, tipped his battered bushman's hat, turned and walked away.

Missy floated the rest of the way home, in perfect time to milk the cow. Neither Drusilla nor Octavia made reference to her bush walk, Drusilla because she had been more pleased at the display of independence than worried about the outcome, and Octavia because she had convinced herself Missy's cerebral processes were being affected by whatever ailed her.

In fact, when by four o'clock there had been no sign of Missy, the two ladies left at Missalonghi had had a small tiff. Octavia thought it was time to inform the police.

"No, no, no!" said Drusilla, quite violently.

"But we must, Drusilla. Her brain's affected, I know it is. When in her whole life has she ever behaved this way?"

"I have been thinking ever since Missy had her turn, sister, and I'm not ashamed to say that when Mr. Smith carried her in, I was terrified. The thought of losing her to such an unfair, unjust thing—I was never more glad than when Uncle Neville told me he didn't think it was serious. And then I began to wonder what would happen to Missy had it been me? Octavia, we must *encourage* Missy to be independent of us! It is not her fault that God did not endow her with Alicia's looks, or my strength of character. And I began to see that a whole lifetime's exposure to my strength of character has not been good for Missy. I make the decisions about everything, and it is her nature to acquiesce without a fuss. So for far too long I have gone on making her decisions. I shall do so no longer."

"Rubbish!" snapped Octavia. "The girl's got no sense! Shoes instead of boots! Romances! Bush walks! It is my opinion that you must be more severe in future, not less."

Drusilla sighed. "When we were young women, Octavia, we wore shoes. Father was a very warm man, we lacked for nothing. We rode in carriages, we had plenty of pin-money. And ever since those days, no matter how hard life has been, at least you and I are able to look back and remember the pleasure of pretty shoes, pretty dresses, coming-out parties, *gaiety*. Where Missy has never worn a pair of pretty shoes, or a pretty dress. I'm not castigating myself for that, for it isn't my fault, but when I thought she might be going to die—well, I decided I was going to give her whatever she wanted, so long as I could afford it.

Shoes I cannot afford, especially if there are going to be heavy doctor's bills. But if she wants to walk in the bush, or read romances—she may."

"Rubbish, rubbish, rubbish! You must go on as you have in the past. Missy needs strong direction."

And from that viewpoint Drusilla could not budge her.

Unaware of her mother's soul-searching, Missy decided she had better not read one of the new novels after dinner; she elected to tat instead.

"Aunt Octavia," she said, fingers flying, "how much lace do you plan to set into your new dress? Is this going to be enough, do you think? I can easily make you a lot more, but I'll need to know now."

Octavia held out her knobby hand and Missy deposited the bunched-up lace in it, leaving her aunt to spread out each piece on her lap.

"Oh, Missy, it is beautiful!" breathed Octavia, awed. "Drusilla, do look!"

Drusilla plucked a scrap out of her sister's lap and held it up to the weak light bulb. "Yes, it is beautiful. You're improving all the time, Missy, I must say."

"Ah," said Missy gravely, "that is because I have finally learned to unknit the sleeve of ravelled care."

Both older ladies looked utterly blank for a moment, then Octavia cast a significant glance at Drusilla and ever so slightly shook her head. But Drusilla ignored her.

"Quite so," she said majestically.

Cutting a dash at Alicia's wedding won out; Octavia put Missy's brain storm aside. "Is it enough lace, Drusilla?" she asked anxiously.

"Well, for what I had originally planned it's enough, but I've had a better idea. I'd like to let in some of the same lace all the way around the hem of the overskirt—*so* fash-

636

ionable! Missy, would you mind doing so much extra work? Do be frank if you'd rather not."

Now Missy looked blank; in all her life her mother had never deferred to her before, nor stopped to think whether what she asked was excessive. Of course! It was the heart trouble! How amazing! "I don't mind in the least," she said quickly.

Octavia beamed. "Oh, thank you!" Her face puckered. "If only I might help you with the sewing, Drusilla. It's so much work for you."

Drusilla looked at the heap of lilac crêpe in her lap and sighed. "Don't worry, Octavia. Missy does all the fiddly bits like buttonholes and hems and plackets. But I do admit it would be wonderful to have a Singer sewing machine."

That of course was out of the question; the ladies of Missalonghi made their clothes the old-fashioned hard way, every inch of every seam sewn by hand. Drusilla did the main sewing and the cutting, Missy the fiddly bits; Octavia could not manage to hold an instrument so fine as a sewing needle.

"I am so very sorry your dress has to be brown, Missy," said Drusilla, and looked at her daughter pleadingly. "But it is lovely material, and it will make up very well, you wait and see. Would you like some beads on it?"

"And spoil the cut? Mother, you cut superbly, and the cut will carry it without any adornments," said Missy.

That night in bed Missy lay in the darkness and remembered the details of the loveliest afternoon of her entire life. For not only had he said hello to her, he had climbed down from his cart and actually chosen to walk along with her, chatting to her as if she was a friend rather than a mere member of that tiresome gang called Hurlingford. How nice he had looked. Homespun, but nice. And

637

he smelled not of stale sweat, like so many of the oh-so-respectable Hurlingford men, but of sweet expensive soap; she had recognised it immediately because whenever the ladies of Missalonghi received rare gifts of such soap, it was not consumed upon their bodies (Sunlight was quite good enough for that!), but inserted between the folds of their clothes as they lay in drawers. And his hands might be toil-roughened, but they were clean, even beneath the nails. His hair too was immaculate; no trace of pomade or oil, just the healthy gloss one saw on the fur of a freshly licked cat. A prideful and scrupulous man, John Smith.

Best of all she liked his eyes, such a translucent golden brown, and so laughing. But she couldn't, *wouldn't* believe any of the tales hinting at dishonesty or baseness. Instead, she would have staked her life upon his intrinsic integrity and fiercely defended ethics. She could see such a man doing murder, perhaps, if goaded beyond endurance, but she could not see him stealing or cheating.

Oh, John Smith, I do love you! And I thank you from the very bottom of my heart for coming back to Missalonghi to see how I did.

❦

With only a month left until her wedding, Alicia Marshall came day by day closer to the most perfect manifestation of her long and glorious blossoming, and she meant to enjoy even that final frantic month to the top of her bent. The date had been set eighteen months previously, and it had never occurred to her to doubt the season or the weather. Sure enough, though occasionally springs on the Blue Mountains might be late, or wet, or unduly windy, this one, obedient to Alicia's whim, was coming in with the halcyon dreaminess of Eden.

"It wouldn't dare do otherwise," said Aurelia to Drusilla, a nuance in her tone suggesting that just once Alicia's mother might enjoy Alicia's plans going awry.

Missy's Sydney appointment had been set up, but a week later than had been hoped; which was lucky for Missy, because on the Tuesday that Dr. Hurlingford had planned she should see the specialist, Alicia did not make her customary weekly trip to town. For on the Thursday of this week Alicia had scheduled her bridal party, and the preparations for it allowed of no other consideration, even hat shop business. The bridal party was not a humble sort of affair where modest kitchen gifts and girlish chatter prevailed; it was instead a formal reception for Alicia's female relatives of all ages, an occasion upon which everyone would have an opportunity to see and hear what would be expected of them on the Great Day. During the course of the festivities Alicia intended to announce the names of her bridesmaids, and show the designs and fabrics for the bridal party and the church décor.

The only blight came from Alicia's father and brothers, who brushed aside her attempts to enlist their help with a brusque impatience hitherto unknown.

"Oh, for God's sake, Alicia, go away!" snapped her father, more passion in his voice than she certainly could ever remember. "Have your wretched bridal party, by all means, but leave us out of it! There are times when women's affairs are a flaming nuisance, and this is one of them!"

"Well!" huffed Alicia, stay laces creaking dangerously, and went to complain to her mother.

"I'm afraid we must tread very carefully at the moment, dear," said Aurelia, looking worried.

"What on earth's the matter?"

"I don't really know, except that it's something to do

with shares in the Byron Bottle Company. I gather they've been disappearing."

"Nonsense!" said Alicia. "Shares don't disappear."

"Out of the family? Is that what I mean?" amended Aurelia vaguely. "Oh, it's quite beyond me, I have no head for business."

"Willie hasn't mentioned it to me."

"Willie mightn't know yet, dear. He hasn't had much to do with the company yet, has he? After all, he's just finished at university."

Alicia dismissed the whole tiresome business with a snort, and went off to instruct the butler to the effect that only female servants would be allowed in the front of the house, as it was a party purely for ladies.

Of course Drusilla came, and brought Missy with her; poor Octavia, dying to go, was obliged at the last moment to remain behind in all her best clothes, as Aurelia had forgotten to arrange the promised conveyance for the ladies of Missalonghi. Drusilla wore her brown grosgrain, happy in the knowledge that to do so would not be exposing this tried-and-true outfit to an early encore at the wedding itself. And Missy wore her brown linen, on her head the old sailor hat she had been forced to don on every occasion demanding a hat for the last fifteen years, including church each Sunday. New hats would be forthcoming for the wedding, though not, alas, from Chez Chapeau Alicia; the basics were already bought from Uncle Herbert's emporium, and the final furbishings would be done at Missalonghi.

Alicia was looking stunning in a delicate apricot crêpe dress trimmed with lavender-blue embroidery and bearing a huge bunch of lavender-blue silk flowers on one shoulder. Oh, thought Missy, just this once I would love to be able to wear a dress like that! Now I *could* survive that

640

apricot colour, I am positive I could! And I could survive that shade of blue too, it's halfway to pale purple.

Over a hundred women had been invited to the party. They wandered about the house in little clutches, catching sight of faces and catching up on gossip. Then at four o'clock they settled like roosting hens in the ballroom, where they partook of a magnificent tea of scones with jam and cream, petits fours, cucumber sandwiches, asparagus cornucopias, éclairs, cream buns and deliciously gooey Napoleons. There was even a choice between Darjeeling, Earl Grey, Lapsang Souchong and Jasmine tea!

Hurlingford women were traditionally fair, and traditionally tall, and traditionally incapable of frank speech. Looking around the gathering and listening to its chatter, Missy saw for herself the truth of these observations. This was the first occasion of its kind she had ever been invited to, probably because it would have been impolite not to invite her when so many women less closely related were coming. Somehow in church on Sunday the awesome presence of Hurlingford women en masse was watered down by the presence of a roughly equal number of Hurlingford men. But here in Aunt Aurelia's ballroom the breed was undiluted and overwhelming.

The air was thick with participles properly tucked away and exquisitely spliced infinitives and a great many other verbal delicacies largely gone out of fashion fifty years before. Under the splendour and graciousness of Aurelia's roof, no one dared to say "can't" or "won't" or "didn't". And, noted Missy, she herself was literally the only dark-haired woman there. Oh, a few borderline mouses glimmered (the greys and whites did not stand out at all), but her own jet-black hair was like a lump of coal in a field of snow; she quite understood why her mother had instructed her to keep her hat on throughout. Obviously, even when a Hurlingford man or woman married out of the family, he or she chose a blond partner. Indeed, Missy's own father had been very fair, but his grandfather, according to Drusilla, had been as dark as a dago, this term then being conventional and acceptable.

"Dearest Augusta and Antonia, it is the Saxon in us," fluted Drusilla to the sisters she saw least of.

Aurelia was devoting herself almost exclusively to Lady Billy, who had been amputated from her horse for the afternoon, not without bitter protest. And Lady Billy was sitting looking encephalitically expressionless, for she had no daughters of her own and no interest whatsoever in women. En masse they both frightened and upset her, and the greatest grief of her life had been the acquisition of Alicia Marshall as a prospective daughter-in-law. Undeterred by the fact that she fought a lone battle, Lady Billy had loudly opposed Little Willie's betrothal to his second cousin Alicia, declaring that they would never run together as a team, and would breed very poor stock. However, Sir William (called Billy) rode roughshod over her, as indeed he did over everybody; he had always had an eye for Alicia himself, and was delighted at the prospect of looking down his dining table every night to see Alicia's shining flaxen head and lovely face. For it had been arranged that the newlywed couple would reside at Hurlingford Lodge with Sir William and his lady for some months at least; Sir William's wedding present was prime land, ten acres of it, but the house being built upon it was nowhere near finished.

Left very much to her own devices, Missy looked around for Una. She found Aunt Livilla, but no Una. How odd!

"I don't see Una here today," said Missy to Alicia when that ravishing creature drifted by with a bright and wonderfully condescending smile.

"Who?" asked Alicia, stopping.

"Una—Aunt Livilla's cousin—she works in the library."

"Silly girl, there's no Hurlingford by that name in Byron," said Alicia, who had never been known to read a book. And off she went to spread her glorious presence as thinly across the surface of the gathering as the layer of jam on a boarding school pudding.

At which point the penny dropped. Of course! Una was *divorced!* An unheard-of sin! Stirred to the extent of providing a roof over her cousin's head Aunt Livilla might have been, but her humanitarian instincts would never extend to allowing that cousin—that *divorced* cousin—to enter Byron society. So it seemed Aunt Livilla had decided to keep quiet about Una altogether. Come to think of it, Una herself had been the sole source of Missy's information; on the rare occasions since Una's advent that Missy had found Aunt Livilla in the library, Aunt Livilla had never mentioned Una's name, and Missy, who was afraid of Aunt Livilla, had not mentioned Una either.

Drusilla bustled up, her sister Cornelia in tow. "Oh, is this not splendid?" she asked, speech patterns perfect.

"Very splendid," said Missy, shifting up on the sofa she had found behind a large potted Kentia palm cluster.

Drusilla and Cornelia sat down, replete with at least one specimen from every kind of delicacy offered at the buffet.

"So kind! So considerate! Dear Alicia!" waffled Cornelia, who regarded it as a great privilege to be permitted to work for a pittance as Alicia's sales dame, and had no idea how cynically Alicia traded on her gratitude and devotion. Until Chez Chapeau Alicia had opened its doors, Cornelia had worked for her brother Herbert in his alteration room, so there were grounds for her illusions; Herbert was so stingy he made Alicia look like a Lady

Bountiful. In the same way as Octavia, and with the same result, Cornelia had sold her house and five acres to Herbert, only in her case it was to help her sister Julia pay her tea room off when Julia bought it from Herbert.

"Hush!" breathed Drusilla. "Alicia is going to speak."

Alicia spoke, cheeks glowing, eyes sparkling like bleached aquamarines. The names of the ten bridesmaids were greeted with squeals and claps; the chief bridesmaid fainted clean away from the honour of it, and had to be revived with smelling-salts. According to Alicia, the dresses for her attendants were to be paired in five shades of pink, from palest through to deep cyclamen, so that when the white-clad bride stood at the altar she would be flanked on either side by five attendants who gradually shaded from palest pink at the bride's end to rich dark pink at the farthest end.

"We are all very nearly the same height, all very fair, and of much the same figure," explained Alicia. "I think the effect will be remarkable."

"Is it not a brilliant concept?" whispered Cornelia, privileged to have been a party to the preliminary planning of the entire bridal. "Alicia's train will be of Alençon lace, twenty feet long, and cut on the full circle!"

"Magnificent," sighed Drusilla, remembering that the train on her own wedding gown had been of lace and even longer, but deciding not to say so.

"I notice Alicia has kept her choice to virgins only," said Missy, whose stitch had been bothering her ever since the seven-mile walk from Missalonghi, and now was growing worse. To leave the room was impossible, but nor could she sit still and silent a moment longer; to keep her mind off the pain, she started to talk. "Very orthodox of her," she continued, "but I'm *definitely* a virgin, and I didn't get picked."

644

"Ssssh!" hissed Drusilla.

"Dearest little Missy, you're too short and too dark," murmured Cornelia, feeling very sorry for her niece.

"I'm five feet seven in my stockinged feet," said Missy, making no effort to mute her voice. "Only among a collection of Hurlingfords would that be called short!"

"Sssssh!" hissed Drusilla again.

In the meantime Alicia had passed to the subject of flowers, and was informing her enthralled audience that every bouquet would consist of dozens of pink orchids that were coming down in chilled boxes on the Brisbane train.

"Orchids! How ostentatiously vulgar!" said Missy loudly.

"Sssssh!" from Drusilla, despairingly.

At this moment Alicia fell silent, having shot her bolt.

"You'd wonder that she's happy to give the whole show away at this early stage," said Missy to no one in particular, "but I suppose she thinks if she doesn't, half the details she's so proud of won't even be noticed."

Down swept Alicia upon them, laughing, glowing, her head full of limelight and her hands full of bridal sketches and swatches of fabric.

"It's such a pity you're so dark and so short, Missy," she said, very prettily. "I would have liked to ask you, but you must see that you wouldn't fit in as a bridesmaid."

"Well, I think it's a pity that you're not dark and short," said Missy, equally prettily. "With everyone around you of similar height and colouring, and all that gradual shading of pink, you're going to fade into the wallpaper."

Alicia gasped. Drusilla gasped. Cornelia gasped.

Missy got up in a leisurely manner and attempted to shake the creases out of her brown linen skirt. "I think I'll be off now," she said chirpily. "Nice party, Alicia, but

645

utterly undistinguished. Why does everybody have to serve the same old food? I would have appreciated a really good curried egg sandwich for a change."

She had gone before her audience managed to regain its breath; when it did, Drusilla was forced to hide a smile, and turn a deliberately deaf ear to Alicia's demand that Missy must be fetched back to apologise. Served Alicia right! Why couldn't she have been kind just this once, marred her perfect bridal group by including poor Missy in it? How amazing! Missy's analysis was spot on; Alicia *would* fade into the wallpaper, or rather into the pink and white bows and bouquets and bunting with which she intended to deck the church.

Just outside the front door of Mon Repos, the awful pain and airlessness struck. Deciding she would rather die in decent seclusion, Missy left the gravel drive and darted round the side of the house. Of course Aurelia Marshall's notions of garden layout did not permit a hint of thicket, so there were very few places wherein Missy might huddle undetected. The closest of these was a large clump of rhododendrons beneath one of the downstairs windows, so into the middle of the clump Missy crawled, and half-sat, half-lay with her back against the red brick behind the shrubs. The pain was unbearable, yet had to be borne. She closed her eyes and willed herself not to die until she could die in John Smith's arms, like the girl in *The Troubled Heart*. What a depressing place to be found all stiff and stark, Aunt Aurelia's rhododendron bushes!

She didn't die. After a little while the pain began to recede, and she began to stir. There were voices nearby, and, since the rhododendrons were still rather bare from their autumn pruning, she didn't want the talkers to come round the corner and find her. So she rolled over onto her knees and started to get up. That was when she realised

646

that the voices were coming from the window just above her head.

"Did you ever see such a monstrosity of a hat?" asked a voice Missy recognised as belonging to Aunt Augusta's youngest daughter, Lavinia; of course Lavinia was a bridesmaid.

"All too often, in church every Sunday to be exact," said Alicia's tonelessly harsh voice. "Though I think the person underneath the hat is a far worse monstrosity."

"She's so *drab!*" came a third voice, belonging to the chief bridesmaid, Aunt Antonia's daughter Marcia. "Honestly, Alicia, you're according her far too much importance by calling her a monstrosity. Nonentity is a much better word for Missy Wright, though the hat, I grant you, is indeed a monstrosity."

"You have a point," conceded Alicia, who was still smarting from the unexpected flick of Missy's observation about fading into the wallpaper. Of course she was wrong! And yet Alicia knew that never again would the visual splendour of her wedding quite please her; Missy had planted her barb with more deadly skill than she realised.

"Do we really care about Missy Wright one way or another?" asked a more distant cousin called Portia.

"Due to the fact that her mother is my mother's favourite sister, Portia, I'm afraid I have to," declared Alicia in ringing tones. "Why Mama persists in pitying Auntie Drusie so, I don't know, but I've given up hoping I'll ever wean her from it. Oh, I daresay Mama's charity is laudable, but I can tell you that I try never to be at home on Saturday mornings, when Auntie Drusie comes to gorge herself on Mama's cakes. Lord, can she eat! Mama has Cook make two dozen fairy cakes, and by the time Auntie Drusie has gone, so have the fairy cakes, every last one."

Alicia produced a brittle unamused laugh. "It's become a regular joke in our house, even among the servants."

"Well, they are dreadfully poor, aren't they?" asked Lavinia, who had been good at history at school, so aired her superiority by saying, "It always puzzled me why the French rabble guillotined Marie Antoinette, just because she said they should eat cake if they had no bread. It seems to me anyone dreadfully poor would adore the chance to eat cake for a change—I mean, look at Auntie Drusie!"

"Poor they are," said Alicia, "and poor I am afraid they are going to remain, with Missy their only hope."

That raised a general laugh.

"A pity one cannot have people condemned the way one can have houses condemned," said another voice, a mere fourth or fifth cousin, by name of Junia; disappointment at not being chosen as a bridesmaid had concentrated all her natural venom down to one or two deadly drops.

"In this day and age, Junia, we are too kind for that," said Alicia. "Therefore we must all go on putting up with Auntie Drusie and Auntie Octie and Cousin Missy and Auntie Julie and Auntie Cornie and the rest of the spinster-widow brigade. Take my wedding. They will quite spoil it! But Mama rightly says they must be invited, and of course they will come the earliest and be the very last to go home. Haven't you noticed how pimples and boils always pop up when they're least welcome? However, Mama did have a brain-wave that will spare us from those hideous brown dresses. She bought my household linens from Auntie Drusie for two hundred pounds. And I will admit that they do the most remarkably fine and dainty work, so Mama's money was not wasted, thank God. Embroidered pillow-slips closed with little covered buttons, and every last button embroidered with a tiny rose-bud! Very beautiful! Anyway, Mama's scheme worked, because Uncle Herbert slipped the word to her that Missy came in and bought three dress-lengths—lilac for Auntie Drusie and blue for Auntie Octie. Any guesses what colour for Cousin Missy?"

"Brown!" chorused every voice, and then there was a gale of laughter.

"I have an idea!" cried Lavinia when the merriment ceased. "Why don't you give Missy one of your own cast-offs in a shade that will suit her?"

"I'd rather be dead," said Alicia scornfully. "See one of my lovely dresses on that dago-looking scragbag? If you feel so strongly about it, my dear Lavinia, why don't you donate her one of your cast-offs?"

"I am not," said Lavinia tartly, "in your cosy financial position, Alicia, that's why! Think about it, since you're so peeved at her appearance. You wear a lot of amber and old gold and apricot. I imagine anything in that sort of range would look all right on Missy."

At which point Missy managed to get herself on hands and knees out of the rhododendrons and onto the path. She crept on all fours until she was well clear of the window, then got to her feet and ran. The tears were pouring down her face, but she wasn't about to stop and dry them, too angry and shamed to care who might see.

She hadn't thought anything anybody might say about her could hurt, for a thousand thousand times in her imagination she had catalogued the various pitying or contemptuous things that might conceivably be said about her. Nor did it hurt, really. What stabbed to the quick were the dreadful things Alicia and her friends had said about her mother and all those poor spinster aunts, so decent and honourable and hard-working, so grateful

651

for any attention, yet so proud they would accept nothing they suspected might be charity. How dared Alicia speak of those infinitely more admirable women so scathingly, so unfeelingly! Let Alicia see how she would fare if she were placed in the same pinched shoes!

As she hurried through Byron with the stitch again burning in her side, Missy found herself praying that the library would be open, for Una would be in occupation. Oh, how she needed Una tonight! But the premises were dark, and a sign on the door simply said CLOSED.

Octavia was sitting in the kitchen of Missalonghi, changed back into her workaday clothes, with the small provender of their meal simmering away in a pot on the stove. Stew. Her misshapen hands were busy with knitting needles, magically producing the most fragile and cobwebby of evening shawls as a wedding present for the ungrateful Alicia.

"Ah!" she said, laying her task aside when Missy walked in. "Did you have a nice time, dear? Is your mother with you?"

"I had a wretched time, so I left ahead of Mother," said Missy briefly, then seized the milk bucket and escaped.

The cow was waiting patiently to be let into the shed; Missy reached out to stroke the velvety dark muzzle, and looked deeply into the big sweet brown eyes.

"Buttercup, you're *much* nicer than Alicia, so I just don't understand why it's such an unforgivable insult to call a woman a cow. From now on, the women others call cows, I shall call Alicias," she told it as she led it into the shed, where it moved of its own accord into the milking stall. Buttercup was the easiest cow to milk, letting down without a struggle, never complaining if Missy's hands were cold, as they often were. Which of course was why its milk was so good; nice cows always gave nice milk.

Drusilla was home when Missy returned. It was cus-

652

tomary to pour most of the milk into the big flat pans which lived on the shady side of the back verandah; as she poured, she could hear her mother enthusiastically regaling her aunt with a full description of Alicia's bridal party.

"Oh, I'm so glad one of you had a good time," said Octavia. "All I could get out of Missy was that she'd had a wretched time. I suppose her trouble is lack of friends."

"True, and no one is sorrier for it than I. But dear Eustace's death removed any chance of brothers and sisters for Missy, and this house is so far out of Byron on the wrong side that no one ever wants to come and see us regularly."

Missy waited for her sins to be divulged, but her mother made no reference to them. Courage seeping back, she went inside. Ever since the heart trouble came on it had become easier for her to assert herself, and apparently also easier for her mother to accept these signs of independence. Only it wasn't really the heart trouble caused the change. It was Una. Yes, everything went back to Una's advent; Una's forthrightness, Una's frankness, Una's unwillingness to be sat on by anyone. Una would have told a supercilious twerp like James Hurlingford to go bite his bum, Una would have given Alicia something verbal to remember if she condescended, Una would always make sure people treated her with respect. And somehow this had rubbed off on such an unlikely pupil as Missy Wright.

When Missy walked in, Drusilla leaped up, beaming.

"Missy, you'll never guess!" she cried, reaching round to the back of the chair where she had been sitting and plucking a very large box off the floor. "As I was leaving the party, Alicia came and gave me this for you to wear at her wedding. She assured me that the colour would suit you beautifully, though I confess I would never have thought of it for myself. Only look!"

Missy stood turned to stone while her mother scrab-

653

bled in the box and unearthed a bundle of stiff and crushed organdie which she proceeded to shake out and hold up for Missy's dazed inspection. A gorgeous dress of a pale toffee shade, not tan and not yellow and not quite amber; those in the know would have understood that its frilled skirt and neckline put it at least five or six years out of date, but even so it was a gorgeous dress, and with extensive alterations it would suit Missy down to the ground.

"And the hat, only look at the hat!" squeaked Drusilla, clawing a huge cartwheel of pale toffee straw out of the box and twitching its artless piles of matching organdie into place. "Did you ever see a more beautiful hat? Oh, dearest Missy, you shall have a pair of shoes, no matter how impractical they are!"

The stone dropped away from Missy's limbs at last; she stepped forward, arms extended to receive Alicia's bounty, and her mother placed dress and hat in them at once.

"I'll wear my new brown satin and my home-made hat and good sturdy boots!" said Missy through her teeth, and took to her heels out the back door, the masses of organdie billowing up about her like the skirts on a swimming bêche-de-mer.

It was not yet fully dark; as she raced for the shed she could hear the frantic cries of her mother and aunt somewhere behind, but by the time they caught up with her, it was too late. The dress and hat were trampled beyond repair into the muck of the milking stall, and Missy, a shovel in her hands, was busy heaping every pile of dung she could find on top of Alicia's grand gesture.

Drusilla was unspeakably hurt. "How could you? Oh, how could you, Missy? Just this once in your life, you had a chance to look and feel like a belle!"

654

Missy laid the shovel against the shed wall and dusted her hands together in complete satisfaction. "You above all people ought to understand how I could, Mother," she said. "No one's pride is stiffer than yours, no one I know is quicker than you to interpret the most well-meaning gift as charity in disguise. Why then are you denying me my share of that pride? Would you have taken the gift for yourself? Why then take it for me? Do you honestly think Alicia did it to please me? Of course she didn't! Alicia is determined to have her wedding perfect down to the last guest, and I—I *spoiled* it! So she decided to make a silk purse out of Missy Wright the sow's ear. Well, thank you very much, but I'd rather be my own sow's ear in all its natural homeliness than any silk purse of Alicia's making! And so I shall tell her!"

And so indeed she did tell her, the very next day. Though Drusilla had crept out in the dead of night armed with a lamp, the dress and hat had disappeared from their vile resting place, and she never saw them again; nor did she ever discover what had happened to them, for no one who knew remembered to tell her, so shocking were the other events of that memorable Friday morning in the Marshall residence.

Missy arrived at the front door of Mon Repos about ten o'clock, hampered by a large and exceedingly well-wrapped parcel which she carried rather gingerly by a string loop. Had the butler any idea of the consternation already reigning in the small drawing room, it is doubtful whether Missy would have got any further than the front stoop, but luckily the butler did not have any idea, and so was able to contribute his mite to the general atmosphere of disaster.

The small drawing room, not really small, was nonetheless rather full of very large people when Missy

655

sidled round the door with her parcel on its string. Aunt Aurelia was there, and Uncle Edmund, and Alicia, and Ted and Randolph, and the third Sir William, and his son and heir, Little Willie; Lady Billy was not there, as she was assisting a mare to foal.

"I don't understand it!" Edmund Marshall was saying as Missy gave the butler a smile and a gesture which indicated she would announce herself as soon as maybe. "I just don't understand it! How could so many shares escape us? *How?* And who the hell sold them and who the hell bought them?"

"As far as my agents can gather," said the third Sir William, "every share not held by a Hurlingford proper was bought up for many times its actual value, and then the mystery buyer began to make inroads on shares held by Hurlingfords. How or when or why I don't know, but he managed to discover every Hurlingford in need of money and every Hurlingford not tied to Byron, and he made offers no one could refuse."

"It's ridiculous!" cried Ted. "For the sort of money he's been paying, there's absolutely no way he can ever recoup his outlay. I mean, the Byron Bottle Company is a very nice little enterprise, but it's not gold we're taking out of the ground, nor is it the elixir of life! Yet the prices he's been paying are the sort of prices a speculator might pay on receipt of an infallible tip that the ground is solid gold."

"I agree with all that," said Sir William, "but I can't give you an answer, because I just don't know it."

"Are we reduced to minority shareholders, Uncle Billy, is that what you're trying to say?" asked Alicia, who was fully acquainted with the practices and terminology of the business world—and a not inconsiderable share-holder in the Byron Bottle Company herself, since Chez

656

Chapeau Alicia had put capital in her hands and an acquisitive nature had tempted her into the safer realms of speculation.

"Good God, no, not yet!" cried Sir William; then, with less confidence, he added, "However, I admit it's going to be touch and go unless we can either stem the tide of shares we're losing, or buy more ourselves."

"Aren't there any stray small shareholders living here in Byron whom we can get to first?" asked Randolph.

"A few, Hurlingfords on the distaff side mostly, and two or three of the old maids who accidentally inherited shares they weren't really entitled to. Naturally they've never been paid a dividend."

"How did you manage that, Uncle Billy?" asked Randolph.

Sir William snorted. "What do they know about shares, silly old biddies like Cornelia and Julia and Octavia? I didn't want them thinking they were hanging onto something valuable, so as well as never paying them a dividend, I told them the shares were worthless because they belonged by rights to Maxwell and Herbert. However, rather than make a big fuss, I merely told them they could best rectify the mistake by willing the shares to the sons of Maxwell and Herbert."

"Clever!" said Alicia admiringly.

Sir William gave her one of his hot lusting glances; she was beginning to wonder privately how easy it was going to be to keep Uncle Billy at arm's length after she married and moved into Hurlingford Lodge—but cross that bridge later.

"We'll have to acquire the old maids' shares now," said Edmund Marshall, looking very gloomy. "Though, Billy, I must be frank and admit that I don't know how I'm going to find any ready money. I'd have to retrench drastically, which would be most disagreeable for my family—Alicia's wedding, you know."

"I'm in the same boat myself, old man," said Sir William, the words sticking in his gullet. "It's all this flap over a big war in Europe, dammit! Rumour-mongering is all!"

"Why *buy* the shares?" asked Alicia, just the smallest tinge of contempt for their stupidity in her voice. "All you have to do is go to Auntie Cornie and Auntie Julie and Auntie Octie and *ask!* They'll hand them over without a murmur!"

"All right, we can do that with those three, and with Drusilla as well, I imagine. What on earth possessed Malcolm Hurlingford to leave shares to his daughters, I ask you? He always was soft over his girls, though thank God Maxwell and Herbert don't take after their father in that regard." Sir William sighed impatiently. "A pretty pickle we're in! Even if, as Alicia says, the old biddies hand over their shares without a murmur, we've still got to deal with the various ne'er-do-wells and half-Hurlingfords who most certainly won't want to part with what shares they have for nothing. Oh, we'll manage, I have no doubt, just as long as they don't get wind of the mystery buyer. Because we can't match his prices."

"What can we sell in a hurry to raise cash?" asked Alicia crisply.

They all turned to look at her, and Missy, as yet quite unnoticed, shifted stealthily from her spot in front of the door (against which her brown dress and person didn't show at all) to a safer spot behind one of the potted Kentia palms Aunt Aurelia had placed everywhere inside her lovely house.

"There's Lady Billy's bloody horses, for a start," said Sir William with relish.

"My jewels," said Aurelia with great resolution.

658

"And my jewels," said Alicia with a nasty look at her mother for getting in first.

"The thing is," said Edmund, "that this mystery buyer, whoever he—or they—might be, seems to know more about who owns shares in the Byron Bottle Company than we do, and we're the board of directors! When I consulted our list of shareholders I discovered that in a great many cases the shares had passed from the person listed as owning them into other hands, mostly sons or nephews, admittedly, but strange hands nonetheless. It never occurred to me that *any* Hurlingford would sign away his birthright this side of death!"

"Times are changing," sighed Aurelia. "When I was a girl, Hurlingford clannishness was a legend. Nowadays it seems as if some of the young Hurlingfords don't give a tuppenny bumper about the family."

"They've been spoiled," said Sir William. He cleared his throat, slapped his hands on his thighs, and said with great decision, "All right, I suggest we leave matters as they stand over the weekend, then on Monday we get down to raising some cold hard cash."

"Who is to approach the aunties?" asked Ted.

"Alicia," said Sir William instantly. "Only not until a bit closer to her wedding, I think. That way she can hoodwink them into thinking they're giving her a wedding present."

"Won't the mystery buyer get to them first?" asked Ted, who always worried about everything, and so had drifted into accounting quite naturally.

"One thing you can be absolutely sure of, Ted, is that none of those silly old chooks would dream of parting with anything Hurlingford to anyone outside the family without first asking me or Herbert. The buyer could offer them a fortune, and they'd still insist upon consulting me

661

or Herbert first." So positive was Sir William of his ground on this point that he smiled when he said it.

Taking advantage of the general melée as several worried and overwrought people endeavoured to find the right way to break off their meeting, Missy slid out the door and came back inside very noisily. And they all noticed her at once, though none of them looked pleased to see her.

"What do you want?" asked Alicia rudely.

"I came to show you how I feel about your charity, Alicia, and to tell you that I am happy to come to your wedding in good old brown," said Missy, marching across the room and dumping her parcel on the table in front of Alicia. "There! Thank you, but no thank you."

Alicia stared at her much as she might have stared at a dog turd she had almost stepped in. "Please yourself!"

"I intend to, from now on." She glanced up at the much taller Alicia (who admitted to five feet ten but was actually six feet one) with a puckish grin. "Go on, Alicia, open it! I dyed it brown just for you."

"You what?" Alicia began to fumble with the knots in the string, so Randolph came to her rescue with his pocket knife. After the string was cut the wrapping parted easily, and there lay the beautiful organdie dress and the ravishing hat, unspeakably smirched with what looked—and smelled—like fresh, sloppy, healthy cow and pig dung.

Alicia let out a squeak of horror that kept on growing and swelling until it became a long thin screech, and jumped away from the table as her mother, father, brothers, uncle and fiancé crowded round to see.

"You—you disgusting little trollop!" she snarled at the beaming Missy.

"Oh, I am not!" said Missy smugly.

"You're worse than a trollop! And you may count

662

yourself lucky indeed that I am too much of a lady to tell you exactly what I do think you are!" gasped Alicia, hardly knowing which had shocked her most, the deed, or the doer of the deed.

"Then you may count yourself unlucky that I am not too much of a lady to tell you exactly what I think you are, Alicia. I am only three days older than you, which puts you a lot closer to thirty-four than it does to thirty-three. Yet, here you are, mutton dressed up as lamb, brazen as brass, about to marry a boy hardly more than *half* your age! His father's years are more suitable! And that makes you a cold-blooded cradle-snatcher! When Montgomery Massey died before you could haul him to the altar—thereby escaping a fate worse than death—you couldn't see anyone on your horizon who was a tenth as good a catch. And then you spied poor Little Willie, still with all his baby-curls, playing with his hoop in his sailor suit, and you decided to be Lady Willie one day. I have no doubt that had the circumstances changed, you'd have been just as happy to be Lady Billy instead of Lady Willie —happier maybe, since the title's already there. I admire your gall, Alicia, but I do not admire you. And I feel very sorry for poor Little Willie, who is going to lead a wretched life, a bone between his wife and his mother."

The object of her pity was standing, with the rest of his relatives, gaping at Missy as if she had jumped stark naked out of a gigantic cake and proceeded to do the can-can. Aurelia had mercifully gone into hysterics, but so mesmerised was the rest of Missy's audience that it had failed to notice the fact.

Sir William recovered first. "Get out of this house!"

"I'm on my way," said Missy, looking very pleased.

"I will never forgive you for this!" cried Alicia. "How dare you? How *dare* you?"

"Oh, go bite your bum!" said Missy, and laughed. "It's big enough," she added, and departed.

This was the proverbial last straw; Alicia stiffened until she became utterly rigid, gave a gurgling moaning shriek, and fell over with a crash to join her mother on the floor.

Oh, how *satisfying* that had been! But as she walked away down the gradual hill of George Street that led into the main thoroughfare of Byron, Missy's elation faded. Compared to the topic under discussion during her first and unnoticed tenure of the drawing room, the presentation of Alicia's violated clothing was picayune. Those poor women! Missy knew as little about the world of company business as her mother and aunts, but she was fully intelligent enough to have caught the drift of Sir William's words. She even knew of the shares, for Drusilla kept hers and Octavia's both in the small tin cash-box that lay inside her wardrobe and held things like the deeds to her house and five acres of land. Ten shares each, twenty shares altogether. Which meant that Aunt Cornelia and Aunt Julia probably had ten shares each as well. Dividend. That was obviously some sort of periodic payment, a share in the company's profits.

How very despicable most of her male relations were! Sir William, eager to keep that disgraceful policy of the first Sir William's going, so that the hapless female members of his family who pinched and scraped in grinding but genteel poverty should have none of the fruits that accrued from the bottling of what was, after all, in God's gift rather than in any Hurlingford's. Uncle Maxwell, who was the worst kind of thief, rich in his own right, yet stealing the eggs and butter and orchardings of his poor relations because he had bullied them into believing that to sell elsewhere would be an unforgivable act of disloyalty. Uncle Herbert, who had bought up many of those houses on five acres in his time, always for a great deal less than they were worth, being the same kind of bully as his brother Maxwell. Only he was worse, because he stole back the little he paid out as well, by telling his victims that the investment schemes designed to make that little a little more had failed.

Not only the male relations were despicable, Missy amended, in a mood to dish out criticisms fairly. If the Aurelias and Augustas and Antonias had brought pressure to bear, having married on the inside of the clan fortunes, maybe they might have succeeded in changing things, for the worst bully is vulnerable to being bullied by his wife.

Well, something must be done. But what? Missy debated carrying her tale home, then decided she would not be believed, or if believed, that her mother and aunts would still end in being bullied out of their just due. Something *had* to be done, and done soon, before Alicia came smarming round to secure the shares, as secure them she undoubtedly would.

The library was open today; Missy glanced through the window expecting to see Aunt Livilla's grim form behind the desk, but there instead was Una. So she slowed down, turned round, and backtracked.

"Missy! What a treat! I didn't expect to see you today, darling," said Una, smiling as if she really did think it a treat to see the family trollop cum scragbag.

"I'm so angry!" cried Missy, and sat down on the hard chair provided for browsers, fanning herself with her hand.

"What's the matter?"

Suddenly realising she couldn't possibly expose that small clutch of close blood-relations to the contempt of a

665

person as remotely connected to the Byron arm of the clan as Una, she had to compromise with a lame, "Oh, nothing."

Una didn't attempt to probe. She just nodded and smiled, that lovely radiance emanating from skin and hair and nails subtly soothing rage.

"How about a cup of tea before the long hike home?" she asked, getting up.

A cup of tea assumed the proportions of a life-giving elixir. "Yes, please!" said Missy with fervour.

Una disappeared behind the last bookshelf at the back of the room, where in a small cubicle there lay facilities for making tea; there was no toilet, the norm in Byron shops, for everyone was expected to use the toilets in the Byron Waters Baths, and be quick about it.

To investigate the novels while she waited seemed like a good idea to Missy, so she moved to the back of the room and inched along the shelf that came hard up against the edge of Aunt Livilla's desk. And her eye in moving sideways round the desk to where the shelf continued on its far side encountered a familiar-looking sheaf of papers lying there. A packet of share certificates in the Byron Bottle Company.

Una emerged. "Kettle's on, but it takes time to boil from scratch on a spirit stove." Her eyes followed Missy's, then came to rest on Missy's face. "Isn't it lovely?" she asked.

"What?"

"The money that's being offered for Byron Bottle Company shares, of course. Ten pounds a pop! Unheard of! Wallace had a few shares of mine, you know, and when we separated he gave them back to me—said he didn't want anything that reminded him of the Hurlingfords. I only have ten shares, but I can definitely use a

666

hundred quid at the moment, darling. And just between you and me, Auntie Livvie is a bit on the short side too, so I've persuaded her to give me her twenty shares to sell while I'm selling mine."

"How did Aunt Livilla manage to acquire shares?"

"Richard gave them to her when he couldn't pay her back in cash the time he needed money so desperately he actually borrowed from her. Poor Richard! He never can bet on the right horses. And she's such a stickler for repayment of loans, even when it's her only beloved son on the borrowing end. So he signed over a few of his shares in the Byron Bottle Company to her, and that shut her up."

"Has he got more?"

"Naturally. He's a male Hurlingford, darling. But I do believe he may have sold out completely, because it was Richard put me onto this godsend of a buyer."

"How can you sell someone else's shares?"

"With a Power of Attorney. See?" Una held up a stiff foolscap form. "You get it at the stationer's, like a will form. And you fill it out with the details, and you sign it, and whoever is giving you permission to act on her behalf signs it, and someone signs it as a witness."

"I see," said Missy, forgetting all about perusing the novels. She sat down again. "Una, do you have an address for whoever is buying Byron Bottle shares?"

"Right here, darling, though I'm taking the whole kit and kaboodle down to Sydney in person on Monday to sell them, it's safer. That's why I'm minding the library today, so I can have Monday off." She got up and went back to make the tea.

Missy thought hard. Why couldn't she, Missy, have a try at getting hold of the aunts' certificates before Alicia came asking for them? Why should Alicia fill her with defeat when in their sole clash just concluded, Alicia had been the loser?

By the time Una came back with the tea tray, Missy had made up her mind.

"Oh, thank you." She took her cup gratefully. "Una, is it imperative that you go to Sydney on Monday? Could you possibly make it Tuesday instead?"

"I don't see why not."

"I have an appointment with a Macquarie Street specialist next Tuesday morning," Missy explained carefully. "I was going with Alicia, but . . . I don't think she's going to want my company, somehow. It's possible I may have some of these shares to sell, and if I could go with you, it would be easier. I've only been to Sydney a couple of times when I was a child, so I don't know the place."

"Oh, what fun! Tuesday it is." Una fairly glittered, so bright had the light in her become.

"I'll have to ask you for another favour, I'm afraid."

"Of course, darling. What?"

"Would you mind going next door to the stationer's and buying me four of these Power of Attorney forms? You see, if I go myself, Uncle Septimus is sure to want to know what I need Power of Attorney forms for, and the next thing he'll mention it to Uncle Billy, or Uncle Maxwell, or Uncle Herbert, and—well, I'd rather keep my business to myself."

"I'll go the minute I finish my cup of tea, while you're here to mind the shop for me."

And so it was arranged, including Una's driving out to Missalonghi on Sunday afternoon at five o'clock to witness the signing of the forms. Luckily this time Missy had her own little money-purse with her, and luckily it contained two shillings; the forms were expensive, at threepence each.

668

"Thank you," said Missy, stowing the rolled-up forms in her shopping bag.

She had decided upon some books as well.

"Good lord!" exclaimed Una, glancing at the titles. "Are you sure you want *The Troubled Heart?* I thought you said you read it to death all last week."

"I did. But I still want to read it again." And into the bag alongside the forms went *The Troubled Heart.*

"I'll see you at Missalonghi on Sunday afternoon, and don't worry, Auntie Livvie never minds lending me her horse and sulky," said Una, accompanying Missy to the door, where she deposited a light kiss on Missy's unaccustomed cheek. "Chin up, girl, you can do it," she said, and pushed Missy out into the street.

"Mother," said Missy that evening as she sat in the warmth of the kitchen with Drusilla and Octavia, "have you still got those Byron Bottle shares Grandfather left you and Aunt Octavia in his will?"

Drusilla looked up from her beading warily; though the altered pecking-order was of her own making, she still found it a little difficult to accept the fact that she was no longer the boss-chook. And she had learned very quickly to spot the more subtle, oblique approach Missy employed, so that she knew something was in the wind now.

"Yes, I've still got them," she said.

Missy put her tatting in her lap and looked across at her mother very seriously. "Mother, do you trust me?"

Drusilla blinked. "Of course I do!"

"How much is a new Singer sewing machine?"

"I don't honestly know, but I imagine at least twenty or thirty pounds, perhaps a great deal more."

"If you had yet another hundred pounds besides the two hundred pounds Aunt Aurelia paid for Alicia's linens, would you buy yourself a Singer sewing machine?"

669

"I would certainly be tempted."

"Then give me your shares in Byron Bottle and let me sell them for you. I can get you ten pounds a share in Sydney."

Both Drusilla and Octavia had ceased working.

"Missy dear, they're worthless," said Octavia gently.

"No, they are not worthless," said Missy. "You've been duped by Uncle Billy and Uncle Herbert and the rest, is all. You should have been paid what's called a dividend upon them every so often, because the Byron Bottle Company is an extremely prosperous concern."

"No, you're wrong!" insisted Octavia, shaking her head.

"I'm right. If you two and Aunt Cornelia and Aunt Julia had only taken yourselves off to a disinterested solicitor in Sydney years ago, you might be a lot richer today than you are, and that's the truth."

"We could never go behind the menfolk's back, Missy," said Octavia. "It would be a breach of faith and trust in them. They know better than we do, which is why they look after us and watch out for us. And they're *family!*"

"Don't I know it?" cried Missy from behind clenched teeth. "Aunt Octavia, your menfolk have been trading on the fact that they're family ever since the Hurlingfords began! They *use* you! They exploit you! When have we ever got a fair price from Uncle Maxwell for our produce? Do you honestly swallow all those hard-luck stories of his about being done down in the markets himself, so how can he afford to pay us more? He's as rich as Croesus! And when have you ever seen proof that Uncle Herbert actually did lose your money in an unlucky investment? He's richer than Croesus! And didn't Uncle Billy tell you in person that those shares were worthless?"

The fixity of Drusilla's silent regard had passed from shock to doubt, from unwillingness to listen to a distinct desire to hear more. And by the end of this impassioned speech, even Octavia was visibly wavering. Perhaps had it been the old Missy sitting there destroying the old order, they might have dismissed what she said without a qualm; but this new Missy possessed an authority which lent her words the ring of unequivocal truth.

"Look," Missy went on more quietly, "I can sell your shares in the Byron Bottle Company for ten pounds each, and I know that kind of opportunity is as rare as hen's teeth, because I was there when Uncle Billy and Uncle Edmund were talking about it, and that's what they said. They didn't know I was listening, otherwise they'd not have said a word of it. They spoke of you as they think of you, with utter contempt. Believe me, I did not misinterpret what I heard, and I do not exaggerate. And I made up my mind that there was going to be an end to it, that I was going to see that you and Aunt Cornelia and Aunt Julia got the better of them for once. So give me your shares and let me sell them for you, because I'll get you ten pounds each for them. But if you offer them to Uncle Billy or Uncle Herbert or Uncle Maxwell, they'll bully you into signing them away for nothing."

Drusilla sighed. "I wish I didn't believe you, Missy, but I do. And what you say comes as no surprise, deep down."

Octavia, who might have battled on in blind loyalty, instead decided to switch allegiances; for she was a little bit of a child, and craved firm direction.

"Think what a difference a Singer sewing machine would make to you, Drusilla," she said.

"I would enjoy it," admitted Drusilla.

"And I must confess I would enjoy having a hundred

pounds all of my own in the bank. I would feel less of a burden."

Drusilla capitulated. "Very well, then, Missy, you may have our shares to sell."

"I want Aunt Cornelia's and Aunt Julia's as well!"

"I see."

"I can sell their shares for the same amount of money, ten pounds each. But like you, they must be prepared to give me their shares without one word to Uncle Billy or any of the others—not one word!"

"Cornelia could certainly do with the money, Drusilla," said Octavia, feeling more cheerful every moment, and consigning her male relatives to limbo because it was better to do that than grieve over their perfidy, bleed from their hurtfulness. "She could afford to have her feet done by that German bone specialist in Sydney. She does so much standing! And you know how desperate Julia's case is, now that the Olympus Café has put in that extra room out the back, with marble-topped tables and a pianist every afternoon. If she had an extra hundred pounds, she could afford to make her tea room even swankier than the Olympus Café."

"I'll do my best to talk them into it," said Drusilla.

"Well, if you do talk them into it, they have to be here at Missalonghi on Sunday afternoon at five o'clock, with their shares. All of you will have to sign a Power of Attorney."

"What's that?"

"A piece of paper that authorises me to act in your name."

"Why at five o'clock on Sunday?" asked Octavia.

"Because that's when my friend Una is coming to witness the signing of the documents."

"Oh, how nice!" Inspiration struck Octavia. "I shall bake her a batch of my plain biscuits."

Missy grinned. "For once in our lives, Aunt Octavia, I think we can treat ourselves to a slap-up Sunday high tea. We can have plain biscuits for Una, of course, but we'll have fairy cakes and melting moments and cream puffs iced with toffee, and—*lamingtons!*"

No one gave her any argument about that menu.

When Missy arrived at the Byron railway station at six o'clock on Tuesday morning, she carried forty shares in the Byron Bottle Company, and four duly signed and witnessed Powers of Attorney. Una, it turned out, was a proper Justice of the Peace in spite of her sex (she said it happened in Sydney from time to time), and had fixed a most official-looking seal to the documents.

She was waiting on the platform, and so was Alicia. Not together, for Alicia was at the engine end, where the first class carriages would stand, and Una was at the guard's van end, where the second class carriages would stand.

"I hope you don't mind travelling second class," said Missy anxiously. "Mother has been most generous, I have ten shillings for my expenses and a guinea for the specialist, but I don't want to spend any more of it than I can help."

"Darling, my first class days are long over," soothed Una. "Besides, it's not a terribly long journey, and at this time of a cold morning, no one is going to insist that the windows be opened to let in the soot."

Missy's eyes encountered Alicia's; Alicia sniffed and deliberately turned the other way. Thank heavens for that, thought Missy unrepentantly.

The rails began to hum, and shortly afterwards the train came in, a huge black monster of an engine with a stubby stack clunking past in torrents of grimy smoke and fierce gushes of thick white steam.

"Do you know what I like to do?" asked Una of Missy as they found themselves a couple of vacant seats, one a window.

"No, what?"

"You know the overhead bridge at the bit of Noel Street near the bottling plant?"

"I do indeed."

"I love to stand right in the middle on top of it, and hang over the edge of the parapet when a train goes underneath. Whoosh! Smoke everywhere, just like descending to hell. But oh, such fun!"

And so are you fun, thought Missy. I've never met anyone like you, nor anyone so full of life.

By the time the train drew into its terminus at Central Station, the hands of the platform clock said twenty minutes to nine. Her appointment in Macquarie Street was for ten, but Una said that left them plenty of time for a cup of tea in the railway refreshment rooms. Alicia swept by them in the main concourse; she must have been lurking in wait just to do it, for the first class passengers were normally well ahead of those at the back of the train.

"Isn't that the famous Alicia Marshall?" asked Una.

"Yes."

Una made an untranslatable sound.

"What do you think of her?" asked Missy, curious.

"Obvious and flashy, darling. Keeps all her goods in the shop window, and you know what happens to goods in shop windows, don't you?"

"I do, but tell me in your own words."

Una giggled. "Darling, they *fade!* Constant exposure to

676

the glaring light of day. I give her another year at most. After that, no amount of lacing her stays tighter will keep her figure trim. She'll grow enormously fat and lazy, and she'll develop the most dreadful temper. I believe she's going to marry a mere lad. Pity. What she needs is a man who will make her work very hard, and treat her like dirt."

"Poor Little Willie is too limp, I fear," sighed Missy, and had no idea why Una found that remark so exquisitely funny.

In fact, Una laughed in fits and starts all the way down Castlereagh Street on the tram, but she refused to tell Missy why, and by the time they reached the building on Macquarie Street where the specialist had his rooms, Missy had given up.

At ten on the dot, Dr. George Parkinson's haughty nurse took her into a room plentifully endowed with movable screens of terrifying cleanliness and whiteness. She was directed to remove all her clothes, including her bloomers, place an indicated white wrap around her scrawny person, and lie down on the couch to wait for Doctor.

What an odd way to meet anyone, she couldn't help thinking when Dr. Parkinson's face loomed over hers; she was left to wonder what he looked like when the hairy caverns of his nostrils were not his most prominent feature. With his nurse in silent attendance, he thumped her chest, stared at her pitifully under-developed breasts with the rudeness of utter indifference, listened to her heart and lungs through a far sleeker stethoscope than Dr. Hurlingford's, took her pulse, stuck a spatula down her throat until she gagged dangerously, felt both sides of her neck and under her chin with impatient hard fingers, then went rolling round her flinching belly with his palms.

"Internal examination, Nurse," he said curtly.

"Pee ar or pee vee?" asked Nurse.

"Both."

The internal examinations left Missy feeling as if she had undergone some sort of major operation without benefit of chloroform, but there was worse to come. Dr. Parkinson flipped her over onto her front and then went poking and prying along the cordillera of her backbone until, somewhere around the spot where her shoulder blades stuck out like pathetic wings, he grunted several times.

"Ahah!" he exclaimed, striking treasure-trove.

Without any warning, Missy was grabbed around head and heels and hips by doctor and nurse combined; what they did was over so quickly she had no positive idea what they did, except that there came the sound of a grinding, sickening crunch all the more horrifying because she heard it inside her ears as well as outside them.

"You may get dressed now, Miss Wright, and then go through that door," ordered Dr. Parkinson, and went through that door himself with his nurse still in attendance.

Shaken and diminished, Missy did as she was told.

The right way up he turned out to have a very pleasant face, and his light blue eyes were kind and interested.

"Well, Miss Wright, you may return home today," he said, fingering a letter that lay on his desk along with quite a number of other papers.

"Am I all right?" asked Missy.

"Perfectly all right. There's absolutely nothing wrong with your heart. You've got a badly pinched nerve near the top of your spine, and those vigorous walks of yours kinked it into a vigorous protest, that's all."

"But—I couldn't breathe!" whispered Missy, aghast.

"Panic, Miss Wright, panic! When the nerve kinks the

678

pain is very severe, and it is just possible that in your case it inhibits some of the respiratory musculature. But there's really no need to worry. I manipulated your spine myself now, and that should fix it up as long as you slow down the pace of your walking a little when you're going some distance. If it doesn't clear up, I suggest you rig yourself up a sort of chinning bar, have someone tie a couple of house-bricks to each of your feet, and then try to lift yourself up to your chin on the bar against the weight of the bricks."

"And there's nothing else wrong with me?"

"Disappointed, eh?" asked Dr. Parkinson shrewdly. "Come now, Miss Wright! Why on earth would you prefer to have heart trouble instead of a kinked spinal nerve?"

It was a question Missy had no intention of answering aloud; how could one die in John Smith's arms of a kinked spinal nerve? It was as romantic as pimples.

Dr. Parkinson sat back in his chair and regarded her thoughtfully, tapping his pen on the blotter. It was obviously his habit to do this, for the blotter was pocked with many little blue dots, and at times, perhaps from boredom, he had begun to join up the more scattered dots into a meaningless cat's cradle.

"Periods!" he said suddenly, apparently feeling he ought to cheer her up a little by investigating every avenue. "How often do you have a period, Miss Wright?"

She blushed, and hated herself for blushing. "About every six months."

"Lose much?"

"No, very little."

"Pain? Cramps?"

"No."

"Hmmmm." He began to join up some dots. "Head-aches?"

"No."

"Are you a fainter?"

"No."

"Hmmmm." He pursed his lips so successfully that the top one actually managed to caress the tip of his nose. "Miss Wright," he said at last, "what really ails you can only be effectively cured if you find yourself a husband and have a couple of babies. I doubt you'd ever have more than a couple, because I don't think you'll fall easily, but at your age it's high time you got started."

"If I could find someone willing to start me, Doctor, believe me I would start!" said Missy tartly.

"I beg your pardon."

At this precise and uncomfortable moment Dr. Parkinson's nurse thrust her head around the door and wiggled her brows.

He rose immediately, semaphored away. "Excuse me."

For perhaps a minute Missy sat immobile in her chair wondering whether she ought to get up and tiptoe out, then she decided she had better wait for a formal dismissal. Dr. Neville Hurlingford's name leaped at her from the top of a letter on the desk, midway between a constellation of joined dots and a globular cluster of unjoined dots. Quite independently of her brain, Missy's hand reached out, picked up the letter.

"Dear George," it said,

"Odd that I should have to send you two patients within the same week, when I haven't sent you any in six months. But such is life—and my practice—in Byron. This letter is to introduce Missy Wright, a poor little old maid who has had at least one attack of chest pain and breathlessness following on a long, brisk walk. The single attack witnessed was rather suggestive of hysteria except that the patient was grey and sweating. However, her return to normal was dramatically sudden, and when I examined her not long afterwards, I could find no sequelae of any kind. I do indeed suspect hysteria, as her life's circumstances would make it a most likely diagnosis. She leads a stagnant, deprived existence (vide her breast development). But to be on the safe side, I would like you to see her with a view to excluding any serious illness."

Missy put the letter down and closed her eyes. Did the whole world see her with pity and contempt? And how could pride contend with so much pity and contempt when it was so well meaning? Like her mother, Missy was proud. "Stagnant". "Deprived". "A poor little old maid". "With a view to excluding any serious illness", as if stagnation and deprivation and old maidenhood were not serious illnesses within themselves!

She opened her eyes, surprised to discover that they contained not one tear. Instead, they were bright and dry and *angry*. And they began searching through the litter on Dr. Parkinson's desk to see if among the pieces of paper there might be at least the start of a report on her condition. She found two reports, neither distinguished by a name; one had a list of findings on it that all said "normal", the other was a technical litany of disaster, all to do with the heart. And she discovered the beginning of a letter to Dr. Hurlingford.

"Dear Neville," the letter said,

"Thank you for referring Mrs. Anastasia Gilroy and Miss ? Wright, whose Christian name I am afraid I do not know, as everyone including yourself seems to add a 'y' to her marital status and leave it at that. I am sure you will not object if I send you my opinion about both patients in this one"—

And there it ended. Mrs. Anastasia Gilroy? After sifting through a few of the non-Hurlingford faces in Byron, she came up with a sickly-looking woman of about her own age who lived in a rundown cottage beside the bottling plant with a drunken husband and several small, neglected children.

Was the second clinical report about Mrs. Gilroy, then? Missy picked it up and tried to decipher the jargon and symbols which filled the top half of the sheet. Though the bottom half was clear enough, even to her.

It said, "I can offer no course of treatment able to change or modify this prognosis. The patient is suffering from an advanced form of multiple valvular disease of the heart. If no further cardiac deterioration takes place, I give her six months to one year of life. However, I can see no point in recommending bed rest, as I imagine this patient would simply ignore the directive, given her nature and home situation."

Mrs. Gilroy? If only there was a name on it! But it would be hers, saved to put in with the letter to Dr. Hurlingford. There were no other reports amid the confusion. Oh, why wasn't Missy Wright's the bad report? Death, snatched from her, seemed suddenly very sweet and desirable. It wasn't fair! Mrs. Gilroy had a family who needed her desperately. Where Missy Wright had no one to need her desperately.

Voices sounded on the other side of the door; Missy folded up the report still in her hand neatly and swiftly, and stuffed it into her purse.

"My dear Miss Wright, I am so sorry!" cried Dr. Parkinson, breezing in with sufficient flurry to send the papers on his desk flying in all directions. "You can go, you can go! Leave it a week before you go back to see Dr. Hurlingford, eh?"

Sydney was warmer and moister than the Blue Mountains, and the day was fine and clear. Emerging onto Macquarie Street with Una at her side, Missy blinked in the brightness.

"Nearly half past eleven," said Una. "Shall we go and sell our share certificates first? The address is in Bridge Street, which is only round the corner from here."

So they did that, and it was remarkably easy. However, the small office and its surly clerk offered no clue as to the identity of the mystery buyer; the most intriguing aspect of the sale was that they were paid in gold sovereigns rather than in paper money. And four hundred gold coins were very heavy, as Missy discovered once she had put them in her bag.

"We can't walk far loaded down like this," said Una, "so I suggest we lunch at the Hotel Metropole—we're only a hop skip and jump away from it—then catch a tram back to Central and just go tamely home."

In all her life Missy had never eaten in a restaurant, even her Aunt Julia's tea room, nor had she ever been inside the Hurlingford Hotel. So the opulent vastness of the Metropole staggered her, with its crystal chandeliers and marble columns; it also reminded her of Aunt Aurelia's house, because it was beautifully greened and silenced with potted Kentia palms. As for the food—Missy had never tasted anything as delicious as the crayfish salad Una ordered for her.

"I think I might be able to get fat, if I could eat food like this every day," said Missy ecstatically.

Una smiled at her without pity, but with a great deal of understanding. "Poor Missy! Life has passed you by, hasn't it? Now me, life ran over like a through train. Bang boom crash, and there's our Una flat on her face in the water. But cheer up, darling, do! Life won't always pass you by, I promise. You just hang onto the thought that every dog has its day, even the bitches. Only don't let life run you over, either—that's equally hard to deal with."

Wanting to tell Una how very much she liked her, but too inhibited to do so, Missy sought around for an acceptable topic of conversation. "You haven't asked me what the doctor said."

Una's bright blue eyes gleamed. "What did he say?"

Missy sighed. "My heart is as sound as a bell."

"Are you sure?"

Knowing exactly what Una was implying, she smiled. "All right, yes, it is a bit affected. But not by a disease."

"I think it's the worst disease in the world!"

"Not in a doctor's book."

"If you like John Smith so terribly much, why don't you show him you like him?"

"*Me?*"

"Yes, darling, you! You know, your real trouble is that you've been brought up—along with that whole town— to think that if you don't look and act like Alicia Marshall, no man could ever be interested. But my dear, Alicia Marshall does not slay every man who meets her! There are many men with more taste and discrimination than that, and I happen to know that John Smith is one of them." She smiled impishly. "In fact, I think you'd suit John Smith extremely well."

"Is he married?"

"He was at one time, but he's respectably single now —his wife died."

"Oh! Was she—was she nice?"

Una thought about that. "Well, at any rate *I* liked her. There were plenty who didn't."

"Did he like her?"

"I think he probably liked her well enough in the beginning, but not nearly well enough in the end."

"Oh."

Una commandeered the bill and would hear none of Missy's protests. "Darling, your transactions this morning have been quite without personal reward, where mine have netted me one hundred wonderful pounds that I intend to fritter away like a king's mistress. Lunch is therefore my treat."

A very exclusive-looking dress shop occupied the corner where they waited for the tram, but to Missy's surprise, Una displayed no interest.

"First of all, darling, a hundred pounds wouldn't buy the smell of an oil rag in there," she explained. "Besides which, their clothes are as deplorably dull as their prices are deplorably expensive. No red dresses! It's far too respectable a shop."

"One day I shall have my scarlet lace dress and hat," said Missy, "no matter how unrespectable I look."

"So I don't have heart trouble at all," said Missy to her mother and aunt. "In fact, my heart is perfect."

Both the big pale faces turned anxiously to Missy fell instantly into repose.

"Oh, that is good news!" said Octavia.

"What is the matter, then?" asked Drusilla.

"I have a pinched nerve in my spine."

"Good heavens! Does that mean there's no cure?"

"No, Dr. Parkinson thinks he may already have cured me. He almost screwed my head off, there was a horrible sort of crunch, and I should be quite well from now on. He referred to what he did as a manipulation, I think. But if I do get more attacks, I have to get you to tie two bricks to each of my feet, and I have to hang in the air with my chin resting on a bar!" She grinned. "The mere thought is enough to cure any complaint!" Only with a hefty swing

685

did she manage to deposit her handbag on the table. "Here's something a lot more important—look!" And she withdrew four neatly wrapped cylinders. "One hundred pounds for you, Mother, all in gold. And the same for Aunt Octavia, Aunt Cornelia, and Aunt Julia."

"It's a miracle," said Drusilla.

"No, it's a little tardy justice," contradicted Missy. "You will buy that Singer sewing machine now, won't you?"

Prudence warred with desire in Drusilla's breast until she declared a temporary truce with the outcome undecided. "I said I would think about it, and I will."

When bedtime came around Missy found herself sleepless, despite the day's novel exertions; she lay contentedly in the dark and thought about John Smith. So he had been married, but his wife was dead. There could surely have been no children, or he would surely have them with him for at least part of the time. That was sad, so too was Una's opinion of the union, that he had not liked his wife nearly well enough in the end. Sydney society, decided Missy, was not conducive to happy marriages, what with Una and her Wallace, and John Smith and his dead wife. Still, Mrs. John Smith had not had to suffer the stigma of divorce; at which point, Missy wondered for the first time in her convention-hedged life whether the stigma of divorce might not be preferable to the finality of death.

By midnight her plan was all worked out, and her mind was made up. She would do it, and she would do it tomorrow. After all, what did she have to lose? If her scheme did not bear fruit, she would simply have to continue for the next thirty-three years as she had gone on for the last thirty-three years. Certainly it was worth a try.

Somewhere in her suddenly sleepy brain a little

thought was spared for John Smith, the unsuspecting victim. Was it fair? Yes, came the answer. Missy turned over and went to sleep with no further misgivings.

Drusilla elected to bear the four hundred pounds into Byron without assistance, and set off the next morning at nine o'clock, the heavy burden of her bag seeming as a feather. She was very happy, not only for herself, but for her sisters also. In the last few weeks more good fortune had come her way than in the last almost four decades, and she was beginning to dare to hope that the good fortune was a trickle building into a rivulet rather than a splash draining into the sand. But it cannot be for me alone, she vowed. Somehow I must ensure it embraces *all* of us.

While Octavia pottered happily in the kitchen, Missy quietly packed her scant clothing into the battered carpetbag which served all the ladies of Missalonghi on the rare occasions a bag was needed. On the top cover of her bed she left a note for her mother, then she let herself out of the front door, walked down the path to the gate, and turned left, not right.

This time she didn't timidly explore the start of the descent into John Smith's valley; she walked down it with decision and purpose, using a strong stick and the carpetbag to keep her balance on the treacherous rubble. At the bottom of the landslide the going became easier as the road plunged into the forested flanks below the cliffs. It was not nearly as cold as she imagined it might be, for the ramparts far above took the brunt of the wind; down on the valley floor, all was still and calm.

Four miles from the commencement of the descent the more open woodland of the sloping flanks turned into a kind of jungle, thick with vines and creepers and tree-ferns, even several varieties of palm. There were bellbirds everywhere, though try as she would, she couldn't see them; but their calls filled the air with the most delicate silvery chimes, thin and clear and elfin, utterly unbirdlike. And other birdsongs wove through the chimes, long carols from magpies, joyous trills from tiny fantails which fluttered only inches from her face and seemed to be welcoming her into their home.

That third hour of walking was very damp, the sun hardly showing through the canopy of leaves above, the track slippery from moss and mud and decaying forest detritus. When the first leech dropped on her and immediately attached its skinny slimy wriggling body to her hand, Missy's impulse was to screech and run in demented circles, especially after all her frantic efforts to dislodge it proved vain. But she made herself stand absolutely still and absolutely silent until the hair on her neck and arms subsided, then she gave herself a severe lecture; if these disgusting things lived in John Smith's forest, then she must cope with them in a way that would not brand her in his eyes as a silly woman. The leech had begun to swell up plumply, and, as she discovered when she began to feel areas of exposed skin on neck and face, had been joined by several equally vampirish brothers. Wretched things! They wouldn't let go! So she moved on in the hope that she would encounter fewer leeches moving than standing in one spot, a hope that was right. Replete, the first one to land detached itself without fuss and flopped to the ground, as did its brothers. She then learned that staunch the wounds as she would, they kept on bleeding away. What a sight she must look! Covered in blood. Lesson number one about dreams versus reality.

Shortly afterwards the sound of the river began to fill the distance, and Missy's courage started to bleed away as rapidly as her leech wounds; it took more resolution and strength to walk those last few hundred yards than to mount the whole expedition.

There it was, just around the next bend. A low small cabin built of wattle-and-daub, with a roof of wooden shingles and a lean-to off to one side that looked to be of more recent construction. However, the cabin had a sandstone chimney, and a thin blur of smoke smudged the perfect blue of the sky. He was home, then!

Since it was no part of her plan to pounce on him unaware, Missy stopped at the edge of the clearing and called his name several times in her loudest voice. Two horses grazing in a fenced-off yard lifted their heads to gaze at her curiously before going back to the endless business of feeding, but of John Smith there was no sign. He must be off somewhere, then. She sat down on a convenient tree stump to wait.

The wait wasn't long, for she arrived a little before one o'clock, and he came merrily whistling back to the cabin to get himself some lunch. Even after he entered the clearing he didn't see her; she was sitting in line with the horses, where he struck off towards the river flowing in noisy cascades behind the cabin.

"Mr. Smith!" she called.

He stopped in his tracks, did not move for a moment, then turned. "Oh, bloody hell!" he said.

When he reached her, he scowled at her horribly, not a scrap of welcome in his eyes.

"What are you doing here?"

Missy gulped in a big breath of much-needed air; it was now or never. "Will you marry me, Mr. Smith?" she asked, enunciating very distinctly.

His anger fled at once, replaced by unconcealed mirth. "It's a long walk down, so you'd better come in and have a cup of tea, Miss Wright," he said, eyes dancing. A finger flicked at the blood on her face. "Leeches, eh? I'm surprised you lasted the distance."

His hand went under her elbow and he walked her at a sedate pace across the clearing without saying another word, just muffling his laughter. The cabin had no verandah, unusual in that part of the world, and, as Missy saw when she entered its dimness, the floor was of packed earth, the fittings spartan. However, for a bachelor establishment it looked remarkably neat and clean, no dirty dishes, no untidiness. A new cast-iron cooking range filled half the chimney, an open fireplace the other half; there was a wooden bench for his washing-up dish, as well as a long rough-hewn table and two straight kitchen chairs. He had made his bed from timber slabs, piled what looked like at least three mattresses on top, and a feather quilt that ought to keep him warm in any weather. Some cowhide stretched across a chunky wooden frame served him as an easy-chair, and his clothing hung on wooden pegs hammered into the wall next to his bed. There were no curtains on the one window, which looked as if it had been recently glazed.

"But why have curtains?" Missy asked aloud.

"Eh?" In the act of lighting two kerosene lamps from a spill he had thrust into the stove, he looked at her.

"How splendid to live in a house that doesn't need any curtains," said Missy.

He put one lamp on the table and the other on an orange crate beside his bed, then busied himself making tea.

"There's really enough light," said Missy, "without lamps."

"You're sitting in front of the window, Miss Wright, and I want some light on your face."

So Missy lapsed into silence, letting her eyes wander

wherever they chose, from John Smith to his dwelling and back again. As usual he smelled clean, though dust and earth on his clothing and arms suggested that he had been doing something fairly strenuous all morning, as did a long superficial graze on the back of his left hand and wrist.

He served the tea in enamel mugs and the biscuits still in their huge gaudy tin, but he did everything without apology and with no physical awkwardness. After he had served her and she had indicated she wished for nothing else, he carried his mug and a fistful of biscuits to the leather easy-chair, which he pulled round so he could sit facing her at close quarters.

"Why on earth, Miss Wright, would you want to marry me?"

"Because I love you!" said Missy, her tone astonished.

This answer threw him into confusion; as if suddenly he didn't wish her to see what might lie in his eyes, he removed his gaze from her person to the window behind her, frowning.

"That's ridiculous," he said at last, chewing his lip.

"I would have said it was obvious."

"You can't possibly love someone you don't even know, woman! It's ridiculous."

"I know quite enough about you to love you," she said earnestly. "I know that you're very kind. You're strong on the inside. You're clean. You're different. And you—you have enough *poetry* in you to want to live here of all places."

He blinked. "Christ!" he exclaimed, and laughed. "I must say that's the most interesting catalogue of virtues I've ever been privileged to hear. I like the clean bit best."

"It's important," said Missy gravely.

For a moment he looked as if amusement might get the

691

better of him again, but with an effort he remained sober, and said, "I'm afraid I can't marry you, Miss Wright."

"Why?"

"Why? I'll tell you why," he said, leaning forward in his chair. "You are looking at a man who has found happiness for the first time in his life! If I were twenty, that would be a stupid statement, but I'm pushing fifty, Miss Wright, and that means I'm entitled to some happiness. I'm finally doing all the things I've always wanted to do and never had the time or the chance—and I'm *alone!* No wife, no relations, no dependents of any kind. Not even a dog. Just me. And I love it! To have to share it would spoil it. In fact, I'm going to put a bloody great gate across the top of my road and keep the whole world out. *Marriage?* Not in a fit!"

"It wouldn't be for very long," said Missy quietly.

"A day would be too long, Miss Wright."

"I understand how you feel, Mr. Smith, and I do mean that most sincerely. I too have spent a confined life, I too have chafed against it. But I cannot imagine for a moment that your life has been as dull, as drab and uneventful as mine has always been. Oh, I don't wish to imply that I've been mistreated, or treated one iota worse than the other ladies of Missalonghi. We all live the same dull drab uneventful life. But I am tired of it, Mr. Smith! I want to live a little before I die! Can you understand that?"

"Hell, who couldn't? But if you're in a proposing mood, why not put the hard word on some of the widowers or bachelors in Byron? There must be a few around somewhere." His shell of hardness was setting with every word he said, and he was beginning to feel as if he might extricate himself from this most embarrassing situation without losing either his freedom or his self-respect.

"That would be a fate worse than Missalonghi, because it would be no different. I've chosen you because you're living exactly the kind of life I want to live—away from people, away from houses and smugness and gossip. Believe me, Mr. Smith, I have no intention of cramping your style—on the contrary, I want you to free up mine! I won't be a millstone around your neck. In fact, I'll guarantee to leave you alone most of the time. And it wouldn't be forever, I promise you. A year. Just one little year!"

"So after a year of living the sort of life you're dying to live, you're going to pick up and tamely go back to the life you hate?" His tone was sceptical.

Missy drew up her meagre form with profound dignity. "I only have a year to live, Mr. Smith," she said.

He looked desperately sorry for her, as if he now knew everything about her there was to know.

She pushed her advantage relentlessly. "I understand very well your reluctance to share this paradise—if it were mine, I too would guard it jealously. But try to see my side, please! I am thirty-three years old, and I have never known any of the things most women my age either take for granted or wish they didn't have at all. I am an old maid! That is the most dreadful fate a woman can suffer, for it goes hand in hand with poverty and lack of beauty. If I had suffered one without the other, some man would have been prepared to marry me, but to suffer both is to be completely undesirable. Yet I *know* that if I can only get past these handicaps, I have a great deal to offer that most women don't, because they have no need to. You would enjoy all the advantages, Mr. Smith, for I would be tied to you by the bonds of gratitude and thankfulness, as well as by love. I wish there was some way right at this moment whereby I could show you how little you'd lose by marrying me, and how much you'd gain you don't even know about. I have good sense, and no puffed-up notion of my own importance. And I would try with might and main to be the nicest of companions for you, as well as the most loving."

He got up abruptly and went to stand looking out the door, his hands clasped behind his back. "Women," he said, "are liars, cheats, connivers and fools. I wouldn't care if I never saw another woman as long as I lived. As for love —I don't *want* to be loved! I just want to be left alone!" This cry from the heart he seemed to think was enough, then, rethinking, he added harshly, "How do I know you're telling me the truth?"

"Well, Mr. Smith, you are not exactly at the top of the list of Byron's most eligible men! I have heard you described as everything from a jailbird to an eccentric, and it is common knowledge that you are not rich. Why therefore should I lie?" She opened her purse and fished out the neatly folded piece of paper she had appropriated from Dr. Parkinson's desk, then got up from her chair and walked across to join him at the door. "Here. Read this. You do know I'm ill, because you were there when I had my first bad turn. And when I met you the other day on my walk, I'm sure I told you I had to go to Sydney to see a heart specialist. Well, this is his report on my condition. I stole it, first of all because I don't want my mother and aunt to know I'm so sick. I don't want to become an object of worry for them, I don't want to be forced into bed and fussed over. So I told them I had a kinked spinal nerve, and if I can keep up the deception, that's what they're going to go on thinking is wrong with me. My second reason for stealing it concerns you. I knew I was going to ask you to marry me and I knew I'd need proof of my sincerity. There is no name on it except the doctor's, I know, but if you look at it carefully, you will see no patient's name has been erased from it, either."

He took the paper, unfolded it, read it quickly and turned to face her. "Aside from being awfully skinny, you look healthy enough to me," he said doubtfully.

Missy did some fast thinking, and prayed he was no medical expert. "Why, between my turns I am healthy enough! Mine is not the sort of heart trouble that saps the strength, it's more like—like—like having little strokes. The valves—stick—and—and when they do, the blood stops flowing. That I gather is what's going to kill me. I don't know any more than that—doctors never want to tell you anything. I suppose they find it hard enough to tell you you're going to die." She heaved a sigh, and began to scale histrionic heights with the aplomb of an actress. "I shall just go out like a light one day!" Her eyes lifted to his wistfully. "I don't want to die at Missalonghi!" she cried pitifully. "I want to die in the arms of the man I love!"

He was a born fighter, so he tried a different tack. "How about a second opinion? Doctors can be wrong."

"What for?" countered Missy. "If I only have a year to live, I do not want to spend it traipsing from one doctor to another!" A big tear fell down her cheek, while others still swimming with telling effect threatened to follow its lead. "Oh, Mr. Smith, I want to spend my last year *happily!*"

He groaned the groan of a condemned man. "For God's sake, woman, don't cry!"

"Why not?" sobbed Missy, scrabbling up her sleeve for her handkerchief. "I think I have every right to cry!"

"Then cry, damn you!" he said, goaded beyond endurance, and marched out of the door.

Missy stood mopping her tears, eyes following him through them as he strode to the far side of the clearing and then disappeared from view. Head down, she returned to her chair and finished her cry with no more appreciative audience than a large blow-fly. After which, she didn't know what to do. Was he coming back? Was he hiding somewhere watching to see her leave before coming back?

Suddenly she felt very tired, utterly dispirited. All that, and no result. So much for Una's encouragement. So much for stolen reports. So much for her bright vision of emancipation. She sighed, and had never meant a sigh more, or sighed more. No use staying here. She wasn't wanted.

She let herself out of the cabin quietly, and made sure that she closed the door. It was gone two o'clock, and she had a nine-mile walk, all uphill, all difficult terrain; it would be late before she arrived back at Missalonghi.

"Yet I don't feel sorry I tried," she said aloud. "It was worth a try, I *know* it was."

"Miss Wright!"

She turned, hope kindling and blazing.

"Hold on, I'll drive you home."

"Thank you, I can walk," she said, not stiffly or huffily, just in her old colourlessly polite manner.

By this he had reached her side, and put his hand beneath her elbow. "No, it's too late and too hard a walk, especially for you. Sit here while I harness up." And he deposited her on the same tree stump where she had sat waiting for him.

She really was too tired to argue, and perhaps too tired to face the walk, so she made no demur. When he was ready, he lifted her up into the cart as easily as if she had been a child.

"This only goes to prove what I've been telling myself lately," he said as he turned the horses out of the clearing onto the track. "I need a smaller vehicle, a sulky or a gig.

698

It's a damned nuisance to have to use both horses and a big cart unless I've got a heavy load."

"Yes, I'm sure you're right," she said meaninglessly.

"Angry?"

Her face turned to his, its expression purely surprised. "No! Why should I be?"

"Well, you didn't meet with much luck, did you?"

She laughed, not very heartily, yet still a genuine laugh. "Poor Mr. Smith, you don't understand at all."

"Obviously I don't. What's the joke?"

"I had nothing to lose. Nothing!"

"Did you really think you might win?"

"I was sure I would win."

"Why?"

"Because you're you."

"And what does that mean?"

"Oh—just that you're so very kind. A decent person."

"Thanks."

After that little was said; the horses plodded reluctantly along the jungly track, obviously not understanding why they were proceeding away from home. But even when they came to the switchback up the landslide they plodded on without visible protest, which to the country-wise Missy indicated that they knew their master better than to baulk. Yet he was pleasant to them, and didn't ply the whip; he dominated them by the force of his will.

"I must say that it shows, your not being a Hurlingford," he said abruptly as the journey neared its end.

"Not a Hurlingford? What makes you assume that?"

"Lots of things. Your name, for a start. Your appearance. The godforsaken position of your home, and the lack of money in it. Your nice nature." He sounded as if he grudged this last admission.

"Not all Hurlingfords are rich, Mr. Smith. As a matter

of fact I am a Hurlingford, at least on the distaff side. My aunt and mother are the sisters of Maxwell and Herbert Hurlingford, and first cousins of Sir William's."

He turned to stare at her while she explained this, then whistled. "Well, that's a smack in the eye! A nest of genuine Hurlingfords all the way out at the end of Gordon Road, and scraping to make ends meet. What happened?"

So for the rest of the way home Missy regaled John Smith with an account of the perfidy of the first Sir William, and the compounded perfidy of his successors.

"Thank you," he said at the end of it. "You've answered a lot of questions for me, and given me quite a bit to think about." He pulled his horses up outside the front gate of Missalonghi. "Here you are, home again, and well before your mother would be worried."

She jumped down without assistance. "Thank you, dear Mr. Smith. It's as I still maintain—you're a very kind man."

In answer, he tipped his hat and flashed her a smile, then began turning his horses.

❦

Octavia found Missy's note when she went to investigate Missy's whereabouts. There it sat, very white against the brown coverlet, with the single word MOTHER printed across its surface. Her heart thudded down into her boots; notes that said MOTHER never contained good news.

So when she heard Drusilla letting herself in through the front door, she scuttled into the hall with the note in her hand and her protuberant pale blue eyes all geared up to shed as many tears as the contents of the note dictated.

"Missy's gone, and she's left this note for you!"

Drusilla frowned, unalarmed. "Gone?"

"Gone! She has taken all her clothes, and she has taken our carpetbag."

The skin over Drusilla's cheeks began to prickle and stretch uncomfortably; she snatched the note from Octavia and read it aloud so Octavia could not misinterpret the contents.

"Dear Mother," it said,

"Please forgive me for going off without a word, but I really think it is better that you do not know what I plan until I know whether or not it's going to work. I will probably be home tomorrow or the next day for a visit at least. Please do not worry. I am safe. Your loving daughter, Missy."

Octavia's tears overflowed, but Drusilla did not weep. She folded the letter again and carried it into the kitchen, where she propped it very carefully on the shelf of the chimney.

"We must call in the police," said Octavia tearfully.

"We will do no such thing," contradicted Drusilla, and moved the kettle to the front of the stove. "Oh, dear, I need a cup of tea badly!"

"But Missy might be in danger!"

"I very much doubt it. There's nothing in her note to indicate any kind of foolishness." She sat down with a sigh. "Octavia, *do* dry your eyes! The events of the last few days have taught me that Missy is a person to be reckoned with. I have no doubt that she is safe, and that, probably tomorrow, we will indeed see her again. In the meantime, we do not so much as mention to anybody that Missy has left home."

"But she's out there somewhere without a soul to protect her from Men!"

"It may well be that Missy has decided she would rather not be protected from Men," said Drusilla dryly.

"Now do as you're told, Octavia, stop crying and make us some tea. I have a lot to tell you that has nothing to do with Missy's disappearance."

Curiosity overcame distress; Octavia poured a little hot water into the teapot and set it to stand by the stove. "Oh, what?" she asked eagerly.

"Well, I gave Cornelia and Julia their money, and I bought myself a Singer sewing machine."

"Drusilla!"

And so the two ladies left at Missalonghi drank their tea and discussed the events of the day more thoroughly, after which they went back to their routines, and eventually retired to their respective bedrooms.

"Dear God," said Drusilla on her knees, "please help and protect Missy, keep her from all harm and give her strength in all adversities. Amen."

After which she climbed into her bed, the only double one, as befitted the only married lady. But it was some time before she managed to close her eyes.

The organ had saved Missy from detection when John Smith dropped her back at Missalonghi; no one heard his cart arrive or depart, and no one heard Missy as she crept around the side of the house and headed across the backyard towards the shed. It held no place capable of concealing her, but she managed to tuck the carpetbag down behind a sack of fodder, and then she left the shed for the shelter of the orchard until after her mother had milked the cow. Of course the cow knew her step and began to low pitifully to be milked, but before Buttercup became really agitated, out came Drusilla with the bucket.

Missy huddled down behind the fattest-trunked apple tree and closed her eyes and wished she did have terminal heart disease, preferably severe enough to ensure she would never see the morning.

Not until after full darkness had fallen did she stir; it was the penetrating Blue Mountains cold spring air drove her from the orchard at last, into the relative warmth of the shed. Buttercup was lying with feet tucked under, placidly chewing cud, udder comfortably empty. So Missy put a clean sack down on the ground next to the cow, and curled up on the sack with her head and shoulders lying against Buttercup's warm rumbly side.

Of course she should have gathered up her courage and walked into the house the minute John Smith had gone, but when she tried to make her feet mount the front verandah steps, they just would not. How could you tell your mother that you'd proposed marriage to a near-stranger and been refused for your pains? Or failing that one, what convincing story could she have concocted? Missy was not a story spinner, she was only a story reader. Maybe in the morning she could confess, she told herself, gasping at the ache and sorrow of it; but how much worse would that be, with a night spent elsewhere than under the roof of Missalonghi to be accounted for? Who would ever believe she had spent it sleeping with a *cow?* Go inside at once, whispered her better self; but her worse self could not find the courage.

The tears began to gather and to fall, for indeed Missy was exhausted, not so much from her physical exertions as from the terrific burst of will that had sent her to see John Smith.

"Oh, Buttercup, what am I going to do?" she wept.

Buttercup merely huffed.

And shortly afterwards, Missy fell asleep.

The Missalonghi rooster woke her about an hour before dawn, screeching his clarion from the beam right above her head. She leaped up, confused, then subsided against her living pillow in a fresh agony of pain and

703

bewilderment. She wasn't hungry, she wasn't thirsty. What to do? Oh, what to do?

But by dawn she had made up her mind what to do, and rose then to her feet with purpose in her movements. Pulling comb and brush from the carpetbag, she tidied herself as best she could, but at the end of her efforts was dismally aware she smelled strongly of cow.

No sound of stirring life came from Missalonghi as she crept past it, and faintly from out her mother's window came a series of little snores. Safe.

Down once more into John Smith's valley, not with the dreamy enchantment of yesterday, nor with the irrepressible happiness of yesterday, when nothing had seemed impossible and everything had seemed bound to end well. This time Missy marched with little hope but iron determination; he would not say her nay again, even if it meant she had to spend every night of the next year in her mother's shed with Buttercup for a bedmate, and every day marching down to the bottom of John Smith's valley to ask again. For ask again she would, and tomorrow if he said nay today, and the day after, and the day after that. . . .

It was going on for ten o'clock when she came at last to the clearing and the cabin; there rose the same rippling blur from the chimney, but, as yesterday, no John Smith. Down on the tree stump she sat to wait.

Perhaps he too had passed beyond hunger; when noon came and went without a sign of him, Missy resigned herself to waiting the whole afternoon as well. Indeed, the sun had long gone behind the great walls above, and the light was fading rapidly, before he came home. More seriously than yesterday, but just as blind to Missy sitting on her stump.

"Mr. Smith!"

"Bloody hell!"

He came across immediately to stand looking down at her, not angrily, but not pleasantly, either. "What are you doing back here again?"

"Will you marry me, Mr. Smith?"

This time he didn't put his hand beneath her elbow and walk her across to the cabin; he turned to face her fully as she rose to her feet, and looked down into her eyes.

"Is someone putting you up to this?" he asked.

"No."

"Does it really mean that much to you?"

"It means my life, literally. I am not going home! I'm going to come here every day and ask again."

"You're playing with fire, Miss Wright," he said, lips thin and tight. "Hasn't it occurred to you that a man might resort to violence if a woman refuses to leave him alone?"

She smiled up serenely, sublimely, seraphically. "Some men, maybe. But not you, Mr. Smith."

"What do you really stand to gain? What if I did say I'd marry you? Is that the sort of husband you want, a man you've worn down until he doesn't know what else to do for peace than give in—or strangle you?" His voice dropped, became very hard. "In this big wide world, Miss Wright, lives a malignant thing called *hate*. I beg of you, don't uncage it!"

"Will you marry me?" she asked.

He screwed up his mouth, blew air through his nose, and lifted his head to stare above hers at something she couldn't see. And said nothing for what seemed like a very long time. Then he shrugged, looked down at her. "I admit I've thought a lot about you since yesterday, and even the heaviest work I could find didn't stop my thinking about you. And I started to wonder too if maybe I was being offered a way to atone, and if my luck might disappear because I ignored the offer."

"A way to atone? Atone for what?"

"Just a figure of speech. Everyone has something to atone for, no one is free of guilt. In forcing yourself on me, you're creating a cause for atonement, don't you see that?"

"Yes."

"But it makes no difference?"

"I'll take whatever comes to me gladly, Mr. Smith, if I can take you along with it."

"Very well, then. I'll marry you."

All of Missy's pain and numbness flew away. "Oh, thank you, Mr. Smith! You won't regret it, I promise!"

He grunted. "You're a child, Miss Wright, not a grown woman, and perhaps that's why I've given in rather than strangled you. I can't honestly believe there's woman's guile in you. Only don't ever give me reason to change that opinion."

. And now his hand went under her arm, the signal to walk.

"There's one thing I must ask, Mr. Smith," she said.

"What?"

"That we never refer to the fact that I'm going to die, nor let it influence our behaviour. I want to be free! And I cannot be free if I am to be perpetually reminded by word or deed that I'm going to die."

"Agreed," said John Smith.

Not wanting to push her luck, for she sensed she had gone about as far in that line as was prudent, Missy entered the cabin and went to sit quietly in one of the kitchen chairs, while John Smith swung round inside the door and stood staring out of it at the beginnings of a thin blue night's ground mist.

Silently she watched his back, which was long and broad and, at the moment, extremely eloquent. But after about five minutes she ventured to say, her voice very small and apologetic, "What happens now, Mr. Smith?"

He jumped as if he had forgotten she was there, and went to sit opposite her at the table. His face in the gloom was full of shadows, heavy, deadened, a little daunting. But when he spoke, it was cheerfully enough, as if he had decided there was no point in making himself more miserable than the situation called for. "My name is John," he said, and got up to light his two lamps, both of which he placed on the table so he could see her face. "As to the main business, we get a licence, and we get married."

"How long will it take?"

He shrugged. "I don't know, if banns aren't called. A couple of days? Maybe even sooner, with a special licence. In the meantime, I'd better drive you home."

"Oh, no! I'm staying here," said Missy.

"If you stay here you're likely to start your honeymoon prematurely," he said, hope blossoming. What a good idea! She might decide she didn't like it! After all, most women didn't. And he could be hard about it, not rape her exactly, just force her a little; a virgin of her age was bound to be easy to frighten. At which point he made the mistake of looking at her to see how she reacted. And there she was, poor little dying thing, just gazing at him with blinded foolish affection, like a puppy awash with love. John Smith's sleeping heart moved, felt a bitter and unaccustomed pain. For indeed she had haunted him all day, no matter how hard he worked to drive out her image and replace it by emptiness hacked out of physical labour. He had his secrets, some of them buried so deep he could tell himself in all truth that he had never suffered those secrets, that he was reborn in all the newness and naked-

707

ness of a life begun again. But all day things had nibbled and whispered and gnawed, and the utter pleasure he had found in his valley had vanished. Maybe he did have to atone; maybe that was why she had come. Only he honestly didn't have one thing to atone for so large, so depressing. He didn't. Oh no, he didn't, he didn't!

Maybe she wouldn't like it. Take her to bed, John Smith, show her what it's like in the wasteland of the body, fill her with yourself and with disgust for it. She's a woman.

But Missy liked it very well, and demonstrated a surprising aptitude for it. Another nail went thudding into John Smith's coffin, as he wryly admitted to himself about three hours after he and Missy had retired dinnerless to bed. Wonders never ceased. This ageing spinster virgin was made for it! Though dreadfully ignorant at first, she was neither shy nor shamed, and her affectionate responses warmed him, touched him, made it impossible for him to be cruel or unkind to her. The little baggage! None of your lying there passively with your legs open for her! And how much *life* there was in her, just waiting to be tapped. Suddenly the thought that the end of her life was imminent shocked him; it was one thing to pity someone he didn't know, quite another to face the same dilemma with someone he knew intimately. That was the trouble with beds. They turned strangers into intimates more quickly than ten years of polite teas in parlours.

Missy slept like a log and woke before John Smith did, probably because sleep eluded him long after it had claimed her. He had more to think about.

A faint light filtered through the window, so she eased herself carefully out of the bed and stood shivering until she donned the dressing gown out of her bag. How lovely it had been! More of a realist than she had suspected, she dismissed the initial unpleasantness of pain and remembered instead those big strong work-roughened hands stroking and soothing and comforting. Feelings and sensations, touches and kisses, heat and light—oh yes, it was lovely!

She moved as quietly as she could about the cabin, hotting up the stove and moving the kettle to a place where it would boil. But of course her activity woke him, and he got out of bed too, quite unconcerned at his nakedness; Missy was given an unparalleled opportunity to study the anatomical differences between men and women.

Even more delightful than this was his reaction to her presence. He walked straight across to her, folded her in his arms and stood rocking gently, still half-asleep and thus heavy against her, his beard scraping her neck.

"Good morning," she whispered, her smiling lips pressing little kisses on his shoulder.

"Morning," he mumbled, evidently liking her response.

Of course she was ravenous, having had virtually nothing to eat in two days. "I'll get breakfast," she said.

"Want a bath?" He sounded more awake, but made no attempt to move away from her.

He could smell Buttercup! Oh, poor man! Hunger fled yet again. "Yes, please. But a lavatory too?"

"Get your shoes on."

While she slid her feet into her boots, not bothering to lace them, he rummaged in a big chest and produced two towels, old and rough, but clean.

The clearing sparkled with frost and was still in heavy shade, but as Missy looked up, the great sandstone walls of the valley were already glowing red with the sunrise, and the sky was taking on the muted milky radiance of a pearl—or of Una's skin. Birds called and sang everywhere, never more prone to give voice than at dawn.

"The lavatory's a bit primitive," he warned, showing her where he had dug a deep hole and placed some stone blocks around it for a seat, with newspaper tucked into a box to keep it dry; he had not enclosed it with roof or walls.

"It's the best-ventilated lavatory I've ever seen," she said cheerfully.

He chuckled. "Long job, or short?"

"Short, thank you."

"Then I'll wait for you. Over there." He pointed to the far side of the clearing.

When Missy joined him a minute later she was already shivering in anticipation of an icy plunge into the river; he looked like the kind of man who would relish freezing ablutions. Maybe, she thought, I'll be hoist with my own petard, and keel over stone dead from the shock.

But instead of steering her towards the river, John Smith drew her into the middle of a thicket of tree-ferns and wild clematis in feathery white flower. And there before her was the most beautiful bathroom in the entire world, a warm spring that trickled out of a cleft between two rocks at the top of a small stony incline, and fell, too thinly to be called a cascade, into a wide and mossy basin.

Missy had her robe off in a flash, and two seconds later was stepping down into a crystal-clear pool of blood-heat water, tendrils of steam rising languorously off it into the chilly air. It was about eighteen inches deep, and its bottom was clean smooth rock. No leeches, either!

"Go easy on the soap," advised John Smith, pointing to where a fat cake of his expensive brand sat in a small niche alongside the pool. "The water obviously gets away, because the level of the pool never rises any more than the spring stops flowing, but don't tempt fate."

"Now I understand why you're so clean," she said, thinking of Missalonghi baths, two inches of water in the bottom of the rusting tub, hot from a kettle and cold from a bucket. And that one miserably inadequate ration of water was used by all three ladies, with Missy, the shortest straw, last in line.

Quite unaware how alluring she looked, she smiled up at him and lifted out her arms until the small buff nipples of her slight breasts just rode clear of the water. "Aren't you coming in too?" she asked in the tones of a professional temptress. "There's plenty of room."

He needed no further encouragement, and appeared to forget his strictures about the production of suds, so assiduous was he in making sure every part of her was thoroughly explored with his hand and the bar of soap; nor did she think that his thoroughness had much to do with Buttercup. She submitted with purring pleasure, but then insisted upon returning the service. And so bathtime occupied the best part of an hour.

However, over breakfast he got down to business. "There must be a registry office in Katoomba, so we'll go on in and get a marriage licence," he said.

"If I go only as far as Missalonghi with you and then walk on into Byron and catch the train, I imagine I'll get to Katoomba almost as quickly as you will in your cart," said Missy. "I must see Mother, I want to shop for food, and I have to take a book back to the library."

He looked suddenly alarmed. "You're not by any chance planning a big wedding, are you?"

She laughed. "No! Just you and me will do very well. I left a note for Mother, though, so I want to make sure she's not too upset. And my dearest friend works in the

711

library—would you mind if she came to our wedding?"

"Not if you want her there. Though I warn you, if I can persuade the powers that be, I'd like to get it over and done with today."

"In Katoomba?"

"Yes."

Married in *brown!* Wouldn't it? Missy sighed. "All right, if you'll promise me something."

"What?" he asked warily.

"When I die, will you bury me in a scarlet lace dress? Or if you can't find that, any colour but brown!"

He looked surprised. "Don't you like brown? I've never seen you wear anything else."

"I wear brown because I'm poor but respectable. Brown doesn't show the dirt, it never goes in or out of fashion, it never fades, and it's never cheap or common or trollopy."

That made him laugh, but then he went back to business. "Do you have a birth certificate?"

"Yes, in my bag."

"What's your real name?"

Her reaction was extraordinary; she went red, shifted around on her chair, clenched her teeth. "Can't you just use Missy? It's what I've always been called, honestly."

"Sooner or later your real name is going to have to come out." He grinned. "Come on, make a clean breast of it! It can't be that bad, surely."

"Missalonghi."

He burst out laughing. "You're pulling my leg!"

"I wish I were."

"The same as your house?"

"Exactly the same. My father thought it was the most beautiful word in the world, and he loathed the Hurling-

712

ford habit of using Latin names. Mother wanted to call me Camilla, but he insisted on Missalonghi."

"You poor little bitch!"

꠸

This time Missy's feet experienced no trouble mounting the steps to the front verandah of Missalonghi; she banged on the door as if she was a stranger.

Drusilla answered, and looked at her daughter as if she really was a stranger. Definitely there was nothing the matter with her! In fact, she looked better than in all her life.

"I know what you've been doing, my girl," she said as she led the way down the hall to the kitchen. "I wish you'd stuck to reading about it, but I daresay that's crying over spilt milk now, eh? Are you back for good?"

"No."

Octavia came hobbling, and received a kiss on either cheek from the sparkling Missy.

"Are you all right?" she quavered, clutching at Missy's hands convulsively.

"Of course she's all right!" said Drusilla bracingly. *"Look* at her, for heaven's sake!"

Missy smiled at her mother lovingly; how odd, that only now the cord binding her to Missalonghi was broken did she understand the depth of her love for Drusilla. But maybe now she had opportunity to stand back and see Drusilla's worries, heartaches, difficulties.

"I thank you very much, Mother," she said, "for according me the dignity of assuming I know what I'm doing."

"At going on thirty-four, Missy, if you don't know what you're doing, there's no hope for you. You tried it

713

our way for long enough, and who's to say your way won't be better?"

"Very true. But what you're telling me now is a far cry from dictating the kind of books I might read, and the colour of my clothes."

"You put up with it tamely enough."

"Yes, I suppose I did."

"You get the government you deserve, Missy, always."

"If you can admit that, Mother, don't you think it's more than time you and the aunts and all the other manless Hurlingford women banded together to do something about the glaring injustices and inequalities in this family?"

"Ever since you told us how Billy has lied to us, Missy, I have been thinking along those lines, I assure you. And I have been talking to Julia and Cornelia too. But there is no law that compels a man—or a woman—to leave property equally divided between sons and daughters. In my book, the worst offenders of all have been Hurlingford women with money to leave—nothing goes to their daughters, not even a house on five acres! So I have always felt there was no chance for us, when our own female kind stand so solidly behind Hurlingford men. It is sad, but it is true."

"You're speaking of the Hurlingford women who will lose a great deal if you win. I'm speaking of our fellow sufferers, and I know you can get them moving if you really try. You do have legal grounds to seek compensation for those unpaid dividends, and I think you should institute proceedings against Uncle Herbert to compel him to disclose the full details of his various investment schemes." Missy shot a demure look at Drusilla from under her lashes. "After all, Mother, you were the one who said it—you get the government you deserve."

She walked from Missalonghi into Byron. What a beautiful, beautiful day! For the first time in her life she felt really well, the bursting-out-of-one's-skin sensation she had read about but never experienced; and for the first time in her life she was looking forward to living a long life. That is, until she remembered that the full measure of her happiness depended upon one John Smith, and John Smith only expected to put up with her for a year at most. She had lied and cheated and stolen to feel this happy, and she wasn't at all sorry for it. The Alicias of this world might snap their fingers and conjure up the men of their choice, but no use pretending a man like John Smith would have looked sideways at a Missy Wright, snap though she would. And yet she *knew* she could make John Smith the happiest man—if not in the world—at least in the town of Byron. She had better! Because when her year was up, he had to want her to live so badly he was prepared to forgive her the stealing and the cheating and the lying.

Time was getting on, and she had to make sure she caught the eleven o'clock train into Katoomba, where John Smith had promised to be waiting for her at the station. Groceries she could put off until tomorrow, but somehow she had a feeling Una could not be postponed. To the library it was, then.

A magnificent motorcar was purring sedately down the middle of Byron Street as Missy hurried along in her brown linen dress, inconspicuous as ever. Which was more than could be said for the motorcar, also brown; it had collected an admiring audience down both sides of the road, locals and visitors alike. Glancing at it in amusement, Missy decided the chauffeur had a definite edge over the two occupants of the tonneau when it came to haughty aloofness. The chauffeur she knew from hearsay; a handsome fellow with more love for cutting a fine figure

715

than hard work, and a reputation for treating his many women badly. The occupants of the tonneau she knew from bitter experience: Alicia and Uncle Billy.

Alicia's eyes met hers. The next moment the sumptuous car had slewed sideways into the kerb, and Alicia and Uncle Billy were tumbling out well ahead of the startled chauffeur's attempt to open a door for them.

"What do you mean, Missy Wright, taking Aunt Cornelia's shares and selling them out from under our noses?" demanded Alicia without preamble, two bright red spots burning in her alabaster cheeks.

"Why shouldn't I?" asked Missy coolly.

"Because it's none of your damned interfering business!" barked Sir William, stiff with outrage.

"It's as much my business as it is yours, Uncle Billy. I knew where I could get Aunt Cornelia ten pounds a share, and what use were they to her when you'd led her to believe they were quite worthless? Aunt Cornelia badly needs an operation on her feet she couldn't afford because, Alicia, I gather you refused to give her either time off or a little extra money. So I sold her shares for a hundred pounds, and now she can have her operation. If you wish to terminate her employment, at least she has a sum in the bank to tide her over until she can find another position —I'm sure there are shops in Katoomba just dying to engage someone of her calibre. You might like to know that I have also sold Aunt Julia's shares, and Aunt Octavia's, and Mother's."

"What?" squawked Sir William.

"All of them? You sold all of them?" faltered Alicia, the red spots in her cheeks draining away in a second.

"I most certainly did." Missy stared at her cousin with a malice she had not known she possessed. "Why, Alicia, don't tell me forty little shares in the great big Byron Bottle Company were enough to tip the balance!"

716

For a confused moment Alicia fancied Missy had grown horns and a tail. "What's the matter with you?" she cried. "You've got to be off your head! Soiling my dress, saying insulting things about me in front of my family, and now selling that family into ruin! You ought to be locked up!"

"I only wish what I did had resulted in your being locked up. Now if you'll both excuse me, I must dash. I have an appointment to be married." And Missy walked away with her nose in the air.

"I think I'm going to faint," announced Alicia, and suited action to words by flopping against Uncle Herbert's window, the one full of work clothes.

Sir William seized the opportunity to put his arms around her, head turned to call for assistance from his chauffeur; but somehow as they supported Alicia between them back to the car, it was the chauffeur's ungloved fingers that managed to ascertain the delicious size and shape of Alicia's nipples. By this time the crowd had swelled to include all of Uncle Herbert's sons and grand-sons, so Sir William dumped Alicia unceremoniously on the seat and ordered the chauffeur to drive off immediately.

When her prospective father-in-law attempted to loosen her stays by lifting up her dress and groping inside her fine lawn drawers, Alicia revived in a hurry.

"Stop that, you lecherous old man!" she snapped, forgetting the need to be tactful, and leaned forward to press her cheeks between her palms. "Oh, Lord, I feel awful!"

"Would you like to go home now we don't have to drive out to Missalonghi?" asked Sir William, red-faced.

"Yes, I would." She lay back against the seat and let the cool air fan her skin, and finally relaxed a little, and sighed. Thank heavens! She was beginning to feel better.

Right in front of her but on the other side of the glass

that separated the tonneau from the open driving compartment, the chauffeur's proudly shaped head sat upon his strong smooth neck; what lovely ears he had for a man, small and set right against his skull. He was handsome, as dark as Missy, and as alien. It took a brawny man to heft her around as easily as he had, and his hands on her breasts—she felt her nipples pop up at the memory of them, and squirmed achingly on the seat. What was his name? Frank? Yes, Frank. Frank Pellagrino. He used to work at the bottling plant until he got the post as Uncle Billy's chauffeur.

A sidelong glance at Sir William revealed him sitting bolt upright, a very worried man.

"Do those forty shares make so much difference to us?"

"All the difference in the world, now we know Richard Hurlingford sold out a month ago." Sir William sighed. "And it explains why the mystery buyer thinks he has sufficient clout to call an extraordinary meeting tomorrow."

"The little fool!" snarled Alicia. "How could Missy be such a little fool?"

"I think we're the fools, Alicia. I for one never even noticed Missy Wright, but I see now that I should have. And been more attentive to all the ladies of Missalonghi. Did you take in how she looked this morning? As if she'd got to the cream ahead of every other cat in the district. And did she say she had an appointment to be married, or was that my imagination?"

Alicia snorted. "Oh, she said it, but I suspect it was *her* imagination." A more urgent grievance came to mind. "Silly old Auntie Cornie!" she muttered savagely. "Oh, how I wish I could have had the satisfaction this morning of sacking her when she came prattling about her shares and the time she was going to take off for her operation!"

"Well, why didn't you sack her?"

"Because I can't, that's why! My hat shop may well end up my only source of income, if things at the plant keep going from bad to worse. And I'll never find anyone else half so good to run the salon end of it, even if I paid them ten times what I pay Auntie Cornie. She's—indispensable."

"You'd better pray she never realises it, or she'll ask for ten times what you currently pay her." A tinge of satisfaction coloured his voice as he added, "And then, my dear, if you can't afford it, you'll have to go into the shop as your own sales dame. You'd be even better at it than Cornie."

"I can't do that!" gasped Alicia. "It would *ruin* my social standing! It's one thing to be the creative genius behind a business of that nature, but quite another to have to peddle my wares in person." She tugged at the lapels of her pale pink coat, her lovely face set into the lines of sullen discontent its construction made fatally easy. "Oh, Uncle Billy, suddenly I feel as if I'm walking on ice, and it's going to crack any minute, and I'm going to go under!"

"We're in a pickle, it's true. But don't give up, we're not finished yet. Pounds to peanuts, when the mystery buyer turns up to his extraordinary meeting tomorrow, he'll turn out to be some self-made yokel easily manipulated by his betters. And for that sort of exercise, you will come in very handy."

Alicia did not reply, merely flicked him a glance of mingled doubt and dislike; her eyes reverted to the back of the chauffeur's head, a far nicer prospect than Sir William's choleric countenance.

When Missy walked into the library she fully expected to find Una, even though it was not one of Una's days. And sure enough, there was Una.

"Oh, Missy, I'm so glad to see you!" she cried, jumping up. "I have a surprise for you."

"I have a few surprises for you too," said Missy.

"Wait right there, I'll be back in two flicks of a dead lamb's tail." Una vanished into the tea cubicle, and came out bearing a large white box and hatbox, each tied up with white ribbon. "Happy anything, dearest Missy."

They smiled at each other in complete understanding and great affection.

"It's a scarlet lace dress and hat," said Missy.

"It's a scarlet lace dress and hat," agreed Una.

"I shall wear it to my wedding."

"John Smith! You've picked exactly the right man."

"I had to resort to trickery and deception to get him."

"If you couldn't get him any other way, why not?"

"I told him I was dying of heart trouble."

"Aren't we all?"

"That," said Missy, "is splitting hairs. Can you come to my wedding?"

"I'd love to, but no."

"Why?"

"It wouldn't be appropriate."

"Because of your divorce? But we're not getting married in a church, so who can object?"

"It has nothing to do with divorce, darling. I don't think John Smith would appreciate a face from the past at his wedding."

That made sense, therefore Missy left it alone. And there was nothing really left to say; her gratitude was quite beyond words, her need to go quickly was great. Una stood watching her painfully, as if with her she was taking something so precious the quality of Una's life would suffer ever afterwards—and that something was not so tangible as a scarlet lace dress and hat. On an impulse she didn't understand, Missy returned to the desk, leaned over it and put her arm about Una's shoulders, her lips against Una's cheek. So frail, so cold, so weightless!

"Goodbye, Una."

"Goodbye, my best and dearest friend. Be happy!"

Missy made the train with a minute to spare, and saw John Smith on the platform in Katoomba before the train came to a standstill. Thank God for that. He hadn't changed his mind during his slow amble along the highway, then. And in fact, when he saw her alight from her carriage, he even looked quite glad to see her!

"They'll issue us with a licence and marry us today," he said, taking Missy's boxes from her.

"And I don't have to be married in brown," said Missy, retrieving her boxes. "If you'll excuse me, I'll pop into the platform toilet and change into my wedding dress."

"*Wedding* dress?" He looked down at his grey flannel work shirt and his old moleskin trousers in comical dismay.

She laughed. "Don't worry, it's not traditional. In fact, I guarantee that you're going to look a great deal more appropriate than I am."

Her dress fitted perfectly. What an eye for size Una had! And what a wonderful colour! Her eyes swam with the strain of looking at it. Where on earth had Una managed to find a garment so elegant in style yet so wanton in colour?

The mirror on the wall seemed to own a touch of magic, for whoever it reflected, it lent a slight patina of beauty; adjusting her preposterous scarlet hat, Missy decided she looked very well. Her darkness was suddenly interesting, her thin body was suddenly merely slender as a young tree. Yes, very well! And certainly not spinsterish.

Once he recovered from the shock of that red, John Smith thought she looked very well too. "Now this is my sort of wedding! I look like a hayseed, and you look like a madam." He tucked her arm through his gleefully. "Come on, woman, let's get the deed over before I change my mind."

They strolled into Katoomba Street, the cynosure of all eyes, and actually quite pleased with the sensation they were creating.

"That was easy," said Missy after the deed was done and they were sitting together in John Smith's cart. She held out her hand to see her ring. "I am now Mrs. John Smith. How nice it sounds!"

"I must say this time was a lot better than the last."

"Was your first wedding a big affair, then?"

"It could have passed for a circus. Two hundred and fifty guests, the bride with a thirty-foot train that needed a whole regiment of runny-nosed little boys to lift it, twelve or fourteen bridesmaids, all of the men stuffed into tails, the archbishop of something presiding, a massed choir—God Jesus, at the time it was a nightmare! But compared to what followed, it was an idyll in paradise." He looked sideways at her, one eyebrow raised. "Do you want to hear this?"

"I think I'd better. They say the second wife always has to contend with the ghost of the first, and that it's a lot harder to fight a ghost than a living person." She paused to gather her courage. "Was she—dear to you?"

"She may have been when I married her, I honestly can't remember. I didn't know her, you see. I only knew of her. She must have meant to have me, because I'm sure I didn't do the proposing. I'm obviously the sort of bloke women propose to! Only I didn't mind your way of proposing, at least it was honest and above-board. But her—one minute she was all over me like a rash, the next minute she was acting as if I had the plague. Blowing hot and cold, they call it. I think women think it's expected of them, that if they don't do it, they're going to make life too easy for the bloke. Now that's where I like you very much, Mrs. Smith. You don't blow hot and cold at all."

"I'm too grateful," said Missy humbly. "Do go on! What happened after that?"

He shrugged. "Oh, she decided she was entitled to make all the decisions, that what *she* wanted was all that mattered. Once she'd landed her fish, the fish didn't matter a bit. I was just there to prove she could catch a fish, to lend her respectability, to give her an escort here and there. She didn't exactly have lovers, she had what she called cicisbeos, pansified twerps with gardenias in their buttonholes and a better shine on their hair than on their patent leather shoes. If anyone was ever branded by the company she kept, my first wife certainly was—her women friends were as hard as nails and as tough as old boots, and her men friends were as soft as butter and as limp as last week's lettuce. She liked to mock me. In front of anyone, everyone. I was dull, I was stodgy. And she never kept our differences private, she'd get set on a quarrel no matter how public the place. In a nutshell, she held me in utter contempt."

"And you? What light did you hold her in?"

"I *loathed* her." Evidently he still did, for the feeling in his voice did not belong to an experience buried in the past.

"How long were you married?"

"About four or five years."

"Were there any children?"

"Hell, no! She might have lost her figure. And of course that meant she was a great one for teasing, for kissing and cuddling, but to get my leg over her—it only happened when she got drunk, and afterwards she'd scream and howl and carry on in case anything came of it, then she'd pop out and visit the tame doctor they all patronised."

"And she *died?*" asked Missy, scarcely able to credit that such a woman could have had so much consideration.

"We had a terrible fight one evening over—oh, I don't know, something small and idiotic that actually didn't matter a bit. We lived in a house that had a waterfrontage onto the Harbour, and apparently after I'd gone out she decided to go for a swim to cool her temper. They found her body a couple of weeks later, washed up on Balmoral Beach."

"Oh, poor thing!"

He snorted. "Poor thing, nothing! The police tried in every way they knew to pin it on me, but luckily the minute she'd done shouting at me, I went out, and I met a friend not twenty yards down the road. He'd been kicked out of bed too, so we walked to where he'd been going, the flat of a mutual friend—a bachelor, the wily bastard. There we stayed until past noon of the following day, getting drunker and drunker. And since the servants had seen her alive and well more than half an hour after my friend and I arrived at our mutual friend's flat, the police couldn't touch me. Anyway, after the body turned up the post-mortem revealed that she'd died of simple drowning, with no evidence of foul play. Not that that stopped a lot of people in Sydney reckoning I did kill her

724

—I just got a name for being too smart to get caught, and my friends for being bought to alibi me."

"When did all this happen?"

"About twenty years ago."

"A long time! What have you done with yourself since, that it's taken you so long to do what you've always wanted?"

"Well, I quit Australia as soon as the police let go. And I drifted round the world. Africa, the Klondike, China, Brazil, Texas. I had to live through almost twenty years of voluntary exile. Since I was born in London, I changed my name by deed-poll there, and when I did come back to Australia, I came as that bona-fide citizen of the world, John Smith, with all my money in gold and no past."

"Why *Byron?*"

"Because of the valley. I knew it was coming up for sale, and I've always wanted to own a whole valley."

Feeling she had probed enough, Missy changed the subject to the skulduggery going on at the Byron Bottle Company, and told her husband about the plight her mother and aunts were in because of it. John Smith listened most attentively, a smile playing round the corners of his mouth, and when she had ended her tale he put his arm around her, drew her across the seat against his side, and kept her there.

"Well, Mrs. Smith, I really didn't want to marry you when you first brought the subject up, but I confess I'm growing more reconciled to it every time you open your mouth, not to mention your legs," he said. "You're a woman of sense, your heart's in the right place, and you're a Hurlingford of the Hurlingfords, which gives me a lot of power I didn't expect to have," he said. "Interesting, how things turn out."

Missy rode the rest of the way home in blissful silence.

725

The next morning John Smith donned a suit, a collar, and a tie, all remarkably well cut and oddly smart.

"Whatever it is, it must be a lot more important than your wedding," observed Missy without a trace of resentment.

"It is."

"Are you going far afield?"

"Only to Byron."

"Then if I'm quick about it, may I come as far as Mother's with you, please?"

"Good idea, wife! Wait there for me until sometime late this afternoon, and you can introduce me to my in-laws when I pick you up. I'll probably have a lot to say to them."

It's going to be all right, thought Missy as she rode in her bright red dress and hat alongside her unfamiliarly elegant husband up to the top of the ridge. I don't care if I got him by trickery and deceit. He likes me, he really does like me, and without even realising it himself, he's already moved over a little to fit me in alongside him. When my year is up, I'll be able to tell him the truth. Besides, if I'm lucky, I may well by then be the mother of his child. It hurt him badly when his first wife didn't want any, and now he's closer to fifty than to forty, so children will be even more important to him. He will be an excellent father, because he can laugh.

Before they set out for Byron he had taken her across the clearing and round its bend to where he intended to build his house. The waterfall, she discovered, fell so far that on a windy day it never reached the valley floor, spinning away instead into nothingness, and filling the air with clouds of rainbows. Yet there was a huge pool below it, wide and calm until it poured through a narrow defile and became the cascade-tortured river, a pool the colour

726

of a turquoise or of Egyptian faience, opaque as milk, dense as syrup. The source of all this water, he showed her, was a cave below the cliffs, out of which issued a very large underground stream.

"There's an outcropping of limestone here," he explained. "That's why the pool is such a bizarre colour."

"And this is really where we're going to live, looking at so much loveliness?"

"Where *I* will live, anyway. I doubt you'll be here to see it." His face twisted. "Houses don't get built in a day, Missy, especially when they're built single-handed. I don't want a horde of workmen down here, pissing in the pool and getting drunk on Saturdays and then telling any curious bystander what's going on in my valley."

"I thought we had a bargain, not to mention my condition? Anyway, you won't be building single-handed, you'll have my hands as well," said Missy cheerfully. "I'm no stranger to hard work, and the cabin is so small it won't keep me busy. From what the doctor said, it makes no difference whether I lie in a bed or work like a navvy— one day it will happen, that's all."

At which he took her in his arms and kissed her as if he enjoyed kissing her, and as if she was already a little precious to him. They finally set out for Byron somewhat later than originally intended, but neither of them minded.

Octavia and Drusilla were in the kitchen when Missy walked in unannounced. They stared at her in astonishment, trying to take in the full glory of that outlandish scarlet lace dress, not to mention the huge lopsided hat with its graceless plume of scarlet ostrich feathers.

She hadn't turned into a beauty overnight, but there

was certainly an eye-catching quality about her, and she held herself too proudly to be mistaken for a trollop. In fact, she looked a lot more like a sophisticated visitor from London than one of the inhabitants of Caroline Lamb Place. There was also no doubting that the colour suited her down to the ground.

"Oh, Missy, you look lovely!" squeaked Octavia, sitting down in a hurry.

Missy kissed her, and kissed her mother. "That's nice to know, Auntie, because I admit I feel lovely." She grinned at them triumphantly. "I came to tell you that I'm married," she announced, waving her left hand under their noses.

"Who?" asked Drusilla, beaming.

"John Smith. We were married yesterday in Katoomba."

Suddenly neither to Drusilla nor to Octavia did it matter a scrap that the whole town of Byron called him a jailbird, or worse; he had rescued their Missy from the multiple horrors of spinsterhood, and he must therefore be loved for it with gratitude and respect and loyalty.

Octavia positively leaped up to put the kettle on, moving with more flexibility and ease than she had in years, though Drusilla didn't notice; she was too busy looking at her girl's convincingly massive wedding ring.

"Mrs. John Smith," she said experimentally. "Why, bless my soul, Missy, it sounds quite distinguished!"

"Simplicity usually is distinguished."

"Where is he? When is he coming to see us?" asked Octavia.

"He had some business or other in Byron, but he expects to be done late this afternoon, and he wants to meet you when he picks me up to take me home. I thought, Mother, that to fill in the day, you and I might walk into

728

Byron. I have to buy groceries, and I want to go to Uncle Herbert's to choose some materials for me to make into dresses. Because I am done forever with brown! I won't even wear it to work in. I'm going to work in a man's shirt and man's trousers because they're a great deal more comfortable and sensible, and who's to see me?"

"Isn't it lucky that you bought a Singer sewing machine, Drusilla?" asked Octavia from the stove, too happy at the way things had turned out to worry about the trousers.

But Drusilla had something so important on her mind that neither Singer sewing machines nor trousers could loom larger. "Can you afford it?" she asked anxiously. "I can make for you for nothing, but the materials at Herbert's are so expensive, especially once one gets away from brown!"

"It seems I can indeed afford it. John told me last night that he was going to put a thousand pounds in the bank for me this morning. Because he said a wife shouldn't have to ask her husband for every little penny she needs, nor account for every little penny she spends. All he asked was that I didn't exceed the allowance he makes me—a thousand pounds every year! Can you imagine it? And the housekeeping is separate from that! He put a hundred pounds into an empty Bushell's coffee jar and says he'll keep it replenished, and doesn't want to see the dockets. Oh, Mother, I'm still breathless!"

"A thousand pounds!" Octavia and Drusilla stared at Missy in thunderstruck respect.

"Then he must be a rich man," said Drusilla, and did some rapid mental gymnastics in which she saw herself finally able to cock a snook at Aurelia and Augusta and Antonia. Hah! Not only had Missy beaten Alicia to the altar, but now it began to look as if she might also have made the better bargain.

"I imagine he's comfortably off," temporised Missy. "I know his generosity to me suggests real wealth, but I suspect it's more that he's a truly generous man. Certainly I shall never, never embarrass him by overspending. However, I do need a few decent clothes—*not* brown!—a couple of winter dresses and a couple of summer ones is all. Oh, Mother, it's so beautiful down in the valley! I don't have any desire to lead a social life, I just want to be alone with my John."

Drusilla looked suddenly troubled. "Missy, there's so little we can give you for a wedding present. But I think, Octavia, that we could spare the Jersey heifer, don't you?"

"We can *certainly* spare the heifer," said Octavia.

"Now that," said Missy, "is what I call a handsome wedding present! We would love the heifer."

"We ought to send her to Percival's bull first," said Octavia. "She's due to come on any time now, so you won't have to wait long for her, and with any luck she'll give you a calf next year too."

Drusilla consulted the clock on the kitchen wall. "If you want to go to Herbert's as well as to Maxwell's, Missy, I suggest we make a start. Then we might be able to fit in a bit of lunch with Julia in her tea room, and tell her the news. My word, she'll be surprised!"

Octavia twitched herself gently, and experienced no pain. "I'm coming too," she announced firmly. "You're not going without me today of all days. If I have to crawl on hands and knees, I'm coming too."

Thus in the late morning Drusilla strolled through the shopping centre with her daughter on one arm, and her sister on the other.

It was Octavia who spied Mrs. Cecil Hurlingford on

the opposite side of the road; Mrs. Cecil was the wife of the Reverend Dr. Cecil Hurlingford, Byron's Church of England minister, and everyone went in fear and trembling of her tongue. "Dying of curiosity, aren't you, you old besom?" muttered Octavia through her teeth, smiling and bowing so frostily that Mrs. Cecil thought the better of crossing the road to see what was what with the Missalonghi gaggle.

Then Drusilla completed the routing of Mrs. Cecil by suddenly shouting with laughter and pointing one shaking finger in Mrs. Cecil's direction. "Oh, Octavia, Mrs. Cecil hasn't recognised Missy! I do believe she thinks we've got one of the Caroline Lamb Place women in tow!"

All three of the ladies of Missalonghi dissolved into laughter, and Mrs. Cecil Hurlingford tottered into Julia's tea room to get away from so much unseemly mirth, all apparently directed at *her.*

"What an uproar!" crowed Octavia.

"The bigger the better," said Missy, entering Herbert Hurlingford's clothing emporium.

That whole experience was a terrific tonic, between Uncle Herbert's flabbergasted imitation of a codfish when Missy proceeded to buy men's shirts and trousers for herself, and James's tonguetied terror when she proceeded to buy lengths of lavender-blue taffeta, apricot silk, amber velvet, and cyclamen wool. Recovering somewhat after Missy left him to go to James, Herbert debated as to whether he should relieve his feelings by ordering the hussy from his premises; then when she paid for her purchases in gold, he changed his mind and humbly rang up the sale. Staggering as Missy's visit was, he really only had half a mind to pay to it and her, for the other half was occupied in wondering what was going on up at the bottling plant, where the extraordinary meeting of share-

733

holders was taking place. The shopkeeping Hurlingfords had despatched Maxwell as their representative, acknowledging that Maxwell had the best and bitterest tongue, and understanding that he would fight as hard for them as for himself. Business must go on as usual, after all, and if the bottling plant and its corollary activities like the baths and the hotel and the spas was going to go west, then the shops became more important than ever to their respective owners.

"You may deliver these to Missalonghi this afternoon, James," said Missy grandly, and slapped a gold sovereign down on the counter. "Here, this is for your trouble. And while you're about it, you can go into Uncle Maxwell's and pick up my grocery order as well. Come, Mother, Aunt Octavia! Let us go to Aunt Julia's for lunch."

The three ladies of Missalonghi swept out of the shop more royally than they had swept in.

"Oh, this is such fun!" chuckled Octavia, whose walk was just about normal. "I have never enjoyed myself so much!"

Missy was enjoying herself too, but less simply. It had been a shock to find the promised thousand pounds had actually been deposited for her, and even more of a shock to be treated with great civility by Quintus Hurlingford, the bank manager; John Smith had instructed him to pay Missy's withdrawals in gold, since the deposit had been in gold. A thousand pounds!

Well, she had her dress materials and her shirts and her trousers, and several pairs of pretty shoes into the bargain. She really didn't need anything else. If she kept a hundred pounds of that amazing thousand, it would be more than enough to last her until her allowance was replenished at this same time next year. After all, when had she ever owned more than a shilling or two? She would therefore

734

use the bulk of her allowance to buy Mother and Aunt Octavia a little pony-and-trap. The pony wouldn't eat the place out the way a bigger horse would, they could manage its harnessing with ease, and never again would they have to walk anywhere, or humble their pride by begging that a conveyance be sent for them. Yes, they should go in style to Alicia's wedding in a smart pony-and-trap!

The hundred pounds Julia had realised from the sale of her shares was already being spent; half the tea room was roped off, and two workmen were toiling at stripping and sanding.

Once she ceased apologising for the mess, Julia gathered her wits together sufficiently to absorb the full splendour of Missy's outfit. "It's a superb dress and hat, dear," she said, "but isn't the colour a little *lairy?*"

"Definitely lairy," admitted Missy, without shame. "But oh, Aunt Julia, I am so sick to death of brown, and can you name a colour further from brown than this? Besides, it suits me, don't you think?"

Yes, but does it suit my tea room? was the question Julia burned to ask, then decided it would be unpardonable to criticise her benefactress. And due to the renovations there weren't many patrons today; she would just have to hope no one would decide she had thrown open her doors to the likes of Caroline Lamb Place. Oh! That must have been what Mrs. Cecil Hurlingford was gobbling about! Oh, dear! Oh, dear dear dear!

In the meantime she had ushered the ladies of Missalonghi to her very best table, and shortly thereafter served them an assortment of sandwiches and cakes, and a big pot of tea.

"I'm going to have a striped paper on the walls in cream and gold and crimson," she said, sitting down to join her guests, "and my chairs will be reupholstered in a matching but brighter brocade. I'm having the moulding on the ceiling picked out in gilt, canaries in gold cages, and pots of tall palms everywhere. Let Next Door"—her head tilting scornfully towards the wall she shared in common with the Olympus Café—"compete with *that!*"

Drusilla's mouth was open to unburden herself of the news that Missy was married to John Smith and that John Smith was a rich man rather than a jailbird, when Cornelia Hurlingford erupted through the doors and descended upon them, her various scarves and ribbons trailing behind her like moulting feathers from a peacock's tail.

Cornelia and Julia lived together above the Weeping Willow Tea Room, which Julia did not own outright. She paid a large rent to her brother Herbert, who regularly assured her that one day she would have paid enough, between the rent and what her house and five acres had fetched, to buy the premises.

As well as sharing their living arrangements, the two maiden sisters also shared and relished every morsel of information their public occupations garnered, but mostly Cornelia, the less excitable of the two, could wait until Chez Chapeau Alicia closed its doors for the day; Alicia did not permit her to leave the shop while ever it was open. Obviously whatever she had to impart was urgent enough to run the risk of incurring Alicia's wrath, and so bursting was Cornelia with her news that Missy's scarlet outfit got no more than a cursory glance.

"Guess what?" she gasped, plumping herself down on a chair and forgetting she was supposed to be the formidably elegant and snooty sales dame of a formidably elegant and snooty one-off millinery establishment.

"What?" asked everyone, well aware of these various facts, and therefore prepared to be tremendously impressed.

736

"Alicia ran off with Billy's chauffeur this morning!"

"What?"

"She did, she did! She eloped! At *her* age! Oh, what a circus is going on at Aurelia's! Hysterics and tantrums all over the place! Little Willie nearly tore the house apart looking for Alicia because he refused to believe what her note to him said, and Billy was roaring like a gale because he had to go to some important meeting at the plant when what he really wanted to do was set the police onto his chauffeur! They carted Aurelia off to bed as stiff as a board, and had to send for Uncle Neville when she kept holding her breath until she passed out, and then Uncle Neville gave her such a wallop across the ears because he was cross at being called out for nothing, and he called her no better than a spoiled baby, so that set her off screaming, and she's still screaming! Oh, and Edmund is sitting on a chair just twitching, and Ted and Randolph are trying to pull him together so he can go to the meeting at the plant. But the worst of it is that Alicia and the chauffeur went off in Billy's brand-new motorcar, for all the world as if they owned it!"

Cornelia ended her breathless recital with a bellow of laughter, Missy joined her, and one by one the others came in to ring a peal of glorious mirth over the events at Mon Repos. After that catharsis everyone felt absolutely tiptop, and settled to a quieter but no less enjoyable dissection of Missy's marriage and Alicia's elopement, not to mention lunch.

John Smith arrived at Missalonghi just before five o'clock, looking very pleased with himself. He shook his mother-in-law's hand with great affability, but refrained from kissing her, a piece of good sense she heartily approved of. The handshake he also offered Octavia disappointed her, but she had to admit, looking at him properly

737

for the first time, that he was a fine figure of a man. Of course the suit aided her impression, as did the fresh haircut and neatly trimmed beard. Yes, Missy had nothing to be ashamed of in her choice of a life's partner, and to Octavia's way of thinking, his fifteen years of seniority made him just the right age for a husband.

He seemed a nice man on the inside too, for he made himself easily at home in the kitchen and sniffed at the scent of roast lamb appreciatively.

"I hope you and Missy will stay to dinner?" asked Drusilla.

"We'd love to," he said.

"What about the road home? It isn't going to be too risky after dark?"

"Not at all. The horses know it blindfold."

He leaned back in his chair and raised one eyebrow at his wife, who was sitting opposite and just beaming at him with a pride in him his first wife had certainly never owned. What fools men were! They always went after the pretty women, when their intelligence should tell them the homely ones were much better bets. However, she looked all right in that bright red getup, not beautiful, certainly not pretty, but interesting. In fact, she looked like the sort of woman most men would want to get to know because they weren't sure what went on inside. Attractive, bumpy nose and all. And as she sat there sparking with life, it was difficult to believe she could die at any moment. His heart twisted, an odd sensation. Tomorrow, tomorrow! Don't think about it until it happens! You are beginning to dwell on it, and you mustn't! Don't think of her death-sentence as a cosmic revenge on you!

Maybe if he could make her happy enough, it wouldn't happen at all. There were such things as miracles, he had seen one or two in his travels. Getting rid of his first wife undoubtedly fell into the category of a miracle.

"I want to talk to you ladies," he said, dragging his eyes and his mind away from his present wife.

Three faces turned to him with interest. Drusilla and Octavia ceased fussing at the stove and sat down.

"There was a shareholders' meeting at the Byron Bottle Company today," he said, "and management of the company has changed hands. In fact, it passed into my hands."

"You?" squeaked Missy.

"Yes."

"Then you're the mystery buyer?"

"Yes."

"But why? Uncle Billy said the mystery buyer had outlaid the kind of money for shares that no one could ever hope to get back! So why?"

He smiled, not attractively; for the first time since meeting him Missy saw a different John Smith, a powerful and flinty John Smith, a John Smith who might not know the meaning of the word mercy. It didn't frighten her and it didn't take her aback; rather, it pleased her. Here was no defeated refugee from life's insistent pressures, here was no weakling. On the outside he was so delightfully relaxed and easygoing, and there were people who might mistake that for weakness even after they knew him very well, perhaps intimately well. Like his first wife? Yes, she could understand how a wife might come to judge him as less than he actually was, if that wife was a rather stupid, self-centred kind of woman.

But he was answering her, so she paid attention to him.

"I had a bone to pick with the Hurlingfords. Present company excluded, of course. But by and large, I have

739

found the Hurlingfords so damned smug, so sure that their quasi-noble free-settler English origins put them much higher than people like me who have the rattle of leg-irons on their mother's side and full Jew on their father's. I admit I set out to get the Hurlingfords, and didn't care how much it cost me to do it. Luckily I have enough money to buy out a dozen Byron Bottle Companies without ever feeling the pinch."

"But you don't come from Byron," said Missy, bewildered.

"True. However, my first wife was a Hurlingford."

"Really! What was her name?" asked Drusilla, who was one of the clan experts on Hurlingford genealogy.

"Una."

Fortunately Drusilla and Octavia were far too interested in what John Smith was saying, and John Smith himself was far too interested in saying it, to pay any attention to Missy.

She sat in stony stillness, unable to move the smallest part of her. Una. *Una!*

How could her mother and aunt sit there so unresponsive to that name, when they had met her and entertained her in this very house? Didn't they remember the biscuits, the documents?

"Una?" Drusilla was asking herself. "Let me see now . . . Yes, she would have to be one of the Marcus Hurlingfords from Sydney, which would make Livilla Hurlingford her first cousin and her closest relative here in Byron. Humph! I never did meet her, but she died a long time ago, of course. A drowning accident, wasn't it?"

"Yes," said John Smith.

Was that it, then? Was that why she glowed? Was that why every time Missy had needed her, she had been there? Was that why so many small incidents had hap-

740

pened so fortuitously in the library? The novels, all leading up to the one about the girl dying of heart trouble. The shares on the desk. The Power of Attorney forms. Una the conveniently handy Justice of the Peace. The impudence and the gay carelessness, so hugely attractive to one as repressed as Missy had been. The scarlet dress and hat *exactly* as it had flowered in Missy's imagination, and exactly the right size too. The curious significance she had managed to give all her words, so that they sank into Missy like water into parched soil, and germinated richly. Una. Oh, Una! Dear, radiant Una.

"But her married name definitely wasn't Smith," Drusilla was saying. "It was much more unusual, like Cardmom or Terebinth or Gooseflesh. He was a very rich man, as I recollect, which was the only reason the second Sir William approved the match. Yes, I see how they would have insulted you, if you were he."

"I was he, and they did indeed insult me."

"We," said Drusilla, reaching out her hand to clasp his, "are delighted to welcome you into this branch of the family, my dear John."

The hard John Smith had gone, for the eyes resting on his mother-in-law were soft, amused in a gentle way. "Thank you. I've changed my name, of course, and I'd prefer you didn't speak of all this ancient history."

"It will go no further than Missalonghi," said Drusilla, and sighed, assuming he had changed his name to sever all the painful memories. The sordid ramifications Missy knew of from John Smith himself were obviously not a part of Hurlingford history in Byron.

"Poor thing, drowning like that," said Octavia, shaking her head. "It must have hit you hard, John. Still, I'm very glad things have turned out the way they have, the

743

bottling plant and all. And isn't it interesting that you've gone and married another Hurlingford?"

"It was a great help today," said John Smith calmly.

"There are Hurlingfords and Hurlingfords, like any other family," said Drusilla with truth. "Una may not have turned out the right sort of wife for you, so perhaps it's better she died so young. Where Missy—*I* think she will make you happy."

He grinned and reached his arm across the table to take hold of Missy's cold clammy hand. "Yes, I think she will too." He managed to kiss the trembling fingers in spite of their distance from where he sat, then he released the hand and gave all his attention to Drusilla and Octavia.

"Anyway, now I'm in control of the Byron Bottle Company and its auxiliary industries, I want to make some much-needed changes. Naturally I shall sit as chairman of the board of directors and Missy will be my vice-chairman, but I also require eight other directors. Now I need a group of busy, interested individuals who will be as concerned about the town and people of Byron as about the bottling plant itself. Today I received the necessary votes to enable me to restructure the board any way I want, and I want to do something so different that when I announced my intentions, I acquired a few more shares! Sir William, Edmund Marshall, the brothers Maxwell and Herbert Hurlingford, and some dozen others sold out to me when the meeting concluded. Their spleen got the better of their judgement, which only confirms what I've suspected for a very long time—they're fools. The Byron Bottle Company is going to get bigger and better! It's going to become more civic-minded, and it's going to diversify its interests."

He laughed, shrugged. "Well, no point in dwelling on the likes of Sir William Hurlingford, is there? I want *women*

744

on my board, and I want to start with you two ladies and the Misses Julia and Cornelia Hurlingford. All of you have coped magnificently with your hardships, and you certainly don't lack courage. It may be a radical departure to staff a board of directors with women, but in my opinion most boards already consist of women—*old* women."

He lifted that magical eyebrow at Drusilla and Octavia, who were listening to him in spellbound silence. "So? Are you interested in my offer? Naturally you'll be paid directors' fees. The previous board paid each of its members five thousand pounds per annum, though, I warn you, I shall cut that figure to two thousand pounds."

"But we don't know what to do!" cried Octavia.

"Most boards don't, so that's no handicap. The chairman is John Smith, remember, and John Smith will teach you every rope. Each of you will have a specific area to deal with, and I know you'll look at hoary problems with fresh eyes and new problems with the kind of unorthodoxy a usual board can't match."

He looked at Drusilla sternly. "I'm waiting on your answer, Mother. Are you going to join my board, or not?"

Drusilla shut her gaping mouth with an audible snap. "Oh, indeed I am! And so are the others, I'll see to that."

"Good. Then the first item of business you have to deal with is who we're going to appoint to the remaining four board places. Women, mind!"

"I must be dreaming," said Octavia.

"Not at all," said Drusilla, at her most majestic. "This is real, sister. The ladies of Missalonghi have come into their own at last."

"What a day!" sighed Octavia.

What a day, indeed. The last of it was going on outside the open back door, which faced west. So did Missy's chair. She could see the great fanning ribbons of high cloud dyed as scarlet as her dress, and the apple-green sky between them, and the mass of blossom on the fruit trees in the orchard, drifts of white and pink gone pinker in that lovely waning sun. But her mind and her eyes, normally so receptive to the natural beauty of the world, were not preoccupied with that glory. For Una was standing in the doorway, smiling at her. Una. Oh, Una!

"Don't ever tell him, Missy. Let him believe his love and care cured you." Una chuckled gleefully. "He's a darling man, darling, but he has a terrible temper! It's not in your nature to provoke it, but whatever you do, don't tempt fate by telling him about your heart trouble. No man likes to be the dupe of a woman, and he's already had a fair taste of that. So mark what I say—don't ever, ever tell him."

"You're leaving," said Missy desolately.

"With knobs on I'm leaving, darling! I've done what I was sent to do, and now I'm going to take a well-deserved rest on the softest, fattest, pinkest, *champagniest* cloud I can find."

"I can't do it without you, Una!"

"Nonsense, darling, of course you can. Just be good, and especially be good in bed. Look after his stomach and Little Willie, and you can't go wrong. That is, as long as you heed my warning—*don't ever tell him the truth!*"

That exquisite radiance welling from within Una had fused with the last of the sun; she stood a moment longer in the doorway with the light pouring through her and out of her, then she was gone.

"Missy! Missy! Missy! Are you all right? Are you in pain? Missy! For God's sake, answer me!"

John Smith was standing over her, chafing her hands, a look of desperate horror in his eyes.

She managed to smile up at him. "I'm quite all right, John, truly. It's been the day. Too much happiness!"

"You'd better get used to too much happiness, my little love, because I swear I shall drown you in it," he said, and caught his breath. "You're my second chance, Missalonghi Smith."

A chill breeze puffed in through the open door, and just before Drusilla reached to shut it out, it whispered for Missy's ears alone, "Never tell him! Oh, please, *never* tell him!"

From Colleen McCullough's classic bestseller,

THE THORN BIRDS

Once a month Meggie wrote a dutiful letter to Fee, Bob and the boys, full of descriptions of North Queensland, carefully humorous, never hinting of any differences between her and Luke. That pride again. As far as Drogheda knew, the Muellers were friends of Luke's with whom she boarded because Luke traveled so much. Her genuine affection for the couple came through in every word she wrote about them, so no one on Drogheda worried. Except that it grieved them she never came home. Yet how could she tell them that she didn't have the money to visit without also telling them how miserable her marriage to Luke O'Neill had become?

Occasionally she would nerve herself to insert a casual question about Bishop Ralph, and even less often Bob would remember to pass on the little he learned from Fee about the Bishop. Then came a letter full of him.

"He arrived out of the blue one day, Meggie," Bob's letter said, "looking a bit upset and down in the mouth. I must say he was floored not to find you here. He was spitting mad because we hadn't told him about you and Luke, but when Mum said you'd got a bee in your bonnet about it and didn't want us to tell him, he shut up and never said another word. But I thought he missed you more than he would any of the rest of us, and I suppose that's quite natural because you spent more time with him than the rest of us, and I think he always thought of you as his little sister. He wandered around as if he couldn't believe you wouldn't pop up all of a sudden, poor chap. We didn't have any pictures to show him either, and I never thought until he asked to see them that it was funny you never had any wedding pictures taken. He asked if you had any kids, and I said I didn't think so. You don't, do you, Meggie? How long is it now since you were married? Getting on for two years? Must be, because this is July. Time flies, eh? I hope you have some kids soon, because I think the Bishop would be pleased to hear of it. I offered to give him your address, but he said no. Said it wouldn't be any use because he's going to Athens, Greece, for a while with the archbishop he works for. Some Dago name four yards long, I never can remember it. Can you imagine, Meggie, they're flying? 'Struth! Anyway, once he found out you weren't on Drogheda to go round with him he didn't stay long, just took a ride or two, said Mass for us every day, and went six days after he got here."

Meggie laid the letter down. He knew, he knew! At last he knew. What had he thought, how much had it grieved him? And why had he pushed her to do this? It hadn't made things any better. She didn't love Luke, she never would love Luke. He was nothing more than a substitute, a man who would give her children similar in type to those she might have had with Ralph de Bricassart. Oh, God, what a mess!

Archbishop di Contini-Verchese preferred to stay in a secular hotel than avail himself of the offered quarters in an Athens Orthodox palace. His mission was a very delicate one, of some moment; there were matters long overdue for discussion with the chief prelates of the

Greek Orthodox Church, the Vatican having a fondness for Greek and Russian Orthodoxy that it couldn't have for Protestantism. After all, the Orthodoxies were schisms, not heresies; their bishops, like Rome's, extended back to Saint Peter in an unbroken line.

The Archbishop knew his appointment for this mission was a diplomatic testing, a stepping stone to greater things in Rome. Again his gift for languages had been a boon, for it was his fluent Greek which had tipped the balance in his favor. They had sent for him all the way to Australia, flown him out.

And it was unthinkable that he go without Bishop de Bricassart, for he had grown to rely upon that amazing man more and more with the passing of the years. A Mazarin, truly a Mazarin; His Grace admired Cardinal Mazarin far more than he did Cardinal Richelieu, so the comparison was high praise. Ralph was everything the Church liked in her high officials. His theology was conservative, so were his ethics; his brain was quick and subtle, his face gave away nothing of what went on behind it; and he had an exquisite knack of knowing just how to please those he was with, whether he liked them or loathed them, agreed with them or differed from them. A sycophant he was not, a diplomat he was. If he was repeatedly brought to the attention of those in the Vatican hierarchy, his rise to prominence would be certain. And that would please His Grace di Contini-Verchese, for he didn't want to lose contact with His Lordship de Bricassart.

It was very hot, but Bishop Ralph didn't mind the dry Athens air after Sydney's humidity. Walking rapidly, as usual in boots, breeches and soutane, he strode up the rocky ramp to the Acropolis, through the frowning Propylon, past the Erechtheum, on up the incline with its slippery rough stones to the Parthenon, and down to the wall beyond.

There, with the wind ruffling his dark curls, a little grey about the ears now, he stood and looked across the white city to the bright hills and the clear, astonishing aquamarine of the Aegean Sea. Right below him was the Plaka with its rooftop cafés, its colonies of Bohemians, and to one side a great theater lapped up the rock. In the distance were Roman columns, Crusader forts and Venetian castles, but never a sign of the Turks. What amazing people, these Greeks. To hate the race who had ruled them for seven hundred years so much that once freed they hadn't left a mosque or a minaret standing. And so ancient, so full of rich heritage. His Normans had been fur-clad barbarians when Pericles clothed the top of the rock in marble, and Rome had been a rude village.

Only now, eleven thousand miles away, was he able to think of Meggie without wanting to weep. Even so, the distant hills blurred for a moment before he brought his emotions under control. How could he possibly blame her, when he had told her to do it? He understood at once why she had been determined not to tell him; she didn't want him to meet her new husband, or be a part of her new life. Of course in his mind he had assumed she would bring whomever she married to Gillanbone if not to Drogheda itself, that she would continue to live where he knew her to be safe, free from care and danger. But once he thought about it, he could see this was the last thing she would want. No, she had been bound to go away, and so long as she and this Luke O'Neill were together, she wouldn't come back. Bob said they were saving to buy a property in Western Queensland, and that news had been the death knell. Meggie meant never to come back. As far as he was concerned, she intended to be dead.

But are you happy, Meggie? Is he good to you? Do you love him, this Luke O'Neill? What kind of man is he, that you turned from me to him? What was it about him, an ordinary stockman, that you liked better than Enoch Davies or Liam O'Rourke or Alastair MacQueen? Was it that *I* didn't know him, that *I* could make no comparisons? Did you do it to torture me, Meggie, to pay me back? But why are there no children? What's the matter with the man, that he roams up and down the state like a vagabond and puts you to live with friends? No wonder you have no child; he's not with you long enough. Meggie, why? Why did you marry this Luke O'Neill?

Turning, he made his way down from the Acropolis, and walked the busy streets of Athens. In the open-air markets around Evripidou Street he lingered, fascinated by the people, the huge baskets of kalamari and fish reeking in the sun, the vegetables and tinsel slippers hung side by side; the women amused him, their unashamed and open cooing over him, a legacy of a culture basically very different from his puritanical own. Had their unabashed admiration been lustful (he could not think of a better word) it would have embarrassed him acutely, but he accepted it in the spirit intended, as an accolade for extraordinary physical beauty.

The hotel was on Omonia Square, very luxurious and expensive. Archbishop di Contini-Verchese was sitting in a chair by his balcony windows, quietly thinking; as Bishop Ralph came in he turned his head, smiling.

"In good time, Ralph. I would like to pray."

"I thought everything was settled? Are there sudden complications, Your Grace?"

"Not of that kind. I had a letter from Cardinal Monteverdi today, expressing the wishes of the Holy Father."

Bishop Ralph felt his shoulders tighten, a curious prickling of the skin around his ears. "Tell me."

"As soon as the talks are over—and they are over— I am to proceed to Rome. There I am to be blessed with the biretta of a cardinal, and continue my work in Rome under the direct supervision of His Holiness."

"Whereas I?"

"You will become Archbishop de Bricassart, and go back to Australia to fill my shoes as Papal Legate."

The prickling skin around his ears flushed red hot; his head whirled, rocked. He, a non-Italian, to be honored with the Papal Legation! It was unheard of! Oh, depend on it, he would be Cardinal de Bricassart yet!

"Of course you will receive training and instruction in Rome first. That will take about six months, during which I will be with you to introduce you to those who are my friends. I want them to know you, because the time will come when I shall send for you, Ralph, to help me with my work in the Vatican."

"Your Grace, I can't thank you enough! It's due to you, this great chance."

"God grant I am sufficiently intelligent to see when a man is too able to leave in obscurity, Ralph! Now let us kneel and pray. God is very good."

His rosary beads and missal were sitting on a table nearby; hand trembling, Bishop Ralph reached for the beads and knocked the missal to the floor. It fell open at the middle. The Archbishop, who was closer to it, picked it up and looked curiously at the brown, tissue-thin shape which had once been a rose.

"How extraordinary! Why do you keep this? Is it a memory of your home, or perhaps of your mother?" The eyes which saw through guile and dissimulation were looking straight at him, and there was no time to disguise his emotion, or his apprehension.

"No." He grimaced. "I want no memories of my mother."

"But it must have great meaning for you, that you store it so lovingly within the pages of the book most dear to you. Of what does it speak?"

"Of a love as pure as that I bear my God, Vittorio. It does the book nothing but honor."

"That I deduced, because I know you. But the love, does it endanger your love for the Church?"

"No. It was for the Church I forsook her, that I always will forsake her. I've gone so far beyond her, and I can never go back again."

"So at last I understand the sadness! Dear Ralph, it is not as bad as you think, truly it is not. You will live to do great good for many people, you will be loved by many people. And she, having the love which is contained in such an old, fragrant memory as this, will never want. Because you kept the love alongside the rose."

"I don't think she understands at all."

"Oh, yes. If you have loved her thus, then she is woman enough to understand. Otherwise you would have forgotten her, and abandoned this relic long since."

"There have been times when only hours on my knees have stopped me from leaving my post, going to her."

The Archbishop eased himself out of his chair and came to kneel beside his friend, this beautiful man whom he loved as he had loved few things other than his God and his Church, which to him were indivisible.

"You will not leave, Ralph, and you know it well. You belong to the Church, you always have and you always will. The vocation for you is a true one. We shall pray now, and I shall add the Rose to my prayers for the rest of my life. Our Dear Lord sends us many griefs and much pain during our progress to eternal life. We must learn to bear it, I as much as you."

At the end of August Meggie got a letter from Luke to say he was in Townsville Hospital with Weil's disease, but that he was in no danger and would be out soon.

"So it looks like we don't have to wait until the end of the year for our holiday, Meg. I can't go back to the cane until I'm one hundred percent fit, and the best way to make sure I am is to have a decent holiday. So I'll be along in a week or so to pick you up. We're going to Lake Eacham on the Atherton Tableland for a couple of weeks, until I'm well enough to go back to work."

Meggie could hardly believe it, and didn't know if

she wanted to be with him or not, now that the opportunity presented itself. Though the pain of her mind had taken a lot longer to heal than the pain of her body, the memory of her honeymoon ordeal in the Dunny pub had been pushed from thought so long it had lost the power to terrify her, and from her reading she understood better now that much of it had been due to ignorance, her own and Luke's. Oh, dear Lord, pray this holiday would mean a child! If she could only have a baby to love it would be so much easier. Anne wouldn't mind a baby around, she'd love it. So would Luddie. They had told her so a hundred times, hoping Luke would come once for long enough to rectify his wife's barren loveless existence.

When she told them what the letter said they were delighted, but privately skeptical.

"Sure as eggs is eggs that wretch will find some excuse to be off without her," said Anne to Luddie.

Luke had borrowed a car from somewhere, and picked Meggie up early in the morning. He looked thin, wrinkled and yellow, as if he had been pickled. Shocked, Meggie gave him her case and climbed in beside him.

"What is Weil's disease, Luke? You said you weren't in any danger, but it looks to me as if you've been very sick indeed."

"Oh, it's just some sort of jaundice most cutters get sooner or later. The cane rats carry it, we pick it up through a cut or sore. I'm in good health, so I wasn't too sick compared to some who get it. The quacks say I'll be fit as a fiddle in no time."

Climbing up through a great gorge filled with jungle, the road led inland, a river in full spate roaring and tumbling below, and at one spot a magnificent waterfall spilling to join it from somewhere up above, right athwart the road. They drove between the cliff and the angling water in a wet, glittering archway of fantastic light and shadow. And as they climbed the air grew cool, exquisitely fresh; Meggie had forgotten how good cool air made her feel. The jungle leaned across them, so impenetrable no one ever dared to enter it. The bulk of it was quite invisible under the weight of leafy vines lying sagging from treetop to treetop, continuous and endless, like a vast sheet of green velvet flung across the forest. Under the eaves Meggie caught glimpses of wonderful flowers and butterflies, cartwheeling webs with great elegant speckled spiders motionless at their hubs, fabulous fungi chewing at mossy trunks, birds with long trailing red or blond tails.

Lake Eacham lay on top of the tableland, idyllic in its unspoiled setting. Before night fell they strolled out onto the veranda of their boardinghouse to look across the still water. Meggie wanted to watch the enormous fruit bats called flying foxes wheel like precursors of doom in thousands down toward the places where they found their food. They were monstrous and repulsive, but singularly timid, entirely benign. To see them come across a molten sky in dark, pulsating sheets was awesome; Meggie never missed watching for them from the Himmelhoch veranda.

And it was heaven to sink into a soft cool bed, not have to lie still until one spot was sweat-saturated and then move carefully to a new spot, knowing the old one wouldn't dry out anyway. Luke took a flat brown packet out of his case, picked a handful of small round objects out of it and laid them in a row on the bedside table.

Meggie reached out to take one, inspect it. "What on earth is it?" she asked curiously.

"A French letter." He had forgotten his decision of two years ago, not to tell her he practiced contraception. "I put it on myself before I go inside you. Otherwise I might start a baby, and we can't afford to do that until we get our place." He was sitting naked on the side of the bed, and he was thin, ribs and hips protruding. But his blue eyes shone, he reached out to clasp her hand as it held the French letter. "Nearly there,

Meg, nearly there! I reckon another five thousand pounds will buy us the best property to be had west of Charters Towers."

"Then you've got it," she said, her voice quite calm. "I can write to Bishop de Bricassart and ask him for a loan of the money. He won't charge us interest."

"You most certainly won't!" he snapped. "Damn it, Meg, where's your pride? We'll work for what we have, not borrow! I've never owed anyone a penny in all my life, and I'm not going to start now."

She scarcely heard him, glaring at him through a haze of brilliant red. In all her life she had never been so angry! Cheat, liar, egotist! How dared he do it to her, trick her out of a baby, try to make her believe he ever had any intention of becoming a grazier! He'd found his niche, with Arne Swenson and the sugar.

Concealing her rage so well it surprised her, she turned her attention back to the little rubber wheel in her hand. "Tell me about these French letter things. How do they stop me having a baby?"

He came to stand behind her, and contact of their bodies made her shiver; from excitement he thought, from disgust she knew.

"Don't you know anything, Meg?"

"No," she lied. Which was true about French letters, at any rate; she could not remember ever seeing a mention of them.

His hands played with her breasts, tickling. "Look, when I come I make this—I don't know—stuff, and if I'm up inside you with nothing on. it stays there. When it stays there long enough or often enough, it makes a baby."

So that was it! He *wore* the thing, like a skin on a sausage! Cheat!

Turning off the light, he drew her down onto the bed, and it wasn't long before he was groping for his anti-baby device; she heard him making the same sounds he had made in the Dunny pub bedroom, knowing now they meant he was pulling on the French letter. The cheat! But how to get around it?

Trying not to let him see how much he hurt her, she endured him. Why did it have to hurt so, if this was a natural thing?

"It's no good, is it, Meg?" he asked afterward. "You must be awfully small for it to keep on hurting so much after the first time. Well, I won't do it again. You don't mind if I do it on your breast, do you?"

"Oh, what does it matter?" she asked wearily. "If you mean you're not going to hurt me, all right!"

"You might be a bit more enthusiastic, Meg!"

"What for?"

But he was rising again; it was two years since he had had time or energy for this. Oh, it was nice to be with a woman, exciting and forbidden. He didn't feel at all married to Meg; it wasn't any different from getting a bit in the paddock behind the Kynuna pub, or having high-and-mighty Miss Carmichael against the shearing shed wall. Meggie had nice breasts, firm from all that riding, just the way he liked them, and he honestly preferred to get his pleasure at her breast, liking the sensation of unsheathed penis sandwiched between their bellies. French letters cut a man's sensitivity a lot, but not to don one when he put himself inside her was asking for trouble.

Groping, he pulled at her buttocks and made her lie on top of him, then seized one nipple between his teeth, feeling the hidden point swell and harden on his tongue. A great contempt for him had taken possession of Meggie; what ridiculous creatures men were, grunting and sucking and straining for what they got out of it. He was becoming more excited, kneading her back and bottom, gulping away for all the world like a great overgrown kitten sneaked back to its mother. His hips began to move in a rhythmic, jerky fashion, and sprawled across him awkwardly because she was hating it too much to try helping him, she felt the tip of his unprotected penis slide between her legs.

Since she was not a participant in the act, her thoughts were her own. And it was then the idea came. As slowly and unobtrusively as she could, she maneuvered him until he was right at the most painful part of her; with a great indrawn breath to keep her courage up, she forced the penis in, teeth clenched. But though it did hurt, it didn't hurt nearly as much. Minus its rubber sheath, his member was more slippery, easier to introduce and far easier to tolerate.

Luke's eyes opened. He tried to push her away, but oh, God! It was unbelievable without the French letter; he had never been inside a woman bare, had never realized what a difference it made. He was so close, so excited he couldn't bring himself to push her away hard enough, and in the end he put his arms round her, unable to keep up his breast activity. Though it wasn't manly to cry out, he couldn't prevent the noise leaving him, and afterward kissed her softly.

"Luke?"

"What?"

"Why can't we do that every time? Then you wouldn't have to put on a French letter."

"We shouldn't have done it that time, Meg, let alone again. I was right in you when I came."

She leaned over him, stroking his chest. "But don't you see? I'm sitting up! It doesn't stay there at all, it runs right out again! Oh, Luke, please! It's so much nicer, it doesn't hurt nearly as much. I'm sure it's all right, because I can feel it running out. Please!"

What human being ever lived who could resist the repetition of perfect pleasure when offered so plausibly? Adam-like, Luke nodded, for at this stage he was far less informed than Meggie.

"I suppose there's truth in what you say, and it's much nicer for me when you're not fighting it. All right, Meg, we'll do it that way from now on."

And in the darkness she smiled, content. For it had *not* all run out. The moment she felt him shrink out of her she had drawn up all the internal muscles into a knot, slid off him onto her back, stuck her crossed knees in the air casually and hung on to what she had with every ounce of determination in her. Oho, my fine gentleman, I'll fix you yet! You wait and see, Luke O'Neill! I'll get my baby if it kills me!

Away from the heat and humidity of the coastal plain Luke mended rapidly. Eating well, he began to put the weight he needed back again, and his skin faded from the sickly yellow to its usual brown. With the lure of an eager, responsive Meggie in his bed it wasn't too difficult to persuade him to prolong the original two weeks into three, and then into four. But at the end of a month he rebelled.

"There's no excuse, Meg. I'm as well as I've ever been. We're sitting up here on top of the world like a king and queen, spending money. Arne needs me."

"Won't you reconsider, Luke? If you really wanted to, you could buy your station now."

"Let's hang on a bit longer the way we are, Meg."

He wouldn't admit it, of course, but the lure of the sugar was in his bones, the strange fascination some men have for utterly demanding labor. As long as his young man's strength held up, Luke would remain faithful to the sugar. The only thing Meggie could hope for was to force him into changing his mind by giving him a child, an heir to the property out around Kynuna.